A PLACE WITHOUT PAIN

A Place Without Pain

By Simon Bourke

First published 2023

Printed in

Cover Design by Design for Writers

Edited by Elaine P Kennedy

This is a work of fiction. Unless otherwise indicated, all the names, characters, businesses, places, events and incidents in this book are either the product of the author's imagination or used in a fictitious manner. Any resemblance to actual persons, living or dead, or actual events is purely coincidental.

For Joseph, Ned, Michael and Vera

PROLOGUE

2015

How easy it would be to step forth, let go, and shatter their idyll. To come crashing down to earth, right there in the middle of them all. To bring an abrupt end to the hustle and bustle, to dash my brains out on the pavement and ruin their day. This is my latest fantasy: taking my own life.

I peer out the large bay window in the living-room of my sixth-floor apartment and imagine climbing out onto the sill; standing there, savouring the moment, taking flight and landing, face first, onto the concrete below. It would be violent and shocking, a spectacle not to be missed. Those unfortunate enough to be in the blast radius would be picking bits of me out of their hair for days. The bystanders and onlookers would merely be traumatised, require counselling, a few days off work. My name would be enshrined in history. I would go down in folklore: the guy who went splat outside the Milky Moo milkshake shop on a balmy Tuesday in June. That's why I'll never do it. I couldn't bear the fuss.

I do want to die, though. I want this to end. I haven't tried to kill myself yet, but it's all I think about. It's my obsession and, ironically, the only thing keeping me going. There are a couple of problems though. Problem number one: the methodology. I don't know how to go about it. It sounds simple: take a scissors to your wrists, jump off a building, neck a load of pills; pain and suffering over. What if I mess it up, though? What if I don't cut deep enough, or cut too deep? What if I smash my body to pieces but somehow survive the hundred-foot drop to the ground, or swallow enough pills to turn my insides to mush but not enough to switch the lights out? If I get it wrong I might not get another go; life in a wheelchair or a hospital bed the reward for my haplessness. And if I fail, people will know what I've done. I'll be the suicide guy. Aidan Collins, your man who jumped out the window and broke nine vertebrae in his back, half his pelvis and four of his toes, and now can't go to the toilet unaided. That eejit. A failure at life, a failure at death.

I have failed in life, of that there can be no dispute. I am thirty years old, unemployed and single. I have no qualifications and no skills. I excel at nothing. I have no friends, no social life and no hobbies to speak of. I am overweight, with bad skin and worse hair. I've never had sex. I suffer panic attacks every time I go outside, do nothing but watch television from morning till night, and my cat left me to live with one of the neighbours. I'm also an alcoholic. Someone like me can't be trusted with their own death. Not that it matters, because I'm too scared to do it anyway. Problem number two: the thought of inflicting harm upon myself terrifies me. I don't like pain. So I'm left in limbo, too unhappy to live, too cowardly to do anything about it. The whole thing just gives me a headache, not one bad enough to kill me - more's the pity - but one which makes me understand why most people don't bother with suicide, no matter how unhappy they are.

If I were to do it, if I were less scared and I had to choose a method, I'd choose drowning. It's not overly violent and I could do it away from prying eyes. They'd have no way of knowing whether it was an accident or not, whether I'd been out for a late-night swim and lost my bearings, or willingly allowed myself to be submerged by water until I could no longer breathe. There'd be no collateral damage, either. It'd probably be a hardy fisherman or a lone dog-walker who would discover me, rather than a child or some sensitive sort. It would still physically hurt, of that I have no doubt, but there'd be great peace of mind with it too, the knowledge that I'd be sinking to the bottom where I belong, my lungs slowly filling with water as I suffocate to death.

If I fulfilled my task successfully people would think it was suicide, whisper it among themselves, note how I was 'always a morose sort', how depression 'ran in the family', but they'd never come out and say it. They would never say, 'Oh yeah, Aidan Collins killed himself, jumped in the Suir one night and washed up a couple of days later.' Instead there'd be a question mark hanging over me, an air of mystery: did he or didn't he?

It makes me think I shouldn't do it locally. A beach - I'd like to do it at a beach; to be more precise, I'd like to do it in the sea. I'd like to just walk into the sea and keep walking and walking until my feet no longer touched the ground, until I was surrounded by water and sky, until I slowly went under, to the seabed, my deathbed. If I do it at the beach, it would be obvious I'd gone in on purpose. No one falls into the sea, unless it's from a boat. They'd know. However, if I put on a pair of swimming togs I could swing the odds back towards accidental death and have them guessing again, retrieving that air of mystery I lost when I started wading into the water. I plan on having a good few drinks beforehand, though, and who goes swimming at night in their togs after drinking a couple of litres of vodka? That would all come up in the coroner's report: 'his blood levels showed high toxicity of alcohol'. There's so much to consider.

PART ONE

2006

1

After sitting my Leaving Cert and accumulating enough points to go to any college in the country, I spent the next three years playing video games, watching films and sleeping till the early afternoon. I rarely left the house. Once a week I went to the post office to collect my Jobseeker's Allowance, and once a month I went into town to sign on. I lived rent-free, my meals were cooked for me, my room tidied, bed made, clothes washed and bills paid. If, on my last day of school, someone had told me this was what I had to look forward to, I would have been entirely satisfied.

With no place to be on any given day I kept social interaction to a minimum, shutting myself in, sinking deeper and deeper into my own little world. There was no one to bother me. I could stay right where I was for as long as I wanted. If I'd been drinking in those days it might have been different, I might have been encouraged to venture outdoors, but alcohol didn't interest me at that time; I didn't see the point of it. I'd had my first drink on the evening of my eighteenth birthday, my father had insisted.

We rarely did anything together, but he made such a big deal of it, explaining how his first legal pint had been bought by his father and how important it was to maintain the tradition. I went along with it out of politeness. I sat in *The Fiddler's Elbow* alongside half a dozen regulars and allowed him his moment; *his* moment, not mine. He bought me a Guinness and I brought it to my lips as they all watched, took a slug and hid my displeasure as best I could. It was rotten. I didn't like it, it was a real struggle to finish it. I'd hoped that would be the end of it, but one of his friends insisted that he buy me one too.

The second one wasn't as bad. I felt a little tipsy, but those men were terrible company, the worst kind of people: pub bores. They shouted rather than spoke, their conversational skills in keeping with men who'd spent their entire lives sat in those same seats, talking about the same things, without anyone to tell them how boring they were. After the second pint I decided I'd had enough; I wanted to get back to my room, maybe watch a film. But my father was in his stride now, was all excited at being out and swelling with pride as he introduced me to the owner, to the couple who'd come in for a quiet one, to anyone who'd listen.

I should have humoured him a little longer. It wasn't often I gave him reason to be proud. I'd grown tired of the charade, though, of middle-aged men cracking unfunny jokes, recounting their escapades with my father when they were younger. I'd given him what he wanted: a chance to show off in front of his pals, an opportunity to parade me around, the next great Collins to come off the production line.

"I'll head off home now, Dad," I said, while one his friends bought another round.

He wheeled round in his seat, eyes disbelieving, already half-drunk.

"What? Sure we're only after getting here! Is it money you're worried about? I'm buying for the night."

"Nah, Dad. I've just had enough."

A flash of anger crossed his face, and for a moment I thought he was finally going to give me the dressing-down I'd long since deserved, right here in front of everyone; but he just shrugged in resignation and returned to his drink.

"Sorry, Dad," I said, rising from my seat, saluting the others and heading out into the night, knowing this wouldn't affect our relationship as we didn't have one. When I got home I watched a film, listened to some music and went to bed. And the following morning life returned to normal. I was eighteen, legally allowed to drink, but had no inclination to do so whatsoever.

That was my last encounter with alcohol until the summer of 2006, when, at the age of twenty-one I found out why everyone was so interested in going to pubs and nightclubs, getting shit-faced and falling home in the early hours. Yet even that discovery was manufactured on my behalf. Left to my own devices, I might never have developed a taste for the drink and recognised its ability to obscure pain. It was all my mother's doing. She was the one who introduced me to Dan, and it was he who introduced me to everything else.

2

TECHNICALLY SPEAKING, I'D ALREADY BEEN introduced to Dan. He was my cousin, the son of my mother's brother, Uncle Bobby. We didn't really know one another. They lived in Galway, the other side of the country, far enough away that we only crossed paths at family get-togethers and occasional weekends away. Dan was a few months older than me, but in terms of life experience we were worlds apart. Upon finishing his Leaving Cert he'd immediately gone travelling, backpacking across Europe and Asia, his adventures funded by the part-time job he'd held since the age of fifteen.

I'd received an email from him while he was away, a rambling missive about life in the monasteries of India; accompanied by pictures of him with the local farmers, impoverished children and a German girl called Birgitte. Although well meant, that email served only to remind me of the things I could and should have been doing. It instilled in me a hostility towards my cousin, a deep-seated bitterness born of jealousy and self-loathing. I wanted to be like Dan and all the rest of them, I always had, but I didn't know what to do, couldn't negotiate the world like they could. So instead I stayed in my room, where it was safe.

Once he returned from his travels, bronzed and urbane, Dan used the 400-odd points he'd got in his Leaving Cert to enrol in a primary teaching course at Dublin City University. Having seen the world and broadened his horizons, he had begun his journey to what would surely be a rich and fulfilling career. If I'd had a larger extended family, dozens of cousins, a flock in which to conceal myself, Dan's achievements wouldn't have been so galling. There were really only the two of us, and so everything he did brought my inertia into greater focus. It got to the point where the very mention of his name enraged me. He was my nemesis and I would have given anything to see him fail, to hear he'd dropped out of college and was a homeless rent boy selling himself on the streets of Galway. He wasn't, though, he was thriving, making a show of me.

In the summer of his second year in college, Dan brought his good self to the south east of Ireland, to a school in Waterford city, some thirty miles from our family home in rural Kilkenny. Upon hearing the news I realised I'd most likely have to see him at some time over the summer; he'd probably call to the house, all radiant and worthy, and sit beside me on the couch so that everyone could compare us: the success and the failure, both ends of the spectrum. The reality was far worse than an occasional visit. My mother was a stoic woman, a solid, unwavering presence. She wasn't one for excitement. But when it was mooted that Dan might come and stay with us during that summer of 2006, she developed a spring in her step.

"How would you like a lodger for a few months, Aidan?" she asked one afternoon, trying to act casual. My first reaction was to panic. Anything which might change my circumstances and tamper with my small, self-contained existence was cause for concern.

"A lodger?"

"Yes. Just for the summer."

"Why do we need a lodger? Are we broke?"

"No, we're not broke," she laughed.

I was glad someone found it funny.

"We have that spare room so we may as well use it," she continued.

"Okay, Mam," I said, shakily taking a sip of my tea, starting to palpitate, my heart racing as a whirlwind of possibilities circled through my mind. What if it was a woman, an attractive woman? The spare room was right beside mine, what if we bumped into one another on the landing? Suppose I had to take a shit in the bathroom and she went in after me? A man might be worse, though, he might try to befriend me, come into my room and start asking me questions.

"Dan is coming to stay with us, your cousin Dan. Isn't that fantastic?"

My heart rate slowed and the lightness in my head began to evaporate. I exhaled in relief. I knew Dan. He was a known quantity, but maybe that was worse. He'd have expectations of me. They all would. I'd have to show him round, keep him entertained, make sure his stay was pleasurable. This was selfish of them, foisting someone on me like that. All they saw was the glamour and excitement Dan's presence would bring; they didn't see the chaos, the potential dangers.

"When is he coming?" I asked, resigned to my fate, already planning ways to limit the damage.

"So you're okay with it, then?"

I shrugged my shoulders.

"Wonderful. I'll ring Bobby now."

Two days later I sat nervously on the couch awaiting Dan's arrival. It wouldn't have been too bad if my sister Sally had been here, the onus wouldn't have been solely on me. But she'd moved to London, a success story in her own right. Dad was out somewhere, using any excuse to avoid Bobby. They didn't get on. It was just me and my mother; her checking the drive every time a car came down our road, me feeling sick, angry and depressed.

"They're here! They're here, Aidan. Sit up now."

She opened the door to greet them: Uncle Bobby, Aunt Stephanie and, of course, my cousin Dan. There was the usual fawning and hugging, high-pitched greetings and awkward handshakes, and before I knew it Dan was on the couch beside me, with Bobby across from us in one of the armchairs, while the two women made the tea.

"How's Aidan?" asked Bobby, managing to make this most innocuous question sound like a threat.

I knew what was coming. My uncle was a forthright man, a member of the Defence Forces, an imposing moustachioed presence. He saw the world in black and white, and my work status and living arrangements were an affront to his sensibilities.

"I'm all right."

"What are you doing with yourself these days?"

"Still looking for work," I said meekly.

"You're looking a long time now, Aidan."

"Yeah."

He shook his head despairingly, muttering under his breath.

"Would you consider joining the army?"

He asked me this every time we met, had done so since I was nine years old.

"Maybe."

"A fantastic career, you get to see the world and serve your country, no previous experience required. It's high time another member of the family joined up."

This was a barb at Dan, who was on his phone and not even listening. I could have joined the army. The thought of pleasing Bobby and gaining his respect was motivation enough. I would instantly become a man, an army man, and he and I would spend all family occasions sneering at all the other men, the limp-wristed wastrels with their dull, non-life-threatening professions. Dan could circumnavigate the world ten times over, earn five doctorates and become president of the universe, but Bobby would still prefer me because I was an army man.

The only problem was that the prospect of joining the army made me nauseous: all that shouting and prancing about in uniforms, the machismo, brotherhood and patriotism. It was a farce. Plus, I hated Bobby. He was a dullard, a boorish cretin.

"Jilly might join in a few years," I suggested, referring to Dan's fourteen-year-old sister, a young madam with impossibly delicate tastes and as unlikely a candidate for life in the armed forces as you could possibly get.

Dan chuckled quietly to himself, whether at me or something on his phone I couldn't tell.

Bobby gave me a flinty stare, scrutinising me.

I stared straight ahead, saying nothing.

The tension was broken by the return of my mother and Stephanie. They'd finalised Dan's room and it was time for the big reveal. We all trooped up the stairs to take a look, Dan ushered to the front of the queue by my almost rabid mother. It was nice, tasteful and homely. They'd done a good job, had brought a few of Dan's personal effects: a rugby jersey hanging in the wardrobe, his hurling helmet, a picture of him and our grandmother, books, CDs and a framed poster of Che Guevara. They'd also got him cards wishing him well in his new job, and an array of treats: chocolate, minerals, crisps, biscuits. The only thing missing was a cake.

"Aw, you guys," he said, enveloping them both in a hug, his strong forearms wrapped around their necks.

Dan crossed the threshold into his new abode and took a look out the window.

"Perfect. I couldn't have asked for more. Thanks, Aunt Avril, honestly."

His cloying sincerity and easy charm just heightened my sense of inadequacy. If the roles were reversed and I was staying with the Hennesseys in Galway, I'd have mumbled my gratitude and sat nervously on the bed until everyone stopped looking at me. Dan, though, was entirely comfortable in the spotlight, entirely comfortable in general. He was streaking into adulthood at full speed, while I pottered round in a wretched netherworld.

Later, after an uncomfortable dinner in which Dan's career prospects were dissected in full and mine repeatedly alluded to by the wilful Bobby, he and Stephanie announced it was time they were getting back; they had a three-hour drive ahead of them. In between the protracted goodbyes and final round of hugs I managed to slip off, silently extricating myself from the clamour and sneaking upstairs to the sanctity of my room. This was a statement on my behalf, one which said: 'Do your own thing, Dan, because I will be doing mine.' I knew my mother would be up the stairs after me, scolding me for my rudeness, but she'd got enough out of me for one day.

Yet when the knock came, it wasn't her. It was Dan.

"What are you up to, cuz?" he asked, smiling, awaiting permission to enter.

I cringed. I was playing my Xbox, sitting in my recliner, snacks on one side, drink on the other.

"Ah, *Halo 2*!" he said, entering the room and taking a seat on the footstool I sometimes employed as an auxiliary table. "One of the lads in college has this but I never got a proper game of it. Do you have a second controller?"

I was taken aback. Dan had travelled the world, had slept under the stars in Thailand, befriended street urchins in India, seduced German backpackers and God knows what else. He'd spent the last two years living in Dublin, sharing a house with five other students, learning about life, growing, maturing. What interest could he have in a video game about interstellar warfare? Plenty, it would appear.

I handed him the second controller and waited for him to pick his character.

"I'll go with the red guy," he said, pulling the footstool closer to the screen. His earnestness was almost endearing.

It quickly emerged that Dan was not skilled in the art of video games, nor in the art of war. He had no regard for his own safety and constantly charged ahead, Rambo-style. This led to repeated deaths and a 'game over' screen. Eager to ensure that his visit to my room was enjoyable, I risked life and limb to protect him, taking heavy fire in the process. "Cheers, Aidan," he said, immediately rushing forward and succumbing to another hail of bullets. With anyone else I would have made my displeasure known, but I wanted this to go well. In spite of myself, I was having a good time. Eventually, after I'd rescued him at least a dozen times, the penny dropped. Dan hung back, picked his moments, used cover and followed my lead. Within half an hour we were working in perfect tandem, flanking the enemy, aiding and assisting one another - he even rescued me at one point.

After another half an hour we'd completed the level, annihilating the boss with a clinical display of measured aggression. We shared a high-five and moved straight on to the next level. I opened the big box of Maltesers I'd been saving for later and we dipped in and out of them as we played. Our success continued; we ploughed through the game's most difficult sections, decimating everything in our path. What a team we made. It was the most fun I'd had in months, but after finishing three levels and playing for more than two hours, sanity returned.

"Shit, man, I'd better get to bed. New job in the morning," said Dan as I refilled his glass with Coke.

"Oh, yeah. Okay," I replied.

"We'll continue this tomorrow night?"

"Yeah, sounds good."

"Night, cuz."

"Night, Dan."

I continued playing for a while after he'd gone, but it wasn't the same. I only wanted to play with Dan now. Perhaps when we'd finished *Halo 2* we could start on my other games. I had loads, but it was best to wait until we'd completed *Halo 2* before mentioning anything else. There was no point in getting ahead of myself.

3

THE NEXT EVENING AT DINNER I watched Dan slowly work his way through the shepherd's pie, wondering if he wanted to play straight away or if he'd prefer to wait a while. He hadn't mentioned it when he came in, it had been all about his new job, the kids, the other members of staff and the commute.

"Thanks, Avril, that was delicious," he said, rising from his seat and bringing his plate out to the kitchen.

I followed suit, mumbling my thanks and joining Dan at the sink.

"So, what do you do for fun of an evening round here?" he asked, looking out the window doubtfully.

The answer was that I played my Xbox. Dan didn't want to hear that, though; he'd moved on. He wanted to know where the young people of the area hung out, where he might go for a drink, meet girls and live a little. I didn't know the answer to those questions.

"There's a pub down the road," I said.

"Ah, we can't be drinking on a Monday night, Aidan, come on now."

Relieved, I racked my brain for other ideas. If only I could remember what my classmates in school used to do every night while I sat at home. I knew they went somewhere: a lake, or a field. They used to always hang out.

"There's a chipper, and a shop," I said.

Dan rinsed off his plate, put it in the draining rack and took me by the shoulder.

"Come on," he said, "let's just get out of here and see where we end up."

We announced our departure to my mother, whose look of smug satisfaction suggested that this had been the plan all along, and within seconds we were in Dan's car, a 1994 red Mondeo. I was starting to palpitate; it had all happened so fast. I wasn't used to unplanned trips outside, flights of fancy to lands unknown. He started up the engine, saluted my mother and we were away, out of the driveway on to the little country lane - fields and farms on one side, the detached homes of the middle classes on the other. Soon we were into the village, passing the church, the primary school and the closed butcher's shop before coming to the hub of all life in Cruinníth: The Tree.

The Tree was a hulking eighty-foot oak which, according to local historians, was at least a thousand years old. Those same historians believed the village had formed around this tree, that it served as a meeting point before becoming a hub for the area's fledgling communities. It now resided upon an impeccably manicured square of grass, accompanied by a handful of benches, the official village sign, a post box, a sculpture of a local man who had fought in the 1916 Easter Rising, and a fading map detailing amenities which no longer existed. If you were to take a seat on one of those benches you could survey the entirety of life in Cruinníth; the local shop on one side, the two pubs, the chipper, and the road which had to be navigated if you wished to enter or (more likely) leave our bypassed village.

There had been some great moments at The Tree, though. It was where we had all gathered when the Tour de France came through Cruinníth in 1998, where Barry Everett had been hoisted onto the shoulders of the drunken masses when the junior hurling team won the county final in 1986, and where a witch by the name of Angelica Montrose was allegedly beaten to death by a gang of bearded men sometime in the sixteenth century. It had sheltered sleeping drunks, teenage fornicators, and weary wanderers, been pissed on, climbed up, and trimmed back; but still it remained, resolute and unmoved, a symbol of our united strength. Tonight it stood alone, the village around it deathly quiet, devoid of activity and life.

"Not much doing here," Dan said, slowing down to cruising speed as he peered out the window.

I blanched at his tone, suddenly protective of Cruinníth, a place I'd yearned to escape for as long as I could remember.

"Do ye have a hurling pitch? Ye must have a hurling pitch?"

"Course we do," I replied haughtily, "just turn left up there and carry on for about half a mile."

And so it was that I found myself standing in goal, just Dan's spare hurley for protection, while he practised his free-taking, his penalties and his finishing from in close. I didn't do sports, had spent a lifetime avoiding them, yet here I was in one of the most specialist, dangerous sporting roles of them all: hurling goalie. Dan was happily honing his skills, pointing frees from the halfway line and beyond, moving in close to send the occasional missile right at me, oblivious to my discomfort. I noticed him tutting his disapproval when I threw the ball back instead of pucking it out, but, that aside, it felt like we were bonding again.

"Try and save this one," he called, standing on the twenty-metre line and firing an Exocet right down my throat.

I ducked just in time, the *sliotar* barely missing my head as it flew into the net. That didn't feel very fair. I'd spent much of the previous evening chaperoning this Galway prick through *Halo* 2 and now he was trying to decapitate me. I was about to voice my displeasure, maybe even stage a sit-down protest, when I saw why my cousin had adopted this sudden aggressive streak. There were two girls watching on the sidelines; young wans, maybe seventeen or eighteen. I thought I recognised one of them as Declan Fenlon's younger sister, the other I'd never seen before. Why they were hanging round the GAA pitch on a Monday night I didn't know, but their presence was all the motivation Dan needed.

What had been a gentle knockabout between two cousins became Galway versus Kilkenny in the All-Ireland Final. Points weren't enough for him anymore, it was goals, goals and more goals. He stood on the twenty again, leathering the *sliotar* into the four corners of the net, waiting patiently for me to retrieve it, throw it back out to him so he could repeat the process all over again. Meanwhile the two young wans watched on, no doubt impressed by Dan's form, by his tanned legs, toned arms, wide shoulders, unerring accuracy. The useless slug in goal didn't merit a second glance. He was a bit-part player in this scene, an extra in *The Dan Show*.

After a while he went back to scoring points, moving further and further out the field. A sixty-five sailed over the crossbar and the fence behind. Having retrieved it, I returned to see Dan in conversation with the girls. He had the hurley across his shoulders, his arms draped over it, while he regaled them with a story about the Spanish Arch or some other Galway shite. I sat down in the goal, my back against one of the posts, wondering how I'd get home if Dan and the girls went off to wherever people went.

"Aidan, come over!"

Fuck's sake. I didn't want to 'come over', could think of nothing worse. Girls hated me, they found me repulsive. Because of that, I preferred not to be in their company.

"Aidan!"

I could hear the girls laughing. I'm sure they found the whole notion of me hilarious. Embittered, I got up and began walking towards them, eager to get it over with, wishing more than anything they'd disappear and we could just drive back home. As I got closer, I could make them out more clearly. One of them was definitely Declan's sister, she was pale and blonde, all elbows and angles, head held high, coquettish, aggressive. The other one was more demure, plump and short, with curly hair and a strong, almost rugged, jaw. Everything about the situation depressed me.

"This is Breffni and Gail," announced Dan.

I said nothing. Just stopped a few feet away from them and took to staring at the ground.

"And this is my cousin, Aidan," he said on my behalf, to the girls' amusement.

"We were thinking about going for a drive. The girls know a few nice spots, don't ye?"

The blonde girl nodded in agreement. Her friend looked as unenthusiastic as I felt. I didn't want to go for a drive, not this evening, not with a cousin I hardly knew and two complete strangers. I wanted to go home, to my room, to watch telly or play a game. But I already knew that wasn't an option. I was going for a drive, even if it meant Dan frog-marching me to the car and bundling me in the boot.

As we traipsed back to the car, Dan sidled up to me and whispered, "You get in the back with your wan," then continued on his way. I assumed, correctly, that he was referring to the less attractive of the pair and did as I was told, sitting as close to the door as possible while my back seat companion did the same. It struck me that she and I had something in common; we were both used to being overlooked, relegated to the margins, seen as a triviality, someone not worth bothering with. Maybe that was presumptuous on my part, she wasn't as unattractive as I was, probably had a boyfriend once, or had at least kissed someone at some point in her life.

I had never had a girlfriend, and the closest I'd come to kissing someone was when one of my sister's friends suggested they practise on me to hone their technique - a suggestion which, to my eternal regret, was instantly shot down by my sister.

Up top, Dan and the blonde were getting along famously. She was mocking his accent, repeating everything he said in an exaggerated fashion, making him out to be a big culchie - ironic, considering she was from Cruinníth. He was pretending to be offended, acting all hurt and upset, proposing we just drop the girls off and head home. This sounded great to me, but I knew he was having her on. She was taken aback, momentarily uncertain, she apologised, said she hadn't meant it and became almost tearful. Dan laughed, called her gullible, and received a dig on the thigh for his transgression.

I'd seen encounters like this before and knew enough to understand this meant they liked one another. Instead of being nice, saying sweet things and revealing their true thoughts, they would do the opposite; engage in spiteful, critical conversation, chide and cajole the other, more like bickering siblings than potential partners. They would slag one another, maybe even get physical; punch, poke and pinch each other, then one of them would grow subservient, accede, show a softer side and the mood would shift, becoming more playful, warm and tender. That was how it went.

Dan and his soon-to-be were now at the 'mocking one another' stage. She was cackling hysterically at his little GAA shorts and the hairy legs beneath, and he was denouncing her nose-ring, saying she looked like a washed-up punk rocker. Each insult was met with a slap, a grab or a tickle, one tedious scuffle almost caused us to swerve off the road. Breathless, the blonde girl proposed we pull in at Turk's Pass, a little lay-by where lorry drivers stopped to get something from the chip van. It overlooked Cruinníth and the neighbouring villages of Besborough and Breanor.

No sooner had we pulled in when Dan stretched out in his seat and suggested, in the nicest possible way, that myself and the other girl should get out and take a walk around. We did as we were told. She immediately walked off in the opposite direction, as if to say, 'Don't be getting any ideas, boy'. I had no ideas. I wasn't like Dan, I had some decorum and knew how to keep my distance.

I sat on one of the benches and stared at the horizon. It was dusk. A light fog hung over the smattering of houses, the fields, the farms, the trees and the river Nore. We were into June now, summer was upon us and the evenings were becoming longer and warmer. It felt like the start of the school holidays: that time when anything seems possible, when three months of freedom stretched out before you like unexplored terrain. Well, that was how I imagined it felt. For me, it had always been a time of respite and relief, an opportunity to recover from the stresses of my life in school.

This meant long, lazy days spent in bed, sleeping well into the afternoon, it meant avoiding the outdoors and limiting human interaction. As the summer progressed, I nervously counted down the days till I had to return to St. Mark's and suffer the resumption of my stifling anxiety, my insomnia and compulsions, the paranoia, fear and dread. The school-work didn't bother me all that much, it was the people, the other students, the teachers, the boys in my class, the boys in the classes above me, below me, the girls from the school down the road, the woman in the shop, the bus driver, the headmaster.

The shouting, laughing, talking, squealing, whispering and sniggering meant I was constantly on edge, always mindful, always watchful. I knew they weren't all talking about me, all laughing at me, but some of them were. Those who looked closely would have seen how pitiful I was, how abhorrent. They would have seen an awkward shambling mess of a boy with dark greasy hair, shifty eyes, a gormless expression and ill-fitting clothes. They would have smelled his stench, heard his stupid voice and known exactly what he was: an imposter. A waste of space. Someone who didn't deserve to be on this earth, whose presence was an affront to the human race.

Every morning I awoke tense, uneasy, at the thought of having to walk through corridors full of people, sit in classrooms with my peers, make myself invisible at break times, and do everything in my power to go unnoticed until such time as I could step off the bus and hurry home to safety. The mental torture was bad enough, but it also manifested itself in physical ways. I would sweat a lot, by noon my armpits were sopping. I'd go into the toilets, find a stall and dry them with paper, but it would only be a temporary reprieve. I'd be soaked again by lunchtime.

I tried every antiperspirant on the market to no avail, and the more I sweated the more self-conscious I became. I was paranoid about having a bad odour, convinced that my classmates were laughing at me behind my back. If I ended up having to sit near the front in class my sweating would get even worse, dripping down my back so that my shirt stuck to me. Each class became an ordeal, forty-five minutes I had to endure before I could race to the toilets and try to dry myself before the next one started.

I spent a lot of time in the toilets, another physical manifestations of my crippling anxiety requiring frequent trips to the lavatory. My stomach was in constant turmoil, leading to bouts of diarrhoea and violent vomiting. There were days when I'd spend entire afternoons sitting on the toilet in school, weeping in frustration, knowing they were already looking for me, wondering where the fuck Collins had got to this time. Rather than drag myself back into whatever class I was supposed to be in, I'd leave the building, sneaking out the side entrance, hoping no one saw me. Someone always did. Detention would be my reward, meaning more time spent in the place I least wanted to be.

I thought life would become easier when I left school. I thought once I was free of all those people, I would simply be free. I quickly discovered that, although I'd escaped them, I couldn't escape myself. They weren't the problem - I was. My anxiety, which had once been confined to the halls of St. Mark's CBS, was now a constant companion. It didn't exist within the school like I'd thought, it existed within me. It quickly infiltrated my home life, switching from the classroom to the place where I now spent the majority of my time, my bedroom. It followed me wherever I went. And I couldn't shake it.

The things I'd always taken solace in; my video games, my films, books and music, became at best temporary distractions. Sometimes they even made things worse, my inability to concentrate and relax making a ninety-minute film a trial of strength. Even so, this restricted existence was far easier than the alternative; going outside, interacting with other people, getting a job and having a normal, fulfilling life. That simply wasn't possible.

As I waited on the bench, resisting the temptation to turn round and see what was happening in the car, I asked myself if this was a normal evening's entertainment - hanging around at Turk's Pass while my cousin ravaged a girl he'd met less than a hour ago? If so, then the normal people were welcome to it. Some good had come out of it, though, my anxiety, the terror I'd felt at being whisked away from my comfort zone at a moment's notice, had begun to subside. During the hurling, where my focus had been on survival, it had disappeared completely, only to return with a vengeance during the drive here.

Right now the fresh air and solitude, the sense of enduring something and surviving unscathed, had calmed me. I heard a cough and glanced to my left. The other girl was sitting on the bench across from me, her head buried in her phone, no doubt sending angry texts to the blonde. She gave me a baleful stare and I returned my gaze to the horizon. I was blameless in this situation, there was no need to take it out on me.

After listening to giggles and yelps emanating from the car for at least another half an hour, the doors opened and the two paramours emerged. Dan joined me on my bench, and the blonde sat alongside her friend on the other. My cousin wore a satisfied smirk, he looked ready to share the details of their coupling.

"Well, did you try your wan?" he asked, nodding in the direction of the other girl.

"Nah," I said, in the manner of someone who'd given it deep consideration but had ultimately decided to keep his powder dry.

"Shame, if she's anything like her friend…"

I nodded and continued staring down at the darkening vista. Dan chuckled to himself and shook his head in apparent admiration. I looked over at the girls, the blonde was trying to reason with her friend, explaining something, but the other girl didn't want to know. I got the feeling this would be our one and only double date.

We all got back in the car, me in the front this time, and drove back to the village. The girls were dropped off at The Tree and we continued on to my house. As soon as we stepped inside the door my mother was out to greet us, eager to know what we'd been up to. When Dan casually informed her that we'd been out hurling she seemed puzzled, a bit disappointed, but she perked up when he added that we'd also been for a drive and made some new friends. As we mounted the stairs and made for our respective rooms, I thought I saw her wink in my cousin's direction. I was glad things were working out for her, I really was.

4

I SPENT MUCH OF THE following day in a state of near-panic, what was Dan going to suggest we do next? Would he be offended if I said I didn't want to join him on another of his drives? What if he brought those girls here, and my mother thought the curly-haired one was my new girlfriend? But my greatest fear was that Dan no longer liked me, that he'd seen me for what I truly was and had no more use for me. Because, despite my reservations, his arrival had cheered me up. I liked being around him and was keen to spend more time with him.

When he came in from work, he was the same as ever. We sat down for dinner, made small talk and then went up to my room. There was no talk of the girls, no suggestion we go for a drive or for a few pucks of a *sliotar*. The previous evening's events seemed already forgotten. I was still on tenterhooks though, nervously sat in my gaming chair while he looked around my room in awe.

"Fucking hell, Aidan, where did you get all this stuff? How many DVDs do you have? You could nearly open up your own shop."

I had almost two thousand DVDs, although a lot of those were replacements for old VHS tapes.

"Have you seen *all* of these?" Dan asked, as if such an achievement was unimaginable.

"Yeah. Some of them more than once."

"Which is your favourite? I mean, your favourite of all time?"

There were two possible answers to this question. I could give him the more palatable response and say *Platoon*, or I could tell him the truth.

"Well, I really like Asian cinema and French stuff," I said, checking to make sure he didn't think that was weird. He seemed to be intrigued so I continued, keeping my head down so he wouldn't see my face while I talked.

"And although I love a lot of Japanese horror, *Ringu, Uzumaki, Audition,* and Michael Haneke's *Funny Games*; my all-time favourite is *Battle Royale*."

I looked up, awaiting his reaction.

"*Battle Royale*. What's it about?"

"There's a group of school-kids. They get brought to a remote island and instructed to fight to the death. They're each given a weapon, rations, and a map of the island. If they refuse to participate, they're killed by the government."

"And that's it?" he asked, bemused.

"Yeah."

"Will we watch it?" Dan asked, a grin on his face.

"Okay," I replied, matching his grin. I'd seen the film more than twenty times, but that didn't matter.

"Just let me get the chair from the other room," he said, hurrying off.

He returned, breathless, with a bean-bag, cushions and some of the treats my mother and aunt had got for his new room. This was almost as good as playing *Halo* 2 together, and if he liked *Battle Royale* I could slowly introduce him to the rest of my favourites. We could get through a sizeable chunk of my collection over three months.

"This is subtitled, right?" he asked as I inserted the disc.

"Yeah."

"Okay. It's just . . . I haven't seen many subtitled films."

He seemed hesitant, almost bashful.

"There's nothing to it, you just read the words at the bottom of the screen," I said.

"Grand," he replied, popping open a tube of Pringles.

The film started and we lapsed into silence. I was nervous, and spent much of the first ten minutes trying to gauge Dan's reaction, hoping he'd stay with it long enough for the killing to begin. When it did, when Kitano killed Fujiyoshi by throwing a knife into her forehead, I relaxed. Murmuring his satisfaction, Dan settled back into the beanbag. He was on board. I knew he'd love it.

About halfway through, we paused for a toilet break.

"You should come out with us in Dublin some weekend," Dan said as we readied ourselves for the second half. "You'd get on well with my friends. You're an interesting guy, Aidan."

His words created a strange sensation in my stomach: a lightness, an airiness. *I was interesting. I'd get on well with Dan's friends*. For a moment I was someone else, a person who accepted invitations, who went on nights out in Dublin, met new people and thought nothing of it. Then reality hit: I hadn't been out of this village in three years, had barely even left the house. I'd almost had a meltdown when we'd driven a couple of miles to the hurling pitch. A trip to the capital would render me catatonic, yet I still wanted to imagine I could be this other person, this person that Dan thought I was.

"Yeah, that sounds good," I said softly, pressing play on the remote and bringing the conversation to an end.

Pushing Dan's suggestion to one side, burying his declaration that I was 'interesting' somewhere deep in my soul, I returned to the film, hoping to experience it vicariously through my rapt cousin. It was no use, he'd ruined it. Now all I could think of was how to extricate myself from his invitation, and I knew that as soon as I wriggled out of one there'd be another, and another, until this budding bromance ended up like all my other friendships: dead in the water. The prospect upset me so much I fell into despair, no longer taking pleasure from Dan's little proclamations of delight as the film geared up for its grand finale. Why couldn't we just watch films and play games every evening? Why was everyone so obsessed with going out and doing things?

"Brilliant," Dan announced as the final credits rolled. "Just brilliant."

I smiled in recognition, but my heart was no longer in it. Our friendship was doomed. He started talking about the film, theorising and hypothesising, but I was gone now. I'd been reminded of who I was: a pathetic, hopeless loser who panicked about everything, had never kissed a girl, never worked a day in his life and couldn't live without his mammy and daddy. While every other twenty-one-year-old in the country was out living their life I was stuck here in my room, my only achievements the closing credits of whatever game I was playing on the Xbox. The sooner Dan realised this, the sooner he left me alone and did his own thing, the better it would be for all concerned.

Any hope that the film had made him forget his earlier suggestion was dashed when he began detailing plans for a night which had already acquired a date, a venue and a list of invitees. There was talk of bars and nightclubs, gigs, drinks, women, sessions, a spare room, a hostel, a couch for me to sleep on. Names rolled out of his mouth, people, places, streets, restaurants, pubs. I nodded dumbly while he continued to talk, wanting more than anything, for him to leave so I could draw the curtains, get into bed and put on my headphones and listen to some Joy Division, Slipknot maybe even Nine Inch Nails.

Given time to think, I could devise a strategy to bring this relationship to an amicable end. I could tell Dan I'd contracted a highly contagious disease and had to be put in quarantine. He would no longer be allowed into my room and I would not be allowed to leave it. This would ensure we remained friends and immediately end all talk of excursions. It would also finish our gaming and film nights, but I would just have to live with that. The most important thing was we didn't fall out.

The tone in Dan's voice had changed, he was asking me a question. Reluctantly, I tuned back in.

"What do you reckon?"

"Yeah," I said reflexively.

"Deadly. I'll find out who's around and what the situation is with somewhere to stay. I'll let you know tomorrow."

"Okay."

Then he was gone, his head full of plans and excitement. I shut the door behind him, locking it, and drew the curtains. Throwing off my clothes, I crawled into bed, realising too late that I'd forgotten to bring my Walkman. It didn't matter. I was going to go sleep now and I wouldn't wake for quite some time.

5

SATURDAY WEEK, IN ELEVEN DAYS' time: that was when we were going. We were getting up early in the morning, having breakfast and then driving up to Dublin, aiming to arrive before noon. Dan had a friend who lived in Garristown. We'd stay with him, Dan in the spare room and me on the couch, although according to Dan, there was really no telling where we'd end up. Once we'd settled in there we'd go for a few afternoon pints in one of the local pubs before returning to the house for food, a few cans and a bit of a sprucing up.

Then it was a bus into town to meet the others. There would be at least ten of them, hopefully more, hopefully double that. I absorbed this information as if it were my last rites. There was no way I could go. And yet I yearned for it, wished more than anything there was a way I could banish my fears and stride confidently into this brave new world. But just thinking about it moved me to tears.

Each time Dan launched into one of his spiels about the wonders which awaited us I felt a chill down my spine, a lump form in my throat and a weight gather on my chest. My breathing faltered, I became dizzy and had to quickly excuse myself as I rushed to the bathroom. There I'd sit on the toilet, not knowing if I was going to puke, piss or shit, until eventually my breathing slowed, the world stopped spinning and I was able to rejoin my cousin. If he continued where he'd left off I'd just tune him out, nodding when it seemed appropriate, replying in the affirmative whenever I thought he'd asked a question.

As the day drew nearer and our plans began to solidify I became mired in misery, spending entire days in bed, tearful and feverish, rising only when I knew Dan was on the way home. I would join him for another evening of gaming and films, putting on a brave face until he retired for the night and I could return to my bed. The weekend before we were due to go, he went home to Galway to see his family. This allowed me a little respite, an opportunity to take stock of the situation.

I thought about going to my mother and telling her the whole Dan thing wasn't working out, that she should call up his parents and inform them that he wasn't welcome back. I could tell her about the young wans he'd brought off in the car, make out he was some kind of pervert, a sexual deviant who was leading me astray. It'd create a bit of tension within the family for a while and Dan would hate me for it, but it'd get me out of this predicament. I couldn't blacken his name like that, though, it wouldn't be fair. Besides, my mother would never believe me; Dan was second only to the Lord Jesus in her eyes, with the Pope a close third.

I thought about waiting till the night before and feigning illness, I even practised putting my fingers down my throat and making retching noises. I devised a story where I got robbed on the way back from the post office, a hooded gang grabbing my wallet and shoving me to the ground; the cuts on my cheek, carefully administered in the back-yard, adding extra veracity. I considered saying I'd lost all my money, mislaid it, and had no way of affording an expensive night out in the capital. But he'd just lend me the money and tell me I could pay it back whenever I had it.

I thought about hiding in our shed for two days until it was too late to go to Dublin. I thought about slashing the tyres on Dan's car and then calling both Bus Éireann and Irish Rail and telling them there was a bomb on all their Saturday services from Kilkenny. My last idea was to drug Dan and lock him in his room, or drug myself and lock me in my room, or drug both of us and lock every door in the house. I didn't know what drugs did what, though, and besides, Dan's room had no lock on it.

In the end I had to accept that I had but two choices, and neither was any use to me. I either had to go or not. With a week left, in a sudden act of Saturday night bravery, I decided I was going. I puffed myself up in the front of the mirror, banished all negative thoughts from my mind and declared a new era in the life of Aidan Collins. From here on in things were going to be different. I was going to be an active member of society. I was going to emulate Dan, make my parents proud, and talk to and kiss as many girls as I could. But first I needed a little assistance.

Dan loved drinking. Every story he told began and ended with booze: the time he and the lads stole a fishing boat and went for a midnight sail, the time they Sellotaped a mate to a bed and carried him on to the roof of the house, a 5-km charity race they all did in women's underwear, a bonfire, a mystery tour, a lad's holiday, a stag do, Amsterdam and so on. Then there were the conquests. I showed no reaction when he told me about all the women he'd been with, but inside I burned with jealousy. How could one person be so prolific and so flippant about it? It didn't seem fair.

Yet, to his credit, Dan seemed keen to involve me in his lady-killing adventures, peppering his anecdotes with promises to introduce me to girls he knew, girls who 'weren't shy about coming forward', as he put it. That was what tipped me over the edge: the women. If I could just have a conversation with a girl, a successful chat which didn't end with her walking away in disgust, I'd be happy. That would be my starting point, from there I could work on becoming intimate with someone, maybe even a relationship.

But it would have to start with alcohol, that much was clear. If it was as transformative as Dan made out I'd be a man reborn, a sweet-talking Lothario who made girls swoon with just a nod of his head. There would have to be a few trial runs, though, I couldn't leave it to chance on the night. I had to get drunk before we went, properly drunk. I considered raiding my father's drinks' press and sampling some of the spirits he kept stored in the cabinet beside his armchair. But that stuff was for seasoned drinkers, oul' lads. Instead I went to the local shop and assessed the moderate fare in its off-licence.

It felt empowering just standing there, perusing the gaudy coloured cans and bottles like any other young lad on a Saturday evening. I was part of things now. If people saw me they'd think I was getting a six-pack before going into town, or preparing for a night in with the lads, watching the football, the boxing or some other sporting occasion; just one of the lads, one of the normal lads. After some deliberation I went for four cans of weak American beer. It was a brand I knew, one which regularly featured in advertisements on the television. It would be safer than some of the others. Hurrying home, I readied myself for a night of decadence.

Throwing on some Bowie, I opened the first can and took a slug. It made me question how such a thing could be so popular. Nevertheless I forged ahead, ignoring the acrid tang, finishing it within twenty minutes.

I didn't feel any different. Slightly concerned, I opened the second can and drank with gusto, resolute in my determination to experience whatever it was everyone raved about. Lo and behold, about halfway through the second can I began to feel something. *The Jean Genie* sounded different, more rocking, more up-tempo. I'd always loved that song, but had I ever really listened to it before? I turned it up and began to sing along, stamping my feet, nodding my head.

When that track was over I turned off Bowie and put on some Led Zeppelin. It was great. By the third can, I was on my feet, strutting round the bedroom like the showman I'd never realised I was. I was drunk. It was brilliant. That can was consigned to the bin and on I went, popping open the fourth, now well into my stride. But what would I do when they were all gone? I didn't want to stop now. Turning the stereo off, I carefully stowed the remaining can up my sleeve and went out the front door.

I would get more drink before the shop closed, just a couple in case I needed them. I meandered my way into the village, head held high, no longer afraid. Usually I would actively avoid the centre of Cruinníth on a Saturday evening, but now I savoured the moment. I hoped there'd be people loitering around The Tree or coming in and out of the two pubs so I could engage them in conversation, tell them how great it was to be drunk and share some of my can with them.

Alas, the only people sat on the benches outside *The Fiddler's Elbow* were a middle-aged couple and a handful of smokers. Further on at The Tree were a group of youths, perhaps a dozen in total. They were hanging out, smoking fags and trying to look tough. They were mostly young lads but in their midst were three girls, one of whom I instantly recognised. She was at the centre of the action; hanging out of one of the young lads, play-fighting with his friend, grabbing a bottle of wine from one of the other girls, taking a swig, catcalling at someone passing by in a car.

It was the girl Dan had been with, the tall, skinny blonde; Declan Fenlon's sister. Her more demure friend was nowhere to be seen. I had been eager for a chat but now I resorted to type, skulking in the shadows, hoping to make my way in and out of the shop without being noticed. I achieved the first half of my goal, procuring two more cans in the process. However, as soon as I stepped outside she clocked me.

"Hey, you! You!"

I ignored her and kept walking. The Tree was about twenty metres away from the entrance to the shop, I guessed she wouldn't have the heart to pursue me. I was wrong. She was straight across the road after me, all high and mighty, a bone to pick.

"You! You're from the other night. You're his cousin. You are!"

I stopped in my tracks. She had me on all counts.

Once she realised I was no longer running away she slowed down, suddenly uncertain. One of the other girls had followed her, anxious to see what all the fuss was about. Buoyed, the blonde turned to the friend and informed her of my transgression.

"Remember that fellah from Galway I was telling you about, Gina? This is his cousin, he was there. We're gonna find out now, we're gonna find out everything."

Intrigued, I took a seat on the wall outside the hairdresser's, pulled the can out of my sleeve and waited for the two girls to approach.

"Hey," said the blonde, "remember me?"

"Breffni," I said.

"Yeah. Where's that fucking cousin of yours?"

"He's in Galway."

Gina joined us and was quickly brought up to speed. Now they both stood before me, agitated and aggressive.

"And is he coming back?" Breffni asked.

"Yeah, tomorrow night."

This seemed to cheer her up.

"I see," she said, giving Gina a knowing look.

"He spoke very highly of you," I said, not really knowing why I was talking or what I was hoping to achieve by doing so.

"Did he now? D'ya hear that, Gina? And what exactly did he say?"

The menace was back in her voice. Gina looked angry too.

"He said you were nice," I offered.

"*Nice? Nice?* NICE!"

I thought I'd been doing a good thing here, easing relations between Dan and Breffni, setting the scene for a romantic reunion, but she was more incensed than ever.

"And lovely," I added, wondering what type of adjective it would take to placate her.

"You think you're fucking funny, don't you, fat boy?" she snarled, putting her face close to mine, grapes and vomit on her breath.

"I'm only telling you what he said," I countered, getting up off the wall, keen to escape a showdown.

"Yeah. Well, tell him I said he's a fucking prick," she spat.

"I will," I replied, retreating.

"And tell him his knob is fucking tiny and all!" she shouted after me, much to Gina's delight.

"Grand," I shouted back, laughing, falling into a fit of hysterics. This was mad. This was what being drunk was like, you got into all sorts. Imagine what being drunk in Dublin would be like, with all those people. I continued laughing all the way home, then decided to ring Dan to tell him what had happened. He'd love this.

"DAN!" I shouted as soon as he answered.

"What's up, cuz?!"

He was drunk too, I could hear it in his voice. There was music playing in the background and the hum of a large crowd of people. More than anything I wished I was there with Dan now, up in Galway, having the craic.

"DAN!" I shouted again, forgetting why I'd rung him, just happy to have someone to talk to.

I could hear him laughing on the other end of the phone.

"You all right, Aidan?"

"I am. I'm flying it!"

"Had a few drinks, have you?"

"Yes. Just getting in the mood for next weekend."

"Good man. We're going to have some laugh."

"We are, Dan. Hey, Dan?"

"Yeah?"

"We get on well, don't we?"

"Ah, we do, Aidan, definitely, man."

"We have a good time, playing *Halo* and that?"

"Yeah, we're some fucking team."

"We are, Dan, we really are. I'm fucking delighted you came to stay with us, Dan. It's great having you around."

"I'm delighted to be there, Aidan."

A voice drifted in from the background, someone was telling Dan to drink up, they were going to O'Connor's.

"Aidan, I'm going to have to go. I'll see you tomorrow evening, though. Have a good one, cuz!"

The phone went dead. Dan was great, though. I'd text him later. I'd forgotten to tell him about Breffni; what an idiot. Undeterred, I opened another can, my fifth of the evening, and, after a little deliberation, I put on some Pink Floyd. The next hour or so was a blur but I recalled my mother walking in on me as I sang along to *Wish You Were Here*. I think she was annoyed, there may have been a heated discussion, and the end result was the music went off. Then I definitely watched something on television, something funny, or something which seemed funny at the time, and scoffing either Pringles or one of those big bags of crisps. Then I went out the back for a bit of fresh air, came in and lay down on the bed and thought about what to text Dan. And that was the last thing I remembered.

*

I'd heard about hangovers, but all those stories had been laced with gallows humour, a fatalistic attitude. If anyone had bothered to tell me what they were really like, about the headache, the sick stomach and the seediness, I might have thought twice about experimenting with alcohol. And those were only the physical ailments; mentally, I felt worse than ever. I was so depressed, so down, and when I tried to recall the previous evening's events I began to feel light-headed, my anxiety threatening to spill over into a full-blown panic attack.

Initially I couldn't remember much, but as the day progressed I began to experience flashbacks: Breffni Fenlon doorstepping me outside the shop, the smell of her breath, her demented eyes as she interrogated me. Fear washed over me. What if I'd irked her? What if one of her yobbish mates now had it in for me? And what if I'd got Dan in trouble? Dan. I grabbed my phone, panicking, had I texted him? Had I told him how afraid I was of going to Dublin but that everything was okay now because I'd discovered alcohol? Had I said that his arrival was the best thing to happen to me in years? That had certainly been my intention.

I searched my sent messages. Nothing. I was in the clear. Jesus, what had come over me? Who was I? A few drinks and I'd been ready to reveal my deepest, darkest secrets, open up to a person I didn't know at all. Yet it hadn't all been bad. I'd managed to go into the village on a Saturday night, something I hadn't done in years. I'd spoken to two girls, casually, as if their presence meant nothing to me. And I'd discovered that music, especially that of David Bowie, sounded way better when you were drunk. Unfortunately, upon going downstairs to look for some painkillers, I discovered that my actions had repercussions beyond my own selfish world. My mother wasn't happy with me.

"Since when did you start drinking beer, Aidan?" she asked as soon as I stepped into the kitchen.

"I just had a couple last night is all."

"It seemed like more than a couple."

There was no point in arguing so I left it at that, abandoning my search for medication and returning upstairs. It was ironic in a way, my mother would surely equate my sudden interest in 'beer' with Dan's arrival, and perhaps this would shift, ever so slightly, the halo which resided above his perfect, curly-haired head. If I wanted to persuade her that he was a bad influence, this would be the time. I would never do that, though, we had a night out in Dublin to plan.

By the time Dan arrived back that evening I'd begun to feel a little better, a Sunday roast and an afternoon nap helping to revive me. We didn't really get a chance to talk, the long drive and the effects of his own night out sending him to bed early. This was probably for the best because, in the cold light of day, I had begun to feel nervous about Dublin again. There was really only one thing for it; I would have to keep drinking for the entire week, straight through till Saturday morning. Out of all the plans I'd concocted this was the best one, the most sensible one.

6

Obviously I didn't carry out that plan. That would have been foolish. But I did return to the shop for cans three times during the week. This time, when I drank them, I was more discreet, waiting till everyone had gone to bed, taking it nice and slow, and only listening to music on my headphones. And the more I drank, the less anxious I felt. A solution had been found.

Yes, things returned to normal the following morning, and I had a headache to boot, but the point stood: alcohol cured my anxiety. With that in mind I stocked up in advance of our drive on Saturday morning, deciding I would hit the booze early and hope everything else looked after itself. The thought of travelling so far away from home still made me nauseous but I reminded myself that, once drunk, my fears would evaporate, and so long as I kept drinking I would be okay.

Sleep didn't come easy on the Friday night, and I rose early on the morning of our expedition, busying myself with packing and preparing as I tried to take my mind off what lay ahead. It didn't work. As I stood in the shower, focusing on the sensation of the water as it drummed upon my head, doing my best to stay in the moment, my breathing became ragged and my chest began to constrict. I tried to stay calm but the more I fought it, the more I pushed it away, the stronger it became. Frustrated, I beat my fists against the bathroom wall, my tears washed away by the water. It was no good. I couldn't go.

I whimpered as my head began to swim and my legs began to falter. I slowly slid down to the shower floor, sitting there as the water continued to pound down, incessant and deafening, sending me over the edge. Pulling my knees up to my chest and wrapping my arms around them, I began to weep, kicking my feet back and forth like a toddler having a tantrum, causing the water to splash into the air.

I'd been so stupid. How could I have believed I could ever go on a night out? And to Dublin, to fucking Dublin? I didn't know anything about Dublin, didn't know where we'd be going, who we'd be going with or what we'd be doing. It was madness. You didn't go from living like a hermit for three years to a night out in the capital with a bunch of strangers. You took small steps, a night out in the local, into Dooncurra for one or two, work up to a big session in Maraghmor, gradually build your confidence. What I was doing was ridiculous and probably quite dangerous.

I'd been avoiding any thoughts about what might happen during the night out, but now they all came tumbling out: I could have a full-blown panic attack, one where I couldn't breathe, where I became frantic and desperate, start freaking out in an unfamiliar bar in an unfamiliar town with unfamiliar people, far from home, surrounded by strangers. It would be much worse than anything I'd experienced before. I'd probably end up in hospital or in jail, Dan and his friends at my bedside, outside the barracks, nervously waiting to see if I was okay. My parents would have to come and collect me. They'd be looking for an explanation, a reason why I'd brought shame on the family. And by the time I got back to the sanctity of my room I'd be utterly broken, a shell of a man, a fool who'd thought he could conquer his fears with booze.

I stopped crying, turned off the shower, and got out. The worst part was over now, the panic had given way to a numbness, a deadening acceptance. I'd wait for Dan to get up and gently break the news to him: I couldn't go, it was too much too soon. How about a night down in *The Fiddler's Elbow* next weekend? Invite your friends but not too many of them, just one or two? Yes, that would be a start. And Maraghmor was supposed to be good, that would be enough to sate a carouser like Dan, at least for a while. Casting aside the clothes I'd intended to wear for the day, I put on my manky tracksuit bottoms and hoodie and went to see if he was up.

"Jesus, you're finally out!" he said, appearing in the hallway. "I thought I was going to have to wash myself under the hose."

He barged his way past me with a grin and shut the door behind him, leaving me standing in the hallway. The door opened an inch and Dan's eyes appeared in the gap, "Get dressed, man, we're hitting the road for nine, yeah?"

I nodded dumbly and shuffled down to my room.

Dan was right, we were hitting the road for nine, the two of us. Instead of knocking on the bathroom door and explaining myself, I went and got dressed. When he came out of the shower I was sitting in the living-room, ready to go. When he asked if I had everything, I said I did, and when he said it was time to go I rose to my feet, followed him out the door and got into the car. No sooner had the key turned in the ignition than I opened my first can. By this point, it was the only hope I had.

*

The first hour of the drive was horrendous. Dan wouldn't shut up talking. I was barely holding it together, fighting to stay afloat, and just needed some peace and quiet, but on and on he went. On a couple of occasions I thought about opening the door and jumping out; into a ditch, over the side of a bridge, into oncoming traffic - anything to get away from him. And when he insisted I roll up the window, when the fresh air was the only thing keeping me sane, I nearly smashed my half-empty can into his stupid curly head. That half-empty can was quickly emptied though, as was the next one, and the one after that. I felt a bit better then.

We were only going for a drive, what was I so worried about? And what a lovely country we lived in: Carlow, Kilcullen, Naas, Johnstown. I did suffer another attack of the jitters when the green fields and countryside gave way to the outskirts of the capital, when the cows and sheep were replaced by cars and people, but I shoved those feelings to one side, drowning them in a sea of alcohol. At some point I began talking to Dan, his inane ramblings getting more interesting with each slug of beer. And by the time we turned off the N7 and made our way towards Garristown, he and I were in the midst of a very deep, very insightful conversation. It was about me, my life and what I was doing with it.

"I mean, you're an intelligent fella, Aidan. Why didn't you go to college? You had the points."

I couldn't recall ever telling Dan how I'd fared in my Leaving Cert, which meant my mother must have told him. I didn't like the idea of her and Dan discussing my career prospects. He was supposed to be on my side.

"I might still go," I answered.

"Oh, really? Which college? What course?"

"Not sure. Maybe Cork. Maybe history."

I did like history, but I knew nothing of Cork or its colleges.

"What kind of job would you get out of a history degree?" Dan asked, starting to sound like his father.

I pondered this for a moment.

"I dunno. A historian?"

Dan laughed, so I laughed too. But I didn't feel like laughing. He'd pissed me off now. Why was he asking me all these questions? I thought he'd accepted me for who I was, but now it appeared he wanted to turn me into another of his college buddies. Was this what I was going to have to put up with for the night: people quizzing me on my academic qualifications?

"Well, I might not do history," I said, hearing the petulance in my voice and hating it.

"I didn't mean to put you on the spot, lad. Just looking out for you, that's all."

We drove in silence for a while, me drinking steadily, my anxiety gradually morphing into depression. Dan said nothing, probably thinking I was overreacting to a routine conversation. Feeling guilty, I asked Dan to explain again what was in store for us tonight. He'd told me a dozen times already, but I saw how excited he got when he talked about his friends and I knew it'd cheer him up and lighten the mood. Straight away he repeated his promise to find me a woman, vowing to introduce me to half-a-dozen potential suitors who'd all be perfect for me. He listed all the pubs we'd be going to, the types of music they played and the clientele they attracted, and then he described how the presence of such-and-such a person would lead to almost nuclear levels of *craic*.

I tried to match his enthusiasm, and the thought of meeting a woman did genuinely excite me, but the closer we got to our destination the more I realised I didn't belong here, in this car, heading to this town to meet these people. They weren't my people. I didn't know who my people were, but they weren't them. If I was drunk, though, I could pretend they were my people, no one need know any different.

I turned up the radio, shifted the dial until I found something suitably rocking, and began to sing, quietly at first and then rising in decibel as the chorus came in. When it did, myself and Dan shared a look, a look that could surely only be shared by two good friends, and sang in unison.

I'm a creep! I'm a weirdo. What the hell am I doing here? I don't belong here.

We sang our way through the rest of the song and then I opened another can, sharing another smile with Dan as I took a deep, luxurious slug.

Other songs we liked came on after that one, and we sang along to each of them. And as we pulled into the driveway of Dan's friend's house, our duet of Aretha Franklin's *Respect* destroying the idyll of this quiet housing estate, I noted how different the last hour of the journey had been from the first. I'd had a great time singing those songs with Dan, had existed outside of my head, forgotten who I was, where I was and where I was going. But now that part was over and we were into another new environment, one where I would not be able to turn up the radio and sing my way to oblivion.

Dan's friend was called Fergal and he lived in a proper house, not some shabby student accommodation. It was one of those new builds, the type which had sprung up throughout the country over the last decade. And while it needed a lick of paint, and the front lawn could have done with a mow, it promised a level of comfort and style which I hadn't anticipated.

Fergal opened the door. He was tall, athletic and confident, just like Dan.

"How are the lads?" he said with a grin, inviting us in.

He shook my hand and said he was pleased to meet me.

The inside of the house was minimalistic, low-maintenance. A black leather three-piece suite dominated a living-room with a large glass coffee table in its centre, a plasma television in the corner and what looked like a drinks cabinet on the back wall. The floor was wood, buffed and polished, and the walls a nondescript colour: beige or cream, one of those inoffensive shades of yellow.

"You're on the couch, mate. Is that all right?" he asked.

"At the rate Aidan is drinking, I don't think it matters," said Dan.

I sheepishly looked at the can in my hand, but I was delighted. Fergal's first impression of me was that I was a big boozer, I would endeavour to maintain that image. It wouldn't be easy, though, I was already feeling a bit woozy. Keeping this up for the rest of the day and into the night would be a challenge for a seasoned drinker, never mind a novice like me. However, I had size on my side. My body mass was finally coming in useful; I'd become the archetypal chubby guy who could drink.

I could also eat, which was what the lads suggested we do first. "Line the stomach," they said. An artisan pizza house was our port of call, Dan and Fergal politely working their way through their Sicilian slices, me pigging out on a calzone like someone brought in off the street. From there we took up residence in one of Fergal's locals, a bustling bar with a selection of sports on its screens, bright, airy and modern; a place for young go-getters like us to have a relaxing pint before the real business began. It was beside a bookie's and the two lads were keen to bet on a Gaelic football game taking place later that day. I left them to it, the pub marginally less intimidating than the hyper-masculine betting office.

I nervously scanned the taps for something recognisable, but it wasn't like back home where you had a choice of two, maybe three, ales and lagers, with stout as an additional option and a glass of wine for the lady. Here there were taps from one end of the bar to the other, fridges full of bottles, fancy, eye-catching spirits, buckets of ice and attractive bar staff, one of whom was staring right at me, awaiting my order. Panicked, and seeing no sign of my usual light beer, I plumped for the first thing I saw: a German-sounding drink which came out of a shiny silver tap.

It was handed to me in a vase-like glass with a slice of lemon on the rim. Perturbed, I handed over the money, got back far less change than I'd expected and found a seat away from the bar, away from the television screens and away from the other patrons. I tasted the drink. It was delicious, far nicer than the stuff I'd been drinking on the way up. I immediately decided this was my drink of choice from now on. Here I was, in the big smoke, drinking fancy beers in a pub all by myself. The night ahead would be just the start for me. Once I got home I'd make plans for further nights out, start embracing the world instead of hiding from it. Life was made to be lived, after all.

Dan and Fergal returned, full of talk about corner-forwards and 'swarming the midfield'. Fergal commended me on my choice of beverage and once more I flushed with pleasure; but when he tried to engage me in conversation, our differences became apparent.

"So, what do you do, Aidan?" he asked when Dan went to get their drinks.

There it was again, that question. The thing they fell back on every time.

"Just taking some time off at the moment," I replied.

Fergal nodded knowingly. Perhaps he'd taken time off at some point in his life too.

"What did you do before?" he asked.

This was hopeless. They wouldn't be satisfied till I told them I'd never done anything, at any point. That I'd finished school and spent the next three years sitting in my bedroom watching films. That this trip to the capital constituted the high point of my life so far, and I'd really only come because Dan had promised he'd find me a woman. Dan returned with the drinks, sparing Fergal from uncovering the odious truth, and they lapsed into familiar, jovial conversation. They mostly talked about other people, friends of theirs; sharing anecdotes, in-jokes, casual asides which to me, an outsider, meant nothing, but were a source of relentless hilarity to them.

I tried to keep up, to absorb some of the details in the hope of gaining access to their world, but it was too difficult, like trying to learn a year's worth of school work for an exam the next day. After a while I just zoned out and let the alcohol do the work. Not bothering to ask the other two if they wanted a pint, I returned to the bar, more confidently this time, and ordered another. The barman did as instructed without batting an eyelid, in fact, no one was taking any notice of me. I was just one more punter, enjoying a few pints with his mates of a Saturday afternoon. And I was happy with that.

As with the drive up, however, as soon as I got settled we were on the move again. This time it was back to Fergal's. They wanted to get ready before going into town. This meant a shower, a change of clothes, styling their hair until it was just right and then applying cologne to every available pore. While I waited, I put on the shoes I'd worn to my great-aunt's funeral the previous winter and the shirt I'd dug out from the back of my wardrobe. I opened another can and sat out on the front step.

A lot of the houses in the estate weren't occupied. Some of them didn't even look finished. It was as if the builders had decided to down tools one day and head off on another job. There were no recreational areas or plant-life anywhere, just white concrete and asphalt. This, combined with the growing heat of the late afternoon sun, gave the place an otherworldly feel, as if we'd been transported into the future, into a bleak, post-apocalyptic universe.

The bounce of a ball and the shriek of a child brought me back to reality. Across the way there was a house with a car in the driveway, a red people-carrier, and from behind it emerged two kids, a boy and a girl. They raced for the ball, the girl, slightly older, got there first, and scampered away with her bounty, the boy giving chase determinedly. The game consisted of them aimlessly running around, occasionally voicing their displeasure, their jubilation, as rules were added and abandoned by whoever had the ball. I watched them through my drunken stupor, envying the simplicity of their lives. They had no idea what was ahead of them, and if I told them they wouldn't believe me.

Dan was the first to emerge from the cloud of steam and scent, shining from head to toe, hair, eyes, teeth, clothes all perfect. Here was an object of attention for all who crossed his path. Fergal followed shortly after, not quite so striking, operating at a lower level, but a catch in his own right. We got a bus into the city centre. There were other groups of lads and young wans on the upper deck, their intentions similar to ours: to give themselves to the night, let alcohol be their master.

I'd brought a can with me and drank it silently as I looked out the window, detached from it all, no longer afraid, just numb. We'd fallen into a tacit agreement now, myself and the two lads; I was with them and would remain so, but there was no common ground and no point trying to involve me. They were free to do their thing without worrying about my well-being. I was a passenger, a silent face in the background.

The bus dropped us into the heat and clamour of the city, and immediately we ducked down a laneway for a piss, a lad from one of the other groups joined us, sharing our relief. Then, led by Fergal, we were taken down one street, across traffic, into a park, out of a park, and into a pub. Except I didn't go in. I was instructed to secure a table in the beer garden out front, ensure we had a good spot in what, even at this early evening hour, was a busy, bustling spot. I found as good a berth as could be expected and awaited my fruity pint. It came moments later, accompanied by two more of Dan's friends, a man and a woman; a couple by the look of things.

"Aidan, this is Greg and Máiréad."

I stood up to greet them, almost knocking the table over. Greg wasn't like Dan and Fergal, he was rounder, pudgier, not nearly so physically intimidating. But as he shook my hand, throwing in a little wink for good measure, his broad grin making the gesture seem almost avuncular, I recognised in him a different quality, one which couldn't be honed through hours in the gym or time spent in front of the mirror. He had a looseness about him, a self-confidence which didn't tally with his appearance.

There'd been one or two lads like Greg in my school, people who, at face value, didn't appear to have a whole lot going for them but had the personality to overcome any shortcomings. They were popular with everyone, even the outcasts like me, their charisma giving them the sort of mass appeal attained by very few. In Greg's case that charisma had enabled him to acquire a significant other who, to my untrained eye, looked at least two leagues above him.

Máiréad was very attractive, in an elegant, well-off kind of way. Long chestnut hair, round friendly eyes, great skin, a silver necklace round her thin neck, a bangle on her wrist, light, tasteful clothing, which revealed long tanned legs but didn't cling to her figure enough for you to imagine what she might look like naked. Even shaking her hand made me feel ashamed.

She was nice, though, they both were, funny too, especially Greg. He was a natural story-teller and ensured that everyone at the table was included when he spoke, looking everyone in the eye, engaging them, inviting them into his warm, friendly little heart. Usually when someone looked me in the eye I felt incredibly uncomfortable, but with Greg it was okay, I could look right back at him, there was no weirdness or discomfort. He immediately started calling me 'Aido' and made gentle fun of my choice of drink, dishing out a bit of a slagging, bringing my place of residence into it, labelling me 'the cat'. But there was nothing hurtful in it, no chance of my sensitivities being pricked. He seemed to instinctively know how far to push it, where to draw the line. Even when the dreaded "What do you do?" question came up it didn't pose a problem. I didn't even mind him asking. I simply shrugged, said, "Not much", and we continued on our way, Greg's laughter rendering the moment inconsequential.

I was wary of Máiréad though, terrified the other three might dive into a deep, esoteric discussion and leave me to talk to her. I was drunk and getting drunker, but not so drunk that I could share her airspace with any sort of comfort. Once or twice I saw her lean in my direction, a beautiful Máiréad-shaped question forming on her lips, and I hastily buried my head in my pint, drinking until the moment had passed. That was something else I was discovering about alcohol, and pints in particular: they served as a great prop. You always had something to do with your hands when you had a pint.

I was drinking mine too fast, though, trying to keep pace with these seasoned drinkers, going into rounds with them, bringing up the rear no matter how quickly I went. And it was starting to take its toll. I couldn't say exactly when I strayed from drunk to too drunk, but it came hard and fast and without real warning. There was a spell of joyous mirth, of freedom and merriment, in which I still retained my senses, in which I even managed to engage Máiréad in conversation and became charming, maybe even suave, at least in my own mind. That didn't last long. Shortly thereafter I began to lose control, subconsciously aware I was acting out of turn, but powerless to prevent it.

I became loud, too loud. Lairy. Bored of Dan and the lads, I went for a wander inside. I knocked over someone's drink, trod on someone's foot, apologised, became too familiar, too pally, and was told to fuck off. In the toilets I started cackling for no apparent reason, trying and failing to explain my good humour to my fellow men. Then, as I mingled at the bar, looking around for girls, I heard the music. There was a jukebox. It would have Led Zeppelin, Steely Dan, The Who, and *Bowie*. Recalling how fantastic he'd sounded while drunk, I hurried back outside, several light bulbs glowing above my beery head. I didn't even bother to sit down, just inserted myself between Dan and Greg, and began explaining why we needed to go inside and listen to Bowie, to sing, dance and clap our hands. They rejected my idea out of hand, insisting they were fine where they were.

Shocked, crestfallen, I tried to get across the monumental importance of the moment but the words wouldn't come out. So I sat down again, giving Máiréad a baleful look as I drank my pint. My unhappiness was fleeting, though. The fresh air helped clear my head, allowed me to overcome the growing confusion in my brain. I carefully assembled my thoughts and waited until a reasonable amount of time had passed (I tried counting to five hundred but lost my way in the early eighties). Then I repeated my idea, this time underlining its significance, stressing that it wasn't a flippant notion, it meant something, held great weight. To my surprise they went along with it, maybe out of pity or to just shut me up, it didn't matter.

Thrilled, revelling in my status as group leader, I marched through the pub, casually easing people out of the way as I led the gang to the jukebox. It was in a crowded area, amidst tables and chairs, but I wasn't going to let that deter me. Checking to make sure the lads were still with me I fell upon my prey, shoving a two-euro coin in the slot and encouraging Greg to select some tunes with me. Unfortunately, Greg and I didn't share the same taste in music and, after letting him choose two god-awful dance tracks, I put on the first three songs of *Hunky Dory*, aiming to recapture the spirit of my bedroom right here in this bar.

However, I hadn't reckoned for the other patrons and their desire to hear their favourite songs. We had to wait our turn, sit through a steady stream of Oasis, Queen, The Killers and, inexplicably, Abba. As each song ended and another few minutes passed I willed Greg's cheesy tunes to come on, knowing their appearance would bring me that bit closer to my own choices and our moment of magic. Frustrated, I went to the bar to ask how long it would be before my songs came on, receiving a shake of the head and a dismissive eye-roll by way of response.

Then more of Dan's friends arrived: two guys and two girls. This just confused things even more. They didn't know what songs I'd chosen or why we were standing there waiting. Throwing everything into chaos, these new people suggested we go elsewhere, declaring themselves tired of this pub despite only having just arrived. I resisted stubbornly, informing them that I hadn't paid good money just for someone else to listen to my David Bowie songs. At this point Dan quietly took me to one side, gesturing to the others in a placatory manner as he and I moved to a less populated area of the bar.

"Aidan, you'd want to relax a bit for yourself. Have a pint of water or something."

I looked him squarely in the eye, wondering what the fuck he was on about. "But the songs ... " I began.

"Never mind the songs," he said, grabbing me by the shoulders. "Are you going to be okay?"

"Course I am," I answered, shaking him off, making to leave, thinking twice about it, and hugging him instead. "Where are we going next?"

The answer was an upmarket place nearer the centre of town: a brightly-lit collection of wide, open rooms with high ceilings, vintage furniture and long sleek bars operated by trendy gents and winsome ladies. It was hell on earth. There wasn't one person who looked like me. It was full of women like Máiréad and men like Dan: beautiful people who knew they were beautiful. I'd had no idea that so many of these people existed. It was like a Mensa meeting, but instead of a high IQ you had to have a killer smile and cheekbones to die for. What were we doing in here? What was I doing in here? It was farcical.

One of the new people, Hugo or something, suggested we go out to the beer garden, a rooftop terrace overlooking the city. And to be fair it was nice out there, nice to listen to the traffic below, the whoops and shouts of those working their way from one bar to the next. The view was great, the sunset in the distance and the descending darkness contrasting with the garish lighting of the restaurants and bars, the seagulls puncturing the tranquillity as they drifted in from the Liffey, their caws and squawks still audible over the din of an evening about to turn to night.

And then I got sick.

The fervour I'd experienced at the previous bar, the desire to get up and dance, had evaporated. I'd become light-headed, breathless, dizzy. My willingness to converse, my *ability* to converse, left me. I just wanted to lie down, take a little breather and assess my options. Instead I was sitting in a wicker chair surrounded by Ireland's most gorgeous people, listening to the laughter and conversation of Greg and Máiréad, Fergal and Dan, and some women they'd invited to our table. The cool night air sent chills through me as I contemplated a quiet exit and a return to the house, wherever that was.

I tried to get up, felt the world revolve on its axis, and sat back down with a jolt. Things were spinning, my head hurt, I felt over-encumbered, sweaty and cold. Realising what was happening, I lunged towards a potted plant and vomited into the damp, fluffy earth, leaning my head against the tall shrub as I went down on all fours and retched violently. There was a lot of vomit, it filled the dusty, redbrick pot so that the plant stood mired in it, like the last living thing in an inhospitable planet of sick.

When it was finally over I shakily got to my feet and wiped my mouth, aware that the eyes of all these beautiful people were upon me. Dan was by my side, propping me up, rubbing at my clothes with a tissue. I briefly glanced in the direction of his friends, seeing the look of disappointment on Máiréad's face and the disgust of those people I'd never bothered to introduce myself to, as my cousin escorted me to the bathroom. He was talking to me as we went, he sounded pissed off, like I'd ruined his night. I knew then I wasn't cut out for this drinking lark, and I certainly wasn't made for socialising in a place like this. I didn't say any of this to him, though, I just let him clean me up, like a baby who's spat out his dinner.

He told me to throw some water on my face while he went to the bar to get me a coffee. A coffee? What kind of pub served coffee? While he was gone I went into one of the cubicles and sat on the lid of the toilet, my head in my hands, everything still spinning. If I could have stayed like this a while, an hour or two, I would have been fine again. Dan and his friends could have continued their lovely, gorgeous night and I'd have caught up with them when I was ready. I wasn't afforded that luxury. He was back again within seconds, knocking at the door, instructing me to open up, warning me about something or other, just generally wrecking my head.

I tried to explain my situation, put into words what I was feeling, but all I could manage was a garbled, "Go away!"

His voice got closer then, imposing, like a deity. He'd gone into the cubicle beside me and stood on the toilet so he could look in at me.

"Aidan, what the fuck?"

He sounded exasperated. I had exasperated him. I grunted an apology.

Other people had come into the bathroom. I could hear them.

"Open the door," he said, whispering.

"No."

"Aidan..."

"No."

I wasn't going to open the door. I wasn't going to go back out into that stupid, beautiful pub. I was going to stay here until it was all over, until it was safe to emerge and I could go home.

"Jesus fucking Christ!"

Dan was giving out yards now, effing and jeffing as he considered his next option. I peeked out from between my hands and saw he'd mounted the cubicle wall and was coming in to join me. What were we going to do in here, the two of us? He landed in beside me and immediately opened the door, exposing me to all the badness out there.

"Come on," he said, lifting me up, a little less gently this time.

"I don't want to!" I pleaded, fearful of seeing Máiréad again.

But we were going downstairs, away from the beer-garden, from my puke and their looks of horror. Was it possible Dan was bringing me home, back to Cruinníth? I could only but hope. We spilled out into the street, to the sounds of heels clicking, cars beeping and men shouting. I shielded my face, my eyes, determined not to let them see me.

"Wait there," Dan instructed, pushing me onto the windowsill of a shop.

I felt sick again, the walk downstairs, the blast of fresh air, had sent me into another spiral. Unsure of my location, but knowing there wasn't a potted plant in the vicinity, I leaned to one side and had a little vomit. There wasn't much, it was just the dregs now, but that didn't stop my stomach from convulsing, sending whatever bits of pizza and breakfast it could find in the general direction of my mouth. I retched loudly, one of those dramatic ones you have no control over, but nothing came out.

"Aidan, for fuck's sake! How am I going to get you a taxi if you're like this?"

That was Dan. He was back. I hiccuped.

"It's all gone now, Dan," I said, dragging myself upright and looking him in the eye. "All gone."

And it felt like it was. My head wasn't spinning as much, it was merely listing now. The blood was returning to my legs and my cheeks felt flushed. I was back. If I could just compose myself, I might even be able to go upstairs and apologise to Máiréad.

"Are you sure?" Dan asked.

"Yes," I said, emphatically.

"Okay."

And off he went, with his curly head, white shirt and light blue jeans. I hoped there wasn't any sick on his shirt, that would really ruin his chances with the ladies.

"Come on," he said, returning and pulling me towards a car.

"No," I protested, "I'm okay, Dan. Let's go somewhere else, just me and you . . . and Greg."

He was having none of it. I was bundled into the back of the taxi and sent packing. This was no good.

The taxi driver wound down the rear window. He knew what he was dealing with, knew the dangers involved. But I was fine now. There was no more vomit to come. As we sped through the streets of Dublin, I contemplated asking him to leave me out somewhere, to drive me to a bar of his choice. I could have my own night out, I didn't need them. I didn't fit in with them anyway. I'd find my own crowd, my own bar, one which played Bowie and Joy Division all night long. But I was tired and a little scared. It had been an eventful day, a long one, and I needed a rest.

7

"THIS IS YOU, SON," SAID the voice. "Your pal paid so you're all right."

Vaguely aware I needed to get out of the car, I mumbled my thanks and staggered out on to the footpath. This was me, the man had just said so. I walked up the pathway of the house in front of me and knocked on the door. There was no one home. So I sat on the step and dozed for a while, tried to get comfy on the mat. But it was no use. I wasn't staying there for the night, sitting on a step like a cat waiting to be let in. I'd go off for a walk and, hopefully, by the time I came back there'd be someone in. Making a note of the area's defining features, I set off with renewed purpose. I was starting to come round a bit.

I remembered now, I was in Garristown, at Fergal's house. There were pubs near here, we'd been in one earlier that day. The one beside the bookies, that's where I'd go. But after ten minutes of walking, all I'd encountered were houses and a takeaway. I peered into the distance; there were no pubs ahead, just darkness. Obviously I'd gone the wrong way. Loath to retrace my steps, I turned ninety degrees and headed in a new direction. This reaped almost immediate rewards. Within minutes I'd escaped the grey drabness of suburbia and found a park, and on the other side of the park I could see lights, signs of life. Excited, I hopped over the little wall surrounding the park and strode towards salvation.

It was closer than I thought.

Inside the collection of moderately tall trees, bushy plant-life and winding paths were benches. Beside those benches were tall lights, illuminating the way for nocturnal types like myself. From one of those benches, underneath those lights, I could hear voices: loud voices, young voices, several of them. It may have been my first time on a night out in Dublin, but I knew enough to steer clear of groups of people sitting in parks late at night. I kept my head down, hunched up my shoulders and hurried forward, hoping to escape the park without being seen.

"Hey! You! Where're ya going?"

I ignored them.

"Hey! You deaf? Come over for a second."

"We won't do anything to ya, boy. Come over."

"Hey, baby, let the free birds fly."

Laughter, then, jeering male laughter.

"C'mere ta fuck."

"Is that Willie Murphy?"

"Willie! Willie! We have drink, Willie."

The idea of drink, of assuming a false identity, appealed to me but still I walked, hoping they'd grow tired of me. Instead, the tone shifted, became menacing.

"If you don't fucking come over here now, we're gonna come after ya. Don't be such an ignorant cunt."

I slowed. If they chased me I was fucked. The exit was nowhere in sight and I couldn't run in these shoes.

"Yeah, come on, boy," the voice said, all friendly again. "We're not going to do anything to ya."

I decided I would go and talk to them, explain I wasn't Willie Murphy. They would know where the nearest pub was, maybe we could go together. I would buy them all a pint to make up for not being Willie Murphy. There were five of them, all males, younger than me, but not by much. Two were sitting on the bench, the others stood around it.

"That's not Willie," one of them said, sounding genuinely upset.

"Who is it?" asked another.

The ringleader, the one who'd threatened to come after me, sized me up. He was tall and thin, with cropped hair, intimidating, but when he opened his mouth I relaxed.

"What's the big deal, boy? We only wanted to talk to you is all."

"Sorry, I don't know the area."

"What's your name?"

"Aidan."

"Aidan," my inquisitor repeated, turning to his pals. "Aidan."

One snickered with laughter, another politely said hello.

"Where you from, Aidan?"

"Kilkenny."

"What you doing up here?"

"On a night out with my friends."

This got them all laughing.

"Where are your friends now?"

"I don't know."

"Sounds like they ditched you."

"No, I ditched them."

More laughter.

"Can I have a can?" I asked, pointing to the bag on the ground.

One of the other kids took out a can and handed it to me. They were all right, these lads.

"So, where're you staying tonight?" the tall one asked me.

"In a house back there somewhere," I replied, nodding my head in its general direction.

"Who's there now?"

"No one."

"Lads!" he said, turning to his friends.

A ripple of excitement passed through them. I could feel it. And I was the one who'd created it.

"How about we hang out there for a while until your friends come back, keep you company, like?" suggested my new pal.

That sounded like a great idea. Just one problem: I couldn't get in.

"I can't get in."

"What? Why not?"

"I've no key. The taxi just dropped me there."

Key: the word stirred a memory. Dan pressing an object into my hand, changing his mind and giving it to - the taxi driver? No. Jamming it into my pocket, warning me about something, his eyes intense, hair all curly. I put my hand in my pocket: wallet, coins, a note, no key. The other pocket: phone. Then the little pocket beside the other pocket: key.

"Oh, hold on," I said, "here it is."

I held it aloft like the Golden Fleece. And my flock gathered round, ready to be led to their destination.

*

Jinx. That was my new friend's name. Although he wasn't being friendly with me at the moment.

"Fuck's sake, man, where's this house? We're after being up and down this road three times!"

We were standing outside the takeaway I'd passed before I'd chosen to alter my route. I knew we hadn't gone completely off track. But all the houses looked the same to me, in fact everything looked the same to me. That was Dublin for you. We'd looked at the key, examined it for any distinguishing features, but that hadn't thrown up any clues. And now Jinx and the lads were growing impatient.

"Ring your buddies, Aidan. Find out the address?" suggested one.

But I didn't want to do that. Dan would only start lecturing me again.

"Let's just walk down this way," I said. "I know I passed this takeaway."

My increasingly disgruntled followers fell into line and we marched off down the road, into an estate with characterless, semi-detached houses, dream homes for the right family. *Family*. I felt a surge of inspiration. The two kids playing outside earlier - their house had a car in front of it, one of the few inhabited houses in the estate. If I could just find that house I'd have it all figured out. Deciding not to reveal my brainwave to my companions, I remained silent while Jinx and the boys moaned and complained. I'd already drunk two of their cans, they deserved something in return.

We passed two houses with cars outside and on each occasion I stood on the opposite side of the avenue, tried to envisage those children playing while I idly surveyed the scene, and knew it wasn't right. By this point the lads were questioning my sanity, the friendships I'd struck up were turning sour, and I thought I heard one of them mutter something about 'kicking the shit out of me' and 'robbing all my money'. Ignoring the negativity, I continued to lead the way, carefully examining each house, certain I'd eventually find what I was looking for. We turned into another section, a wide cul-de-sac, bare earth, bollards and a car – yes, a car, in one of the driveways. I stopped in the middle of the road and held my hand aloft until they were silent.

"I think it's one of these ones, lads."

More sighs and groans.

Quickly, I moved to the houses opposite the one with the car, pausing outside each one. I could just have tried the key in all of them, most were vacant as far as I knew. But I wanted to get it right first time. So, after further consideration, after being brazen enough to sit on the step of the premises I believed I possessed the key for, I told them what they'd been waiting to hear.

"It's this one, come on."

Still unconvinced, they slouched up to the front door.

"We could always just break in," one opined as I fumbled in my pockets for the key.

I swept their misgivings away with one twist of my right hand. The door swung open and we were in. The session had begun.

8

I'D NEVER BEEN AT A session before, but this seemed like a good one. As soon as we got inside the lads were straight into the fridge, rooting in the presses, laughing away to themselves like children, returning with cans, bottles, crisps, bread, stretching out on the couch, their battered runners resting on the coffee table. Fergal wouldn't be happy, neither would Dan, but I pushed those thoughts away, deciding to let the future take care of itself. Someone put on music, dance music, it was loud and hard. It wasn't my jam, not in the slightest, but I moved to the stereo and turned it up a notch anyway, doing a silly little dance in the process. The lads liked this. I was back in with them now.

Jinx had taken a seat in the big armchair, overseeing things, watching his minions at play. He was rolling a cigarette, a big one, burning something into it. I knew what that was. I'd try some when he lit it up. For now I was making do with the budget can of beer I'd been handed by way of reward. They'd found some vodka and had poured it into mugs and glasses. I chose not to indulge, I'd done enough puking for one night.

We'd only been there twenty minutes when I heard a banging at the door, a raucous din. I froze, looking to the lads for guidance. Was it the guards? Were we in trouble? No, it was just some more of their friends. In they came, half a dozen of them, big, grizzled-looking fuckers, more men than boys. There was a young girl with them, a thin waif of a thing with dark, sad eyes and ruby red lips. She sat between two of Jinx's mates, sinking into the couch with a nervous smile. I hadn't considered this, that they might bring girls.

"Any more young wans around?" I asked Jinx.

He smiled indulgently, "Gwan ouwa that, Aido, ya dirty bollix, coming up here, trying to rob our women!"

"No, no, I didn't mean it like that," I protested.

But he just laughed and returned to his drink.

The new arrivals were just as friendly as Jinx and the lads. They all came up to me, shook my hand and said how sound I was for hosting the session. One of them offered me a pill. I didn't want to upset him so I politely accepted and put it in my pocket. A couple of them started dancing, dragging the girl up from the couch and draping themselves over her while they bopped and bounced around the room. She didn't look like she was enjoying herself, and on a couple of occasions had to fend them off when they got too handsy. No one said anything, though, so I remained quiet. Eventually there was just one guy trying it on with her. He was a bear of a man, as wide as he was tall, a leather jacket stretched around his bulk despite the stifling heat in the room. He looked wild, eyes rolling in their sockets, mouth askew as sweat poured down his brow.

I didn't want to look at him lest we make eye contact, but there was something fascinating about him, something which made you stare. And the way he danced: head back, shoulders hunched, legs barely moving, like Stevie Wonder when he's in the groove. Every so often the bear man paused, rubbed his hands vigorously on his face, gazed across the room and then returned to his trance. No matter how vacant he appeared, how dazed, he made sure the girl was always within reaching distance. By now the other men had lost interest, sat back down or taken to dancing by themselves, but this guy was persistent and willing to stay the course.

For her part, the girl looked like she was attempting to get into the mood: swaying her hips, raising her arms to her chest and slowly moving her head from side to side. But then she'd stop as if momentarily blinded, swallow and breathe deeply for a few seconds. Someone handed her a cigarette which she gratefully accepted and began chugging on immediately. That seemed to calm her but she didn't look well. I wanted to ask her if she was okay but I dared not go near her. Anyway, the bear had her fully in his grasp now.

He was behind her, his massive arms hung over her shoulders while he nuzzled her neck and tried to negotiate her dress with his sausage fingers. She was resisting but in a distant sort of way, like when you tickle someone's nose when they're asleep and they half-heartedly wave you away. It was distressing to watch. She couldn't have been more than sixteen; he looked at least ten years older. Again I looked to the others, to his friends, to Jinx, but no one seemed to care. They were all lost in their own little worlds, content to let this play out right in front of them.

Apparently bored with dancing, the bear-like guy instructed one of his friends to move from the couch so he could sit down. As he did so he pulled the girl onto his lap, sitting her on his knee like a child. For a second she stayed like that, sitting on his knee and dumbly looking around the room, before he pulled her towards him, draping her legs over the side of the couch, her dress riding up so you could see her underwear. He began kissing her, slathering her face with spittle, holding the back of her head so she couldn't escape. When he tired of this he let her go, cradling her in his arms as he grinned in triumph. Somewhere during the ordeal she'd fallen asleep, or lost consciousness, but this didn't deter him. Indeed, it gave him the impetus to go that little bit further.

I saw his hand go between her legs, his eyes now fully focused as he concentrated on his task. Sensing it was open season, one of the other men tried to put his hand down the girl's top to fondle her breasts. The bear-man shook his head at him, mouthed something and began slapping the girl on the face, trying to wake her up. At first she was unresponsive. The two lads looked panicked. But then her eyes flickered open, she pawed the air in irritation until someone placed a drink in her hand and she knocked it back.

Relieved, I hoped they'd leave her alone now. There was no way I could do anything about it. Not me, not on my own, but if it carried on, if it got any worse, I was going to ring Dan. I'd have to explain what had happened, how stupid I'd been, but once he understood what these guys were doing, that they were taking advantage of this girl he'd come straight back. He'd bring Fergal and Greg and they'd sort this mess out. And if I couldn't get through to Dan, if he thought I was just being dramatic, I'd call the guards. That would be the best option. Call the guards, make sure the girl was okay, get everyone out of here, and be in bed asleep by the time Dan and Fergal got back.

I was considering all of this as I watched the girl slowly return to her senses, when someone tapped me on the shoulder.

"Here bud, is this your house?" asked a voice.

"No, it's my friend's."

"Grand," he said, grinning.

I thought I saw him nod to one of the others then, in a conspiratorial kind of way. But I was probably just being paranoid. He went out to the back garden to make a call, saying it was impossible to hear over the music. I got up to follow him, deciding some fresh air would make things better; but as I went to go out a hand pressed against my chest, guiding me away from the door, until I was sat on a chair in the kitchen.

"Keg on the way," the first guy said, winking as he took a seat across from me.

That was good. More beer.

But no, I had to check to make sure the girl was okay, call Dan, the cops. I started to get to my feet and once more felt hands restraining me, one of the guys beside me was holding me back, encouraging me to stay with them a while.

"Here, try this," he said, holding a cigarette in front of me. Except it wasn't a cigarette, not the kind I knew.

"I'm okay," I said, shaking my head, looking over my shoulder towards the sitting-room.

"Try it," he insisted.

"Give him a blow-back," one of the others said.

I shuddered at that. If I was getting blown I certainly didn't want any of these lads to do it. A face appeared before me, a dirty male face with its lips puckered. I recoiled.

"Relax, ya eejit," he said, cupping his hands over my face. He blew smoke into my mouth and then departed with a grin.

It appeared I had been blown, by a young fellah from Dublin no less. I felt dizzy and light-headed, it was like the scene in the pub all over again. What a day I was having. I'd crammed all the experiences I'd missed out on as a teenager into a few short hours. The next time the joint came around I took it myself, deciding that if I was going to get fucked up I'd do it on my own terms. It was worse than I expected. My head was totally gone. I needed to lie down. The boys were talking, either to each other or to me, I couldn't tell. I couldn't really see them either.

This time when I got to my feet they didn't stop me, in fact, they actually laughed at my decision to leave their little soirée. I went out the back, the air helped a little. I was so tired and hot, really hot. I lay down in the nice cool grass. It was slightly damp, it cooled my brow, soothing me.

I saw some feet and heard a man pissing.

"What's up with yer man?" someone asked.

"Whitener," came the response, followed by a laugh.

Was that the next thing they had planned for me, a whitener? I didn't care what they did, so long as I didn't have to move.

I'd only made myself comfortable, felt my senses return, when I began to feel cold. Chills ran through me and I shivered involuntarily. I could think of nothing more inviting than a warm, cosy bed. I wasn't going to get that here, not with all these fuckers around. I sat up and took stock. It sounded like half of Dublin was in the house. The lights were on upstairs, voices, shouting, laughing, coming from every direction. I thought of the people living in the house opposite, and their children. How had they not complained yet, or called the guards? They must have gone away for the weekend. No one could endure this. It had escalated beyond all reason.

I'd only intended to have a few cans with Jinx and the lads, be sitting there with them when Dan came back so he could see I didn't need him, that I had my own friends. That reminded me. The girl. The bear man. I had to make sure she was okay. I got to my feet unsteadily, feeling woozy, and made for the living-room. It was awash with people. More had arrived; a couple of girls, which was a good thing, but also a lot more lads. They were all dancing, beatific smiles on their faces, cans, bottles, flagons, naggins, pint glasses, cups, mugs in their hands. Someone had brought a bigger stereo, a louder one, with speakers which thumped out the bass and made the whole house throb.

I looked around for the girl. She was nowhere to be seen. The couch she'd sat on had been pushed back into the corner, a couple of gurning teens thrown across it. The bear man wasn't there, nor were his cronies. I went back into the kitchen; no one there but a couple of stray dancers and the guys who'd given me the blow-back. The downstairs toilet was impregnable, not locked, just jammed - that would be a problem for later. A couple of young wans sat on the stairs, conversing intensely, holding one another and intermittently hugging.

"Where did the girl go?" I asked, my voice sounding fuzzy and faraway.

"What you say, love?" one asked turning in my general direction, chewing gum feverishly.

"The girl, where is she?"

She shrugged her shoulders good-naturedly and went back to hugging her friend.

There were loads of people in the front garden, some lay flat on the ground, staring at the stars, others danced to the muffled music coming from inside, but most were shouting and whooping for no apparent reason.

As I stepped outside, scanning the crowd for signs of her, a car pulled up. Its occupants immediately spilled onto the path, clambering over one another as they made for the house. But it appeared they weren't welcome. The guy I'd spoken to in the kitchen stood by the driveway, blocking their way. My party was now so exclusive it had a guest list.

The newcomers weren't taking no for an answer though. There was a heated exchange, threats were made and voices raised. Those guarding the premises were doing their best to keep the peace, to mollify the interlopers and get rid of them without resorting to violence. A scuffle broke out. One lad broke the line, shoving me out of the way as he raced inside, apparently hoping to get lost in the crowd. He was swiftly followed by one of the 'bouncers' and moments later he returned, shielding himself from the blows as he was sent back from whence he came.

I was in way over my head here. Anxious about a retaliatory assault, I went back inside, sidling up the stairs away from any further violence. The best thing I could do now was hole up in one of the bedrooms until all this was over, until Dan and the lads came back and sorted it out. I stood on the landing outside the bathroom, outside the three bedrooms, wondering which would be quietest. The door of one had been kicked in, its interior ransacked. That wasn't good. A smaller, more intimate party had sparked up in the middle one, the box room; music emanated from inside, low voices, a relaxed vibe. A chill-out room? As host I should have had access to every room going, but having seen how the unwanted guests outside had been treated I was reluctant to invite myself in.

The last bedroom, the one facing the back of the house, had people in it too. They were quieter even than those in the chill-out room, but not so quiet that I couldn't hear them. There was a lot of heavy breathing and grunting, the creak of a bed, urgent whispers. More than two people, maybe three or four, and all male. It sounded like . . . a gay orgy? Was that why those lads had been so friendly downstairs? Had they been coming on to me? But then, amidst the hushed masculine tones, I heard an anguished moan, a gasp of pain, which sounded distinctly feminine.

I knew it was none of my business, that I should either have gone into the wrecked bedroom or back downstairs, but I was curious. It sounded like something I needed to see, and deep in the back of my mind - no, right at the front of my drunk, confused mind - was the thought that maybe

I could join in with whatever was going on in there, that if those moans belonged to one or more girls, perhaps the person responsible for organising this shindig could have his fill. I crept towards the door, expecting it to be locked or at least closed, but it was ajar, allowing me to open it an inch and see inside.

The first thing I saw was a man standing on the far side of the bed, his body illuminated by a lamp on the bedside locker. He was completely naked, his penis erect. He was stroking himself, face tense as he stared down at the bed. There I saw the back, the arse and legs of the big bear-like man, the bumbling oaf who'd been mauling the young girl on the dance floor, molesting her on the couch. She was beneath him, her legs at either side as he pounded his flabby torso against her tiny frame. Were it not for the light cast by the lamp, I wouldn't have known it was her. But there she lay, her head propped up on a pillow, lolling to one side, those round eyes staring into space, devoid of emotion, almost of life. The bright red lipstick had been smeared across her face, and her mascara ran in streaks down her cheeks.

She emitted a gasp as he began to increase the pace. I heard another voice mutter an expletive from the other side of the room, outside my eye line, someone urging clemency, pleading for the assailant to go easy. And then for a split second we locked eyes, the girl and I. Life flickered back into her as she focused on the stranger at the door, perhaps wondering if I were a potential saviour, someone who might rescue her from this tyranny. Then the shutters came down again and she returned to oblivion, to a place where she couldn't be harmed. I was just another man coming to join them, ready to heap more misery upon her.

I drew away from the door, my breath hitching as I stumbled down the stairs and out into the front garden. There I fell to my knees, head reeling, thoughts spiralling, and vomited up everything I'd drunk since my last emission. Everything went black. I blinked in terror, twisting my neck wildly from one side to the other, but there was only darkness. I couldn't feel my arms, my legs, my face, the only sound the incessant thud of my heart and a distant rasping wind. I listened to that thud, focusing on it, until it began to slow, gradually steadying, returning to its normal rhythm. The wind grew louder. It was me, my breathing, my ragged gasps and wheezes catching in my throat as the clouds lifted and I returned to the world of the living.

I was on my knees in the front garden. Music continued to blare from the house. A couple of people stood nearby, smoking, a few more sat on a wall drinking cans. For what felt like the umpteenth time I hauled myself to my feet, the ground unsteady as I sought my bearings. None of these people would be able to help, that much was clear. It would be pointless even trying to explain it to them. It was me, and me alone, who would have to stop this.

For the first time in my life I was about to do something good. Best of all, I wasn't even afraid. I went back into the house and ascended the stairs, my mind blank, devoid of thought or emotion. I went to the room, waited outside a moment, composed myself and pushed the door open. The guy with his back to me, the one who'd been standing guard, spun round in surprise. I shoved him aside. Another fella was sitting on a chair, topless, watching the action, presumably waiting his turn. I shot him a glance which said 'Don't even fucking think about it'. The bear man still lay on top of the girl, looking back at me, reluctant to stop what he was doing.

"Get the fuck off her," I instructed, my voice commanding, authoritative.

"Fuck off," he said dismissively, still on top of her, still in her.

I stepped towards the bed.

"Look at her, she's out of it," I said.

"No she's not. She's grand," he said, slapping her on the face until she whimpered in response.

Unable to control myself any longer I sprang forward, using my entire body weight to haul him off the bed, my fingers kneading into his flabby haunches as he toppled over the other side. I found myself momentarily lying on the girl's limp frame, on her legs. Not waiting for him to react, I scooped her naked body from the bed and strode out of the room with her in my arms. I reached the bottom of the stairs. The two girls who'd been chatting jumped to their feet in terror, not knowing if I were saint or sinner. Others gathered round, someone brought a blanket. There was a commotion, accusatory words. People began to leave. "We have to get her to the hospital," a man said angrily. I walked away then, casting a glance back to make sure she was okay, that no one else was going to harm her. I'd done a good thing. I'd ended her suffering, for now at least.

That was what I should have done. That's what I imagined myself doing as I knelt in the garden, listening to the clamour, the shouting, the voices, the mayhem coming from inside. But I didn't do any of it. I didn't go back inside, I didn't end the girl's torment. Instead I did what I always did: I gave in to fear, I withdrew into myself, and did everything in my power to ensure my own safety, no one else's, just mine. I got to my feet, tearful, full of self-loathing, and slowly walked away from the house, away from the music, away from the shouting, the voices, and, most importantly, from the horror I'd witnessed in that bedroom.

9

I WENT TO THE PARK and walked around in circles, concocting ways to avoid the inevitable fallout. I thought of getting the train home, the bus, feigning ignorance when Dan came back later in the evening, telling him I'd woken up in the park and gone straight to the station. But I had no money, I'd lost my wallet and my phone. I thought about hitching, but I didn't even know which direction was home. And then I thought about staying in the park, finding a quiet spot under the bough of a tree and waiting it out for a few days. But then I'd still have no money, and I'd be hungry and thirsty. It was that thirst which eventually drove me back. The sun had been up for a few hours and I'd walked myself to a standstill. There was nothing else to do but go back and face the music.

My hope was that Dan and Fergal had returned before things escalated any further, before someone had set fire to the house. They were confident lads, not much fazed them. What chance they'd arrived back and cleared the place in that assertive manner of theirs, the revellers obliging without too much resistance? Maybe it would all be okay. I'd return to a quiet house, the two lads asleep, no sign of a party save for a few bin liners full of cans. I'd get a few hours kip on the couch and drive back with Dan later on. Nothing would be said. After all, they were used to mad sessions - they went on about them often enough.

Really, though, I knew I was heading back to a shitstorm of my own making. The only question was how bad it would be, nuclear or atomic? And how damaging, how lasting, would the fallout be? There'd surely be a financial cost, maybe a physical one, but it was the emotional impact I feared most: the hate, the anger, the pain I'd caused. I turned into the cul de sac. The initial signs were promising. There wasn't any music, and I couldn't see any people outside the house. The party was over. The lads had succeeded in ending it. With any luck they were in bed or gone out for food.

As I drew closer, however, I saw that the front door was open and someone was sitting on the step. It was Fergal, the gatekeeper. His head was in his hands, it looked as if he might be asleep. There was little point in trying to sneak past him. I coughed, announcing my arrival, scuffing my feet on the ground in case the cough wasn't loud enough. Like something out of a cartoon he jerked awake, confused at first then very much focused. He looked at me, I looked at him, and I knew that having just had my first session I was now about to have my first hiding.

I watched him get to his feet and approach me, rage in his eyes, no, not rage, hate, pure hate. His mouth was set in a grimace, teeth clamped down, shoulders tensed, back hunched as he prepared to unleash his fury. The last thing I saw was the chain around his neck as it leapt from underneath his shirt. It was gold. It looked expensive. A symbol hung from it, like letters intertwined. Maybe it was a family heirloom and had sentimental value, or perhaps it was just his initials, a present from a loved one. I would ask him about it another time. There was an impact, a smack, flesh on flesh and then I was on the ground, my sight blurry, pain spreading across my face.

He was quite a wiry chap, Fergal, but he sure packed a punch. Retaliation wasn't an option, so I curled into the foetal position and awaited the onslaught. But he was practising great restraint. Rather than subject me to the volley of punches and kicks I deserved, he grabbed me by the shoulders quite brusquely and shook me, pushing me as he shouted expletives, insults, indecipherable aspersions, into my face. He was letting it all out, unloading his emotions in a controlled way, far too classy to hit a prone opponent. Even now, as they dished out my punishment, they were better than me.

After what felt like an age Dan appeared and dragged Fergal off me, attempting to placate him. But Fergal was upset. He turned on Dan, lashed out at him. That hardly seemed fair. Yet Dan, to his credit, to his eternally noble fucking credit, didn't respond. He waited for the storm to pass, for Fergal to remember who the real enemy was, then, after a tearful apology, a manly hug and a pep talk, they went back inside. Dan's parting words a dagger to my heart.

"Leave him, man. He's not fucking worth it."

I lay there for some time, dabbing at my nose with a tissue, wondering if it was broken. I listened, trying to judge the mood. I was keen to help with the clean-up, to do my bit. But I also wanted to see the level of destruction for myself. For them to react like that it had to be bad. I could hear the two of them inside, their voices low and muted, respectful, as if in mourning for the house. They had started tidying up but with no great enthusiasm. There was the occasional clink of a bottle as they cleared debris away, a moan of disgust, a sigh of resignation.

It was up to me to lead this operation, to inject some energy into this miserable after-party. I couldn't possibly make things any worse at this stage, but maybe I could make them better. Carefully, gingerly, I stepped inside, my feet crunching on broken glass. Dan appeared in the doorway.

"Happy?" he asked sarcastically, gesturing at the carnage like an estate agent showing off an open-plan living area, but instead of tasteful decor, a modernised kitchen unit and a homely three-piece suite, I was entering a bomb site. That's what it was like. It reminded me of those images on the news, of a smoke-filled street in the Middle East with junk everywhere, people emerging from the wreckage with soot on their faces, confusion and panic, sirens wailing in the distance. I went into the kitchen first. It was fucked. Everything was broken. Everything.

There was a keg in the sink and bottles and cans on every available surface. The fridge had flooded, its waters partially diluting the gunk which had formed on the floor, a sticky residue comprised of alcohol, piss, mud, vomit, ash and God knows what else. Teabags, sugar, pasta, rice, the few foodstuffs in the house, lay atop broken plates, inside filthy mugs, half-eaten and unwanted, just left there for the fun of it. There was a space where the microwave had been. The kettle had exploded, leaving burn marks on the wall. A fire extinguisher had been set off, the foam leading outside to the back garden, the empty can discarded in the grass.

Not content with a microwave, someone had tried to take the washing machine too. It had been pulled out from its place beneath the worktop but then left there, its weight deterring the would-be thieves. Someone had put the toaster inside it and filled her up, causing another flood, this one with suds, crumbs and bits of old toast.

By comparison the living room wasn't too bad. The television was gone, and the stereo, but in terms of damage only the coffee table (cracked down the middle) and the armchairs (ripped at the seams, their insides spilling out) had suffered. The rest was just surface; dirt and grime, nothing that a mop and some industrial-strength cleaning products couldn't rectify. My spirits lifted. We could do this. I'd go to the shop, get some bleach, a few scouring pads, and we'd get straight into it. If I led the way and did most of the donkey work, it would show them how sorry I was. Actions spoke louder than words, after all.

"And then there's the toilet," Dan said, pointing me towards the downstairs loo, the door of which was firmly shut. I looked at Dan for reassurance. What was in there? He cast his eyes downward, offering neither encouragement nor warning.

Tentatively, I opened the door and looked inside. The smell hit me first: shit, sharp and pungent, mixed with piss, vomit and maybe a hint of blood. Eyes watering, I pushed the door open fully. It was a tiny room, just a toilet and a sink, a little window. The toilet, naturally enough, was flooded, wads of discoloured loo roll floated in water which lapped at the edges of the bowl. That hadn't stopped one person or maybe two, it was hard to tell, from squatting in the general direction of the cistern and evacuating their bowels. Unfortunately this person appeared to have acute digestive problems and a jet-propelled arse.

If the shit had been consigned to the general toilet area it might not have been so bad, but they had somehow managed to get it on the wall behind the toilet, on both walls either side and even on the ceiling. There was more on the floor but it was different to the rest, more solid. Thankfully the sink had escaped, it only contained vomit. There was dried blood on the mirror and on one of the walls. I couldn't see the piss, but I knew it was there.

"And then there's upstairs," Dan said.

This was getting to be too much. I couldn't handle upstairs. I'd been avoiding the thought of what I'd seen up there, hoping that if I simply ignored that part of the house I could pretend it had never happened, that it had been a drunken hallucination. Dan was determined to give me the full tour, though, so up we went.

Fergal was in his room, the master bedroom - *that* room - so we left it till last. First we visited his housemate's room, some Scottish guy called Vic who had gone home for the weekend. I hoped he never came back. I also hoped he'd brought anything of value with him, because his was the room which had been completely ransacked: mattress flipped, wardrobe emptied, locker on its side, bags turned inside out. It just looked like an all-out robbery. The bedclothes had been hastily rearranged on the floor, probably by an amorous couple, but there was no sense of fun in here, just dark intentions.

"His laptop is gone and a couple of suits, a coat and runners. They took the telly and DVD player," Dan informed me, going from estate agent to sombre policeman in the space of a few minutes.

"I'll pay for everything," I said.

He didn't respond, instead briefly opening the bathroom door to reveal more destruction, more despair, before leading me to the middle bedroom, the one Fergal used as a study. I'd heard people in there at the party speaking in hushed tones, quiet folk, the more chilled guests at Aido's Big Bash. I'd been misled, they were as bad as the rest. Vomit on the floor. A broken window. A singed rug. An upturned chest of drawers on which, according to Dan, Fergal's desktop computer had once resided.

"I wouldn't go in there yet, if at all," advised Dan as we lingered outside Fergal's room. I could hear him inside, sorting the rubbish, going through the wreckage. It must be a very intimate type of outrage to know that a bunch of strangers had run riot in your place of rest. But they'd done more than run riot in there. I felt a sudden urge to tell Dan what I'd seen. I could unload my burden, get him and Fergal to carry it too, but then I'd have to tell them I walked away, that I let it happen. So I let the moment pass, and stood outside the room listening to Fergal's sobs until Dan signalled for us to go back downstairs.

*

It was early evening when we finally left. Vic, the Scottish guy, was due back at eight p.m. and Fergal wanted us gone by then. I'd taken the lead on the clean-up, but only after Dan had shelled out for a new bucket and mop, bottles of bleach, scouring pads, rubber gloves, kitchen and bathroom spray, bin liners - anything which might make the house habitable once more. I did the downstairs toilet first. It was unspeakably grim. I worked in two-minute bursts, doing as much as I could before the stench sent me hurrying out the front door for air. Once I got the filth off the walls and unclogged the toilet it got easier, and there was a certain satisfaction in seeing it returned to its former state, seeing that, despite appearances, it was nothing a bit of hard work couldn't fix.

Once we'd cleared away all the empties and swept up the broken glass, we set about eliminating the viscous gloop which had formed on the living-room floor. It took five buckets of hot water and a full bottle of bleach. I marvelled at the coffee table, a solid glass construct with a marble stand. Yes, it had a sizeable crack which stretched right across its length but it had survived the night, come out the other end of an ordeal which had left its contemporaries gathered in a sorry pile at the end of the back garden. As we slid it back to the centre of the room, you could almost forget what had taken place here. Sadly, the broken three-piece and a fireplace which looked like a bomb had detonated in its hearth, spoiled the scene.

The kitchen was easy in comparison, the floor requiring a couple of buckets before we polished down the worktops, scrubbed the presses and plugged the fridge back in. There was a strange smell, like dead animals, but that would fade in time. We did the upstairs bathroom and tidied two of the bedrooms as best we could. I didn't get to see Fergal's room, the only hint to its condition coming when he emerged with a bundle of bedsheets, put them in a bin liner and threw it out the back door. When we'd finished I looked over our work with a hint of pride. We'd made a decent fist of it, we really had, and I would replace the stolen items and pay for any associated costs.

Given how bad things had appeared this morning, it was all rather heartening. I still had to maintain an air of gloom, out of respect for Fergal, because although we'd done a good job the emotional trauma was something I would never be able to fix. Vic's trauma when he returned and saw what they'd done to his room. Dan and Fergal's trauma when they'd returned to the house and found the party to end all parties in full swing. The further trauma of seeing what they'd done to the house, and the trauma of having your personal space invaded, your small part of the world destroyed by people who didn't give a damn, each would linger long after I waved Dublin goodbye.

I never found out what happened in those hours, between the time I left and the time I returned, but I knew it hadn't been good. I knew from the looks on their faces it had turned ugly. There was no mention of the girl, that must have been over by the time they arrived. Or maybe the people in the room dispersed when they heard the ruckus, leaving the girl lying on the bed, broken and afraid, grateful to be on her own but knowing she wasn't safe yet, listening out, wondering if they were coming back. And then, when enough time had passed, quietly gathering her clothes, wincing as she bent to pick them up, hastily dressing herself, ignoring the blood, and creeping down the stairs. Squeezing to avoid the passing couple who giggled as they made a beeline for the room she'd vacated. Pausing outside the living-room, wondering about her jacket, the jacket she'd got for her birthday, which contained her phone, her keys, her purse. Knowing it was in there somewhere, on the couch, someone sitting on it, crushing it under their weight, stuck between the cushions, stained with drink, burned by ash, dirty and ragged. And deciding to leave it, carrying on out the door, unable to face them, their leering and jeering, reasoning that it was only a jacket, only a phone.

Walking home on her own, head down, trying to make herself small, hoping to pass unnoticed. Starting as a car honked its horn and slowed down alongside her, its occupants shouting at her, more leering, filthy talk from filthy boys. Until eventually they grew bored and continued on their way. Making it to her house, the one she shared with her mother and three younger siblings, and tapping on the back door until her eleven-year-old brother, hair tousled, eyes blinking, let her in. And then finally retreating to the solace of her room, crawling in to the bed, kicking off her clothes, unable to get warm. Crying silently so as not to wake the others, her soft snuffling receding gradually until she drifted off to sleep, to a place of safety, to a place of respite, where she didn't have to think about men and the things they did.

10

ONCE DAN GOT ME IN the car alone, just the two of us, I learnt a bit more. At first he said nothing, concentrated on negotiating the traffic, his senses blunted by the sleepless night. But once we got out of Dublin, onto the relative peace of the M11, he let me have it.

"What the fuck were you thinking, Aidan?"

I was tired too. All I wanted was my own house, my own room, my own bed. But I had to answer for my crimes.

"I don't know," I said, aware of how inadequate it sounded.

"How did you . . . where did you meet those people?"

"In the park."

"The park?! What were you doing in the park? You could hardly stand when I left you."

"I was looking for that pub. Look, Dan, I'm really sorry . . ."

He shook his head dismissively. Apologies were no use to him.

"Do you have any idea what you did? Do you?"

He turned to look at me, now a mirror-image of his father.

"I saw the house, Dan," I said defensively.

"You didn't see it when we did, when we came back," he countered.

"Were there many of them there?"

Another shake of the head.

"And where the hell were you, Aidan? You declare open season on Fergal's house and then fuck off! Went for another walk in the park, did you?"

Funnily enough, he was right.

"I had to get some fresh air."

"There was fresh air in the front garden, and the back."

"I just had to get away," I said.

"Yeah, and leave us to deal with it."

There followed another period of silence, occasionally punctuated by Dan's angry mutterings.

"He needs that computer for work."

"The *state* of the toilet."

"You stupid fuck, Aidan."

"Jesus."

"Only for the guards."

And so on. Until an hour or so from home, he issued a warning.

"There's to be no mention of any of this when we get to your house," he said.

"What about my face?" I asked, pointing to the cut on the bridge of my nose and the blackening eyes on both sides.

"You bumped into a door, fell over. Make something up."

"Okay."

"And whatever money you get on the dole goes towards paying Fergal and Vic back."

"Of course."

"And as for this," he said, waving his hand between the two of us."As for you and me, hanging out, going out, you can forget about that. Don't come knocking on my door asking for a game of *Halo*, or to watch a Chinese film, I'm doing my own thing from now on. If your mother asks why we're not hanging out I'll tell her I'm busy, you can tell her what you like. I just want to get through this summer and get back to college."

"Japanese. The films were Japanese," I replied, a lump forming in my throat.

*

We did hang out again that summer. We went to the pub a couple of times and even watched a few films, but it wasn't the same. We were like a couple seeing out the last days of an unhappy marriage, waiting for the divorce papers to arrive so we could go our separate ways, trying to end it amicably for the sake of the kids. In our case, the divorce papers were the end of the summer and the kids were my parents. As July gave way to August and it succumbed to autumn, Dan's mood lifted considerably. Some of the old warmth returned and we had a bit of a laugh again.

On his last night before heading back we got royally pissed, fall-down drunk, and this time I didn't make a fool of myself or fuck things up. We went to *The Fiddler's Elbow* in Crunníth, played pool, darts, sang songs with the regulars, and then stumbled out onto the street singing as we meandered our way home arm-in-arm. The next morning, after he'd packed his stuff and said goodbye to my parents, he shook my hand, gave me a half-hug and told me to look after myself.

Then he got in his car, started the engine and offered one final salute before returning from whence he came. I knew I'd only ever see him again at funerals, weddings, and christenings, and that our conversations would be always be stilted and awkward, but I was okay with that. I had no place in Dan's world nor he in mine. It had been an interesting experience, but I was relieved it was over. Now that he was gone, things could return to normal. I didn't need to pretend any more, I could live the life I wanted, free from interference.

But I was haunted by that night in Dublin. Haunted by what I'd seen in that bedroom. In the days and weeks that followed I waited for my guilt to be proven, leaping out of my skin whenever the phone rang, expecting to hear the stern, officious tone of a guard, a solicitor, at the other end. I constantly checked the news, poring over every paper, watching the bulletins at one p.m., six p.m. and nine p.m., expecting to see something about a rape trial, to see four men hurrying into court, their faces obscured by hoods. It never happened. If she had gone to the guards or pressed charges, they hadn't contacted anyone at the party and it hadn't made the news. Maybe it was still going through the courts, maybe the call would come soon, maybe they were still gathering evidence.

Deep down I knew why I hadn't received a phone call or seen it on the news: the girl hadn't done anything. She hadn't gone to the authorities. She had remained silent. I understood why. It was easier that way, easier to absorb the blows and move on to the next thing. Sometimes, while drunk, I imagined myself taking revenge on her behalf: travelling up to Dublin to that same housing estate and working my way backwards, hanging round the park and the newsagents, looking for Jinx and his friends and using them to track down the perpetrators. But no, my part in that story had already concluded, and it was a miserable, insignificant one.

That summer left me with more than just a few bad memories, a couple of black eyes and a scar on my nose. It left me with a burgeoning taste for booze, an appetite for alcohol which didn't disappear with Dan's departure. If anything it increased in his absence. And that appetite rapidly progressed from being a crutch to help with life's difficult moments to an almost daily dependence, the foremost presence in my life. Blaming everything on Dan would have been churlish, but I couldn't help wonder if my life might have been different had he chosen to spend that summer elsewhere.

PART TWO

2010

1

"AIDAN, YOU HAVE TO DO *something* with your life, you can't just spend your days holed up in that room."

We were having one of our chats, myself and my father. It was a massive undertaking for him, a drain on his limited resources, but he had to do it, if only for a quiet life. Cursing myself for coming downstairs before they'd gone to bed, I pondered my response; something worthy, something he could bring back to my mother as proof of his efforts.

"I was looking at courses in the paper the other day," I said.

"Oh yeah, which ones?" he asked, his eyes bright and hopeful.

"There was a computer one, something about a European Computer Driving Licence."

"That sounds good, Aidan. It's all computers nowadays."

"Yeah. I must get the form and send it off. Are there any envelopes around?"

He opened one of the presses and began sorting through bits of paper: old bills, receipts, manuals for toasters and kettles.

"I could have sworn there were envelopes in here," he said, as he plucked out a postcard with the Coliseum on the back and began reading it. "Remember this? Sally was going out with that Richard guy at the time. I wonder what became of him?"

My father's heart wasn't really in it, and neither was mine. Yes, he would have liked to see me make something of myself, but he was content to let me be. It was my mother who drove him to it, who silently made her displeasure known until he was forced to act. I knew how it worked. If I gave him something to bring back to her, we could all resume our lives as normal until the next time. There wouldn't be any computer course, or any type of course at all. We were experts at living in denial, had been for years.

My relationship with my mother was a case in point. We were cordial, exchanged pleasantries, but there was nothing there. There had been no tipping point, no flare-ups, we had just gradually grown apart, if we had ever been close at all. She was a haunted, haggard figure, a ghost who silently moved from room to room, stalked by the same demons that I fought, but she was further down the line in her battle. All that I was I inherited from her. We could have helped one another, but it was up to her to make the first move and she never did.

I left my father with his memories and returned upstairs with my drink. He would find the envelopes and there would be one sitting on the kitchen table in the morning, beside the newspaper clipping containing details of the computer course. Depending on my mood, I would either remove the offending items and stash them in my room or leave them where they were, to be frowned over the following evening. The latter would seem like an act of petulance, a petty response designed to frustrate and irritate. But it wouldn't be anything of the sort. It would be a cry for help.

From the outside it looked as if I were an overgrown man-child, still reliant on his parents at the age of twenty-five, a lazy good-for-nothing, a drunken loser. And I was, but not by choice. I wanted to change, to be better, to get out and start living. I just couldn't. If my parents could see how paralysed I was, how the simplest of tasks completely overwhelmed me, that my behaviour wasn't churlish defiance, then maybe I could get better. But we didn't discuss our feelings, so my only way of communicating my despair was by disengaging completely, by sinking deeper into alcoholism, abandoning all reason and hoping one of them would throw me a lifeline.

I wanted to do that course. It was exactly what I was looking for. It would help me to get a place as a mature student on a degree course at the nearby Institute of Technology. From there, if I knuckled down, I could get a job as an application designer at the software company in town. That was a job I'd be good at, one I could flourish in. With that job I would have made something of myself, I would have enough money to buy my own house, find a wife, a dog, have children. Have a life.

All I needed was a little help, a push in the right direction, someone to tell me it would all be okay, that there was nothing wrong with being scared. If I could just get that, an arm around my shoulder, I felt like I could tackle it, I could make a start and move things in the right direction. Tonight was rum night, though, and rum night was usually followed by rum morning or, to be more precise, rum afternoon, so the course and my future would have to wait a while longer.

It was after two p.m. when I woke up. The house was empty. Dad was at work and Mam at the community centre where she did administrative stuff three days a week. I went downstairs, poured myself a mammoth bowl of cornflakes and sat looking at the envelope. How did I get the form to apply for the course? Did I have to ring and ask for one to be posted out? There was no chance of that happening today. I was in no shape for talking to strangers. Leaving the bowl in the sink, I took the envelope and the torn-out page and went back upstairs. That would be enough for one day. I had the number now. I would ring them later on in the week, on a day when I wasn't feeling quite so seedy. Sure the closing date wasn't for another ten days.

"You sent off the form anyway, lad, did you?" asked my father when I came down with my plate after dinner.

I nodded, incapable of lying outright.

"That'll be good for you, son," he said agreeably, bringing his tea into the living-room. My mother had already retired to her room for the night. She had her own television in there, watched her own programmes. No one disturbed her. I would go to my room and do the same, leaving Dad to his own devices, to another evening of solitude with his family. He hadn't even realised there was no form, that I had to get it from somewhere before it could be sent off. He didn't get it, didn't get any of it, just thought I was a quiet lad who kept to himself.

I knew he was mildly perturbed by my drinking - he'd made reference to the amount of empties in the recycling bin on a couple of occasions - but he had no comprehension of the extent of my problems. If I were to expose him to it, to sit him down and tell him the thoughts that had begun circling round my head in recent months, the fantasies of ending it all, of her finding me hanging in my room, of him trying to shake me awake, and the pleasure I would derive from their guilt, he'd be horrified.

The next day, my head a little clearer, I prepared myself for a phone call. I stared at the piece of paper, reading it over and over again.

Fancy a career in IT? Need to learn office skills? Then why not enrol in our ECDL (European Computer Driving Licence) course today. The course is split into different modules that focus on subjects such as Microsoft Excel, Word, PowerPoint and IT fundamentals. Also includes four weeks of work experience designed to give you an opportunity to practise your new skills in a suitable environment. All the modules are designed to give you the skills you need to fit your future career plans. This is a full-time six-month course provided by FÁS and is only available for those in receipt of social welfare payments. To learn more, and to receive an application form, contact us on this number.

I'd easily be the best candidate on the course. Most of the people who went for these things had barely been to school, were just going to keep the dole office off their back for a few months. The lecturers would be thrilled to see me; someone who actually had an interest in IT and planned to use the course as a springboard for his future career. I'd be top of the class, their brightest student, but only if I could get to class every day, only if I could control my anxiety, my stomach, my racing thoughts.

Things were different now, though. I was older and a little more knowledgeable about the ways of the world. Yes, I still sweated whenever I was in a public place, but the vomiting and diarrhoea had mostly stopped. This would be a more relaxed setting, too, an adult environment. I wouldn't be wearing that itchy school uniform and there wouldn't be a room full of posturing young lads making me feel uneasy. Instead, I'd be in my own comfortable clothes surrounded by people just like me, people who'd somehow lost their way and found themselves doing a FÁS course for reasons they'd rather not divulge. Maybe I'd make some friends, even a girlfriend.

But, every time I thought about the course, my stomach took a turn. I took that as a sign. I allowed a couple of days to pass, then a week, till the closing date grew near. Occasionally, after a few drinks, I'd get a burst of positivity and vow to ring the number first thing in the morning, planning out what I'd say and the questions I'd ask, only to awake the next morning in a cold sweat, reminded of my limitations. Until eventually the closing date passed and I relaxed. There was nothing more I could do, no more decisions to make, it was out of my hands. The course was consigned to history, an idea I'd toyed with but one I'd chosen not to pursue. My father did bring up it a while later, asking if I'd heard anything about that 'computer thing'. I told him I hadn't and that was that.

I would come to regret not availing of that opportunity when it presented itself. Because, unbeknownst to me, the social welfare office had been updating their files and noticed that there was a chap called Aidan Collins who had done nary a day of work since leaving school seven years previously. He had signed on as soon as he'd turned eighteen and had been in receipt of Jobseeker's Allowance ever since. Yet, according to their records, he hadn't been doing much job seeking at all. From what they could see, all he'd been doing was sitting on his fat arse, taking handouts without ever threatening to give something back. Well, that simply wasn't good enough. It was high time Mr. Collins explained himself and his actions, or lack thereof.

2

RECEIVING POST FROM THE SOCIAL welfare office was nothing new for me, they'd been sending me stuff for years. Usually it was a selection of job opportunities suitable for an unskilled school leaver with no experience, or a course being held in the local community centre. Those went straight in the bin, my own bin in my own room in case anyone saw them. There were also letters asking me to verify my living arrangements, to prove I was eligible for whatever few quid they were giving me. I had to reply to these letters, as failure to do so would see my money stopped.

After I'd jumped through their hoops and done as instructed, they means-tested me and I ended up losing a fiver here, a tenner there. That just deepened my resolve, they weren't going to make me do anything I didn't want to, fuck them and their forms. I would sign on once a month and do whatever was necessary to keep them off my back, but I would never engage with them and their pissy suggestions that I apply for this job or enrol in that course.

But the letter I received on September 19, 2010 was different to anything I'd received before. They wanted me to come in and meet them, to discuss my next move - or my first move - with a view to applying for jobs or taking one of their courses. Failure to turn up for this meeting would automatically see my payment stopped. Once I'd discussed my moves, I had to be seen to be actively seeking work or further education, otherwise my payment would be stopped. I considered ignoring it, calling their bluff and seeing what would happen.

Surely they couldn't just cut me off like that? There had to be a law stating that every citizen was entitled to a certain amount of money, regardless of their compliance. But ignoring it would lead to more meetings, more paperwork, and by the end of it I'd still end up in their offices, talking to a bored, middle-aged woman about my 'career prospects'. I considered saying 'To hell with it', allowing them to cut me off and striking out on my own, but I knew I had to answer their call. The only hope I had was emerging with my life still intact, without finding myself in a factory or doing a crochet course in the community centre.

They wanted me in that Thursday at 11.30 a.m. It gave me just three days to prepare, and prepare I did. I drank for two days solid, then, on the night before I was due to go in, I went cold turkey, to bed, early, panicking about the bus in the morning, about the meeting, about being sent straight off to work with no way of getting home, nothing for my lunch, having to sleep on a park bench. After a restless night I got up and readied myself, put on my most eager, compliant face and walked down to the bus stop. When it arrived, I handed the money to the driver and made my way to the back, focusing on my breathing, reminding myself that in a few short hours I'd be on my way home again and this would be all over.

At the social welfare office I handed my letter to the woman at reception and she gestured towards a blue door opposite. This was different, usually I went into the main hall with all the hatches, the metal seating areas, the winding queues, the arguments, the laughter, the worried faces. I'd never gone through the blue door. On the other side, half-a-dozen people sat on wooden chairs with cushions on them. There were magazines, potted plants and a water cooler, it was almost cosy, like a real place for real people. There was still a person in authority, though: someone sitting on the other side of a Perspex barrier. I went up to her, showed my letter, and was instructed to sit down and wait my turn.

None of the magazines interested me, so I decided to assess the other candidates. There were four men and two women. I recognised one of the men, he'd gone to St. Mark's as well: Barry Browne. He'd been a couple of years below me but had hung around with lads from my class. He was lying almost prone in one of the chairs, with his feet stretched across the carpet. He caught me looking at him and gave a nod of recognition which made me feel better, like me and Barry were in this together. I wish I could have been relaxed about it as he was, though.

One of the other men was middle-aged, like my father, and was taking his appointment very seriously. He'd put on a nice jumper and had a plastic folder with sheets of paper inside. Every so often he coughed nervously and checked his watch. I hoped he'd have a successful meeting. The last two men looked like they'd come directly from the pub, their eyes were bloodshot, their chins stubbly; receding, thinning hair scraped back in an effort to look presentable. The older of the two women, possibly in her late thirties, was making sure everyone knew she didn't want to be here. She did this by sighing deeply at regular intervals and shaking her head in annoyance. The rest of the time she stared at her phone, furiously tapping at the screen whenever a message came in. The other woman was younger, nearer Barry's age, she bore no expression and had scarcely moved since my arrival. She seemed a bit dozy and vacant, as if they'd had to drug her to make her come in.

The impatient woman was the first to be called. She disappeared through a different door, a normal brown one, and emerged ten minutes later, an arched eyebrow leaving us to guess what had gone on back there. The man in the nice jumper was next. He was in there for ages, at least twenty minutes, and when he came out he was still locked in conversation with a staff member. One of the drunk lads went next, leaving me, Barry, the other drunk and the young woman. I started to get nervous then.

I was last in, so the only question was who would be left sitting here with me at the end. When we were all together there'd been no pressure to make conversation, but once you get down to two people the atmosphere changes. I didn't want to be left with Barry. We'd made contact when I came in, but I was intimidated by him and didn't want to talk to him. The safest bet would be the drunk, we had no common ground and I imagined he'd be equally content to sit in silence. If it were the girl, the onus would be on me to say something. I didn't know why, that was just the way it was. Judging by her slackened jaw and heavy eyes, there was no telling what way that conversation would go.

Barry was called next. I breathed a sigh of relief. When he came out he gave me a smug nod and carried on out the door, then we waited for the next name out of the hat. It was the man, leaving me alone with the girl. I wasn't used to being alone with girls but, as girls went, this one seemed fairly harmless so I decided to do the gentlemanly thing and make some sort of contact. I glanced at her, trying to catch her eye, but she was staring at the pictures on the wall, moving her gaze from one to the next, really slowly, like a sloth, a sloth with an interest in cheap art.

After several glances our eyes briefly met and I raised mine to heaven: the universal sign of 'What's this all about, then?' She immediately stared at the floor. Did I detect a touch of redness in her cheeks? Was she actually embarrassed by our innocent encounter? Usually I was the one flushing red, stammering and stuttering like a half-wit, yet here she was, getting in a state over nothing more than a bit of eye contact. Before I had a chance to digest this and interact further she was called in, meekly gathering her belongings and joining the man at the door. It gave me an opportunity to check her out. Despite my apparent chivalry I was still a man, and one who reflexively gave women the once-over whenever the opportunity arose. She was quite small and thin, I'd hoped to get a look at her arse but there wasn't a whole lot to see there, or indeed anywhere; just a puffy pink jacket, light blue jeans and white runners. Even her hair didn't seem to be any particular colour, maybe brown or dark blonde, I couldn't say. As soon as she'd disappeared from sight I instantly forgot what she looked like, couldn't have pictured her in my mind's eye if my life depended on it.

She came out a few minutes later, accompanied by an exasperated-looking man. He gestured for me to join him, distracting me from getting a proper look at the girl before she left. And then I was in the little office space, sitting on one side of the table while the man gathered up my pitiful files and prepared for our discussion.

"So, Aidan, my name is Joe," he said.

Informal. Clearly a company policy.

"Hello, Joe," I said.

He continued looking over my files, a confused look on his face, as if he were being asked to solve the greatest riddle known to man. We sat there like that for some time, me wondering where this was all going, him continuing to tussle with this great brainteaser. Until, eventually, he returned to the land of the living.

"Aidan, sorry about that," he said, putting the papers on the desk. "How are you?"

"I'm okay."

He moved forward in his seat, indicating that the serious part was about to begin.

"Aidan, I've been looking over your records," he said, gesturing at the puzzle laid out before him. "It says that you signed on the day you turned eighteen and have been doing so ever since. Is that right?"

He knew it was right. It said so in front of him.

"Yes."

"You did your Leaving Cert, didn't you?"

"Yes."

"How did you get on?"

"Okay."

"What marks did you get?"

I exhaled deeply.

"Nearly 450 points."

"What? 450! Sure that would have got you into most of the universities in the country. Did you not apply for any courses?"

"No."

"How come?" he asked, looking genuinely sad.

I shrugged my shoulders, getting defensive now.

"Jesus, that's an awful waste, Aidan, if you don't mind my saying so."

"I don't mind," I replied, appreciating his forthrightness.

"What are you interested in? You could still go as a mature student, what are you – twenty-five?" he said, checking my file for confirmation.

I didn't want to tell Joe what I was interested in, didn't want to expose myself like that. He'd only laugh at me.

"I don't think college is for me," I said.

"Well, what then? You're clearly a bright lad. We have some courses coming up that might be suitable for you."

Great. Here came the courses.

"I mean, are you good with your hands? Do you want to learn a trade? Or maybe you'd like to work in hospitality? There's a huge range of options," he said, producing a sheath of papers and placing them in the space between us.

"Why don't you take those home with you, have a read through them and meet me back here next week to see where we're at?"

That seemed fair. I could work with that. There'd been no threats of cutting my money off, no ultimatums, just a friendly man doing his best to help me out.

"What time next week?" I asked.

"Same time. I'll get a letter sent out to you to confirm."

He got to his feet and picked up the papers, handing them to me.

"See you next week, Aidan."

"Okay."

I was free to go. It hadn't even been that bad.

I walked out of the office onto the street, feeling liberated, as if I'd achieved something.

*

The courses looked great. There was an IT Skills QQI Level 4 one starting in town not six weeks from now. There was a definite process at play, a pathway to success for those who wished to walk it. In all likelihood there would be other courses after the ones listed here, follow-ons from the beginner stuff. If I did a couple of those I could get a job as an entry-level engineer. If I really took to it, I could go to college. It was all there for me, all I had to do was summon up the courage to take what was on offer. But within a couple of days, after the sense of glory had faded, I was back to fretting once more. I couldn't do it, I hadn't the strength. It was as simple as that.

However, whereas previously I had been free to throw the scrap of paper to one side and carry on with my life, I was now being held accountable. Joe was expecting something of me. If I didn't deliver, he would be upset. He was probably assessed by the number of people he got on courses, and how many of those found work thereafter. His livelihood was on the line here. So, after some careful deliberation, I decided to tell him I'd do the IT Skills course. Then I'd have six weeks to figure out my next move. Not surprisingly, he was thrilled.

"Good man, Aidan, good man," he said, scooting his chair across the floor in search of a form.

That form contained my future, it felt like signing my death warrant.

"Now you'll still be able to get all your money, you'll also get a travel allowance, and there's free dinners at the training centre . . ."

This was a rare victory for Joe. I let him savour it.

"So, any questions?" he asked, his face almost radiant.

"No. Thanks, Joe."

"Here's my number," he said, handing me his business card. I put it in my pocket, thinking that maybe I could place it beside my suicide note and spread around some of that guilt.

3

THERE WERE JUST TWO WEEKS left until the course started. Several letters had been received and posted. An irreversible chain of events had been set in motion. There was no escape. I was considering heading for the hills, living off the land and sheltering in a cave until it all blew over, then news came from Galway. Bobby had taken a turn. If I hadn't been so preoccupied with my own affairs I might have taken some interest in his welfare, maybe even reached out to Dan with some consoling words, but it barely registered. My focus lay elsewhere.

Even the news that my mother was going to go there, up to Galway for a couple of weeks, made little impact. I hadn't told either of them about the course, didn't need the extra pressure. She and my father set off one morning before I awoke. They'd barely been gone a few hours when I got a phone call from my father.

"Aidan."

"Yeah."

"Listen to me."

"Okay."

"Your mother's after forgetting her pills."

I didn't even know she had pills.

"You're going to have to post them up to her, and you're going to have to do it this afternoon before the post office shuts."

"Can it not wait?"

"No, Aidan. She needs these by tomorrow evening at the very latest."

"Can't a doctor up there give them to her?"

"No, Aidan. She doesn't like seeing any doctor other than Doctor Flynn."

It sounded serious so I acquiesced.

"Okay, where are they?"

"Go into our room," he instructed.

I did as I was told.

"Now, go into the en-suite."

"Yeah. Now what?"

"See the little locker down by the sink, open that up."

"Okay."

"Now on the top shelf . . . what?"

I heard my mother's voice in the background, strained, impatient.

"Sorry, on the bottom part there should be a plastic container with a few bottles of pills in it."

I looked into the locker, and sure enough there was a blue tray with five different bottles of pills. Some of them were shop-bought, large white bottles, vitamins and the like, but there were two which bore the hallmark of a doctor's surgery: orangey-brown with a white sticker on the front. It would be one of those she was after.

"Have it," I confirmed.

"Good. Now, in that container there's two brown bottles with your mother's name on them. I want you to get the one that says 'Diazepam 10 mg' on the sticker. Do you see it?"

My ears pricked up. Diazepam: I knew what that was. It was like Valium, a kind of sedative.

"I have it."

There were a lot of tablets in the bottle. It was almost full.

"That's the one, Aidan. Now we need you to get it sent by express delivery, and make sure it's recorded too. Do you know how to do that?"

"I dunno."

He started to explain but I cut him off, now far more interested in the contents of the bottle than any postal instructions.

"There's money in the top drawer in the cabinet in the hallway, okay?"

"Yeah," I said, scrutinising the bottle as I walked out of the room and sat down on my bed.

"And send them straight away. Your mother needs them urgently."

"Okay, Dad," I said absent-mindedly as I hung up the phone and went on my computer to see what these things did to you.

The very first thing I saw was that diazepam 'typically produces a calming effect'. I continued my research. It said that it was used to treat anxiety, muscle spasms, and fits. My muscles were fine and I'd never had a fit, but anxiety – God, yes. The most common side effect was feeling drowsy. I was okay with that. It was recommended that you didn't drive machinery or use tools while taking it - I had never done either in my entire life.

There were some worrying details; you couldn't take it while drinking alcohol or while trying to get pregnant, but other than that it sounded like a panacea for all that ailed me. There was something about dosage too, a warning not to exceed a certain daily amount and to take it only for four weeks in succession, but I knew how to regulate my intake. I'd been doing it with alcohol for years.

Once I'd stopped thinking about myself and what these tablets could do for me, I thought about the person they'd been prescribed for: my mother. I had always known she wasn't well, that she suffered with her nerves, but hadn't understood the extent of it. This cast her in a new light. I felt a pang of guilt and a lump form in my throat. I'd been selfish. The world didn't revolve around me. Just because she was my mother didn't mean she had no problems of her own. While I'd been hiding away in my room, fighting my demons, she was doing the same just across the hall. And instead of seeing her gloominess, her inability to communicate her innermost feelings, as a cause for concern, I took it as an attack, a sign she was upset with me.

It was such a mess. If she and I could just sit down and discuss our issues maybe we could make a breakthrough, maybe this household could be a whole lot happier. She was in Galway now, though, and she needed her tablets. I counted them out on the kitchen table: there were twenty-nine in total. I took five out of the bottle and put the rest back, then I took out another two. That'd be fine: twenty-two for her, seven for me. I hurried to the post office to send the package, already thinking about the night ahead and my first foray into the world of benzodiazepines.

*

I ate my dinner, had a cup of tea and readied myself mentally. I was a little afraid of the tablets. What if they were dangerous? According to the Internet one in every thousand people got constipation after taking them, and a further one in every ten thousand lost control of their bodily movements. But if my mother could take them, then surely they were harmless enough. As an anxious person, I was a prime candidate for these tablets; I needed them. So I swallowed one down and went upstairs to play *Bioshock* on the Xbox, hoping it would prove a distraction until the drug took effect.

For the first half an hour I checked the time constantly, assessing my state of mind, waiting to feel relaxed and just making myself more anxious. After a while, though, I forgot about the time; I forgot about everything. Nothing really mattered, not even the game. My character, whose name I'd forgotten, was getting shot a lot, beaten with a crowbar, set on fire and electrocuted. I didn't mind, it was only a game, after all. Even when he came back to life, I didn't go in search of vengeance, I was more preoccupied with the world created by the game's designers, the lush colours and vivid environments. Just as I was immersing myself in this beautiful world, an enemy with a machine gun would come along and mow me down. There was no need for that. So I turned off *Bioshock* and put on a game I'd picked up in the bargain bin a couple of weeks previously. It was called *Viva Pinata* and, from what I could gather, involved gardening and creating a self-sustainable farm. This would be more pleasant.

The game started and a woman gave me a shovel, a watering can, some seeds and instructed me to plant some grass. I did as she said. Then I made a pond, and did a little digging, it was very soothing, just digging. Two worms appeared and a graphic came up to say they'd got married and were starting a family. I was happy for them. They were joined by some birds and I built a birdhouse for them, just like that, without being asked. There were butterflies, buttercups and a village shop where I could spend chocolate coins. I wanted some pigs but the woman didn't know anything about that.

The game ran in a twenty-four-hour cycle, and when night fell a fox appeared and started sneaking round the verge, bothering the hedgehogs. I gave him a belt with the shovel. Then it started to rain and some carrots began growing in the grass, I couldn't even remember planting them. By the third day there were animals everywhere; moles, rabbits, mice, badgers, squirrels, and a horse. And the garden was slowly getting out of control. The woman was nagging me to build more fences, the fox had reappeared with one of his mates, and there were carrots everywhere.

I decided to take a step back from the garden and let nature take its course. That was much better. It was still chaos, but it was no longer my responsibility. I looked at my watch. Two hours had passed since I'd taken the tablet, and not once during that time had I found cause to check my breathing, to quell the rising panic in my chest or push away thoughts of fear and tension. Even now, as I pondered these things, they were of little concern. What was there to be afraid of? Sure wasn't I breathing grand?

Delighted, I went off to the toilet for a piss. That felt nice too. I went downstairs, stood outside for a while and admired the nice weather we were having. I thought about all the insects I'd collected as a child, the hours spent in the dirt, rummaging round for slugs and whatnot, and wondered if I should take up gardening in the real world. It would be my new hobby, the thing I'd tell people about when they asked me what I did with myself. Maybe I could get a job as a gardener or a person who collected insects. Feeling sleepy, I went back upstairs and put on some Hall and Oates. It was groovy. It was nice, everything was just nice. If I could be like this all the time everything would be okay, there'd be no need to worry about anything.

There were a couple more albums played before I went to bed at the uncharacteristically early hour of one a.m. I was feeling good and I still had five more pills, or was it six? Whichever, I'd take another one in the morning, and then maybe one in the afternoon. I'd make them last until my mother came back and then take some of hers again, or get some off the doctor myself. It really didn't matter. It was all sorted now, the whole anxiety thing had been a problem there for a while but it would soon be behind me, a silly phase in my life that I'd laugh about some day.

4

I SLEPT DEEPLY AND AWOKE feeling groggy. At first I thought this was a good thing, that the pill was still working. Then I got a headache and suddenly I was anxious again; shaky, jittery, just like always. It had been an illusion, a temporary reprieve. And it had seemed so real. The only thing for it was to take another one. But I only had six left. Supply was going to be a serious problem. This wasn't like alcohol, where I could go down to the shop and stock up every night. I was going to have to save these things for special occasions, for particularly stressful days or perhaps an occasional treat. Or for the start of something life-changing like, say, an IT course which required me to turn up at a training centre five days a week, every week, for six months.

While I considered this I heard the front door open.

"Hello? Aidan?"

Dad was back.

I went down to say hello.

"How is he?" I asked, knowing my father disliked Bobby even more than I did.

"Ah, sure," he said, "he'll live."

I thought I detected a twinkle in his eye as he said it but couldn't be certain.

"The pills arrived this morning before I left, thanks for that," he said.

No mention of any of them being missing. She probably hadn't even noticed.

"Have you had any lunch? I'm starving," said my father as he went into the kitchen.

Those other six pills lasted a week. Each time I took one I'd tell myself that was the last one and I needed to save some for emergencies, but I felt so good when I was on them, they washed away all my worries and made me forget about my life. It was like alcohol, minus the messiness and regret. When they ran out I just increased my drinking for a few nights but it wasn't the same, wasn't as good.

Finally Bobby was allowed home from the hospital and my mother was freed from her duties in Galway. Dad went to collect her and I sat at home, wondering how many tablets she had left and whether I'd get a chance to rob a couple tonight. I was waiting for them when they came back, sitting in the living-room as if I'd missed them or something. Dad boiled the kettle while my mother went upstairs to unpack.

"Is everything okay, Aidan?" he asked.

"Yeah. Why?"

"We don't usually see you down here at this hour."

"I can go back upstairs if you like."

"No, don't be silly. I was just saying, that's all."

I poured myself some tea and brought it into the living-room. There was a reason I was being so sociable. I was testing the waters, seeing if she'd say anything about the tablets. She wouldn't say anything directly, but she had a way of letting you know she was onto you. I also wanted to assess her behaviour. I'd lived with this woman for my entire life but I'd never really watched her, never looked to see what was going on behind the veil of misery and martyrdom. Now that I knew there was more to it, I was curious.

She came down ten minutes later, wordlessly accepting a cup of tea and sitting on the couch.

"How's Bobby?" I asked off-handedly.

"Oh, he's fine," she replied, indicating she didn't wish to discuss it any further.

"And the rest of the lads?"

"They're good. Dan asked after you."

"Is he still working at the swimming pool?"

She nodded curtly. I knew this irked her, it irked the whole family. Dan, the great white hope, had gone travelling again after finishing his degree. Upon his return, the expectation was that he'd do his master's degree or a get a teaching job, but instead he'd become a lifeguard in a local aquatic centre. This was not what Bobby and Stephanie had envisaged for their son. At every opportunity they explained that it was only a temporary gig, a way of saving money while Dan pondered his next move.

But he'd been there two years now and, according to my father, had moved into an apartment with two of his work colleagues. One of them had a child which, again according to my father, may or may not have been Dan's. Knowing Dan, he'd be happy enough with his lot, he was the kind of person who went with the flow and didn't think about the bigger picture. His parents, though, would be horrified. It was probably why Bobby had ended up in hospital with a suspected aneurysm.

We sat in silence for a while, Dad flicking through the channels and my mother staring at the screen absent-mindedly. Was she on the tablets now? I couldn't tell. She looked the same as ever; long-drawn face with a slightly curled upper lip, deep lines around her mouth and slate-grey hair held back in a bun, a woman in her early fifties who could have passed for someone a decade older. I didn't detect any calmness there, just a complete lack of life.

"Thanks for posting up the tablets," she said suddenly.

"No probs," I replied.

We shared a look. And in that moment I saw it. She knew. There was pity in her eyes, a hint of recognition. Not only did she know, she understood. That look told me she didn't mind that I'd taken the tablets, and if I wanted to take some more they would be where I'd found them. Slightly unnerved, I stayed where I was for another few minutes before making my excuses and going back upstairs. I wasn't going to go straight in and look for the pills, that would be rude. I'd wait until the morning, when she went off to the community centre.

*

As soon as I heard the door go, I jumped out of bed and ran to the front of the house to look out the window. There she was, in that beige coat she wore every autumn, getting into her car, the one she'd owned for as long as I could remember and was only ever driven to and from the centre. A thought struck me: should she be driving a car while taking those pills? It was a mechanical vehicle, after all. But that was her decision. I went into their bedroom to the en-suite, and to that locker I'd first encountered a week before.

I opened the door, pulled out the blue tray and there on top was the same brown bottle I'd sent to Galway. At the time, there'd been more than twenty pills left, now there were only eight. This presented me with a dilemma. It was all well and good taking a few when the bottle was almost full, but with just eight left she'd immediately know if some had been taken. Still, I hadn't misread the signs, I knew what that little look meant. I took two, just to see if anything would be said. With any luck, she'd be getting a fresh delivery soon.

That evening I remained in my room. If anything was going to be said, she would have to come here and say it. But nothing happened. My mother had become my *de facto* drug dealer. And when I checked back a couple of days later, I discovered that she *had* received a fresh delivery. The bottle was full again. Where she was getting them? No doctor would prescribe so many tablets. Was my mother part of a drug ring? Were the mammies of Cruinníth dealing benzos at bingo every Tuesday night? Well, so long as they kept coming I didn't care where she got them. Mindful that my course was starting in just a few days, I shook ten pills out of the bottle and stowed them away in my room.

5

It had seemed so easy when I'd agreed to do the course, but with just two days to go it had suddenly become very real. I had to be at the training centre for nine-thirty every morning, which meant getting a bus at eight-forty-five and being up and out of bed by eight. If I was getting up early every morning, I couldn't stay up all night drinking. Getting up and catching the bus was the easy part, I then had to go the centre and mingle with other people. I had to sit in a room with my new classmates, interact and learn. Thinking about it made me hyperventilate. The diazepam would be my saviour, it would get me through this course, all six months of it.

On the Sunday afternoon before I was due to start the course, I decided to tell my parents about it. We had dinner together every Sunday, sat down at the kitchen table and played happy families for an hour once a week. After my mother and father had exchanged opinions on the quality of the beef, I cleared my throat and delivered my bombshell.

"So, I'm starting a FÁS course in the morning."

"Really? That computer one?" asked Dad.

"Well, it's a computer course, but it's not the one out of the paper. It's a better one."

"Where is it on? Will you need a lift? I can bring you."

"It's on in town, but it doesn't start till half-nine, I can get the bus. They give us travel allowance."

"That's good of them. So tell us about the course. What will you be doing?"

While I explained the content of the course, the modules and their proposed outcomes, I stole a glance at my mother. She was hanging on my every word, fully engaged, chewing on her food thoughtfully.

"God, if you learn all that, Aidan, there'll be no stopping you," she said when I was finished. "Will there be a job at the end of it for you?"

"I hope so, Mam."

She made that face she always made when something wasn't quite up to standard, a sort of dismissive pout.

"Let him finish the course first, Avril, no need to think too far ahead," said my father.

"You'll be looking for ham for your lunch, I suppose?" she asked.

"They do dinners at the centre, Mam."

"So you won't want a dinner when you come home, then?"

"I don't know. I'll have to see what the dinners are like in there."

"Well, let us know in advance, if I'm to start cooking for two, I'll need to know. Oh, and have you clean clothes? You can't be going in there looking like a tramp."

"Yeah, Mam. I'll text you tomorrow afternoon to let you know about dinner."

And that was that. I went back upstairs and whiled away the evening, going to bed at ten p.m. having laid out my least trampy clothes for the morning.

I didn't sleep well, I wasn't used to going to bed sober, and even less used to getting up at a set time. But I managed to crawl out of it a few minutes after the alarm went off. I had breakfast, took a shower and put on my clothes. Dad was already gone to work, my mother was up but in her room, wisely deciding to stay out of my way. I didn't have to bring anything with me, just money for the bus and my diazepam. Taking a deep breath, I opened the door and stepped out into the autumn morning, like an ordinary, functioning member of society heading off to contribute something to the world.

That world seemed different at this hour; fresher, brighter, unsullied. The dewy grass glittered in the morning sun, which refracted off a spider's web in the bushes and warmed my cheeks as I walked to the bus stop. If I weren't so tired and anxious, so desperate for a drink, I might have enjoyed it. As things were, I took the diazepam out of my pocket, swallowed it dry, and joined the handful of people waiting for the eight-forty-five bus to Maraghmor.

It arrived on time, about half-full, and I took my place towards the back. There were three more stops before we reached town; Bessborough,

Breanor, and Limmyvara, neighbouring rural villages which relied on Maraghmor for many of its jobs, schools and opportunities. They were similar to Cruinníth, once busy communities which had slowly disintegrated, bypassed by the road networks and left to flounder by the local authorities. They had one or two pubs, a shop, a church and a GAA club, but there was nothing there for the young people - no prospects, nothing to keep them beyond school age. The only people who stayed in places like these were single mothers on welfare or sad, lonely saps like me.

Recently, though, I had noticed a change, a sign that these rural villages might be able to sustain themselves in the future. Improved roads and shortened commutes made them attractive to young families looking for somewhere quiet to bring up their children, professional couples who worked in town and welcomed the sleepy, dazed atmosphere of places like Cruinníth, willing to drive forty-five minutes each way if it meant they could get a mortgage on a three-bed semi in a nice area. And the more who came, the more life returned to the villages. There was some hostility, a fear that these 'townies' with their townie ways might take over the villages with their big mouths and big ideas. That never materialised, life went on as normal, the increase in population even allowing a few more businesses to open, to eke out a living in the digital age.

I didn't know what kind of people would be on my course, where they would have travelled from, whether they'd be townies, culchies, single mothers or the saddest of saps. But as we approached Maraghmor, crossed the bridge and moved swiftly through the mid-morning traffic, I no longer cared. The tablet was working its magic, I was getting that nice, warm glow. Life felt easy. In an ideal world I would have been sitting at home on the Xbox, but this was okay too. The day would take care of itself, and if it didn't I had another diazepam in my pocket just in case.

*

We were all gathered in a room full of desks with computers on them. There were sixteen of us, ten women and six men. I was one of the men. The women were of all ages, shapes and sizes. There were a couple of middle-aged ones who were acting all giddy and excited, mad for blackguarding by the looks of them. There was a really old woman - I hoped I wouldn't end up sitting beside her - and four intimidating townie girls. They were accompanied by another girl who was younger and less battle-weary. She had long blonde hair, big blue eyes and massive boobs. She was a little overweight, her stomach spilled out over her jeans, but I was spellbound. I hoped I wouldn't end up sitting beside her either. That would be too much, even in my current mellow state.

There was an unremarkable tall woman around my age and then, to my surprise, there was a familiar face. The girl from the waiting room at the social welfare office was here, the lazy-eyed one who'd blushed when I'd tried to communicate with her. She was standing apart from everyone else, staring out the window as if wondering how she'd got here. I didn't recognise any of the other males. There was one guy in his forties or fifties who looked like a country-music singer, he had a curly auburn mullet and wore expensive-looking clothes. He was entirely relaxed in his surroundings and had already engaged one of the townie girls in conversation.

There were a couple of younger lads, track-suited and nonchalant, a guy with a shaved head and a goatee, and a simple-looking fella who was already trying to latch on to the country-music guy. Out of all of them, the only ones I thought I'd be comfortable sitting beside were the two middle-aged wans and the goatee lad. But as Geraldine, the tutor - female, late twenties, stick thin, alabaster skin - nervously urged us to settle down, it became obvious we were going to be allowed to choose where we sat, and with whom.

Immediately everyone fanned out. There were eight desks: four on each side, two chairs and two monitors at each. The two young lads took the back row on the right, cool as a breeze as they flopped into their seats. Country-music man took a seat across from them and was quickly joined by the simpleton. The middle-aged women had paired off in one of the middle rows, and the four townie girls had done the same. That left me, the goatee guy, the girl with the large breasts, the old woman, the tall, unremarkable one and the lazy-eyed girl from the welfare office. Big boobs quickly linked arms with the old woman and led her to a seat at the front.

I glanced hesitantly at the goatee guy but he'd been talking to the tall woman, they'd formed a connection and were now occupying two front-row seats. Not even bothering to look at my friend from the dole office, I slid into the one of the two remaining chairs and waited for her to follow suit. I sat there staring at the monitor, expecting to feel her presence at any moment, but she didn't come. Did she not want to sit beside me? Was this going to be like school all over again? No, she was just sorting something out with the tutor, signing her name on a piece of paper.

Now that I thought about it, a few of them had been talking to the tutor and writing on that piece of paper.

"What's your own name?" Geraldine asked me, finally catching my attention.

"Aidan."

"Have you signed in, Aidan?"

I got up, wrote my name where instructed and returned to my seat. By this time, the girl had joined me. She looked uncomfortable, had probably been hoping to end up beside anyone but me. Well, there was nothing she could do about it now. She'd have to put up with me for the next six months, or at least until I dropped out of the course. I hadn't been this close to a girl in a long time, and yet I wasn't even sweating. I tried to think about sweating, focused on my armpits, but nothing happened. My stomach was grand too; no churning, no worrying rumbles. I was just sitting there, not bothered about anything.

The girl shifted nervously in her seat. She needed to relax, it was only a FÁS course, nothing to be afraid of. I was going to say something to that effect but my mouth felt rubbery. If I spoke, or tried to, there was no telling what might come out. Instead I tried to put her at ease by being at ease myself. I remained entirely still, staring at the blinking cursor on the screen. Geraldine was saying something. I tuned in for a moment.

" . . . and hopefully by the end of this course you'll all have acquired new skills and be capable of . . ."

Boring. I went back to looking at the cursor on the screen. I was happy to do this for the day: sit in a comfy chair beside a young wan and stare at a computer screen. My body felt warm, my limbs loose and my mind completely empty. I was daydreaming, imagining what it would be like to work in the office of a major games developer, work on the new *Mass Effect* game, have brainstorming meetings with American and Canadian people who drank coffee all day and were always upbeat. Then I slowly became aware of my surroundings.

Not only was Geraldine looking at me, but other people were too, even the girl beside me. I pushed myself up in my chair, mildly aware that my mouth was open and my expression vacant.

"So, what about yourself?" Geraldine asked with practised patience. She'd perched herself on the side of her desk, skirt riding up to reveal long, bony legs.

"What about me?" I asked.

The goatee guy turned round in his seat, flashing me a look which, if I wasn't mistaken, seemed to be a warning of some kind. I looked to the girl beside me for assistance, thinking we were in this together and she might bail me out. No such luck, she was staring right ahead, even more nervous than before. Geraldine was getting flustered now as well, casting her eye around the room for assistance. If anyone needed assistance, it was me. After a few seconds, which were probably excruciating for her but were just downright confusing for me, the moment passed and the same question was put to my desk mate.

"Hi, I'm Ellen. I'm from Dooncurra and I decided to do this course because I'm interested in computers . . . and that's it, really."

Ah, so that's what we were doing. We were introducing ourselves. I'd missed the whole thing, missed everyone's stories. I genuinely felt bad, I had wanted to know more about these people. Geraldine smiled agreeably at Ellen and moved on to the front desk, to goatee man and his new wife. I raised my hand.

"Sorry, I wasn't paying attention. Can I have my go now instead?"

"Of course," she said, happy to be back on good terms.

I hadn't really thought of anything so I just started talking and waited to see what came out.

"I'm Aidan. I'm 25. I'm from Cruinníth. I came on the bus here today. This is my first time doing a course like this. I'm doing it because it's about time I did something. If I can manage to finish this course, I'd like to do another one, what's the name of the one that comes after this? I can't remember. But I'd do that one. Try and get a job. If I wasn't qualified enough by then I'd go to college as a mature student, get a degree and then get a job, possibly at – ah, I can't think of the name of the place, the one out by the industrial estate, and then . . ."

I tailed off, unsure of where I was going with this or how I was meant to end it. Geraldine stared at me and I gave her a little nod to confirm I was done. She smiled amenably and shifted her gaze to the tall woman in the front row. Ellen was looking at me, as were the people on the other side of the room. I shrugged contentedly and focused in on the tall girl's life story. I'd already missed most of the introductions, I couldn't afford to miss any more. The tall girl said something about 'gaps in her CV' and 'new career paths', she sounded well-heeled, had one of those mid-Atlantic accents. That wouldn't go down well with the townie girls, I could tell. Then it was the goatee guy.

"Hey, everyone. I'm Aaron, I'm 29, I'm from Kilkenny city and I started this course because I wanted to build on the work I've been doing myself. Last year I set up my own website, it's a news site which I run with a couple of friends, but I need to find out how to monetise it."

"What's the website called?" Geraldine asked.

"Well, um, it's only in beta mode at the moment, but it will be ready to go live soon, I hope."

"Can we look it up?" she asked hopefully.

Aaron made a sucking noise with his teeth. He'd been found out.

"Ah, it's not properly set up," he said, furiously back-pedalling.

Geraldine nodded non-committally, she'd sussed him now as well. I moved in my seat to get a look at Aaron's face, he was flushed. The tall girl had edged away from him. Maybe I could become the alpha male in this assortment of people. Aaron was clearly all mouth and no action. The cowboy was too old, too avuncular to be the big dog, and the half-witted lad wasn't even in the reckoning. That just left the two young lads at the back. They'd be doing their own thing, skitting and laughing like a pair of jackals. Then there was me. I could be the dominant one. All I had to do was sit here and keep to myself, remain quiet and speak when spoken to. And I had to display my skills in IT, show Geraldine and everyone else that this was second nature to me.

Someone passed over a sheath of papers from behind, I took one for myself, and handed them over to Ellen. It was our first little assignment. I looked at the contents. Even in my altered state of mind I could breeze through this stuff, no worries. I decided to try and finish it before everyone else and then say nothing, just sit back in my chair as if bored. I logged on to the desktop. She wanted us to create a new folder and transfer files from one she'd made earlier. It really was simple stuff, a child could do it. We'd even been given instructions. The old woman was calling for assistance already. The two lads at the back hadn't even turned their computers on.

I right clicked and made a folder. Easy. But then the fog descended. What was I supposed to do after that? I checked the sheet again. It said something about a folder called XYZ. Where was that? On my computer? I stared at the screen, trying to recall what I was doing. This was too much hassle. I just wanted to chill out and listen to people do more introductions. I could hear the townie girls chattering away, they'd finished already. Jesus, if I didn't hurry on I'd be last, bettered by an oul' wan and a half-wit. With great effort I sat up in my seat, narrowed my eyes and concentrated intently. It wasn't easy, having to read the instructions, go onto the screen and then read the instructions again. But I did it. Or at least I thought I did. A few minutes later, just when I'd started to relax, the tutor was calling out my name once more.

"Aidan, I didn't get your files. Have you finished?"

"Yeah," I said. And I had finished. Hadn't I?

"I don't see any file with your name on it here," she said.

"Sorry," I sighed, returning to the computer. I'd forgotten to send them on to her, forgotten the most important part of the task. I was last in the class; worse than Aaron, the oul' wan and the half-wit. Alpha male? I wasn't even a beta male or whatever came after that. It dawned on me then that I had a decision to make. I could either medicate myself every day, keep my anxiety at bay and spend the next six months in a stupor, failing this course for dummies. Or I could ditch the diazepam, risk total mental collapse, and try and get out of here with whatever low-grade qualification was on offer. Neither option sounded great. I'd much sooner have been at home, taking diazepam and doing whatever I liked. But those were thoughts for another day. Right now I was in my sweet spot, that hour or two where the mellow buzz reached a lovely plateau and nothing really mattered.

After another assignment, we did some theory. There was a whiteboard. Geraldine began talking, pointing at words, letters. None of it made sense. So I spent some time wondering about Ellen. I'd been so preoccupied with my work I'd almost forgotten she was there. I couldn't recall her moving since we'd sat down, or making any noise. She must have completed the assignments through telekinesis: moving the mouse with her eyes, one blink for left click, two for right. She was now sitting upright in her chair, her hands in her lap, staring in the general direction of the whiteboard. I couldn't tell whether she was engrossed or uninterested.

During our previous encounter I'd noted how she gazed at the paintings on the wall, devoid of expression. Maybe she was a half-wit, too. Maybe this was a course for half-wits, and I was one of them. She appeared to exist in a bubble of her own. The average human felt the need to move some part of their body every few minutes, to sigh, clear their throat, run their hand through their hair, scratch their nose. With her there was nothing. I turned my attention to her physical characteristics. She had taken off her jacket this time, revealing a modest figure: small but not quite petite, thin but not skinny, no curves or contours to speak of.

Her clothes didn't help. They were faded and dull, colourless. They simply lay upon her body. She wore no jewellery and any make-up had been subtly applied. It was as if she was purposely trying to deflect attention away from herself. I wasn't going to do anything, I was just having a look at the person I'd be sitting beside for the next six months. Surely at some point during that time she would reveal part of her personality, prove she wasn't an empty vessel.

Lunchtime arrived and Geraldine brought us down to the canteen. There were already lots of people there, more than a hundred, most of them either young lads from the engineering course or young wans from the hairdressing course, all in their late teens, early twenties, and full of vim and vigour. It was like school all over again; good-looking lads and pretty girls, preening and posturing, trying to impress one another without letting on they cared. Then there was us, a rag-tag bunch of old women, cowboys, and beta males. The townie girls found a free table. The two young lads took one look at the scene before them and cleared off. Aaron, the cowboy and the half-wit went off to the counter, having received instructions from the middle-aged women.

I couldn't see Ellen anywhere, she was probably still sitting at her desk, staring into space. I went up to the counter for a look. I was hungry. What had I said to my mother about lunchtime? I couldn't remember. The best course of action was to eat now and ask questions later. So I got the roast beef and mash with carrots and gravy. By the time I got to the end of the line, the cowboy and the others had returned to their seats. They didn't seem to be in any hurry to invite me, so I went down to the end of the room, far away from everyone else, and found a table all to myself - classic alpha behaviour.

No sooner had I swallowed my first mouthful of spud when two people joined me. It was the cowboy and the half-wit - they sounded like a movie duo: Smokey and the Bandit, Crocket and Tubs, The Cowboy and the Half-Wit. The shittest movie duo of all time.

"We saw you sitting on your own and thought we'd join you," said the cowboy, all friendly, sounding more like someone from Laois than The Wild West. The half-wit nodded in agreement, saying something agreeable which I couldn't make out. His teeth were wonky and his mouth didn't work properly.

"Thanks," I said, returning to my beef.

"You got the dinner," the half-wit said.

"Yeah. It's nice, man. You got a roll," I replied, gesturing towards his sandwich.

"Mmm," he said, taking a massive mouthful. He ate with an abandon usually not seen outside a pigsty. I was glad we were down here, out of sight.

"What do you think of the women?" the cowboy asked with a grin.

"What women?"

"The ones in our class. I'd say that tutor is filthy."

I looked at the cowboy. He was older than I thought, maybe fifty, too old to be talking like that.

"And those girls at the front!" he continued. "You should be getting in there. Although you pulled a fast one getting that little wan to sit beside you."

Why wasn't this fucker married? Out earning for his wife and kids, instead of here on a FÁS course, perving on young wans? He appeared to be well-off and had the tanned, healthy look of a man who could afford to take a holiday in the depths of winter. If it wasn't for the ridiculous mullet and the big thick Irish head, he could have passed for one of those high-rollers you saw strutting round Monaco.

"I'm just here to get my qualification," I said.

I didn't want to be in cahoots with this lad, become his wingman or co-conspirator.

The half-wit - I had to stop calling him that - nodded through a mouthful of sausage and bread. There was ketchup smeared across his face.

"Oh yeah," said the cowboy, "but it's nice to have a few ladies in the class, be a bit boring if it was just us lads. Isn't that right, Derek?"

He jabbed the half-wit in the ribs.

Derek coughed, almost choking on his breakfast roll, but regained his composure long enough to swallow a lump of pudding which teetered on his lips before being pulled back into the abyss. He had a bag of crisps and a can of orange on the table. I couldn't wait to see how he tackled those.

"I'm going out to the car for a smoke. Coming?" asked the cowboy.

"Yup," said Derek, rising and heading towards the exit in one motion.

I had most of my dinner eaten so I decided to join them, they were entertaining, certainly entertaining enough to have a TV show named after them.

The cowboy's car turned out to be a massive SUV, a black behemoth with wheels so large you needed the footrest to climb aboard. I'd been right to suspect he was 'of money'. This wasn't the vehicle of your average FÁS trainee. The interior was leather, plush with retractable seats and the latest gadgetry. He hadn't wanted to have a smoke at all, just show off his motor. Although, having said that, he did flick open a box of Silk Cuts, offering myself and Derek one before lighting up.

"You don't smoke at all, Aidan?"

"Nah, never bothered."

"Drink?"

"A bit."

The cowboy smiled, Derek guffawed.

"What about hash?"

"Never tried it."

That was a lie. I had tried it once, up in Dublin, at that house party.

"I thought ye youngsters were mad into drugs these days," the cowboy said.

Was he a narc? Was that was this was all about? Maybe he and Derek were undercover detectives - that would actually make for a decent TV show. But him bringing up drugs reminded me that the effects of mine were starting to wear off. I'd never taken them in the morning before, it had always been at night. Today was different. It had been almost five hours since I'd taken one. Soon I would start to feel normal again, and my version of normal was anything but.

The cowboy turned on the car radio. It was loud and tuned in to a local station which played nothing but the hits. The vehicle pulsed with the vibrations of US rap, one of those club-friendly tracks with crossover appeal. I looked back at Derek. He was sitting inches away from the bass speakers, his head visibly vibrating with each thudding beat. But he was smiling away to himself, oblivious to the ear-splitting noise. No way was he a detective. The cowboy had rolled down one of the windows and was puffing his cigarette, staring at the young wans going in and out of the training centre. This was too much for me. I couldn't be associated with these two any longer.

"Just going to the toilet. See ye upstairs," I said, clambering down from the Jeep and going back inside.

I located the gents and took my second diazepam of the day. I was slightly concerned about being too out of it, but it was easier this way, at least for now. I could decide on my long-term plan that evening, or maybe at the weekend.

There was a team exercise after lunch where Ellen, Aaron, the tall girl and myself were grouped together. We had to try and survive on a desert island. We were given a list of twenty items and asked to choose five. I wasn't sure how this would help us gain skills in IT but I was grateful for the break, especially now that the diazepam was kicking in and that lovely warm feeling was back. Aaron had recovered from his earlier embarrassment and took the lead, arguing that you couldn't hope to survive on a desert island without a pen-knife. Relying on my years of video-game experience, I told him you could just as easily fashion a cutting instrument out of a tree or the tusk of a boar. He countered by asking how I hoped to cut down a tree or kill a boar without a knife.

I lost interest after that and spent the rest of the session drawing the four of us seated by the camp-fire, myself and Ellen on one side eating chicken wings, Aaron and the tall girl on the other, looking sad. We lost the challenge anyway; according to Geraldine the toothbrush was the most important item, followed by the tarpaulin and the torch. That didn't sound right to me, and when Aaron protested I considered backing him up, but instead I joined the rest of the room in shouting him down. I liked seeing him squirm. The team with the old lady and the girl with the big tits won. I wished I'd sat on that side of the room.

We were given another assignment then and this time I kept an eye on Ellen, just to see what she did. Without shifting her position she studied the piece of paper, her eyes moving up and down the list of instructions slowly. There was definitely an intelligent life-form in there. After a couple of minutes she moved forward, placed her right hand on the mouse and began the assignment. She was methodical in her work, following each instruction to the letter, pausing at the end of each task, studying the paper, and then moving on to the next.

There was a moment of slight hesitation towards the end, when she was required to save something to an external memory drive, but that aside it was plain sailing. It had taken her longer than was reasonable, and at no point had she used any natural intuition, but the task had been completed, comprehensively. While I'd been watching Ellen's progress Geraldine had begun a circuit of the room, checking in on people, answering whatever queries they might have. She arrived at our desk without any prior announcement, and as I stared at Ellen's screen Geraldine stared at me.

"How are you getting on with it, Aidan?" she asked, interrupting my reverie.

It took a real effort to switch my attention to her, to process what was being asked of me. I slowly moved my head from Ellen's screen to Geraldine's face, narrowing my eyes as I focused on her. I was aware I was out of it, but I didn't care.

"Huh?"

"The assignment," she said.

"Yeah."

"Have you done it?"

"This?" I asked, picking up the piece of paper.

"Yes," she said.

I could see she was getting annoyed.

"I'll do it now," I said, stretching forward in my desk, leaning my elbows on the table and making a great effort to appear studious.

She moved on to Ellen, showering her with praise, the two of them sharing a moment. As Geraldine walked away, I caught Ellen looking at me. There was no judgement in her look, just curiosity. To be fair, I was acting oddly. And this at least confirmed that she was aware of my presence. But Geraldine was looking at me too, eyeing me with suspicion. I could tell I'd fucked up. Even though no one took these courses seriously I couldn't turn up out of my head on diazepam, at least not every day.

I stifled a massive yawn and switched my attention to the assignment, vowing to make a better impression in the time we had left. But before I could make a start on it, people began gathering their belongings, putting on their coats. The day was over. It had flown by. Aside from Geraldine's questioning looks, and a small bit of paranoia during lunchtime, I thought it had gone fairly well. As I switched off my computer and got to my feet, Ellen did the same. She gave me a half-smile, pushed in her chair and said, "See you tomorrow."

"Yeah, see you," I replied automatically.

She fell in with the others then, everyone filing out the door, all firm friends after a few hours spent together. I was last to go, last except for Geraldine. She was seated at her desk, doing something on her laptop, pretending not to notice my lingering presence.

"See you tomorrow," I said as airily as I could muster.

She looked up from the screen, knowing full well who it was.

"Bye, Aidan," she said coldly.

I'd gone three years without even speaking to a woman, now here I was flirting with one and pissing off another. If that wasn't alpha male behaviour, I didn't know what was. My good mood lasted all the way home, until I got in the door. The smell of dinner hit me straight away, reminding me that I'd been supposed to tell my mother about my eating arrangements. I'd had a massive roast at lunchtime, and had nipped out for a bag of crisps and some chocolate during the afternoon. I was in no way hungry. But you didn't waste food in our house. If something was served to you, it was eaten. So I sat down, and began picking at the chilli con carne.

Dad asked me questions about the day, getting all excited when I told him the course material was pretty easy. My mother just looked at me. She knew I'd already had a dinner. Usually I demolished whatever was put before me like a farmyard dog. Now here I was daintily nibbling on her offering like a lady out for afternoon tea. Just to spite her, I ate every bit of it and then went upstairs to lie down and recuperate. I would have to tell her about the dinners at FÁS, I couldn't afford to put on any more weight. Before I could do that, I had to decide on my strategy for the rest of the week. However, before I could do that I had to listen to some Marvin Gaye. I needed something relaxing after the day I'd had.

The following morning's decision was made for me as soon as I woke up. I felt wretched, on edge, uneasy. The thought of going anywhere, let alone into a room full of people, made me nauseous. So, I took a tablet. And by the time I got to the training centre things seemed okay again. Once more the day passed me by in a blur. There were assignments, a question-and-answer session and some more group exercises. At lunchtime I sat with Derek and the cowboy again, but I wasn't really there. I was detached from proceedings, listless and remote.

The rest of the class seemed to be getting along famously. The room rang with the sounds of laughter, with the chatter of blossoming friendships, so much so that Geraldine had to intervene and tell them to keep the noise down. Yet while everyone else conversed and became familiar, myself and Ellen had barely spoken two sentences to one another. Shortly after my second pill of the day, I resolved to change that. If we didn't talk soon it would become a thing, we'd settle into our non-speaking roles and stay there forever.

Ellen wasn't going to initiate a conversation, that was for certain. It wasn't just me she didn't speak to, she didn't speak to anyone. Neither of us did. We were the two outcasts in the group, all we had was one another.

"What do you think of it so far?" I asked as we settled into our third assignment of the day.

Her body jolted in surprise. She glanced at me and did a double-take, checking to make sure I was talking to her. My steady gaze told her I was. She immediately became flushed, her cheeks went red, and her eyes cast downward. I wondered what had happened to make Ellen so insecure.

"It's okay," she replied quietly, as if relaying a secret.

"What do you make of them?" I asked, indicating the rest of the room.

She had a look of desperation on her face, like an animal caught in a trap.

"I dunno," she said, shrugging her shoulders.

"That cowboy guy is weird," I said, stifling a laugh.

Ellen smiled. The effect was startling: for the briefest of moments, she was radiant. Her mouth opened, revealing porcelain white teeth, downy fluff on her upper lip and a small indent in her chin. This set off a chain reaction across her face, her cheeks filled out, making her look dainty and feminine, drawing one's attention to her hair, the way it flowed to her shoulders. An image flashed through my mind: Ellen naked from the waist up. I noticed her neck for the first time, it was slender and slight, its skin flawless.

Yet, amid this sudden blossoming, there was a darkness. Although she tried to hide it, I could see it in her eyes. They narrowed as if consumed by mirth, her brows doing a funny little dance to help carry off the act. But in their depths I saw a deep sadness, a vulnerability. She quickly regained her composure, brought the shutters down again, returned to her normal state.

"You're weird," she said flatly.

"How am I weird?"

"You just are."

And she smiled again.

It was intoxicating.

I couldn't think of anything else to say after that, but the ice had been broken. And even though we were now seated in silence again, it didn't feel awkward. After a while I remembered how I'd made her smile.

"Have you seen his car?" I asked, lowering my voice in case the cowboy overheard.

"Whose car?"

"The cowboy's!"

She laughed this time, a gentle little titter which reminded me of the Teletubbies.

"Who's the cowboy?" she asked.

"The guy at the back, the oul' lad with the cowboy boots."

She stole a glance at the back row where Derek and the cowboy sat.

"They're not cowboy boots," she said.

Now it was my turn to laugh.

"How do you know what cowboy boots look like?" I asked.

"I dunno," she said, shrugging her shoulders again.

"Well, he's a cowboy and he has a massive Jeep. I was in it yesterday."

She had nothing to say to this.

"And he's weird," I reminded her.

"Okay."

I would have to find some new material. Talking to girls was difficult, you really had to entertain them. I glanced her way to see if she was looking at me but she was staring intently at the screen, diligently carrying out her task. This was how it was going to be. I was going to have to do all the running, come up with new and interesting things to say every few minutes. I decided to let it happen organically, not to force things. Besides, I was now deep in the diazepam fog, so it was best I said as little as possible. I must have drifted away for a few minutes, allowed myself a momentary lapse, because the next thing I knew Ellen was talking to me, harshly this time.

"Have you even started it yet?"

"What?" I asked.

"The assignment."

"Oh," I replied, looking at the screen, not sure where the last few minutes had gone.

Geraldine was doing the rounds again, checking in to see how everyone was doing. I needed to hurry up. Ellen shook her head, staring at me in wonder.

"What?" I asked.

"Nothing," she said.

I tried to make a start on the assignment but I was too slow, and when Geraldine came around I wasn't even halfway through. She spoke briefly to Ellen, complimenting her, and then switched her attention to me. I pretended to focus on the screen, as if lost in thought, and after a pause she moved on. That hurt. I'd been rejected, considered not worthy of her attention. I was the dumbest person in a room full of dummies. I focused as hard as I could, determined to submit my work before the end of class. I just about managed it, and then waited until everyone had gone before approaching her desk.

"Hi, Geraldine. I submitted that assignment there, sorry for the delay."

"Thanks, Aidan," she said, even colder than the day before.

"It's not that I'm not interested, I'm just finding it hard to adjust to the classroom environment," I said, surprised by my frankness.

This caught her off guard.

"Is everything okay, Aidan? If there are any issues please let me know."

"No, no, it's fine. It'll just take me a few days to get used to it, that's all."

She tilted her head and regarded me with what I presumed was sympathy.

"Okay, Aidan. But if you've any problems, just tell me."

"I will. Thanks."

It had gone well. I'd made a vague reference to something or other without actually naming it. She was probably thinking all sorts now, wondering if I'd flip out at the merest hint of criticism, start strangling the oul' wan and threatening to stab the cowboy to death with a pen. Well, let her think that. As long as she left me alone and gave me my certificate at the end, I didn't care either way.

The rest of the week carried on in much the same vein. I continued taking my tablets and floated through the days, chatting with Ellen, being weird and taking liberties with Geraldine. I was going to re-evaluate at the weekend, come up with a strategy which would enable me to spend at least part of the week with a clear head. I'd been taking the pills for a little over a fortnight now and was already dependent on them. They were worse than alcohol, the hangovers were more severe, the need far greater.

Although I still enjoyed that wonderful feeling of nothingness, some of the side-effects listed on the bottle had begun to manifest themselves. My appetite was on the wane. Even junk food like chocolate and crisps, things I'd always loved, did nothing for me. I could barely eat one dinner now, never mind two. I found it hard to focus on anything and had become increasingly forgetful. I was constantly fatigued, and no matter how much I slept I never felt fully rested, but the only way to make these symptoms disappear was to take more tablets.

When the weekend came I tried to cut down, to see how I coped with just one a day or even none. I woke up on the Saturday, full of resolve, and decided to go for a walk to get some exercise. I never would have done this before I'd started the course, but if I could get the bus into town every day then a stroll down the lane should be easy. I'd only been gone ten minutes when a familiar foe reared its ugly head. My breath began to shorten, my chest hurt, I felt dizzy.

I strode forward, trying to walk off the panic, but it just got worse. I couldn't do it, I couldn't do anything without the tablets. So I went home, I went back upstairs and I drank. I drank all day and into the night, drank myself into a stupor and passed out on the bed, fully clothed. On Sunday I drank a little more, just enough to keep me ticking over. And then, when the coast was clear, I sneaked into my parents' room to get some more pills. This time I took a few extra. I had a long week ahead of me.

6

THE SECOND WEEK WENT MUCH like the first. A pattern began to emerge: the worse I performed in class, the better I got along with Ellen. It was true what they said about girls liking bad boys. And that's what I was now, a bad boy. I didn't care about anything, and Ellen seemed impressed by that. Geraldine was less impressed, but every now and again I caught her looking at me in concern. That was perfect. She was worried about me.

That's how it was with these courses. They guided you through them, aware that life had dealt you a bad hand, that the qualification at the end was worthless and it didn't matter if you hadn't earned it, because employers didn't take it seriously anyway. I'd noticed it with Derek, he'd really begun to struggle now and was constantly calling for assistance. It was the same with the elderly lady, except in her case it was the girl with the big tits and those around her who were helping out. Essentially our futures had already been written: we were coming out of here with a Level 4 qualification in IT Skills. All we had to do was turn up every day and behave ourselves.

I was managing to do that. And I was being helped by a growing tolerance to the pills. They weren't affecting me in the same way now. I wasn't zonked out like I had been before, was getting a more mellow high, still carefree and unconcerned but not so dopey, not so wiped out. It was better. I could be more sociable, interact a little. The assignments and the classwork still posed a challenge, but only because I didn't want to do them. When it came to the theory, putting my hand up and answering questions, I excelled and showed them all that I wasn't the moron they had thought I was.

The Thursday of the second week was in essence my coming-out party. That was the day I announced myself as not just a bad boy, an alpha male, but also an intellectual, a communicator and a public speaker. Geraldine was doing her usual thing, writing stuff on the whiteboard, asking us what it meant, calling upon the dimmer ones when she grew tired of Big Tits answering everything. I'd been sitting there, not really present, not really in the moment, when I emerged from the mist, her words piercing my cloud, as if spoken solely for me.

"How has technology impacted the working lives of rural Irish people?"

That was the question. It was open-ended, too abstract for this room full of rote learners and their dull, unimaginative brains.

"Well, for a start, it's changed the way farmers do business," I offered.

Everyone turned to look in my direction. I stared them down.

"In what way, Aidan?" asked Geraldine.

"Broadband in rural Ireland is still pretty patchy but even so, from an agricultural perspective, farmers can register their calves online, they can set up monitoring devices to keep an eye on their livestock. There's milking robots, and they get hourly weather reports on their phones. It's not just the farmers, either. Small businesses can trade online, where they would previously have relied on their local community to keep them going. They can ship orders across the country, even to the continent, through their websites. There's one of those digital hubs out near us and people work remotely there instead of going to the office. It's always full. But it's not just their working lives, IT is changing the way older people live too. There's this thing being rolled out for pensioners, a sort of smart device, which allows them to log their details to the hospital at the end of each day, there's an alarm built into it which they can use if they need assistance. It's amazing, really."

I wanted to keep talking, had plenty more to say, but decided to pause and gauge the reaction. They were all still looking at me, some of them with what appeared to be grudging admiration - except for Aaron; he was livid.

"That's great, Aidan," said Geraldine, a grin on her face. She was gazing at me with genuine affection, as if I was her favourite singer serenading her out of a crowd of thousands.

"Anyone like to expand on that?" she asked, looking around the room.

They didn't. They knew better.

Concerned I'd ruined my bad boy reputation, I stole a glance at Ellen. Her grey eyes stared right back at me. If anything, she seemed even more entranced. I shrugged by way of explanation. I was an enigma now, that was even better than being a bad boy.

At lunch I sat in my usual spot, in the corner, away from everyone else. Derek and the cowboy had grown bored of me and just did their own thing now, a most unlikely couple as they hurried about the centre deep in conversation. On this day, however, I had a new companion. I didn't see her approach, didn't hear her, until there she was, sitting in front of me, her home-made sandwiches on the table, some orange liquid in a bottle, and an apple. Ellen. My Ellen.

"Thought I'd sit with you," she said nervously, as if awaiting permission.

I smiled agreeably. All I had was a plate of chips which I was nibbling at half-heartedly, my appetite had almost completely disappeared, and that morning when I'd put on my jeans I'd had to go a notch up on my belt. At this rate I'd have a rakishly thin body to go with my enigmatic personality.

"How do you know all that?" she asked. "That stuff you said in the class?

"Dunno. I just started talking and that was what came out."

She smiled again. Her teeth were her best feature, straight and white, perfectly fitting her prim little mouth.

"Mad," Ellen said.

I really wanted to say 'not mad, just intelligent', but nobody likes arrogant people.

"Do you remember seeing me at the social welfare that day?" I asked. "We were the last two in the waiting room."

She nodded.

"He's sound isn't he? The lad in there."

Another nod.

"Was it him who suggested this course for you?"

No reaction. She was eating one of her sandwiches, tuna and lettuce on white bread. I waited for her to finish her mouthful, wondering if what I'd said had registered.

"He suggested lots of courses," she said. "I just chose this one."

"Why?"

"No reason."

It was just as well I was on drugs, a sober conversation with Ellen would be hugely challenging.

"Do you think it's good?"

"It's okay," she said, taking a slug of her orange drink. She paused, took another tiny sip and screwed the top back onto the bottle.

"Are you from town?" I asked, taking a different tack.

"No."

I thought about punching her in the face to see if it might elicit a response.

"I'm from Dooncurra," she added after another bite of her sandwich.

Dooncurra was about twenty minutes outside of town, but on the opposite direction to Cruinníth.

As we sat there, me firing questions at her, Ellen batting them away absent-mindedly, I realised that I was approaching this all wrong. Ellen operated in a different sphere to me. I could ask her all the questions I wanted, and she would answer them with as much or as little enthusiasm as she could muster. Or I could remain silent, like she did. Because she was perfectly content to do that. Just sitting there appeared to be her preference. Every now and again a thought would enter her head and she'd share it with me, but for the most part she said nothing, just ate her sandwiches, took a sip of her drink and looked at the table.

I'd thought her taciturnity in the classroom had been a result of good manners, not wanting to offend Geraldine, but no, this was her default mode. I looked at her, took a good look at the shallow grey eyes, the light translucent eyelashes, the little munchkin cheeks as she took an age to eat two bog-standard sandwiches, and asked myself what made this woman tick. After careful consideration, I decided that the answer was nothing. She didn't tick, she just kind of existed, went along with life in a docile, agreeable way, neither happy nor sad, up nor down, just there. There was a possibility she was medicated too, so stoned that all emotion had been drained out of her, but I didn't think so. She looked too normal, too healthy.

Regardless of her conversational skills, she was the best company I'd had in the entirety of my adult life. Better still, she was a female, and better again she seemed to like me, or at least didn't hate me. And now that we were lunching together, there was no telling how our relationship would develop. The more familiar we became, the more chance there was of something exciting happening. I shooed those thoughts out of my mind, surprised by their arrival.

The drugs had been suppressing my tendency to over-analyse situations, but here I was getting neurotic again, worrying about the future, anxious about making a mess of my relationship with Ellen. It was a constant balancing act with these tablets. I was still shielded from the worst of my anxieties, still felt that cosy warmth in my stomach, but the complete and utter detachment they'd once provided was no longer there. I was more 'with it' but I wanted to be 'without it', that's why I'd taken the drugs in the first place.

So the next day I upped my dose. I took one and a half tablets in the morning while waiting for the bus. And it was just like old times. I floated through the day, languid and loose. Myself and Ellen shared jokes and she called me weird, I told her she was weird and she got annoyed but in a friendly way. We must have been noisy because Geraldine intervened and told us to 'cop on to ourselves'. Ellen went bright red. She was properly angry with me for a while then, wouldn't talk to me. That was fine, too, what did I care? Eventually she signalled a truce, calling me a 'stupid weirdo' after almost two hours of silence. I had taken the power back. It had been easy. But at what cost?

Because when Geraldine called upon me to answer a question about smart technology and how it might cause job losses in the IT sector in years to come, I was completely dumbfounded. What the hell did she mean? I groped around the inside of my head for an answer, but it wouldn't come. A few potentially useful sentences made themselves known, but I couldn't figure out which order to put them in. The entire class had turned to look at me, expecting another nugget of genius from the IT maverick, instead they got a protracted bout of humming and hawing, followed by a defeated shrug and a distracted yawn.

Geraldine moved on, heartbroken. Even worse, Ellen looked upset too. She shook her head sadly and shunned me for the rest of the day. I wished she'd make up her mind: did she like bad boys or swots? She couldn't have both, not from me. I decided not to care what she wanted. All I was interested in was sitting here in the warm classroom, in the comfortable seat, stretching out my legs and listening to the vague chatter of my colleagues, the chirping of the birds from outside, the occasional rev of a boy racer's engine and the blissful nothingness of my own empty head.

7

THE PROBLEM WITH UPPING MY dosage was supply. Having started out taking a handful of pills from my mother's stash once a week I was now emptying entire bottles, leaving a token pill or two by way of apology.

Nothing was said, our tacit agreement remained in place, but I was reaching the point where I couldn't even afford to leave one or two pills behind. I was now taking three a day and barely managing with that. And my mother was an unreliable supplier. Sometimes she'd get two full bottles in a week with twenty-eight pills in each, more than enough to go round, then a week would pass without anything. That was no good to me. I needed some stability where my pills were concerned. It wasn't as if I could complain, though, knock on her door and enquire as to when she was expecting her next delivery. I just had to live on my wits, check back every evening to see if her dealer had come through.

Whereas my mother couldn't, or wouldn't, call me out on my fledgling drug addiction, she was less reticent when it came to my weight loss. In the space of a month I'd lost more than a stone. I rarely ate meals, just grazed on bits of chicken, lumps of cheese, toast, crisps, chocolate. To be fair, I needed to lose a bit, but not like this, not through fasting. As I picked at a specially-made shepherd's pie, my absolute favourite, a dinner I'd been devouring for as long as I could remember, she finally snapped.

"Are you going to eat that at all, Aidan?"

That was her version of snapping.

"Huh?" I said, looking up from the potato field I was expertly ploughing.

"Isn't that your favourite?"

"Had a dinner at the centre. I forgot to say."

I'd been using that excuse a lot. Too much.

"You texted me earlier to say you hadn't," she shot back.

"Did I?"

I looked up and stared into her eyes, her sad, tired eyes. She had no fight in her, neither of us did.

"Yes, Aidan," she replied with such gravitas, such solemnity, I almost felt a twinge of guilt. Then a fresh wave of diazepam-induced loveliness hit me and everything was okay again. I ate a few more forkfuls of the shepherd's pie, excused myself and went upstairs to lie on the bed. There had been a new development in class that day. We'd been asked to work on a week-long project, some kind of case study. It involved going to the library and doing some research, and we were expected to do at least some of it during our free time.

To make things more awkward Geraldine had mixed everyone up, putting me in a group with the cowboy, one of the middle-aged women and one of the townie girls. At the end of the day we'd exchanged numbers, promising to update one another on our progress. But Cruinníth didn't even have a library. How was I supposed to do research? Geraldine had said that some of the materials were available online, but I had enough of looking at a computer screen for one day. I just wanted to relax and listen to some Prince. Then the phone beeped.

It was the cowboy.

Hi Aidan, Geoff here. Just checking in to see if you'd made a start on the project. I think we said you were going to do the part on business operating models?

Geoff: what a ridiculous name for a cowboy. And what was all this about business operating models? I had no recollection of agreeing to that. It seemed to me that Geoff was trying to pull a fast one, getting me to do the hard stuff while he and the women took it easy.

Did we?

I'd barely sent it when the phone rang. It was Geoff, he was actually ringing me, the lunatic. I let it ring out. I got a couple more texts, one from Geoff, another from a number I didn't recognise, and then put the phone on silent. I couldn't have these people invading my private life, it was bad enough seeing them every day. I dozed off for a while. When I awoke it was the dead of night, I was fully clothed and ravenous with hunger. This was new. I had been constipated for a few days, and had finally cleared the backlog earlier on. Maybe that had something to do with it? Either way I had to eat.

So I went downstairs to polish off the shepherd's pie I hadn't eaten earlier. That was another thing about my mother, she never threw anything out. That food would go from the fridge to the freezer and there it would remain until the people of the future discovered it amid the rubble and human remains. She hadn't kept the gravy, though. My father must have had all that, he loved gravy. To give it a bit of moisture, I heated up a tin of beans and poured the whole lot on top.

Even though I was starving I found it difficult to eat, the food was cloying and tasteless in my mouth, and with each morsel I questioned why we had to do this, why humans had to concoct such elaborate dishes when we could just as easily have survived on berries from the trees. Exhausted from the effort I slunk over to the couch and lay down, planning to watch some telly. When I got there I was too tired, too sick to look for the remote, and instead just lapsed into a deep sleep.

*

"Unusual for you to be sleeping down here, son."

I opened my eyes to see my father on the chair opposite in his overalls, a cup of tea in his hand. He'd wisely opted not to open the curtains, but the morning sun still streamed in from the kitchen. My head hurt like it had never hurt before. I felt weak and sick. The pain was everywhere, radiating from my chest and coursing through my body.

"Haven't you got any classes today?" he continued in his jaunty, everything-is-perfectly-normal, manner.

At that moment I wanted to kill him. I wanted to grab him by the lapels of his blue overalls, pin him to the ground and pound his genial little face off the floor. But I could barely get up off the couch, never mind do any grabbing or pounding.

"Day off," I said, wincing as I got to my feet and crawled upstairs.

Hands shaking, I took a pill from my stash and necked it. Then I got into bed, pulled the covers up over my head, and took a break from the world. But sleep could only ever offer a brief respite. There was no real escape.

Once more I awoke to a darkened room, not knowing whether the day was ending or starting or even what day it was. I could hear the sounds of life from downstairs: the television, the gentle hum of the radiators and my father clearing his throat as he had done every couple of minutes for the past twenty years. It was evening. I'd overcome the day, a day, and I didn't feel so bad any more. The headache remained - that was more or less a constant - but the other aches and pains had receded, cured by rest and recuperation.

Buoyed, I got out of bed and stretched my weary limbs. Everything was going to be okay, I'd just been a bit tired, maybe dehydrated. I would eat more from now on, drink lots more fluids, and keep my intake of pills to the bare minimum. I could see everything more clearly now. The course. Ellen. My fears, my needs, my wants. It all seemed so foolish. What was I up to at all? Taking drugs so I could impress a young wan? Was that what

I was about now? All those dopes in the class thinking I was the dopiest of them all? The shame.

I decided I would dispense with the diazepam. I'd proved I could go in to class every day, I didn't need that stuff, it was only a crutch at this point. If Ellen didn't like me for who I was, then that was her problem. And if she really did enjoy the company of stoned, drugged Aidan Collins, then more fool her. I lifted up the mattress and pulled out my stash. There were fourteen pills there, neatly assembled in an old DVD case. I would put them back tonight, prove I didn't need them. They would always be there, in the next room, tempting me with their warm goodness. But I would resist, I would show a bit of backbone for once in my life.

My phone went off. A text. It was from Geoff.

We missed you today, Aidan. Had to do the presentation by ourselves. Geraldine said you can do your part tomorrow if you're back in.

He ended it with a winking emoji.

I threw the phone to the floor in disgust. Who did he think he was, with his passive-aggressive emojis? All I wanted was to get by in life, quietly and without incident. I didn't know anything about a presentation or what my part entailed. I'd taken one day off and now the world and his dog was giving me grief. Staring at the message I toyed with the idea of telling Geoff to fuck off, telling him his hair was ridiculous, his clothes were embarrassing and he needed to get a life. Instead, I typed **Okay, see you tomorrow** and hit send. Then I checked my mini-fridge to see if there were any cans inside, saw I was running low and headed down to the shop for more.

8

Needless to say, I didn't return the pills to my mother's room. If it hadn't been for Geoff's text, I might have gone cold turkey, but he'd put extra pressure on me. Now I had to return to the classroom, explain my absence and give a presentation on a topic I knew nothing about. I would need some assistance so, in addition to my usual morning pill, I stuffed three more in my pocket. Mercifully, traffic was light and I arrived in class before Geoff and the other two people on my team. Geraldine was at her desk, doing something on her laptop, sending emails or whatever. I crept into the room and approached her.

"Hi, Geraldine. Sorry about yesterday. I think I had a bug."

"Oh hi, Aidan," she said gaily.

"Is that okay?" I asked.

"Have you a doctor's cert?"

"I don't."

"I need a doctor's cert or you get docked money."

"Why? I was sick."

She smiled innocently and made a 'them's the rules' gesture.

At least I knew the penalty for missing days now. This was like work, albeit with dole wages. I slunk back to my desk, annoyed at her demeanour. I thought we'd been making progress, that she'd been sympathetic to my needs, but she'd been fairly quick to jump ship. And she wasn't finished yet.

"Geoff, Ursula and Donna did their part of the presentation yesterday. You'll have to do yours today. I can't mark your project until you do."

I looked at her, exasperated.

"Okay," I muttered.

I would have to talk to Geoff and the others, find out what I was supposed to do, go online, do some research, print out some materials, prepare my presentation, take more pills and then speak in front of the class.

Ellen came in and sat down beside me, her usually inscrutable face a picture of concern.

"Where were you yesterday?"

"I wasn't feeling well."

"You missed your presentation."

"I know."

"What did Geraldine say?"

"She said I've to do it today."

"I've to do mine as well today."

That made me feel better. We were in it together, myself and Ellen.

"Have you got anything prepared?" I asked her.

"Kind of," she said, screwing up her face as she handed me a couple of sheets of paper. It was all perfunctory stuff, she'd had to do the statistical part of her project, back up the points her team-mates had made with facts and figures. It seemed like the easiest part, much easier than the bit the other pricks had given me.

"What about slides, Powerpoint and that?"

"Aaron did all that for us," she said.

Aaron. I hadn't realised he'd been on Ellen's team. How noble of him to volunteer his services like that, as if he didn't have an ulterior motive. But there was no time for me to worry about Aaron's altruism, I had concerns of my own. I took another pill to calm me down. At lunchtime I talked to Geoff. He was helpful if haughty. Our project was entitled: *Why Ireland is one of the world leaders in IT.* Was that true? I wasn't sure, but I had to make it sound true.

Geoff showed me what they'd done on the previous day, taking me through Ursula's introduction, Donna's analysis and statistics and his own conclusion. He even gave me a few pointers on what I could do with my section. I'd been entrusted with the history, charting the growth of Ireland's IT sector from its beginning to the present day. I was okay with that. After imparting some final words of wisdom, Geoff left me to get on with it. I was scheduled to talk at two p.m., right after lunch, leaving me with approximately forty-five minutes to put something together, to research and write the content, fashion a few slides and prepare to address the class.

Since starting the course I'd been helped by the drugs, they'd enabled me to converse like a reasonably normal person, but standing up in front of a room, all eyes on me while I read from a script, was uncharted territory. I decided to take another pill, my third in the past four hours. I'd never taken that many in such a short space of time before, but this was an emergency. Hoping I would be in my confident, chilled sweet spot by two o'clock, I googled 'Ireland's IT sector'. That brought me to a page which contained the line: 'Ireland, particularly in the area of technology, often plays a significant role as intermediary between the United States and continental Europe'.

The article also said that the development of Ireland's IT sector had led to a lot of inward migration, which meant people were moving to the urban centres for work. This was perfect. I would take a few quotes, expand a bit on the themes, freestyle and accept the acclaim from my grateful colleagues. There was even a part about the lack of qualified coders and the need for companies to import employees from abroad; I would use that to highlight the opportunities available to us plebs if we furthered our education after finishing this course.

I got so much into the topic that I almost forgot I had to do the presentation. It was only when a couple of the class started ambling in from lunch that I remembered I needed to put some slides together. Luckily, I was familiar enough with Powerpoint to assemble something worthwhile within a few minutes. I inserted a picture of a man on a horse and cart on the first slide to signify the progress Ireland had made, a catchy headline which read, *Ireland: innovators in its field*, and a vivid, vibrant font which made my slides look professional yet exciting.

I'd just emailed it all to Geraldine when she returned from her lunch. There was a sense of anticipation in the room: I could feel it. Whatever had gone on yesterday had whetted their appetites. People had suffered, and now they wanted to see someone else suffer. And who better than the weird guy who made no effort to befriend anyone and seemed a bit up himself? Geraldine gave me a little nod to confirm she was ready.

"Do you not have any notes?" she asked as I joined her at the top of the class.

"No, I'll be grand," I replied.

"Okay," she said.

She pulled up the first slide. Looking at it afresh, I realised there was a typo in the headline. That was okay, though, we weren't here for our grammatical skills. I stepped forward, staring out the window, ignoring their expectant faces.

"Up until the middle of the twentieth century Ireland was predominately known for its farming industry, but as technology developed and we cast off the shackles of the past, a new powerhouse has grown. You might not realise this but IBM, one of the world's largest ICT companies, actually began operating out of Ireland in 1956 and, during the 1980s, it installed the first laser scanner system in a supermarket in Cork. IBM was joined by Intel and Microsoft in that same decade, and by then the die was cast.

"These global conglomerates initially incorporated their business into third-level campuses, offering students an opportunity to gain valuable in-house experience before becoming full-time employees. It cannot be disputed that faster internet speeds and increased access to broadband has accelerated the rate at which these company's Irish bases have grown, but it would be overly simplistic to attribute their rise solely to that. No, for the true cause of the sector's importance, we must look at something less intangible: Ireland's geographic position."

I paused. I'd totally forgotten about the slides. Belatedly I nodded to Geraldine, and she moved on to the next one. It had stuff about the industrial revolution, about farmers using tractors and combine harvesters instead of horse and carts. Where had that come from? It had nothing to do with what I was talking about. I nodded to her again. The next slide was a black and white photo of a woman standing beside a massive computer. I decided to disregard the slides completely and focus on my speech, but I'd lost my train of thought. What had I been saying? I looked at Geraldine.

"Ireland's geographic position," she whispered.

"Oh yeah," I said loudly. "It's been said that we are the gateway to Europe, or to America, one of them anyway, and that our position gives us a economical advantage in terms of . . . and if companies see us, and know we can do it, they will arrive here and avail of . . . but also, in essence, it . . ."

I faltered. The third pill was kicking in, or was it the fourth? I couldn't remember. Either way a beautiful fluffiness was descending all around me. I wanted to reach out and touch it, let it cool my face, lie upon the little clouds and be spirited away to the sky.

"I have a question for you, Aidan," said Geraldine.

A question? Yes, that sounded good. I liked questions.

"Being from the country, how do you think we can revive our towns and villages in the digital age?"

It was a good question. She wasn't trying to trip me up, I could sense that, but I was swimming against the tide now. Everything was becoming blurry and pleasant, and I really wasn't interested in her question. Yet I knew if I could just overcome this final hurdle I would truly be free. What was her question again? Something about reviving rural Ireland? I opened my mouth to speak, unsure of what was going to come out.

"The problem with rural Ireland is its ageing population and their unwillingness to change," I began with deadly seriousness. "You have people there who have lived in the same houses, and in the same way, for generations. How do we reach those people? Explain to them how beneficial the internet could be? We can't. Those people will never adjust to this new way of living. So instead we must build for the future."

I had no idea how we built for the future. What could we build - a library? That'd be great for the village. Better roads? That new bypass had completely cut Cruinníth off, and led to the closure of one of the chippers. How about a big phone mast? I had to go out the back to send text messages sometimes.

A gentle cough from Geraldine brought me back to the room.

"Only by improving connectivity in these areas can we build for that future," I continued. "Where I live, in Cruinníth, the fastest speed I can get on a good day is 2MB download. That's okay for me if I'm just going about my day, but how can businesses be expected to rely on that if they're ordering products and processing deliveries online? It's impossible to operate a business without good internet speed nowadays, so instead of trying to attract yet another multinational to Dublin or wherever, why don't the government focus on bringing the rest of the country up to speed, allow those of us living in the sticks to compete on an equal playing field? If this country is serious about being a global leader in IT it needs to ensure everyone is brought along, not just those who happen to live in the right areas and can avail of the best services."

My shoulders slumped in sheer exhaustion. That was it. I was done now. I wanted to stretch out on a couch somewhere and listen to Prefab Sprout, but I had to finish this, I had to show them I could do it, talk more about IT, horse and carts, and libraries. I was beginning to feel really sleepy. If I could bring in a bean bag and use that as my chair from now on, this course would be so much better. I yawned and rotated my head along my shoulders, as I did so, a phrase popped into my head: 'inward migration'.

"An unexpected and perhaps unwelcome side-effect to our flourishing IT sector has been an unprecedented rise in inward migration across the country. Inward. Migration."

I enunciated the words for effect. Let the phrase roll off my tongue as if it were the secret to eternal life.

"Inward. Mi-gray-chun."

It felt so comfortable, just standing there. I didn't mind it at all. My feet were so snug in my runners, I really wanted to wiggle my toes. Everything just felt so *snug*. Unable to resist, I did a big stretch, the kind a dog does after a twelve-hour nap. I flattened my hair with my hands, rubbed my shoulders and looked out at all the staring faces. I was perplexed. What did they want? I saw an empty chair through the fog. It looked comfy, so I walked towards it. The girl beside it was staring at me too and said something as I sat down.

"Bloop," I replied and lay back in the chair. It was a sin to be this comfortable, it really was.

*

It's an incredibly strange feeling to wake up in a public place, not knowing how you got there, how long you've been asleep and what you've been doing. This is made worse when you're a disgusting sleeper, a drooler, a grunter, a pig. My chin was soaked, the top of my chest was damp and there were stalactites of spittle connecting the two. People were gathered round examining me with concerned looks on their faces. I recognised Geraldine. That was fine. But there was another person, a man, older, in a suit, with harsh eyes and a red raw complexion. Another woman stood to the side, plump and fretful, and then there was Geoff. I looked to my right: there was no sign of Ellen. In fact the room was empty, save for me and my inquisitors.

"Welcome back," said Geraldine, sounding relieved.

That was good. They were worried about me.

"Are you okay?" asked the older man. He didn't sound so sympathetic.

I stretched out again, I couldn't help it. I looked at the clock on the wall; it was half four. I'd been asleep for a while.

"Bit of a headache," I said, wincing. "Could I have a glass of water?"

Geoff went off to get me the water while I pulled myself together.

"What happened, Aidan?" asked Geraldine. "You were doing your presentation and then you just . . . fell asleep."

My mind was still cloudy. I recalled preparing for the presentation and standing up before the room, but everything thereafter was hazy.

"I'm tired," I said.

"I can see that," she replied, attempting to lighten the mood.

But the man wasn't having it. He knew there was something amiss.

"Okay, Aidan," he said. "When you're ready, come down to my office so we can have a bit of a chat."

He gave Geraldine a meaningful look and departed for his office. The plump lady stood in the background, observing.

"I'd better go too, Geraldine," she said finally. They whispered their farewells and then it was just me and my tutor.

"And your presentation had been going really well," said Geraldine, smiling. "It was so well-prepared. I was ready to give you an A. You can finish it tomorrow if you like, or whenever you're feeling better."

There was no tomorrow. I just wanted to go home.

Geoff came back with the water. I took a sip and shakily got to my feet.

"You're a popular man, Aidan," he said. "Everyone finished early because of you."

Geraldine put an arm around me. I could smell her perfume, the shampoo she used. I promptly got an erection; it was the only part of my body that seemed to know what was going on.

"Are you okay to go down to Frank's office?"

"Yeah," I said, hoping that meant she would continue to hold me.

Instead she escorted me as the far as the hallway, pointed in the direction of Frank's office and set me free, like a bird with only one functioning wing. Frank's office: I didn't like the sound of that. He was the stern guy from earlier, the one who'd looked at me suspiciously, who'd correctly surmised that I wasn't narcoleptic, that I hadn't been up all night studying for my presentation. Frank was no fool. He'd looked like a guy who'd been involved with FÁS for a long time, who'd seen all types of miscreants come through these doors. So, instead of going to see Frank, instead of explaining my actions, I walked straight past his door, down the stairs and out of the building. I'd left my jacket upstairs, and my bag, but I had my phone, keys and wallet. I didn't need to go back there and I definitely didn't need to see Frank.

9

When I got home I went straight to bed. I had a throbbing headache, worse than ever. There was a ringing in my ears too, which was new, but rest would cure everything. I lay there, dozing, lapsing in and out of sleep, gradually returning to the surface, to the true reality of my existence. The clearer things became, the less I liked them. The course, my chances of progressing in life, it was all gone. I couldn't go back there, I wasn't going back there, that was the only certainty. I hadn't just burned my bridges, I had incinerated them. All that was left was to extricate myself from this mess with as little damage as possible.

By the time I got up it was well into the afternoon and I needed a pill in a bad way. Of course the sane thing to do would have been to just stop taking them, to endure whatever sickness I'd brought upon myself and ride it out till I was clean. But I needed them. After hauling myself out of bed, taking a tablet and drinking four cups of tea, I looked at my phone for the first time. Ordinarily it was a barren wasteland, the odd text from my mother, a few cold calls, but in the space of twenty-four hours I had become hot property.

Geoff, who had assigned himself the role of chief protector and friend, had called me three times, leaving two voicemails and a number of texts. They began with the standard **How are you feeling?** before progressing to **Are you coming in today? Is everything all right?** and **If you need to talk, just give me a call.** Geraldine had called twice, and there were missed calls from numbers I didn't recognise. A quick Google search revealed that one of those was the FÁS office, probably Frank or some other henchman tasked with tracking me down. There were also mobile numbers.

One read **Hope you're feeling better pal, you gave us a fright yesterday - Aaron.** Fucking Aaron, kind, considerate Aaron, he made me sick. Derek had texted me too, I knew it was him because it was barely legible. A couple of the young wans had taken the time to get in touch which made me feel bad, guilty and slightly aroused all at the same time. The text I most treasured, though, came from Ellen. **Are you okay? Let me know as soon as you get this.** Poor, sweet Ellen; deceived by my pretence, taken in by my loutishness.

I was incapable of dealing with this outpouring of goodwill, so I switched off the phone and went downstairs. Hunger assailed me. There was no one home, so I helped myself to the pasta bake I found in the fridge and ate three yogurts for dessert. This was better, this was what I was used to. I should never have dallied with the outside world, it only made life worse. When my mother got home I told her I wasn't feeling well and would need to take the rest of the week off. She was midway through telling me I'd lose out on money when I closed the door on her face.

She was right, though. Each day I spent at home, absent from a course I'd committed myself to for six months, was costing me money.

But even the thought of informing the powers-that-be I was finished with the course had me reaching for the tablets. I knew enough about the system to know that leaving would be a long and arduous process. There would be more forms, more meetings, explanations would be required, they would fight with me, cajole me, do anything to get me back on that course. And if I didn't return to that one there would just be another, and then another.

How could I explain my situation, that I would happily do every course in the brochure if only I was able? That I was so mentally fragile I couldn't sit in a room full of people without wanting to slit my wrists? If I did tell the truth they would probably find somewhere for me to go, a place full of other blubbering idiots who couldn't function in real life. I didn't want to be grouped with the rest of the nut-jobs, they might as well put me in the asylum. So I did what I always did; I buried my head in the sand and waited for the problem to go away.

I didn't reply to any of the texts, not even Ellen's. I didn't return any of the phone calls and I didn't formally announce my departure from the course. After a week or so my mother stopped asking me when I was going back, and my father simply sighed in resignation any time we crossed paths. While they were away at work, doing whatever it was they did all day, I sat at home, taking diazepam, playing on the Xbox and wondering when the letter would come. It took its time. A full two weeks passed before it arrived. It told me that my repeated absence and refusal to return any phone calls or emails had led them to the conclusion I no longer wished to study IT Skills QQI Level 4.

Offering me one final chance, it said that if I wished to continue my studies I was to ring the number listed below and explain my absence. I didn't ring the number. Shortly thereafter the social welfare office started calling me on an almost daily basis. I didn't answer the calls. Until, finally, they sent me a letter, saying that I needed to come and see them immediately. I was well aware of this as I had no income now, hadn't received a cent since leaving the course. In an ideal scenario I would have disappeared off the grid altogether, but I missed my booze, my snacks and the few other luxuries my social welfare money allowed.

So with no little effort and a headful of diazepam I made my way into town, to the social welfare office, to explain my recent activities. When I got there I gave them my PPS number and took a seat while they sorted me out with an appointment. I'd hoped to get this resolved in one visit, but it was never easy with this crowd. To my surprise and dismay, Joe appeared; Joe who'd sorted me out with a place on the course, Joe, who'd been so pleased to see me engage with the options on offer. Joe.

"Aidan, do you want to come in with me?" he said, gesturing to a door at the far side of the main hall. This one was grey, like a prison door.

I got to my feet and followed him. We went through the inner sanctum, past the worker bees, the decision-makers. I spotted the guy who used to give me my signing-on sheet, he nodded in recognition. Then we reached Joe's office. He led me inside and sat down in his chair. As before, he took his time, shuffling his papers, reading his notes, before he turned to look at me. There was still sympathy in his eyes, still a hint of the big brother trying to encourage me to make the most of myself, but he was annoyed now. I could see it.

"What happened?" he asked, opening out his palms as if I were going to place my answers inside them.

"It didn't work out."

"I spoke to Geraldine, she said you were doing great."

"I wouldn't go that far," I replied, wondering if she really had said that.

"And then," he said, looking back at his papers, "there was an incident where you just fell asleep - into some sort of coma, it says here. There were going to get an ambulance, you know."

"Problems at home," I said, hoping that would throw him off the scent.

"What kind of problems? Are you taking anything, Aidan? You don't look all that well. We can get you into a programme if that's what you need."

What was it with these people? They had a solution for everything: a course, a programme, a chat, an appointment. All I wanted was a few bob a week to buy some cans and to be left alone.

"Nah, it's grand," I said.

"Well, we can't just set you loose. We can't put you back on Jobseeker's until this is resolved."

He sat there scrutinising his papers, contemplating his next move, the next round of torture.

Then he sighed heavily. "I don't know, Aidan. My hands are tied here, there's not a whole lot I can do."

What did that mean? Was I going to dole prison? Three months of detention and hard labour until I proved myself worthy of state aid.

Joe stepped out of the room and left me on my own. What could they do to me? Surely it was my legal right to claim benefits? I was an Irish citizen, a proud son of Éire, I had a right to be looked after, same as everyone else.

Joe returned with yet another sheet of paper.

"Sign that," he said, now completely officious, all warmth gone from his voice.

I scribbled my name where instructed, not even bothering to read the document.

"That's just to confirm you've left the course for personal reasons," Joe said. "It'll take a couple of weeks for your money to come through, but you can sign on again now."

"Right now?" I asked.

"Yes."

He swivelled in his chair and began typing something on his computer. Were we finished?

"You can go," he said coldly.

I got up and left without a word. Walking back through the offices, into the main hall and up to the booth, I did what I'd been doing for all but two months since I'd left school: I signed my name on the dotted line. Mission accomplished.

10

THE SENSE OF ACCOMPLISHMENT DIDN'T last. I'd failed again. I knew my limitations now, what the future held for me: I would stay indoors, living a simple life, avoiding the world and all responsibility. Whatever fantasies I had about progressing, about making a life for myself, were just that: fantasies. In the words of Brian Wilson, *I just wasn't made for these times*. With any luck, the booze and drugs would claim me in my sleep and do everyone a favour. In the weeks following the course I fell into a deep depression, an incapacitating emptiness unlike anything I'd experienced before.

There'd always been a low-level hum of sadness in me, a weariness which ebbed and flowed depending on my circumstances, but anxiety had been king. That was my defining illness. Now though the depression took hold, it consumed me, consumed everything, even my anxiety. Every emotion, every feeling, every thought, drained out of my system. It went beyond misery or unhappiness, torment or woe. There was just a void, a black hole, with me somewhere deep inside.

Days were spent in bed, staring at the walls and reaching for my pills whenever the thought occurred to me. I didn't even bother drinking, it was too much hassle. Dad brought me food sometimes and forced me to take a shower so he could change the bedsheets. As soon as he was finished I'd crawl back into the bed, on to the fresh new sheets, my hair still wet. He'd speak for a while then, sitting on the footstool at the side of the bed and offering words of encouragement. His voice sounded far away, as if coming from another dimension. After a while he'd get to his feet and place a hand on my shoulder. Once he kissed the top of my head and I felt something flicker into life, an emotion, a feeling, but it disappeared as fast as it came.

There was nothing from my mother, no visits. She might have come to the door a couple of times - I thought I heard her - but she never crossed the threshold. This neither upset nor disappointed me. Time lost all meaning: I was aware only of brightness and darkness, of day and night, a beginning and an end. I was an organism, a mass of flesh and gristle. Once, I stared into the void and saw myself at the bottom of a deep hole, lying in the bed, curled up as if hibernating for the winter. I hated that sad, lonely little creature. Hated its insistence in living, its stubborn refusal to sink completely out of sight. Shortly afterwards I switched everything off. My mind ceased to function. There was no brain activity. I was incapable of thought. I wasn't Aidan Collins, I wasn't even a person, I was just a thing.

A doctor came: Doctor Flynn, the family physician, the man I'd been going to since childhood. He baulked at the scene, at the pungent air and stifling heat in the room. I turned my back on him, let his words fritter into the air. When he left my father took his place, speaking in urgent, desperate tones. Two sunrises later, I turned to find a box of tablets on my locker. They weren't diazepam. I regarded them for a moment, saw a name written there, recognised it as my own, and then went back to staring at the wall. But they must have intrigued me because later I made the effort to read the box: venlafaxine, an anti-depressant. I didn't have the energy to investigate further. I had my diazepam, I didn't need those ones.

He came back again, the doctor. Spoke for a bit - to my back. Opened some windows and pulled the curtains. I'd almost forgotten he was there when a word, a sentence broke through the endless, meaningless patter: *Vengeance. The Vengeance Trilogy.*

"I like those films. *Oldboy* is obviously the best."

What was an old boy? A distant memory rekindled. Someone else had liked that. Was it me? Why would anyone like old boys? No, it was a film. A series of films. There was a man in a recliner, a can of beer in his hand, watching the television. That man was me. I was watching the television, because I liked doing that; and films, I liked those. That's what *The Vengeance Trilogy* was: a collection of films. This doctor, this middle-aged man, James or Jim, had said something about those films. I turned on my side, the exertion making me light-headed, and looked at him askew. How could he, a GP in a rural village in the south-east of Ireland, have heard of Park Chan-wook's seminal trilogy which explored themes of revenge and retribution in sickening, often horrific ways. He looked back at me, this doctor, and our eyes met for a moment. Grief and shame washed over me and I burrowed back into my hideout, still aghast at the thought of Jim sitting down to watch *Oldboy* with Mrs. Jim.

My father came in then. He and the doctor talked for a bit, quietly, as if I were listening. And then it was just Dad again. Nothing he said struck a chord, I knew for a fact he had never heard of Park Chan-wook. But something had awoken in me. A hint of reality had returned. I still felt disconnected from the world, as if I were looking down at myself from afar, but at least now I understood that the person I was watching was me, Aidan Collins.

*

Several more sunsets passed before he returned again, but I didn't turn my back the next time. I was still way off listening or engaging, but having identified who I was I quickly discovered that these people, the doctor, my father, the others (I thought I'd heard a female voice, maybe a neighbour or a cousin) were here out of concern. They wanted to help. I didn't want their help, I wanted to be left alone. However, I realised that the only way to achieve the peace I required was to show them they were helping me. That made me anxious, which in turn eased my depression for a few hours.

The last thing I wanted was a steady stream of visitors coming in here, staring at me and talking behind my back. So I began to fight, not with any great strength or determination, but enough to keep them happy. I sat up in the bed, nodded my head and took the tablets they gave me. Speech was still beyond me so I didn't get the opportunity to ask Jim about *The Vengeance Trilogy*, but I noticed how he regularly browsed through my film collection, making little faces as he did so. He caught me looking once.

"Quite the film buff, Aidan," he said, "and a lover of foreign cinema too. I don't think I've ever seen such an eclectic film library."

His words evoked a feeling, a tiny movement in my stomach, and then I resumed my catatonic state. But I had to keep showing signs of progress, to get to the point where neither he nor the others felt the need to come and visit. The female voice I'd attributed to a cousin belonged to our neighbour, to Mrs. M. It had been a long time since Mrs. M had been allowed in our house. She'd fallen foul of my mother's moods and been banned many years ago - but when you have an ailing young man in the house I guess even the worst of hostilities can be put on ice.

I remembered liking Mrs. M because there were no angles to her. She wasn't from around here originally; she'd arrived sometimes in the 1990s with her two dogs, no husband, no kids. This made her an immediate source of suspicion, someone not to be trusted. A single woman, she was regarded as bohemian and free-spirited, a danger to the hard-working middle-class families of the area. To us kids, she was great. We'd go over and play with her dogs, a St. Bernard and a Newfoundland, and she'd give us glasses of orange and biscuits.

She was artistic, both in mind and spirit. She wore flowing clothes and spoke with an accent, using harmless swear words like 'feck' and 'shite' and 'arse' which we'd never heard an adult say. She had come from 'somewhere up the country' and had lived and worked abroad for a number of years. No one knew where her husband was, because surely a woman of that age had to have a husband: how could she afford a house in such an affluent part of the village on her own? She did oil paintings, dramatic sweeping works which left the locals scratching their heads but commanded five-figure sums in the art world. She also made ceramics, had a potter's wheel, and sold many of her creations right from her front door. This set tongues wagging.

Who were these people calling to her house at all hours of the day and night? Many of them were men. Were they there to buy art or for some other reason? She held parties too, lavish soirées which involved expensive cars lining up outside her house and urbane guests laughing long into the evening. The local community didn't like it, this peculiar woman inserting herself in their lives with no forewarning. She didn't fraternise, never appeared at any of the events held in the parish hall, and kept conversation to a minimum on the rare occasion someone managed to corner her in the village shop.

Now here she was, my old friend, the woman who'd introduced me to the works of David Lynch, Hunter S. Thompson, Charles Bukowski and Kurt Vonnegut. She still looked the same, free, open and expressive, not a hint of cunning or deceit.

"Hi, stranger," she said softly as she propped up my pillows.

I was suddenly embarrassed. Mrs. M might not have changed, but I had. I was no longer a wide-eyed kid, I was now an incompetent mass of hair, blood and sweat. We were equals, two adults with adult experiences and adult thoughts. Being observed in my lair, in my sticky pyjamas, hadn't been an issue when it was just the doctor and my father, but in the presence of Mrs. M I became self-conscious, almost prudish. I pulled the duvet a little tighter around me, hoping to obscure myself, my adultness.

"You're looking a lot better now," she said. "Here, I brought you some books. I don't know what you read these days but you might like them."

I glanced down at the bag beside her. It bulged pleasantly with books of all shapes and sizes. She had always been a voracious reader and had been a great influence on my literary choices. Introducing a fourteen-year-old to *Fear and Loathing in Las Vegas* might not have been the most responsible thing to do, but that was why I liked Mrs. M; she didn't care for convention.

"I have new dogs now. You should come over and see them when you're well enough. There's Ghandi, he's a Labrador, and Mercury, a spaniel. Do you remember my old dogs, Patsy and Cooper? The hours you and Sally spent with them."

She looked out the window, reminiscing. It was odd, I'd spent endless days in the company of this woman without ever realising she was just that: a woman. She'd been our auxiliary aunt, that cool lady who let us hang out and watch MTV, but she wasn't that old - maybe forty-five. That put her in her late twenties or early thirties when we were kids, not much older than I was now.

I remembered her going on dates back then with transient men whose presence I resented. And I remembered the stories she told me about her youth, her childhood in the south of England, the school she went to in Dublin when the family moved home and the excitement and vigour of her days at college. There'd always been a gap, a time unaccounted for between her early forays into the workplace and her arrival in Cruinníth. And despite only selling a few of her creations on the side, she always seemed to have money and lived in a house big enough for a family. Yet for all her glamour, her means, and her education, she remained alone.

We sat in silence for a while, my discomfort easing with each passing moment. It was almost like old times, apart from the lack of music, films or any form of communication. As the room grew dark and shadowy, she got up to leave.

"I'll be back later on in the week," she said. "Do you still like cheesecake? I'll make you one."

She lingered a moment, perhaps debating the correct way to bid farewell to a catatonic mute, before carefully leaving the room and closing the door behind her with a soft click. I waited until I was sure she wasn't coming back and switched on the lamp. Unsurprisingly Mrs. M's taste in literature was as refined as ever. There were books I'd heard of but never read, books I'd never heard of but instantly wanted to read, and books I'd long wanted to read but never had the chance. I started with *Stoner* by John Williams. It was the first time I'd done anything other than eat, sleep, or go to the toilet since taking to my bed.

11

I WAS COMFORTABLE IN MY depression, barely aware of the outside world or my own sense of self. It seemed as good a way to live as any other. But then the numbness, the emptiness, gave way to something else. It started when I absent-mindedly put my hand under the mattress for my diazepam and discovered I'd run dry. Rather than panicking I saw it as a mild irritation, a bit of a nuisance. I waited until Dad had gone to work and crept into the hallway, listening out for the sound of my mother's television. It was quiet; she must have left earlier.

I went into her bathroom, to the shelf in the cabinet where her array of medications usually sat, but it was empty. That was a puzzler. I fumbled round the cabinet, picking up random boxes and tumblers, opening them, turning them upside down. I unearthed nothing of any use. Perplexed, I returned to my room. So that was the end of the diazepam then.

When next I awoke, I wasn't so flippant. It began with a sense of longing, a gnawing desire. At that point I merely *wanted* a pill. It was like unrequited lust, seeing an unattainable woman and wishing you could fuck her; frustrating, saddening but manageable. That want soon gave way to need. My dependence, the chemical process I had inadvertently set in motion, creating a craving unlike anything I'd ever experienced.

My body screamed for diazepam, banged its fists on the table for diazepam, shouted 'Diazepam!' over and over again at full volume right into my ears. It tugged at my hair, my ears, pulled the skin on my face, all for diazepam. It was a like a child throwing a tantrum only far, far worse. And whereas a parent can accede to their child's demands when all else fails, I could not. My body could shout and scream all it liked. There was no diazepam. That shouting and screaming intensified, became more aggressive. My brain, fed up of it all, tried to squeeze itself out of my skull, pushed against my eyeballs, my temples, my ears, expanding, contracting, going to extraordinary lengths to escape. The rest of my body took this as a signal, a call to arms: "Hey lads, the brain is jumping ship, let's get out of here." My heart, my poor exhausted heart, took off at a gallop, not sure what the big hurry was but determined not to be left behind. That set my stomach off, rocking and rolling, bubbling and boiling.

The cramps came like contractions: piercing pains every thirty seconds, causing me to spasm in agony each time, to retch with such ferocity I thought I'd be ripped in two. I emptied my bin and laid it beside the bed. I couldn't even drink a glass of water without it coming straight back up, so alcohol was no use. When my head wasn't pounding, chest hurting, or stomach reeling, there was an all-round pain to keep me company, a jack-of-all-trades agony which stepped in to the breach while the others gathered their strength. It flowed from one end of my body to the other, jabbing and poking here, punching and kicking there, exploring my every inch, determined to find the most sensitive area and give it a good going over.

I was shaking and sweating, gritting my teeth as I awaited the next chapter in this hellish tale; burping, barfing, trying not to scream in case Dad heard. When someone came into the room I stayed still and pretended I was in my catatonic state. It was easier that way, there was less to explain. Someone removed the bin, cleaned it out and brought it back. A wet flannel was placed on my forehead. They spoke among themselves, sounding like sentries at the pearly gates, debating whether or not to let me in. If only they'd open those gates, I'd be free to endure in peace.

Yet as my pain waxed and waned, peaked and peaked some more, I not only accepted it, I embraced it. I was going through something, a real-life experience. It was horrendous but it was authentic, it meant something. My body, this sluggish mass which weighed me down from one day to the next, was undergoing a transformation. I was shedding my old self and becoming reborn. The old Aidan Collins was congealing in the bucket before me, evaporating into the ether. Once I shook him off, life would begin again. Maybe I was delirious but it felt like a second coming. My body was cleaning itself, glad to be rid of the drug I had leaned upon so heavily for the past four months. That this cleaning process was being carried out with industrial-sized scouring pads by an army of spiteful roughnecks was besides the point; I was being remade. My joy was fleeting. For a few hours I suffered the pain like a true martyr, content in the knowledge it was for the greater good. Then the darkness descended and my mood soured. Dirty and soiled, inside and out, I lapsed into self-pity and self-loathing. Why was I here? What was the point of this? Such a foolish practice, such a waste of time.

I lay there, whimpering, clawing at the air, and a familiar ghost made her presence known. It had been a while since I'd seen her. No, that was a lie. I saw her all the time but I always pushed her away, covering my eyes until it was safe to look once more. There was no escape this time, though. Even closing my eyes, squeezing them shut made no difference: there she was, her head on that pillow, that vacant expression on her face, looking into the distance as if remembering something from long ago. The image began to expand, filling in around the edges. I saw her little feet, not much bigger than a child's, jiggling up and down in the middle of the bed. I didn't want to see any more, but I had no choice.

I saw his back, wide and pink, rivulets of sweat running down his spine and his shoulders flexing as he loomed over her, lowering his head to hers, kissing her, licking her like a dog. His backside, ploughing forward, like a piston, in and out, in and out. The slapping noise as flesh clashed with flesh, and the barely audible whimper which accompanied each thrust. That was enough, I didn't need to see any more. But still it came, the picture now almost complete: her thin torso, the ribs visible beneath her skin, her breasts red with bite marks and hand prints, her slender neck as brittle as a twig.

The other men stood to the side, naked, awaiting their turn. They stroked themselves in anticipation, their faces illuminated by the bedside lamp. And then back to the girl, to the image which haunted my dreams. Her eyes meeting mine, a brief flicker of hope as she saw an end to her torment, that hope quickly fading as she realised that at best I was just a curious onlooker, at worst someone whose desire would also have to be sated.

She'd been right, of course, she'd seen into my soul and known all there was to know in those couple of seconds. I had been a curious onlooker, no better than the man lying on top of her, his hands pressed against her shoulders, pinning her to the mattress as he took what he desired. I was no better than those men standing by the side of the bed, leering, waiting their turn, eager to heap more misery upon her. I was just as guilty as they were.

I found sleep, or at least a version of it. But it brought no respite. The girl followed me there; the girl who'd dressed up for a night out, done all her make-up, put on her new outfit, and met up with her friends. The girl who'd been separated from those friends, convinced to come to a house party, to take the drugs and been left alone with a predator, a man who knew exactly what he was doing. The girl whose night had been ruined, whose life had been ruined, all because of my stupidity, my inaction and cowardice. She was taking her revenge now, taking great pleasure in my predicament. No longer a helpless waif for others to use and abuse, she had undergone a sexual awakening, was all powerful and merciless. The men were still there, but they had been joined by dozens of others, each knelt before her, their penises tucked ashamedly between their legs. As I stood once more at the door she beckoned me in, her mouth twisted in a wicked smile, her eyes mocking as I shuffled into the room. She was standing on the bed, dressed in black, like a dominatrix, as she summoned me forth. Dutifully I did as I was told, my head down like the other men who were now sobbing in fear. I crept to the edge of the bed and awaited further instructions.

"Lie down," she commanded.

I lay on the bed, noticing that I wore nothing but a pair of flimsy underpants like the ones they give you in hospital. Despite myself I felt an urge, a familiar animal desire, but nothing happened; it was as if there were nothing there. Ashamed, embarrassed, fearful, I pleaded for mercy, begged her to leave me alone, but she was only getting started.

Surprisingly nimble, given the length of the stilettos on her boots, she lifted the underpants up with her cane, peered at what was inside and cackled. One or two men squealed in terror. And then she bent forward and gently tore the pants down the middle. When I looked down to see what she'd uncovered I saw - nothing. It was as if I were a newly-minted doll, smooth and hairless, just a little nub of flesh with not even a hole to piss out of. I looked at the girl, hoping for an explanation. She gave me a sad little smile, a look of genuine disappointment, and prodded me with her toe, pushing me off the bed until I landed on the floor with a hefty thud. I got to my knees and joined the others, on my knees, whimpering as I went.

12

I'd always imagined that weaning yourself off drugs would involve a beginning, middle and end. It wasn't like that. On the third day the pain abated and the terror subsided, but there was no conclusion. I didn't whip back the blankets and declare myself better, jump out of bed, a new man. No, I simply lay there, dead inside, feeling wretched, wanting diazepam. This was my new reality. I had rid myself of a dangerous addiction and come out the other side. A fog had lifted, I had clarity of thought and the world seemed real again.

But little had changed. Because right at the centre of my being, in my chest, in my stomach, was that ball of tension which had formed in early adolescence and remained lodged inside me ever since. Months of drug abuse, of floating in a benzodiazepine fantasy, had failed to shift it. I was still the same, maybe even worse. I hadn't been reborn, I still felt like death, like dying. And right now that seemed like the best option available to me.

I decided I needed to get back drinking, and fast. Before I could do that, though, I had to rid myself of my torpor and return to the land of the living. It seemed impossible, even taking a shower was an ordeal. The doctor continued to visit, chiding me when I forgot (or didn't bother) to take the pills he'd prescribed, the antidepressants which had made no difference after weeks of taking them. My dad did his best, sat with me for hours on end, both of us silent. My mother appeared to have washed her hands of me, I hadn't seen her for weeks. That was fine, I didn't mind. I had Mrs. M now. She was a regular visitor, calling at least twice a week. True to her word she had made me a cheesecake, among other things, and she began bringing me dinners, leaving stuff to be heated up on the days she wasn't here. While all this was welcome, it did arouse my suspicions.

At a certain point I had noticed a drop in the quality of food being served to me. Like a hospital patient, I had little else to mark my days and the arrival of my three square meals had become a highlight. These meals were always served to me by my father, my mother clearly continuing her boycott. She and I had retained our connection through the food I ate, the food she cooked, but I hadn't lain eyes on her since this sorry affair had begun. Those plates, hot and full of goodness, represented the only form of care she seemed capable of giving, my ability to clear them the only way I could thank her. But then our connection, her love, disappeared.

My father sometimes took over the reins in the kitchen, so I was used to his unseasoned spaghetti bolognese and overcooked vegetables. I knew his cooking, and when soggy broccoli and nuked sausages became part of my daily diet, my suspicions heightened. Mercifully, Mrs. M stepped in to fill the void, but even a full belly couldn't distract me from this troubling development. As I became more lucid, I began to notice the complete absence of my mother, the little things, the flush of her *en-suite*, the gentle scuttle of her slippered feet, the familiar theme tunes of the evening soaps – they were all gone.

I no longer heard the sound of RTÉ Radio One in the mornings, the gentle chug of her Fiat as she backed out of the driveway and, most tellingly, I didn't hear her voice coldly berating my father for another unforgivable error. More than that, when you've lived in the same house as someone for twenty-five years you can sense their presence, even when all is quiet. My mother wasn't here. She was gone. Yet I was still too passive, too fatigued to fully care, so I pushed these anomalies to the back of my mind and vowed to investigate when I felt stronger. In all likelihood she'd gone to visit her brother in Galway again. Anything to get away from here, away from me. I preferred Mrs. M anyway. She was the mother I'd never had.

I really wanted to discuss the books with her, not just *Stoner* but *Engleby* by Sebastian Faulks, *Amongst Women* by John McGahern, all of them. But it was too soon, too big a step. I could see how those monks got used to living in silence; the longer I did it, the more it appealed to me. So I just read the books, ate the meals and convalesced at my own pace. Because I *was* convalescing, a small sliver of defiance had begun to rise in me. Although I wasn't exactly hopeful for the future or ready to take on the world, I was willing to go on for a while, to slowly recuperate and see where it took me. Mrs. M recognised this and began cajoling me to do more.

On one sunny October morning she convinced me to get out of bed and sit by the window. It made me light-headed and nauseous, but after a while I welcomed the heat of the sun on my face. A week later I was coerced downstairs, bringing my duvet down to the couch where I watched the rugby with my father. I spent the entirety of the game fighting the urge to go back upstairs, wrestling with my thoughts, but managed to see it through to the end. After that I went outside, just to the back garden and just for ten minutes, but it was enough. I was spending as much time out of the bed as in it and I felt stronger, more able to deal with the world, not as fragile or fearful as I'd once been. And after almost ten weeks of silence, I finally spoke again.

Dad had been at work, gone for the day. For a while he'd been coming home at almost hourly intervals, checking on me to make sure I hadn't done anything drastic, but now he obviously felt it was safe to leave me on my own. When he came in the door a little after five I was standing in the back garden looking out at the mountains, at the dull greens and decaying browns of late autumn. A chill swept through the house as he closed the front door and briskly walked into the kitchen.

"Jesus, Aidan, come in out of the cold. I'll turn the heating on," he said.

"Where's Mam?" I asked without turning around.

There was a stunned silence, like when a toddler speaks their first words.

"What?" he asked.

"Mam," I said. "Where is she?"

I walked inside and sat at the kitchen table.

"Is she dead?"

"No, of course not."

"In the nut house?"

"No. Stop it, Aidan. Your mother is fine."

"Where is she, then?"

I looked at him. Even before he spoke, I knew a lie was coming.

"She's up in Galway with Bobby and Stephanie."

"Why?"

"She just needed a break."

"How come she hasn't called?"

I couldn't stop talking now, was better than any toddler.

"Oh, you know your mother, Aidan. Communication isn't her strong point."

I left it at that. The answers would come in good time. Whatever had happened, I wasn't ready to hear it yet.

*

I don't know how toddlers put up with people trying to get them to talk all the time. No sooner had I uttered my first words then everyone started harassing me for more. My father was like a man on a mission, following me around the house, all chat, hanging on my every word. All he was missing was a little notebook to document my progress. Even Mrs. M was pushing and probing, asking me about books, films, music, trying to trigger a response. I'd had thoughts about the books she'd brought and had planned to discuss them with her, but I wasn't going to be forced into it.

Actually, after initially being pleased to see Mrs. M I was already growing tired of her. She was needy, always asking me if I was okay, if I wanted this or that, if I liked one thing or another. And she hovered. Every time I ate something or watched a programme on the television she lay in wait, anticipating the last bite, the end credits, so she could ask me what I thought, whether I wanted more or if she could do anything else for me. It was enough to make me miss the quiet hostility of my mother.

Details on the whereabouts of my mother remained hazy. I'd tried calling her phone but it went straight to voicemail, and I'd texted Dan but had received no response. They were hiding something from me, I was sure of it. I was the child in a room full of laughing adults, not getting the joke, knowing it wasn't meant for my ears. There I would have stayed but for the arrival of someone I hadn't seen or spoken to for longer than I cared to admit: my sister.

I'd been fourteen when Sally left for college. I remembered her coming into my room, instructing me to turn off the Xbox and sitting me down for a serious talk. She'd got a place on a biomedical science course in Cork and told me that once she left here she was never coming back. She said I needed to concentrate in school so I could go to college too. Life had been hard for her, I knew. I was our mother's favourite, a position which spared me the worst of her poisonous tongue, but from a young age Sally had been castigated for the most innocuous behaviour, reproached for being too excitable, too talkative, too loud, too grown-up, too childish, too much, too little.

It got worse when she became a teenager. Then her attire, her demeanour, even her hygiene were called into question. The two of them argued constantly, my mother harsh and severe, Sally defensive and desperate. My father kept out of it, refusing to intervene no matter how hurtful the comments or how damaging the exchanges. I did likewise, realising that if Sally was in trouble it reflected well on me. A lot of children would have rebelled, stayed out late, challenging my mother's authority; Sally did the opposite. She became a model daughter, a model student, a credit to her family and the Collins name. It did her no good. The criticism continued, the reasons more obscure, more pernickety. But while my mother was remarking on her complexion, mocking her figure, Sally was planning ahead.

She had devised an exit strategy. It involved a stellar Leaving Cert and a place on one of the most sought-after courses in the country, then a Master's degree in Dublin and finally a job as a microbiologist in London. She'd lived there for two years now and, judging by the infrequent texts we shared, was doing well for herself. One day, out of curiosity, I'd looked up the average wages for microbiologists and had been suitably shocked:

she was earning at least eighty grand a year, according to the Internet. She'd met a man over there too, a vet, and they'd moved in together. Sally was the success story of the family, the girl who 'done good'. True to her word, she'd never been back, not even once, not for Christmas, birthdays or anniversaries, not for anything.

Unless she came here, she wasn't going to see her brother. I hadn't visited her in Cork during her four years there, nor had I darkened her door during the two years she'd spent in Dublin. She never criticised me, though, just pleaded with me to follow in her footsteps, to get out of the house and make a life for myself. I told her I would. Even now, living in London, she'd said I could come over any time and sleep in their spare room until I got myself set up. Sometimes I fantasised about doing that, living in one of the world's biggest cities, showing everyone how wrong they'd been, returning to Cruinníth years later, dripping in money, a beautiful wife on my arm, adorable kids in tow.

Part of the reason Sally never criticised me was because she knew something was amiss. We never discussed it, never strayed far from trivial matters, but she had the inside track on my mental state. She knew how our mother was, how our father was, and how that could damage a fragile soul. She saw how I took after our mother, how nervous I was as a child, how timid and unsure. Maybe she felt guilty, leaving me there, but I didn't blame her. She had her own life to live, and the last thing I wanted to do was burden her with my troubles.

Even when I took to my bed for weeks on end and lost the will to live, I didn't tell my sister, didn't reach out to her for support, so when I saw her name come up on my phone I panicked. I thought my father or Mrs. M had rung her, told her what was going on, recruited her to drag me out of my malaise. I let the phone ring out. A text swiftly followed.

Answer the phone. It's about Mam.

That was hard to resist: a potential answer to the ongoing mystery.

I went upstairs, closed the door and took a deep breath. I called Sally back, wondering how much credit it would cost to call the UK.

"Aidan," she said.

"Well."

"How are you?"

"I dunno. Why?"

"I know what happened, Aidan. You don't need to pretend."

That annoyed me. They had no right to tell her about me.

"It wasn't that bad. I'm grand, really."

"I'm going to come over," she said.

"Jesus, it's not that bad, Sally. I'm grand, don't worry."

"No, not from London. I'm in town. Myself and Grant came back yesterday."

"What? Why?"

"It's Mammy, Aidan. She's not well."

"What do you mean?"

"She's in the hospital. She had a stroke."

I felt a darkness envelop me, the clouds returned. Fighting for air, I gasped, "Hurry, Sally. Come soon."

13

It was worse than I could have imagined. It had happened about a week after I'd come home from the course, while it was just myself and her in the house. One afternoon, having checked to make sure I was still alive, my father decided to go in to work for a couple of hours. My mother had been complaining of dizziness, of headaches, but that was par for the course for her. She'd taken to her bed with a book and a couple of aspirin.

While I lay there staring at the walls, willing myself out of existence, a rogue blood vessel in my mother's brain was slowly expanding to the point of bursting. At the moment of impact, when the vessel ruptured, preventing sufficient oxygen from reaching her brain, I continued to lie there selfishly wishing for it to be over, for my own pitiable problems to be cured. Did she cry in pain or call out for assistance? I have no idea. I have no recollection of the day in question. All I know is that over two hours later my father returned home, threw his keys on the table on the hall, and then went up to check on me. Yes, my welfare was his priority at that moment in time.

Satisfied there was no immediate threat to my life he looked in on my mother, almost as an afterthought. If he hadn't seen the wide damp patch across the duvet, he might not have investigated further. If the sun hadn't caught the deathly pallor of her skin, he might have continued on down the stairs. As it was he furrowed his brow, called out her name and stepped into the room he had stopped sharing with his wife some four years previous.

By the time the ambulance crew arrived, it had been almost three hours since she'd had the stroke. She was rushed to hospital, to the newly-established stroke unit which had been opened to great fanfare by the mayor a few months before. Without it she would have died. She underwent emergency surgery to repair the ruptured blood vessel. The surgeon, an Indian man recently recruited from a clinic in Calgary, Canada, was considered one of the best in the country, a man at the top of his game who saved lives as a matter of routine. His work was done in just under five hours.

From there my mother was taken to the ICU where she would be monitored for the next ten days before the long rehabilitation process began. In my mother's case, this process was complicated by the severity of her stroke and the length of time it had taken to get her to hospital. Now, six weeks after she had almost haemorrhaged to death, she was in a specialist unit, stable, out of the woods but with her faculties severely compromised. She couldn't speak, had limited movement throughout her body and was on enough pain medication to topple an elephant. For a time our lives had dovetailed in perfect harmony; as she sat on her bed in a ward staring out the window, eyes glazed over, nothing going in or coming out, twenty miles away I was doing the same. But whereas I had slowly clawed my way out of the hole I'd dug myself into, my mother's condition had not changed. She remained in that ward, her condition neither improving nor worsening. The tests were done, the results had come back, and the doctors all agreed; it was up to her now.

The treatment was there, only by engaging with it could she hope to regain some quality of life. They didn't know how stubborn my mother was, how wilfully pugnacious. Even if she knew it would be beneficial and allow her to get out of that bed on her own two feet some day, she would refuse the treatment, purely out of spite. She would stay there until they decided to move her elsewhere, to a nursing home or a healthcare centre. Her days of making decisions were over.

Even a stroke hadn't been enough to get Sally to come to Cruinníth and enter the house. As soon as she'd heard the news she'd booked the next flight over, arriving in Dublin that evening. She and Grant had stayed in a hotel in Maraghmor, alternating between there and my mother's bedside, allowing my father to go home, to come back and check on me and to call over to Mrs. M and ask if she might visit me on occasion. After a week in Ireland, staring into the cold depths of my mother's empty soul, Sally and Grant went back to England. They both had jobs, they were busy people; they would be back in a month.

Obviously Sally had enquired about her brother, asked why I wasn't at the hospital. The contents of that conversation were never fully divulged, but she was told in no uncertain terms not to tell me what had happened to our mother. She could see me soon, when I was feeling better. As far as my father was concerned, though, I was never going to get better, certainly not well enough to receive this news, so my sister had intervened and broken the silence.

Having done so, she broke a promise she had made ten years ago and drove to Cruinníth, through the village, past the oak tree, the shop, the pub and the GAA pitch. She went up the *boreen*, the one she and I had walked down on our way to school as kids, then past the O'Gorman's house, Barry's and Joyce's, into ours; to the house where her stricken brother sat in the living-room, wondering if he'd managed to unwittingly kill his mother.

Sally looked good. She always did. She was an example of what could be achieved with our set of genes. Like me she'd been an ungainly child, an introvert whose presence went largely unnoticed in any social setting. But although she would never be a head-turner or a show-stopper, adolescence had been good to my sister. Whereas I became more ungainly, more awkward, Sally grew into her body, developing at a faster rate than her peers and attracting the attention of boys, older boys and sometimes men. I remember her having her first boyfriend at the age of fourteen and the almost instantaneous transformation she underwent as a result. She knew she had something people wanted, and that gave her confidence. It was easier for girls - I often wondered whether my life might have been easier if I'd been born female.

It wasn't just her burgeoning sexuality which enabled Sally to move through the social classes. She was incredibly intelligent, with an aptitude for all subjects. Learning came easy to her. Best of all, she managed to straddle two worlds. On one side of any school you had the nerds, the kids at the top of the class, the high-achievers. While academically gifted, many of these kids were social outcasts. It wasn't their fault, fate had simply decided to give with one hand and take away with the other. So they had bad haircuts, poor dental hygiene, suffered explosive outbreaks of acne and went clothes shopping with their mothers.

Their counterparts, the cool kids, weren't particularly bright but they made up for their shortcomings by being handsome or pretty, funny or strong. It was a tale as old as time itself. Every now and again, someone came along to break these age-old traditions, and Sally was one such person. She hung out with the nerds and the pretty girls. She had handsome boyfriends, drank cider in the park and still managed to remain at the top of the class. When my turn came I didn't manage to enter either world, never mind straddle them. I was an above-average student who wasn't clever enough to hang out with the nerds, who was too nerdy to hang out with the cool kids and too niche to attract the attention of the kids who occupied the mid-tier stratum. If Sally had been male, I would have been jealous but I was happy for her, happy to see at least one member of the family excel. I hoped some of her stardust might land on me, that I could become successful by association.

That never happened. I remained that odd, forgettable lump whose sister was destined for great things. Her boyfriends ignored me, and on the rare occasion she had friends over my presence barely registered. We lived in the same house and ate the same food, but once we stepped outside that door we entered two distinct stratospheres. Upon finishing school Sally expanded hers yet further, stretched it beyond and away from Cruinníth, while mine contracted, shrank away to nothing. Now she was back, dragged into this distant, miserable existence I'd shared with our parents since she'd escaped all those years ago. We hugged awkwardly, only our shoulders and upper arms connecting, and she took a seat on the edge of the couch.

"You're looking well," she lied.

"You too," I replied, and she was. Her clothes, her hair, her make-up and jewellery were all immaculate. Stylish yet understated, feminine but reserved, Sally had left Ireland a girl and returned a woman. London suited her. It had given her an edge, an air of clinical efficiency and control which was badly needed in a situation such as ours. Up to now my father had been muddling along as best he could, but I had a feeling that was about to change.

Sally waited for Dad to go make the tea and then huddled close to me.

"I wanted to tell you earlier but he kept saying no," she said, nodding towards the kitchen. "If it'd been up to him you'd never have found out."

"How is she? Is she going to die?" I asked.

"No, she's not dying," Sally replied, "but she's not going to be coming home any time soon."

"I should go see her," I said sadly.

"You should. Dad doesn't want you to go, but you can come with me in the morning."

Our father returned with the tea and Sally moved to the other end of the couch.

"So you know everything, then?" he said, looking at me ominously.

"I suppose I do."

"It's not your fault, Aidan. I don't want you thinking that. It's as much mine as anyone's."

"It's no one's fault," said Sally irritably. "Stop being so maudlin about it."

That quietened us. We sat in silence like scolded children, waiting to see what Sally would say next.

"Dad, I'm bringing Aidan in to see her tomorrow, if he's up to it," she said, looking at me for affirmation.

I nodded my assent.

"Are you sure, son?" he asked.

"I'll be okay, Dad."

"No one's forcing you, just remember that. Take as long as you need."

"How is she?" I asked him.

"She's okay now, getting better, I think."

Sally sighed deeply, "Dad, stop."

"What?" he asked.

"She's not getting better and she's not going to get any better. We've discussed this already," said Sally. "Aidan, we're going to have to put her in a nursing unit. I've found one but Dad is dragging his heels. We can't make any decision without your input."

The idea of me being involved in something so important seemed ludicrous when just a couple of weeks ago I couldn't figure out what socks to wear.

"I don't mind. Whatever you think is fine with me."

"No, Aidan, we have to do this as a family."

She took out a brochure then, for a place called Eden Lodge in County Waterford. It looked nice, all the nurses were smiling, the residents too. There was a large garden with places to sit and look out at the sea, and the rooms were spacious and tastefully decorated. I would have liked to live there myself.

"How much will this cost?" I asked.

"Don't worry about the money," she said dismissively.

"Well, it looks perfect, I suppose."

Sally and my father shared a look, there was still an impasse to be breached despite my ringing endorsement of Eden Lodge.

After more cups of tea, some stilted small talk and an agreement to ring Bobby to discuss our decision, Dad broke the tension by turning on the television.

"*University Challenge,*" he said innocently, as if he hadn't known exactly when it started.

Some of my fondest childhood memories, perhaps my only ones, involved all four of us sitting in this room watching *Who Wants to be a Millionaire or The Weakest Link*, arguing over the answers, chastising the cowardice or stupidity of the contestants. Those family occasions gradually became less frequent until Sally left, and then we didn't bother any more - though I would still often hear my father barking out the answers to *Eggheads* of an evening.

"You should be good at this. How many degrees have you got, again?" he asked Sally.

"Two, Dad," she said, smiling.

"Well, come on then."

"What about me?" I asked, hurt.

"If you think you can roll with the big dogs, then bring it on." Dad laughed.

And I did roll with them, helped in no small part by a music round featuring the works of Led Zeppelin and three questions on the flora and fauna of the Amazon rainforest. Much to his delight, Dad got more answers right than either of us, reminding Sally of his truncated education at the local tech each and every time.

For those thirty minutes it almost felt like we were a real family, that we hadn't spent the last decade in habitual silence without ever sharing our thoughts or emotions. A real family would know how to deal with one of their number being consigned to the hospital, though. They would lean on one another for support and make important decisions without resorting to recriminations and finger-pointing. We weren't a real family. We didn't know how to do any of that.

14

THERE HAD BEEN A TIME when my mother had been more vibrant and alive. I remembered a summer afternoon in the back garden, herself and Dad larking about with a hose, the two of them getting soaked, while I looked on, laughing, awed by this rare show of intimacy. A day spent Christmas shopping in the newly-built St. Stephen's Green, lugging bags full of shopping through the car park, Mam humming carols as Sally and I skipped along behind. My appearance in the school play, her brushing my hair repeatedly and then seeing her in the crowd, smiling up at me when I ambled out, shepherd number three of five. A World Cup, when Ireland scored a goal to beat a team they weren't supposed to beat and my mother, who was as uninterested in sports as I was, clapping her hands in celebration at the end, drawn in by the drama of the occasion.

But those were distant, isolated memories. My abiding memory was the fear she instilled in us all. Rarely was a word said in anger or a voice raised, but at some point we became aware that we shouldn't upset our mother, that there was the potential for things to go very wrong unless we tread carefully. It was like living with a time-bomb, and the older we got the more that bomb crackled and fizzed. We saw and heard flashes of pure malignancy, bitter put-downs, caustic, hurtful remarks - the kind of things no mother should ever say to their children. I recalled nights spent on the landing, listening in as Sally was admonished for another heinous transgression.

Our mother would sit Sally down at the kitchen table, under the glaring lights as if in an interrogation room, and lecture her for hours on end. Most of the words have faded over time. It was routine stuff: 'What are you doing with your life?' 'Is this any way to behave?' 'You should be ashamed of yourself.' 'After all we've done for you.' What has stayed with me is her tone, how she would drone on and on incessantly, asking one rhetorical question after another, snorting dismissively whenever Sally dared to speak. Our mother could switch from withering and contemptuous to mocking and vindictive in an instant. And only when she'd had her fill, when she'd tired of the browbeating, was Sally free to go.

My sister rarely fought her corner. Occasionally she might try to state her case or offer an explanation, but it would be rejected out of hand, calmly rebuffed as if it were the ramblings of a madwoman. There was one other voice, though, that of my father. Cast in the role of peace-keeper, he could be heard cajoling my mother in the background, pleading for clemency on his daughter's behalf, working towards an agreeable solution, doing his utmost to limit the damage. My mother ignored him completely. He was an irrelevance, a bystander, a member of the gallery with no say in proceedings. When it finally ended I'd scurry back to my room and listen to Sally mount the stairs, quietly shut her door and go to bed. Sometimes I heard her cry, but we never discussed it. When Sally left for college I feared that I would become my mother's primary target, but instead she just retreated into herself, became less and less communicative, a shadow haunting the halls.

Now she lay before me, greyer than ever, an old woman mummified in a bed three sizes too big for her. Already slight in stature, she was now in danger of wasting away entirely. Her face drooped on the left-hand side and her few movements were slow and deliberate, requiring an effort she didn't seem willing to make. Even in her darkest, most apathetic days there'd always been a little something in her eyes; a death-stare capable of curdling milk, or a wicked dart of spite as she chided you in that easy way of hers. Now there was nothing. Her head was turned to the side, towards the window, where she gazed into the middle distance at nothing in particular and waited to die.

"Look, Avril, Aidan's here," said my dad helpfully. He moved to the side of the bed and stood in front of her, blocking the window view. "He came, look?"

"Well, Mam," I said awkwardly, standing beside my father.

Nothing. Not even a flicker.

"She's looking stronger today," Dad said agreeably. "There's definitely an improvement since the weekend."

Sally resisted the urge to correct him. This was simply another formality to her. She wanted me to see for myself that all hope was lost. Once she got my assent, the plan would be put into motion. Mam would go into the nursing unit, Sally would go back to London, and myself and my father would see out the rest of our days as a pair of bachelors in the family home. I should have been annoyed at Sally for being so clinical, but I didn't care. I felt nothing.

I looked at my mother and tried to feel some compassion, some sadness. I found it, but it was for myself. This woman had brought me into the world and then we had spent the last twenty-six years behaving as if we were strangers. I knew nothing about her. She was just this person who'd lived in the same house as me, who washed my clothes, cooked my dinners and gave me money. Perhaps that was love in itself, perhaps I was simply ungrateful, but staring into those cold dead eyes I only felt discomfort and a desire to get away.

I stayed. I listened to my father's delusions, his insistence that there were signs of improvement. I stayed to meet the consultant and hear his more realistic take on the situation: that my mother's condition had plateaued and there was very little they could do for her. I even stayed to meet the wife of the man in the bed next door, who told us we were in her prayers. Eventually, though, myself and Sally shared a look and rose in unison, signalling an end to this visit, an end to the whole charade. As we walked out of the room, I didn't even turn to say goodbye to my mother, didn't even think to.

*

With my vote secured, Sally went about re-homing our mother with minimal fuss. Eden Lodge was exactly as advertised, if not better. From the outside it resembled a futuristic villa, all curves and contours, but the interior was homely and familiar. The residents were in various states of decay and disrepair - during our visit we heard at least two blood-curdling wails from the on-site abattoir - but all in all, it was a lovely place. Dad was still in denial, convinced it was only a matter of time before his wife suddenly sparked back into life, became reanimated and had us clutching her hand and telling her what a terrible fright she'd given us. But having met the staff at Eden Lodge and heard about the treatments they offered, he relented, reasoning that it might aid her recovery and have her home sooner than expected. We had stopped arguing with him by this point, he needed to believe in something.

My mother wordlessly accepted her fate and allowed herself to be wheeled into her new room, not a flicker of emotion as we showed her all the lovely features contained therein. Her eyes immediately moved to the window, to the sea view, and there they remained until it was time for us to go home. She was still staring out there when we returned the next day, and continued to do so during each of the five visits I managed before giving up the pretence. Sally didn't return after that first meeting and so it was left to my father to make a biweekly vigil to Eden Lodge, to sit with the mother of his children as her life slowly ebbed away.

15

Despite my recovery, Mrs. M continued her visits. This wasn't wholly unwelcome; she was a great cook and continued to share her expansive literary collection with me, but now that I was up and about I could see that her visits weren't solely for my benefit. She was spending a lot of time at our house, more than seemed necessary. In addition to the cooking she was now cleaning, buying groceries and, shockingly, washing my father's clothes. Other neighbours called, other women who'd heard about my mother and wanted to make sure us lads were doing okay, but they didn't linger. Mrs. M lingered. She became a regular fixture in our house, and after a while I got the sense that I was the outsider, not her.

Somewhere between my meltdown, my mother's stroke and the washing of my father's socks, Mrs. M had made herself invaluable, had become a de facto member of our household. I watched her, watched them both, and knew something was up. After dinner in the evenings we would all sit down and watch television together, and the longer I stayed the more agitated they became. They were waiting for me to go. So I would stay right where I was until Mrs. M sighed and announced it was time for her to go. As soon as she left I would go upstairs, which was my way of telling Dad I knew what he was up to. But I didn't know, until I saw it.

My father had been an unashamed soap-watcher prior to Mrs. M's arrival, but now it was all arts programmes, documentaries on Renaissance painters, highbrow stuff which would have bored him to tears a few months ago. Perhaps it was part of their scheme, a way of getting rid of me, but when they announced that there was a programme about the life and times of Caravaggio on the Arts Channel I left them to it. I had recently purchased *The Elder Scrolls* for the Xbox 360. I was back drinking too, not like before, but enough to keep me occupied. I had a taste for the ale on this particular night, however. I'd grown tired of the Xbox and moved on to season four of *Oz*. Then I'd put on some tunes, was having a right little midweek shindig.

With the juices flowing, I decided I needed more booze before the shop closed at ten p.m. I put on my runners and a coat and went downstairs to see if the other two wanted anything. And they did. They wanted each other. It could have been worse, a lot worse, but there was no denying the intimacy of the scene before me. They were on the couch, Dad in his customary position, flat-out, almost ready to slide to the floor, Mrs. M curled into his side like a haughty cat. One of his arms was around her shoulders and both her hands clutched his paunchy flank.

I stood there for a moment, my presence undetected.

"Do ye want anything from the shop?" I blurted out.

They sprang away from one another.

"What? No, you're grand, son," said my father, dusting himself down.

I looked at Mrs. M.

"No, thanks, Aidan," she said breathlessly.

I left the house and walked down the road in a state of shock. I suppose it had been obvious, but still . . . my father and Mrs. M. The dirty bastard. And Mrs. M. I'd always thought of her as a mythical, sexless creature like Mrs. Claus or Smurfette. What had they done so far? And how long had this been going on? Had it pre-dated my mother's illness, or had their love blossomed while she was in the hospital?

Either way it was a desecration of the house, a betrayal of both mother and son. I may have been ambivalent towards my mother and her failing health but I wasn't a turncoat; I had some loyalty. I wasn't going to start calling Mrs. M 'Mammy' just because she'd made me some cheesecake and brought over a few books. Having initially intended to get just a couple of cans, I upgraded the situation to Code Red and purchased a bottle of rum. There would be a reckoning in the Collins household tonight.

When I got back she'd gone and the telly was off. My father was sitting in the kitchen with a cup of tea before him, looking suitably contrite. "We wanted to tell you but there just wasn't a good time," he said.

"Nice," I replied sarcastically.

He cast his eyes downward.

"What about Mam?" I asked.

"You've seen her, Aidan."

"When did it start, you and Mrs. M?"

"A while back, before you started your course. Sure myself and your mother have barely spoken a word to one another in years."

"Drink?" I suggested, placing the bottle on the table.

"No, thanks," he said, shaking his head. "Aidan, there's more."

"Well, I'm having one," I said, pouring a large glass and topping it up with lemonade from the fridge.

"Aidan . . ."

"What?"

"It's costing an awful lot to pay for that Eden Lodge place."

"I thought Sal was helping out?"

I sat down opposite him, enjoying his discomfort, glad I wasn't the only one culpable in my mother's demise.

"She is, but Jesus . . . between that and the mortgage, the bills, the expenses . . ."

Here it came. Time for me to get a job.

"I'm going to have to sell the house," he said.

"What? But we've always lived here."

"It's too big for just the two of us. We don't need all this space."

"Where are we going to go?" I asked. "I'm not moving into Mrs. M's house."

"Aidan, I know you've had a tough time of it recently but this could be an opportunity for you, a chance to strike out on your own."

It took me a second to understand what he was saying, but once the pieces fell into place it all made sense.

"So yourself and Mrs. M are going to move in together and I'm out on the street, is that it?"

"No, Aidan. You'll always have a bed in my house."

"Fucking hell, Dad," I said, draining my drink and picking up the bottle. As I stood over him, our eyes met. He looked scared.

"I'm sorry, Aidan."

"Yeah, me too," I said sadly.

16

I UNDERSTOOD IT WAS TIME, a man of twenty-six shouldn't kick up a fuss at being asked to leave his parental home. I also understood that this wasn't about me and I needed to display a modicum of maturity during such turbulent times. That didn't stop me from hitting the bottle, and hitting it hard. I sat in my room, seething, angry at them and angry at myself, and drank like I'd never drunk before. It was destructive. I polished off entire bottles of vodka in a night, drinking as if it were my punishment. My behaviour changed; I became erratic, unpredictable and temperamental. I would stay up all night, rambling round the house, cooking and watching late-night television at full blast, making an awful racket.

Most of the time I had no recollection of my actions. My worst excesses were a mystery, known only to my increasingly beleaguered father. I could have discussed it with him, he had been making a concerted effort to build bridges since his announcement. He was trying to save me, to hold on to his only remaining family member, but I wasn't interested. I had no desire to talk to him about my feelings or explain my behaviour. If he wanted to confront me about my drinking, he was within his rights to do so, it was his house, after all. A heart to heart, though, that was out of the question.

When he cornered me one evening and asked me to sit at the kitchen table with him, I braced myself for the worst: he had contacted Doctor Flynn and I was to be sent to the sanatorium in the morning. The local Alcoholics Anonymous meeting was that very night and he was going to drive me there and wait outside until it was over. Mrs. M was pregnant (was she too old to be pregnant?), the house had gone 'sale agreed' and I had two days to pack my bags. My mother had regained consciousness, was coming home and I had to take her place in Eden Lodge. It could have been anything.

"How are things, Aidan?" he asked for the umpteenth time that week.

"Fine."

"Have you given any more thought to looking for somewhere to live?"

"Yes," I said decisively.

"It's been two months now."

This was his way; he was one of life's great pussy-footers.

"I'm still looking."

He exhaled and fiddled with one of the table mats.

"Still drinking, too," he said quietly.

It wasn't an accusation, nor was it a question. He just wanted to put it out there, see how it felt.

"Yeah, still drinking, Dad."

He smiled then, to himself. "Do you remember the night I took you out for a drink on your 18th? You had two and then went home."

"Yeah," I said morosely.

"Made up for it since then, eh?"

I looked him dead in the eye. I'd never hated him so much, never hated anyone with the intensity I felt at that moment. He couldn't come out and say it, couldn't ask me why I drank so much, tell me how dangerous it was, or point an accusing finger at me. He couldn't get angry or sad or display emotion of any kind, instead he just pitter-pattered around the issue as he always did; a pathetic shell of a man, spineless, with no heart, no soul.

"What do you want, Dad?"

"I've accepted an offer for the house," he said quietly.

"Oh, right. How much?"

"It's a good offer."

He said it like an apology.

"What happens now?"

"Well, Beatrice and I have seen something we like. We have a verbal agreement with the owner, but there's paperwork and money to be shifted this way and that. It'll be a while yet."

"How long?"

"A few weeks."

He shuffled into the living-room, bombshell delivered.

I went back upstairs to my room, to the only room I'd ever known in the only home I'd ever had. I couldn't live in the real world. I didn't have the life skills, the street smarts, or the know-how. I was incapable of working. I couldn't fend for myself. Then there was the anxiety, the fear of going outside unless I was raving drunk or doped up to the eyeballs. Up to now I'd always had someone to buy my groceries for me and to wash my clothes, to ensure my life ran smoothly.

In the real world no one bought your groceries and made sure the fridge was always full. You had to buy bread and milk with your own money and replenish your own fridge. Not only that, you had to pay your bills and take the rubbish out on bin night. You had to cook your own meals, keep your house tidy and do the dishes. If you didn't, you'd starve, you'd die or you'd end up on the streets. That was the real world and, whether I liked it or not, I was about to enter it.

17

The next day there was a brochure from one of the local estate agents on the kitchen table. I purposely didn't look at it. The very sight of it caused a tremor of panic to run down my spine. A week passed, I continued to drink, to live in denial. Maybe if I kept to myself and hid upstairs, the new owners would let me stay. They could move in, convert the attic into an extra bedroom, stick me up there and begin their new lives. I'd keep quiet, they wouldn't even know I was there. When people came to visit and they saw me skulking around in the background, rummaging in the fridge, they'd say, "Oh, that's Aidan. Don't mind him, he's harmless."

I'd be like their pet, a greedy, ugly pet who liked drink and belly rubs. On birthdays and special occasions they'd give me a good scrub, spruce me up and sit me at the kids' table. If proceedings were slow someone would say, "Will we give Aidan a few drinks?" and I'd be cast in the role of entertainer, thrown into the spotlight for their titillation, bribed into prancing about in exchange for cider. A few days later I'd wake up in my lair, clothes all torn, wondering what had happened. Yes, that would be a fine life, much better than fending for myself in the big, bad world.

But as much as I shied away from that world, I couldn't avoid it forever. And when the great procrastinator of our time began putting the squeeze on me, I knew time was running out.

My father appeared at the door one evening, brochure in hand.

"I circled a few places for you here," he said with a smile.

"Yeah, leave it on the dresser and I'll have a look later."

I didn't have a look later. I didn't have a look at all. The brochure sat there, all evil, all powerful, reminding me of my fate.

Having tried the subtle approach and failed, the lovebirds took a different tack. I hadn't really spoken to Mrs. M - or Beatrice, as she was now known - since I'd seen them snuggling on the couch. She'd stayed over a couple of nights and I'd seen some of her clothes on our washing line, but she'd been respectful, hadn't flaunted her status as the new woman of the house. I wasn't mad at her, just disappointed. She'd gone down in my estimation, and I couldn't for the life of me understand what she saw in my father.

There was a little jealousy there too. She'd been my friend first, and she'd abandoned me for him. The thought of her becoming a constant presence in my life, of going over to Dad and Mrs. M's, didn't fill me with glee either. Yet despite our cooling relations there was still a flicker of that old friendship between us, a recognition of how pally we'd once been. When I came down for lunch one day to find her waiting for me in the kitchen, I didn't resist. She had the laptop open and there were properties on it, carefully selected abodes for a young up-and-comer from Cruinníth.

"You could get a room in town," she said pleasantly, pushing the laptop towards me.

They must have decided that Dad's passive style wasn't getting the job done and a bit of feminine charm was required to uproot me.

"Is there anything in Cruinníth?" I enquired, knowing there wasn't.

"Come on now, Aidan," she said, a hint of sympathy in her tone.

I understood it was a big deal for her, that she'd made an effort to engage, so I sat down at the laptop and perused the available rentals. Straight away I saw a major problem.

"These are all two and three beds."

"So?"

"I can't share with people."

"Well, you won't be able to afford a place on your own, not straight away, anyway."

The terror I'd felt at having to fend for myself paled in comparison to the thought of living with strangers. I would rather live in the shed out the back than with people I didn't know. Ironically, after changing the search setting to one-beds I found a dwelling which looked exactly like the shed out the back. It was in the very centre of town, on the sixth floor of a red-brick building overlooking a busy intersection. There were shops on either side, a milkshake shop underneath, and takeaways across the road. The building might have served a worthwhile purpose at one stage in its life - it looked old, venerable - but now its only role was housing the poor and the destitute, the outcasts and immigrants, those who had nowhere else to go.

Whoever had taken the pictures had tried their best to accentuate the positives of the flat, focusing on the large bay windows, the natural light, but that light only illuminated what should have stayed hidden: the dirt, the sad beige walls and tatty curtains, the kitchenette and 1970s decor, the bathroom with its curling linoleum floor, the stained toilet and the shower crammed inhospitably beside the sink and mirror. The bedroom was a ten-by-eight metre tomb, with just enough room for a bed, an ancient chest of drawers, a wardrobe and bedside locker. Yet the thought of living there didn't faze me. Being thrust into a world of unfamiliarity was terrifying, but where I laid my head at night was of little consequence. Mansion or midden, it was all the same to me.

*

As soon as I told dad and Mrs. M I'd found a place they were offering a deposit, the first month's rent and the use of someone's van to move all my stuff. They could at least have feigned sadness. Their enthusiasm dampened somewhat when I showed them where I intended to live, though. They were unhappy with my choice, saying that area was notorious for crime, was rife with drug addicts and violent types. Why couldn't I live in the suburbs, they asked, share a house with some nice young people my own age? A little back and forth ensued, they argued the merits of a house-share, but I remained resolute. Ultimately their desire to move on with their lives, to kick-start mine, saw me get my way. I would go to Apartment 14, 56 Wolfe Tone Street, and reap what I had sowed.

My confidence growing, I rang the estate agent and arranged a viewing for the next day. My father offered to come with me, to drive me into town, but once more I refused. Something had awakened in me, an independent streak. I began to believe that this *would* be the making of me, that all my problems would be solved once I escaped my parental home. Now, if I wanted to spend a week without going outdoors or lie in bed for days on end, I wouldn't be able to. I'd have responsibilities. I'd have to go to the bank, do the hoovering, pay my rent, and get some spuds. I'd have no choice. If I got a panic attack on the way to the supermarket, I'd have to keep going. It'd be either that or starve.

The first test of this new confidence came when I went to view the flat. Usually my visits to town, when I went to the social welfare office to sign on, were planned with military precision. I would get the bus in, arrive at 1.50 p.m., walk the five hundred metres to the dole office, wait in line for about ten minutes, sign my name, and be done in time for the 2.15 p.m. bus back to Cruinníth. It was an ordeal but it rarely threw up any surprises. Going to meet an estate agent in the middle of town for an undetermined amount of time was different; anything could happen. I completed the first part of my task, arriving outside the building five minutes early, awkwardly leaning against the wall as people, traffic hurried by.

"Are you Aidan?" a voice asked.

He was middle-aged and world-weary, his few strands of hair flying in the breeze, tie haphazardly dangling from his neck.

"Yeah."

"Come on, then."

He opened the door and led me inside to the lobby area. The first things I saw were bicycles, lots of them, propped up against an old washing machine under the staircase. There was no lift. Flats one and two were to the right and there was an open door leading outside, perhaps to a communal garden.

Taking a deep breath, the estate agent began ascending the stairs. They were wooden, as was the banister. Halfway up each flight there was a window with bars, its frame powdered with dust, edges decorated with cobwebs. What were the bars for – to keep us in or everyone else out? There were two more flats on the first floor, two on the second floor, and so on. Each time we reached a new floor the estate agent paused momentarily, sighed to himself and continued on his way. On the third floor I heard noise coming from one of the flats, Number 8: it was an infant crying, a tired mother pleading with it to stop. I could hear hammering and the hum of traffic from outside, cars beeping and people shouting and laughing.

We reached the sixth floor, apartments 13 and 14, the end of the line. Immediately I wondered who was in number 13. The thought of having a neighbour, just us, up here at the top, intrigued me. Maybe he and I would be friends, or maybe he'd torment the life out of me and steal everything I owned. It could have been a woman or a family, but no, this was a prison and the sixth floor was maximum security, where they kept the worst offenders.

"In here," said the estate agent, looking clammy and irritated.

I knew it was going to be bad but the pictures had deceived me, almost given me false hope. I'd thought it was a hovel or at worst a pigsty, but it was actually a shit-tip. There was damp on the walls, great black and brown spirals which bubbled and bulged from beneath curling wallpaper, a two-seater couch with a musty old blanket draped over it to hide the stains, a square of thin, stringy carpet across the middle of the floor and two hard chairs in front of a tiny table with scratches and scuffs all over it. An old storage heater lay face down on the floor, a pale outline on the wall indicating where it had once stood.

"We'll get that fixed," the estate agent told me as he turned the tap in the sink, a look of uncertainty on his face as he waited for the water to come. He hastily turned it off when it juddered out in violent spurts.

The bathroom was like a pond, mould everywhere, insects scuttling underfoot; at one point I thought I heard a frog 'ribbit' accusingly in our direction. The lino was filthy, the kind of filth that doesn't come off no matter how hard you scrub. There was grime on the shower door and all along its exterior. The lid of the toilet was down, probably to keep the crocodiles in, and it stank like a sewer. There was no window to offer some respite, although I did spot an attic door: something to explore later.

Entering the bedroom was like stepping into the Antarctic. We were high up, but even now, in the middle of the afternoon, there was no sign of sunlight or warmth. The bed itself was just a frame, there was no mattress; but there were two bin-liners full of dirty laundry, underpants and T-shirts, stained and soiled.

"We'll get rid of those," I was informed as the estate agent tried to close one of the windows, realised the latch had rusted away, and discreetly left it alone.

"So," he said, gesturing around him, "what's the verdict?"

"If I give you the deposit now, could I move in at the weekend?" I said without flinching.

I thought I saw a hint of pity in his eyes, but that was quickly replaced by his ordinary business-like manner.

"Grand," he said, moving to the living-room and gingerly sitting on one of the chairs. "Sure we may as well do the paperwork here."

While I filled out the forms he engaged in a little small talk, nice and friendly now that the deal was secured.

"Where're you from, Aidan?"

"Cruinníth."

"You working?"

"Not yet."

"Yeah," he said knowingly.

"Who lives next door?" I asked.

He looked into the distance, trying to remember the identity of my new next-door neighbour.

"There was a woman there, but she left. I think there's a Polish couple there now, or maybe just a man on his own. You'll find out soon enough, anyway."

"And downstairs?"

He shook his head tiredly, intimating how impossible it was to keep up with the movements of the lowlifes who came in and out of these apartments. I signed my name at the bottom of the tenancy agreement and handed it back to him, then we went to his office to complete the formalities. I handed over the cash, took my receipt and agreed to return on the Friday to collect my keys. It was official: I now lived at Apartment 14, 56 Wolfe Tone Street. On the bus home, I felt a strange sensation. It was only a small thing but it was there nonetheless: elation. Somewhere deep within my soul, fluttering in my chest, was a lightness of spirit, a tiny voice congratulating me on a job well done. Acknowledging it, examining it, I swiftly dismissed it, embarrassed that something so trivial and insignificant could cause me to feel good about myself.

*

I began packing as soon as I got home. There was a lot to do, an entire life's worth of possessions to sort through. On Mrs. M's advice, I set aside a couple of bin liners for the stuff she could either throw out or donate to charity. But, after two hours of heavy lifting, those bin liners remained empty. Opposite them were an assortment of boxes filled with magazines and books, CDs and DVDs. And there was a lot more to come: my collection of video games and their consoles, my computer, my TV, my clothes, my stereo.

There was no way everything would fit in the boot of my father's car. I would have to do some downsizing of my own, at least initially, so I created a third pile of items which were to remain here: DVDs which I'd since bought the Blu-Ray version of, magazines I no longer subscribed to, old consoles and their games, books I'd read more than once. I would focus on the essentials, the things I couldn't live without.

"Do you need all these CDs?" asked my father when he came up to check on my progress.

He wasn't a music lover so he didn't understand how I might at some point in the future suddenly want to hear The New Radicals sole studio album, which I'd bought on the day it came out, listened to once or twice and ignored ever since.

"I need them, Dad," I said, stepping defensively in front of the box.

"And all these films," he said, gesturing helplessly at my significant DVD collection.

To placate him, I threw a couple of jumpers into the empty bin liners.

"That's a good jumper, Aidan. You might need that in the winter."

There was no winning with him.

Eventually, after much soul-searching, I decided to leave half of my film and music collections behind, but only on the proviso they would be transported to Dad's new house and given a safe location when the time came. It took me two days in total, but finally I had my bags packed, stuff ready for the big move. Only then did the anxiety kick in, did the true enormity of what lay ahead hit me. In just a few short hours, I would be left to fend for myself. My cosseted, comfortable existence was over. Life was about to change, and there was little I could do about it.

18

ON THE MORNING OF THE move I rose from my old bed for the last time, to the calm and tranquil environs of a three-bed detached house in the south Kilkenny countryside, knowing that by day's end I would be crawling into a bed in an entirely less hospitable environment. I had a quick cup of tea and a slice of toast and bundled myself into the car. Mrs. M was busy so it was just me and Dad.

"Have you everything?" he asked as he turned on the engine.

"Mmm," I replied.

"The key to the apartment?"

"Yeah."

"Money?"

"Yeah."

"The dinners Beatrice made?"

"Just drive the car, Dad, will you?"

He did as instructed and with each turn in the road, with each passing junction, I got closer to my new life and further away from the only one I'd ever known. In an attempt to lighten the mood my father hummed a nameless tune, affecting an air of cheeriness as if we were setting out on a road trip. It should have felt like an adventure, but all I felt was dread, helplessness and a complete loss of control.

"Wolfe Tone Street," mused my father as we approached the city limits, "now where would that be?"

"I thought you knew where it was?"

"Ah, I forgot."

"For fuck's sake, Dad," I said, my already frayed nerves stretching towards breaking point.

There followed an agonising twenty minutes in which I assumed the role of navigator while he crept his way through the midday traffic. Twice we went the wrong way down a one-way street and had to reverse our way out. On a further two occasions we were the recipients of angry beeps and gestures after we crossed over lanes of traffic without indicating, and for thirty excruciating seconds we found ourselves stranded in the middle of a four-way intersection after he hesitated at the traffic lights, decided to go for it and then changed his mind halfway through.

Having finally located Wolfe Tone Street we slowly inched down it, hoping to get a spot somewhere near my building. There were no parking spaces, but rather than accept defeat and park somewhere else he insisted on doing a lap of the block and coming back around again.

"Someone will have gone, Aidan, wait till you see."

"Can we not just park on the quay?" I pleaded.

"We'll get a space, don't worry."

He drove along the quay, past all the available spaces, and turned back up towards Wolfe Tone Street, stopping at the intersection and peering ahead while we waited for the lights to turn green. Slowing to a crawl, my father searched for spaces. There were no spaces. We passed another intersection, onto Catherine Street, passing takeaways, a coffee shop, mobile phone repair stores, a Polish supermarket and more gloomy, grey buildings with apartments stacked high. He turned back onto Henry Street, down along O'Connell Avenue and nudged his way into the traffic on the quay. There were spaces galore; all he had to do was turn in and park. It was only a two-minute walk to the apartment.

"I'll just have one more look," he said, turning back towards Wolfe Tone Street.

"JESUS CHRIST, DAD!"

"What?"

I put my head in my hands and sucked in some air. When I lifted my head again we were once more making our way down Wolfe Tone Street. This time, to my father's unbridled joy, there was a space. He reversed into it expertly, beaming with delight.

"See!" he said triumphantly.

We got out of the car and examined our surroundings. The milkshake shop was busy, as was the chemist one door up. There was a butcher's further on and a pub on the corner. Across the road was a child's clothing shop, an off-licence and a string of takeaways. Above all these retail units were flats like mine, with grimy windows, tatty curtains and dusty blinds. Clothes hung out of some, the odd potted plant or window-box rested on others, but there was no escaping the reality of the situation: this was Skid Row, only one step away from sleeping on the street.

Then there was the traffic, both vehicular and human. A constant stream of cars flowed up and down, horns honking irritably as everyone fought to get in or out or town, away from the madness or into its very heart. When the lights went red the noise briefly abated, like those anxious moments before the start of a Formula 1 race; the second they went green the drivers were off again in a crescendo of revs, leaving the street momentarily empty until it all began again. All the while people wove their way up and down the pavement, in and out of one another's way, across the road and between the cars, ignoring the lights, hurrying, ambling, shouting, laughing, spitting. Others stood outside shops or in the middle of the path, yakking and yammering in that way townies did, all business, as if they owned the place.

This was my life now. I was wilfully subjecting myself to this.

I took a box of my belongings from the boot, fished the keys out of my pocket and opened the door to the building.

"This is it," I said.

Dad joined me in the hallway and we began our ascent to the summit. He had brought two boxes, I had one box, two bin liners and an assortment of dinners and pre-prepared foodstuffs. At each floor he stopped and looked at me expectantly. I shook my head and continued up the stairs. When we reached the sixth floor, I laid my box on the floor and opened the apartment door.

"Here we are."

My father, now markedly out of breath, strode inside, leaving the boxes on the couch and taking in his surroundings.

"Okay," he said.

It was even worse than I remembered it, the sunlight exposing additional damp patches and dry rot that I hadn't noticed before.

"I'll open a few windows," he said, as if that would fix everything.

As luck would have it, the window he went to had a broken latch and would neither open nor close. Pretending not to notice, he moved over to the other window and opened that one instead. Immediately the sounds of the street filtered in, loud, alive and invasive. While he tended to the windows I started cramming the food into the freezer. There was enough space for a couple of pieces of lasagne and one of the shepherd's pies Mrs. M had cooked. I would have to eat the rest, the spaghetti bolognese, the chilli and the casserole, within the next day or two.

Dad had begun rooting round in one of the drawers, presumably looking for something to fix the window. I knew this would happen, that he'd take over. I left him to it and went downstairs for more boxes. When I returned, he had a screwdriver in one hand and a piece of twine in the other, and was hard at work on the window.

"The kettle doesn't work, Aidan."

"Okay."

I dropped the boxes and descended for another load. When next I returned my father had acquired a hammer and was attempting to fashion a makeshift latch for the window. I went back down for the duvet and the bin liners containing my clothes. I would drop them in and then go for a walk around town, letting him do whatever he had to do, it was easier that way. I returned to find him underneath the sink, his little pot belly and bandy legs sticking out.

'Dad, get out of the fucking sink, will you?" I said.

He scooched out, his face a picture of confusion.

"I was just checking the pressure, there seems to be an issue with the flow."

"It doesn't matter, Dad," I said. "Just leave it."

"Where are you going to put the clothes horse, Aidan?

"I don't know, Dad."

"But you'll need to dry your clothes. If I was you I'd put it over there beside the heater."

"Dad, I don't give a shit. Will you just leave me alone for a second and stop fussing!"

"All right, all right. I'm only trying to help."

I sat on the couch and looked at him in desperation.

"Please, Dad. I need to get my head around this."

He wanted to fix the water. I could see it in his eyes; but as soon as that was fixed, there'd be something else.

"I'll be grand, Dad. I'll give you a call later."

"Alright," he said dejectedly. "That window opens and closes now."

"Thanks, Dad."

And then he was gone.

I peered out the window, waiting for him to emerge from the building. He came out and looked up hopefully. I gave him a little wave, but he couldn't see me. He got into the car and drove away. That was it. I was alone, I had finally flown the nest. The challenge now was to ensure I didn't plummet directly to my death.

19

THE FIRST TASK WAS TO stockpile my alcohol, to lay it all out so I could make a plan for week one. I'd packed it in its own suitcase, keeping it separate from the other luggage, and compartmentalised everything in order of importance. The cans (forty-eight Belgian Pilsner) had been laid across the bottom, like shock absorbers. On top of those were four flagons of cider, then came the spirits, zipped up and protected by bubble wrap: a bottle of whiskey (700 ml), a bottle of vodka (also 700 ml), and a bottle of rum (1 litre).

It was a fine haul, enough to last me a couple of weeks or more under normal circumstances. But these weren't normal circumstances. My anxiety had been steadily building in anticipation of this day, had reached a crescendo during the search for a parking space, and was now wavering somewhere between 'Lie down on the floor and start crying' and 'Scream at the top of your lungs and punch yourself unconscious'.

What I really wanted more than anything was a good dose of diazepam. Thirty tablets would do it. That would be enough to blur my new reality long enough for it to become normal. I wouldn't get addicted to them again, I'd seen the damage they could do. But the stash was gone. My mother probably had loads of them in that nursing home, and better stuff too. She was completely out of it all the time now. Doctor Flynn had encouraged me to keep taking the antidepressants, but I didn't see the point of them. Apparently they took weeks to work, and even then there was none of the pleasurable effect you got with diazepam. Plus, he'd said it was best not to drink while taking them, that doing so was potentially harmful and would negate whatever benefits they might provide. So I'd given up on them.

Doctor Flynn had also suggested I seek professional help, that I should book some sessions with a counsellor and attend the day centre, Elm House, which offered treatment for those experiencing mental health issues. There was no cost, he said, it was covered by the HSE. All you had to do was turn up, put your name down and you'd be looked after. For a while I considered it, I really did. Some mornings when I woke up, I told myself I would sign up and submit myself to the process, but then I remembered I could just continue to drown my feelings in alcohol. Why subject myself to the humiliation of a 'day centre for those experiencing mental health issues' when I could just drink all day?

Pouring myself a whiskey, I took a seat on the window sill and assessed my new environs. It was a far cry from Cruinníth, from the hills and fields which had greeted me every morning there. There were no hills and fields here, not even any grass. It was concrete and metal, fumes and dirt. For the first time in my life, though, I was the king of my own castle. It was a shit castle, admittedly, but it was mine. If I wanted to walk around the place naked, I could. If I wanted to fall asleep on the couch with an empty bottle of gin by my side, I could. And if I wanted to leave the washing-up for a couple of days, or even a week, I could do that too.

This was what freedom felt like. I was an independent man with the world at his fingertips. No matter how bad things got, I wasn't going home; kings didn't abandon their castles at the first sign of danger. What kings did do was furnish their castles with treasured possessions. So I set up my TV, connected my Xbox and DVD player and tried to make the place feel homely. I didn't have any channels, though, nor did I have the internet. Those things costed money. How much money I didn't yet know. But I would have to find out, and soon. I needed the internet. It helped to distract me from my anxiety.

I didn't like social media, Bebo, Facebook, they were too personal, too invasive. I preferred chat forums and message boards, you could retain your anonymity there, even create a new persona. I spent hours on them: on gaming sites and movie forums, turbo-posting, starting discussions about French cinema or the best *Final Fantasy* characters, whatever random shit was on my mind; replying to any active threads, jumping from one discussion or one forum to the next, spending hours conversing with people I'd never meet, never know. By keeping my mind active and engaged, I could temporarily shut out those anxious thoughts. Better still, some of the people online seemed to like me. On one of the sites I frequented, a forum where users discussed all things Xbox, I had the third-highest reputation of any user.

Some of the people on the site played online together and they constantly asked me to join them in their group chat, but I couldn't do it. I wanted to, had, on a couple of occasions, sat staring at the screen, headset on, my finger hovering over the 'Join Game' icon, ready to chat with Captain Frantic, Useless Hombre, Delicious Lizard and the rest of the gang. But the thought of them hearing my voice, of revealing the real me, brought me out in a cold sweat. So I remained a voiceless entity, albeit a hugely popular one.

That popularity would soon be on the wane, though, unless I got back online. To do that, I needed money. At home I'd been spending approximately a €100 a week on drink, dining out on brand-name beers and ciders and the very best of spirits. That would have to change. From here on in, it would be off to the discount supermarkets with me, foraging around the pallets for ninety-cent cans of lager and two-euro flagons, splashing out on wine if it was on offer. Unless I got rent allowance.

My rent was three hundred euro a month. There would be other bills: electricity, bins, food, household goods, other unknown costs that came with being a king. I currently received €180 a week in Jobseeker's Allowance. Multiplied by four, that was €720 per month which, minus the rent, left €420. Approximately €100 of that would be spent on bills, leaving me with €320 per month, or €80 a week, to feed and clothe myself. By my reckoning, I would need €40 of that for drink. I wasn't sure how much my groceries would cost, whether I could exist on €40 per week, but I would have to find out.

The rent allowance had the potential to change everything. It was an additional payment from the government, designed to help non-working, non-participating souls like myself. However, getting it wasn't straightforward. There was a vetting process, I'd read about it on one of my forums. You had to endure stressful, strained encounters with the staff at the social welfare office, fulfil certain criteria to get that money. They would ask me questions, judging me as I tried to explain why I'd moved out when there was a perfectly good bedroom at my dad's new house. My entire fate would be in the fat, sticky hands of a civil servant. One tick of a box and I'd be back online, boosting my reputation, summoning up the courage to join Captain Frantic for a game of *Halo*. A cross, a rejected application and I'd be out of contention, destined to live off cans of Green Orchard for the rest of my miserable days.

These were all problems for the future, as remote as the sounds of traffic coming from below. Evening was closing in with an autumn chill in the air. I shut the windows, drew the curtains and popped Disc 1, Season One of *The Sopranos* into the DVD player. Who needed the internet when you had all seven seasons of the greatest television show of all time? I watched four episodes before stumbling to bed, reeling from the whiskey. And there I lay, cocooned and comatose on a bed which needed to be fumigated, until noon the following day.

Fear greeted me as soon as I woke, fear and noise. I went back to sleep, trying to drown out the sounds of the city, my new reality, but I couldn't avoid it forever. When I'd finally squeezed every last second of sleep out of my body, I opened my eyes and faced the day. Cold, hungry and afraid, I gathered the duvet round me and slithered into the living-room. This was it, now. This was my new life. This was how it felt to be a king.

I sat on the couch, trying to calm myself, telling myself everything would be okay. It was no use. The maelstrom of emotions, feelings of confusion and fear, panic and desperation, manifested in their usual manner. My heart began beating faster, louder, my breathing became hitched, unsteady and irregular. My ears began to ring and my sight grew blurry. I felt dizzy and sick, I needed to urinate, defecate and vomit. I flopped over on my side, curling into the foetal position, facing inwards so that all I could see was the grimy pattern of the ancient couch, and I began to cry.

I should never have agreed to this. I'm not cut out for life on my own, I'm not one of those people. I need someone to look after me. I need someone to feed me, to shelter me from the real world.

Allowing these thoughts in, admitting they were true, opened the way for further thoughts, further truths.

I'm twenty-six years old and I can't even live without my mammy and daddy. How pathetic am I? There's people my age, people I went to school with, out there doing all sorts. They're seeing the world, starting families, and I'm here lying on a couch, bawling my eyes out because I had to move out. I've never had a job, never had sex and now, after finally moving out, finally taken what should be the first step towards a normal life, I'm having a fucking meltdown.

Who'd employ me? Who'd fuck me? I'm afraid to go outside, afraid to talk to people, afraid to be seen - afraid, afraid, afraid. I'm a freak. All I want is a normal life, to be like everyone else, but I can't do that. I belong here, in this shithole, on this couch. This is where I'll stay, weeping like a baby, until my body gives up, until I go somewhere else and do everyone a favour.

I lay there like that, fighting with my thoughts, listening to the constant thud of my heart; crying, weeping, shuddering, drifting in and out of consciousness, jolting awake, while life on Wolfe Tone Street carried on regardless. It was constant, consistent and unrelenting. But those exterior sounds were only half the problem. There were other noises from within the building, from the people with whom I now shared a communal space: my neighbours. The people downstairs appeared to be Polish, or some class of eastern Europeans, and they were noisy.

As I lay on the couch, wrestling with my demons, they were going about their own daily routines, oblivious to the presence of their new, stricken neighbour. These routines seemed mostly to consist of shouting and banging. They weren't exactly a laugh a minute. I heard his footsteps as he lumbered from one room to the other, bringing to mind a cumbersome ogre, a joint of meat hanging from his jaw as he commandeered his domain. That image was backed up by his voice; loud, authoritative, demanding. Of course I couldn't understand what he was saying but he seemed to be in an eternal state of annoyance, growling at the woman, barking orders and questioning her with increasing force.

She was quiet, soft-footed and softly spoken, and responded to his barks witheringly as if she'd had enough of his shit and was preparing to murder him any day now. Perhaps I could help. We could murder the ogre together and hide his body in the fridge, no one would ever know. I'd move in with her and see if she'd mind me. I could hear their every movement, what they watched on television, when they ate, when they went to the toilet. It was a level of intimacy I wasn't prepared for.

I continued in this semi-conscious state for some time, aware of the outside world, of the noise from below, of the sun gradually moving across the sky, but locked inside my own mind, afraid to move. My phone rang intermittently. I yearned for some diazepam. Just one pill would do. Maybe the people at Elm House would have some? If I called them they might bring me one. I would trade pills for my loyalty and become their best, most frequent, visitor.

Eventually I had to get up and go to the toilet. Hunched, with the duvet still around me, I dragged myself to the cistern and splashed piss in the general direction of the bowl. Daytime had passed, it was now dusk. I went back to bed, I would more comfortable there, more protected. It made no difference. I tried to talk myself out of it, I really did, but the harder I tried the worse things became.

Why are you so afraid? What are you panicking about? Just relax and your heart will slow down, your breathing will return to normal..

I can't relax. I'm trying to. What if this doesn't stop? What if I'm like this forever?

You won't be.

You don't know that.

You've had panic attacks before and none of them have lasted forever.

Yes, but none of them were like this.

There was no answer to that. This was the worst one I'd ever had, and it showed no sign of easing. If anything, it was getting worse. With my every movement a struggle, each step sending a shiver up my spine, I made my way to the kitchen. The vodka I'd been saving for the weekend was in the fridge - I liked it cold. Gathering it to me, I returned to the bed and opened the cap with shaking hands. I took a slug, and then another. Like a child I cradled the bottle beside me, taking a sup every few minutes until I began to feel better.

Stupid anxiety. How foolish.

With the drink inside me, warming me, I decided I needed to eat. Beatrice's chilli con carne would help revive me. I had no appetite, but I put it in the microwave, set it to medium high and twisted the dial. Nothing happened. No life, no heat, no waves. It was plugged in and it made the little ping when you turned the dial, but it didn't possess the ability to make food hot. I could have given up there and then but I persevered, found an inner strength, and turned on the oven. In went the chilli; 200 degrees seemed an appropriate amount of heat. I waited for it to heat up, sitting on the floor in my duvet staring at the food, the warmth on my face reminding me how dead I felt inside.

There was rice somewhere, I'd seen a box of it. That was too much hassle, though. I decided I'd resume my *Sopranos* marathon as soon as I'd eaten. Once I had some food down me I'd feel better. I could go back on the cans, take it easy for the night. But as I waited for the food to heat, I smelled smoke. I opened the oven door and it billowed out, choking me. I opened both windows to clear the air, and after a few minutes it dissipated. Another crisis averted. The chilli turned out fine. I sat there on the floor, eating it straight from the little tray, force-feeding myself, tasting nothing. Then I closed the curtains, took two cans out of the fridge, found a glass for my vodka and put in Disc 2 of Season 1 of *The Sopranos*.

The second day wasn't much better. I was still in a state of high alert, teetering on the brink, but I managed to pour myself a bowl of cornflakes and was eating them on the couch when I heard a knock on my door. What fresh hell was this? I was in no state to converse with another human being. What if it was the landlord, the estate agents, someone who needed to come in and look around, make sure I was behaving myself? All they'd see was empty cans of beer and a half-mad hermit in a blanket.

But if I didn't answer them they'd keep coming back, until there were dozens of them standing outside, hammering at the door and calling out my name, threatening me with all sorts. So I got off the couch and went to the door. It was the Polish guy from downstairs. He was a little older than I'd thought, maybe mid-forties, but I'd been right about the ogre thing; he was a big lump, an awkward bony brute.

"How much you pay?" he asked as soon as I'd opened the door.

"What?"

"How much you pay? Your rent?"

"€300," I said, eager to get off on the right foot.

"€300?" he repeated.

I nodded in confirmation.

"Fack's sake," he muttered, shaking his head and going back downstairs.

I heard his door bang. He had returned to his lair to discuss my rent with the missus.

I resumed my position on the couch. There hadn't even been so much as a hello: 'How are you? Settling in okay? My name's Igor, I live downstairs.' No, just straight into the finances. And why was he so annoyed? Was I getting a bargain on this place? It didn't seem likely. Perhaps I'd go and bang on his door and ask how much he was paying once I'd finished my cornflakes. I didn't want to draw the likes of him upon me, though, so I made a cup of tea, stayed on the couch and prepared myself for another day of drinking. It was the only way to stave off the anxiety and prevent it from completely overwhelming me.

I was mentally exhausted, utterly drained. How long could a panic attack last? Days? Months? Surely it would have to burn itself out at some point. I drank myself into a stupor and went to bed thinking I'd bested it, that good old alcohol was all it took to cure me, but the next morning the anxiety had returned twice as strong, fully rested and ready to do battle with whatever I laid in its path. So I hit it with everything I had. I got reckless. There was vodka, rum, wine, cans, flagons, the lot. I mixed them together, making snakebites, toxic cocktails, and as twilight came I hit my sweet spot - that point where, although lucid, I no longer cared about anything.

Even then, as my burdens lifted and I moved over to the window to watch the world go by, I knew it wouldn't last. In an hour or two I'd pass out and wake up worse than the day before. But for now, I was alive and well, a young man settling into his new home, taking stock and evaluating his surroundings. The traffic had dwindled by this point, just the odd car cruising down the street, taxis looking for fares, kids flitting in and out of side-streets. All the shops had shut, apart from the newsagents on O'Connell Street.

There was a pizza place directly opposite me. I could see the people upstairs; youngsters, families, mothers and little kids, eating their pizza, chatting away, enjoying the treat, the time together. For a moment I worried that they could see me, that I'd be accused of staring at people, being a pervert, but no, I was just a guy sitting at a window, minding his own business. Further down across the street was a more upmarket restaurant, a steakhouse. The people going in and out of there were different, not quite dressed to the nines, but they'd made an effort; the men in shirts, women in heels.

Two doors down was one of the town's livelier pubs, and even on a Thursday night it was busy. Maybe this was the big student night. I could hear the music coming from the bar, intermingling with the street noises, growing momentarily louder when someone came in or out, which happened a lot. There were two bulky bouncers at the door, barricading the way, quietly assessing the condition of each approaching customer. A group of lads got turned away, one of their number deemed a little worse for wear. Rather than carry on without him they simply continued up the street, hoping the next place would be more forgiving. I liked that. There was no question of abandoning their pal, it hadn't even been up for debate.

The girls generally had more luck. The bouncers knew the score. Drunken young lads were boisterous and messy, a liability. They caused fights, upset the atmosphere. Drunken girls sometimes caused fights too, but mostly they just enjoyed themselves, added to the atmosphere, made it more exciting, gave the drunk lads something to focus on. A bar full of happy women was a good place to be. I could have stayed there all night, watching the night unfold, but I was too drunk to even sit by a window in a darkened room. I staggered off to bed, the duvet still draped round my shoulders, what was left of the rum within reach for the morning after.

That was how I spent the first seven days and nights at Apartment 14, 56 Wolfe Tone Street. I would wake in a state of high terror, the hangover making things worse, and lie in bed for three or four hours, staring at the walls, panicking, trying to control my breathing and stay in the now. And then, when I felt I'd endured enough, I would get some food down me and lace into the booze. But the spirits ran out on the sixth night, leaving me with just cider and beer. That was worrying. As much as I enjoyed a can of Pilsner, no amount of it could get me where I needed to be. Alcohol wasn't the only thing in short supply, either. I hadn't been eating much, but I'd worked my way through the stuff Mrs. M had made for me.

The milk was long gone. I had a couple of slices of bread, some cheese and half a tube of Pringles. There was meat: mince and chicken fillets, but I hadn't the wherewithal to start cooking properly. In short, I had reached a critical point and had no choice but to leave the apartment. This might not have been so hard if I hadn't decimated my booze, if I had something to numb me, but it had been an unprecedented week: seven days of panic and confusion. I'd been sloppy. I'd drunk like a lunatic, and now I didn't have enough to get me through the most stressful event of all: my first grocery shop.

There was a newsagent's within a few metres of my apartment. I could have gone there, slipped out under darkness, got what I needed and been back within minutes. But it looked small. The other customers would be right in my face, there'd be nowhere to hide. The person behind the counter would be able to see me, might try to make small talk. Plus, everything would be dearer there, and who knew what their selection of alcohol would be like? It would be handy for emergencies, but my goal was the discount supermarket on the outskirts of town. It was a thirty-minute walk, which would take me through some busy streets and past hordes of people, but once there I'd have the anonymity I needed. I could pick up a basket and take my time, wander down the aisles and fill it up with whatever took my fancy. The selection of alcohol would not only be better, it would be cheaper too.

So, after having my first shower since moving in, drinking four cans and finishing off the Pringles, I put on my coat, took the reusable shopping bag out of the press and opened my door. Straight away I was hit by a fresh wave of anxiety, by the urge to scurry back inside. I stood firm, taking deep breaths, waiting for my head to clear. I walked out to the landing and began my descent downstairs. I feared meeting into someone, a neighbour, the Polish fellah, but the residents of 56 Wolfe Tone Street kept to themselves of an evening. I heard sounds of life from inside the other apartments, televisions, conversations and laughter, but no one accosted me, no one asked me where I was going.

At the bottom of the stairs I took a moment to compose myself and opened the main door, the one which led outside to the world I'd watched quietly for the past seven days. It hit me all at once: the noise, the smells, the kaleidoscope of lights and colours. Like a spooked animal, my senses were heightened, my nerve-endings frayed. Every sound, no matter how small or far away, was amplified: a gang of teenagers jeering and joking, music from a car radio, a misfiring engine, the tick of the traffic lights as the green man slowly departed, a beggar lambasting someone for knocking over his cup, the slam of a door, a dog barking. And even at night, under the cover of darkness, it seemed unnecessarily bright. Street lamps and shop fronts, bars and restaurants, everything was illuminated - you couldn't escape it.

My legs gave way and I fell back against the wall, breathing furious, ragged breaths. The street swam before my eyes, I had pins and needles all over my body. I began to lose consciousness, the world spun on its axis as my stomach slowly unfurled. I held onto the wall for security, easing myself into a sitting position, placed my head between my legs and focused on breathing, just staying alive. I stayed there for some time, until order was restored. Shaky and nauseous, I got to my feet, turned the key in the door and returned to my apartment. Tomorrow was another day.

20

It was another day, but it was one without spirits. A dangerous day. I only had five cans and half a flagon left. Something bad would happen if

I didn't get more drink. I simply had to get some hard liquor. So, having knocked back the cans and flagon in less than an hour, I once more exited the apartment and entered the breach, ready to face whatever the world threw at me. In a sense, I no longer cared what happened to me. If I broke down again, then so be it. I would simply sit there until the end of time, my head in my hands, weeping like a child. And for a moment it appeared as if that was to be my fate. It was the same thing all over again: dazzling sights and deafening sounds, weakness in my legs, an urge to crawl into a safe space and never emerge.

But this time I rode it out. I held onto the wall, steadied myself and breathed in that gritty city air. I put one foot in front of the other and walked towards my destination. Once I got into my stride, it was okay. I kept my head down and tried not to think too much. Walking provided an outlet for my anxiety and pent-up energy. There were more cars, more people but I was able to shut them out, shut everything out as I wound my way through the inner-city streets. Finally, after twenty minutes of power-walking, I saw it shining in the distance: the supermarket, the brightest light of all. I'd left it as late I could, the shop closed in half an hour, but it still looked busy. I made my way across the car park, bracing myself for what lay ahead.

All you have to do is get in and get out. It won't take ten minutes. And think of all the booze, think of how you'll feel when you get home and pour that first cheap whiskey. This is something you just have to do, and it will get easier each time you do it.

Clutching my money in one pocket and the list of items in the other, I entered the supermarket. Except I didn't. Because the door wouldn't open. I looked inside; there were people in there, so they definitely hadn't closed for the night, but no matter which way I approached the automatic doors they wouldn't open. I was just about to turn back, head home for the night and declare the mission a failure, when I noticed the big 'Exit' sign above the door.

You fucking idiot.

Embarrassed, hoping no one had seen me, I approached the correct door, the entrance, and it opened without hesitation. I was in. This was it, the ultimate test. If I could do this, I could do anything. I picked up a basket, my hands shaking, and hesitantly made my way down the first aisle.

I'd written a list: bread, milk, cereal, tea, butter, beans and booze. But as soon as I began walking I was assailed by deals, bargain discounts on things I didn't even know I needed. I couldn't remember the last time I'd eaten a kiwi, but a packet of five for only 49c was too good to refuse. In they went.

They were joined by parsnips, celery and an aubergine. I'd intended to buy a packet of chocolate digestives, nice biscuits to go with my tea, but instead ended up with some *luxury* chocolate chip cookies and a carrot cake. I managed to restrain myself at the cereal aisle, getting the giant box of cornflakes I'd put on my list. A small bag of spuds were purchased to go with my parsnips and aubergine. I got some cheese, tinned goods, toilet rolls, and had to switch my basket for a trolley before I came to the main event, the alcohol section.

There would be no surprises here. I'd been studying the prices in a catalogue. The cans of beer were 89c, the flagons of cider €2.49, the wine started at €4.99 and the spirits began with a litre of vodka for just €12.99. But seeing how much I already had in my basket, I knew I wouldn't be able to carry enough booze to last me the week. I scrutinised what I'd purchased so far, wondering if anything could go back. I needed the spuds, the cake and the tins of spaghetti hoops, or more accurately I *wanted* them. Resigning myself to a return visit in the coming days, I took eight cans, two flagons, a bottle of wine and a bottle of vodka and added them to my trolley. I'd have to buy a second bag now, too. Having picked up two giant bars of chocolate and a bag of fruit gums along the way, I heaved my shopping onto the belt and watched the price add up on the register. It was going fast, past €10, €20, €30. I only had a €50 note. If I went over that, I'd just have to run out of the shop and never come back again. It reached €40 and I began to sweat. There were still a good few things left.

"You pack," the lady announced as I stood there staring at the cash register. My shopping had begun to form a little mountain on her till.

I apologised and began shovelling stuff into the one bag I'd brought. When that was full, I fished one from underneath the belt and added it to my pile. Now I was really nervous.

"€47.58," she said, not appreciating the magnitude of her words.

Smiling, I handed her the fifty and crammed the rest of my items into the new bag. She gave me my change without even looking at me, leaving me to carefully place the bottle of vodka in beside the toilet rolls and hoist the two bags from the ground. They were heavy, incredibly so, but it was a burden I was happy to accept.

*

During the walk home I thought about the dinner I was going to cook, the wine I'd have with it, the chocolate I'd eat and the episodes of *The Sopranos* I'd watch. I even thought about the following day and the possibility of getting the form to apply for rent allowance. If I could get that sorted then I could see about getting broadband, maybe a package deal with one of the TV providers. It was amazing how restorative a simple trip to the supermarket could be. I'd gone from being unable to get out of bed to planning a bright new future for myself in the space of a few hours.

But as I turned the key to the apartment block and began my journey up the stairs, I was brought crashing down to earth. I could hear the arguing even from the ground floor; a man and a woman, a child wailing in the background. It wasn't the eastern Europeans, these people were Irish. The man was doing most of the arguing. His voice bellowed through the building. I couldn't make out every word but the gist was clear. He was accusing her of something, infidelity by the sounds of it.

"you fucking did . . . don't lie to me . . . I saw you . . . get out your phone then, show me . . ."

The woman's replies were apathetic and contemptuous, barely audible over the cries of the child.

They grew louder as I ascended the stairs. I went up the first flight and paused on the landing, listening to see if they'd stopped. They hadn't.

"SHOW ME YOUR PHONE! SHOW ME IT!"

They were on the third floor, either Apartment 7 or 8. I just wanted to get past their floor, back to the sanctity of my own flat. Gripping the bags tightly I hurried up the stairs, trying to close my ears to the distressing scene playing out a few feet away. I practically ran up the stairs, turning sharply to continue up the next flight. The handle on the plastic bag snapped, spilling groceries all over the landing. At this inopportune moment, the door to Apartment 8 was flung open and a woman appeared with a toddler on her hip. She stood at the door, the light from their living-room flooding onto the landing.

I frantically picked up packets of rice and pasta, pretending I hadn't noticed her. She shut the door behind her, her tormentor roaring "Yeah, fuck off, bitch!" by way of goodbye. She set the child down - he was old enough to stand - and turned on the hall light. Wordlessly she began putting items into the bag. The kid, no longer crying, fetched my spaghetti hoops which had rolled into the corner.

"Here go," he said, holding them out for me with both hands.

"Thank you," I whispered.

When we'd picked everything up the woman smiled and took the bag in her arms.

"No, it's okay," I said. "I can carry them up myself."

"You're okay. I'm going that way anyway."

Not sure what she meant, I accepted her help and led the way up the stairs, the kid bringing up the rear. He mounted each step by hoisting a leg over it and dragging himself up.

"Will he be all right?" I asked, looking back.

"He's grand, he's well used to these steps."

The kid grunted triumphantly in confirmation.

On the next landing, she set down the bag and we waited for the little boy to complete his ascent. Once he'd done so, he went straight to Apartment 9 and began hammering on the door.

"Peenay! Peenay! Peenay!" the boy chanted as his mother, or maybe sister - she was young - smiled in acknowledgement.

'Peenay' came to the door. She was black, of African descent, and wore a brightly-coloured dress which hugged her buxom figure. It matched the headscarf which sat above her forehead, obscuring all but a few strands of her hair. Her oval eyes had an almost bovine quality, a deep calmness as they slowly and steadily assessed the situation, moving from the woman to the little boy and then to the newcomer: me.

"I heard," she said to the woman, accepting the little boy into her skirts.

"Is it okay, Anipe? I'm really sorry."

"Don't be sorry, come on," she said, beckoning her inside. The child had already gone in and could be heard singing from the living-room.

Hesitating, the woman turned to me.

"This is our new neighbour, Anipe. Number 14, right?"

"Yeah. Aidan," I said, glad that my identity had been established.

"Nice to meet you, Aidan," said Anipe, offering me her hand.

I had never shaken hands with a black person before.

I shook it. "Nice to meet you, too."

"Thanks for the help," I said to the other woman as she went to join the boy inside Anipe's apartment.

"No worries," she replied, offering a half-hearted smile.

I continued up the stairs to my flat, opening a can of beer as soon as I got in the door. It had been quite the outing. I'd managed to overcome one of my biggest fears and meet some neighbours, all in the space of an hour. And although I knew my anxiety would be back, it felt good to know that I was capable of going outside, of walking to and from the supermarket for provisions. More than that, I'd survived the first week, I'd proved I could go it alone, that I wasn't a total failure. Now that I'd done that, there was no telling what else I could do.

21

THE NEXT DAY I TRIED to clean up the flat. I made a cup of tea and had some of the fancy biscuits, took a shower, threw my dirty duvet cover into the basket and put on some fresh clothes. I put all the empty tins and bottles into a refuse sack, did the dishes, swept the floor, opened the windows and gave the place an airing. I wanted to stay active and busy. I even turned my mattress, discovering a slightly less stained underside. During my tidy-up, I discovered my phone, wedged in between the cushions of the couch, its battery long dead. I charged it up and scrolled through my messages and calls.

My father had been trying to ring me. There were seventeen missed calls from him, text messages asking if I was okay, why I hadn't picked up, to reply as soon as I could, and so on. I saw that three days ago at 2.42 a.m. I had replied to his barrage of messages with a simple **Yeah**. So he knew I was alive, anyway, but if I didn't deal with this now it would just get worse. I rang him.

"Aidan, where have you been?"

"I couldn't find my charger. Sorry, Dad."

"How are you getting on?"

"Grand."

"Do you need anything? We were in the town the other day. Beatrice had dinners for you."

Dinners sounded good, that would save me cooking, leave more money for booze.

"Ah, the next time you're in, let me know and I'll get them off you."

"We can come in this evening, when I'm finished work."

"It's grand, Dad. There's no hurry."

"I'll ring when we're on the way."

This was what I didn't want, the two of them becoming regular fixtures in my new life. I still wanted the luxuries, the free food and whatever else was going, but I didn't want to see them.

"Okay," I said and hung up.

He came that evening, on his own. I met him outside.

"There's some casserole in that, and shepherd's pie," he said, handing over the bag.

I gave him back the Tupperware and dishes that had contained the previous dinners.

"How are things?" he asked, loitering in the street, eyeing the door of the building.

"I'm okay. Settling in."

"Will we have a cup of tea?"

"I'm in the middle of something, Dad."

I saw the hurt in his eyes, the desperate desire to spend some time with his son.

"Come on, so," I said, leading the way.

"You've the place nice and tidy," he said when we got inside.

"What did you expect?"

"Well, if your room at home is anything to go by . . ." he said, grinning.

I boiled some water in a saucepan while he made himself comfortable.

"Is the water running okay, Aidan?"

"It is."

"That's good."

Just then, with perfect timing, my Polish friend launched into one of his tirades. I'd grown used to them, filtering them into the background with all the other noises, but for the uninitiated it was a frightening sound.

"What the hell is that?" my father asked, looking around.

"My neighbour downstairs."

"What's up with him?"

"They're foreign."

Dad paused, motionless, as he listened to the stream of shouting and hollering coming from below.

"Is he okay? Have you checked on him?"

"Jesus, no."

"We'll see if he's all right after the tea, will we?"

"No, Dad."

"Okay," he said good-naturedly. "What are the rest of the neighbours like?"

"They seem all right. Friendly enough."

"What about the person across the way?"

"Still haven't met them."

"Ah, you need to meet your neighbours, Aidan. It's good to be on terms with them."

"I will meet them, Dad. Give me a chance."

I chose not to mention the incident on the stairs. My father would report everything back to Mrs. M, and I didn't want her knowing my business.

"I'm visiting your mother on Wednesday, if you want to come?" he said tentatively.

I shot him a glance, hoping it was sufficiently derisive.

"Is Mrs. M going with you?"

"No."

I had no interest in seeing my mother but I could still make him feel guilty if I wanted.

"I won't come, Dad."

"That's fine, maybe next time," he said.

He stayed for an hour or so, until he got bored of trying to make small talk. I walked him to his car and said I'd see him soon. He told me to let him know when the dinners were gone and he'd bring more. There would be no escape at this rate. It wasn't his fault, I knew he was only trying his best, but I had no interest in him or his life. There was no hate, I'd gone beyond that, he simply meant nothing to me. I was content to accept his food, though. It was the least I deserved. It also meant that I only had to go the supermarket once a week, and therefore only had to go outside once a week. I was still struggling with the whole outdoors thing, I could manage a night-time visit to the shop or a quick circle round the block in the small hours, but I'd yet to brave daylight.

However, when signing-on day arrived I was left with no choice. I would have to walk the five hundred metres to the social welfare office and I would have to do it at eleven a.m. If I didn't keep this appointment, it would spell trouble. I'd done it before, not bothered to show up, thinking it wouldn't matter and it had taken five phone calls, a lot of apologising and two additional signing-on days to rectify my error. I hadn't missed a day since. Now that I lived in town, just minutes away from the office, I had no excuse to miss one again.

It should have made it easier, being so close. Previously I'd had to take a bus in and out of town and time everything to perfection. I could roll out of bed now, throw on some clothes, go up, scrawl my name and be back under the covers ten minutes later. But I still felt nervous. So far I'd managed to avoid bumping into any of my neighbours again, had stolen in and out under the cover of darkness, but mid-morning was a busy time in our building. I was frequently awoken by the comings and goings of the Poles, Anipe, the woman with the toddler, and others I had yet to meet. It seemed almost inevitable that I would bump into one of them on the stairs.

I still hadn't met my next-door neighbour. There had been no signs of life from Apartment 13 so far, its occupant was even more anti-social than I was. As I quietly emerged from my flat, the door opposite remained firmly closed. No sound emanated from inside, no arguments raged nor loud music played. It was lifeless. I continued down the stairs, listening warily, ready to run if I heard a key turn in a door, any door. But no one came and I made it to the bottom unmolested. I took a moment to steady myself, fighting the negative thoughts swirling around in my mind.

I got to the social welfare office in two minutes. Once I was in the queue, I composed myself. I was among my people now: the deadbeats, outcasts and losers. There was less pressure here, I was just another victim of circumstance, another hopeless case who needed the state to look after him. I inched towards the booth, scanning the walls for information on rent allowance. I'd been thinking about it a lot, about the changes it would make to my life. It was worth the gamble. I'd only have to apply once, sit down and speak to an officer once. It would be a yes or a no, and that would be the end of it.

I didn't know where to get the form, though. It had to be in this building somewhere but I didn't want to ask anyone, didn't want them knowing I was looking for more money. I peeped round the handful of people standing in front of me, trying to see who was at the desk. It was the younger fellah. He was sound enough, didn't make you feel subhuman for being unemployed. If there was anyone I could ask, it'd be him. As the queue shortened I practised my question, repeating it over and over in my head.

"Hey, do you know where I'd get the rent allowance form?"

But the queue was too short, I hadn't time to fully prepare myself. Before I could get the words ready, I was standing there in front of him.

"PPS number?"

I gave it to him.

He flicked through the files on his desk, taking his time. Now was the perfect moment.

"Right here, Aidan," he said, pointing to the next line on a page full of my signatures.

"Thanks," I said and signed my name.

"Back here on November 11, okay?"

"Okay."

There were still other people I could have asked: the security guard, the woman on the desk or the friendly-looking gentleman standing by the wall. I could have had a look around; there were information booklets everywhere and noticeboards full of stuff. I did none of those things. To do so would have been to attract attention, to risk being noticed. Instead I put my head down and walked as fast I could until I made it back to the sanctuary of my flat. I didn't meet Anipe or the arguing couple on the way up. It was all quiet again.

Relieved to have completed my mission, but annoyed that I hadn't asked about the rent allowance, I sat down to play on the Xbox. I didn't have any new games and couldn't play online because I couldn't afford broadband, but I would make do; I still had a garden to tend to in *Viva Pinata*, a few locust to kill on *Gears of War*, and other assorted tasks to busy myself with until it was time to start drinking.

I'd been playing for less than an hour when a loud thump came from outside my door. It sounded like a bag of spuds being dropped to the floor. I panicked: it was the partner of the woman with the toddler. He'd come to get me after hearing what I'd been up to, chatting to his missus in the hallway, making moves on her. I hadn't done those things, but you couldn't reason with lads like him - jealous types who flew off the handle if you so much as looked at *their* woman.

I stayed on the couch, game-pad in hand, Marcus Fenix taking heavy fire from enemy forces. There was no further sound. Maybe he'd murdered her and left the dead body outside my door as a warning. No, that wouldn't make sense. If anyone was getting murdered it was me. I carefully got up from the sofa and crept out to the door, peering through the keyhole to see if he was waiting for me. I couldn't see anything, just the creamy white door opposite with the number 13 in metallic gold. I was about to return to my game, writing off the noise as a by-product of living among lunatics, when I heard a groan from the hallway. Maybe he had killed her, or tried to.

I opened the door. There was a man lying face down on the floor, moaning plaintively.

"Hello? Are you okay?" I asked.

No response.

I stood looking at him a moment, wondering if I could go back inside and leave him there. Someone would eventually find him, someone more capable of helping him than I was. As if sensing my hesitation, he rolled on to his side into the recovery position. He was just drunk, that was all. I relaxed. I could deal with that. He was around fifty, a fluffy collection of grey hairs atop his balding head, matching the colour of his scruffy, unkempt beard. His eyes, grey too, bulbous and bloodshot, dark circles around them, stared vacantly into the abyss as he opened and closed his mouth like a fish out of water. Some drool spilled out and rolled down his chin on to his neck.

He suddenly let out a deep baying sound, scrunched up his face as if smelling something unsavoury, smiled in a conspiratorial fashion and then furrowed his brow in confusion. It was like watching an actor prepare for a scene, or a circus clown regale his young audience. His clothes were similarly expressive. He wore a black blazer with a red T-shirt underneath, a box of cigarettes poking out of his breast pocket. There was a slogan on the T-shirt but I couldn't see it from where I stood. He also wore a pair of grey trousers, the knees stained with blood, and red runners. The trousers had ridden up his legs and I could see scratches on his shins. He'd been in the wars.

I crouched down beside him.

"Do you live there?" I asked, pointing at Number 13.

His eyes rolled this way and that as he searched out the source of the voice. It looked like there was more than alcohol at play here, but now that I'd engaged with him I was duty-bound to help him. If I went back inside and he died, it'd be my fault. With a great deal of effort I moved him into a sitting position, propping him against the banister on the landing. He seemed happy enough there. His head lolled on his shoulders as he fought to stay conscious; he had enough about him to know he wasn't quite home yet.

There was still a possibility that he didn't live in Number 13. He could have lived downstairs, beside the Poles, or he could have been a complete stranger, some head-the-ball off the street who'd fallen into our building and was crawling to the top just for the hell of it. The only way to find out was to check his pockets. If he had a key which fitted the lock, the mystery would be solved. Slowly, so as not to scare him, I moved my hand towards his trousers pocket, but as soon as I touched him he roused into life.

"What you doing?" he growled, eyes now locked on mine.

"I was just seeing if you have a key for the apartment."

He looked at me, processing this information, working hard to figure out what kind of a predicament he'd got himself into.

"Keep away from my pockets," he said menacingly.

Now in a right huff, he tried to get to his feet. It was a painful sight. His legs weren't working, and the rest of his body wasn't much use either. First he flopped over onto his side like a broken toy, then, after getting onto all fours and circling 360 degrees, one of his feet got stuck between the railings of the banister. He pulled and pulled, looking at me accusingly as he did so, before yanking it free, minus one red runner. Lastly, having succeeded into getting to his feet and steadying himself, he half jogged, half stumbled into the wall beside my door and fell on his backside. Menacing or not, I had to point him in the general direction of his abode.

"It's this way," I said, putting my hands beneath his armpits and lifting him to his feet. He tried to shrug me off, announcing that he was all right, but I'd had enough by this point and wanted to get him out of harm's way for my sake as well as his. I draped his arm over my shoulders and dragged him over to his door, ignoring his spluttering protests.

"Have you your key?" I asked.

It was already in his hand. Shoving me away he collapsed against the door, using it for support, and twisted the key in the lock. Before I could intervene he fell through the open door and onto the floor inside with a gentle sigh. I went to follow him inside, planning to tuck him in, put a glass of water on his bedside locker, maybe a bucket on the floor, but he kicked the door shut behind him. And that was that. I'd finally met the occupant of Apartment 13.

I returned to my Xbox, enthused. My next-door neighbour was a boozer, and a big one too. I was also a boozer. Surely we'd get along? If I could just meet into him on one of his good days, maybe we'd get to talking, have a few drinks and a friendship could form. I'd never met anyone like me, who liked to drink like I did. This chap had an apartment of his own but still liked to get falling-down drunk of a Wednesday afternoon. He seemed like my kind of person. I would be keeping a steady ear out for him from now on.

22

After a couple of months of living in Apartment 14, 56 Wolfe Tone Street, I began to feel settled. Going outside continued to present problems and I still hadn't summoned up the courage to apply for rent allowance, but I had been granted fuel allowance without even asking for it. That wasn't enough for me to afford to get broadband, but it did allow me to treat myself to a bottle of rum every second week. My only concerns were the interminable noise from the neighbours, the constant wall of sound from outside and my parlous finances.

All of those things bothered me, but man has an unerring ability to adapt to his circumstances, no matter how unpleasant, and I had learned to live with mine. Since my initial meeting with my next-door neighbour, we had run into each other twice. On the first occasion I was going down the stairs and he was coming up. This time he was sober. He'd tidied himself up a bit too, the beard had been trimmed and trousers ironed. I slowed down, waiting to see if he'd recognise me. He walked past without a word. That was fine, I hadn't expected him to remember anything.

A few weeks later, having summoned up the courage to go for a walk in the park one afternoon, I ran into him as he made his way down Parnell Street. On this occasion he was incredibly drunk. Using the wall as a buffer he was bouncing his way forwards, leaning against it for support, propelling himself forward and then colliding back into it when his legs started to go. It was a remarkable sight. He knew exactly where all the shop fronts were and where to take care so he didn't fall in through a window or a doorway. When he came to the butchers, he paused before slowly plotting his way past the window and the open door until he could stick to the wall like a limpet once more.

I had a mind to follow him, to see him home safely, but he seemed to have everything under control. I still hoped we'd become friends, but he only ever seemed to be sober or paralytic, and didn't recognise me in either state. The only chance I had was if I met him while he was somewhere in between and still had control of his legs and his wits. We could get drunk together then, either in my place or his. Alternatively, he could bring me to wherever it was he went and we could stumble home together. That was something to aspire to. Because although I'd settled into my new surroundings and developed a routine which minimised my anxiety, I'd discovered there was another unexpected downside to moving out: loneliness.

In many ways I'd always been lonely, ever since I was a child, but this was different. Back then I'd been lonely while in the company of others, now I was simply alone. When I'd been living with my parents, I'd never appreciated the comfort I'd taken from having them around. Even if we didn't speak every day, or have conversations amounting to more than trivial chitchat, it was still a form of human interaction. Now I was going days and even weeks without speaking to another person, the odd greeting on the stairs the sum total of my communication with others. It added a new layer to my depression. I yearned to talk to someone, to share my thoughts with them.

And juxtaposing it all was the constant hum of activity around me, the flushing of toilets, the shouting from below, the occasional banging of a headboard as hate turned to love. Outside there were cars beeping, people coming in and out of shops or walking up and down the street, chatting and sharing. It was worse on the weekends when they sang and fought, went down the lane for a kiss or a piss, or maybe to get sick. All the while I remained in my own tiny world, silent and alone, with no one to talk to but myself and nothing to do but drink, eat, and watch DVDs I'd seen dozens of times.

I decided to walk in the park more often, reasoning that at least then I'd be among other people; but I chose to go when it was quietest, after lunchtime, before the parents came along with the kids from school. I would hurry up Wolfe Tone Street, across Parnell Street, past the GPO and the courthouse, through the pedestrianised area with the monument to Daniel O'Connell and into the park itself. I'd relax when I stepped inside the gates away from the streets, the people and the world at large. A circuit of the park was exactly one kilometre and I stuck to the route, keeping my head down, ignoring the only bit of greenery in this drab Irish town.

If I heard someone walking behind I would speed up, anxious to be rid of them, to be on my own again. And if I got caught doing laps with someone coming in the opposite direction, I would alter my route so I didn't have to cross them more than once. But doing that brought challenges of its own. There was a play area in the middle of the park, and I didn't want to go anywhere near that in case people thought I was a weirdo watching the children. There were benches where people congregated, a fountain, a pond, a work-out area, communal amenities designed to encourage social interaction. I avoided those too. Some days I spent my entire walk switching from one path to the next, backtracking, reversing round, making myself look far more suspicious than I needed to. I'd started the walks in the hope of feeling part of something, only to go out of my way to avoid other people. It was exercise, though, and I did feel better once I'd got home.

Having taken this major step in my life, having moved out and finding that nothing had really changed, I began to question the point of my existence. Why was I bothering? Happiness would forever elude me. The things I wanted: friends, a girlfriend, a life, a job and a home, would always be out of my reach. My anxiety would prevent me from getting a job. Without a job I wouldn't be able to afford my own home, nor would I find a woman willing to go out with me. I had no social life, was terrified to go inside a pub or even look someone in the eye while they talked to me, so the chances of finding friendship were similarly limited. I didn't enjoy sports, so I couldn't join a team and hope for an outlet there.

The best I could hope for was to live out my days in this flat, maybe apply for rent allowance some day and get back online, talk to people on the internet and fill the void that way. If that were my sole ambition, the sum total of my achievements on earth, then really, what was the point? It was no life, no life at all, and when you have no life you have one option: to end it all. The realisation there was a way out gave me solace. I could call a halt whenever I felt like it.

Yet somewhere deep inside a voice told me that fate would intervene, that a chance encounter, a moment of unpredictability, would come my way and my life would be altered. All I had to do was hang on in there and surely something would happen. Happier times had to be ahead, everyone experienced at least one happy period in their lives. Then I wondered if *these* were my happy times, and maybe I should cherish them while they lasted.

23

I CAREFULLY WALKED UP THE stairs, my shopping bag held close to my chest. It had been an unscheduled trip, I'd had a hankering for something strong, and because it was dole day I'd decided to treat myself. I'd got some bottled beer, some of that IPA stuff, and not only that, I'd bought a bottle of brandy. There was no one on the stairs and I was almost home when the door to Number 13 opened: it was my neighbour, my drunken adversary. Our eyes met and he tilted his head in recognition. I thought that would be the extent of it, but as I turned to let myself in he spoke.

"Is that the brandy out of Tuhl's?"

He was well-spoken, his accent difficult to pin down.

"Yeah."

"That'll get you where you need to be."

I smiled, waiting for the right time to say goodbye, but he just stood there, looking very relaxed and content with himself.

"Do you want . . . would you like to come in for a glass?" I asked.

He pondered this as if he were being asked to embark on a dangerous but potentially rewarding mission.

"Okay," he said, nodding. "Sure we'll have one, anyway."

I showed him in, scooping dirty clothes off the floor as I went, trying to make the place look respectable. He sat down in the good chair without invitation, oblivious to the mess. There weren't any clean glasses so I quickly ran a couple under the tap and filled them with the brandy, handing him his as I sat on the sofa.

"Cheers . . . ?" he said.

"Aidan."

"Cheers, Aidan."

We clinked glasses and took a drink.

He murmured his satisfaction, put his glass on the armrest and eased back into the chair.

"I'm Gerard, by the way."

"Nice to meet you, Gerard."

"When did you move in, Aidan?"

"Three months ago."

"They come and go fast in this place."

"How long are you living here?" I asked.

"A few years."

"What do you make of it?"

He looked at me incredulously, unnerving me.

"It's a fucking shit-hole. End of the road. Only place worse is out on the street."

I wasn't sure what to make of him, but it felt good to have someone to talk to, to share a drink with.

"Top-up?" I suggested, gesturing to his glass.

"Don't mind if I do."

I really wanted to ask him about the day we'd met in the hall, when I'd practically carried him into his apartment, but we were getting on and I didn't want to ruin it.

"Some interesting people living here," I said.

"Fucking crack-pots," replied Gerard. "Watch out for that cunt downstairs, he's a fucking prick."

Although he spoke in measured, well-clipped tones, Gerard swore a lot, wrapping his lips round each word and spitting it out with venom.

"The guy with the kid?"

"Yeah. They're always fucking rowing and fighting. She's as bad. Stay away from the two of them, and don't invite her in for a drink whatever you do."

"Why not?"

"Just don't," he replied, waving me away.

We lapsed into silence, sitting there in the gloom, the only sound the occasional beep of a car from outside. I racked my brain for questions, keeping an eye on his drink, ready to fill it again once it dipped below halfway.

A loud clump from downstairs broke our reverie.

"Fucking cunts," Gerard said, staring at the floor in annoyance. "The most ignorant pair of bastards ever to walk this earth."

"Some noise out of 'em," I replied.

"No respect. That's the problem."

"He came in and asked me how much I was paying," I said.

"That'd be right," scoffed Gerard. "You can bet they're paying less, if they're paying anything at all."

More silence. Making friends was hard.

I motioned to top him up again, but he held his hand over it and drank off the rest.

"I'd best be off. Nice meeting you."

He quickly shook my hand and was gone in an instant. As I closed my door, I heard him thunder down the stairs. I waited for the slam of the main outside door and then stood up on the window sill to see where he went. Head down and shoulders hunched he walked up the street, past the pub, around the corner, out of sight. He was probably going drinking somewhere. I wished I could have gone with him, but having a bit of company, even for a few minutes, had perked me up. I'd finally broken the ice with my neighbour, and properly this time. I knew his name and that he liked brandy. I'd also discovered we shared a dislike of the Poles. It was a start.

I wasn't naive enough to think that we were going to be best buds now, but it was good to be on speaking terms with someone, to feel part of this small, strange community. Now that I'd got to know Gerard a bit, it made me less afraid of everyone else. I wouldn't hurry down the stairs in a frenzy any more, I'd take my time, ready to say hello to whoever crossed my path. Maybe there were some other sound people in the building, people I hadn't met yet. I'd ask Gerard about that the next time we met.

*

But I didn't meet him again, no matter how hard I tried. There was no way of telling what hours he kept. Every now and then I'd hear a ruckus on the landing and quickly hurry out, only to see his door slam shut in my face. This happened at noon, midnight, morning or evening, any hour of any day. The rest of the time there was no evidence of life from his apartment. Occasionally I'd press my ear to his door, listening for the sound of a television, a radio, a kettle on the boil, but there was nothing. From what I could tell he only returned to sleep off his excesses, to get showered and shaved, and then he would disappear for days on end, repeating the cycle until he'd either run out of money or could take no more.

I tried to be more sociable with the other neighbours, saying hello on the stairs, stopping and chatting with Anipe; I found out that she lived with her dad, who was blind and suffered from dementia. I met one of the other tenants, a guy living on the ground floor. He asked me if I played football and invited me to his weekly five-a-side game on Thursday nights. I told him I had a dodgy ankle, an old injury. He nodded and said it was an open invitation, I could come whenever I wanted. I'd been accepted, everyone knew my name, but when I got back to my apartment and closed the door, I was on my own again. It was this sense of loneliness which finally compelled me to act.

Fed up of staring at the same four walls every night, of talking to myself and standing on the window sill looking out at the streets, I went over to Gerard's apartment and knocked on the door. I knew he probably wouldn't be in, or if he was he'd be unconscious, but doing it felt like progress. My mantra had always been to never put in or out on anyone, but that led to a life of isolation. There was no answer on that first day, or the second or third, but on the fourth day I heard a faint rustle coming from inside. He was in there. Suddenly afraid, I stepped back, wondering what the fuck I was going to say to him when he answered. The door opened and Gerard appeared, wearing nothing but a pair of tracksuit bottoms, exposing a hairy grey chest.

"What is it?" he asked, wild-eyed, his hair sticking out at the sides like Krusty the Clown.

I had obviously woken him up.

"How's it going?" I asked.

He stood looking at me a moment, trying to get his bearings.

"Come in," he said finally, turning on his heel and leaving the door open by way of invitation.

I followed him inside, curious to see how he lived. I was surprised by what I saw. Although our apartments had the same dimensions, Gerard had done a lot more with his. A comfy-looking blue plush couch dominated his living room, there was a bookshelf, he had ornaments, family photos and, most surprising of all, a cat, a real-life one. It was black with a streak of white fur which started underneath its chin and ran along the underside of its belly. It lay on the headrest of an armchair, licking its paws.

"I thought you were the fellah come to fix the window," said Gerard as he filled up the kettle and lit a fag.

I took a seat on the sofa, which was as comfortable as it looked. The cat stared at me in that way cats do when they want to fuck with your head.

"Milk? Sugar?" asked Gerard. He had put on a T-shirt.

"Erm, a small drop of milk and one sugar, please."

I never took milk in my tea but I'd panicked.

He returned moments later with two cups and set them down on the glass table in the middle of the room, it had some old newspapers on top of it, *The Irish Independent* open at the crossword page.

"What day have we? Aidan, isn't it?"

"Thursday, and yes."

He nodded to himself, as if he'd known all along it was Thursday and he'd just been checking to see if I knew.

"Did I wake you, Gerard? Sorry if I did."

"You're all right. It's time enough for me to be up, anyway."

"I called the last couple of nights but there was no answer," I said.

"No, I wasn't here."

The cat had descended from its perch and was arching its back against Gerard's legs, winding itself around him, purring expectantly.

"Fuckin' cat," he said, taking a sup of the tea and leaving it on the table. The cat followed him to the fridge, almost knocking Gerard over as he took out a carton of milk and poured its contents into a bowl on the floor.

"I do feed her," he said defensively as he returned to his seat.

"Your flat's nice," I said, looking at the framed photos on the wall. They were mostly of old people, probably his parents, but there was one of a younger Gerard with some kids, a boy and a girl.

"It needs tidying up. Do you want a can?" he asked.

He brought me a can of beer, one of the cheap ones from Tuhl's.

"Chin-chin," he said as he took a slug of his.

It struck me that his approach to drinking had no set pattern. He'd only just woken up, had a cup of tea, and now he was back on it. Or maybe that was his pattern: if he was awake, he was drinking.

"What's wrong with your window?" I asked.

"What? Oh. The timber is rotting to fuck. I tried varnishing it and painting it, but it needs to come out now, I reckon."

The cat came back in, eyeing me warily as it mounted the chair opposite and began cleaning itself.

"What's its name?"

"Gráinne."

I wanted to laugh, or at least comment on how unusual a name that was for a cat, but I didn't want to cause offence - it could have been named after his mother or anything.

"Pay day today," I said airily.

Gerard knitted his brow, not understanding.

"Dole day," I explained.

He sighed deeply, as if only just remembering he was unemployed.

"Sure we might as well go out, so," he said. "No point moping around here when we're flush with cash."

I felt a tremor of excitement. We were going out. He'd invited me to come with him. There was no big secret. All I'd had to do was call over.

"Just give me a few minutes to shower, shave and do me constitutional," he said, leaving me alone with the cat.

Maybe I needed to have a shower too? There was no telling who'd be out, there might be women.

"I'm just going over to my flat. I'll be back in a couple of minutes," I called out.

I hesitated at his door. What if he was ready first and fucked off without me? Or what if he decided not to answer when I came back, just waited till I stopped knocking and then sneaked off on his own? I decided to leave the door ajar, just an inch, so I could let myself back in. I was going to have a very quick shower. I had no need for a shave or a constitutional, whatever that was.

After running around under the shower, changing my underwear and socks and spraying some cheap deodorant on my pits, I was back in Gerard's apartment before he'd reappeared. The door had opened out a bit, but I attributed that to one of the draughts which whistled through our building. As I sat and waited I looked at some more of the pictures on the walls; a black-and-white one of a couple on their wedding day, some kids on a beach with adults laughing in the background, a young boy wearing a football top with a puppy in his arms.

The cat! Where was the cat?

I went out to the kitchen, making that noise you make to attract cats, "Psssh whissh whissh whissh," but there was no sign of her. Of course, I knew what had happened, she'd escaped out the front door, the door I'd left open. Checking to make sure Gerard was still in the bathroom, I went out on to the landing.

"Psssh whissh whissh whissh. Gráinne. Gráinne. Gráinne, for fuck's sake."

I looked down the stairs, out the window, but she was nowhere to be found. Fretting, seeing my day out, my budding friendship with Gerard disappearing over the horizon, I went back into his flat and closed the door behind me. Cats went missing all the time, that's what they were like, they had no loyalty. She'd probably be waiting outside the door for him when we returned from our big session in the pub.

Gerard came out, all spick and span, wearing a pair of classic denims and a grey blazer. He'd shaved too, exposing a bitter little mouth, a dour, sour visage which was better off hidden. With the beard, his pithy comments and mordant disposition gave him an edge, a depth, an air of intelligence; without it, all that disappeared. He looked wicked, vindictive and weak.

"Come on, so," he said.

We departed, the absence of the cat neither noticed nor commented upon as Gerard locked up. I chose not to ask where we were going, leaving it to fate, allowing Gerard to lead the way as we walked in silence, me tagging along behind like an annoying younger brother. We walked for ten minutes through the centre of town, past the park and the schools, then for another ten minutes towards the supermarkets, industrial estates, and residential areas. Until finally, we approached Cois Abhann, a notorious council estate with a reputation which stretched not just across town and throughout the county, but nationwide.

It had been built in the 1970s, earmarked as a place to house those on lower incomes, working-class families who were just starting out in life and needed cheap, affordable housing. That all changed with the recession of the 1980s, when most of the residents found themselves out of work. Some emigrated, their places taken by those desperate for somewhere to live, for an escape from the poverty which had cast a pall over the country. Those who managed to hold on to their jobs suddenly found themselves in the minority, living in an estate where theirs were the only cars, where their neighbours scrimped and saved to get by, where crime and drug use offered an escape from the suffering.

So those people left too, finding houses in a better part of town, in a suburb where they would be flanked not by the unemployed, the destitute, but by people like them. Those who stayed, the original residents who'd helped establish the place and foster that community spirit, did their best to keep it going, to maintain a name which grew more tainted with each passing year. But they were fighting a losing battle.

Mass unemployment, a sense of being ignored, of being forgotten about and being told you didn't matter, left many of the residents losing respect not just for Cois Abhann but for themselves. By the mid-eighties the unemployment rate in the estate was at eighty-five per cent, a staggering figure even by the standards of the time. Crime was rife; it was a running joke that everyone who appeared in the local district court had an address at Cois Abhann. And then there was the alcoholism, the drug use, the violence. You didn't go to Cois Abhann unless you had business there, and even then you practised caution.

Their soccer team, which was one of the best in the county, had to disband after away teams refused to play on their pitch - frequent thefts of their gear, their cars, as commonplace as the mass brawls which erupted on the odd occasion the home side lost a game. In a way it became a badge of honour for those who lived there, you knew that if someone said they were from Cois Abhann they weren't to be trifled with, that they would gut you as soon as look at you, or so I'd been told. Yet here was Gerard, sauntering fearlessly into the estate. I broke the silence, my safety now a concern.

"What are we going here for, Gerard?"

"Cheapest pints in town, lad."

"Where?"

"In *The Three Sisters*. Don't worry," he said seeing the fear in my eyes. "The locals are grand. No one will say anything to you once you're with me."

I felt a real affection for him then. He was going to look after me, but I was still shitting it. The last few months had given me a glimpse of how the other side lived, but I wasn't ready for this. I would stick out a mile, they would sense my weakness and devour me, cough up my bones once they'd torn every piece of flesh from my soft, feeble body.

"Come on," said Gerard, leading the way through the estate.

It was a pitiable place. The houses, lined up in long grey rows, were almost all in a state of disrepair, many of them crumbling, the shoddy workmanship of cheap contractors coming to bear. Those were just the habitable ones. Others had been abandoned, boarded up, and when that hadn't kept out the squatters the windows and door wells had been filled in with bricks. Tufts of grass grew here and there, but mostly it was concrete and dirt. There were no gardens to speak of, just dumping zones where people left their junk, their rubbish, anything no longer of use. And then there were the people.

Men sat on their front steps, smoking, drinking. Women, babies on their hips, toddlers in their skirts, gathered in small clusters, discussing and debating, cigarettes on the go at all times. And the youngsters, scrawny and feral, stared at us, hate in their eyes, ready to attack as soon as the shout went up. I was completely out of my depth. I walked as close to Gerard as I could, hoping some of his streetwise attitude would rub off on me, but it was no use; they had me sussed. And once we were inside the pub, which was now just a couple of hundred metres away, it would only get worse.

The Three Sisters stood alone in the very centre of the estate, on a flat piece of land which had once housed a kids' playground. On this winter day in the lost hours between lunch and dinner, the pub looked relatively quiet, at least from the outside. It was painted black with two red dragons depicted on either side of the main entrance, breathing fire from their nostrils, suggesting that to walk through those doors was to enter a furnace, or maybe hell. Above the door was the pub's name in bold script, also in red, and on top of the flat roof were more youngsters, kids really, sitting there like guardians of the realm. I was almost glued to Gerard's heels as we crossed the threshold, past the couple of old-timers standing outside and into the pub itself.

The first thing that struck me was the smoke. The smoking ban was not in effect here. It applied neither to nicotine, marijuana or hash. Then there was the noise, the beautiful clamour of a busy pub in the middle of the day. After my eyes grew accustomed to the hazy sunlight streaming in through the bars of the big window at the back, I noticed the decor and the patrons. The interior, like the exterior, was almost entirely black. The walls contained a few posters advertising upcoming events and some newspaper clippings of momentous events, but there was none of the flotsam and jetsam you tend to associate with an Irish pub; no framed pictures, old sports jerseys, memorabilia or personal effects which tell the story of your average public house. It made sense, what was the point in decorating the walls when everything would be broken or stolen by the end of the night?

This no-nonsense approach applied to the furniture too. The N-shaped padded seating area which came out from the back window was accompanied by a dozen or so low tables, each of them nailed to the floor. The higher tables and the stools which surrounded them had also been safely secured, making life a little less comfortable for the drinkers but a lot more predictable for the bar staff. The wooden shelf which circled the walls had been reinforced with steel underneath. The only surprise was that the bar itself didn't have a protective barrier, a means of keeping the drinkers out and the staff safe. At this early hour, though, the locals appeared relatively calm, the cloud of thick marijuana smoke a contributing factor.

"What will you have, Aidan?" asked Gerard as he led me to a table in the middle of the floor.

I squinted towards the bar, to the taps contained therein. There was nothing fancy here: no pale ales, German Pilsners or, heaven forbid, craft beers. But there was an unfamiliar name, one which required explanation.

"What's the Grizmo like?"

"Aha, the famous Grzmot," Gerard said, giving it its proper title. "Cheapest pint in town and rocket fuel to boot."

"A pint of that, so," I replied as I nervously took my seat.

While Gerard went to get the drinks I kept my head down, staring at the floor, my body tensed, ready to run at the first hint of trouble. He returned moments later with two pints of Grzmot and I allowed myself to breathe again. The drink wasn't bad. It was slightly sour and there were little bits floating on the top, but considering it was the cheapest pint in town you couldn't complain.

"Here we are now," Gerard said as he nodded to someone seated behind me.

"Am I going to be okay here?" I asked him quietly.

Gerard smiled softly, enjoying my discomfort. "Well, that chap I just said hello to put his brother in hospital last month and is after shacking up with the very same brother's wife, and the fellah with him is just out of Mountjoy after an eight-year stretch for manslaughter, but they're pussy cats, really. It's the younger lads you need to look out for; no moral code whatsoever, evil little fuckers."

"But as long as you're with me, you'll be all right," he added when he saw my reaction to his story.

I wasn't convinced. My guess was that Gerard was overestimating his popularity. He didn't look like the other patrons, either, with his suit jacket and red runners. I would have placed him in one of those upmarket bars, the kind where people got pots of tea rather than pitchers of Grzmot. I chanced a quick glance at the guy who'd got out of Mountjoy, and the one who'd hospitalised his brother. They didn't look anything like pussy cats. One of them was round and fat and wore a black T-shirt about three sizes too small, the other had a shaved head, revealing tattoos which spread down his neck and chest, and dark furtive eyes which continually flitted from one side of the room to the next.

The younger lads Gerard had warned me about were sitting opposite the two felines, a half-dozen of them, dressed entirely in sportswear: tracksuits, sweatshirts, and runners. They reminded me of those lads in Dublin, the ones who'd gatecrashed the party, but if anything, they were more menacing, more intimidating. I'd been drunk that night in the capital, a bit lost in myself. I hadn't noticed the enmity flowing from Jinx and the rest of them, but I noticed it here; I felt the aggressive energy these lads gave off. Even while they laughed and joked you could sense the discontent and resentment. What would they make of someone like me, who'd been given every opportunity in life and now found himself here among them with his stupid overgrown hair, baggy jeans and purple hoodie?

But if they'd spotted me they didn't let on, and after an hour of nervous drinking and timid conversation I relaxed a little. I even managed to get a round in, making it to and from the bar without incident. We were knocking them back, going pint for pint like only seasoned drinkers can; but even the most seasoned of drinkers must empty his bladder from time to time. After spending a few minutes counting the number of people going in and out of the toilet and waiting until it was quiet, I rose from my seat.

It was disgusting in there of course. The metal urinal had been clogged up with tissue and a river of stagnant yellow piss sloshed forwards and backwards, with nowhere to go. That wasn't an issue, though; I was headed for the cubicles. There were two of them, one with a door, one without. I chose the former. At least three different people had emptied their bowels into the toilet since it had last been flushed, and their efforts had been furnished with more piss and a bit of vomit for good measure. I yanked the flush, more in hope than anticipation. It gave a little burp by way of reply. Not to worry, my time here would be brief.

Having done my bit I hurried to the sink, foolishly thinking the taps would work. Before I could attempt to wash my hands, I was joined by one of my fellow drinkers. It was one of the pussy cats, the one who'd taken up with his sister-in-law after beating her husband, his own brother, into a coma. He strolled in, all shoulders and arms, and glanced at me briefly before unzipping and swelling the banks of the golden river.

"Friend of Jez's, are ya?" he said, looking at me over his shoulder as he continued to piss.

I froze. I didn't know any Jez. This was some sort of trick, one which ended with me lying on the floor in a pool of my own blood.

"Gerard," he elaborated.

"Oh yeah, he's my neighbour," I said, relief washing over me.

"A proper piss-can, that fellah."

"He likes a pint all right."

"I bet you do an' all."

"Yeah," I said.

"Well, you're in the right place, pal," he said zipping up and giving me a little smile as he went out the door.

He'd called me 'pal'. This violent reprobate, this stealer of wives and beater of brothers, had referred to me as his pal. I wasn't naive enough to believe we were pals, but maybe I could fit in here, maybe I didn't need to dash in and out of the toilets for fear of meeting someone. Sure we were all just lads drinking pints, after all, and I could do that with the best of them. Infused with confidence, I returned to our table.

"All right, *Jez*," I said, smiling.

His eyes narrowed in annoyance.

"Don't call me that."

"Why not?"

"Just don't."

He was quite firm about it. But I wasn't as much in awe of him as I'd once been. After all, I was pals with the pussy cats now. I let it go, though. Gerard had been good to me, and I was still very much under his wing.

The next couple of hours passed without incident, afternoon giving way to evening as the pub gradually got busier and louder. I was well on by now, we'd switched to pitchers of a German beer which the staff poured straight from the can. In fact, everyone was drinking cans now; safer than bottles, I presumed. And because it was their pub, because it had been built specifically for the people of Cois Abhann, the entire community drank here.

A young lad with a wispy moustache and gold earrings sat beside a middle-aged woman with short, bleached hair and enormous saggy breasts, an old-age pensioner was locked in conversation with a heavily pregnant girl, a swarthy man with slicked-back hair and a toothless grin engaged in a finger-wagging dispute with a tall, tanned handsome guy, someone had brought in their dog, a Staffordshire terrier which was lapping away at a pint of its own, and in the middle of it all sat me and Gerard, slumping further and further down our seats as the drink took hold.

"Another one, G?" I asked. I'd taken to calling him 'G' as the day wore on - he hadn't protested.

He stretched contentedly, scratching his face as he pulled himself upwards.

"We're going to have to change it up again," he announced grandly.

His decision to switch to pitchers had been a wise one, I was happy to trust his judgement.

"A few flagons of cider, that's what's required now, cleanse the palate," he said, sticking out his tongue and running it against his lips.

I didn't ask what ciders they had, just requested two flagons and took what I was given. I didn't know the brand but I'd encountered plenty of its ilk; 6% jobs which powered many an alcoholic through the long dark nights. By the time these flagons were conquered the evening would take on a new hue. Because it was evening now, the curtains had been drawn, the lights turned on and dinners, full dinners, with mashed potato and fried steak, were being handed out to the masses. The smell of the food made my stomach growl. I looked at Gerard but he was focused on the booze, he had no time for food, so neither did I. The only way to stave off hunger was to drink twice as hard. My flagon went quickly and with it went the best part of my senses. I was gone, in that dangerous place where inhibitions disappear and bad choices are made.

Gerard had taken to mingling and was chatting up an amused woman half his age. I looked around the bar, wondering if there were any women for me. This was my first time being around the opposite sex in a public setting since I'd bowed out of the FÁS course. There were some attractive girls sitting with the younger lads, but I knew well enough to keep my eyes away from them. A couple of wans around my age sat smoking in the corner. One of them saw me looking and smiled, or at least I think she did. They looked seasoned. If I was ever to lose my virginity I hoped it would be with someone like that, someone who knew what to do; I could just let them take command and deflower me. I looked over again, but they'd been joined by a man so I quickly averted my gaze.

There were other woman there, older wans who would definitely know what to do, but they scared me. Plus, there was no telling who they were married to or having an affair with, and I was determined not to end the night in hospital. So, while life carried on around me I remained rooted to my stool, nursing a whiskey I couldn't remember buying. A singsong started; traditional Irish numbers, sung lustily and with feeling by everyone in the room. One of the youngsters, arms wide, stood up on his seat for the chorus, closing his eyes as he sang, lost in the moment. Someone started stamping their feet and everyone joined in, creating a wall of noise, a steady, persistent back-beat. A man took to the floor, punching the air as he sang, jaw jutted forward as he belted out the words.

As quickly as it began, it subsided. There were instructions to hush, and silence descended upon the room. A lone voice emerged from the quiet, hesitant and shaky at first, but gathering momentum as it found its rhythm. The voice belonged to an old woman. She sat in the midst of all the mayhem, noble and solid, the youngsters gathered round her like expectant children at Christmas. The song was of old Ireland and courageous Fenian men, great men the likes of whom we'll never see again. Her voice, delicate and beautiful, lilting and precious, quivered, trembled but remained intact, turning this den of iniquity into a place of worship, the simple purity of her words transporting you some place else.

I looked upon her, the gentle tilt of her head, slight shake of her neck, hand gripping the armrest as she softly paid tribute to those who had laid down their lives for us, and I felt my throat bob, my eyes prickle. I wasn't a patriot, had never been one for fighting Black and Tans, but her sincerity, and the way everyone, from the gnarled veterans at the bar to the snarling youngsters in the corner, paid her the utmost respect, moved me to my core. A tear ran down my cheek as she concluded her sermon to rapturous applause. A few people got up to go the toilet, one of them, seeing my tears, placed a knowing hand on my shoulder as he walked past.

They returned to the livelier stuff after that. Others volunteered their services, a guitar was procured, but no one moved the crowd as the old lady had. Like a headline act eager to lend its support to the up-and-comers, she remained in her seat, content to be a backing singer for inferior performers. Eventually, after she'd drained the last of her sherry, she was helped from her seat and guided through the crowd. Again she was afforded great deference: "See ya later, Mrs. Maher." "Look after yourself, Mary." "Are you off, Mary? C'mere to me, love." Hugs were exchanged, kisses, a younger woman whispered something fiercely into Mary's ear, held her face and then grabbed her close.

As she finally departed Mary walked by me, flanked by two men, maybe her sons, still chatting as she left; a local heroine. In her absence there was a void. The softness had gone out of the room. It was just a bar full of drunks again. Despite my fears, no one bothered me. There'd been the odd hard stare, a look that lingered too long, but any curiosity had eventually died down. A call went out for last orders and I immediately got up from my seat. I'd had enough for one day. Gerard was nowhere to be seen. Glancing round the room to see if anyone noticed me, I headed out the door, anonymous and unnoticed.

At night Cois Abhann was probably a fearsome place, but I strolled through this notorious estate with a spring in my step. I passed a group of youngsters, still too young to get served in the pub, and they called out threats in their unbroken voices. I kept on walking, just another drunk meandering his way home. When I got into town I stopped for chips and gorged myself, oblivious to the people walking by. After briefly considering going to a nightclub, I returned home and clambered up the stairs, trying to be quiet, laughing to myself, and fell into bed.

*

I awoke to a drilling sound. A hangover? More roadworks? No, it was coming from within the bed, as if through the mattress. I opened my eyes and was greeted by two eyes staring right back at me, green, intense, neither warm nor comforting. Beneath those eyes was a little pink nose, white whiskers and a face of black fur. Gráinne.

"Jesus, cat. How did you get in here?"

She lay upon the pillow, mere inches from my face, utterly at ease. I reached out to stroke her and she drew her head to my hand, nuzzling it and purring loudly. It was nice to have some company of a morning. Maybe I'd adopt Gráinne. Gerard wouldn't even notice. I'd look after her better than he would, make sure she was fed regularly.

"You hungry, Gráinne?"

I got up from the bed and she dropped to the floor, tailing me as I inspected the fridge for something a cat might eat. I surrendered whatever milk I had, pouring it into a bowl while I examined the options. Did cats eat ham? Cheese? Cream crackers? I put all three on a plate. She fairly savaged the ham then sniffed at the cheese, looking up at me inquisitively as if to say "What the fuck do I do with this?" The cream crackers didn't even merit an inspection. I decided having a pet was too much stress and moved to the couch to rest myself.

Some time later, with Gráinne on my chest and depressing daytime telly in the background, there was a knock on my door. I jumped to my feet, the cat yowling in displeasure. If it was Gerard, we were caught bang to rights. There'd be no point in trying to hide the evidence, we would just have to confess and hope he didn't take the news too badly. I listened, waiting for another knock, and again it came, slightly hesitant and gentle - not the kind of knock I associated with a man like Gerard. Telling Gráinne to stay put and not do anything stupid, I went to answer it. It was the woman from downstairs, the one who'd helped me with my shopping, the one with the toddler.

"Hiya, how's things?"

The first time we'd met I'd been in too much of a frenzy to take any notice of how she looked. Now, with the sun streaming in from the window on the landing, I saw her properly. Small and slight, with her peroxide hair tied back in a ponytail, she reminded me of an animated character from a kids' show, one of those bouncy, cheery sprites who encourages her young viewers to adopt a can-do attitude and never succumb to their demons. Her round eyes looked beyond me, into my flat, with darting movements. She shifted her weight from one foot to the next and back again.

This tiny ball of energy wore a white tank top and a pair of those grey tracksuit bottoms with a pink logo on the hips. She dressed like a teenager but looked to be in her early twenties. As she smiled up at me her mouth parted, revealing tiny sharp teeth like a shark's.

"I brought you this," she said, handing me a dish wrapped in tinfoil.

"What for?"

She flushed a little. "I just made too much. If you don't like it, that's okay."

"No, no, it's grand, I just wasn't expecting anything, that's all."

"It's stir-fry, you can have it with rice or noodles, wraps."

"Great. I mean, thanks."

I knew the polite thing would be to invite her in. And I wanted to. But what had Gerard said about this woman? To stay away from her, to not invite her in for a drink whatever you did. He hadn't said what kind of drink, though.

"Would you like a cup of tea?" I asked.

"I should really be getting back."

"Okay."

"But I suppose I could have a quick cup."

She entered the flat and was immediately enveloped by the cat, giving me the chance to clear away some more of my mess. At the rate I was having visitors, I would have to start doing regular clean-ups.

"Oh hi, Gráinne," said the girl. I thought of her as a girl, even though she was a grown woman with a child of her own.

She busied herself with the cat while I made the tea. Her name was Sonia, she'd lived here for four years. The kid I'd met on the stairs was her son, Casper. There was no mention of the boyfriend. When I opened the fridge, I remembered that I'd given Gráinne the last of the milk. I knew if I told Sonia there was no milk she'd say it was all right, that she didn't mind going without. But she'd brought me a stir-fry, the least I could do was give her a proper cup of tea in return.

"Shit, I've no milk," I said, feigning surprise. "I'll just go over and get some. Back in a sec."

I didn't give her time to argue, just left her there, this attractive woman in my apartment with a cat I didn't own. I now had the social life of Paris Hilton. Hurrying down the stairs, focusing on the task at hand, I burst out the front door and into the mid-afternoon traffic. Dodging in and out of the waiting cars, I crossed the road, did the same at the next road and ducked into the corner shop. I took a litre of milk from the fridge, a packet of chocolate biscuits from the shelf and went up to the counter.

"€3.90," said the man.

I could have bought a quart of milk and a chocolate gateau for that in the German supermarket.

I handed over the money and raced back across the road, entering the building with my items in tow. The entire process had taken less than five minutes. It was amazing what a man could do when motivated. Taking a deep breath to calm myself, I ascended the stairs slowly. What would I say to this woman? What *could* I say to her? I decided that less was more; I would stick to the smallest of small talk and be as friendly as possible without scaring her. It was a good plan.

"I'm back," I said, tapping the door as I entered, offering a warning in case she was going through my stuff - which I wouldn't have minded, she could have done anything she wanted and I would have let her. But she was just on the window sill, staring out at the traffic, Gráinne by her side.

"Your view is way nicer than ours. You can see right over to the river."

"Yeah," I said, standing near her, following her gaze.

"Gráinne is a divil, isn't she? She comes to stay with us every now and again too."

"Oh, does she?" I asked, a bit put out.

"Yeah. Casper loves her."

"How is he, Casper?"

"He's grand. Staying at his nan's for a few nights. It's nice to get a break every now and again."

I brought over the tea and we sat on the armchairs, opposite one another. I noticed her wincing as she tried to make herself comfortable.

"Are you okay? Do you want a cushion?"

"No, no, I'm all right. It's just my ribs."

She settled herself and flashed me a wide smile. It made her look like a wolf, like the big bad wolf.

"Oh, right," I said.

"Sorry about that time, before," she said, rolling her eyes.

"That's okay."

"So fucking embarrassing."

"I didn't mind. Thanks for helping me with the shopping."

She smiled happily. I'd never seen a face so transformed by a smile, and not in a good way. It turned her from innocent pixie to villainous foe in the blink of an eye.

"He's not usually like that, you know," she said, by way of explanation.

"Okay."

"He just gets a bit jealous sometimes, when he sees me on my phone and that."

"Hmph, phones," I said non-committally. I was running out of things to say.

"But it's all sorted now. He's great, really."

Talking about Sonia's relationship made me uneasy. I spotted an out and took it.

"Hey, do you hear that Polish lad shouting all the time? It's so bad."

"*Everyone* hears him shouting, Aidan. It's just part of life in this building," she laughed.

"Is he okay, though? It doesn't sound like it."

"He's away with the fairies," Sonia said, crossing her eyes and sticking her tongue out the side of her mouth. "Where did you live before this, Aidan?" she asked, scrutinising me.

"Erm, at home."

"And where's home?"

"Cruinníth."

"You're not like most of the people who live in this place."

"How so?"

"I don't know," she said, analysing me as if I were a test subject. "You're a bit posh."

"I'm not posh," I mumbled.

I was though. She had me figured. I didn't belong here.

"It doesn't matter," she said. "I don't care if you are or not, it's none of my business."

"I was out drinking with Gerard last night," I said, eager to regain some credibility. "We went to *The Three Sisters*, you know, in Cois Abhann."

"Ugh, Gerard," she said, as if the name tasted of shit.

"Oh?"

"What a creep."

"I don't know him long," I said, now fully prepared to denounce him.

"If I were you I'd steer clear, like Gráinne does," she said, adopting a childish tone as the cat vaulted onto her lap.

"What about the other people in the building?" I asked. "Do you know anyone apart from Anipe?"

"Not really. They keep to themselves. You keep to yourself too, Aidan. We don't know anything about you. Don't you ever have friends over or anything like that?"

"Not really."

"You had a session, though," she said, nodding at the two bulging recycling bags.

"Oh yeah," I said, glad she'd seen them.

"A dark horse, then," she said, satisfied by her conclusion. She picked up the biscuits, opened the packet and slid one out. Maintaining eye contact, she dipped it into her tea and bit into it. I could see the crumbs on her lips.

She placed the cup on the armrest and gazed out the window.

"I never thought I'd end up in a place like this. When I met Steve he was full of plans, we were going to go here, do this and do that, and now look at us."

"How long are ye together?" I asked.

She shook her head sadly, as if unable to calculate how many moons had passed since she met Steve.

"It was grand until Casper arrived. Now all we do is fight. And he's never home, just spends his days in the bookies, losing."

If Steve wasn't careful his missus would find solace elsewhere, with someone who listened to her stories and bought her nice biscuits.

Sonia finished her tea and got to her feet.

"Well, it was nice to meet you properly, Aidan. Enjoy the stir-fry and bring down the dish when you're finished, if that's okay."

"I will," I said, showing her to the door, sneaking a glance at her arse, which had the word 'Peachy' emblazoned across it.

"Thanks again."

"No probs," she said, brightening up and then, nodding at Gerard's door. "Remember, avoid that fucking WEIRDO!"

Then she was gone, back down the stairs with her injured ribs, wolfish smile and unfavourable opinion of my new friend. I would be eating that stir-fry at the earliest available opportunity.

24

It was a couple of days before I saw Gerard again. He called to me this time, fresh-faced and bright-eyed.

"Well, how have you been?"

"Grand," I said, a little more coldly than intended. The truth was I'd expected him sooner.

"What did you make of the *Sisters*? Mad oul' spot."

I perked up at the mention of the pub. I was up for a few pints if he was.

"They're good people in there," I answered.

"They are," he said wistfully then paused, a mischievous look in his eye. "I met a quare wan the other night."

I raised a quizzical eyebrow; surely not that woman I'd seen him talking to, the one twenty years his junior.

"Oh, yeah?" I asked.

"Yeah. I'm only back out of hers now."

Envy consumed me. No matter where I went or who I was with, I always seemed to be the one missing out. Part of the reason I liked Gerard was because I'd thought he was like me: a hapless loser who repelled women. There was a sense of security with him, no one else would have us but we'd always have one another.

"How did you manage that?" I asked, even though I didn't want any details.

"Ah, sure . . . " he said, suddenly coy. Sensing my dejection, he added: "She has friends, you know."

"Really? What are they like?"

"I haven't met them yet, but she said they're sound."

Sound. Mother Teresa was sound, that didn't mean I wanted to have sex with her. I had other concerns too.

"But she's older, right? Older than me, I mean."

"She is."

"So her friends are probably older too?"

"Not all of them. I told her about you and she said she already has someone in mind."

I felt a twinge in my groin. That was how bad things were: the thought of meeting a random stranger was enough to get me going.

"Thanks, Gerard," I said.

"No worries. Now, wait till I tell you about this wan."

With my own love life perking up, I was happy to listen to Gerard's story, but that happiness faded with each passing word. He had met this woman outside in the smoking area. Michelle was her name. She was forty-one (I subsequently learned Gerard was forty-seven) and lived at 189 Cois Abhann with her three children. Wise to the fate of those who messed with the wrong women in the estate, Gerard had made sure to establish her relationship status before making his move. Luckily she was single and more than ready to mingle. After a drunken fumble outside, she'd invited him back to hers.

Taking care not to wake the three kids - ages twenty-three, fourteen and eleven - Gerard had been led upstairs into Michelle's bedroom. That would have been enough for me. I didn't need any further information.

But, barely pausing for breath, Gerard continued onward, recounting how she was 'in good nick for someone who'd popped out three kids', how she'd almost 'sucked him dry before they got down to it', and how 'the dirty bitch pulled out a dildo and stuck it in her rat while I fucked her up the arse'. He was just in the process of telling me what had happened to his own arse when I cut him short with an offer of tea.

"Yes, please."

"And you only got back now?" I asked.

"Yeah. We were in the pub the last two days and in her bed the rest of the time," he laughed. "I had to come home to recuperate."

"What about her kids?"

That quietened him. The kettle boiled and I poured the tea, looking at him for an answer as I placed the cups on the table.

"The younger two aren't a problem. You know youngsters, give 'em a couple of quid for an ice cream and they're your best friend."

"But the older one wasn't so happy?"

"Yeah, the son. He was giving me the evils this morning. Big fucker, too."

"You'll just have to make an honest woman out of her, Gerard. Show the family you're not some chancer only out for himself."

He looked at me sharply, anger in his eyes, saw I was joking and broke into a grin.

"Fuck off," he said, chortling.

"I'm serious, Gerard. A man your age, there can't be too many more opportunities for you."

"Cheeky bastard. Wait till we get you set up with this other wan, you won't be laughing then."

"I hope not."

Two days later we made our way through that same estate towards *The Three Sisters*, and this time we were men on a mission. No longer were we a pair of dishevelled winos in search of cheap ale and questionable company, we were now men of romance, with skin in the game. I'd asked Gerard for some details on my potential paramour: age, name, bust size, but he was as much in the dark as me. Michelle had simply told him to bring me at the allotted time and we would go on from there.

Needless to say, I was a nervous wreck. I'd been drinking since midday, pacing the floors as I dreamt up a whole host of disastrous scenarios and, even scarier, successful ones. What if tonight was the night? What if this woman and I hit it off and she brought me back to her place for some dildo-themed fun? Would I be able for it? I decided that if we were getting on I would take it easy on the booze, just in case.

We got to the bar at a little after seven. It was a Monday, so it was quieter. When we entered, there were only around twenty people dotted around the tables - a busy night for most pubs, but practically dead for *The Three Sisters*. I quickly scanned the room, hoping to be met with a friendly, beautiful smile from the future Mrs. Collins. There were a group of oul' lads playing dominos, some younger fellahs at the jukebox, an unhappy man eating a dinner sent over by Mrs. Maher, then slap-bang in the centre of the bar, positioned so you couldn't miss them, were Michelle and my date.

Now, as a larger gentleman, a man with a bit of weight on him, I was in no position to judge anyone else's size. In fact, understanding my own shortcomings, I had considered the prospect of dating a woman with similar weight issues and declared it my best chance of finding love. After all, how could I fat-shame anyone when I was fat myself? But there were limits to this sentiment. And one of those limits was sitting there in front of me.

As someone who had faced more than his fair share of rejection over the years, I was loath to dismiss someone based on their looks, but, if you make your judgement of a person within five seconds of meeting them, then here was mine. She looked incredibly unhealthy. Her face was scrunched up inside a large round head. She didn't have a neck, just a floating mass of flesh which quivered above her chest. Her shoulders were broad; I imagined trying to hug her and not being able to reach all the way around. And, perhaps most disappointingly of all, underneath the black flowing top she wore were breasts which weren't very big.

I breathed deeply and followed Gerard to the bar. We exchanged glances and I could tell he felt bad, but in a way I was relieved. At least I would be able to talk to this woman without stuttering or palpitating. Michelle was no prize either, with her short hair, stout arms and tattoos I would have mistaken her for a lesbian were it not for the passionate kiss she and Gerard shared as we joined them at their table.

"Aidan, is it?" she asked, proffering a hand.

"Yeah. Nice to meet you."

"This is Marion."

My date for the night stuck out a large pink paw and I shook it delicately. She blushed deeply and I felt like a total cunt. This had been a big deal for her too.

"You look nice," I said to her.

"Thanks," she replied. "I like your jumper."

That was kind of her. It was a nice jumper, one of the nicest I owned.

"On the spritzers?" I said, nodding to her drink.

"Yeah," she said, taking a nervous sip.

Gerard and Michelle were already snuggling up close, pinching and poking one another like teenage sweethearts.

"How do you know Michelle?"

"She's my cousin."

"Herself and Gerard seem to be getting on well."

"It's kind of mortifying," said Marion.

"It *is* mortifying," I replied as Gerard slipped a hand up Michelle's top.

I turned away from the canoodling couple towards my date. We didn't need to be associated with those two. Without any chemistry or romance to concern me, I was able to talk to Marion as a friend, another lonely soul in a world full of them. I was also able to drink with abandon, we both were, and after a few more spritzers she loosened up.

"I hate it so much here, this pub, Cois Abhann. I want to get out, move into town," she said.

"Why don't you?"

"I can't afford it. I don't work, don't have any qualifications."

"Sure neither do I."

"Yeah, but you have your shit together."

"Me?" I asked incredulously. "My shit is all over the place."

"Yeah, well, it's harder for me."

"In what way?"

"Look at me."

I knew enough not to suggest that she go on a diet or enrol in a fitness class. She'd heard all that before.

"It must be tough," I said.

"It is. I know people stare and laugh, and I pretend not to care but it hurts."

"Fuck 'em."

She smiled gratefully. "Thanks, Aidan."

Delighted with myself, at how nice I was, I went to the bar to get another round of drinks. This was grand. I was making a new friend, she was easy to talk to and had so many problems of her own she didn't even notice mine. Maybe I could help her out, offer some advice, use my connections at the estate agents to find her a place in town. I'd never really helped anyone before, had always been too consumed with my own demons to think about others. This could be the making of me. I brought back the drinks. Gerard and Michelle had disappeared, it was just me and Marion now, in the middle of a pub which was gradually filling up with the night crew.

I asked her about her interests, what she was passionate about. After much probing, she finally admitted she liked cooking and baking, anything to do with making food. Because of her size she kept this a secret, thinking it too much of a cliché. She dreamed of being a chef, not one of those Michelin Star guys, just a head chef at a local restaurant, somewhere she could experiment with menus and nurture a relationship with her customers. She had some good ideas, too; I mentioned that I liked Italian food and she reeled off recipes I'd never even heard of, things she cooked on a regular basis for her unappreciative family. She was equally knowledgeable on Indian food, south Asian, even Swedish.

"But then I binge on junk food," she said sadly. "I cook all these lovely meals, spend hours preparing them and a couple of hours later, after we've eaten the lot, I order in chips, burgers or whatever. I bake a lot too; cakes, buns, cheesecakes, chocolate biscuit cake. I've started doing them for some of the local kids' birthdays. We pretend it's Mam who makes them, she takes the orders and delivers them and brings the money back to me. But I always make too much, make sure I have enough left over for myself. While they're celebrating the kids' birthdays, I'm having my own little party up in my room."

It was an addiction, no different to me and my booze or diazepam; a way of making herself feel better, a quick fix.

"I know what it's like, Marion."

She looked at me to see if I was joking, to see if this was another cruel trick in a lifetime full of them. Then, having decided I wasn't taking the piss, she averted her gaze, staring into her drink as she stirred it with her straw. It struck me that she wasn't used to earnest conversation, to having her voice heard. She had been dismissed, written off, considered an irrelevance because of how she looked. Encouraged, she continued.

"I could apply for a catering course, there's one in the FÁS centre, but Mam needs help at home. She's not great on her feet and the younger ones need to be got ready for school every morning. I couldn't leave her on her own, it wouldn't be fair."

"I was on a FÁS course," I said.

"Oh, really? What were you doing?"

"Ah, a computer thing."

"Is that what you want to do, then?"

"Maybe."

I didn't want to talk about me. That was too complicated.

"You should definitely apply for that course," I said. "There's a guy in the social welfare, Joe, he could help you get onto it."

She smiled again, slurping on her spritzer before heading to the toilets. The ladies' was on the opposite side of the bar to the male toilets, and she had to walk past a group of youngsters to get there. They didn't look anywhere near drinking age, but were knocking back pints with abandon. As Marion approached they went quiet, I tensed as she made her way past them, waiting for the inevitable wisecrack. When it came I didn't hear it, but it must have been of the highest wit because the lads were in stitches laughing, knee-slapping, breathless laughter, as if they'd heard the funniest joke in the world.

Something bubbled inside me, an unfamiliar feeling. My mind went blank and for a split second I considered picking up my pint glass and hurling it in their direction; but then they looked over at me, hard and uncompromising, challenging me to protest. I put my head down and waited for Marion to come back. Her return journey passed without comment and she gratefully slid up onto her seat.

"Do you know them lads?" I asked, nodding towards the group of youngsters.

She rolled her eyes and shook her head.

Another loud guffaw came from the wall. I looked over in time to see one of the young lads with his cheeks bulged out, waddling back and forth as if holding an oversized belly. Adrenaline pulsed through me, again my mind grew dark and cloudy. Marion continued to talk, pouring her heart out, but I was no longer listening. I was staring over at the boys, at their sneering little faces, their dead soulless eyes and their heartless charade. I snapped out of it, returning to her story.

" . . . if I did get on that course, I could help Mam out with the kids in the morning or even make their lunches the night before, have their clothes ready . . ."

I was too distracted now. The youngsters were staring over at us, speaking under their breath, laughing and skitting. One of them caught me looking and gave me a sly wink, daring me to react, to maintain eye contact for a little too long.

"You're really easy to talk to, Aidan. Do you think we could meet again? It wouldn't have to be here. It'd be better if it wasn't here, actually."

"What? Yeah. Yeah, that'd be good."

"Great," she said, tapping her feet together. "Where will we go?"

There was movement from the corner of the room. The kid who'd winked at me had got to his feet and was coming towards us, a broad grin on his face. His mates sniggered in the background.

"I wouldn't bother, pal. You'll never find it," he said as he walked by.

I didn't know what he meant, didn't even get the joke, but it didn't matter. A dormant energy slowly uncoiled in the pit of my stomach, flickering into life, a hot, burning sensation which slowly travelled up my spine along the very edges of my nervous system. It lingered there, deciding its next move, and then flung itself into an unexplored part of my brain. The effect was immediate, electric. This hidden force launched me out of my seat and onto the back of the passing youngster. I grabbed him by the scruff of the neck, propelling him over to the other side of the bar in one fluid movement. Drinks went flying into the air, people scrambled to avoid us but the tables and chairs remained steadfastly in place.

I pinned him up against the wall face first, my mouth against his neck. I wanted to push him right through it, past the cheap insulation, the wood, through the concrete, so that we both came tumbling out the other side in a cloud of rubble and asbestos. I wanted to crush him, pulverise him until he was a tiny little square, a cube you could kick around the pub for fun. I wanted to squeeze every last breath out of his poisonous soul, suffocate him and roar down his throat so that my rage reverberated around his rotten guts. I didn't get a chance to do any of those things, because seconds later the blows came.

At first I thought it was one of the women from behind the bar, sent to intervene, but it was his mates coming to his aid. Their feeble, underdeveloped arms threw punch after punch at the back of my head, my neck, my throat, my ears. It felt like a bunch of children playfully clambering over me. I began to laugh, released their mate and turned to face them. They stopped in their tracks, wiry and wizened, dukes up, ready to go. I walked past them, through them, and returned to Marion.

"We should go," I said.

My temper, which had sprung out of nowhere, dissipated as quickly as it had risen and with it went my courage. The bravura was replaced by anxiety as Marion faffed about with her drink, taking ages to collect her stuff. The shock and awe of the quiet chubby lad suddenly turning into Clint Eastwood wouldn't last much longer. I needed to disappear before the patrons came to their senses. The lad I'd pinned against the wall was being brushed down by his pals, who were awaiting further instructions. Marion bent to get her bag and dropped her purse. *Pick the fucking thing up for fuck's sake, you stupid cunt.* She got down on all fours, her massive rear end almost begging to be made fun of. If this had happened two minutes ago the young lads would have been in hysterics, but now there was just an uneasy silence, a sense of impending doom.

Finally she got her stuff together, gathering her coat and bag in her arms. *Come on, come on, come on.* She stopped, placed everything on the table, and drained the last of her drink. *Fucking hell.* Then she gave me a nod of affirmation and we were on our way. I gave it the thousand-yard stare, not making eye contact with anyone but doing all I could to ward off danger, and it worked. We made it outside the pub, across the expanse of barren concrete, passed the scorched playing fields and into the estate proper, the warren of pavements and walkways which connected each of its four hundred and twelve houses.

"I live that way," Marion said.

"What?"

"That way," she said, pausing and pointing a finger in the direction from whence we'd come.

"We'll go the long way round."

"There is no long way round," she said quietly, falling into step.

Neither of us spoke for a while after that. I just wanted to get out of Cois Abhann and never return. All sorts of doomsday scenarios played out in my head: the father of that young lad had been informed of my actions and was gathering a group of vigilantes as we spoke, we wouldn't be hard to find, I was the guy walking round in circles with the fat lass. The youngsters were silently tailing us, gathering new members as they went, ready to pounce at the next corner, determined to make amends for their poor showing in the pub, they all knew where I lived, knew I was Gerard's neighbour and would wait until I'd dropped Marion home and got back into town, until I thought I was safe, then they would strike with great vengeance, bringing knives, tools, bricks and other implements to the fight. Never mind getting out of Cois Abhann, I wanted to get out of town, back to Cruinníth, to my childhood room, they'd never get me there.

"I'm tired, Aidan," said Marion, stopping and plonking herself down on the pavement. "Can I go home now?"

I thought of leaving her there, she'd be safe, no matter what, but my new-found chivalry prevented me from abandoning her while God knows what lurked in the shadows.

"Which way?" I asked.

She jerked her head backwards. It occurred to me that maybe she was afraid of me, that she thought I was a psychopath.

I slowed down so that we walked side by side. "Sorry, I just got a bit panicked there."

"That's okay," she said. She was looking at me with something approaching reverence. Marion didn't think I was a psycho, she thought I was a hero.

"Can we go for chips?" she asked.

I refused to dignify that with an answer.

We made it to her house, Number 89, without incident.

"Do you want to take my number?" she asked, all shy.

"Yeah," I said.

She called it out and I dialled it into my phone.

"Text me, okay?" she said.

"Yeah."

She flung her arms around me, her cold cheek pressed against mine. "Thank you."

Then she toddled up the garden path, turned the key in the door, looked back one more time and disappeared inside.

Now fully restored to my normal fearful state, I hurried out of Cois Abhann, onto the ring road and back towards town. Each time a group of people approached I tensed, ready for the hiding of my life, but they all walked on by, engrossed in their own adventures. When I got to Wolfe Tone Street I walked down the other side of the road, eyeing the doorway to my building, looking for them. I looped around, went up O'Connell Street, down Catherine Street, and along Wolfe Tone twice more, before I summoned up the courage to cross over and advance upon my door. Nothing happened, no one came. I got inside, closed the door behind me and allowed myself a sigh of relief.

I had taken part in my first-ever fight and if I wasn't mistaken I had won it, hands down.

25

I MAY HAVE WON THE battle, but I had lost the war. I could no longer go to *The Three Sisters*. To do so would be to invite certain death. I'd only had one fight in my life, but I knew how these things worked: fights didn't just end when one party chose to walk away. The loser had to avenge their loss. Whether this was via a rematch or a random attack involving multiple additional parties was up for debate, but it didn't end there. Maybe if I'd finished the bout in a more conclusive manner, with a vicious threat and a maniacal cackle, I could have convinced them not to retaliate. But by scuttling out of there as fast as Marion's legs could take me, I'd weakened my hand. No, I was finished with *The Three Sisters* and with Cois Abhann. It had been a brief, wonderful time but it was now over.

Any lingering doubts were dispelled by Gerard a day later.

"What the fuck have you been up to?" he asked by way of greeting as he walked in, went straight to the fridge and took out a can of cider. "Are you fucking crazy?"

"What?" I asked.

"That young lad was one of the Laceys!"

I didn't know who the Laceys were, and I didn't want to know, but he told me anyway. I wished he hadn't. There was a 'shower of them in it', a flock of troublemaking ne'er-do-wells who terrorised their neighbours, made a living out of petty crime, turned nasty when they drank and had a flagrant disregard for the law. Gerard reeled off a list of names and their respective charge sheets. The men were bad, very bad, the tales were chilling, the crimes appalling. Des Lacey, Liam, Tony, Séamus, the list was never-ending, the family tree a giant oak, each branch laden with rotten fruit.

But it was the stories of the women which really stood out. Jolene had assaulted a love rival with a stiletto heel, leaving her partially blind in her left eye. Catríona wasn't just barred from all the pubs in town, she was barred from the town itself; years of street-fighting, dragging unfortunate women by the hair, pummelling them until they bled and then leaving them in the gutter for their terrified boyfriends to carry home, forcing the guards to act. If she was seen anywhere near the town centre after eight p.m., she was arrested. Brídín had been jailed for robbery, resisting arrest and perjury, and so it continued. As a family their reputation preceded them; you didn't fuck with a Lacey or anyone belonging to them. Those who did knew all about it.

"Who was he, the lad I attacked?" I asked.

"Doesn't matter who he is, he's one of them. You can't back there again, you can't go anywhere near the place."

I already knew that.

"Do you think they'll come looking for me?"

"They might."

That was one thing about Gerard, he didn't sugar-coat the truth.

I looked at him helplessly, hoping for some reassurance. It didn't come.

"If there was ever a family to bear a grudge, it's the Laceys. A mate of mine, Mickey Cooper, got into a scrap with one of the brothers years ago. Moved to London shortly after. About ten years later, while he was over for a funeral - a fucking funeral! - they jumped him on his way home from the pub one night. He had to carry the coffin with a black eye and a freshly-laid scar down his cheek."

"Maybe I should just get it over with," I said sadly, "head out there tonight and hang round the streets till they find me."

"They'd respect that," Gerard said sagely.

He drained the can and got to his feet. "Anyway, whatever you do leave me out of it. I've a good thing going with this wan."

Gerard readjusted his crotch for effect and left for another evening of disgusting sex.

In his absence I pondered my new circumstances. I may have floated the idea of going out to Cois Abhann, walking through the streets like an ornery gringo, but that was never going to happen. I wasn't the type to go and take my beating like a man, far better to hide like a mouse. I would stay here for as long as it took, even if it was ten years. I did have one ally in that neighbourhood, though, the fair maiden whose feelings I'd lost so much to protect. I decided to text her, see if she had any tough uncles.

Hi Marion. It's Aidan. How's things?

It wasn't like texting a real girl. I didn't fancy her so I didn't need to make an effort. A few minutes later a reply came.

Crrraaaazzzzy night! Everyone is talking about it.

Fuck. I didn't want to be talked about, I wanted to be forgotten, ignored for eternity.

What are they saying? I heard that young fellah was a Lacey or someone? I asked.

I don't know their names but that gang of young lads are hated around here, my mam said one of them got the shit bet outta him in The Three Sisters the other night! I had to pretend I knew nothing about it.

She inserted a row of smiley faces below her text.

It took me a moment to realise what she was saying: that word of my antics had spread, that apparently I'd bet the shit out of this young Lacey chap.

Does she know who did it?

No. She just said some big lad, that's all.

I was the big lad. I'd gone into the most notorious estate in the town and beaten the shit out of one of its most hated residents. Despite everything, I felt a surge of pride. I decided I didn't want to be forgotten after all, but if they were going to talk about me then the least they could do was remember my name. 'The Big Lad' didn't exactly roll off the tongue.

What are you doing? Marion texted.

About the fight?

No, dummy. What are you doing now?

Nothing much. Gerard was just here. He's gone to meet Michelle. Ew.

Ew, indeed. We chatted for a bit then, but I was preoccupied. Years spent living in fear of the unknown, of intangible terrors, and now I finally had something to be afraid of. Maraghmor wasn't a big place, they could find me any time they wanted. Young Lacey wouldn't have enjoyed being embarrassed in public like that, having the whole place talk about the bating he got. He'd probably want to make an example of me, show that what Gerard had said was true, that nobody fucked with a Lacey.

And so I returned to my hermetical life. Out went the nights in the pub with Gerard, the daily walks in the park, the occasional late-night wanders around town and any hope of building a social life beyond these four walls. I could live without all those. But also gone were my trips to the cheap discount supermarket. It was but a stone's throw away from Cois Abhann, far too close for comfort. There was a rival discount supermarket on the other side of town, but it was two bus rides away and not worth the hassle. So it was the nearby non-German, non-discount supermarket for me: an emporium which offered superior products, but at superior prices.

Yet it wasn't all bad. For a start, I could get there and back in fifteen minutes. Better still, it had self-service checkouts, arguably the greatest invention of all time. I could go in, do my shopping, pay and leave without having to talk to a single soul. It was almost worth the extra Euro they charged for flagons of cider. And as it turned out, I had more than enough social interactions to keep me going anyway.

I began to see less and less of Gerard. He would occasionally call over for an hour, drink some of my cans and then announce he had a hot date. I tried to return the favour, but upon knocking at his door I'd be confronted by Michelle wearing nothing but a T-shirt and a filthy smile. On the plus side, Gráinne had practically moved in with me. I'd begun buying her cat food, even set up a litter tray in the hallway. She wasn't the only female who seemed intent on spending time with me. For the first time in my life I became the subject of a romantic tug-of-war, the apex of a love triangle. On one side of the triangle was Marion: loyal, persistent, patient and undesirable. On the other was Sonia: mysterious, hypnotic and so hot that I fantasised about her on a regular basis.

After that first visit and the stir-fry, I'd waited a couple of days and returned the dish in the dead of night, creeping downstairs and leaving it outside her door while the whole building slept. I thought that would be the end of it, that we'd return to being occasional acquaintances. But no, a week later she returned; this time with a pot of chilli, tight jeans and a crop top revealing a pierced belly button. She immediately took a seat at the window, staring off into the distance, all mournful and melancholic. There must have been a shortage of bras locally, because she never seemed to be wearing one. Not that she had much to show off; her breasts were small, but I could see her nipples through her top. That was enough.

"You been out drinking with Gerard?" she asked, not bothering to hide the contempt in her voice.

"Not recently," I said. "He has a new girlfriend."

"Oh, Jesus," Sonia said theatrically. "She must be fucking blind. And deaf. And dumb."

I laughed.

"Is she?" Sonia asked. "Dumb, I mean. Retarded, even?"

"No. She's rough out, though."

She nodded in confirmation. "That'd be right. Where'd he meet her? In that pub?"

"Yeah."

"And there was no one for you?" she asked, adopting a pitying tone which irritated me.

"There was, actually, but it didn't work out."

"How come?"

"Not my type."

"What is your type, Aidan?" she asked, returning to the vampish Sonia I'd been wanking over.

"I don't know," I said sadly. "There was a girl I liked in a FÁS course, but that didn't work out either."

"Unlucky in love, eh? Aren't we all."

She constantly did this, tried to steer the conversation towards her relationship, willing me to enquire how things were between her and Steve.

"What was wrong with the girl Gerard set you up with?" she asked, changing tack.

"I told you, not my type."

"Yeah, but why wasn't she your type? What did she look like?"

I really didn't want to tell her, but Sonia could have asked me for my PIN number, my social services number and the key to my heart and I would willingly have surrendered all three.

"She was heavy, heavier than me."

"Aw, and you wouldn't go with her because of that?"

"No, it was just - I mean, I know I'm not thin, but she just wasn't - I didn't fancy her."

"Relax, Aidan, I'm only messing. If you didn't fancy her, you didn't fancy her."

She fell silent then, giving me a moment to recover, to turn the tables.

"What about you? How long have you been with what's-his-name, Steve?"

"Ugh, don't talk to me about *him*," she said turning her head right around so I couldn't see her face.

But she did want to talk about him, that was all she wanted to do. She spent the next half-hour talking about him, how they'd got together when she was just sixteen and he was twenty-three, how he used to collect her from school in his Honda Civic and bring her to the garage where he worked, show her off to his workmates and then shag her in the service pit when no one was around. He was her first and only love, and she used to fly into a jealous rage if he even glanced in the direction of another woman. They often spent entire days, nights and weeks just lying in bed fucking, promising they'd be together forever.

When she left school, started going out to the clubs with her friends, things began to change. He'd appear out of nowhere in a drunken rage and make a scene, drag her out of the club and onto the street, yelling, getting rough with her, until someone intervened and the two of them turned on the innocent fucker. Until it slowly dawned on her that a life with Steve would be a series of arguments and fights, make-ups and break-ups, that all the promises in the world wouldn't change him, and if she didn't get out soon she'd be trapped in a never-ending cycle of love and hate until it faded to nothing. And then she got pregnant.

At first it seemed to be a good thing. It was like the old days. He was patient and attentive, calm and considerate. She saw him in a new light as the father of her child, the provider of life. They were going on a journey together, but that journey ended when Casper was six weeks old. Steve lost his job in the garage and they'd moved here, to Wolfe Tone Street. With no work to be had, no opportunities for even the most experienced of mechanics, Steve was cast adrift. Now he left the flat at midday and didn't return until evening, for a quick bite and a shower. Then he was gone for the night. Sometimes he didn't come home at all.

"Seven years, Aidan! Seven fucking years with that bastard."

"It's a long time," I said, wondering if they still had sex and if so, how often.

"And what can I do? I can't move out. I put my name on the housing list - don't tell him that, by the way - but sure, I could be on that for years. And I'm not going back to my mother's."

She could have moved in with me. She could have taken my flat and I'd have slept on the street.

"He never does anything with Casper, barely looks at him. Oh yeah, he might play around with him the odd time when he comes back from the pub pissed up, but kicking a ball, bringing him to the beach, all the things fathers are supposed to do with their kids, there's none of that."

"At least Casper has a good mother," I said.

She looked at me sadly. "You're sweet, Aidan."

'Sweet' was the same as 'nice'. Us sweet, nice lads never got girls like Sonia, they were for the bastards like Steve.

I poured the tea and brought it over. She delicately floated from the window sill to the armchair she'd sat in last time, pulling her legs up under her, holding the mug between her hands, blowing on it as she stared out the window.

"Can I smoke in here?" she asked.

"Of course."

She perched the cigarette between her lips, let it hang there a moment, and then casually flipped open her lighter. She took a long drag and exhaled slowly with great relish. It was like something from a film, back when smoking was sexy and didn't cause cancer.

"He's hit me, you know, in front of Casper."

This revelation lingered in the air a moment, long enough for me to envisage Steve belting her in the face with one of his big meaty fists. I'd never actually met Steve, but he was a mechanic so it stood to reason he'd have big hands.

"Do you want a drink?" I asked.

"Why not?" she answered, brightening up.

I took out two cans of German Pilsner, the cheap stuff, and handed her one.

"Where he is now? Or do you know?" I asked.

"He's down at the bookies or over at his friend's house playing with engines, either that or with one of his whores."

"And the little fellah?"

"At my mam's. She takes him a couple of days, to give me a break."

This apartment block was like an eternal purgatory. Nothing good happened here, nothing good ever happened to its residents, we were all just getting by, hoping to move on to better things.

Sonia and I sat drinking for a while. This was the longest she had ever stayed, and with a drink on board I didn't feel quite so frightened in her company. She mostly just stared out the window, allowing me to take in her profile, her taut legs, midriff and bare ankles. She had two more cans and about eight cigarettes before leaving, lingering in the hall for a second, pausing as if to say something important before sighing and thanking me for the drink. After she'd left I moved over to the seat she'd been on, savouring its warmth, her presence. While I'd been gazing all doe-eyed at Sonia, my other new friend had been beating down a path to my door. There were four messages from Marion on my phone, each more agitated than the last.

2.21 p.m. **Wyd?**

3.05 p.m. **You there?**

3.59 p.m. **Are you ignoring me? What did I do?**

5.11 p.m. **Go fuck yourself, Aidan.**

It struck me that if I didn't reply that would be the end of it, I'd probably never hear from her again. But I felt the need to fight my corner.

Sorry, had a friend over.

I'd barely put the phone down when it buzzed in reply.

Why didn't you tell me?

I didn't realise I had to tell you when I had friends coming over. I replied, fairly battering the buttons as I typed.

Don't be like that. I was just worried, that's all.

We were like a married couple.

She wanted to come over, to 'hang out'. I wasn't short of company at the moment, though. I didn't really need another visitor. Thankfully I had a ready-made excuse.

I can't have you coming here. What if the Lacey lad follows you?

He won't. I'll make sure no one follows me.

But I wasn't for turning. It seemed unlikely they would have spotters out waiting for her, lads sitting in parked cars with walkie-talkies, saying stuff like 'target has left Cois Abhann and is headed southbound, over', but I couldn't be too careful. I would keep Marion on the long finger, delay another meeting for as long as I could. A time would come when I'd need her, and not just for a bit of company. Once Sonia had done whatever she intended to do with me, I would call upon Marion. She was my safe bet, the only thing keeping me from a life of loneliness and solitude. If I ever did invite her over here, I could ask her to stop off at the German supermarket on her way to pick up some booze and a few groceries.

Because after a few weeks of shopping at the one in town, the bog-standard Irish one, the money was burning out of my pocket. I was poorer than ever, and still had no internet. Fate had forced my hand: I would go to the social welfare office and apply for the rent allowance. Driven by a thirst for alcohol and online porn, I made the short walk to the welfare on a Friday afternoon. The staff would be more cheerful on a Friday, less likely to dismiss my claim out of hand. Trying to look casual, I walked past the reception desk and up to the stall full of brochures and leaflets, perusing them as if I was waiting for someone.

The rent allowance thing wasn't there; it was just stuff about back-to-work schemes and community employment programmes. They didn't want you knowing about rent allowance, tried their best to hide it from you. I was about to go home and give it up for another day, but desperation made me stay, made me walk up to the lady behind the Plexiglas and open my mouth to speak.

"Ticket," she said, not lifting her eyes from the paperwork in front of her.

"Eh?"

"Get a ticket. Over there," she said, pointing distractedly at a ticket machine by the wall.

I pressed the button on it and a ticket came out, bearing the number 84. At that moment, an electronic voice announced '76' and a man rose from the benches to speak to the lady. All this hassle, just for a form. Almost an hour had passed by the time my number came up. I returned to the counter.

"Ticket," she repeated.

I handed over my ticket.

"Now, how can I help you?" she asked, looking at me for the first time.

"Erm, can I get a rent allowance form, please?"

She lifted a piece of paper from one of the piles on her desk and slid it under the counter.

"Anything else?"

"No, thanks."

And that was that. Aidan 1, The State 0.

When I got home I left the form on the table without even looking at it. I would wait a couple of days to tackle it. I wanted to savour my victory, enjoy the moment. But after another night of rewatching old films with just four measly cans of beer to sustain me, I woke up on a mission. Taking a deep breath, I opened the form and began filling it out. The first page was the usual, basic stuff: name, date of birth, PPS number, address, employment status, income. I was happy to provide that information. Then came the first curve ball. It asked why I was applying for rent allowance, and left a large white box underneath for me to write my answer. I didn't like this. There was no right or wrong response, no way of knowing what they wanted. After some careful consideration I entered the following:

I moved into Apartment 14, 56 Wolfe Tone Street six months ago, and although I had initially thought I would be able to attain work and pay the rent with ease, I have found it something of a struggle. I am currently unemployed and paying rent of €300 from a monthly income of €720, which barely gives me enough to pay for food and other bills. If I cannot pay my rent I will end up on the street, as I have nowhere else to go following a dispute with my family.

That last line was of the utmost importance. They wouldn't give you the money if they thought you had a bed at your parents' home; people had been refused rent allowance on the grounds that there had been no need for them to move out, no need to request further assistance from the state when Mammy and Daddy could just as easily look after them. Well, I was prepared, had even dreamt up a fictitious domestic conflict if they poked into my background. And it wasn't even that fictitious. I would tell them my mother was in a nursing home and my dirtbag of a father had sold the house and moved in with his new girlfriend. It had caused monumental strain on the entire family and driven me to drink and bouts of deep, unyielding depression. I had no morals. I would sell them all out in pursuit of this money.

Having completed the form I then had to attach two utility bills, along with a receipt for my monthly rent and, most excruciatingly, a letter from my landlord approving my application. This would be the hardest part, having to go into the estate agents' office and admit my shortcomings, admit I was just like all the rest of them in 56 Wolfe Tone Street, a perennial loser reliant on handouts from the government. Again I hesitated, thought about leaving it a couple of days, but the promise of proper broadband, Sky TV and premium lager lifted me out of my seat, down the stairs and across the road to the agents.

The prissy blonde was at the desk, the one whose eyes flickered in annoyance any time I came in to pay my rent or ask about something.

"Hiya," she said, her smile as false as the hair extensions, eyelashes and whatever other amendments she'd undertaken to beautify her fairly unremarkable visage.

"Hi. I just have this form," I said, handing it over.

She handled it like it were a steaming dog turd.

"Oh. One moment," she said, disappearing to the back room to seek advice from her superior.

The other receptionist sat at the desk opposite. She was a prune-faced wench, a real piece of work. On a previous occasion I'd made the mistake of approaching her desk, she'd simply glared at me until Miss Prissy Pants intervened. If I'd been renting one of the fancy places or been a potential buyer, it would have been different. I'd seen how they reacted to those people, how they cooed and cawed, fawning over them because of who they were or what job they had. The younger one came back, still holding the form by the edges as if it might ignite at any moment.

"Now, let me just stamp that for you," she said.

I waited, feeling dirty, sweaty and unworthy, until she stamped the form and slid it across the desk.

"Thanks," I said and high-tailed it out of there.

Another leg of the mission complete. Just one more to go.

26

THIS WAS THE BIG ONE. All the others had been straightforward enough, only my own neuroses making them seem difficult. Now I had to go and see the Community Welfare Officer, the member of staff who would decide my fate. They only processed rent allowance applications and enquiries on Tuesday mornings from 9 a.m. I would need to be there early, these were hotly contested appointments. Get there late, even at 9.30 a.m., and you might not be seen. So, the following Monday evening I went to bed early, after only three cans, and set the clock for 8.30 a.m. I had an advantage in being so close to the office; I would arrive at 8.55 a.m. and be one of the first in, bright-eyed and bushy-tailed for my all-important meeting.

And everything went to plan. I got up on time, took a quick shower, put on the least dirty clothes I could find and strolled up to the centre, my heart rattling in my chest. As soon as I turned the corner, I realised I'd made a huge mistake. The office may have opened at 9 a.m. but that didn't stop people queuing up earlier. It was as if Kurt Cobain had risen from the grave and announced a comeback tour, with all tickets on sale at the Maraghmor Social Welfare Office this very morning. There were people lined up all along the front of the building, winding their way right round the corner and down the other side; women with children in prams, oul' lads, young lads, angry lads, nervous couples whose expressions said 'we don't belong here', down-and-outs, student types, professionals, sad-faced children, and foreign nationals, lots of foreign nationals, entire families of them.

My first inclination was to turn back and go to bed. I would know better next week, I would arrive at 7 a.m., camp out overnight if I had to. But I was here now, I may as well try my luck. I went to the back of the queue and stood behind a fellah not much older than me. He was tall and well-built with cropped hair and designer stubble. He dressed like a rapper from New York, baggy jeans, a puffy Yankees jacket and large Nike runners with the tongue protruding out the top. As I took up my place in the queue his phone rang.

"Yeah," he said in a long drawl. "Well, I am, but there's about a hundred people in front of me."

There was a pause while the person on the other end spoke.

"I didn't fucking know it was going to be like this, did I?" the man said, his voice rising an octave. "Yeah well, I'm here now, I might as well go in."

That was exactly what I'd thought.

He hung up and muttered a few curses under his breath before leaning against the wall and lighting up a cigarette.

"Smoke?" he asked, offering the packet.

"No, thanks."

"This is some bullshit."

"Yeah. Where have all these people come from?" I said, glad of the company.

He looked down the line. "Not from round here, anyway."

There was a clamour up ahead as the doors opened and people began shuffling towards the entrance. Even from around the corner we could hear the security guard warning people not to skip the line or to push forward. We had barely made it around the corner before the line stopped.

"That's enough for now," the security guard called out.

There were still seventy people or more standing outside. Ten minutes passed before the first person exited the building, ten more before the next, but then they started coming in fits and spurts; mostly dejected people who didn't understand what had happened, who didn't understand anything because English wasn't their first language and the people inside had neither the time nor the patience to talk them through this most complex of procedures. I had no time to feel sorry for them, the quicker they came out, the quicker I'd be seen.

By the time we reached the doors, the waiting room was full and people were standing outside in the hallway. We got our tickets and squeezed ourselves in against the wall. A sallow-skinned woman sat on the floor opposite us breastfeeding her child, her friend trying to shield her from the crowd. I could see the baby's face through the friend's legs: its eyes open, staring into space, oblivious to the clamour around it, to the arcane rules and regulations of the Irish State.

A number was announced over the Tannoy system: 56.

I was 126.

My tall rapper companion showed me his ticket: 125.

"I'm going to go up the town for a bit," he said. "No point hanging round here."

He left me there on my own, with the suckling children and anxious applicants, nothing for me to do but count down the numbers and wait my turn.

Sometimes the numbers moved fast: 71 was a no-show, 73 was in and out in no time. At other times they moved slowly. Number 76 took an age. From outside in the hallway I could hear a raised voice, an Irish voice, a woman's, berating a member of staff. She was on about foreigners too, claiming that the staff member was prejudiced against Irish people and that she'd fare better if she was called Mohammed. After five minutes of this she was escorted from the premises, her application presumably in tatters.

I still hadn't even reached the waiting room when my friend came back. He saw me standing against the wall and shook his head in dismay.

"You're still out here?" he said, as if it were my fault. He peered into the waiting room at all the sad, tired faces, noted the number on the electronic screen and left once more.

An hour passed, during which I tried to guess the age of the sixteen people still standing in the hallway, read all the leaflets on the nearby stand and, having held it in for as long as I could, went looking for the toilet. When I located it, there was a queue for that too. Finally, at 12.35 p.m., I made it into the actual waiting room. The only available space was right beside the door, meaning I had to turn my back and twist myself inwards any time someone came in or out. But I was in, and that was the main thing. From my new position I could see that the suckling baby was now asleep and its parents had made it inside too; someone had offered them a seat. Even though everyone in here was close to the finish line, there was no sense of excitement. Everywhere you looked there were worried faces, the faces of people who dared not hope, who'd spent the entire night rehearsing their pitch and just wanted the whole thing to be over.

Because I couldn't see the booths, I had no idea if people were receiving good news or bad. Occasionally you'd hear a pleading tone and a stern, unwavering voice from the other side, but despite our close proximity there was no sense of shared experience. We were all in this alone and if the person before you got bad news, that was their problem. The room began to clear and the last dregs from the hallway made their way inside. After another forty-five gruelling minutes, I found a seat of my own. There were just eight of us left. My rapper pal from earlier, number 125, hadn't reappeared and was in danger of missing out if he didn't return soon.

Number 122 was an older man, maybe in his sixties, well-dressed and well-spoken. Now that I was sitting down I didn't really care how long he took, but he was in and out in less than two minutes, the judge, jury and executioner cowed by his officious manner. After him was an African chap who looked resigned to his fate before he was even called. He started out quietly, his voice barely audible in the deathly quiet room, but as each query was rebuffed by the woman on the other side he grew more animated. I looked nervously at one of the others, wondering if we were going to get a show, but eventually he accepted the outcome with a sigh and a slump of the shoulders.

Number 124 was a woman, perhaps in her thirties, who belonged to the category of people who really didn't belong here. You could pick them out right away: they looked ill at ease, a little ashamed and slightly disgusted. They were stony silent, grimacing as they endured this haunting ordeal. This woman had probably never been in a social welfare office in her life, had been a worker, a contributor, a pillar of several communities. Now here she was with us, the wasters, the no-hopers. I felt sorry for her, she was the kind of person the state needed to help, the type who would be back contributing as soon as things picked up.

I heard her thank the official profusely, saw her signing the dotted line with a shaking, grateful hand and then leave the room with an exhalation of relief. Number 125 was called out once, twice then three times, with no response. The other eejit had either mistimed his return or just not bothered.

"126."

I checked my ticket as if it contained the winning lottery numbers. It was me. I was next.

"Hi," I said, sitting down in the warm chair.

The woman on the other side peered at me through glasses which were perched halfway down her nose. Her hair, greying at the roots, was a strawberry blonde colour, she looked like a librarian, a cross, impatient librarian.

She gestured towards the forms I'd brought with me and I slid them through the hatch; then I waited and watched. She skimmed through the first couple of pages, which I took to be a good sign, but when she reached the page where I'd explained why I couldn't return home she paused.

"Your mother got sick?" she asked.

"Yes."

"What's your mother's name?"

"Avril Collins."

She paused, whispering the name to herself as she read what I'd written. Did she know my mother? Was she a regular at the nursing home? This was all going terribly.

"And where does your father and his - his new partner, live?"

"Railway Hill in Cruinníth, but they're moving to a place in Barnduff."

"Well for them," she replied.

"Yeah."

"And now you're living on Wolfe Tone Street?"

"Yeah."

"How are you finding it?"

"It's okay."

She flipped the pages over again.

"Who was your last employer, Aidan?"

Panic. A river of sweat cascaded down my back.

"I haven't . . . there hasn't . . . I'm currently applying for jobs, you can see it there," I said, attempting to point at the attached rejection letters and jabbing my finger painfully against the Perspex.

"I didn't ask you that," she said, now cold as ice. "Who was your *last* employer?"

I folded. I wasn't cut out for this.

"FÁS," I offered meekly.

"Oh yeah," she said, noting the six-month course that I hadn't even finished. "There's a follow-on course from that one, why don't you do it?"

"Um, I don't know."

She stared at me then, her dark, black eyes seeming to bore right into my soul, stealing my last shred of dignity, spiriting it away to a filing cabinet in head office. Then something broke, she relaxed and, with a flourish, stamped my form and slid out a new one towards me.

"Fill out that form and sign your name at the bottom," she said.

I did as she asked and waited for the next instruction.

"You'll get confirmation of your application in the post within the next three working days," she said.

I remained sitting, mute.

"That's it," she said, "you're finished."

I got up and turned to face the room, to face my fellow soldiers, but they weren't looking, all they cared about was the seat I'd just vacated. I walked out of the building in a daze, still unsure what had happened. As I ambled down the road, I saw number 125 jogging towards me.

"Are they shut?" he asked.

"No, there's still a few people up there," I replied.

"Okay," he said, all business-like as he jogged on. He stopped and turned. "Hey, how did you get on?"

"Good, yeah," I called back.

*

True to her word the letter came two days later. In addition to my €180 Jobseeker's Allowance, I was now to receive €62.26 per week to help pay my rent. I was elated, of course; I could now get broadband, better and more copious amounts of alcohol, and even the odd takeaway. But I also felt ashamed, a bit dirty and sleazy. I'd done it again. I'd conned the world. I'd taken the easy option, asked for further handouts instead of trying to better myself, and now that I had this money there was no chance of me doing anything worthwhile ever again. Still, I collected my first payment the following Thursday and immediately began drafting a new budget for the months ahead.

I now had an extra €249.04 to play with per month. It was mind-boggling, almost too much to take in. My finances were in rude health. My current outgoings per month were: rent €300. Electricity €80 (although this would surely rise when I got back online). Bins €14. Phone €20. Miscellaneous €30. Total €444. My new incomings were: Jobseeker's Allowance €720. Rent Allowance €250 (I rounded this up for ease of use). I kept the €20 per month winter Fuel Allowance separate. So my revised total incomings were €970 per month. Subtract €444 from that and I was left with €526 a month to feed, water and clothe myself. More than enough.

I didn't even need to visit the German discount supermarkets, I could laugh in the face of their cut-price products. I spent around €60 a week on food, so that worked out at €240 a month, leaving me with €286 pocket money. I'd been checking out the deals with the broadband providers and one was offering a TV and broadband package for a starting price of just €40 a month for the first six months. I could get that and still have €246 a month for drink. There was even a chance I could buy myself some new clothes. It was unimaginable wealth, riches beyond my wildest dreams.

A week later the man came to install my broadband and television. He seemed utterly bewildered when I told him I'd lived without any internet or television channels for the past six months. But then I told him I'd been rewatching *The Sopranos* and *The Shield* and he smiled knowingly. His favourite episode of *The Sopranos* was the one in the woods, the one where Christopher and Paulie get lost trying to execute a Russian hitman. I didn't tell him that everyone said that was the best episode and that the best one was actually when Janice murdered Richie Aprile in Season Two. It was good to just talk to someone. I'd been feeling lonely again now that Gerard had abandoned me, Marion wasn't speaking to me (for reasons I couldn't remember) and the visits from Sonia had dried up. But I didn't need them, I had the internet now, and satellite television.

The engineer took an age to leave, showing me how the set-top box worked, running through the channels on the remote. He was ruining it for me, spoiling the surprise; I wanted to see these things for myself. Finally, after running a speed test on my laptop and confirming I was receiving the prearranged speeds, he waved a cheery goodbye and left me to my own devices. I would check out all the channels later, get my planner set up and start recording stuff. But I'd gone six months without the internet, that meant six months without porn. Now I was going to indulge myself.

I'd barely opened up the first site and typed 'big bubble butts' into the search bar when there was a knock at the door. It was Sonia, come to see what all the fuss was about.

"Ooh, do you have MTV?" she asked as soon as she saw the box. "They took that off Freeview ages ago. What time is it?"

Then she was off, browsing the schedules, setting reminders, recording series and putting things on her watch list. I hadn't even set up *my* watch list yet. I should have been angry at this violation of my privacy, at someone else getting the first go of my new toy, but the more stuff she recorded the more time she'd spend up here so I let her off. Sonia found a reality show she liked and immediately became engrossed. She was like a child watching a cartoon; eyes glued to the screen, lost in a world of impossibly beautiful people impossibly far away. I thought about watching porn while she sat there, keeping the screen turned away and the sound down, so she didn't know what I was up to. It would be erotic but also creepy, so instead I just pottered about online, going back on my forums, watching YouTube videos and looking for film recommendations for later that night.

I found a video of the world's angriest guitar player, he was trying and failing to play a song I didn't recognise. The harder he tried to get the right chord, the right key, the angrier he got, until he exploded and made shit of the guitar. It was very funny, I did a little belly laugh, my body shaking in quiet appreciation. I was a quiet laugher, a chortler more than a snorter, but loud enough for Sonia to notice. She momentarily averted her gaze from the television screen, shooting me a quizzical look. I gestured towards the laptop screen, still chuckling to myself. She smiled half-heartedly and returned to the telly. This was great.

I would have happily sat there all day and I got the feeling she would have too, but when her phone started ringing I knew that our idyllic afternoon was about to draw to a close. I could hear the voice on the other end, it was male, abrupt, impatient: Steve. I watched Sonia's face for a reaction, trying to read her mood, assess the chances of her staying a bit longer. She tutted a bit, said "Yeah," a few times and then ended the call with "All right, yeah, no worries. See you in a minute." So that was that, our little date was over.

"I have to go, Aidan."

"Yeah, I guessed that."

"Hold on," she said, picking up the remote again. "I just want to record the rest of this."

"Okay."

"Will you be here tomorrow?" she asked.

"Probably."

"Great. See you then."

Then she was gone. Off to meet Steve to do girlfriend things with him, or maybe mammy and daddy things with their son. Well, let them at it, I thought, at least now I could have a wank in peace.

27

I COULDN'T REMEMBER INVITING HER, had no recollection of my folly, but at some point during a sustained drinking session, a binge which started on a Saturday night and didn't ease until the following Tuesday, I had made plans with Marion. Those plans consisted of her coming to my flat, cooking me dinner and then the two of us watching a film. I didn't like the sound of these plans. However, I was nothing if not a man of my word. Also, I'd been feeling bad for constantly fobbing her off, so I would invite her into my home and treat her like an esteemed guest. I just hoped no one (as in Sonia) would find out she'd been here.

Marion arrived at the appointed time and I traipsed down the stairs to let her in. It had been over a month since our blind date, and my second first impression was that she wasn't *that* fat. She was a big girl, there was no escaping it, but not as big as I remembered. She was dressed entirely in black again and had done something to her hair, maybe changed the colour, I couldn't be sure. We shared an awkward hug and she showed me what she'd brought. We were having duck. Duck. There would be vegetables, too, potatoes and greens with a fancy type of French gravy. She'd even brought wine, as if I could be relied upon to sip a glass of red while eating my dinner.

I showed her round the flat, not commenting when she lingered in the bedroom a little longer than was comfortable. Then she was straight into the cooking, reheating the duck in the oven, getting all the hobs on, ransacking my cupboards for pots and utensils I didn't know I had.

"So, how have you been?" she asked as she hefted a pot of water onto a hob. "You haven't been back to the *Sisters?*"

"Nah."

"I think it's blown over by now, you'd probably be all right."

"I'd rather not chance it."

"I mean, you strike me as someone who can take care of himself. You definitely put that Lacey kid in his place, anyway."

"I don't like violence."

That was good, it made me sound noble rather than cowardly.

"Only when a woman is involved, is it?" she asked suggestively.

"Mmm."

Once she'd got everything boiling and bubbling and had a few minutes to spare, she took a seat on the couch and sat there, smiling away at me.

"What film will we watch later?" she asked.

I'd recorded something called *The Raid* on Film Four. It was an Indonesian action film about a rookie cop who has to infiltrate an apartment block in search of a crime lord. Ultra-violent with lots of shoot-outs and fight scenes, it had the potential to be a five-star film, one I'd watch over and over again.

"Ah, I've a few things recorded there. We can decide later."

"Okay," she said, tapping her feet on the floor excitedly.

As the food neared completion, I set the table. This involved taking two plates out of the press, getting two knives and forks and then opening and pouring the wine. Marion served up and, after tentatively poking at it for a moment, I tucked in. It was sublime: restaurant quality, full of rich and mysterious flavours. The duck was tender and soft and had undertones of citrus. The potatoes were to die for. She'd done something with the skins; they had little red and yellow flakes on them. There was broccoli, green beans and mangetout, all delicious, and the gravy was like nothing I'd had before, light yet thick and spicy. I would have drunk pints of it if there had been any left. Instead I quaffed down the wine, nodding vigorously when Marion noted how it brought out the rosemary and thyme.

As I neared completion, she asked if I wanted more. Stupid question. My plate was restocked and I continued eating. Only when I began to sweat did I slow down and lift my head for air. She had given herself the most modest of helpings: a couple of slices of duck, some tiny spuds and a few vegetables which she was delicately spearing with her fork. In the time I'd eaten one-and-a-half platefuls, she'd barely managed to finish a child's serving.

"What's up?" I asked. "This is amazing. You know that, right?"

She smiled appreciatively, bashfully. "I'm not that hungry."

"At least eat the duck, you'll starve otherwise."

"Hope so," she muttered quietly.

I knew what was going on here, I was no fool, but I wasn't getting into this with her. The moment I laid down my knife and fork she was up on her feet again, promising me the dessert to end all desserts. After that dinner, I was intrigued to see what she'd come up with. It was a chocolate cheesecake, homemade, with frozen yoghurt, salted caramel flavour, which she'd also made. As I let it melt on my tongue, my head reeling with endorphins, I looked at Marion in wonder.

"You're some sort of genius, I think, Marion. Like a food scientist. How do you do all this?"

"I dunno; just look up the recipes and then add little bits here and there."

"But this food is incredible, people would pay good money for this."

"You need qualifications," she said sadly. "Restaurants would never hire me, and even if they did it'd be years before I'd be able to do up my own menus."

"Well," I said, wagging a spoonful of cheesecake in the air, "the world needs to taste this dessert. It's wasted on the likes of me."

"No it's not," she said, beaming.

I did the washing-up. There was enough food left over for me to have another banquet tomorrow. She must have spent a fortune on it all and had hardly eaten a morsel herself. I would break out the gin later on by way of recompense. Better still, I would let her choose what film we'd watch. She could go through my entire DVD collection and pick whichever one she wanted. In a previous life those DVDs had been filed by category, year and genre in the myriad shelves at home. Now they were piled high against the wall like a giant game of Jenga.

"I hardly know any of these," she said, running her finger down the pile which mostly consisted of Asian horror.

"Try over there," I said, pointing to my 1990s Hollywood blockbusters.

"Oh, I love *Independence Day*, let's watch that!"

It wasn't a terrible choice. *Independence Day* was a serviceable action adventure film with a few classic scenes and one-liners from the always entertaining Will Smith. It would be better to watch *The Raid* on my own, anyway. I opened the gin and poured us both a treble. "It's slimming," I said when she baulked at the brimming glass.

"Will you not sit beside me?" she said coyly after I'd drawn the curtains and turned off the lights.

I duly got up and sat beside her. She smiled happily and did that tapping thing with her feet again. Maybe she was hoping to return to Kansas.

I pressed play and the film began.

"I love Will Smith," she whispered in the darkness. "Have you seen that one where he has a dog?"

I had seen *I Am Legend*, but I'd never heard anyone describe it as the one where Will Smith has a dog. Five minutes into the film, the questions and observations continued.

"Do you remember *The Fresh Prince of Bel Air?*"

"Carlton's dance was brilliant."

"Why doesn't Ireland have an Independence Day?"

"Is Ireland independent?"

"God, imagine if New York really was blown up."

"Have you been to America?"

"Why are aliens always trying to kill us?"

"Oh wait, E.T. He was nice."

These general queries were accompanied by visceral reactions to the on-screen action, gasps and squeals as Will, Bill Pullman and Jeff Goldblum saved the planet from destruction. During one of the more dramatic sequences she grabbed me by the arm as if I could rescue her from the clutches of the dastardly invaders. I didn't care. I was drunk, really drunk. The bottle of gin was nearly empty and I couldn't remember Marion asking for a top-up. It was a nice drunk. I'd curled myself into my corner of the couch and lay there, gazing at the screen contentedly. And although initially Marion's constant chattering was mildly irritating, it was comforting to have someone there. I never had company when I felt like this, usually sank deeper into depression the drunker I got. But the sound of her voice and the shifting of her weight on the small couch was soothing. I was safe tonight, no harm would come to me, no matter how much I drank.

The film ended and the lights came on. I blinked against them in confusion, annoyed that my reverie had been disturbed.

"Look at you there," she said, gazing down at me.

"Will we watch another film?" I suggested, eager to return to the darkness.

"I don't really want to," she said, still standing over me, moving from one foot to the other.

"Put on some music," I instructed, burrowing my face into the corner of the couch.

"Aidan," she said pleadingly.

I sat up with a start, assessing my level of inebriation. I knew right from wrong, up from down, I was okay. So, when she held out her hand I took it and allowed her to lead me to my bedroom. It was dark there, dark and cosy. We lay on the bed and kissed for a while. It was fine, relaxing; I wasn't thinking about where it was going or what I might need to do. I moved my hands around her body for a while, found her tits and gave them a squeeze. She took them out and I sucked on them. Then I felt her hands on my belt buckle and inside my pants. I was hard. Happy and hard.

"Don't look," she said, pushing me away and sitting on the edge of the bed. I couldn't look, I couldn't even see.

When she returned there was a complete absence of clothes. I got harder. Feeling reckless and free, I slung off my jumper, wriggled out of my jeans and kicked my runners to the floor. I was a wild man. She lay flat on her back in the middle of the bed. I clambered on top of her and continued to kiss her and feel her tits.

"Aidan, come on," she said, a touch of desperation in her voice.

I didn't know what to do or where to go. In porn it was always bright, the girls were thin and everything was clearly signposted. I moved my hand down to her thighs and then felt my way upwards. Eventually I chanced upon something hairy and wet, my destination; but when I tried to position myself for entry I found that my belly, matched with her belly, made it awkward. I jabbed at the general area a couple of times and felt its heat, but I was like a blind snooker player going for a 147. Frustrated by my efforts Marion took hold of me, pushed my legs closer together, my arse lower down and my torso against hers, then grabbed my cock and began guiding it towards its intended target.

Contact was made. I was on the periphery, almost there. Marion was still trying to position me this way and that, but the feel of flesh on flesh, the touch of her hand and the wildness in me all coalesced into one surge of ecstasy and I came: spectacularly, prematurely. There had been no penetration, no insertion, but my poor, lonely, sex-deprived body hadn't needed it. All it had taken was the gentle caress of another, to be held and loved, valued and cared for. I remained on top of her, recovering from my exertions as the wildness ebbed away from me, while she stroked my hair and softly kissed my ear. And then I got up to go for a piss.

*

Even in my sleep I was aware of what I'd done, the predicament I'd placed myself in. I could feel her weight in the bed, her warmth, and made sure not to stray onto her side. As light streamed in through the curtains and the town stirred to life, she got up and left the room and for a brief minute I thought I was free, that she'd gone. But she returned, slid back under the covers and snuggled up towards me. I turned my back on her and faced the wall. I would wait her out, feign sleep until she left, no matter how long it took. It was no use. She was determined to wait it out too. Every time I awoke I felt that weight, that now stifling heat. I needed to piss but I wasn't getting up; that would mean having to face her, having to acknowledge her presence. I huffed and puffed in annoyance, kicked my legs in frustration and she remained stoically in place, as immovable and unyielding as a monolith. When her phone rang and she began a long and detailed conversation with Michelle, I officially gave up.

"Yeah, he's here beside me," she said.

"Still asleep."

"Wouldn't you like to know!"

"I made us dinner and then we watched a film."

"I'm not telling you, Michelle."

"No."

"Stop it, no!"

I couldn't take it any more. I lurched out of the bed, and in one fluid movement vaulted to my feet and out the door. Naked, I took a dirty pair of tracksuit bottoms and a hoodie from the wash basket, had my piss and retreated to the living-room. I wasn't having this, having her take over, talking about me on the phone while I pretended to be asleep. She'd taken advantage of me, in my fragile state, and was now lording it over me. I'd show her. The bottle of gin was where I'd left it, on the floor beside the couch. There was still a third remaining. She would see the real Aidan Collins now. I took a slug straight from the bottle, and turned on the telly. MTV Rocks were doing an 80s metal week: Megadeth, Slayer, Metallica,

Iron Maiden - angry, insular, inhospitable music. I'd barely got comfortable when she came down. She was wearing my dressing gown. This infuriated me further. I turned up the television.

"Hey," she said gently, smiling.

I moved my head a fraction of a millimetre in her direction.

She sat on the edge of the couch in a defensive position while I sullenly stared at the screen.

"Are you hungry?" she asked.

I grunted in the negative and took another hit of the gin. It stung.

"Is that Motorhead?" she asked, but the airiness had left her voice. She knew what was happening, had probably experienced it before. A voice told me to stop being such a bastard, to be nice to her and treat her as I'd want to be treated myself. I silenced the voice with another gulp of alcohol.

"Well," she said, getting to her feet, "there's enough food in the fridge for your dinner later. It's better if you reheat it in the oven than the microwave; about 180 degrees for ten minutes, okay?"

She bent down and kissed me on the cheek. "Talk later?"

I focused on the television, on Bruce Dickinson and Iron Maiden, until she left me be. She went out into the hall and I heard the front door close. Relief washed all over me, and then humiliation and self-loathing. Now that she was gone I could take stock of what had happened; my first real sexual experience, the first time I'd orgasmed in the presence of another. I couldn't bear to think about it. Hot shame prickled down my spine as unwanted memories played out in my mind. I hadn't even been able to seal the deal, had fumbled my way here and there before exploding like a teenager. The sounds, the smells, the mania which had overtaken me, made me shudder. Who was that person, and how had he made me do what I'd done?

This was why I was better off drinking alone. My real shame, however, was reserved for the morning and how I'd behaved towards her. It wasn't her fault I'd got drunk and done something I'd regretted. She'd been nothing but kind to me. Whatever anger I felt should have been directed inwards, not at her. Yet amidst these feelings of anger and remorse was something else, something strange: a sexual urge, a newly-woken desire. I still didn't fancy her, but if she had been here now I would have brought her back up to the bedroom and fucked her properly, angrily, and with some of that wildness I'd unleashed just a few hours previous. Confused, sad and upset, I tackled the gin with renewed gusto and cranked up the television as loud as it would go.

*

She texted me that evening, of course she did. I'd finished the gin and had moved on to the cheap vodka I kept for emergencies; I was in the mood for an argument, so her timing was perfect.

Got over your grump? she asked.

What grump? I replied.

YOUR grump!!!!

I'm not grump. I wrote, aware, even in my inebriated state, that that made no sense.

YOU ARE!!!!

This was how text conversations went with her. Usually I found these chats trite but the booze had dulled my senses enough to make them interesting.

Fuck off. I wrote, chuckling away at my caddish behaviour.

There was a lengthy delay, ten minutes or more, very unlike her. Until this reply came.

Why are you being like this? I thought you were different.

I'm the same.

Two sad face emojis and a crying emoji were my reward. I responded with the eye-roll emoji.

Fuck you, Aidan.

Okay.

Do you even remember last night?

No.

Another crying emoji and a broken heart one.

I left the phone to one side then. I was tired, I'd been drinking all day. And I continued to drink, destructively, in a way I hadn't done for a long time. I embraced the darkness and welcomed the hate. The vodka made me belligerent and rowdy. I may have started shouting obscenities to myself, growled and groused like one of those ancient alcoholics who lie bearded and filthy in laneways and alleys. The drink gave me power, erased my shortcomings, my failures. I was a champion, but even champions need their rest. So I had a little nap on the couch. Then I got up, still angry, still triumphant, and took out the leftover duck and spuds.

What had she said - reheat it in the oven? Whoever heard of such a thing? I'd show her. I put it in my new microwave, vegetables and all, and when it had been nuked, when the duck and potatoes were like molten lava, I sat on the couch and crammed this elegantly prepared food into my mouth like a spiteful Neanderthal, still staring at the screen, at the 80s metal which had been blaring out since morning. However, I'd been long enough at this game to know that you can never escape reality, you can never outrun it. You can try, and lord knows I had, but eventually it sidles up beside you, barely out of breath, grinning at you and the futility of your efforts.

Reality returned on the third day. I'd been drinking steadily since Marion's departure. It had been a torrid time. I'd committed all seven mortal sins and broken the Ten Commandments. There'd been singing and dancing, roaring and shouting, tears and vomit, regret and remorse, defiance and bravado, until finally I retreated to my bed, to the bed I hadn't gone near since she'd left. Accepting my fate, already sweating and shivering, the first rattlings of anxiety fluttering in my chest, I grabbed onto whatever sleep I was offered, knowing there was nothing but badness ahead, nothing but misery and suffering.

When the badness came it was accompanied by something new, something I'd never experienced before. I'd felt like death on countless occasions, been so sick I thought I was going to die on hundreds more, but I'd never actively wanted to die. When I opened my eyes the familiar nausea, headaches, and paranoia washed over me, but they were accompanied by an unexplored anguish, a dark void. I lay in my bed, helpless, as this darkness enveloped me. It spread all over me like a filthy, poisonous virus, crawling into my veins, clawing at my chest, pulling and poking me like an animal searching for the last shred of meat on a dried carcass.

I cried for a while.

Then I began to punch myself in the head, sitting up, balling my fists and pounding my forehead, the top of my skull, the nape of my neck, my face, my eyes, my mouth. When I'd finished doing that I tore at the flesh on my face, digging my fingers in as I tried to rip the skin clean off. I bashed my head against the wall, hard. I scratched at the skin on my thighs until I bled and then, finally realising what I wanted to do, I went to the kitchen and took out the sharpest knife I could find. I walked back to the bedroom and sat down again, the knife firmly gripped in my right hand. Holding it over my left wrist I sneered at myself, at this wretched fuck and his feeble attempts to resolve his problems.

How obvious. What a fucking baby. Get over yourself.

That voice surprised me. It had never been this hostile before, I'd always been able to reason with it. But now it was merciless.

Suicide? Really? You're just hungover, feeling a bit sad 'cos you couldn't fuck the fat girl. What a loser.

I shouted out in annoyance, pressed my hands against my ears and curled up in the foetal position.

Why don't you start crying again, little baba? That's always a good show. Lie in bed, have a good fucking whinge and then go back to drinking. Oh, and while you're at it, put the knife away; we both know you haven't the balls to do that.

I chucked the knife across the room like a stroppy teenager. The voice was right: I hadn't the balls to do it. I was a coward, a feeble, miserable coward. I couldn't fuck Marion, I couldn't do anything. I deserved to die, but unless someone did it for me I would just have to soldier on. I had nothing to live for, no future. The rent allowance had been the last great victory in my life. What else was there for me to conquer? I could have called Marion, apologised and made amends but I didn't even like her, only tolerated her because she liked me. My parents, Mrs. M and Sally, none of them mattered, they wouldn't miss me and I wouldn't miss them.

Sonia? She was only using me to make herself feel better, only called to watch E! or whatever the fuck it was called. Gerard had abandoned me as soon as he'd found a woman. The cat, Gráinne. That made me feel bad. She had no one to care for her. If I didn't feed her and clear out her litter tray she'd be relying on Gerard for her meals, and he couldn't be relied upon. Gráinne would be out on her own, forced to live with the street cats, and although she acted tough I knew she wasn't cut out for that world. So, for her sake I decided to carry on, with the knowledge that should things take a wrong turn the knife was always there in the drawer, waiting for me.

Sick to my core, I got up out of bed for the sole purpose of feeding the cat, but she was nowhere to be seen. At some point some during the past three days she had surveyed the scene and declared herself tired of my shit. I couldn't blame her. I was living like a tramp, decomposing in my own dirt. I cleared away all the cans and bottles, filling a recycling bag, and washed up the glasses and plates. Then, for the first time since moving in, I took out the vacuum cleaner and gave the place a thorough cleaning. I utilised the mop and bucket for the first time too, but not before cleaning the worktops in the kitchen, my humble coffee table and the television stand. After that I did the bathroom and bedroom, throwing the sinful sheets into the washing machine, opened all the windows and carried the rubbish outside. It took me the best part of two hours but I felt better afterwards. I wasn't able to cleanse my soul but I could at least make my living quarters more hospitable.

If I could only live like this all the time, run a tight ship, eat well and fill my days with meaningful tasks, there may have been hope for me; but no sooner had I sat down in my shiny new surroundings than the first pang of desire hit me. I wanted a drink. I *really* wanted a drink. More than anything in the world, I wanted a drink. I checked the fridge: nothing left. None in the press either. I had gone through my entire stash. There was enough money in my wallet for more but, still riding the high of my clean-up session, I decided that no, I would not go and buy alcohol, I would show some restraint.

That restraint continued into the next day. I walked round the supermarket, got my few bits and strode past the drinks section with barely a glance. I was depriving myself, taking on a new challenge and it felt good. There was a price to pay physically, of course. The shakes came first. They were bemusing, I found them ridiculous. The sweating and the nausea were far from funny. Nor was the anxiety. It seemed terribly unfair. The one benefit was that I was too sick to go out and get booze. Instead I lay on the couch, a vomit-bucket beside me, and played on the Xbox. I had a new game: *Fallout: New Vegas*, bought with my rent allowance. It was a role-playing game, but in my itchy, twitchy state I couldn't follow the story and the violence was too much, it made me tearful, emotional.

I turned it off and put on the telly instead, but I couldn't settle on a channel. Music irritated me even more, and a book was simply out of the question. I sensed something terrible was in the offing as I dragged the duvet down from the bedroom and huddled up on the couch, but that terrible thing never came. It got a bit weird for a while; the room spun, the walls shook and I developed a burning pain in my lower back. There were voices, screaming demonic voices - although that could have been the neighbours - insects on the floor, cobwebs in my hair and a recurring sense of weightlessness, but as detoxifications went it wasn't nearly as bad as I'd expected.

Indeed, it would have been entirely uneventful if *she* hadn't appeared. She'd never gone away, of course, never left my thoughts, but I'd always managed to push her to one side, to keep her at bay through alcohol, drugs, whatever it took. Now I was exposed, and she knew it, she'd been waiting for this moment. It was just before dawn when she appeared. I awoke to see her in the middle of the room staring at me, innocent and chaste in her wedding dress. No, not her wedding dress, she was too young. Her communion dress. She had accessories too: frilly socks and an ornate headdress which fitted her perfectly. She wore make-up, dark eye-liner and deep red lipstick, but it had been ruined. The eye-liner had run and streaked down her cheeks, chased there by her tears. The lipstick was smeared halfway across her chin, widening her mouth into a sly, ugly grin.

She wasn't ugly, though, she could never be ugly. That was why they had taken her, why they wanted her. She lifted her dress, exposing herself to me, her vagina bloody and scarred. Once I'd had a good look, she turned and bent over; more blood, more scars. Her dress remained white, despite her wounds. Lastly, she pulled down the front of her dress. There were bite-marks all along her torso, not playful nibbles but deep sores. She turned, showing me the bruises which coloured her ribs, back and shoulders. There were abrasions on her neck and dozens of blisters, as if lit cigarettes had been pressed into her flesh. On cue she turned her arms outwards so I could see her wrists, the criss-cross designs of self-harm, the deeper, still healing wounds which signified more than a cry for help. I thought that was all, that she'd only come to show me her sores, but there was more. She spoke, her voice flat, with no hint of vengeance or judgement.

"This is what they did to me," she said. "Look at what they did."

I reached out to touch her but she backed away.

"No, don't," she said.

An apology formed in my throat but when I tried to speak, nothing came out.

"You could have stopped it, you know. They'd only started then. You could have saved me. It wouldn't have been so bad if they'd stopped then. Why didn't you save me? Why didn't you?"

I croaked my remorse, tried to make her see how sorry I was.

"There'd only been one of them by then, the first guy, that big fat fucker who sweated and snorted like a pig," she continued. "He was small, though, it only hurt a little. He wasn't twisted like the others, he just wanted to fuck me and be done with it."

I shook my head, tried to close my eyes, but she had me now.

"It was the last guy who really fucked me up. He waited until the others had finished so he could take his time. And he hurt me in every way you can imagine. It got so bad the others just left. They couldn't watch. It's his eyes I remember the most. They were empty, like the eyes of a dead person. I passed out after a while, the pain was too much to take. When I woke up he was still fucking me, monotonously, with no expression on his face. Then he put me on my front and did it in my bottom. I screamed in protest. He knew I was awake then; it only spurred him on."

Gasping, I toppled off the couch trying to reach her, to hold her, to kiss her feet, anything to express my devotion. She evaded my touch and continued her story.

"I thought it would be over after he came, but he was only getting going then. I tried reasoning with him, told him I'd never say a word about what happened. He punched me in the face, then in the stomach and all over. He burned me with fags, bit me until I bled and then whipped me with his belt buckle. He fucked me in my mouth while he choked me, he pissed on me and then, as the sun came up and the room began to brighten, he wrapped me up in the blankets, smiled, and said, 'See you later, kiddo.'"

My breath began to falter, my lungs began to burn. I made one final lunge towards her, but this time she was gone. When I finally found my voice, the only sound I heard was my own screams punctuating the silent, empty room.

28

AFTER I HAD COMPLETED MY detox and was free of all contaminants, the first thing I did was call Marion. She'd been texting on and off during my ablutions, my garbled replies enraging her yet further. Now I was ready to answer for my sins.

"Hello?" she said haughtily.

"Hi, it's me."

"Oh, talking to me again now?"

"Yeah," I said.

"Well, what do you want?"

"I wanted to apologise."

"Oh," she said, softer.

"That wasn't right, what I did. There's no way anyone should treat a person like that."

Her breath laboured as she listened.

"I'm selfish, inconsiderate and weak, no better than that young lad of the Laceys and his friends. You didn't deserve that. You're kind, caring and thoughtful and have so much to give. All I did was take; I took what I wanted and then discarded you as if you were nothing. But I'm nothing, not you. Always remember that. You are someone, Marion, and you can live any kind of life you want."

There was a pause while she waited to see if I was finished. I was.

"Thank you, Aidan," she said quietly.

"I mean it, Marion."

"Thank you," she said again.

"Whatever you do with your life, don't let anyone ever put you down. You're worth a million of them, of anyone."

"Aidan, stop it," she said, now bashful.

"Just remember that. You deserve to be happy."

"So do you, Aidan."

We fell silent. I'd wanted to apologise and then say goodbye, that was all. But it felt like that wasn't enough. I owed her something, a meeting, another date. I didn't want that though, I didn't want to lead her on or use her. I had to be strong, or at least as strong as I could be.

"When can I see you?" she asked.

"I'm sorry, Marion, I don't think that's a good idea."

"Just as friends."

She almost had me. Maybe we could just be friends. But all it would take was another night of drunkenness and the wildness would come back.

"Aidan . . ." she said tearfully.

"No, Marion. I'm no good. Look after yourself, okay?"

"Okay."

I hung up and took a deep breath. There were more calls to make.

The next call went to my father. I enquired after Mrs. M, said that he could call in whenever he wanted and pretended to be interested when he started telling me about their new house. Then I called the nursing home. It wasn't hard to get an appointment; my mother's schedule was pretty light. That evening Sonia called up and we watched *Keeping up with the Kardashians*, *My 600 lb Life*, and *90 Day Fiancée*. She didn't utter a single word during any of them, rising only to run to the toilet during the ad breaks. In truth she was terrible company; she took over the television, barely spoke to me and ate all my goodies. But having a woman like that in my apartment, even being associated with her, was recompense enough.

At 10 p.m. she checked the TV guide, declared there was nothing else worth watching and went home, leaving me to clear away the cups of tea and half-eaten cake I'd opened on her behalf. After I'd done that, I fantasised about her for a while. I imagined her coming up one afternoon and announcing that her washing machine was broken. She'd ask if she could use mine and then strip off, casually placing the clothes she'd been wearing into the machine, and take a seat on the couch.

"Aren't your clothes dirty too?" she'd ask.

"I suppose they are," I'd reply, confident and cocksure.

In my fantasy she'd like my tubby body, my flabby thighs and wobbly arse. She'd find it manly. And when I'd walk over to her, fully erect, she'd be ready for me.

That was as far as the fantasy went. I reverted to porn thereafter, searched 'blonde', 'petite', 'small breasts', anything which reminded me of her, and then imagined it was me banging her in the clip - even though the banger was invariably a chiselled African-American with a totem pole for a penis. That helped me relax, and when I went to bed I slept deep and long, nary an erotic dream to disturb me.

*

They were happy to see me at the nursing home. Even though I hadn't visited my mother in almost a year, there was no judgement. She was in the same room, propped up in bed, staring listlessly out the window. Her condition had worsened, the muscles on her face now drooped markedly and her skin was grey and waxy. Beneath her nightie I could see the long pale shapes of her arms, brittle and withered. Her hair had thinned and her eyes had sunk further into their sockets. According to my father, she had broken her silence on a handful of occasions since those early weeks: to complain about a breeze, to refuse food, and to ask him to leave.

He had continued the pretence, coming twice a week, sitting with her for an hour, doing his best to assuage his guilty conscience. Sally hadn't returned; she was probably saving herself for the funeral. The nurse said my mother had a couple of other regular visitors, some neighbours, women from the community centre, but she wasn't exactly a welcoming host.

"If you need anything, just shout," the nurse said, leaving us alone.

I sat in the hard chair by the side of the bed. My mother continued to stare out the window impassively. A couple of minutes passed in silence. She shot a glance at the door.

"It's just me," I said.

A thought crossed my mind: maybe she'd been awaiting my arrival. Maybe I could restore her, solve the puzzle and bring her back to life.

"I moved out, you know, got my own place."

No response.

"Can you hear me?" I asked, looking her straight in the eyes. A bit of drool pooled in the pocket of her lower lip, spilled over and began slowly descending towards her chest. I got a tissue and wiped it away. Then I stood at the end of the bed, in front of the window, so she couldn't look out. But she still wore that same thousand-yard stare.

"Okay, we can just sit and chill out. I don't mind."

Sitting in silence isn't easy but she was great at it, better than any of those Buddhist monks.

"Will I turn on the telly?" I asked, picking up the remote.

She whimpered in protest.

"So you can hear me. Why don't you want the telly on? You used to love the telly."

My guess was that someone had put it on one day and then left her on her own, unable to switch over. It was all well and good watching telly, but when your favourite show ended you wanted to see what else was on, not sit through another eight hours of arbitrary programming.

"No telly, then."

I checked the time. I'd been here ten minutes. It was only right to put in at least an hour, even if I'd already completed my objective. As I sat there beside the woman who had given birth to me, watching her slowly ebb away, I felt nothing. The guilt I'd felt for contributing to her demise had faded and there was no sadness, no remorse, none of the emotions one associates with the loss of a loved one. I didn't take any pleasure in her suffering, but I didn't pity her either. There was just nothing. She could have been anyone.

My hope had been that the sight of her, wizened and decaying, would spark something in my core, revive a primal bond that only a mother and son can share. But that bond, if it had ever existed, remained soundly asleep, as unresponsive as the sad figure before me. I knew then this would be the last time we would see one another, that I wouldn't be coming back. We had reached the end, me and her. There was nothing more to say. Out of respect I stayed for the full hour, thinking about nothing, just passing the time. And when the clock struck twelve, I got to my feet and announced my departure.

"I'm off now, Mam," I said.

I waited a moment, just to see if there was a response, then gave her a gentle kiss on the cheek.

"Bye, then."

There was no need to turn back for one final look. That picture wouldn't change. She had made her bed and was determined to lie in it until the end. As I walked through the home, pausing to pet the two golden retrievers who roamed the premises, thanking the staff for their work, I felt a gentle unburdening on my shoulders, as if someone had lifted a light knapsack from my person and offered to carry my load for a while.

29

For the first time in my life, I was taking back a measure of control. I had given up the drink and managed to stay off it for over a month. I was settled in the apartment and living comfortably. My anxiety still loomed in the background, waiting to strike at any given moment, but I hadn't had a bad attack in weeks. I was depressed, but not so much that I couldn't function. Best of all, I was getting outside a lot. People always said that exercise and fresh air were the best medicine for ailing mental health. That had sounded like hokum to me, new-age nonsense spouted by tree-hugging vegans and beardies. How wrong I'd been. It was the antidote to my illness, the elixir I'd been searching for all my life.

Every morning, after a bowl of porridge with bananas and blueberries, I would take the first of three walks. I waited till 9.30 a.m., when the kids had been dropped off at school and the workers were in their offices, and then headed out; doing a circuit of the river - walking along the north quayside, crossing the New Bridge to the south quays and then looping back around. That was my favourite walk, the air was new and invigorating, the day full of possibilities. I met people on these walks, usually older types or mothers with small children. I was on nodding terms with some, even exchanged the odd "Hello, how are you? Lovely day, isn't it?" with one or two. And by the time I came back into town to the apartment, I was in fine form.

Yet I discovered that like all stimulants and mood-enhancers, the buzz I got from exercising faded quickly. I would busy myself with some household chores, maybe treat myself to a mid-morning wank, but by afternoon the clouds were descending again. Enter walk two. This one brought me to the supermarket and my daily browse round the shops. The record store was on the way, but I tried to go in there only twice a week, keeping it as a treat. Mostly I just did my grocery shopping and then took the long way home, round the banks of the river. That took me up to approximately 3 p.m. and the most dangerous part of my day.

Now I had three hours to kill until dinner, three hours when town got very busy and going outside was to be avoided if possible. I used this time wisely, making it my main gaming time of the day. If I could get to 5 p.m. without any major incidents, without buckling under the pressure and running down for a feed of cans, I was fine. I'd make my dinner, using my limited skills to fashion a curry, spaghetti bolognese, spuds and goujons, and then get ready for the third walk. This was a big one, the longest walk of all. It generally took an hour-and-a-half, maybe longer, as I left the city limits and walked through the well-off parts of town on the North Circular road.

It was quiet there, all gated properties, salubrious estates. You could see why those houses went for so much on the market; you got all the benefits of city living but none of the noise, overcrowding or air pollution. Sometimes I walked so far I left even the suburbs behind, straying into the first layers of countryside, the open fields and farmlands of rural Ireland. I'd be knackered then, and eventually, no matter how far I walked, I had to go home, back to the hovel, to the three small rooms which contained the worldly possessions of Aidan Collins.

I saw people during these walks too, but, unlike my morning companions, I didn't welcome their presence. Because these people reminded me of myself. They would be walking by the river as I came back into town, down O'Connell Street as I hurried towards my building, aimlessly wandering about. They were all men. All solitary figures. They weren't winos or vagrants, just guys like me: single men walking the streets at night, with nowhere to go and nothing to do. Their presence unnerved me, reminded me of who I was. Where had they come from? How had they got here? Did they walk to stave off depression, alcoholism? When they'd finished walking, where did they go? Back to empty apartments like mine, to shabby furniture, draughty bedrooms and noisy neighbours? It was all too close to home. I didn't want to be like them, to be one of those guys, but I was, and that was what I hated most about seeing them.

It was usually after 8 p.m. by the time I got back. My rule was 'no television until 9 p.m.' So I did the washing-up, went online for a bit and then settled in for a couple of hours of whatever shows I was currently stuck in. By 11.30 p.m. I was ready for bed. That last half-hour of the day, the realisation I'd made it to the end unscathed, was the best of all. I'd almost feel content as I lay there on the couch, utterly relaxed, a sense of satisfaction at the life I'd made for myself. It wasn't glamorous, and by the standards of your average individual it was an empty, meaningless existence, but I'd been at the very bottom and from where I stood right now, it felt like the top of the world.

Not only did my new lifestyle improve my wellbeing, it also helped me lose weight. I had lost weight before during my diazepam phase, but this was different; I was glowing now. I didn't need a scales to tell me I'd become thinner, the answer was there in my clothes: my jeans fell off me, my hoodies were like muu-muus. I had to buy new trousers, new T-shirts, new underwear, the lot. With this came a modicum of self-respect. I still walked along the street with my head down, still felt awkward and embarrassed whenever I was within five feet of an attractive person, but I could admit I wasn't as repugnant as before.

Sonia noticed it too. We had settled into our own little routine. She would come up two afternoons a week (Tuesdays and Thursdays) and three evenings (Mondays, Wednesdays, and Fridays) when her son was with his grandparents. She would take command of the remote control and plough through her recordings while I browsed the internet. I knew she was using me for my television, but I didn't care. In a sign of my growing confidence, I told her to make her own tea when, for the umpteenth time, she drowsily told me to stick the kettle on during an ad break. She looked at me in surprise, and for a dreadful moment I thought she was going to get up and leave. Instead she grinned knowingly and did as she was told. You had to take a firm hand with these types of women every now and again. Although I still let her open the good biscuits.

I'd been off the drink a whole two months before she twigged that something was different.

"Did you get a haircut?" she asked me one afternoon as we sat through another turgid episode of *The Real Housewives of New Jersey*.

"No."

"There's something off with you," she said, arching a sly eyebrow.

"No there isn't," I said, enjoying her gaze.

"There is! What have you done, Aidan? Are you seeing that girl again? What was her name? Ella Louise?"

"No, I'm not," I said dismissively. This wasn't the time to be talking about Marion.

"Well, there's something up," Sonia said. "I'm keeping an eye on you, Aidan Collins."

The ads ended and so did our conversation, but I flushed happily as she returned to the TV. I couldn't be so easily disregarded any more. I was no longer the bumbly fool in the apartment upstairs, there was something about me now, something undefinable. I needed to work on this mysterious edge, get her wondering about me more often. And I needed to make her stop mentioning Marion. That episode belonged to my past life. I'd moved up in the world now.

She wasn't the only one to remark on my appearance. I'd reduced my father's visits to a couple of hours on the first Monday of every month. He'd bring me dinners, we'd sit and chat, make some small talk, and then he'd start exploring the confines of the flat, looking for things to fix, things to break so he could fix them. His latest fascination was an outbreak of mould on the ceiling. First, he'd offered to paint it, then he'd suggested checking the pipes, and recently he'd said he knew a guy who could strip back the plaster and improve the heat retention in the room by 25%, or something like that. But I'd managed to keep him at arm's length. I took the same approach when he began probing me with questions, little queries about my life, my day-to-day existence, my plans for the future. He was a terrible inquisitor, though, displaying all the subtlety of an elephant in a tutu as he absent-mindedly pulled at his sideburns and asked me if I'd given any more thought to becoming a computer programmer, if there were any nice women in the building or whether I fancied going for a spin some day, with me as the driver.

I reckoned Beatrice armed him with a list of questions before he left the house, and he was dutifully working his way through them to keep her off his back. So, when I responded to one of his suggestions not just in the affirmative but with a definite plan, he seemed totally taken aback. They had moved into their new home in Barnduff a couple of months prior, and I'd been invited out numerous times already. The thought of going there, of seeing the little life they'd built together repelled me. I wanted no part of it. But after drawing a line under my relationship with my mother, I was keen to do likewise with them. So when Dad lazily stretched out on the couch and pretended to remember that he and Beatrice were free on Sunday and would love to have me over for dinner, I said, "Yeah, why not? Sounds good."

"What? Really?" he said.

"Yeah. Will you collect me? What time do ye usually have dinner at?"

"Jesus, I dunno."

He began fumbling for his phone, expecting to find the answers in there.

"Sure, ring me tomorrow when you know," I said.

"Yes. Yes, I will," he said, regaining his composure. "It'll be great to have you out, Aidan. We're only five minutes from the beach. We can go for a walk after dinner, there's a cliff-side trail, you'd love it, the views are amazing."

"Okay, Dad."

"We'll have roast chicken, stuffed."

"That sounds good, Dad."

He got so excited he forgot all about the mould on the ceiling, leaving the tin of paint and the roller behind him. I suppose he couldn't wait to go back and tell Beatrice, have his belly rubbed, prostate milked, or whatever perverted shit they were into. It turned out they had dinner at two on a Sunday, which was as good a time as any. Dad collected me at noon and chatted excitedly on the drive out to their love shack. The house was everything I'd expected from Beatrice. Although small and compact, it had oodles of charm. Originally whitewashed to protect it from the spray of the ocean, she, in her infinite wisdom, had painted it a pale blue with a navy trim. All the rooms - because yes, I got a full tour - were light and airy, elegantly designed yet homely and comfortable, none more so than the sun-room which looked out onto the expansive garden and the garage which the lady of the manor had converted into an art studio. My father seemed utterly content here, relaxed and at ease in a way I'd never seen him at home. Then again, he didn't have the stalking presence of my mother to deal with; in her stead was the attentive and affectionate Mrs. M, who catered for his every need and treated him with kindness and care. He had it made.

Beatrice instructed us to remain in the living-room while she put the finishing touches to the dinner. There was Premier League football on the television.

"We have all the channels," Dad announced proudly.

They had a three-piece suite with extendable footrests. He flipped his out with a grin.

"Go on, do it. It's comfy," he said.

"No, I'm fine."

I sat awkwardly on the edge of the sofa, wondering if I was in Beatrice's spot and if they snuggled up here in the evenings.

"It's a nice house, Dad," I said, noting Sally's and my communion and confirmation photos on the wall - the solo shots obviously, there was no trace of my mother. There were also pictures of Beatrice's family, her sisters and nephews. They'd created a perfect little hideaway, covered all bases.

"What would you like to drink, Aidan?" asked Beatrice, appearing at the open plan doors.

"Just water, thanks."

"Sparkling or still?"

"I don't mind."

She returned moments later with a bottle of water taken straight from the fridge. What was this madness? Not only had my father moved house, he'd moved at least three rungs up the social ladder. Beatrice left us on our own again, ruffling Dad's hair as she went back to the kitchen. He wiggled his toes in appreciation.

"I went to see Mam," I said.

He tensed.

"Yes, the nurses said."

"Are you still going?" I asked.

"Yes," he said.

"How long do you think she has left?"

"Ah, Aidan," he said, as if her death was unthinkable.

"I don't think I'll go back."

"That's fine, go whenever you can. I'll be going every Wednesday and Saturday, if you ever want to come."

Beatrice's head appeared at the door again.

"Come on, lads," she said sweetly. She looked as if she'd been at a health spa all day, not slaving over pots and stoves.

"Would you like a glass of wine with yours, Aidan?" she asked as I waited to see where I'd be seated. They had decided to assign me the head of the table, with them at either side; the father, the son and the holy ghost.

"I won't, thanks. I'm actually off the drink."

"Are you, Aidan?" Dad asked, encouragement pouring out of him.

"Yeah."

"See, Tom, didn't I tell you?" Beatrice said.

"What?" I asked.

"I told him you looked different, more grown-up. I thought you were after getting yourself a girlfriend."

"Have you, Aidan?" asked Dad expectantly.

"No, I'm just off the drink."

"Well, that's good enough for anyone. Well done, son."

I felt a surge of pride. I *had* done well. It wasn't easy giving up the drink, and I deserved a little bit of praise. Although when I saw Beatrice pouring out a glass of white wine for herself, it took all my power not to snatch the bottle out of her hand and neck the whole lot.

Needless to say, the dinner was a delight. Roast stuffed chicken with both roast and mashed potatoes, roast parsnips, carrots and peas, Yorkshire puddings, croquettes and lashings of gravy. It was the first decent meal I'd had since Marion's visit, and it struck me how sobriety enhanced one's taste buds. I savoured every morsel, barely pausing for breath as a dessert of chocolate fudge cake with ice-cream swiftly followed. We retired to the living-room for tea and coffee then, Dad in his armchair by the telly, me on the couch and Beatrice on the chair opposite.

"That was amazing, Bee," said Dad.

"It was," I echoed.

Out of nowhere an unwelcome image entered my mind: Dad bending Beatrice over the couch and doing her from behind. I glanced over at him uncomfortably, he was smiling away to himself, quietly exhorting some footballer to 'hit it first time'. Beatrice was reading the Sunday papers. There was no hint of a sexual atmosphere, but now that the thought had come into my head I couldn't get rid of it. Was she the dominant kind? I bet she was. I bet she let Dad have his fun at the start before turning the tables on him and assuming command. She probably straddled him in that godforsaken chair of his and slapped him round his sweating face while shouting obscenities at him.

Maybe if she rode him hard enough he'd have a heart attack, then I could move in here and take over. Because that's what this was really about. I was jealous. I'd always had a thing for Mrs. M, even as a child, before I knew what having a 'thing' for someone meant. I wanted to be around her, to have her hold me, to look after me. She'd been absent for much of my adult years, but when she'd returned as I lay on my sickbed those feelings had come flooding back - accompanied by new adult feelings. She looked well for her age. There'd been no children, no marriage, none of the events which traditionally put years on women. Then there was my father, almost ten years older, thirty years of marriage behind him and ready to go again with a new and improved love interest. It knocked me sick. What did she see in him, and how come I hadn't managed to inherit any of it?

The match ended and my father stretched out.

"Will we go for a walk on the beach?" he asked hopefully.

"You two go," said Beatrice.

Or let him go on his own and I'll show you what the young Collins can do.

It was no use, though, he had his jacket on and was waiting for me at the door.

"See you in a bit," I said to Beatrice.

We only had to walk down the lane and through a car park before reaching the beach. Dad energetically scaled the dunes and disappeared over the top. I was fit now and capable of scaling all sorts but I took my time, sullenly dragging my feet as he called for me to hurry on. The beach was busy with young families, couples with dogs, older folk power-walking with big grins on their faces. Of course, Dad knew them all and wanted to stop and talk to everyone. It was like being a kid when your mother meets one of her friends and you have to linger in the background while they prattle on about the latest births, deaths and marriages in the village.

On the fourth conversation I just left him there, went off up the beach on my own, past all the walkers, until only a sole runner in the distance separated me from oblivion. I gazed back and saw him still talking to those people, and thought about sneaking back to the house and maybe murdering Beatrice, or shagging her, whichever came easiest. Instead I scrambled up one of the dunes and sat down in the scraggly grass. I was a bit old for hide-and-seek, but I just wanted to be away from him, away from his new life, his new friends and all the happiness he'd found.

I watched him say goodbye to his friends, pause and look around. After checking his pockets, presumably for his phone, he carried on in the direction he'd last seen me. Even his walk had changed, he walked with his head up now, like someone embracing the day. The wind was in his face but he didn't let it deter him. He drew close to my vantage point, so that we were almost parallel, and looked around once more. I shrank into the grass, obscuring myself, and after one more glance around he went back from whence he came. I could have been in the sea for all he cared.

I decided to put my new-found fitness to good use and get back before him. Staying low, I navigated the dunes until I found a spot where I could descend safely. From there I went as fast as I could, sinking into the sand as I sought the path of least resistance. When I got to the car park I slowed to a brisk walk, but there was no sign of him. I made it back to the house, let myself in and went to the kitchen to get a drink.

"Back already? That was quick," Beatrice called out.

I didn't reply. I filled a glass with water and slugged it off.

"Hi," I said as I entered the living-room.

"Where's your father?"

"Dunno. He was talking to his friends, so I just left him there."

She shook her head in annoyance. "He's like a fucking puppy, you can't bring him anywhere."

I laughed. No one ever swore in our old house.

"Have ye invited Sally over?" I asked.

"Yes, herself and Grant are due to come in the summer."

I wondered what Sally would make of this whole set-up. She'd probably be happy for him, for them both. Happy people liked it when their loved ones were happy.

"I'd say I'll head home when he comes back," I said.

"Well, make sure this isn't a once-off. We want you here at least once a month for your Sunday dinner."

"Of course," I replied. But I'd already made my mind up. I'd seen enough. I wanted no part of this place, this happy little home where my father got rode like a rag doll by the deceptively sweet Mrs. M every evening after the six o'clock news. They could keep their bottled water, wine with dinner and walks on the beach. They could shag each other senseless in those sand dunes if they liked, and Sally and Grant could join them. I'd had enough of them and their lies. We talked about French cinema for a while, but it wasn't like before; our mutual passion for *auteur* film-making had been sullied. As I listlessly explained the plot of *Polisse* to Mrs. M, I saw my father hurry up the garden path looking vexed.

"Here you are," he said as he bundled into the living-room. "What happened?"

"Ah, I just went off for a wander."

"Why didn't you wait for me?"

"I *did* wait."

He rubbed the nape of his neck absent-mindedly.

"I might go home now, if that's okay?" I said.

"Will you not have a cup of tea before you go?" he asked.

"No, thanks."

"Beatrice has some stuff made up for you. Don't you, love?"

She got up from her chair and wordlessly drifted out to the kitchen.

"So many people out walking. I must have got distracted," said my father. He hung up his jacket and sat on the armrest of his favourite chair as if waiting for permission to fully relax.

"It's a nice beach, you're very lucky," I said.

"You're not mad at me, are you?"

"No, no. I just want to go home. Have things to do."

"Okay, as soon as Bee . . . Beatrice gets everything together, we'll head off."

She returned with leftover chicken and some homemade dinners she'd frozen and kept for me.

"Thanks, Mrs. M," I said. "Are we right then, Dad?"

"Okay. I'll just get my keys."

He went out to the hallway to look for keys which were most likely in his pocket, on the floor, the kitchen table, anywhere but the hallway.

"Thanks again for these," I said to Mrs. M, lifting up the bag of food.

"It's no problem. I was cooking, anyway."

"Beatrice, where are my keys?" my father called out.

She shook her head and rolled her eyes at me, as if our mutual suffering at the hands of this man was unending. It made me feel nauseous.

"It's okay!" he shouted. "I have them."

He went straight out the front door and got into the car. Mrs. M and I stood before one another. I wanted to turn on my heels and go, but she felt a gesture was required.

"Well, then, we'll be seeing you," she said, moving close to me. She held out her arms. When I didn't reciprocate, she placed them awkwardly around my shoulders and brushed her cheek against mine. She smelled of wine and sin.

"Bye, Mrs. M."

I joined my father in the car. One goodbye over, one more to go.

We drove in silence all the way home. It was neither awkward nor uncomfortable.

"We'll see you again soon?" he asked, more in hope than anticipation, when he dropped me off at Wolfe Tone Street.

"Yeah. I'll give you a shout next week."

As with my mother, I felt that a line had been drawn, that I had shed a part of my old life. He wasn't dying, my father, but whatever attachment I had to him had slowly withered and fallen away. I wouldn't be going back, not even for the food.

30

SOMETHING WAS STIRRING INSIDE ME. A growth of some sort. I felt uneasy, restless, and it wasn't just anxiety. It took me a while, but eventually I figured out what it was: fear. Not fear of addiction, of going outside, of being laughed at or exposed, but fear of wasting away. In the cold light of day, as a sober man, I could look back upon my life objectively and it terrified me. I had done nothing. If I were to die tomorrow, the sum total of my achievements would read as follows: Aidan did his Leaving Cert, drank a lot of booze, and went to Dublin one time. He watched loads of films, played nearly all the Xbox games and almost had sex with a girl. That was it. That was all I had to show for my time on this earth. My 27th birthday was coming up, my golden decade, the one you're supposed to enjoy the most, was nearly over, and I had wasted the entire thing. It was time to act, time to get real.

I was more confident now, more capable, I could do things, talk to people, utilise my skill-sets, and not just in a FÁS course either. I was better than that. Could I go to third-level, to the local institute of technology, get a degree? Probably, and I wouldn't need diazepam to do it. I had a brain, a good one, and I could use it. So, I went onto the college website. It had a variety of courses that I knew I'd be good at, too many in fact, but after some careful consideration I opted for a Bachelor of Sciences in Information Technology. It was a three-year degree course and would give me a good grounding, enough to get a decent job in a local software company or, if I took to college life, to prepare me for a post-graduate course.

There was no fear this time. Yes, I felt anxious, worried about going into a big lecture hall full of strangers, having to converse with my fellow students, but it wasn't all-consuming. I knew I could handle it. And, in a sign of my growing maturity, I didn't even have a drink to celebrate when I sent off my application. It was just another task I'd completed, the first step towards a better life. I did want to share my news, though, share it with one person in particular. Sonia was still calling in five times a week, still using me for my television. I was currently trying to be mysterious and aloof in her presence, acting confused when she asked me about my weight loss, my new clothes and my healthy glow.

Obviously, I hadn't come up with this strategy by myself. I'd read a blog written by a handsome man who knew how to manipulate women. He said it didn't matter what you looked like or how much money you had; what really drove women wild was being ignored, a complete lack of interest. I'd been trying these new tactics for a while with minimal success. One night I'd left the room unannounced, disappeared for an hour and then returned in what I hoped was an aggrieved state. She didn't even notice, just asked me to put the kettle on during the ads. It seemed to me that Sonia didn't go for mystery and intrigue, and that I would have to be more forthright. Becoming a mature student, an educated fellow with a future beyond Wolfe Tone Street, might impress her, make her realise I wouldn't be around forever and she should place more value on these long evenings we spent together.

"College? What are you doing that for?" was her response.

"Because I want to do something with my life."

She was aghast, as if I'd told her I was joining the Taliban.

"Yeah, but college," she said. "That takes ages."

"Have you seen my life recently? It's not like I'm going anywhere."

"And what will you study?"

I told her the name of the course and she screwed up her face even more.

"Doesn't college cost a load of money?" she asked. "Students are always broke."

"The government pays your fees and I still get to keep my dole and rent allowance."

"Fuck off!" she said, suddenly alert.

I nodded smugly.

"Maybe I'll go to college too," she said, curling up like a cat as her show came on.

It took her ten minutes to start worrying about how my change in circumstances might impact upon her life.

"Will you move out of here if you get a place on that course?" she asked.

"I don't see why I would."

"Ah, good."

"Would you miss me?" I asked.

"Oh, yeah."

Five more minutes passed.

"If you're off in college during the day, can I still come up and watch telly?" she asked.

"I suppose so."

"Could I get my own key?"

"Mmm."

"Will you be studying here during the evenings, or would you do that in your bedroom?"

It was impossible to make an impression on this woman, not in the way I wanted anyway. She viewed me as a friend, an amenable friend who allowed her to do what she wanted. There was no sexual energy, I might as well have been gay. Maybe I would tell her I was gay, I'd see what the bloggers had to say. Yet if I had focused on our friendship instead of my libido, I might have realised that here was a good person, a loyal and considerate companion who did actually care for me, despite my insecurities.

On the day of my 27th birthday, I opened the card sent by my father and Beatrice, called them to say thanks and then stared out the window, wondering how to mark my special day. There was nothing special about it so far. I had been invited out to their place for dinner that evening but politely declined. And that was the only offer I'd had. But I didn't need anyone else. I could have my own party. So I went to the supermarket and bought myself a cake, a small one, but a cake nonetheless. Then, when dinner time came along, I ordered a takeaway, an Indian curry with naan bread, poppadoms and all the dips. I ate the curry, cut myself a massive slice of cake, and played a bit on the Xbox.

I was just about to settle in for the night with a few episodes of *Homeland* when there was a knock at the door. It wasn't one of Sonia's scheduled nights. My father would hardly call in unannounced. Could it have been Gerard, looking for a drinking companion after being dumped by his beau? But it wasn't him. It was my other friend, my real friend.

"Happy birthday, Aidan," said Sonia, brushing past me with a cake, the candles all lit.

"Sonia! What are you doing here? How did you know it was my birthday?"

"Facebook, dummy."

Facebook. I never even used it. I'd set up an account a couple of years ago and had only logged in a handful of times since. I did recall accepting a friend request from Sonia, though, and immediately going on to her page to see if there were any pictures of her in a swimsuit or some revealing outfits, which there were.

"I didn't know what kind of cake you liked so I went for chocolate, everyone likes chocolate."

It was the same cake I'd bought earlier, the one I'd just eaten a slice of and left in the fridge.

"There are twenty-seven candles on there, though. Look!"

She was right; twenty-seven candles, although only about half of them were lit.

"I lit them in the hallway. They must have gone out when I was coming up the stairs," she said sadly.

"It's okay. I mean, thank you."

"You're welcome. Happy birthday," she said again, holding out her arms.

I bent down to hug her, enveloping her. Her hair smelled nice but she reeked of cigarettes and there was a faint of odour of sweat from her clothes.

"What will we do to celebrate?" she asked.

"I don't know. Watch TV?"

"Ha ha, brilliant idea."

She cut us both a slice of the cake and we settled into our usual spots.

"Because it's your birthday I'll even let you choose what we watch," she said with a wicked smile.

"Well, thanks," I said haughtily.

I put on *Homeland* and we sat there in silence, scoffing the cake as Claire Danes ran about in a frenzy and Damien Lewis acted all suspicious. He knew how to do it, how to pull off the mysterious angle; then again, he was a big, tough soldier.

"God, look at us," said Sonia.

"What?"

"Your big birthday night, we're in our twenties and we're sitting here eating cake and watching telly."

"So?"

"Do you ever feel like life is passing you by? We should be living our best lives, going out, partying, being young."

This was unusual. Normally I was the introspective one.

"Maybe we're not just those kinds of people," I said.

"Maybe you're not, but I never got the chance to be," she said. "I've been with Steve since I was sixteen, been a mammy since I was twenty. I never got the chance to be young at all. Every day of my life is the exact same thing. I'd love to go out and get hammered, or go on one of those sun holidays with all the lads, spend a fortnight clubbing and lying on the beach. I've never done any of those things and I probably never will."

It occurred to me that Sonia never opened up like this when *her* shows were on, only when I wanted to watch something. I discreetly paused the episode and offered a considered response.

"Yes, but you've got something else; you've got Casper. All the sun holidays and nights out in the world couldn't replace him."

"I know," she said tiredly. "But still, just once I'd like not to be a mother or *his* missus. Men still look at me, you know. I see them. I could just as easily dump him and find someone better, someone who'd treat me right, and live somewhere nicer than this. We've never been on a holiday, not once. We went to Rún Derg one day a couple of summers ago, all three of us on the bus, but no holidays. My boy should be going to Disneyland, not stuck in a flat or at his Nan's all the time."

"Sure, break up with Steve, then."

"And go where? Back to my Mam's?"

I shrugged my shoulders, she wasn't half ruining my birthday.

"It's just easier to carry on as we are," Sonia continued. "If I broke up with him, he'd probably take me to court over Casper. We'd have to arrange visitation, support, all that shite. And where would I live? If we can't get a house with the three of us, what chance have I as a single mother?"

The more she went on, the more grateful I was for my own life of relative comfort. Maybe it was better to be alone.

"I don't know, Sonia. You don't want to look back on your life and wonder what might have been."

"I already am," she said sadly.

"You could have an affair, spice up your life a bit."

That produced a smile, a sad one but a smile, nonetheless.

"You paused your programme," she said.

"Yeah, well, we were chatting, weren't we?"

"Go on," she said, nodding at the screen.

I pressed play and we returned to *Homeland* in silence. It was a great show, the best new thing I'd seen in ages, but I was otherwise occupied. That had been an illuminating conversation. She had really poured her heart out. If it had carried on she might have cried, I might have had to console her. That would have entailed physical contact, an arm round the shoulder, me patting her hair and telling her things could only get better. While I was loath to see anyone cry, I did like the idea of being there for her, of being her rock. I bet Steve didn't even notice if she cried, didn't even care. Was it really any wonder she was up here looking for companionship?

Strangely, despite forming a solid friendship with his girlfriend, I had yet to meet Steve in the flesh. I had heard him a few times, shouting, slamming doors and stamping downstairs, but our paths had yet to cross. According to Sonia, he spent days at a time at his mother's house and whenever he was home he always left early and returned late. Suspicious, a bit enigmatic, like the bloggers said. But it was obvious he didn't care about Sonia and that she didn't care about him. All they needed was a reason to break up, a little nudge in the right direction.

A few days after my birthday, on one of the afternoons that Sonia didn't come up to watch television, I was walking through town when I saw them coming towards me: all three of them, a perfect family scene. It was Casper who noticed me first. He was smiling and waving at me as they drew closer, shouting something inaudible over the loud city traffic. Sonia saw me then and slowed down as they drew alongside me. But my eyes were firmly trained on the third cog in the wheel, on the beloved partner and dedicated father: Steve. I took an instant dislike to him. He was the kind of man I'd been intimidated by all my life. Tall, taller even than me and muscular with it. It wouldn't have been so bad if he hadn't been so handsome. He had a sallow complexion, big round green eyes and a taut jawline which showed off his manly visage. The look was completed by a shaved head, white T-shirt, baggy jeans and desert boots. He walked with a certain flow, the easy stride of a man who knew what he was about; he was king of the jungle and would always be - unless of course, you removed him from his natural habitat and forced him to rely on his intellect. He had the air of a schoolyard bully, someone who'd been throwing their weight around since childhood.

"Oh hi, what are you up to?" asked Sonia, looking a little flustered.

"Hello," said Casper, squinting in the sunlight.

"Just getting something for the dinner," I said, gesturing to my canvas shopping bag.

"This is Aidan, from upstairs," she said to Steve.

"Ah, Aidan," he said, breaking into a big grin. "So you're the lad trying to rob me girlfriend?"

I flushed red and stared at the ground.

"Stop it, Steve," said Sonia.

"No, I want to know more about this fellah, this mystery man of yours."

I caught Sonia's eye; she looked as uncomfortable as I felt.

"So, what do ye be doing upstairs in number 14?" Steve asked both of us. He was enjoying himself. Now that he'd seen me, the notion of anything happening between me and Sonia seemed ludicrous.

"We talk," said Sonia. "Something you wouldn't know anything about."

Steve feigned annoyance, adopting a forlorn expression as he defended himself. "I can talk," he said, "but you don't ever fucking listen. Am I right, Aidan?"

I looked away again.

"Doesn't say much, does he?" Steve continued. "I can see why ye get on. With your mouth and his silence, you're a match made in heaven."

"Come on, for fuck's sake," said Sonia, ushering Casper forward. "Talk to you later, Aidan."

"Yeah, I bet you will," Steve replied, and then, to me: "Remember, buddy, I'm watching you, so no funny business."

He laughed at his own humour, at the idea of the awkward geek from upstairs doing anything with his girlfriend, the girlfriend he had long since taken for granted, the girlfriend whom every man in the town knew not to go near because she was going out with him, the great Steve Lyons, the big head-basher from Raven's Villas. He was still laughing as I walked away, humiliated, injured, subjugated by a superior being, by a real man from the real world. Fuck him and all the men like him, I thought. The men who strutted through life without ever questioning their worth. The men who'd never had any reason to doubt themselves. And, most importantly, the men whom the women always wanted, the alpha males, who thought they could take, take, take and leave nothing behind for the rest of us. I was sick of those men, with their genetic advantages and animal magnetism. Maybe it was time I took something for myself, struck a blow for the underdog, for the beta boys. I didn't have the chiselled jaw or the confident swagger but I had something else; I could listen, I could communicate. I was good at those things. Hadn't Steve said as much himself? And while his looks would fade, I'd always be a good listener. While he was out living it up, doing God knows what, his long-suffering missus was finding solace elsewhere. Let him laugh, let him think I wasn't a threat, his arrogance would be his downfall.

31

She was full of apologies when she called up next.

"Steve isn't always like that. He's a good person, really. It just takes a while to get used to his sense of humour."

I nodded, like the good listener I was, but it sounded like she was telling herself these things, not me. It was starting to bore me, the soap opera of her life. She wasn't going to do anything, she just wasn't going to change. She'd sit here in this flat, watching my telly, letting her youth pass her by, until suddenly she was thirty and her options were running out. Steve would probably have left her by then, impregnated someone else and been forced to choose; opting for the younger, less bitter option. Leaving Sonia, still attractive but pushing on, to try her luck as a single mother, incorporating men into her life, always mindful of Casper, prioritising his needs, and having her heart broken time and time again.

She would go on believing that all men were bastards when, really, it was just all *her* men that were bastards. And when they weren't bastards, when they were kind and considerate, and caring and nice to Casper, nice to Sonia, she would grow tired of them, leave them at home with her son while she went on the town, searching for the youth she'd never had. At forty she would no longer care, would take affection in whatever form she could get it. Maybe then, when the hope had been drained out of her, she might settle down with one of those safe bets she'd always rejected, but that sense of loss would never fade. She would always wonder about the life she could have had, the free, unencumbered existence of her peers, the reckless, irresponsible partying and pulling she'd missed out on, that she'd envied from afar.

That wasn't for her, though, just as it wasn't for me. You had to make your peace with these things, not dwell on them. That did no one any good.

"It's all right, Sonia," I said, feeling very noble. "He was only having a laugh."

"Yeah," she said, pleased. And that was that.

She went back to her programmes and it was never mentioned again. What was mentioned again, frequently, was her growing disquiet. Her defence of Steve forgotten about, she resumed her complaining, how she never had any fun and was missing out on everything. Although keen to maintain my status as listener-in-chief, I eventually broke ranks and challenged her.

"Why don't you just go on a night out?" I asked during another of her laments.

"I can't afford it," she said. "Anyway, I can't go out without him."

"Why not?"

"I just can't," she said, shaking her head.

"Just call up your friends, organise a time and meet them in the pub. He doesn't have to know."

"That's not how relationships work, Aidan," she said, talking to me as if I were a child.

"That's how normal relationships work," I said under my breath.

"What?"

"Nothing."

An idea came to me then, a solution to all her problems.

"Why don't you and I go out?" I asked.

She laughed in my face. That hurt.

"But that's just silly."

"Why is it? Steve doesn't mind you spending time with me. I'll be sober. You can get drunk, do whatever you like and I'll look after you, make sure you get home."

She was looking at me oddly. I think it was the bit about me looking after her.

"You're gas," she said, returning to her programme.

I thought that was the end of it, but a couple of days later she brought it up.

"I've been thinking about your idea, Aidan."

"Oh, yeah?"

"The one about going out in town."

My ears pricked up, there was a slight motion in my groin.

"I think it could work," she continued.

"Really?"

"Yes."

"What about Steve?"

She laughed awkwardly. "He - erm - he thinks you're gay, Aidan."

I felt both offended and empowered.

"So you're going to be my fag hag, then?"

"Ha ha! I think so."

So it came to pass that myself and Sonia were to have a night on the town. We would go for dinner at the Chinese restaurant across the road before drinks in *Betty Boo's*, her favourite pub. Then, depending on how the night was progressing, we'd either go to a late bar or a nightclub. I would be her chaperone and companion. Was I gay? Were we a couple? Who could tell? It would be just the two of us, and that was all that mattered. Strangely, as I prepared for our date (I had officially declared it a date, at least inwardly) I didn't feel all that nervous. I would have Sonia with me. We were together. There was no pressure.

There would be pressure of a different kind, though. I'd been off the booze for three months now, managing it day by day, but not once during that time had I been surrounded by alcohol, by temptation. Now it would be everywhere. As the night progressed and Sonia inevitably detached herself from me in search of fun, would I revert to type, seek solace in a bottle? I resolved to take my role as her protector seriously, like a bodyguard, a solemn, strait-laced presence with watchful eyes.

When she appeared at my door all dolled up, I had to take a step back. I'd never seen her like this before, never seen her make an effort. She looked stunning in a figure-hugging silver dress which accentuated her shapely legs, slender frame and pert backside. Her hair had been done especially for the occasion, and she wore silver eyeshadow and earrings to go with the dress. I had made an effort myself, splashed out on a pair of chinos and a shirt, but I looked like an ogre standing next to her. As we left the building, she draped an arm inside mine and we stepped into the night.

It felt like a covert mission that only she and I were in on. We were hiding in plain sight and it was fantastic. As soon as we entered the restaurant, the looks started. I saw how the waiter gave her a quick once-over before leading us to our table, and the other patrons, the lads out with their own girlfriends, followed Sonia with their eyes as she walked across the room, then did a double-take as they saw the lumbering oaf accompanying her. *How did he get her? Must have loads of money. Either that or a massive cock.* I had neither, I was just a good listener who seemed a bit gay.

The food was great, the company even better. Away from that grotty flat, from the reality of our depressing existence, Sonia came to life. She was no longer the whiny, mournful woman who came up to watch my television and eat my biscuits. Now she was actually engaging, a good conversationalist as well as the best-looking woman in the room. We talked about my college course, my plans for the future, whether I'd like to be a father, how many kids I'd like, how much she loved Casper, how he was getting on in school, the life she wanted for her son. It was perfect, it was positive.

She did try to talk about Steve, about how she was determined to make it work with him, but I stayed silent until she moved onto something else. As we left the restaurant and walked through town, the looks became less subtle, more pointed. Men had drink on board now, they didn't feel the need to hide their desire. It didn't matter that we weren't an item, just having them thinking we were was enough for me. I felt proud, like a real man. Was this how people like Steve felt all the time?

Betty Boo's was loud and thronged. It was a battle to get to the bar, but I managed it and returned triumphantly with our drinks. In the few minutes I'd gone someone had already moved in for the kill: a young lad with a pink shirt and spiky hair was shouting into Sonia's ear as I placed the drinks on the little counter we'd found. Clearly relieved to see me, Sonia nodded in my direction and the young lad backed off.

"Sorry, man," he said.

He walked off then, wholly unperturbed, ready to try his luck with someone else. He was just the first of many. Whenever I went to the bar, or either of us went to the toilet, she was approached by someone, by men eager to make her acquaintance. I found it exhausting, but she seemed happy enough. Then there were her friends, all the people who knew her. And it was *all* the people - it was like going out with a celebrity. Every couple of minutes our conversation was interrupted by high-pitched screams as another woman she hadn't seen for ages made her way over for a hug and a frenzied exchange. After the initial excitement they would all look in my direction, thinking: *Who's your man? What the fuck is she doing with him?* Sonia dealt with it in a classy manner, giving nothing away.

"This is Aidan, he's my neighbour," she told them.

When they asked after Steve she said he was minding Casper for the night, deepening the intrigue, the sense of mystery, although they probably all just thought I was gay too. Some men came over too, friends of hers, probably friends of Steve's too. I felt threatened by them but held my ground and didn't look away when I caught them staring. My job was to sit with Sonia and that's what I was doing. Inevitably, though, as the drinks started flowing and more and more of her old friends came over to talk, Sonia got a little restless. I could see she wanted to hang out with them, to be with a group of girls in a way she hadn't been for years.

"It's okay if you want to go over to them," I said. "I'm grand here."

"No, that's not fair, Aidan. I came out with you."

"Sure, we can both go over," I suggested.

"You don't mind?"

"Not at all," I lied.

So I ended up sitting on a small stool on the edge of a group of women, beside three blokes who were having a conversation of their own. I didn't even bother trying to engage with them, there was no point. Their curiosity had been piqued, though, and they wanted to know more about the strange guy who had brought Sonia, boyfriend of Steve Lyons, on a night out.

"Are you Sonia's cousin or something?" one of them asked.

"No, I just live upstairs from her."

That wasn't a satisfactory answer. He probed further.

"Does Steve know you're out together?"

"Yeah," I said, nodding firmly.

"Are you *his* cousin?"

"No."

"All right," he said respectfully. "You looking for yokes?"

"No, thanks."

He left me alone then, they all did. I was with them but not really with them. Sonia was happy, though, happier than I'd ever seen her. At around midnight it was decided we would go on to a nightclub, and we exited the bar *en masse*. Once more my date for the night sought me out and linked arms with me for the five-minute walk to the club. She was pissed by now.

"Thanks for this, Aidan, you're very good. You're just so, so good. There's a goodness in you, you know? A real goodness."

Her high heel got caught in the pavement and she lost her footing, but it was easy to steer her back on course, she was as light as a feather.

She continued talking, not missing a beat. "I mean, and I've never said this before but I've been meaning to, you're a real good guy, a good guy. You're my friend, Aidan, do you know that? My good friend, and thank you."

"You're my friend too, Sonia," I said, wishing she hadn't been so adamant about us being friends.

"I'm having such a good time. Will you have a drink? Will we have a drink, together? I know you're off it, and that's very important, but will we have just one drink? That would make the night for me, Aidan, it really would. A Jagerbomb, that's what we'll have. Yeah? Okay?"

"We'll see when we get in," I said as I saw the neon sign of the club in the distance. A Jagerbomb sounded like the perfect remedy. I had never been inside a nightclub and had hoped to keep it that way, but a man will do anything for love and so I paid in for myself and Sonia, got stamped, handed in my coat and entered a dark, noisy, boozy auditorium. The first thing that struck me was the dance floor. It was full of young, happy people lost in the moment. Seeing them, so carefree and joyous, made me immensely sad. We were only separated by a matter of feet, but our worlds couldn't have been much further apart.

I shook those morose thoughts out of my head and dutifully went to the bar. I'd bought Sonia dinner and most of her drinks but that was okay, the state paid me well.

"Where's yours?" she asked when I returned.

"Here," I said, showing her the mineral water.

"Ah, Aidan."

She flung her arms around me and started shouting into my ear. Most of it was unintelligible but I picked up snippets.

" . . . and then I realised it was me that was the problem, not him . . . but look it, this is how it's got to be and I don't really give a fuck . . . you can change it, Aidan, that's what it's about . . . the only thing that matters is we're here now and they can't stop us . . . you're one of the good ones and so am I . . ."

It went on and on. It was boring listening to her but she was hanging out of me now, her dress riding up so that her bare, supple thighs rested against my hip. She had kicked off her shoes and one of her earrings had fallen out.

" . . . you won't leave me, Aidan, will you? . . . start learning all those things in your fancy college . . . all the money and then you'll be too posh for me . . . left with Steve in that fucking apartment, I'll go mad . . . a course that I could do in the college . . . or I am too stupid? You would tell me if I was . . . I know . . . I don't care."

Her hair was tickling my neck, her hands clasped together on my back. It was more than I could take. I was frozen with fear. From beneath this show of affection I spotted one of her female friends looking over at us in disgust, and I felt my breath hitch, chest tighten and stomach churn. It was coming. The panic attack. I delicately disentangled myself and made a beeline for the toilets. The cubicles were all taken so I lay back against the cool wall and waited for it to pass. When two lads piled out of one of the cubicles, snuffling and grinning, I rushed in and bolted the door behind me.

Not now, not now. Don't let her see. Just get through the next hour. It'll be over then. It'll be okay. You're here to mind her, to show her how good you are. It'll be over soon. Forget about everyone else. It's just you and Sonia. Don't worry about the others.

I fought it for a while, taking deep breaths, but it was impossible to regain my composure in this environment. So much noise, lads shouting and jeering, the blare of music every time the door opened. Then someone started hammering on the door of my stall.

"Come on, man, for fuck's sake! I've to take a shit."

It was pointless trying to wait him out. The man had to take a shit, after all. So I let him in and went to the sink, throwing water on my face as my reflection swam before my eyes. Just one hour, I said to myself, just one hour. When I went back out, Sonia was gone. It was just the three lads again, the boyfriends. All the drinks had been gathered on one table and the girls' handbags were on the seat beside the boys.

"Out dancing," said the one from earlier.

That was better. I could sit on my own for a while. I took a seat away from the lads and looked out on to the dance floor. There she was in the middle of it all, head thrown back, singing along to a song I didn't recognise. She and her friends had formed their own little circle, a safe zone, but that didn't stop the interlopers. Along they came, each with a different tactic. Some shimmied their way in from a distance, plotting a course from the other side of the floor, until they suddenly found themselves beside Sonia or one of her pals, and then they would dance there for a while, staring intently at the group of women, waiting to catch someone's eye.

Having gone unnoticed they would change tack, moving uncomfortably close, pushing up against them, until the women shared a look and moved a little to the left, a little to the right, away from the unwanted guest. Others, less inhibited, simply marched over and draped themselves over the women, jammed their head inside the circle of trust and smiled at them happily. Those ones were shoved away, the girls laughing at what seemed like a harmless intervention. There were creepy ones too, though, guys who came over and wouldn't go away, stood still and stared at them until eventually Sonia and her friends were forced to leave the floor and come back to base.

"Aidan," said Sonia breathlessly as she collapsed into the seat and picked up a drink, "what is this?"

She started laughing hysterically and knocked it back in one.

"Dance with me!" she said.

I recoiled in horror.

"Now! Let's go."

She was on her feet, dragging me by the arms.

"Come on," she said, gritting her teeth and digging in her heels, which she'd put back on.

"Dance with the woman, for fuck's sake," shouted one of the lads.

I got up and went to the dance floor. I'd done loads of dancing in my time, all of it in my room while drunk out of my mind, and all of it to classic rock and funk from music's golden age. I'd never danced in public, and never while sober. In a panic, and with the lines between reality and insanity starting to blur, I joined her on the floor. The music was just noise, a jumbled cacophony in my tormented mind, but as we shoved our way into the mass of bodies and I looked down at Sonia's radiant face, a sense of calm came over me. It was just the two of us out here in the middle of this madness. We didn't need anyone else.

I smiled at her and slid my shoulders from side to side, getting my arms going. I was part of their world now. I could come out here and dance and live just like them. They didn't know anything about me, what I had or hadn't drunk or that I'd just had a panic attack. I could be as free as I wanted to be.

"I'm tired now," Sonia mouthed as she stuttered forward and lay against my chest. Someone behind me jumped up in a moment of excitement and elbowed me in the back of the head.

"Sorry, man, sorry. Are you okay?" A face appeared, friendly and apologetic.

"Yeah, yeah, no worries."

He found my hand and shook it.

But this was no place for a woman on her first night out in years, a frail, fragile little thing who'd had too much to drink and had been fending off suitors all night. I guided her back to our seats and eased her down. Her head lolled on her shoulders for a moment and then popped back up, like a toy robot whose batteries have been replaced.

"Where's my drink?" she hollered good-naturedly.

A drink was handed to her and she took a slug, pulling a face as she placed it back on the table.

"Aidan!" she screamed, not realising I was right there beside her. "Oh, there you are. Did you have a drink? Will we have a Jager? Just one little bitty Jager? Go on, I'll pay."

She looked around for her bag, saw it on the floor and went down on all fours to get it, drawing some admiring glances from the next table.

"Two Jagers," she said, waving a tenner at me.

"Ah no, I'm grand."

"Aidan, please, a Jager, just one Jager. Look, the bar is about to shut," she said as the lights flashed. "Get them quick."

She shoved the tenner in my hand and pushed me off the seat, sticking her foot in my arse as I stumbled away. Of course I wasn't going to get a Jagerbomb, I'd lasted all night without drinking, there was no need to spoil it at the death. I got one for her, though, and a ginger ale for myself, and she was positively thrilled when I returned with the drinks.

"You got them! I can't believe it. Woohoo!"

We knocked back our drinks in one and shared another hug. She tottered off to the toilet just as the lights came up and I allowed myself a deep breath. It was almost over. By the time she returned, the bouncers were shepherding people towards the exits and we allowed ourselves to be ferried along with the crowd. As soon as we hit the night air, Sonia began shivering. I draped my jacket around her and we began walking towards Wolfe Tone Street in silence. She'd had enough now, those last few drinks had taken their toll. Aside from the odd hiccup, she was quiet the whole way home. I opened the outside door and carefully guided her up the stairs, but not carefully enough to prevent her falling to her knees on a handful of occasions. Finally we made it to her apartment where she stood looking at me hazily, her eyes half-shut, a vague smile on her lips.

"Keys, Sonia."

She pursed her lips together and blew out.

"Are they in your bag?"

I reached for the bag and she playfully pulled it away from me, hiding it behind her back.

"Sonia, for fuck's sake let me see if you have your keys."

"I can do it," she said smartly, opening the bag and peering inside. She chuckled to herself, lost in a drunken daze, while I patiently waited for her brain to start working. Eventually she handed me the bag and rolled back against the wall, crumpling into a corner, exposing her underwear. I couldn't help but look, couldn't help but notice the black lace of her knickers, couldn't help but feel a twitch, a yearning. Averting my gaze, I rummaged through lipsticks, tissues, tampons, coins and notes, until I found her keys. I turned them in the door and opened it. There was no one home; Casper and Steve were at his mother's house. I really didn't want to go in, to see how they lived but, ever chivalrous, I was determined to get Sonia fully home, safe and sound.

"Come on," I said, holding out my hands for her to get up.

"I'm gonna be sick."

That was all I needed. I moved fast, pulling her to her feet and carrying her inside. I wasn't going into their bedroom, that was too much. Instead I laid her down on the couch, finding a cushion for her head and a throw to keep her warm. Next I went to the kitchen, hoping to find a bin, a bucket, a suitable vestibule for the spew which was probably only minutes away. Their bin was nowhere to be found and there was no bucket so I improvised, taking the basin out of the sink and placing it by the side of the couch where she was already out for the count. I filled a glass of water and laid it on the table beside her. She would be needing that. Satisfied I'd done all I could, I leant down to check on her. She was breathing, anyway, that was the main thing.

Only then did I take in my surroundings. The apartment was surprisingly old-fashioned, like that of a couple fifty years their senior. There was a gaudy rug on the floor, tartan curtains and a sideboard with a clock and lots of photos. They had a little electric heater in the middle of the room and a tiny television, an old telly, not like the modern flat screens. Some of Casper's books and toys lay in a little box behind the door, and a clothes horse laden down with tired, faded garments stood in the corner. It wasn't old-fashioned, it was poverty. These people had nothing, they had even less than I had. I looked down at Sonia, this beautiful sleeping girl, and rubbed my hand against her cheek. Then I left the apartment, quietly clicking the door behind me.

32

Sonia never had credit on her phone, so there was no point in texting her. I just had to presume she was alive and wait until she called up to me. Monday night at eight was one of our allotted slots. I waited until nine and then put on *Homeland*. I wasn't worried about her, not really. She was probably still hungover, or spending time with Casper out of guilt. Perhaps Steve had given her a hard time, though, given her a few digs. I pressed 'pause' on the TV. I would go down and check on her. Make sure she was all right. She might be waiting for me to call, might be lying battered and bruised on the floor in desperate need of salvation. If that fucker had laid a finger on her, there'd be hell to pay. I was just about to get up and put on my runners when I heard the familiar knock on the door.

"Oh, God," she said, brushing past me and going straight to her seat. I followed her inside.

"So sick, so, so sick," she said ruefully. "All day yesterday and last night. I'm only starting to come round now."

I smiled knowingly.

"How did I get home?" she asked. "I remember leaving *Boo's* but after that, not much."

"I brought you."

"Was I bad?"

"Ah, you were grand."

"Was it you that left the basin out for me?"

"Yeah," I said, laughing.

"Don't even ask," she said, shaking her head.

"What did Steve say?"

"A *lot*. He must have had spies on the town, 'cos he got about sixty texts from people telling him what I'd been up to."

I wondered what his spies had made of my performance. Had I been gay enough?

"They were all like 'Sonia was out with this weird-looking fellah last night. Out dancing with him, hanging out of him, pissed out of her brain,'" she said. "You can't do a thing in this fucking town."

"You got your night out, though," I said reassuringly.

"Oh, I did, and I'm fucking paying for it since."

I would have liked her to remember. But I knew how it went. And even though her memories of the night had been doused in alcohol and set aflame, I felt our bond had deepened. Somewhere within her consciousness lay a distant dream of me carrying her into the apartment, gently laying her down on the couch and caressing her cheek as she slept. Alongside that dream were further fragments, flickering images like those from an old 8-mm camcorder: us dancing in the club, me buying her drink, listening to her stories, being there for her and never once flinching no matter how drunk, loud or lairy she got. You couldn't burn those memories, there wasn't enough alcohol in the world to do that.

"Your friends seem nice," I said.

"Them? They're not my friends," she said dismissively.

She had been hugging and kissing those people all night.

"I'm not sure they liked me."

"You're worth ten of them, Aidan."

It was such a strange world she lived in; effortlessly popular, an object of desire, admired and envied in equal measure; attractive, charming, part of a social elite, existing in a space accessible to few. Sonia could go out every night of the week and never have to pay for a drink. She could go to any pub, any nightclub, any party and be welcomed inside without a moment's hesitation. She was untouchable, royalty among the gentry. In a small city like this a woman like her was headline news, spoken about in hushed tones by lonely men on Sunday afternoons. And yet, like a tragic *femme fatale,* she was just as lonely as they were, lamenting her youth before it had ended.

When her programmes ended, she stretched out and lay lifeless in the armchair.

"Tell me I don't have to go back there, Aidan."

"You don't have to go back," I replied dutifully.

She pouted girlishly.

"If you ever want to stay here, you're more than welcome," I offered.

A giant sigh brought her to her feet.

"Would you give me your bed?" she asked.

"Of course."

"You'd better!"

And then she was gone, leaving me alone with my thoughts, with a vision of her staying over, sleeping in my bed in her delicates. I locked the door behind her, clicked on the laptop and began a search for petite blondes in lingerie.

33

A LETTER CAME IN THE post inviting me for an interview at the college. It said there were only a certain number of places for mature students and I would have to compete against others to pursue my third-level education. That was fine. This was my choice, my decision. If I didn't get in, I would simply apply again next year. No pressure. That's what I told myself, but as I sat outside the interview room, sizing up the opposition, I felt an inordinate amount of pressure. They were better prepared than me; two of them were wearing suits and one had a briefcase. I'd put on my smartest shirt, my best shoes and had a folder with my CV inside, but these guys were serious operators. They probably had families, careers which had been curtailed by the recession. They needed this more than me, they deserved it and would represent the college well when selected.

A lady in a dark grey business suit and a white blouse appeared at the door.

"Aidan Collins," she said.

I followed her into the room and took the seat offered. There were two other people seated opposite me, a chunky bald man with a dent in the side of his head and another woman dressed similarly to the first. The second woman was older and not as good-looking, but she was the friendliest of the three.

"I'm Elaine, this is Trevor and this is Clare," she said. "Water?" she asked, pushing a bottle towards me.

"Thanks," I said, unscrewing the cap and taking a sip.

"So, Aidan," said the man whose name I'd already forgotten, "why do you want to join us here in the IT Department?"

A nice easy one to start.

"Well, I've always been very interested in technology from a young age, and have trained myself in a lot of software. I want to get a formal education in this field, learn from the experts and then progress to the next level."

"You trained yourself in JavaScript?" he asked, raising an eyebrow.

"Yes."

"How did you do that?"

"Online tutorials."

"Okay," he said wearily.

Clare spoke then.

"You're twenty-seven now, Aidan. Is that right?"

I nodded, knowing exactly where this was going.

She scrutinised my CV.

"You had a very strong Leaving Cert," she said, "strong enough to have been accepted on this course when you left school."

"I know. I didn't feel ready for college at the time, didn't know what I wanted to do with myself."

"And what have you been doing with yourself?" she asked.

I had practised this, learned it by rote.

"Well, you see, my mother was quite unwell at the time, had been suffering very badly with her nerves. I was the only one at home and I was worried about leaving her. I had plans to go abroad, to maybe work part-time, but she was very vulnerable and prone to bouts of deep depression. My father had to work all day and my sister lives in England, so I kind of took it upon myself to look after her. In the meantime I was working on up-skilling myself online, learning software and programmes that I hoped would stand me in good stead in years to come."

Clare was implacable. The man was looking down at his stomach. Only Elaine, the friendly one, seemed moved by my tale.

"How's your mother now?" she asked.

"We admitted her to a nursing home a few months back."

"I see," she said, averting her gaze.

They tested my knowledge then, asking me some fairly routine questions about programming, web design, databases. I answered them all without hesitation, looking them straight in the eye as I did so. When it was over Elaine thanked me for my time, showed me to the door and said they'd be in touch.

I tried to tell Sonia how it went but she didn't want to hear it.

"You and your big fancy college, woo woo," she said drearily.

She was even less impressed when, two months later, I got a letter confirming I'd been accepted onto the course.

"That's that, then. You'll be off with your college mates all the time now, I suppose."

"Ah, no."

"You will, Aidan."

"I won't."

"You will," she said vehemently.

I was secretly delighted by her reaction. She was afraid of losing me, afraid our friendship was coming to an end; either that or she was worried about not seeing her programmes. And she had constructed an imaginary life for me, one involving a gang of new and interesting friends. Her version sounded far more appealing than the life I was imagining, where I was shunned by the other students, ignored by the lecturers, made no friends and dropped out after three weeks. But that was the old me talking. This was something I could do. And with four months to wait until the course started I focused on getting my affairs in order.

I sent my confirmation letter back to the college, applied for my grant, enquired about text books and purchased them nice and early. I would get a head start, establish myself as a force from day one. I told my father about college, keeping it curt, ignoring his gushing congratulations and offer of a celebratory dinner. I was on my true path now. I didn't need anyone. However, as the weeks ticked by and summer began, my other needs, my carnal needs were alerted to a change in the atmosphere, to a possibility which outstripped any academic ambitions I had begun to harbour.

Sonia was acting strangely. It had taken me a while to notice it, but there was a definite shift in her behaviour. For months she'd sashayed into the apartment, flopped down in her chair and wordlessly flicked from one programme to another. Now she seemed distracted, uninterested in the television, in even her favourite shows. Repeatedly, she would switch off the telly, turn to me and begin talking, asking me earnest questions about life, the future and the meaning of it all. Her general demeanour had changed too, there was something in the way she moved now, a caution, a deliberation. It was summer so her attire was minimal, clingy, insufficient for the job; short shorts, vest tops, and skirts exposing more of her than I could deal with.

If it had just been that, just skimpy outfits and deep conversations, I would have thought nothing of it, would have continued to fantasise about her at night, nothing more. But there were other things. The first time it happened, I eventually had to look away, was shamed into prudishness. She decided she wanted to watch one of my DVDs and made a great show of choosing one from the bottom of the pile. This involved her bending over as she tried to read the titles of old slasher films from the 1980s, treating me to a view of her little arse as she twisted her head from side to side. It was so close I could have touched it, could have reached out, pulled down her denim shorts and had my wicked way with her.

Maybe she was oblivious. We were such good pals that she didn't even think of me like that. But then it happened again, and again. While I was making the tea, she would come over and reach up into the press so that her chest was inches from my face, so that I could feel the heat of her body next to mine. She would brush up against me in the hallway, initiate contact whenever possible, resting her hand on mine when I passed her the biscuits, making me queasy with one of those lingering looks of hers.

If she was trying to make me forget about college, she was succeeding. During the days when she wasn't here I would open up my books, ready for a day of third-level studying, and drift back to the moment she asked for my opinion on a new skirt, twirling so that it lifted and offered a glimpse of the pink underwear beneath. It got so that I couldn't go five minutes without having to close all my tabs and watch yet more porn. She was driving me demented. The sooner I started college, the sooner autumn came and I didn't have to deal with her summer outfits, the better.

But it was as if the gods knew how tormented I was. After two months of the normal damp, cloudy Irish summer we got a heatwave, a proper one. Ordinarily anything over 20 degrees was enough for Irish people to strip off, to stand in the shade, fanning themselves, complaining of feeling faint. That summer, for ten successive days the thermostat hovered around the 30 degree mark. It was relentless: 29 degrees, 28, 30, 31, 32 and 28 again. Old women were dropping dead in the post office, dogs were jumping off bridges, the rivers ran dry, and the main street in Maraghmor got so hot it melted and had to be relaid. I had never done well in hot weather. I didn't like wearing T-shirts or shorts, exposing my body, so I stayed indoors, sweating, slowly baking, waiting for the sun to go down.

"Will you come to the park with me and Casper?" asked Sonia on day six of the insanity.

"I won't, thanks."

"Come on, the sun is good for you. Vitamin D!"

She stared at me, willing me to come up with a good reason to stay put.

"Okay, okay," I said, "just let me change."

The only shorts I owned were swimming togs I'd had since I was a teenager, part of a short-lived plan to swim for an hour before school every morning and lose weight. I did have a polo shirt I'd bought in case Sonia ever wanted to go for a night out again, so I put that on with the loosest pair of jeans I owned.

"Where's your summer clothes?" Sonia protested when I returned.

"I don't have any."

"You'll roast in those."

"I'll sit in the shade."

"First bit of sun we've had in years and you want to sit in the shade!"

We collected Casper from Anipe and went outside. Even I had to admit that the town came alive when the sun shone. There was an air of expectancy, a sense of freedom; people were already sitting outside the pubs, pints of cider in front of them, not bothered that it was only one o'clock, thinking no further than their next sup. I would have liked to join them, but I had Sonia and Casper for company. Needless to say, she was dressed in next to nothing: a luminous yellow bikini top, tiny orange shorts and flip-flops. She wasn't the only one. Everywhere you looked there were semi-naked women, braless, tanned, long-legged, alluring. It was just as well I wasn't drinking, I would have gone completely mad.

"Hey, eyes over here," said Sonia, twisting my head towards her.

"Hey," chimed Casper from beneath his sun hat.

Someone called out a greeting to her from across the road. She waved and then muttered some expletives under her breath.

"Where's Steve?" I asked.

"Fuck knows."

"Fuck knows," repeated Casper.

"Is he okay with this, with me coming to the park?"

She made a face and we continued on our way. This was on another level. Now it looked as if I had a hot girlfriend and a three-year-old son. People might wonder why Casper looked nothing like me, why he was so fair while I was dark, but that often happened with kids, he might grow to look like me when he got older.

"Park!" said Casper excitedly when he saw the gates up ahead.

We both held his hands as we crossed the road and entered the safety of the town park. The playground was already heaving with children. These were the poor kids of the town, the kids whose parents had nothing else to do of a weekday afternoon, the kids who never got brought to the beach, never went on holiday, had nowhere else to go but this park, day after day, year after year. Sonia and I sat on the grass while Casper weaved his way around the amusements. All the good stuff was being used, the swings, the see-saw, the little rocking horses, but he found a space in the queue for the slide and waited patiently for his turn.

"I'd better go down," said Sonia, running over.

She waited for him to climb up the ladder and then held his hand as he positioned himself at the top of the slide. It was so greasy from all the children, so hot from the sun, that he couldn't even slide down it. Sonia almost had to pull him to the bottom, but as soon as he got there he ran around and joined the back of the line again. This carried on for some time until he got bored and started running around aimlessly, latching onto other kids doing the same, all of them screaming at the top of their lungs. We passed an hour there until Casper announced he was thirsty and we marched out of the park towards the shop down the road. The pubs had put out chairs, drinkers occupied them, sunglasses atop their heads, slowly boiling in the heat. It was like being out foreign, although I'd never been out foreign so I had nothing to base this on.

"Casper, would you like a drink in the pub?" asked Sonia.

He stuck out his tongue and panted like a dog.

"Come on, then," she said, flashing me a look as if to say *I dare you.*

And sure what harm would it be? How often did we get weather like this? The whole country was out drinking. We entered the dark coolness of the pub. The barman's shirt was unbuttoned, exposing his fluffy belly.

"Jaysus, sorry, love," he said, trying to make himself decent.

"You're grand," said Sonia. "I might do the same meself."

"Don't let me stop you," he laughed, glancing at me to make sure it was okay.

"I'll get these," I said to Sonia, nodding towards the beer garden out the back.

"Small bottle of cider with ice and a 7up," she said.

Casper did his dog impression again and they left me at the bar.

"Fierce weather," said the barman, mopping his brow.

"Savage."

"What will I get you?"

"Small bottle of cider with ice, a 7up and a pint of Hoegaarden."

I did it without thinking, reflexively. There was no guilt, no regret. It felt good. I was at the bar buying the drinks for the missus and the young lad. It'd only be the one, maybe two, it wasn't like we could stay out all day, after all.

"A pint!" said Sonia when she saw me coming.

"For the day that's in it," I said.

Casper slugged off half a glass of 7up and let out a monumental burp, laughed and then knocked back the rest.

"You'll make yourself sick," his mother scolded.

"He's grand," I said, taking a sip of the pint. It felt good, too good.

I got Casper a bag of crisps and we played around in the beer garden for a while. He was still thirsty after his 7up so I got him a Coke, and seeing as Sonia had nearly finished her cider I got a round for us too. The second pint was even nicer than the first, it was as if I'd never been away. I was about to go for a third when Sonia stopped me in my tracks.

"I'd better not have any more. I've to bring him to Steve's mother's soon."

She'd got me back on the drink and was now calling a halt to the session before it had even begun.

"Sure bring him now and come back, we'll have a few more."

She smirked slyly. "The sun has you driven mad."

"Go on," I said. "I'll wait here."

"Casper, want to go to Nanny's?"

"Adi coming?" he asked, looking at me.

"I can't, Casper, but we'll go to the park tomorrow."

He looked at me and then his mother, assessing the situation.

"Nanny will have ice cream," said Sonia.

Casper licked his lips in anticipation. "Okay," he said reluctantly, giving me a hug by way of apology.

I watched them go; my surrogate son and his beguiling mother. She would come back, there was nothing surer. The sun had *her* driven mad.

*

She took her sweet time, though. I was on my fourth, maybe fifth, when she reappeared. She'd spruced herself up a bit, done something with her eyes, washed off the grubbiness of the park. I went straight to the bar, eager for her to catch up. It was late afternoon now, a few working men had got off early and were propped up on stools, savouring that first icy sup after a hard day's graft. I ignored them and their tired, grateful expressions and got the drinks. Sonia had moved to a different table, escaping the shadow which was slowly creeping across the garden. She lay back in her chair, closing her eyes as the sun beat down on her face.

"Mmm," she purred contentedly.

Her skin had turned deep bronze, her hair golden yellow, she looked younger, like a teenager. We were a strange country, all the same, capable of producing big floury lummoxes like me, loping lotharios like Steve, and little nymphets like this wan before me. There was probably a bit of Viking in her, some stray Scandinavian blood left behind after all the rampaging and destruction. That was the only explanation.

"I thought you were only having a couple," she said dreamily, her eyes still closed.

"This is probably my last one now."

"Yeah, right."

But it wasn't my last one, or anything like it. We stayed in that beer garden until the sun dipped behind the roof of the building opposite and the music echoed from inside the bar, then we tumbled out on to the street, much the worse for wear.

"Where to next, chief?" asked Sonia.

The town had grown rowdy in our absence; there were loud voices, people shouting, a sense of excitement, frustration, and desire, as the heat slowly faded.

"Why don't we get a few cans, head back to mine and listen to some tunes?" I suggested.

"We go boogie-woogie?"

"It's Tuesday, there is no boogie-woogie."

Sonia looked up and down the street, as if expecting to find a line of people doing the conga.

"What about *The Grotto*?" she said.

The Grotto was the on-campus student bar.

"Are you mad? We'd have to get a bus out there."

"I thought you were a student," she said mockingly.

"Not yet. Anyway it's summer, most of the students aren't here."

"Oh, yeah," she tutted and sauntered off down the road.

I stood where I was, wondering if she was serious about going out there, whether the bus still ran at this hour.

She turned around. "Are we getting cans then, or what?"

At some point in the off-licence an executive decision was made. We got cans, but only six of them. Our main outlay was on a bottle of vodka.

We fussed over the price, counting out pennies like two old biddies, then strode triumphantly through town, royally drunk. A passing car tooted at Sonia and someone in the back seat shouted something at her. She shouted back, gave them the finger and kicked the ground in disgust. I'd never felt prouder. Those lads thought she was my woman, thought this little fireball of energy was the property of Aidan Collins - and so did I. There was no Steve any more. No one spoke of him. He didn't exist.

"Don't turn on the light," she said, taking her customary seat by the window when we got inside. "It's better like this."

I poured us two handy vodkas and stood poised at the stereo.

"What are we thinking?" I asked.

She had kicked off her flip-flops and was staring out at the traffic.

"I want to sing. I want to sing!"

There was only one album for a situation like this. I pulled the CD out of its case, hit 'play' and turned it up as loud as it would go. As the opening riff of *Welcome to the Jungle* sounded out across Wolfe Tone Street, I knew I'd made the right decision. Sonia got to her feet and began to dance in the dark. I joined her, the two of us going mental in this little room in the shittiest part of the shittiest city in the country. We tried singing, but could only remember the chorus and the bit about going to your *shanananana knees, knees*. It didn't matter, though; she was Axel and I was Slash, and we were rocking the shit out of it.

The Polish bloke was banging on the ceiling, giving out yards, we laughed and roared the line from *It's so Easy* in his direction: *Why don't you just . . . FUCK OFF!* By the time we got to *Paradise City*, we were flagging.

"Taking a break," said Sonia breathlessly.

I turned down the music and joined her on the sofa.

"Guns 'n' Roses," she said.

"Yeah."

I opened a can and we wordlessly passed it back and forth in the darkness. By the time *Sweet Child O' Mine* came on we had recovered enough to resume our dancing, but it was slower now, less manic. We swayed from side to side, serenading one another. Sonia put her hands out towards me and I held them as we danced. I could feel the sadness in her, it matched my own. We were two lonely souls cast together by circumstance. This was as close as we'd been, as intimate as we'd allowed and as far as we could go.

I finally understood that she could only ever be a fantasy, that there was no possibility of anything happening, and it was better that way. She would only hurt me more than I'd ever been hurt before. The thought of never being with her deepened my sadness, but it was a beautiful sadness, an aching melancholy, because while I would never be with her I would always have her, we would always be friends and she would always be there for me.

Suddenly the lights came on and a voice boomed out.

"SO THIS IS WHAT YOU'RE FUCKING UP TO!"

I blinked in confusion, initially thinking the stereo had switched CDs and put on some angry rap music. But it was Steve, here to gate-crash the party.

"Come on, you," he said, grabbing Sonia roughly by the arm.

"Ow! Stop it, Steve," she protested, twisting away from him.

I stood in silence as the opening lines to *You're Crazy* blasted out from the kitchen top, too stunned to act, to even think. He continued to grapple with her, shaking her violently, shouting over the music. And all I could see was her face, eyes shut tight, mouth set in determination as she resisted him with all her little might. Steve pulled hard again, yanking her towards the door, her knee hit the coffee table and she winced in pain. I felt that thing uncoil in me once more, that latent energy which had infused me with an alien power in *The Three Sisters*. Fuck Steve. Fuck him and all the men like him. They took and they took, and anything they couldn't take they destroyed. Well, he wasn't going to destroy this. I picked up an unopened can and moved in his direction.

"Leave her alone, you cunt!" I roared.

Steve paused, momentarily easing his grip on Sonia; she slumped to the floor like injured prey.

"Ha! This fucker. You're not gay at all, are you?"

With his full attention on me, his imposing bulk looming over me, I felt my alien power retreat, slide back down my spine. This wasn't a fight I could win. But I didn't have to win, I only had to strike a blow for the underdog, leave my mark and let him know he couldn't keep taking with impunity.

"Fuck you, Steve."

"No, fuck you," he said, picking Sonia up from the floor and half-lifting, half-dragging her out the door. She squealed her resistance, her feet sliding on the lino as she fought gamely on. My temper returned. I launched myself at him, smacking the can off the back of his skull. It burst, sending beer spraying over the two of us. Again Sonia was dispensed with, this time she scurried to the corner of the room like an insect.

"Would you ever fuck off!" said Steve, shoving me hard in the chest so that I skidded backwards and landed in one of the chairs with a thump. Sonia was hiding now, had sought refuge behind the clothes horse, her frightened eyes peering out beneath my socks and jocks. Steve sighed in annoyance. This was all just an inconvenience to him.

"Sonia, get the fuck out," he said, in one of those voices which suggested there would be consequences if you didn't obey.

She stayed where she was, her eyes darting back and forth like those of a cornered animal. And she was the weakest of animals, incapable of fending off a large predator like Steve. He hoicked the clothes horse into the air, sending damp T-shirts and jeans flying. A pair of my boxer shorts landed snugly over the kettle.

"Come on!" he growled, uprooting her once more.

He adopted a new technique, taking her by the hair this time, eager to bring this silly game to a conclusion. Sonia's shrieks didn't deter him, nothing was going to stop him now. They made it out of the living-room to my front door, but no further. I was after him, chopping at his arms, forcing him to release his grip. Sonia once more fell to the floor and remained there, all the fight knocked out of her.

"If you don't stop . . ." Steve said, turning to me, his mass obscuring the light from the hallway.

I shoved him this time, as hard as I could, hoping to get him out the door and lock it behind him. He shifted a few inches and then resumed his position.

"This guy!" he exclaimed, as if addressing an audience.

It occurred to me that he didn't even know my name.

With one sweep of his left arm, he plucked Sonia from the floor and flung her out onto the landing. I tried to follow her, to protect her, to place my body over hers so she wouldn't feel any more pain. But I was stopped in my tracks, knocked flat on my back by a sharp, jolting right hand. I had been punched in the face before, by Dan's friend in Dublin, but not like this. It was like being hit with a sledgehammer. And because I'd been moving forward at the time, the impact was increased. I may have been unconscious for a few seconds, it was hard to tell.

When I opened my eyes, I couldn't see through the tears. I could hear, though, hear Sonia being dragged down the stairs, hear the whimpers as another part of her body connected with something sharp. I tried to get to my feet, to find one last surge in my depleted reserves, but the punch had taken it out of me. An old jacket had landed on top of me in the furore. I lay beneath it, listening as Sonia's cries slowly receded into the distance and the last strains of *Rocket Queen* faded out from my stereo.

34

I DIDN'T SLEEP, JUST LAY there in shocked silence. Then I remembered there was drink. So, I crawled into the living-room, picked up the can I'd burst off Steve's head and supped whatever was left in it. When that was gone, I found another. Then I found the vodka. Soon the heat of the morning began to spread across the room. I listened out for a tap at the door, her tap, a sign that everything was okay. There was no tap, only traffic and noise, so I stayed where I was, drinking, not feeling. When the drink was gone and the sun was shining directly upon me I crept up to the bedroom, pulled the curtains and clambered onto the bed. Once sleep took me I'd be safe.

But it offered no relief. My dreams were sad and empty, the dreams of a useless man. And when I awoke to the throb of another balmy evening I knew there was trouble ahead. All the drink was gone. The town was alive with the sounds of summer, just as it had been yesterday and the day before. I had been part of it then. It seemed like a lifetime ago. I got up, looked in the mirror, saw the mess he'd made of my face and felt a fresh wave of anger. How dare he. Coming up here, causing a ruckus, giving me two black eyes. It wasn't my fault his girlfriend hated him.

For a second I considered going downstairs, barging in there, taking him by surprise and doling out some retribution; but that would only end in more pain, more punches with me on the receiving end. It would cause further distress for Sonia too, and she was the real victim here. I wanted to ring her, or to text, but he'd probably taken her phone and was waiting for me to get in touch. It would only inflame the situation, cause her further suffering. I could have called the guards, reported Steve, helped Sonia get a place in the women's refuge, but that wasn't my job. I had caused enough trouble already. Whatever we had was over now. It was best I kept out of it.

For the time being I had to focus on getting some drink, just enough to get me over the trauma of the event, enough to help me deal with the stress. After that, I could assess the situation again. But to get more booze I would have to go down the stairs, past their apartment. That was a risk I couldn't take. I knew Sonia brought Casper to her mother's at ten every morning. That would be my opening. Steve's movements were less predictable, but oddly I was less scared of bumping into him.

So at 9.55 a.m. I sat on the window sill and waited for the familiar slam of the outside door. It came at 10.02, swiftly followed by mother and son. She was bedraggled, sparsely dressed and wore a baseball cap. I couldn't see any bruises from up here but she walked with a pronounced limp. I heard her reprimand Casper, and his whining response, as they disappeared round the corner. At 10.20 I gathered my sturdiest shopping bags and headed to the supermarket. Even at this early hour, the heat was oppressive. I walked in the shadows, head down, avoiding the happy, sun-kissed faces and their big beaming grins.

It was 10.28 when I got to the shop. I stood by the off-licence and waited for someone to open the gate. A man appeared at 10.32 and gave me a knowing nod as he opened up. He probably thought I was heading off to the park for the day, slugging flagons with the boys while we lay out in the sun. If only. I was clinical and efficient with my purchases: a slab of beer, a bottle of vodka, and two bottles of wine. It would be enough. I would think about my next step when that was all gone.

"Where's the session?" the man joked as I made my way towards the checkout.

Another man had to take the tags off the bottles before I could scan them through. He didn't give any nod or mention any session. I preferred him. By 10.39 I was out of the supermarket and on the way home. I lugged the heavy bags as fast as I could until I reached the front door. I got inside, climbed the stairs and reached my flat without incident. I was safe again, at least for a few days. I took to the couch and began to drink, pacing myself, aware that in my situation I couldn't afford to get sloppy.

The sun rose to its highest point, so high that it bathed my entire living room in bright light. As it made its way across the sky, it cast a shadow on the floor. I watched that shadow creep across the room until it disappeared altogether and darkness fell. The vodka was gone, and a bottle of wine. I couldn't remember drinking them. Maybe I dozed off for a while, it was hard to tell, but by the time I started on the second bottle of wine the sun had returned. I was watching the shadow creep across the floor again when there was a knock at the door.

Sonia? My heart leapt. It was okay. She'd explained everything to Steve and was coming up to watch her programmes. It hadn't sounded like her knock, though. Maybe she had a new knock? That was the kind of thing people did when they wanted to make a fresh start. It could have been Steve. I didn't know what his knock sounded like. He wasn't the knocking type. But it was my old drinking buddy, Gerard. I hadn't seen him in months.

"What the fuck happened to you?" he asked.

No such thing as, 'Well, how it's going?' or 'Sorry I haven't been around much lately,' just straight to the gossip.

"Fighting," I said sourly.

"Any cans?"

I pointed at the fridge, pleased to have a drinking partner, but annoyed at myself for being a pushover.

He popped open the lager and sat opposite me, awaiting the news.

"Where have you been?" I asked.

"Busy out, man. Been working."

"You don't work," I said incredulously.

"I built half the houses in this country, boy."

"Where's your woman? That Mary, or whatever her name was."

"Jaysus, she's long gone."

Satisfied with these updates, I offered an explanation for my black eyes, a version of the scuffle which painted me in a more heroic light.

"He got jealous. Thought I was trying to steal his missus."

"And you were," Gerard replied.

"Yeah."

We shared a look then, a look I'd often seen men share but had never been part of. He was all right, Gerard. I wished he'd call over more often.

"I told you she was trouble."

"You did, Gerard."

"But you didn't listen."

"I did not."

"You're lucky he didn't kill you. He's a dangerous bastard."

"I'm dangerous too," I told him, slugging off my can. "Want another?"

"Can't. I've places to be."

"Where?" I asked, annoyed he was leaving me in the lurch again.

"I'm going out to Kiltubbern, looking at a dog, a greyhound."

"For what?"

"To buy him! Always wanted to own a racing dog."

I waved him away; if that was how he spent his days, then it was probably best we remained mere acquaintances.

"You could get a part-share for five grand," he said.

"I'll talk to you later, Gerard."

I was discovering that good friends were hard to find these days.

35

THE SUN WAS STILL SPLITTING the stones when my booze ran out. The heat was relentless, a harsh and unforgiving scourge. But I would outlast it. Again I waited until Sonia had left the building before making my pilgrimage. I skulked in the shadows, kept my head down and made it to the supermarket without any drama. The same fellah was at the off-licence; he gave me a different look this time, one of disgust, with a hint of pity. As I collected my booze I could sense him lurking in the background, keeping an eye on me, making sure I didn't quaff a naggin of vodka when no one was looking. I was one of those guys now, a down-and-out, not to be trusted.

"You going to be able to pay for all that?" he asked.

"Yeah."

"Prove it."

Letting on I was mortally offended, I opened my wallet for him.

"All right. Had to check, you know how it is."

I didn't know how it was, but I nodded anyway. As I hefted the drink over to the checkouts, a thought struck me: food. I hadn't been eating much of late, that was probably the sun, it killed a man's appetite. I went down the nearest aisle. It was a meat one. They had microwaveable food there, lasagne, shepherd's pie. I stuffed a few into my basket and proceeded to the checkout. Job done once more, I returned home and continued my session.

As luck would have it the weather broke at almost exactly the same time as my will to keep drinking. I woke up on the couch one afternoon, completely spent. I didn't reach out for a can, a bottle, I just lay there, waiting for God to take me. I had alcohol poisoning, possibly brain damage. A decision was made; I would lie here indefinitely, wait to see how it panned out. If I died, which seemed quite likely, it would be a relief from the pain if nothing else. Maybe I was dead already. I checked to see if I was still breathing. I couldn't hear anything, couldn't feel air going in or out. So that was that, I was dead. If this was the afterlife it was shite, worse than being alive.

With no proof I was breathing, I listened out for my heart. A gentle pulsing sound, like someone kicking a ball off a wall a few streets away, came back by way of response. I was alive, then. This realisation was swiftly followed by another: I was thirsty, so thirsty I could have drunk the River Suir in one slug and then come back for the Barrow and Nore. I moved my eyes to one side. It didn't hurt so I did it again. There was a bottle of orange on the table. If I leaned over I could get it. But it seemed too much of a risk. I'd only just established that my heart was beating. I stayed where I was, motionless, fantasising about bottles of orange with big orangey bits in the middle of them.

The rest of me started to wake up. I had to piss. I was hungry. The big toe on my right foot was sore. I needed to shit. I was cold. One of my teeth felt wonky. My brain damage was better, though. Everything was clear, too clear. All the thoughts were back, all the bad ones, and now they had some new material, an LP full of classics which would never grow old.

You should have stopped him. You should have protected her. You just let him walk in here and take over, let him drag her out by the hair, wreck the place and punch you in the face. And did you call the guards or try to get her help? No. You just sat up here drinking, like you always do.

That was side one. You had to flip the record over for side two.

What did you expect to happen, carrying on with that psycho's girlfriend? If you'd just left her alone, like Gerard said, everything would have been all right. He's probably been beating the shit out of her every night, and it's all your fault. How pathetic. Hanging around with her in the hope she might eventually fuck you out of pity.

There was even a bonus track for those who bought the deluxe version.

You're fucked. The only friend you had, and you can't talk to her any more. Her boyfriend wants to kill you. The neighbours will all know by now. The whole building knows about you, that you tried to get off with her and got a hiding for your efforts. Everyone hates you. You'd better not go out. Stay here where it's safe.

These hits played on a constant loop, getting louder and louder. With each rotation my chest grew tighter. It all came back. The palpitations, churning stomach, racing heart, panic, anxiety, paranoia - the whole fucking lot. I put my hands over my face and tried to cry, but I was too dehydrated. No tears came. All hope was lost. I was tired, tired of myself and my bullshit. Some people weren't meant to live, they brought nothing to the world. I was one of those people. There was a reason no one liked me, that no-one had ever liked me: I was a parasite. Even if I'd wanted to give, I had nothing anyone wanted.

So I gave up. I stopped trying to live a better life. Instead I would fester, wallow and decay. It would be liberating. In this new existence it wouldn't matter how much I drank, whether I shaved, showered or had a balanced diet. Exercise, getting outside, maintaining a positive state of mind: that was all a waste of time. Now, if my state of mind wasn't positive I would drink until it was. If my state of mind was already positive, I would drink to make it even more positive. And if all the drink in China couldn't make it positive, then I would drink anyway. It would be a fine way to live.

During one of my covert missions to the supermarket, I saw a letter had arrived from the university. I ripped it up without opening it. A week later another one came, and then another. They kept coming until the leaves turned brown and the nights grew cold, then no more letters came. I bunkered in for the winter, relishing the long, dark nights. Gerard, my old pal, my oldest of pals, visited from time to time. We would share a drink, a hurried conversation, and then he'd disappear. He'd lost his job, spent all his money and was back drinking at *The Three Sisters*. There was no mention of the dog he'd bought a share in.

There was no mention of Gráinne either, the cat who'd left Gerard for me and was now rumoured to be living with the fellah in Flat Number Two.

I didn't need that cat, though, I didn't even need Gerard and I certainly didn't need my father. One evening, however, as I sat slurping a pint of orange and vodka, I heard shouting from outside. This was nothing new, people were always shouting around here, but I recognised the voice: it was my father. I turned down the telly.

"AIDAN! ARE YOU IN THERE? I NEED TO TALK TO YOU!"

What did he want? I peeped outside. He was standing on the path, looking up at my flat.

"AIDAN! AIDAN! Jesus Christ."

I heard another voice: Mrs. M, trying to calm him, suggesting a different approach. There was silence for a minute or two.

"AIDAN, IT'S IMPORTANT! CALL ME, PLEASE."

When they got back into the car and drove off, I returned to my drink. How could I call him? Sure I hadn't seen my phone in months. I thought that would be the end of it, but the next day I was rudely awoken by a knock at my door. Maybe it was Sonia this time, or Steve again, or maybe Sonia and Steve and Casper. Whoever it was, they could keep knocking. I wasn't accepting visitors at the moment.

"Aidan, it's me, your father. I spoke to the people in the estate agents and they said you were still here. Let me in, I need to talk to you."

Had they given him a key? Was that not a breach of privacy? If they'd given him a key for the outside door, there was nothing stopping them giving him a key for my door. I decided to answer it, to resolve the issue and get rid of him. I turned the lock and drifted back into the living-room, not bothering to welcome him in.

"Jesus, Aidan, what's going on?" he said as he followed me inside.

I sat on the couch, duvet wrapped around me, staring into the distance. He stood motionless, taking in his surroundings. It was probably a mess, but there was no need for all this drama.

"Christ above, you can't live like this. This is . . ."

He was off then. First he drew the curtains and opened the windows. Then he began clearing up the empties. After that he tackled the piles of dirty dishes. There was sweeping and mopping, scrubbing and cleaning, bleach and sprays, and all the while he muttered under his breath about how much of a disgrace it was. Luckily I had a few cans to hand so didn't need to move from my position, although he did ask me to move my feet when he was doing the floors, a request which was denied. When he was finished he disappeared up to the bedroom for a while, and then into the bathroom.

I fully expected him to pick me up and start cleaning me next. Instead he sat down opposite me with that earnest face he had acquired since shacking up with Mrs. M.

"What's going on, Aidan? I thought you were going to college."

"Was I?"

"Yes, an IT course. You rang me about it months ago."

"Oh, yeah."

"Jesus, look at the state of you."

That seemed a little harsh. Yes, I'd been slacking off on the old exercise and hadn't been grooming as often as one should, but a 'state'?

"You should see a doctor. I can arrange for Doctor Flynn to call in."

An errant thought floated across my mind, something about medication, pills, a nice feeling in my belly.

"I'm okay."

He stared at me, studying me in that way people do when they're making unwanted decisions about your future.

"Anyway," he said. "I had to see you. It's your mother."

He paused for effect. I took it as an opportunity to open a can.

"She hasn't got long left, Aidan."

All this hullabaloo for that.

"They're saying it'll only be a week or two now."

I shivered against the cold and glanced askance at the windows he'd opened.

"You won't fit into your old suit, I'd say, but Beatrice might be able to let out the waist and we can get you a shirt. Have you some decent shoes?"

I got up, the duvet still wrapped around me, and closed the windows.

"Sally is staying in a hotel. She said she'd call later," he continued.

"Can you go now, Dad?"

"What will I tell Sally? She tried ringing you but there was no answer. Where's your phone? Do you need credit?"

I yawned.

"What about food? Feck it, I should have brought the dinners, but we'll have loads at the house afterwards. Don't worry about the arrangements, we have everything sorted."

"Good man."

He was still asking questions and making suggestions as I ushered him out the door. When I got rid of him I locked it, putting the chain across for extra security. That would be the last time I welcomed visitors into this place.

*

Needless to say he was at my door a couple of days later, droning on about my mother being dead, how important it was I be there for her, for the family. He kept mentioning Sally, but I didn't hear her voice. She probably wasn't even home. It would just be Dad and Mrs. M at the funeral, the adulterer and his mistress, one as compliant as the other; a splendid send-off for the old bird. His last futile attempt came of a morning, early, so early I'd only just got to bed.

Through the haze of my dreams, my drunken stupor and a pounding headache I heard my father crying, apologising for some unspoken crime, for the sins of the world. It went on for some time, getting very bothersome, until I heard another voice, gruff, irate: Gerard. There was an exchange of words, muffled and indecipherable through the concrete walls; Dad offering miserable explanations, Gerard abrupt at first but then amenable. Some common ground was reached, maybe even kinship. And then Gerard was knocking at my door too. His appeals were more manly, more stern. He was most likely banging on about my responsibilities as a son, my duty to the family. If I'd been able, I would have shouted something back about him not even looking after his own cat, but instead I put two pillows over my head and curled up into a ball.

I thought the whole building would end up outside my door, maybe a guard, a fireman, an ambulance crew, like that scene from *There's Something About Mary*. But no, it was just those two goms. Gerard got aggressive, threatening to kick the door in and drag me out. He didn't need that hassle, though. And time eventually won out. With one last plaintive plea, my father hammered on the door, repeating my name over and over as if it were me that had died. Then there was silence; sweet, sweet silence.

36

Out of common courtesy I spent some time thinking about my mother. I thought about the past, about my childhood, and tried to mourn her but nothing happened. Thinking it might hit me all of a sudden, I carried on as normal, but I just forgot her. I didn't even feel sad about not feeling sad. I was a child of the drink now, it cared for me in a way she never had. Unfortunately, the booze was proving an abusive parent, taking as much as it gave. In my rare moments of clarity I noted my body was starting to revolt. It had been happy enough to comply with my excesses when I was a youngster, but, now nearing thirty, it was sending out distress signals. The most obvious manifestation was my gut. It had doubled in size and was solid, like a hard-boiled egg. My face was blotchy and red, the beard I had dispassionately grown only obscuring part of the problem. Those were the jaunty, jolly side-effects. The diarrhoea was more concerning, as were the stomach cramps, the sharp, jagged pain in my lower back and the occasional spots of blood in the bile I regularly vomited into the toilet after a rough few days.

Occasionally, I felt genuine fear for my health. I worried about those pains, about what I was doing to myself and what the end result would be. If I got too worried, so worried I began to feel anxious, I would drown those worries with more alcohol until my health didn't matter, until those pains were distant fears belonging to someone else. And so I continued through another summer, not as hot as the last, an autumn, a winter and another year.

Sonia and Steve moved out. I saw them leave and wondered if they were breaking up, whether he was going to his mother's and Sonia to a new council house. Their body language gave nothing away. She stood to the side with Casper while Steve and some other lads loaded the van. I felt an overwhelming sorrow as they drove away, a sadness I hadn't felt in a long time. There was a finality to it now. Even though I'd spent eighteen months avoiding her, I'd held out hope that one day we might meet into one another and everything would return to normal. There was no chance of that happening now. This must have been what break-ups felt like.

Someone else moved in, another single man around my age. I briefly thought about being his friend, but I was too tired for new people now, too tired for it all. The pains got worse. It was taking more and more alcohol to make them go away. Sometimes I had to drink to unconsciousness to make them stop. Those pains would kill me eventually, unless I got there first. It was time to accept defeat, to hold my hands up and say 'no more', to burn out instead of fading away. The only questions now were when and how.

PART THREE

2016

1

Today will be different. Today will be my last day. No more fighting. This is where it stops. I have chosen death by drowning, death by the sea. I'm afraid of the physical sensations, of the water filling my lungs and being unable to breathe, but I remind myself that those few minutes of discomfort and pain are nothing compared to what I've already endured and what I'll continue to endure if I don't do this now. I've tidied the flat, because people will be in here, rooting through my stuff, looking for clues and suchlike.

I've binned anything likely to cause shame; old porn DVDs, a book entitled *Britain's Deadliest Killers,* the rope I'd bought to hang myself when that was still an option, and the unopened pack of condoms I'd bought during one of my confident spells. I brought all the empty bottles and cans to the bottle bank, shredded all my bank statements and social welfare payment receipts, cleared the search history on my laptop, deleted all my bookmarks and painstakingly went through all my emails, deleting any I didn't like. They'd try and learn more about me through social media, but I hardly used those. I hadn't written a note. Who would I be writing it for: my father? My sister? If I was going to be writing anything it would have been for my landlord; I'd fallen a bit behind on my rent, which wasn't like me. I'd leave out the few quid I had left by way of apology.

I ate a good breakfast, showered and shaved, put on some clean clothes and made sure I had my wallet. There was no one I needed to say goodbye to, not at this stage, so I left the money on the kitchen table and shut the door on the place I'd called home for almost five years. Before going downstairs, I stopped outside Gerard's flat. I wondered would he miss me, would he feel bad. People tended to blame themselves in situations like this, but Gerard wasn't that type. He had a marvellous sense of indifference towards the world. His only concern would be if I'd left any booze in the fridge.

If Gerard wasn't going to miss me, then my others neighbours certainly weren't. My death would barely register with them. They'd all have a new neighbour in the coming days. Would they tell the person moving in that Number 14 was the dead guy's flat? Would that be a problem? I couldn't see why it would. It wasn't like I'd died in the flat or anything. This new tenant could bring some happier memories to the place, maybe bring his girlfriend over, have sex with her in my bed. They could cook for one another in the kitchen, him laughing as he held out the spoon for her to taste, her burning her mouth but agreeing that yes, it was delicious. Then they could sit on my couch and watch a film, curled up in each other's arms, making happy memories in a place which had never known anything but sadness.

That was an exaggeration, of course. There'd probably been all sorts happening here before I moved in, murders, orgies, pagan rituals and the like. But as I reached the ground floor and walked through the foyer one last time, it all ceased to matter. Apartment 14, 56 Wolfe Tone Street was just a subtext in the sad story of Aidan Collins, the place where he'd finally stopped fighting, where he'd thrown in the towel and headed for pastures new. Reaching those pastures wasn't going to be easy, though.

I'd chosen to die at a quiet beach thirty miles outside of town called Farragorm. It was the place most suited to my task. Although a fairly big beach, with a long shoreline and surrounding hilly area, it had very few amenities; therefore it was only ever busy during good spells of weather. On a day like today, you could easily find a quiet spot to reflect on the disastrous decisions you'd made in your life and then quietly wade into the waters, never to return.

To get there I needed to get the Number 370 bus. I'd have to wait at the stop, near other people, exposing myself to the possibility of seeing someone I knew while I waited for the bus to arrive. Then I'd have to queue up, stand in an orderly fashion while the pensioners got on first, the mammies with prams, and finally the deadbeats like me; the losers who should have cars, should be at work, but because they were incapable of living like normal folk were stuck on the bus with the elderly and the infants.

Once I'd got on, I'd have to face the driver, show him my social services card – because I didn't have to pay, I was, according to the government, disabled, so depressed, so incapable of existing, they'd given me a card to prove it – and then shuffle down the bus, praying for an empty seat near the back, away from the friendly chatter of my fellow travellers, the wails of the griping toddlers and the mumbled apologies of their flustered mothers. All I wanted was a nice, unoccupied place for me to carry out my last journey or, to be more precise, my second-last journey.

I left my building and began making my way down the street. It occurred to me that I hadn't gone through my normal routine before leaving the house. Usually when I went anywhere I carried out a lengthy and complex set of checks and assessments, ensuring that all the windows were shut, all the lights and taps were off and of course that my door was firmly locked. It could take me half an hour to leave, sometimes more, but I hadn't bothered today. Not only that, I didn't even feel anxious.

If I'd walked down this road a few days previously, past the vape shop, the butchers, the old sweet shop, I'd have cowered in fear, awaiting something terrible and unexpected, praying I could make it to my destination unnoticed and ignored. On this day, however, my last day, I felt okay. There was a slight twinge in my chest, a tremor in my step, and I obviously wasn't making eye contact with anyone, but it was manageable, I could do it. Perhaps later on when the time came, I would once more be gripped by fear, but for now my neuroses were gone and I was cured.

I reached the bus stop and saw people huddled under the shelter, women, children, old people, at least a dozen of them. I stood to the side, an aloof young man just off to the beach for the day, to meet a girl perhaps, or some friends. My only source of anxiety now was the bus. What if it didn't come and I had to wait an hour for the next one? An hour was a long time when you were in a position like mine, long enough to reconsider, to quietly walk back up the road, back to the flat. But no, I'd left the key inside the building, discreetly placed on the shelf where our communal mail gathered. There was nowhere else for me to go. That flat, this city, these oppressive streets - I was never going to see them again. Once this bus came I was out of here and I wasn't coming back.

I peered up the Quay, it was a long street, taking traffic in from the New Bridge and depositing it in the city centre via a series of side streets and roundabouts. There was no sign of the bus, just the usual mid-morning traffic, easy and light; people late for work or school or early for shopping. It was 10 a.m. now, the clock tower, which stood halfway up the Quay and gonged on the hour, every hour, told me so. The bus shouldn't have been late, it had no right to be late. I'd specifically chosen this bus, reasoning that no one of any importance would have anywhere to be at this time, that there'd be very little traffic, almost no delays, and that I'd be seated and settled by 10.01, ready to carry out the next step of my mission. Yet here we were, 10.01 and no bus.

I stole a glance at the people waiting, looking for signs of disquiet or unease among their ranks. They seemed pretty calm, even the elderly ones who had less time to waste than most. They were chatting away about the latest part of their bodies to start acting up, a friend who had recently passed, the usual miserable stuff. No one had noticed that the bus was late, that the hour had struck ten and it hadn't arrived. That placated me. If they could be sanguine about the bus's lateness, then so could I. As I listened to them talking, keeping my distance, I felt a pair of eyes upon me. There was someone looking at me, someone on the bench inside the shelter. I dared not look their way, terrified of whom I might see.

"Aidan! Is that you?"

I recognised the voice immediately: Mrs. M.

Heart sinking, I turned to face her. She was already up on her feet coming towards me.

"It is you! How have you been? I haven't seen you since . . ." her voice trailed off.

"Hi, Mrs. M. I'm grand, thanks," I replied, as she gazed up at me expectantly.

"How are you, Aidan?" she asked softly.

She had always known how to sweet-talk me, a skill she had successfully employed with both the Collins men.

"I'm okay."

"We haven't seen you in a while."

"No."

"Are you still living on Wolfe Tone Street?"

"Yeah."

I was reluctant to tell her anything because if I completed my task successfully she'd spend the rest of her life wondering. And, unlike Gerard, she would blame herself, think she could have done something differently, changed the course of history.

"I'm just going to the beach," I said.

"Which one?" she asked hopefully.

To get to Farragorm you had to go through Barnduff, where Mrs. M and Dad lived. She was waiting for the same bus as I was. Where was her car? Had someone told her about my suicide attempt? This was all my father's doing. He'd planted her here to stop me going through with it. I paused, frantic. There was a bus in the bay behind us. It was going to Rún Derg, the biggest seaside village in the south east with a horrible, busy beach full of people and dogs.

"Rún Derg," I said.

"Ah, that's a pity, you could have come up to the house. I know your dad would love to see you."

I maintained my strongest poker face, giving nothing away.

"I'd better go," I said as the last of the passengers boarded the bus to Rún Derg.

"Well, give us a call when you . . ."

I didn't hear the rest. I ran across the forecourt and hopped onto the bus just as the driver was about to close the doors.

"Single for Rún Derg," I said, showing him my card.

I moved towards the back of the bus. I knew she was watching me, hoping I'd wave, give her something positive to bring back to my father, but I stared dead ahead as the bus pulled off. Now, instead of nice, quiet Farragorm with its long, empty swathes of sand, I was going to hellish, noisy Rún Derg, with its arcades, amusement park, pubs, water slides and, worst of all, perennially busy beach. *Fucking Mrs. M.* I'd spent months formulating a plan to end my life, picking a specific day, a specific time, summoning up the courage to go through with it, only for her to appear and scupper everything.

I could have got another bus to Farragorm when I arrived in Rún Derg, but there was no direct route. I'd have to go back into town and start all over. It'd be nearly lunchtime by then. Yet if I was truly determined to go through with this I had to be prepared for all eventualities. I couldn't let this put me off. There was a beach at Rún Derg, the sea was just as deep there, just as capable of flooding one's lungs and causing one's death. I'd just have to wait till later, until the evening, when it had calmed down and everyone had gone home. I knew that beach went on for miles, knew if you walked far enough and long enough you could find the kind of isolation you got at Farragorm. The plan was still on. It had just taken a little detour.

2

HALF AN HOUR LATER, THE bus pulled into the station at Rún Derg and I alighted. The meeting with Mrs. M had shaken me up a bit. I didn't want her to be the last person I ever spoke to, it wasn't right. However, I wasn't dead yet and, thanks to my new plan, I wouldn't be for another eight hours or so. That left plenty of time to find someone else to talk to; a lonely old man sitting on a bench, an attendant in the arcades, one of those gypsy fortune-tellers in a rickety old caravan. I could have a dozen conversations between now and high tide.

The original plan had been to get off in Farragorm, wander down to the tiny shop and purchase a bottle of vodka and a bottle of whiskey, head to the beach, walk to its northernmost tip, its most remote area; over the rocks, past the small pools and cave and down to where the beach faded away and was replaced by a jutting shoreline, by treacherous outcrops of stone and rock, slick with seaweed and spray. Once there, I'd intended to find a cosy inlet, open the vodka, stare out to sea and wait for the water.

I'd figured out the tides and everything, mapped out my day right down to the minute I'd enter the water, estimating how long it would take to finish the booze, hoping it would strengthen my resolve, clear any lingering doubts, give me the courage to go through with it. I was going to drink the vodka first; it made me ballsy and defiant, just what was needed in a situation like this. The whiskey would add a touch of wistfulness, elicit a song or two, perhaps a few tears as I reflected on my life and the decisions that had brought me here.

Then, with just the dregs remaining, the water would lap at my feet, wetting my backside. That would be my cue to stand up, carefully set the bottle to one side, and march out to sea. That had been the plan. It would have looked like I'd just gone down there for a quiet drink and lost track of time. That, realising the errors of my ways, I'd tried to make it back to safety and been caught by the tide, sucked out to sea against my will, my cries for help unheard as I lost my battle with the elements. Now I had to make a new plan. I didn't know where the beach ended in Rún Derg, whether there were quiet spots with slippy rocks and deceptive tides. I would just have to find out.

*

The amusement park was up and running, even at this early hour; its cacophony of noise, bleeps and horns encouraging anyone within shouting distance to bump on the bumpers, roll on the coasters and whirl in the gigs. Across the road, the arcades were open for business too, bells and whistles drifting out onto the street as I made my way to the beach. There were a few families ambling about, some youngsters idling around the car park, but summer was over and in a few days Rún Derg would shut down completely. Its pubs and cafés would remain open, its hotels still accept bookings, but life would take on a very different feel. Another tourist season over, the locals would sleepwalk their way through the winter, leaving the beach to the swimmers and surfers in search of high winds and big waves, to the walkers and joggers keeping in shape while the rest of the country hibernated.

The tide was neither in nor out. I knew it took approximately six hours to go from high to low and that it would be high at Farragorm at 10.32 p.m. Surely it would be the same here? I would assess it properly later on in the evening when things quietened down. First I had to purchase some alcohol. I didn't know the lay of the land here, where to get drink, what the prices were like. In Farragorm they had a small little shop where discretion was of the utmost, bottles handed out and brown paper bags provided. Here, though, I was exposed. I'd have to go to an unfamiliar supermarket or an off-licence, wouldn't know which aisle to head to, which shelf they kept the premium stuff on.

I thought it'd be easy enough to find a shop selling alcohol, a cosy little off-licence tucked away from the main strip, but locating anywhere with even a dram of booze proved difficult. I walked past pubs and hotels, B & Bs, phone repair shops, more pubs, a tourist centre, a gift shop and a plethora of places with loud, banging music. There was no supermarket. Not even a newsagent's. What did people do for food around here? You couldn't live off chips and tomato ketchup. This was no accident, though; the supermarkets were hidden in the outskirts for a reason. The last thing anyone in Rún Derg wanted was for local businesses to suffer, for the chip shops and candy floss men to lose custom to the giant supermarket chains. If you put a supermarket near the beach, no one was going to bother going for a €5 pint in that quaint seaside bar. So they hid the shops where visitors couldn't find them. Well, I wasn't going into the *The Fisherman's Arms* asking if they did carry outs, embarrassing myself in front of all the cheery tourists digesting their full Irish. I was going to find a supermarket and buy the drink I was entitled to buy, and if the local publicans didn't like it that was their tough shit.

3

THERE WAS A SUPERMARKET AT the other end of town, far enough away to ensure most people didn't bother trying to find it. But I wasn't most people. My need was great. And because it had taken me so long to discover, I'd managed to while away an hour, bringing myself a little bit closer to the end. It was a big store, bigger than the one I usually went to. It looked like an airport hangar, with entire aisles dedicated to cheese, to nappies, a DIY section near the front and a corner devoted to televisions, laptops and other electrical goods.

A situation like this; an unfamiliar supermarket in broad daylight, surrounded by lots of people, would usually have been cause for a severe panic attack, a complete meltdown, concluding with me stood outside the shop, bent over, ashen-faced and covered in sweat, with not a drop of alcohol to my name. Now my anxiety, that fearsome beast which whispered expletives in one ear, negative thoughts in the other, was quiet as a mouse as I made my way inside the shop and began my search for booze.

Perhaps the beast was gone now. It had won, it and all the other beasts: the depression, the OCD, the insomnia, the paranoia. They had set out to destroy me, whittle me away until there was nothing left, until I either had myself sectioned, upped my medication, was away with the fairies or threw in the towel altogether. The beasts didn't care which of these options I went with, only that I succumbed one way or another. I had done that. I had given up. Some of the beasts were still there: the one who looked after the self-loathing was present and accounted for. And I felt empty and numb, devoid of hope, worthless, a disgusting, shameful creature slithering my way through society. Pretty soon, though, that beast would be gone too. They'd all be gone. And me. The whole lot of us.

While the supermarket itself was moderately busy, the drinks aisle was deserted; I had the run of the place. I wasn't in the mood for idle fancy, though, I was here on business, to purchase two large bottles of spirits and be on my way. For once, I wasn't on a budget, nothing but the finest of beverages for my last supper. Instead of looking for the cheapest stuff or whatever was on special offer, I went straight for the good stuff; imported Russian vodka, four times distilled, three times filtered and single malt Scotch whiskey, the best. It would almost be a shame to have it swilling around inside me as I sank to the ocean floor. I placed the two bottles in my basket and headed towards the self-service checkouts, pleased there was no one around to judge me or my purchases.

"Self-services are down, pal. You'll have to use the normal ones."

It took me a moment to realise the voice was aimed in my direction. Its source was a man in a white shirt and dark trousers, the uniform of the modern security guard.

"They're not working, see?" he said, pointing at the self-service checkouts.

He was right, they weren't. They all had angry red crosses on their screens.

"Go up there to Yvonne. She'll look after you."

The security guard walked away, leaving me alone with my drink. This wasn't part of any plan. I'd braced for myself for a brief chat with the kindly old woman at the shop in Farragorm, not a showdown with a stern checkout operator at a supermarket. I couldn't talk to Yvonne, couldn't rock up and make small talk about the weather, not without any prior warning. The whole point of the self-service checkouts was to minimise human contact, to allow social misfits like myself to pass through life unnoticed.

My initial reaction was to call back the security guard and ask him why the self-service checkouts were down and when they'd be up and running again, but he was long gone, roaming the aisles with watchful authority, securing and guarding for all he was worth.

I thought about dropping the basket and leaving, quietly placing it on the floor then making my way to the exits and outside to safety, far away from Yvonne or anyone else. I wouldn't have any drink then, though, I'd have to abandon the plan altogether. Another idea briefly flickered through my mind: I could make my way to the exits and outside to safety *with* the drink. No Yvonne, no awkward conversations and no judgement. The security guard was fatter than me, if he came after me I'd outrun him easily, even with the drink. But there was no telling what lengths he'd go to in order to apprehend me. He could be one of those head-cases who'd always wanted to join the army but lost interest when he discovered the job mostly consisted of keeping the peace and making sure your shoes were clean. He could be the type of person who lived for opportunities like this, who, upon seeing me rumbling across the car park, booze in tow, would briefly look to the heavens, whisper 'Thank you, God,' and spring into action, calling for back-up on his walkie-talkie as he hurdled over the checkouts past the frightened customers, in pursuit of his target.

He might be the type of person who, although carrying a little extra timber, had a level of fitness in keeping with someone who spends the day on their feet, someone who could shift through the gears when he needed to. Who, upon giving chase, would quickly realise that he needn't have called for back-up at all, that he could take down this pathetic slug all by himself. The type of person who wouldn't just tickle the collar of the felon but would launch himself at the staggering, stumbling fool, bringing him thudding to the ground, knocking the air clean out of him and smashing his precious cargo in the process; and then roar in triumph, adrenaline coursing through his veins, as he clambered all over his quarry, determined to ensure there would be no escape. It goes without saying that a person such as this would not be content to smack the thief on his rear end and let him continue with his day. Certainly not. The guards would be called, names would be taken and only then would the scoundrel be set free. But not before he had paid for the alcohol destroyed in the skirmish, frogmarched back into the store by the hero of the hour and made to count out every last cent for the, now, frankly appalled, Yvonne.

So no, I wouldn't choose that option. I would do the decent thing, the thing any normal human being would do. I glanced nervously towards the checkouts, hoping against hope that Yvonne wasn't young or attractive. I couldn't deal with an attractive woman right now, far better for her to be old and decrepit, a faint smell of wee wafting up from beneath her chair. Yvonne was none of those things. She was about my age, pleasing to look at, a friendly familiarity about her. And she was waving at me, smiling, beckoning me towards her, practically begging for my company. I began the slow walk to Checkout Nine, Yvonne's features becoming clearer as I drew closer. What struck me wasn't so much her profile but her size; she seemed a little chubby, even cuddly. She wore it well though, and looked at ease with herself and life in general.

"They've been down all morning," she said apologetically.

Now, with just a few feet separating us, I could see her properly. Her hair was dyed a dark metallic red; shoulder-length, straight, stylishly cut. You could tell she was proud of it. Coupled with the small stud in her nose it suggested a rebellious streak, an adventurous side held in check during business hours, unleashed after dark. Her skin was olive, almost oily, her cheeks and jaw line round and puffy, bringing to mind one of those Russian nesting dolls. Her slight double chin was offset by a wide, pleasant mouth, opening out into the most welcoming of smiles. Eyes, light blue, genuine and honest, her whole countenance spoke of kindness and decency. This was a person who would do me no wrong, I was sure of that.

"Not to worry," I said shakily, placing my drink on the counter. My voice sounded unfamiliar, as if it belonged to someone else.

"Off to a party?" she asked, nodding at the drink.

I felt the sweat prickle on my back, conscious of the sheer awfulness of my fat, blistered face, the abhorrent mass of my gut, the worn state of my clothes. I looked like shit, I knew I did; how could I be going to a party?

"Just a few friends," I whispered, trying to escape within myself, to get out of there before I infected her with my filth.

"Well for you," she said, "I'm stuck here till six. Do you want a bag?"

"Yes, please."

She scanned the bottles and totted up the price. I had the money ready, hadn't expected to be passing it into the hands of another.

"And €2.43 change," she said, smiling as she placed the coins into my clammy palms.

"Thank you," I said, now truly humiliated.

"You're welcome. Enjoy your party!"

"I will," I replied, already feeling the dampness on my brow, down my back, in my crotch, the pressure threatening to overwhelm me as I trudged out of the store, the bottles jangling in the seventy-cent bag.

Outside at last, I relaxed. That had been an unexpected challenge, but I'd overcome it. Not only that, I'd spoken to a new person, a stranger, had a genuine conversation, however brief, with a woman my own age. Even though it had reduced me to a quivering wreck, it actually felt quite nice now, I'd almost got a buzz from chatting away to Yvonne about drink and fictitious parties. It made me yearn for more conversations, more human interaction, but no, I was too far gone now. I had detached myself from society for a reason.

No one needed to get to know me, be taken in by my apparent ordinariness, the unassuming personality which might lead them to believe I'm a decent person. Conversations like the one I'd just had with Yvonne only served to remind me why I couldn't go around speaking to people, run the risk of familiarity developing into acquaintance and maybe even friendship. I'd had friends before, and I'd lost them all. On the plus side, this meant I no longer had to worry about my last meaningful interaction on this earth being with Mrs. M. Yvonne would never know how helpful she'd been.

4

I WALKED BACK THROUGH TOWN to the promenade, to the beach and the amusement park. It had grown busier, but this was still a quiet day at Rún Derg, a day of little opportunity and few takings. I certainly wouldn't be adding to anyone's coffers, My focus now was on leaving all this noise behind and finding a quiet place to be by myself. I made my way past the casinos, the arcades and the pedalo lake and circled round the edge of the park, past the oddities which clung to its outskirts: the virtual reality ride, the man selling counterfeit jewellery, the ice cream man, the hot-dog man and the burger woman, until I finally stepped on to the beach, the uneven, uninviting beach with its large flat rocks perfect for skimming and assortment of extravagantly coloured shells which had been picked up, marvelled at and replaced over and over again. Some of these stones and rocks had been deep in the ocean, miles from the coast, surrounded by fish and underwater life; now they'd made it to the beach, ready to start their journey all over again.

I moved in closer to the water itself, where the grains of sand finally began to outnumber the stones and you could walk without having to check your footing every couple of moments. But this was where those who had come to enjoy the seaside had gathered; they were sitting on towels shivering uncomfortably, or strolling, walking, jogging and running by the water's edge. They were loving life, enjoying the elements, relishing the sea air, the spray, feeling at one with nature, their gormless faces staring into mine, hoping to catch my eye so they could holler some inanity about how lovely or unlovely the day was.

I kept my gaze fixed firmly on the sand, waiting until I reached the point where there were no more happy walkers and it was just me and the sea. That took a while. After twenty minutes of walking, twenty minutes of keeping my head down, ignoring the shoes and sandals of passers-by, scowling at dogs who came up for a sniff and positively bristling at the father and son with the kite which almost got entangled in my jacket, I still wasn't free of them. The sand had grown softer and more yielding, to the point where I was almost sinking in it, and I'd passed a few dunes but still they came: the runners with their heavy breathing, the watersports enthusiasts with their wetsuits and wind-propelled bits of plastic and carbon fibre, and the dog-lovers with their sticks and soaking wet canines who were drawn to me no matter how many bad vibes I gave off.

Eventually though, after powering through deep heavy drifts of sand, tiptoeing through muddy, shallow waters, and negotiating yet more stones and pebbles, their numbers dwindled. I went five minutes without seeing anyone, then ten, until, after daring to lift my head and looking this way and that, there wasn't a soul to be seen. No one came up this far, because there was no conceivable reason to do so. The beach had narrowed to almost nothing, just a bare strip of sand which gave way to scrub and grassy marshlands, a foreboding terrain which stretched all the way to the horizon. Further on, the sand disappeared altogether, outdone by mud and stone, grassy outcrops and rugged rock formations.

This was the spot. No one would bother me here. I had the sea in front of me, a vast expanse of mud and brush behind me and the world's end to my left. I found a dry area where the grass sprouted in tall, unruly tufts and made myself comfortable. The tide was still a long way out, the sun, although obscured by the clouds, still high in the sky. It was around one in the afternoon, I guessed. I had a few hours left yet, but I was scared now. I reminded myself this was what I wanted, that I'd prepared for it mentally and emotionally, that it would bring relief, rid me of my pain and suffering, but I was still scared.

Rather than dwell on it I opened the vodka, the expensive vodka which I'd shelled out nearly forty quid for, and took a swig. It tasted no better than the €12 stuff I usually got. That was an alcoholic talking, though, one with no appreciation for the finer things. A whipping breeze gathered round me, forcing me to draw my knees up to my chest, wrap my arms around my legs, compact, like an embryo. I wondered how cold it would be in the water, whether hypothermia might take me first, but then I remembered something about the water being warmest at this time of year, how the weeks of sunshine brought its temperature up, until by late August, early September it was lovely and tepid, perfect for swimming.

It wouldn't be like that at night, though, when I was going in. It would be dark, murky and chilling. More vodka. It was going down well, its charms becoming apparent with the passage of time; a fine vintage. More importantly, it was improving my mental state, guiding me where I needed to be: to oblivion. First, though, came the maudlin thoughts, I started to reminisce, to look back at the good times, or at least the better ones, and imagine what might have been.

5

I AWOKE WITH A FAMILIAR sense of dread. To a soggy dampness: I'd pissed myself. No, it was the sea, reaching out towards me, reminding me the time was nigh. The tide had come in and the water now lapped against my feet, between my legs, seeping into my jeans. I instinctively backed away, as if it were a dangerous predator and I its quarry. I wasn't ready. My final hours were supposed to have been spent in quiet contemplation, not laid out flat on my back, unconscious. I wanted to be prepared for this moment, ensure I was in the correct state of mind to complete my task. Now I was disorientated, confused, afraid. Suddenly everything felt very real. Panicking, I searched for the alcohol. There was still time, I could still do this, but I needed the drink.

The vodka was there, in the grass, almost empty. The whiskey stood where I'd left it, wedged into the sand. I glugged down the remains of the vodka, winced, and immediately switched my attention to the whiskey. With shaking hands I unscrewed the bottle and tilted it back, intending to drain it in one go. I got a third of the way down before I came spluttering up for air, coughing and retching. And still the tide came, teasing me, reminding me that time was of the essence.

I got to my feet and surveyed the scene. It was dark. The only light came from the moon as it peeked out from behind passing clouds, and the stars as they glittered in the black sky. Somewhere in the distance came the faint sound of the amusement park, people at play, lives being lived. And before me lay the sea, an expanse of nothingness slowly rolling towards me, ready to take me away. This was my moment. Everything was in place. Taking one last hit of the whiskey, I stepped forward.

The first wave took my breath away, almost knocking me over as it rushed against my knees. I strode ahead, teeth clenched, mind blank as the water snaked its way inside my clothes, against my flesh, sending chills through my body, waking me up, bringing me to my senses. I didn't want that, I wanted to be senseless. Resistance rose in my gut, the voice of reason telling me to turn back. Pushing it away, annoyed by its presence, I forged onwards, silent and stoical, determined to win this one last battle. The water swelled to my midriff, to my chest, hindering my progress. My legs were heavy now, reduced to slow, sluggish steps as I pitter-pattered towards a most shameful death.

I thrashed at the water in defiance, flailing at it impotently as a wave knocked me on my heels. Pausing, I allowed the cadence of the tide to rock me back and forth. The water was on my side. This was nature, I just had to work with it. I resumed my advance, using my hands to propel myself until, with the water lapping against my chin and splashing into my mouth, I began to swim. Which was odd, because I didn't know how to swim. But my feet weren't touching the seabed and my body was moving forward, so I could only have been swimming.

I remained there a few seconds, head above water, suspended in the ocean, perfectly still. Then the laws of physics reasserted themselves. I felt myself slip, start to go under. My arms weren't doing whatever it was they'd been doing and my legs had become dead weights. Floundering, I clawed at the surface, fought to maintain my buoyancy as the water revealed its true strength. It came up to my chin, then my nose, until I was fully submerged. The sea rushed into my mouth, my ears, I closed my eyes and allowed myself to sink to the bottom, to the ocean floor with the rest of the garbage.

For a second or two it was as peaceful as I'd imagined. I felt faint, a little delirious; if this was death, there was nothing to it. Then came the pain. My lungs filled with water and I began to slowly suffocate. It was worse than anything I could have imagined: an unbearable, unspeakable pain. My nerve-endings shrieked in protest, my head felt as if it were about to explode, my brain like it was trying to squeeze its way out through my ears. Blocking out the excruciating pain I searched for somewhere safe, a place where I could observe all this from a distance, a place where pain didn't exist. But it couldn't be found.

There was nowhere to go. This was all there was, and it was getting worse. Panicking, fearing that relief might never come and I would be stuck forever in this broiling ball of agony, I made a conscious decision: I would fight this. I would try and escape. I would try and get myself out of this unmerciful mess and see what happened. It was probably too late and I was probably still going to die, but at worst it would take my mind away from the pain, at best it might stop it completely.

No longer capable of determining left from right, up from down, I simply pushed, gathered whatever strength I could muster and forced my entire being in that direction. Nothing happened. The pain was still there, I was still underwater, in a dark, empty void, a grave of my own making. I pushed again. Nothing. Just fear and darkness. Another push, a weak one this time. Same result. But the pain was starting to diminish, replaced by numbness. Cheered, I resolved to have one more go and if nothing came of it I would succumb to this numbness, this new sensation which hinted at an ending. So I pushed again, with legs I could no longer feel, arms I could no longer perceive. And then everything changed.

Precious life flowed into me as I emerged from the water and returned to the land of the living. I sucked in air, gasping, spluttering, choking, desperate to grab one more second of the life I'd tried so hard to escape. That was all I got, one second, before the water took me once more; but I had a taste for freedom now. Energised, I rose to the top once more, mouth wide open, eyes ablaze, ready for that oxygen, to suck it into my soul. I got barely a mouthful before going under again. Up I came. And back down. Over and over, up and down, tumbling under, bursting forth, until gradually my trips to the surface grew longer.

I was getting more air now, getting some of the feeling back in my body, a second wind, an unknown reservoir of strength taking command, until finally, magically, something halted my progress to the bottom, something solid and unyielding. It took me a few seconds to comprehend what was happening, that my feet had come into contact with the sea floor. I planted them there firmly and waded to the shore, as far up the beach as I could manage, away from the tide, right into the grass and reeds, and collapsed to the ground.

I vomited, coughed and convulsed, bringing up all that expensive alcohol, pulling the night air into my burning lungs. Eventually the convulsions subsided, my breath steadied and I began to dry heave. Only then did I realise how cold I was, how wet I was. If I stayed here, lying in the damp grass in soaking wet clothes, hypothermia would take me. And having fought so valiantly to escape death, I wasn't going to let it creep up on me again. Exhausted, I dragged myself to my feet and began walking. I was cold and in pain, and I wanted to live. Survival was my aim. I was angry at death, piqued at its audacity, at the nerve it had shown in trying to take me before my time. This galvanised me, gave me the drive I needed to keep going.

There was no plan; I was incapable of anything so complex. My only hope was to be discovered, to fall upon a stranger and allow the normal way of things to take over, to pass the responsibility of keeping me alive to someone else. I knew I was going in the right direction, but the beach seemed to have grown overnight. Perhaps I'd inadvertently swum across the channel and was now in Dover or one of those places; how else could this unending expanse of sand and stone be explained? Even the sound of the funfair had died down. Now there was only the gentle rush of the tide to accompany me. On and on I went, head down, eyes closed, only altering my path when I felt the water lap at my toes. Until, I felt heat on my face.

It was subtle at first, like a candle on the other side of the room, an ember in the morning ashes. Initially I thought that dawn had come and the autumn sun was riding to my rescue, ready to burn me back to life with an unseasonal scorcher. I halted my progress, unwilling to open my eyes, to lift my head, or get my spirits up. I listened, hoping the warmth was emanating from a generator at the funfair, that I was seconds away from being spotted by a group of excited teens on their way home from a night of festivities. Everything was still. I walked a bit more. The heat increased and I heard something in the foreground: voices, low and murmuring. There was another sound too, harder to define, belonging to nature, like the sea, but not the same.

I pushed myself on towards the heat. It intensified, spreading from my face down through my body, into my veins, my bones, offering deliverance. This was life. This was - fire! I could hear it, raging, crackling. I lifted my head, opened my eyes and there it was: an inferno, a beautiful beacon of hope. There were six or seven people sitting around it, having a party, probably an end-of-summer gathering; one last hurrah before everyone went home. It was most likely an emotional occasion, one they wished to mark in a fitting manner, remember for reasons other than the arrival of a drunken, hypothermic hobo. Still, I had a life to save: my own.

6

THE VOICES GREW LOUDER, THE heat stronger, until it felt as if I were about to walk straight into the gates of hell. Maybe they couldn't see me, maybe I'd died in the water and these were just the first of many people I would haunt in my days as the Ghost of Rún Derg. Then the voices grew querulous as the convivial atmosphere of their late-night soirée was disturbed by my arrival. I couldn't hear what they were saying, but it didn't sound like they were laying out a 'welcome' mat for me. Fearful of them trying to run me off, send me back from whence I came, away from the fire, I staggered as far as I dared and slumped to the sand, an imaginary white flag sticking out of my fist.

Their tenor immediately changed; concern, shock, panic, all on my behalf. I was hoisted onto someone's back and brought hurriedly to the fire, dumped to the ground. Blankets were put over me, then taken off again. Someone pulled at my jumper, then at my jeans: I was about to be sexually assaulted. It didn't bother me, as long as I was warm. The blankets came back on, this time with jackets, a hat. It was brilliant, so warm, so snug. Soothed by their voices, the hushed reverence as they debated what to do next, I drifted away and lost consciousness. It felt good to allow these strangers to take command and determine my fate.

As I slowly sank into a carefree slumber, I was once more hoisted into the air. Unhappy at being taken away from the heat, I grumbled my discontent. But I understood I couldn't stay there forever. These people knew what they were doing. After a bumpy few minutes, I found myself lying in the back seat of a car, my head in someone's lap, our slow, easy speed telling me I was safe; I was going to make it, we weren't headed for the emergency room. My companions were speaking to one another calmly, their voices respectful and considered. I could smell marijuana. My blankets were adjusted, my hair stroked. A car whooshed by, but mostly we had the road to ourselves. I recognised the sounds of that hour before dawn, the time when the night gives way to day and the world comes back to life. I usually went to bed at this time.

When next I awoke I was in a bed, not my own, this was a nice bed, with crisp, clean sheets and a duvet which didn't stink of sweat and urine. Guilt washed over me. I didn't want to defile someone's home with my dirty, quivering stink: my exposed genitals, my greasy hair, my rancid, protruding gut, my feet and my general filth. That feeling passed. The good people were in charge now, and if this was where they wanted me to be, then who was I to argue? So I slept. At one point I was awoken by someone opening the door, they stood there a moment and then closed it again. I slept some more, aware of voices from downstairs, music, and an urgent need to piss. I went from a deep stupor into a restless doze and then into full wakefulness. The spell had been broken, I could no longer hide, I had no choice but to emerge from my bubble and face reality.

I opened my eyes and lay staring at the ceiling a while, then I sat up and looked around. I was in a woman's room, a master bedroom. Weak light crept through thick red curtains on the window to my left. The duvet was also red, as was the carpet. The walls were a lighter colour, perhaps pink. A white locker stood on the right-hand side of the bed; a Betty Boop alarm clock on top of it, some jewellery and a picture of a woman and a young girl. The woman seemed familiar but I couldn't place her. A large built-in wardrobe accounted for the right-hand wall. Clothes hung from its doorknobs. There was a dresser by the wall facing me, a mirror on top with various accoutrements arranged on either side. A bin stuffed with tissues sat underneath. Beside that was the door, and on that a hook with a dressing-gown, and more clothes. To the left a large, flat-screen television, forty inches or more, was attached to the wall; a wire hung from the back, a DVD player on the floor beneath. Beside me, to the left, a chair, clothes hung on its back, a uniform of some sort. And on the floor shoes, socks, underwear, more clothes, handbags, shopping bags, empty energy drink cans, magazines, a schoolbag.

Chaos, but a life lived well. Right there in the middle of it all was me, naked and afraid in a stranger's bed. One thing the room didn't have was an *en suite* bathroom. I needed to piss in a bad way. It was impossible to think straight, to plot my escape with a full bladder. My clothes were nowhere to be seen. Under different circumstances, this scenario could have been quite arousing, I could have draped some of the underwear over my erect penis and gone for a wander round the house. Now I just wanted to find something to maintain my dignity, something I could drape round my midriff while I went in search of the bathroom.

I got out of the bed, accidentally treading on a can of hairspray, and plucked a dressing-gown from the back of the door. It was a light, flouncy number, like a kimono, something a geisha might wear. It barely covered my thighs and, because of my gut, didn't tie at the front, but it would have to do. Edging the door open, I peered out. There was a landing with three other doors, two to my right, one to my left, all closed. The stairs were almost in front of me. I'd been in houses like this before; they were all laid out the same way. Two of the closed doors would lead to bedrooms, one to the bathroom. The one to my left had large plastic letters stuck to it, spelling the name ISABEL. It seemed unlikely that anyone would call their bathroom Isabel so I ruled out that door, and you wouldn't put a bedroom either side of a bathroom, so it had to be the one furthest away.

Wincing from the pain in my bladder, I tiptoed across the landing. I glanced down the stairs and saw light coming from a room. A sudden laugh sent me scurrying inside what I hoped was the bathroom; it was. I closed the door behind me, turning the lock as slowly and silently as I could. And then, in an attempt to minimise splashing, I sat down on the toilet and pissed like a woman. It went on for quite some time, a couple of minutes at least, and when it was over I felt brand new. The question then was whether to flush the toilet or not. The polite thing to do was to flush it, thoroughly wash my hands and leave the room as I'd found it, but doing so would alert my rescuers. They would know I was awake and stirring, and within minutes they'd be up to check up on me. I could always leave it and hope someone else got the blame, there were men in the vicinity and men were renowned for their inability to flush toilets. No, I'd already caused myself enough shame, I didn't need to let myself down even further. So I flushed it as gently as I could, which was ridiculous because every flush is as loud as the next one, and waited for them to come hurrying up the stairs.

No one came. I waited a while, then I washed my hands and looked out onto the landing. Nothing had changed; the other doors were still shut. It was gloomy and getting gloomier, and my room, the room I'd woken up in looked exactly as I'd left it. So I crept across the landing, sneaked into the room, tore off the dressing-gown, hung it back on the door, hopped back into the bed and waited. Any second now they'd be up for a look. Time passed. I sat there, listening. There was a television on downstairs, that must have been where the laugh had come from. I heard shouts from outside; young people, a football hitting a wall, a dog barking.

More than anything I wanted to take a look and see where I was, but I dared not move. If they came up and saw me staring out the window, at a load of kids, naked, they might get the wrong idea. I needed them to come up soon, though, because, with the drama of my visit to the toilet over, and the pain in my bladder no longer the focus of my attention, I'd begun to feel quite unwell. I was thirsty and I was hungry, and I was also very, very sick. My head hurt, my chest hurt and my body hurt. I was cold, yet also hot. The weak light which had been coming through the curtains had faded yet further so it was night-time. Presumably I'd been here since morning, which meant I hadn't had a drink in almost twenty-four hours.

It had been a long time since that had happened, and my body didn't like it. I didn't like it either. I needed a drink. I needed to be back home. I scanned the room once more, looking for anything which might pass for male clothing; a hoodie, a tracksuit, something with 'one size fits all' on the label. But it was all dresses and jeans, skirts and T-shirts: clothes which would burst at the seams if I tried to work myself into them. I stared at the dressing-gown I'd worn on my sortie to the bathroom. That fitted me, I just needed something to go with it.

A creak on the stairs brought me back to reality. I froze. Someone was coming. Footsteps across the landing and then a gentle knock on the door. I remained silent, couldn't have spoken even if I'd wanted to. After a pause, a head appeared.

"You all right, man?" said the head.

I breathed by way of response.

"Can I turn on the light?"

A croak confirmed that he could.

The room was illuminated, the mess more vivid under the harsh ceiling light. I gathered the bedclothes round my shoulders like a shy bride on her wedding night.

"She's a messy bitch, isn't she?" said my visitor. He looked a little younger than me. Slender with rock-band hair, delicate features and soft brown eyes, he had a languid way about him, a soothing presence.

"I have your clothes here. We washed them."

I nodded my thanks, increasingly aware of my nakedness.

"Do you want something to eat? A cup of tea?"

"Do you have any drink? Alcohol, I mean."

"Yeah, we've a few cans downstairs," he said with a smile.

I smiled back. This lad was sound.

"You have to take a shower, orders from downstairs," he said. "There's fresh towels here too."

"Okay."

Just as he was about to leave, he turned. "Are you sure you're okay? You had a fairly rough night back there."

"Mmm," I said, nodding with all the enthusiasm I could manage.

No sooner had he closed the door then I was out of the bed. A shower. There was no way I could do that quietly. But those were my orders. I would do as instructed, get showered, get dressed, see if there were any cans going, and then make my excuses and leave. This time I turned the light on in the bathroom, exposing more mess, more chaos. An array of ointments, moisturisers, and creams stood assembled on the window sill. Beneath them, on a shelf, were sprays, razors, combs, tampons, tubes and cylinders containing unknown substances, tweezers, pencils, brushes, and a tanning mitt. There were towels on the floor, towels draped over the shower door, and towels covering the radiator. I stepped inside the shower and was confronted by ten bottles of shampoo and conditioner, shower gel and body wash. There was no need for me to use any of those, I would just get in and out with a minimum of fuss. After washing the sea, sand and grit from my body, I put my freshly-cleaned clothes on and descended the stairs, briefly considering carrying on through the door and into the night in my stockinged feet, but I desperately needed a drink. Light came from the closed door to my left, voices from inside. That's where they were, my long-haired friend and his companions. I'd have one can, maybe two, apologise profusely and be on my way.

I tapped on the door. It opened, and I came face to face with the woman whose bed I'd spent the best part of a day in. There was an instant flicker of recognition. Dyed red hair, shoulder-length and straight with a metallic sheen. A small stud in her nose. Olive skin. Light blue eyes. A wide, pleasant mouth. It was the woman from the shop, the woman I'd bought the alcohol from. The last person I'd spoken to before my unsuccessful suicide attempt.

"Come in and sit down," she said. "Do you need anything? You must be starving. I could make you soup?"

I cautiously positioned myself on the edge of the couch. My friend from upstairs was in an armchair in front of the television, with another man, a youngster, in the seat across from him. Again there was a smell of marijuana.

"Um, I'd take a can if you have one," I said to the woman, whose name escaped me.

She looked at me disapprovingly, the warmth of her initial welcome replaced by despair, maybe disgust. I was used to that look, but it still stung.

"No, actually, what kind of soup is it?"

The smile returned.

"Chicken soup, of course. Do you want tea?"

"Please."

Off she went, happy to feed this strange, shabby man, this man she'd brought into her home and let sleep in her bed.

"Here," said the long-haired guy, producing a can from behind his chair. "Say nothing."

I greedily accepted the drink, sinking half of it in one frantic slug. The taste calmed my nerves.

"You scared the shit out of us last night, man," he said.

I grimaced. This wasn't something I wanted to discuss. If he persisted, if they tried to turn this into some sort of intervention I'd be out the door, chicken soup or not.

"Just one of those nights," I replied.

The other young man snorted in derision.

I flinched, ready to take flight at the first sign of confrontation, but it made me realise that a little gratitude wouldn't go amiss.

"Thanks," I ventured. "I don't know what would have happened to me if ye hadn't found me."

"You'd be lying face flat on the beach, seagulls pecking your brains out," suggested the more scornful of the two.

The kind chap gave him a look of reproach and the discussion ended there. The silence was broken when the woman reappeared with four cups of tea, and a tray with the soup and a plate of bread. She placed the tray on my lap and sat at the other end of the couch.

"Looks great, thank you," I mumbled, placing my can on the floor.

Awkwardness set in straight away. There was a sizeable elephant in the room, one so big its arse was jammed up against my face, its trunk draped over my shoulders. With each passing moment I expected one of them to broach the subject, to stare that elephant right in its tiny little eyes and ask me what the fuck I'd been doing last night. And then there was the soup. If she'd brought me something more manageable, a sandwich, a banana, a bar of chocolate, I could have munched away quietly; but no, it had to be soup, the noisiest, slurpiest food in the world.

It mattered not that it was delicious, perhaps the nicest bowl of soup I'd ever tasted. Nor that the soda bread accompanying it was utter heaven.

I just wanted to finish it and go. To make things worse, she'd turned the television down so that the only audible sounds were the clink of my spoon, the smack of my lips, the slow, endless chewing as my parched mouth searched for enough saliva to make the bread go down. The first good meal I'd had in months, and I couldn't even enjoy it. When I finally finished, I rose to my feet and asked where the kitchen was. I was going to wash up but really I just needed a breather, an excuse to escape.

"No, you're fine," said the woman, taking the tray from me. "I'll wash it."

"No, let me do it," I persisted, eliciting a dubious look from the aggressive young man.

"Come on, then," she said. "I'll show you."

She led me out to the modest kitchen; table and chairs, fridge, washing-machine, its sole window overlooking a garden which backed out onto someone else's. There were pictures on the wall, framed ones of her and a girl whom I presumed to be Isabel, and others of Isabel on her own: as a baby, a toddler, starting school, in a Halloween costume, on her bike. The truculent young man from the living-room featured in a couple, looking much happier, more carefree. There were none of the other guy.

"They're not much for conversation," she said, nodding towards the living-room.

"Me neither," I replied.

"Do you remember me from the shop?" she asked.

"Yeah, of course."

"How was the party?"

I gave her a wry smile.

She left the dishes on the side and opened the back door. It was night now, the porch light illuminated the threadbare garden; a coal bunker, a shed with the lock hanging off the door, white clothes on the washing-line, reflected by the moon.

"Smoke?" she asked, offering me a cigarette.

"No, thanks," I said, joining her on the step, wondering if it was too late to go back for my can.

"What's your name?"

"Aidan."

"I'm Yvonne."

"Yes. I remember."

"Oh yeah," she said, blowing smoke into the cool autumn air.

"Thanks for letting me sleep in your bed."

"You're grand."

"There was no party," I said.

"Is that why you came to our one instead?"

Her tone was playful, sardonic.

"I'm messing with you," she said, apologetically.

"That's okay."

She stubbed the fag out against the wall and returned to the kitchen.

I followed her back inside, joining her at the table where she put a large glass of cranberry juice in front of me.

"Drink that, it has antioxidants in it," she instructed.

"Thank you," I replied, wincing at its bitter taste.

"You can't stay here tonight."

I recoiled, preparing myself for a browbeating.

"I mean, my father will be here with Izzy in the morning. Even Noel can't be here when she arrives."

"No, no, I'll be off now. I just wanted to say thanks for everything before I went."

"You're grand," she said, smiling. It was a good smile, made her eyes shine.

"I'll just say goodbye to Noel and the other fellah," I said, rising to my feet.

"I didn't mean right away," she said.

"I need to be getting back now, anyway."

"Where do you live?"

This was a problem. I didn't want to risk them offering me a lift. The tension in the car would be unbearable. They might even order me a taxi, offer to pay for it, make me feel like even more of a nuisance.

"Not far from here," I replied.

"Do you even know where we are?" she asked, smiling again.

"Rún Derg," I said hopefully.

"Where do you live? I'll get Noel to drop you off."

"No, no, it's fine, honestly. I can make my own way now, you've done enough for me as it is."

"And how do you intend to do that without any shoes?" she asked, pointing to my feet.

"I don't know what happened to them," I said sheepishly.

Despite my protestations, moments later I found myself in the passenger seat of a car. Noel, who was the man with the long hair, was driving, with Yvonne in the back. The other guy had chosen not to accompany us. We were in a village called Castleblaney, about ten minutes outside of Rún Derg and a further twenty minutes away from Maraghmor. Noel and Yvonne chatted idly as we drove, filling the silence, trying to put me at ease. But I was far from at ease. With the scent of home in my nostrils, my thoughts had turned to drink and how to procure some. There was money in my apartment, the cash I'd left for my landlord, but I'd left my keys inside, without those keys I couldn't get in. The estate agents had a spare set but they didn't open till the morning. I didn't tell my companions that, they'd probably have offered to pay for a hostel for the night.

"Whereabouts in town you living, Aidan?" asked Noel.

"You can drop me on the quay. I'll be fine from there."

"You sure?"

"Yes. Thanks, Noel."

We stopped and Noel turned on the inside light. This was it, they were finally going to lecture me on the dangers of late-night swimming. Instead, Noel just shook my hand and said, "Take it easy, man," and Yvonne gave me a little hug and shoved a piece of paper into my coat pocket.

"If you're ever in trouble, just give me a call," she said.

I nodded, offered my thanks and got out of the car. Then I watched them drive off, Yvonne waving goodbye, Noel somehow managing to sound friendly even while beeping the horn. As I walked towards my apartment, I took the piece of paper out of my pocket. It had her name and number on it.

7

It was late at night, after ten, and even though I knew I wouldn't be able to get in I walked toward Wolfe Tone Street anyway. If I waited outside the main door for long enough, someone would be coming in or out. Who would be coming in or out at this hour, though? It was all families and quiet types living here now, working people who'd either be in bed or winding down for the evening. The golden days of myself and Gerard living it up had long since passed. I barely communicated with my neighbours these days, had become the strange loner everyone avoided.

I needed them now, though. I needed one of them to go out on a late-night errand, to return home from an evening of overtime or a match in the pub. I needed that door to open so I could get in out of the cold. I stood outside the grey old building, with its big black door and crumbling paintwork and willed someone to appear, knowing the longer I waited the less likely it was that someone would come. There were lights on in a few of the apartments, I could have shouted at them to let me in, I knew all their names. That would have created a scene, though, so I waited. On several occasions I thought I saw someone familiar approach; a lone drunk, a downtrodden shift worker, a couple who could easily have been Polish, but they all kept on walking. Then the light in the lobby area came on and I moved to the side of the door, ready to slip inside. No one came out; it must have been someone bringing down the rubbish.

I gave up after that. It was close to midnight on a Tuesday, no one would be stirring until the morning. Resigned to my fate I went for a walk, glad of the runners Yvonne had found for me, even if they were a size too big. I wished she'd found a couple of jumpers for me, too, I had a long night ahead of me. There was a homeless shelter nearby, but I could never stoop that low, I wasn't like those people, the rough sleepers, the beggars on the street. If I ever did end up on the street, cup in hand by day, under the stars at night, I'd be back out at the beach ready for another go. Avoiding the city centre, I made my way through some of the inner-city tenements, the old buildings which had been re-purposed for the rental market.

These streets were all takeaways, corner shops, barbers and phone shops, but now and then I passed a pub, the doors shut but a dim light coming from inside, and had to fight the urge to knock and ask for a few cans on tick. Not really thinking where I was going, I skirted round the edge of the park which was barricaded at night to keep out the junkies and oddballs. Those barricades weren't all that effective, though; I could hear shouting and cackling from within as I navigated its wall and carried on up the hill towards an area known as Knock Arch. It had its own little shopping mall, its own pubs, and a swathe of new housing developments, modern homes purposely located just outside the city.

Knock Arch was also home to one of the county's most successful GAA clubs, a senior hurling team which had won the last three All-Ireland Club Championships and produced countless Kilkenny hurlers. In keeping with their fine traditions, they also had the best facilities money could buy: a recently renovated clubhouse, and a pristine, well-manicured pitch with two covered stands to keep the rain off the patrons during the winter months. If those stands were good enough for GAA supporters, then they would be good enough for me.

In my naivety I thought I could just stroll onto the pitch, pick a seat and while away the hours, but those GAA boys are fiercely protective of their land. A six-metre gate, painted in the club's green and black colours barred my way, an imposing presence which even in my younger, more sprightly days, I would have struggled to scale. On either side of that was a wall, equally tall, equally imposing. Undeterred, I circled the premises, hopeful of finding a chink in the armour, and sure enough the wall came to an abrupt end fifty metres down. It was only a front, a grandiose attempt to make Knock Arch GAA seem more glamorous than it was.

One side of the complex was protected by nothing more than trees, those large evergreens which look a bit like Christmas trees and never seem to grow. Delighted with myself, I shoved my way through a gap in the foliage, ready to gallop onto the lush turf like a full-forward on All-Ireland Sunday. Unfortunately my enthusiasm was misplaced, the trees were on top of an embankment and I instantly tumbled to the bottom of it, coming to a rest in a pile of stones and dirt. Dusting myself down, I discovered a further impediment to my progress: a mesh fence with barbed wire on top. I shook the fence, testing its strength. I couldn't climb it, nor could I knock it down.

Annoyed, I traipsed round the perimeter, noting that even if I gained access I still wouldn't be in the actual complex; this was the old pitch, the one they used for the under-age games. The new pitch with the stands was on the other side, presumably surrounded by a minefield with a team of snipers perched on the roof. The old pitch had dugouts, though, and they would be arguably even cosier than the covered stand. I'd snuggle up on the bench where all those famous hurler's arses had sat, and I'd be sorted for the night.

Kicking the fence, I reasoned there had to be a point of entry somewhere. Surely the local toerags would have made a hole, a part where you could climb underneath? But there was nothing. Only another iron gate, smaller than the main one but similarly imposing. I shook it, leaned against it, barged it, kicked it. It buckled a little, but it was secured with a chain. I saw now how the kids got in, though. If you pushed the gate enough a little gap appeared in the middle, one wide enough for a scrawny teenager to squeeze through but too small for even one of my fat legs.

Tired and depressed, I meandered towards the clubhouse, fantasising about finding an unlocked door and gaining access to the bar. But everything was shut. A security light came on and spooked me, sending me dithering into the shadows. I'd had enough of Knock Arch and its hallowed turf, and just wanted to escape its environs in one piece. However, as I made my way back to the trees I encountered what would surely be my last hope: the old scoreboard. I'd always wanted to see what was up in those little enclaves, what secrets lay behind those numbers and letters. This was my chance. I peered up into the little hollow. It was far too high for me to reach without assistance. They must have used a ladder to get up there on match days. So, I looked around for a ladder; there wasn't one, but there was a wall behind the scoreboard, with netting attached to prevent balls flying out onto the road.

This wall wasn't like the one outside, it was crumbling, scored by years of sliotars hopping off it. It had footholds aplenty, the older kids probably sat up on it to watch matches. So I climbed the fucker, scrambling a bit at points but making it to the top with relative ease. Now the scoreboard was but a short jump away. I still had to be careful, though, the only way in was by the side, meaning I had to angle my leap a bit. I lined it up, took a breath and practically soared through the air, landing flush in the box, my momentum almost causing me to continue out the other side.

I sat there a moment, panting, sweating but feeling good, then checked out my environs. There weren't any numbers lying around, just empty cans and fag butts, a filthy old jacket and a broken hurley. It was a great spot for a rough sleeper, though, and unlike those fools in town I wouldn't be disturbed by road sweepers and traffic at first light. Using the jacket, which smelled of petrol and dirt, as a pillow, I laid my head down and stretched out, not bothered whether I slept or not. After all, I wasn't long up. I'd been in Yvonne's bed all day: Yvonne, the woman who'd given me her number and asked me to call her. I wondered what we'd talk about if I did call her, and whether it was worth buying a phone solely for that purpose. I thought it might be.

She was an attractive, seemingly normal member of the opposite sex who wasn't repelled by me. There weren't many of those around. Maybe it was fate. In years to come when people asked how we got together, we would have one hell of story for them. Of course, I would never tell Yvonne what I'd intended to do that night, would offer a toned-down version if asked, but even so it was still a powerful tale, one for the romantics of this world. I stopped myself. What was I thinking? Why would Yvonne want anything to do with me? She'd only given me her number out of pity. It was a gesture, nothing more. If I did ring her she'd feign ignorance, hang up and block my number. She had a child to protect, a daughter to rear, what use would she have for an alcoholic virgin with no shoes? She was probably already regretting giving me that number and hoping I didn't remember the name of the estate she lived in. No, it was enough that I'd met her, that she'd given me her phone number, whatever the motive. To take it any further would be foolish. All the same, as I snuggled up in that little scoreboard box I repeatedly checked my pocket to make sure the piece of paper was still there, finding warmth in its presence, even hope. She had written on it, she had given it to me, and for that alone I was grateful.

8

THE NEXT MORNING I WENT into the estate agent's, acquired the spare key and let myself back into the flat. I felt no great emotion in seeing it, no thoughts of a second chance in life, none of that. All I saw was the money on the table and the little note I'd left for the landlord. There was €211 there. I could buy a lot of drink with that. I could also buy a phone. Because even in the cold light of day, I harboured dreams of contacting Yvonne, of seeing if she really had just given me the number out of pity. I now realised my fantasy of us being drawn together by fate was, well a little fanciful, but we could be friends; I could hang out with her and Noel and that other grumpy little shit.

After some careful consideration, I decided I would buy a phone, the cheapest they had, and then, obviously, go get some drink. Whatever change

I had left over would go towards the rent. They sold phones in the supermarket, thus halving the number of stores I had to visit, and after waiting for the thing to charge and the SIM card to activate, I was up and running. Not only that, I'd got a load of booze, cans of beer and bottles of wine - I was staying off the spirits for a while. As I settled down for a nice, relaxing drinking session, I reflected upon the set of circumstances which had led me here, back to square one, drinking cans and staring out the window.

The first thing I asked myself was whether I was still suicidal, or whether I'd really been suicidal to begin with. As I'd walked into that water I'd certainly wanted to end it all, yet here I was, living and breathing with the best of them. There'd been no epiphany, no sudden realisation I had something to live for. It was much more simple than that, it was the pain. I hadn't liked the pain, and I'd been afraid of dying. This act of defiance had been born of cowardice, a desire to escape something unpleasant. In short, I wanted to die but I didn't want any of the nasty stuff that went with it. However, now I had something to focus on, perhaps even something to live for.

I entered Yvonne's number into my new phone and considered my next move, my first move. Even I knew you didn't call someone the day after the night before. If there was to be any contact it would be a simple text, something short, a testing of the waters. In order to summon up the courage to do that, I needed more drink. So I drank a little more and thought about what I could say to a woman who'd rescued me from death, brought me into her home and fed me chicken soup. At 8.24 p.m. I bit the bullet. She would have had dinner by then, and if she was helping her daughter with her homework that would probably be done too. It wasn't so late in the night that it could be classed as disturbing her. All that was left was to decide what to say.

Hi, Yvonne. This is Aidan, the guy from the beach.

No. I deleted that. I wasn't the guy from the beach. I didn't know who I was.

Hi, Yvonne. This is Aidan. Thanks for the soup. I hope I didn't put you out too much last night.

I deleted that too. It sounded stupid. I was stupid.

Hi, Yvonne, this is Aidan. Just wanted to say thanks for last night, and apologise for everything.

That was a little dramatic, but I was on the right track.

In the end I kept it simple, leaving no room for mixed messages or hidden meanings.

Hi, Yvonne, this is Aidan. I just wanted to apologise for last night and to thank yourself and the lads for looking after me.

I pressed send, wincing as I did so. What an idiot. Then I waited. What was the normal response time for texts these days? I was out of practice. Every person was different though, weren't they? Yvonne might have been someone who went hours without checking her phone, or someone who heard a message and said she'd get to it later. Ten minutes passed without a reply. My hopes began to falter, my spirits diminish. I skulled a can, put the phone on silent and hid it under a cushion. But I kept checking it, pulling it out for a look every couple of minutes. Finally I had to go out for a walk, leaving the phone behind me, reasoning that if she hadn't replied by the time I came back I would move on with my life. I pounded the streets, trying not to think of my phone, of its blank screen and empty inbox.

After walking all the way through town, down by the quay, across one bridge and back over another, I went home. A good hour had passed; if she hadn't replied by now, then that was that. I opened another can and stared at the cushion where the phone was. It would be easier not to check, to just leave it till the morning, the week after, to never check it, to just die without ever knowing if she'd replied. After an agonising few minutes I took it out and looked at the screen: nothing. The fucking bitch. Why had she given me her number if she'd planned on ignoring me? She was just like all the rest of them, a bullshitter. All that talk about looking after myself meant nothing. I drained the can and opened up a bottle of wine. Fuck her. I stuffed the phone down the back of the couch and sat staring into space until I got drunk enough for the sadness to go away.

As was the norm, I woke up with no recollection of going to bed or how my night had ended. It was midday, early for me, and my hangover seemed manageable. I went down to the living-room; a few cans littered around the place, an empty bottle of wine, nothing too crazy. I'd conducted myself well, for a change. The phone,where was the fucking phone?! After rummaging behind the cushions for a couple of minutes, and finding €1.45, I located it beneath one of the broken springs. I went to check my messages, but nothing happened. It was dead. I'd obviously switched it off in disgust before retiring for the night.

While I waited for it to reboot I cleared away the drink, wondering if I could bring the phone back to the shop for a refund; but no sooner had it come back to life when I heard three pings go off in quick succession. I grabbed it and stared at the screen. Three text messages. Jesus. My first thought was that I'd sent her something abusive and she was mad; no one sent three messages in response to the kind of innocuous text I'd sent. Yet that was precisely what she'd done. This was too much. I had to sit down and compose myself before reading them.

The first one was sent at 1.34 a.m.

Hi, Aidan. Sorry for the late reply, been one of those nights. Good to hear from you. So you got home all right then? No need to apologise, I'm just glad we found you when we did. How are things? Any more parties? ;)

She had sent another at 1.41 a.m.

God, I hope you don't think I was taking the piss about the parties. I have a weird sense of humour. Sorry. Speak soon.

And one final text at 7.12 a.m.

Just realised I was texting you at some ridiculous hour last night, sorry if I woke you. Have a good day.

I sat back on the couch, trying to take it all in. She was just a normal person, a nice, normal, kind, thoughtful person. It warmed my heart to think of her. I thought of the seven minutes between the first and second texts, wondering what had led her to text me again; the sudden realisation her joke may have been in bad taste. And I thought about her waking up, checking her phone, noting the time she'd sent the texts and then messaging me again. It was truly endearing, all of it. The warmth in my heart quickly chilled, however, when I realised I now had to formulate a worthwhile response, something which would charm her in equal measure. It was too much pressure to bear. I looked out the window, town was busy, I couldn't go for a walk, and it was too early to start drinking. So I sat down with the phone and began working on my reply.

Hi, Yvonne. No need to apologise for the late texts, I'm a heavy sleeper anyway. Yeah, I got home grand thanks to yourself and Noel. Everything is good here. No more parties, I'm keeping a low profile for the time being!

New paragraph.

No, I knew you were only joking, don't worry about it. Your sense of humour is fine. And you didn't wake me, like I said, deep sleeper. You have a good day too.

That was good. I paused, finger hovering over the 'send' icon. It wasn't good, it was bland, lifeless, shite. It had none of the whimsy of her texts, none of the authenticity. I needed to add a bit of life to it, give her something to smile about, but I had no life to add. Be yourself. That was it. That was what they always said. In the end I presented her with a jazzed-up version of myself, a less maudlin, less morose version. Aidan Collins 2.0.

Hi, Yvonne. No need to apologise for the late texts, I'm a heavy sleeper as you probably guessed (how long was I asleep in your house, by the way?). Yeah I got home grand thanks to yourself and Noel. All good here. No more parties, I'm keeping a low profile for the time being!

New paragraph.

I knew you were only joking, don't worry about it. Your sense of humour is fine. And you didn't wake me, deep sleeper, remember? My day promises to be a quiet one, but hopefully I'll make the most of it. Are you working today? Hope it's a good one.

I sent it. I felt I'd done all right. I'd made reference to my sleeping in her bed, but not in an apologetic kind of way. I'd alluded to the vast emptiness of my life, but without giving too much away, and I'd thrown in a couple of questions so that she would have something to respond to when she saw the text. Contented, I cracked open a can by way of special celebration, perched myself on the windowsill and watched life pass me by. I'd figured I wouldn't hear from her again until later that night. But at four p.m. my phone pinged.

You are a deep sleeper, Aidan, a very deep sleeper indeed! You were conked out from about six in the morning till eight that night, must have been some party all the same. :P

I waited for her to reply to my other question, the one about whether she was working or not, but there were no further texts. So that was it, then, she'd grown tired of me already. Annoyed, I went to the fridge for another can. I drank aggressively, with abandon. Only when I felt the numbness, the loss of all sensation and feeling, did I slow down. I was in my safe space then, the place where no one could touch me. I turned off the lights and played some music, not loud. When the album ended I sat in silence, not thinking, not listening, in a sort of drunken meditation: an alcoholic Buddhist.

From somewhere in the distance my phone made a sound. It was a text. I didn't reach for the phone, the contents of that text mattered not, its message, whether positive or negative, was of no consequence. I was all alone in perfect harmony. Let them text away, I had no need for their childish discourse. When I woke up on the couch sometime later, however, my outlook had changed. The phone, where was the phone? It was nearby this time and still switched on. The text was from her. It had been sent at 10.12 p.m. It was now 4.36 a.m.

What a fucking day! Just finished now. Had to work till ten. Some dose. How was your day?

My spirits immediately lifted. It had all been a simple misunderstanding. She had probably been too busy to answer my other question earlier. And now here she was, just finished her shift, messaging little old me. That clearly counted for something. I thought about replying but it was the middle of the night, she would be sleeping. Anyway, it was better not to seem overly keen. I would go to bed and text her as soon as I woke up. With a spring in my step, I went to the bathroom and brushed my teeth, already thinking up things to say to her.

9

Yvonne's texts became my lifeline, my sole reason for being. Every time my phone beeped my heart soared. As soon as I replied, I would fret until it beeped again. When I went two days without receiving a text, I spiralled into despair. When she responded to one of my jokes with a smiley face, I danced round the living-room. It was unhealthy, I knew that, but this had never happened to me before; I was entitled to be excited. It was hard thinking up things to say so I kept it light-hearted, talked about music, film, literature, drink, the past, family, the future, anything but my current circumstances and the void she had filled.

There was no mention of how I'd come to be traipsing along the beach in the early hours of the morning, how they'd rescued me, undressed me and put me to bed. No more mention of me sleeping in her bed, eating her food and drinking her drink. In fact, there was no mention of that night at all. Instead, she told me about her daughter, Isabel, fifteen years old, dark, moody and rebellious. She told me about her job and how tedious it was, her colleagues and their lives, her bosses and their bullshit. She revealed that Noel, far from being Izzy's father or an on-again/off-again lover, was simply a childhood friend, part of an extended group of pals she'd hung around with for years. The hostile prick who'd added to my discomfort on the night in question was her younger brother, Gavin. He'd recently returned from a two-year stint in the army, unexpected and unannounced, and informed them he wasn't going back. Since then he'd been withdrawn and uncommunicative, spending most of his time indoors, chain-smoking joints.

Tentatively, not really wanting to know the answer but feeling obliged to enquire, I asked about Izzy's father, hoping maybe he was dead, that I could step in and become the man of the house. But he was still around. He saw his daughter as often as he liked, or as often as she liked, which wasn't very often.

He's a fucking prick. Izzy is starting to realise that for herself now too.

No competition there, then. By way of return I told her about my parents, how my mother had got sick and died and my father had run away with a neighbour. It added a bit of mystique to my life, showed I was capable of discussing deep issues. That wasn't enough to win her over, though. Yvonne saw me as a peculiarity, a charity case. I needed to impress her somehow, erase the memory of me being rescued from the ocean and replace it with a more positive, reassuring image. I didn't know how to do that, though. I didn't know how to be impressive. The only time a woman had been wooed by my actions was when I'd tackled those young lads in front of Marion.

Maybe I could go to the supermarket where Yvonne worked and bash up a few shoplifters with that security guard. No, Yvonne was more discerning than that, she had the air of someone who'd had her fill of knuckleheads in fast cars, the Steve Lyons of this world. She knew men like that didn't last, that they brought only empty promises and broken dreams. That was probably why she was texting me; I was unassuming, non-threatening, a nice guy. If I didn't act fast, though, I'd be 'friend zoned', sitting in her living-room with Noel and Gavin while she was out getting her heart broken by another handsome, callous bastard who'd promised so much. I had to change her opinion of me, become a viable contender. My heart was too faint for this fair lady, though. All I could do was drink and be there for her at all times. If that wasn't enough, then so be it. So I stuck it out, becoming the text buddy she never knew she needed.

Sometimes she didn't feel like chatting, sometimes she took ages to reply, sometimes she seemed distracted and bored, but I never wavered. I was only ever a text away, her most loyal servant. Solid and dependable, that was me, and it must have worked because, after three weeks of sticking around, I was invited to what she described as a 'shindig' in their local bar, *Cullen's*. There was no fanfare, no suggestion it was anything other than a casual invite, but it was the breakthrough I had been waiting for. She said to be there at around eight p.m. on Saturday where they would be going out to hear a local band play a selection of classic and modern rock hits. It sounded like I had finally found my people, a group of chilled-out beach bums who enjoyed rock music and beer.

10

It wasn't really a date but it was a big deal. Drinks in *Cullen's* with the lads, with Yvonne and her pals. I would have to get a bus out there and then fork out €20 for a taxi home, but that was a small price to pay. On the day, I was nervous, but not as nervous as I'd expected. Things had changed since I'd had a go at the suicide. Having plumbed the depths and emerged unscathed I was more fatalistic, more willing to expose myself to dangerous situations just to see what would happen. There was a lot on the line, though; if the night went badly and Yvonne washed her hands of me, then I would be alone in the world again. There was no possible way to prepare for a night of such significance, so I just did what I always did: I had a drink.

After a few cans to warm up I attempted to get ready. It was no easy task. A few years ago, when I'd been out walking every day and off the drink, you could have made a strong argument for me being average-looking. I'd been in my prime then. Now I was like one of those celebs from Sonia's reality shows, who'd had a breakdown and been pictured coming out of Walmart wearing a baseball cap over greasy hair, looking like they stunk of fag-butts and old socks. Like those celebs what I really needed now was a bit of TLC, a two-month spell in rehab, a holiday in the sun and then a triumphant return to form, ending with a workout DVD featuring a tanned, smiling version of myself on the cover. I didn't have two months, though, I had less than an hour.

After showering, I took a deep breath and looked at my naked self in the mirror. It was horrendous. I was so fat. Not like I'd been in my youth, that had been a jiggly, friendly fatness. This was beer fat, mud fat, the unhealthy, obnoxious girth of someone who no longer cares. My belly was big and round and looked impossibly pleased with itself. If I sucked it in and held my breath I looked normal, quite buff, but as soon as I exhaled the illusion was shattered. I had moobs too, hairy, clammy things which needed taming with a reliable bra, nothing fancy, just something with good upholstery. I'd heard on the radio that there were special T-shirts for lads like me, tops made out of Spandex which magically held all your unseemly bits in place and made you look like Johnny Sexton or one of them rugby lads. It would take some T-shirt to contain me, though. It would have to be reinforced with steel.

Things weren't much better beneath it. My entire undercarriage area needed a makeover, a crack, back and sack cleanse from a sturdy little Filipino lady who didn't care how loud I screamed. Odour was another concern. I wasn't used to being clean, and as soon as I'd showered my body fought valiantly to return to its natural state, that of a stinky fat guy who lived in his own filth. Determined to fight back, I sprayed an excessive amount of anti-perspirant on my pits, my nuts and my problematic undercarriage area, then moved on to the next step. What to wear. We were just going to the pub, it wasn't anything fancy, she'd emphasised that, but I couldn't turn up in a hoodie and a pair of tracksuit bottoms.

So it was into the wardrobe, time to go digging, see if there was anything remotely smart. I found a shirt from the old days. It smelled musty, but it had a brand name and would benefit from an iron. It was light blue, though. If I perspired, and I surely would, the patches would appear and she'd think I was a freak, a big sweaty freak. No, the shirt needed to be either very dark or very light, capable of absorbing moisture without any change in colour. That ruled out the blue one, the red one, the nice light purple one and the striped green one. There was a white shirt, but when I tried it on one of the buttons popped out. Eventually I found a perfectly black shirt, one probably ten years old. It was as crinkled and unkempt as my ball sack but I sprayed it with air conditioner, gave it a good ironing and made the best of the situation. I had one pair of half-decent jeans that fitted me, and I matched those with my good shoes - my feet had remained the same size.

I hoped that I could at least get as far as the pub in Castleblaney without being bathed in sweat, but there were other issues to concern myself with. My years of drinking had given me a pot belly and the complexion of a sea captain; it had also been quietly chipping away at my health, destroying my organs, sending out distress signals by way of chronic ailments, concerning maladies which were only going to get worse. The worst of these were the unpredictable emissions produced by my gut. All the bile created by the alcohol had to go somewhere and often it chose to come out of my mouth, not in solid form but in loud, unsavoury belches that I could just about quell if I caught them in time. I hadn't been checking, but I was pretty sure this meant my breath was far from pleasant.

Occasionally I would wake up and smell the bile in my throat, the stale cheesy stench of a poisoned stomach. Who would want to kiss that guy, kiss that mouth? In spite of myself, I was thinking along those lines. She had said she was looking forward to seeing me, and she had seen me before at my lowest ebb. It had been dark most of the time then, though. Her memory was probably hazy. When she saw this giant, bleary joke waddle into the pub, stinking of cheese and arse-crack, she'd be looking for the first exit. The cruel irony was that if I gave up the booze I would be less stinky, but then I wouldn't have the strength to meet her or to do anything, really.

I pulled my jacket off the latch, smoothed down my beard and hurried down town for the 7.15 p.m. bus to Castleblaney. Of course I got there early, so early I had to find a quiet place to sit down and wait until 8 p.m. and then 8.05 and finally 8.10, before making my way to the pub. My biggest fear was Yvonne being late, of walking in and seeing Gavin there with a group of strangers, him looking over at me and whispering to the person beside him, sharing a knowing look while I slunk off to the bar, humiliated. She was there, though, just her and one of her friends.

"Here he is now," she said as I bumbled over to their table and stood over them awkwardly.

She looked lovely. She was perfect in every way. I'd only ever seen her in her uniform and in a baggy jumper the following day, but here she was in full bloom. Her hair was even shinier than before, glossy, like the hair of a cover model from a magazine. Those pale blue eyes, offset by her sallow skin, sparkled and gleamed, her subtle make-up bringing them to life, enhancing her soft features, her cheeky smirk. Some men might have thought she needed to lose weight, dress differently or wear her hair longer, but it was more than her physical appearance that attracted me: it was her manner, her disposition. She had something which went beyond a flat stomach, perfect breasts or shapely thighs, there was a warmth and goodness which seemed to radiate from her.

"This is Dervla," she said, gesturing to her friend.

I shook a hand, barely registering the person it belonged to, and continued to stand, staring down at Yvonne, lost in the moment.

"Are you going to sit down?" she asked.

"Um, I think I'll get a drink. Would you like one?"

Yvonne gestured to her bottle of beer and the full glass beside it. Dervla made a noise. I took that as two 'no's and made for the sanctuary of the bar. So far, so terrible. While the barman poured my pint, I tried to compose myself. Once I got my drink I would sit down beside them, smile and ask how they were. *Hello, Dervla, how are you? Hello, Yvonne, I love you.* And so on. I arrived back with my pint, sat opposite them on a stool, and drank off almost half of it in one go.

"Hope you brought your shoes this time," Yvonne said, laughing.

I grinned, tried to lift up a foot to show I was wearing shoes and knocked over a stool. By the time I'd picked it up the two of them were staring at me, like children at a circus waiting for the clown's next act. Rather than try anything clever, I took off my jacket and laid it down carefully on the upright stool.

"What time are the band on?" I asked.

"Supposed to be nine but they're always late," replied Dervla.

I hadn't really been asking her, wasn't interested in anything she had to say. It suddenly occurred to me that this could be a repeat of the night with Gerard, Michelle and Marion. Was I being set up here, with Dervla?

The mere thought of it was like a kick to the bollocks. There was no one else I wanted, only Yvonne. I looked at Dervla for the first time and felt a wave of relief. She was far too good for me, not that Yvonne wasn't too good for me also, but Dervla was a little stunner and she was younger too, early twenties, maybe late teens.

"Noel is in the band. You remember Noel?" asked Yvonne.

"Of course. What does he play?"

"I dunno, bass or something."

That made sense. Noel seemed like a bass player, quiet and unassuming, keeping the groove going while everyone else went mad.

"Is your brother coming out?" I asked.

Yvonne shrugged. "Who knows? He comes and goes as he pleases, that fellah."

In my nervousness I'd already finished my first pint, draining it in less than ten minutes. At home on my own that was normal behaviour, but I was among ordinary, everyday people here. These people didn't drink pints like they were shots, they took their time, savoured the drink and enjoyed their night out.

"Thirsty," I said by way of apology as I went to the bar for another. I considered getting two and drinking one on the sly before coming back with the other; but no, I would just have to fit in, regulate my intake and act like a normal member of society.

When I returned, Yvonne was gone.

"In the toilet," said Dervla, not looking up from her phone.

"Right," I said, taking the opportunity to survey the bar for the first time. It was nice here, friendly and cosy but modern and spacious. The old boys who'd been in to watch the racing were still hanging around, probably toughing it out until the music started, and there were a few middle-aged groups of men and women, couples out for the night, having one in the local before heading into town. In the younger crowd, there was none of the menace and antipathy of the town pubs; the lads were harmless-looking, easy-going, and the girls were different too; not so provocative, dressing more conservatively, a bit laddish in their behaviour but still distinctly feminine.

This was where I belonged, in a community like this, one of those small 'tight-knit' places you heard about on the news any time someone from rural Ireland got killed. The door opened and two lads came in, they were around my age, indie types with flares and army-style jackets. To my horror, they came towards our table.

"Hi, Dervla, who's out?" said one.

"Yvonne," she said. "And this is Aidan, Yvonne's friend."

I could have hugged her then. Good old Dervla, introducing me in such a delicate yet offhand manner.

"All right, man," said the first guy. The other lad gave me a brief nod and went to the bar. The first one took off his jacket and sat on a stool. He was pale and thin with a big mop of hair, like a budget Richard Ashcroft but not as tall. What was his relationship to Yvonne? Was he her type, skinny with cool hair? Or maybe she'd been with the other guy? He was stockier, more solid, with big chunky sideburns and a pair of glasses which made him look a bit like one of the Thunderbirds. She must have been with some of them, Castleblaney was a small place and they'd all been hanging round together for years. I tried not to think about it, focusing on not drinking too fast and keeping my breathing in check, but when she came back and greeted each of them with an enthusiastic hug, my spirits sank. She had been with them. It said it all there in the hugs. You didn't go round hugging people in that way unless you'd been intimate with them. But then she switched her attention to me, made me feel like the most important person in the room.

"So, lads, this is Aidan, the merman of Rún Derg," she said, formally introducing me to the boys.

"Ah," said Ashcroft, breaking into a grin, "the late-night swimmer."

"One and the same," confirmed Yvonne, smiling at me.

"Mad fucker," said the stocky one.

This was great. They all thought I'd been out swimming. No one suspected a thing. As the pub slowly filled up, Yvonne came round the table and sat beside me. She smelled incredible, like the cake shop my mother used to bring me to as a child.

"How are things?" she asked, turning to face me.

My stomach lurched, a massive burp travelled up my oesophagus and paused in my throat, while it waited for me to give it the green light. I twisted away from Yvonne, quelled the belch with my hand and returned to face her.

"I'm okay. Not the best with new people."

"Don't worry, we'll just get pissed," she said, giving me a friendly little poke in the ribs.

She made everything seem so normal, so natural. We *would* just get pissed. Sure, weren't we in a pub? To that end I went to the bar for another drink, getting Yvonne a bottle of cider in the process, trying to think up topics we could discuss, questions I could ask. This time when I got back someone else had commandeered her, an older man from one of the other tables. They were having a right old natter, like two best friends reuniting after years apart. I burned with jealousy. He was making her laugh, flirting in that casual way people did when there was no sexual tension between them. I'd almost finished my pint by the time she came back and refilled her glass.

"That's Tony. He was a regular in the bookies when I worked there; a degenerate gambler."

"Poor Tony," I said.

"Ah, don't worry about Tony, he always gets by. What have you been up to?"

This time I didn't burp. But I might as well have, because what could I possibly say to this woman about my life which wouldn't sound pathetic? Oh, I've just spent the last few weeks drinking to excess, watching films and playing video games. Work? No, not for me. I've never had a job, I'm a prisoner of the state. Anything planned: holidays, weekends away? Not really, don't do those either. It was tragic. I was tragic.

"Just been busy with stuff," I said.

"Stuff," she repeated.

"How about you?"

"Well, work is a fucking nightmare, my daughter hates me, my brother is after turning into a sociopath and the last fellah in my bed was some class of merman from the sea."

I laughed. It had been a long time since I'd laughed.

The band were setting up, doing their sound test. Soon it would be too loud to talk.

"Why is work a nightmare?" I asked her.

"Ah, it just is. Shower of bastards in there."

She was about to expound on this when the drummer hammered on his hi-hats and drowned her out. Then the guitarist practised a few riffs, the sound man began tampering with the levels and Yvonne ended her story before it had even started. The lights went down, a few whoops went up from the crowd and the band launched into a rendition of *Baba O'Riley*. Judging by the audience reaction, Black Daze (which I'd been informed was the latest in a long line of names Noel and his mates were operating under) were quite a big deal round these parts. Our group, which had swelled in numbers, was very enthusiastic in its appreciation, pumping fists, rocking heads and playing air guitars as Black Daze effortlessly segued into a Metallica medley of *Blackened, Master of Puppets* and *One*.

They were talented guys, especially Noel, who was the glue that kept it all together. I would have preferred to have been talking to Yvonne but she was still sitting beside me and that was good enough. And when I nipped off to the bar for another pint she didn't leave her station. I liked that. Someone looking over might assume we were a couple, himself and herself out to watch the lads after a hard week of work.

"Brilliant, aren't they?" she shouted over the chorus of *I Bet You Look Good on the Dancefloor*.

"Class!" I shouted back.

"Just going out for a fag."

"Okay."

Half the table suddenly departed, leaving me with Dervla, the Ashcroft guy from earlier and a handful of unfamiliar faces. One of them, a creepy-looking man with a receding hairline, smiled over at me. I gave him the briefest of nods before returning to the music. This gang of hers contained all sorts of people and of all ages. They couldn't all be her friends. There must have been just one or two who were her close friends. When Yvonne came back, I asked about her the man who'd smiled at me.

"Who's the balding fellah over there, with the white T-shirt?"

She sniggered to herself. "Why, was he eyeing you up?"

"I hope not. Who is he?"

"That's Conrad. You're exactly his type."

I chanced a quick glance over at him, he was drinking his gin through a straw. Now I was being set up with a man, this night was going from bad to worse. Yvonne saw my reaction and burst out laughing, shoving me in the chest reproachfully.

"He's harmless enough. Go over and talk to him!" she shouted.

If anyone else had jokingly tried to pair me off with a man, and a slimy, toad-like man at that, I would have been raging; but Yvonne had a way of making everything seem fun, of normalising my hang-ups and loosening my inhibitions.

"Maybe I will!" I shouted back, deadly serious.

She made an "Oooh!" face and purposely turned her back on me.

The band took a ten-minute break, giving me the opportunity to have a decent conversation with her, but before I could open my mouth she was out smoking fags again. The smoking ban was the worst thing to ever happen to this country. I would rather have died from second-hand smoke than be left on my own every twenty minutes with Conrad making eyes at me. Yvonne did invite me out a couple of times, but I had to stand on my own two feet here. I couldn't be tailing along behind her every time she needed a nicotine fix. I was on my own, staring into my drink, pretending to be carefree, when my old friend Noel came to join me. A member of the band, sitting down to chat with me, I must have looked very important.

"Hey man, good to see you," he said amiably.

"You too. Ye're playing some serious tunes up there."

He shook off the compliment, preferring to focus on me and my well-being.

"You were okay after that night, then? Did you go to the doctor or anything?" he asked.

"No, just needed a bit of rest and I was fine again."

"You gave us some fright," he said, laughing at the memory. "What were you doing in the water, anyway?"

It was the first time someone had come right out and asked the question. I had presumed we'd come to an understanding that we wouldn't discuss the details.

"I was drinking up the beach with my friends and I fell asleep."

"And they just left you there?"

I nodded; my friends were clearly terrible people.

"You were lucky, man. You could have been dragged out to sea, happened to a mate of mine," Noel said.

"I was lucky I met into ye," I said.

"We did nothing, it was all Yvonne, really."

"Yeah, she's unreal. Hey, Noel, what's the story with . . ."

"NOEL, WE'RE BACK ON!"

He gave me a friendly pat on the shoulder and ambled back to his band mates, slinging the bass over his shoulder as he consulted the set list. I'd been about to ask him, subtly, about Yvonne's relationship status. It was probably just as well we'd been interrupted, he'd have told her, she'd have thought it hilarious and I'd have ended up going home with Conrad. The smokers returned just as the band started into *Lithium*. Black Daze were really good. I was getting pissed and really wanted to get up and dance, to jump up and down, but no one was into it, not like that. Yvonne was chatting to Dervla and two other women, the two lads from before were singing but not dancing, and the rest of the gang were either knocking back drink or going to and from the bar. Maybe these weren't my people after all. If they had been, they'd all have been out dancing.

Feeling fed up, a little annoyed, I went to the bar myself and dispensed with all formalities.

"Double Jack with ice," I instructed the barman.

I watched him pour the drink, it looked a healthy measure. After the first sip I calmed down. When the glass was empty my mood markedly improved. I got another. This was more like it. This was how I drank, I didn't need to pace myself for these people. I could drink more than anyone else in this bar, and if they didn't like it that was their problem. My problem, however, was I wasn't used to drinking in the company of others. At home I could get as drunk as I liked and not have to worry about the consequences, about embarrassing myself, about the public's reaction to my behaviour. Here, though, I was in the wild. And with each visit to the bar my defences weakened. Growing increasingly agitated, I vacated my seat and stood in the middle of the group, of my group, looking for someone to talk to. One of the guys from earlier, the short stocky guy, was on his own. The band was playing *Fire* by Jimi Hendrix.

"Some fucking song!" I bellowed into his ear, taking him by surprise.

He nodded good-naturedly, so I continued on.

"Mitch Mitchell, best drummer ever!"

He smiled, but didn't look convinced.

"Everyone says John Bonham or Keith Moon, or even Dave Grohl, but Mitch is the fucking man!"

I drummed along to the solo to emphasise my point, my new pal took a step back, perhaps worried one of my imaginary drumsticks would hit him in the face. He was no craic, but I didn't want to hurt his feelings so I told him I was going to the toilet. I wasn't really going to the toilet, I was going over to the seats near the stage. I wanted to see Black Daze up close because from where I stood, they sounded like they could be the greatest band of all time. True enough, from my new vantage point I could see their full array of skills: the virtuosity of the lead guitarist, the deftness of their keyboard player, how Noel and the drummer kept everything together, and the sweat on the rhythm guitarist's brow as he struggled to keep up. They were really going for it, playing as if it were Woodstock rather than *Cullen's* bar in Castleblaney, and their audience were just not reciprocating. At the end of *Fire* I made a great show of applauding them, letting out a few cheers, showing them that at least one person here appreciated good music. Noel gave me a little thumbs-up as he prepared for the next song.

"What are you doing all the way over here?"

It was Yvonne. I'd almost forgotten about her. Did I even need her any more, now that I had the band?

"Ah, I just wanted to hear them properly, the lads didn't seem too bothered," I said, nodding dismissively at my former friends.

Yvonne sat down beside me. She'd brought her drink with her and sipped it thoughtfully as the band began playing *Last Nite* by The Strokes. That was disappointing, I hated The Strokes, so when Yvonne suggested we go outside I readily agreed and followed her, trying not to look Noel in the eye in case he saw how upset I was.

"Can't believe they're playing The Strokes," I said as we stood under the outdoor heater.

"Shush Aidan, stop shouting."

I didn't think I was shouting, was almost sure I was talking normally, but I chose not to argue. Under the lights I could see Yvonne properly, and she looked great, divine really. I hadn't really noticed her figure before, had been preoccupied with the smoothness of her skin, that big wide smile and her red hair. But she was buxom. That was the only way to describe her: buxom and petite, with wide hips. I wanted to take a look at her arse, thought about absent-mindedly walking behind her to sneak a glance, but decided I'd wait until we went back in and take a peek then.

"What you staring at?" she asked.

"Nothing."

"Hmph," she replied, tipping her fag into the ashtray on the wall.

I was such a flirt.

The other people in the smoking area went back inside, leaving just the two of us. Yvonne shivered against the cold.

"Do you need a jacket?" I offered, keen to show I could be chivalrous as well as flirty.

"You're grand," she said, moving closer to the heater. "You having a good time?"

"I am, but your friends aren't much for chatting."

"Why don't you talk to Conrad, like you said?"

"He's probably too chatty."

She laughed at that.

"I was talking to Noel."

"Oh, yeah?"

"Yeah, I told him what happened the night ye found me."

"And?"

"I fell asleep and my friends left me."

The lie felt good as I said it, felt solid, true.

"What kind of fucking friends are they?" she asked, incredulous.

"I don't know."

"Sound like a shower of bastards."

"I think they were hammered and just couldn't find me," I said, eager to stand up for my fictional friends.

"I see," she said in a way which unnerved me, made me think the lie wasn't as solid as I'd thought. "And where are they tonight, these friends of yours? Why didn't they come with you?"

"Ah, I only see them now and then."

"Not real friends, then."

"Probably not."

I had denounced them now, abandoned them completely.

"Is someone looking after Isabel?"

"Hardly. She looks after herself, that wan."

"Where is she?"

"At home, or at least she was when I left."

"Where does she go?"

"Where do teenagers go? She says she's going 'out' and I don't see her again until bedtime."

"Does she have to be in at a certain time?"

"Supposedly."

I thought of my own life at that age, how I'd spent my entire teenage years holed up in my bedroom. Girls like Isabel, the ones who had friends and social lives and went out and whispered and giggled in little clusters, had been a mystery to me. Even now the thought of meeting one of them terrified me.

"Will we go back in?" she asked. "I'll introduce you properly to the lads."

"Including Conrad?"

"*Especially* Conrad."

I allowed her to lead the way, taking the opportunity to have a look at her arse. It was wide and round but in a nice firm way. Back at the table I was fully integrated into the group courtesy of Yvonne's easy charm, and before long I was locked in conversation with a lad with a shaved head and a tattoo of a snake winding round his neck. He liked the really heavy metal bands of the 80s and 90s: Slayer, Anthrax, Megadeth, Pantera. Those weren't my favourites, but we were having a proper chat about the best drummers of all time when I became vaguely aware of a presence at the other end of the table.

Distracted for a moment, I looked over and saw Gavin, Yvonne's brother. He was on his own at the head of the table like a pygmy king; ignoring the music, the people, the entire pub, and staring at me with real enmity. Fucking Gavin. What was his problem? I'd only begun to make friends, and here he was bringing the mood down with his negative vibes. I tried to return to the conversation with my mate, listening as he made a valid argument for Dave Lombardo being the greatest of all time, but it was no use, Gavin had soured the mood. He was just sitting there, hostility pouring out of him. Why go to a pub if you were going to be like that?

I saw Yvonne go over to him, with her big smile and open heart, and he brushed her off like she was nothing. And all the while he kept his eyes fixed on me, as if hoping he could intimidate me enough to make me leave. He reckoned without my insatiable thirst for alcohol. Ignoring him, I returned to the bar just as they were calling last orders. My last order was a treble rum and coke. See how Gavin liked that. He could stare all he wanted but he couldn't stop me from enjoying a drink with my new pals as we listened to the best band of all time. I'd missed a few of their songs while I'd been mingling, but with the night drawing to a close they were preparing for their finale, a song which was, apparently, their trademark: *Where is my Mind* by Pixies.

Finally, after a night of pretending to be too cool for school, Yvonne's friends took to the floor. It wasn't all of them, and Conrad appeared to be the instigator, but it was enough for me to let loose. Placing my drink on the table I joined the lads as they drunkenly pogoed, moshed and stumbled across the pub's hardwood floor. I felt a shove in my back and turned, expecting to see Gavin with his fists up, but it was the shaven-headed guy joining the scrum. Someone else put their arms around me and we all linked up as the lead singer screamed out the chorus.

It was one of the most liberating experiences of my life: being here with these people, pissed out of my brain, singing a song I loved, knowing that the night wasn't done yet, that there might be a session somewhere, and that a girl I liked might come too. This was real life, this was living. The music ended and we applauded Black Daze off the stage like the heroes they were. We reconvened at the table, talk immediately turning to our next port of call. Some of them were intent on going into town, were ringing taxis on multiple phones, negotiating prices, ordering and cancelling mini-buses. Others, including Dervla and her little boyfriend, said they'd had enough for the night and were going home. Then there was Noel and his little tribe, the skinhead among them, who I learned went by the name 'Mutt'. They wanted to go to Mutt's house, drink a few cans, smoke a few joints and listen to tunes, maybe have a jam. This sounded perfect, but I wanted to see what Yvonne was doing.

She was currently drifting round the pub, stopping to talk to people as she slowly made her way towards the toilets. What was her plan, her preference? The last thing I wanted was to go back to a session with Noel and Mutt and find that Yvonne was in a minibus on the way to town. She'd end up in a nightclub then, surrounded by handsome men, I might never see her again.

"Aidan, are you coming?" asked Mutt, as he hauled two carrier bags full of drink from behind the counter.

"Just one sec," I said as I watched Noel and two other members of Black Daze disappear out the door with some girls.

"We're heading into town in five minutes if you want a lift?" offered Conrad, speaking to me for the first time.

"Oh, maybe, hold on."

I had to see what Yvonne was doing, but she'd disappeared into the ladies'. I hurried over and waited at the entrance. I could hear Yvonne in the bathroom talking to another woman, chatting away as if the night was still young and there was simply no need to be hasty. By the time she came out, Noel, Mutt and the boys were long gone and those heading into town were outside waiting for their taxi.

"It's weird to stand outside the ladies', you know," she said as she came out.

"I was waiting for you," I said. "Are you going into town?"

"Town? Jesus, I never go into town. Sure, we're going back to Mutt's, aren't we? Where are they, anyway?"

And so it was that myself, Yvonne and her friend Gabby, exited into the chilly autumn evening, another bag of drink in tow, trying to catch up with the rest of the crew. I'd hoped to have more chats with Yvonne, to talk about serious stuff, show her how deep and soulful I could be, but it quickly became apparent that Gabby was appropriately named. She began talking from the minute we left the pub, rattling on about her ex-boyfriend and his new girlfriend and how incompatible they were, how she'd paid for the television in the house they shared, how the two of them had tried to keep the dog Gabby and her ex had bought together, how Gabby was seeing a new man now, and how he was a *real* man, a good man who treated her right and just hadn't been able to make it out tonight because he was having issues with *his* ex-girlfriend.

Yvonne listened intently throughout, following the narrative, voicing her assent or dissent when required. When Gabby paused for breath, stopped talking for about 1.4 seconds I pounced, asking Yvonne if she was all right, if her heels were hurting her. Gabby looked at me as if noticing I was there for the first time and then resumed her verbal onslaught. By the time we reached Mutt's place, I knew more about Gabby than I did about myself. She'd had two miscarriages in the last three years and blamed it on an abortion she'd had when she was seventeen, an abortion she'd been pressured into having by her boyfriend at the time; this was a different boyfriend. He was now happily shacked up with a long-term partner and they had four kids together.

That rankled with Gabby. She said she hated him but then admitted she sometimes rang him late at night, hiding her number, waiting till he answered and then hanging up. But it was the other ex, the one who'd tried to steal her dog, for whom she reserved her deepest disdain. To get back at him she walked the dog, the dog they'd once shared, by his house at night and instructed it to shit in their garden. I wondered how the dog was able to shit on command, but it was pointless trying to ask. She had just started on another story about her boss and how she suspected he went for wanks in the bathroom every morning when Yvonne quietly informed me that we'd reached Mutt's flat.

It was situated above a newsagent's; we had to go round the back and up a set of metal stairs to get inside. It was much nicer than my place, he had a little patio area and a set of sliding glass doors. Inside, the square living-room was modern and minimalistic, the furniture expensive, newly-purchased. I wondered how much his rent was and whether he fancied a swap. Noel and two of Black Daze were on the couch with Ashcroft, there were a couple of girls I didn't remember seeing earlier, and then Mutt and Gavin. Cans were being popped open, joints being rolled, and one of the musicians had got out his acoustic guitar.

"Come in, lad, come in," instructed Mutt as I lingered on the patio.

There weren't any seats left so I sat on a metal box by the fireplace, making sure I was as far away from Gavin as possible. I wanted to be on the couch, though, or at least near it; that was the heart of the session, where all the best people were. Determined to make my presence felt, I quietly took a bottle out of the bag I'd brought and enquired whether anyone fancied a drink.

"Is that rum?" asked Ashcroft, his eyes widening.

"Yeah," I said, looking around for glasses, seeing there were none and excusing myself.

Yvonne was in the kitchen with Gabby. They were locked in a tearful embrace, Yvonne consoling Gabby as she wept softly on her shoulder. I gave Yvonne a little smile, whispered "Where are the glasses?" and plucked half a dozen out of the press. Upon my return I measured out some rum for everyone except Gavin, who declined my offer, and basked in the acclaim. I'd contributed to the session now, proved myself. Clearly impressed, Mutt handed me a bag of weed and some cigarette papers and invited me to 'skin up'. I wanted to do it, to skin up and blow smoke rings into the air, but I didn't know how.

"I'm okay, thanks. I don't really smoke it."

He looked a little surprised, so I quickly knocked back the rest of my can.

"I used to smoke it but had to give it up," I added hastily.

"I hear ya," Mutt said, understanding even if I didn't.

One of the band guys was over by the stereo, going through what looked like a significant collection of CDs. I wanted to join him, to look through Mutt's music and make a decision on what best to listen to, but Gavin was sitting beside the stereo in an armchair about four sizes too big for him. He was sunk back into it, taking deep pulls on a joint, and even through the smoke I could tell he was staring at me. I'd always thought hash or weed or whatever it was called was supposed to make you mellow. He seemed far from mellow. The singer - or the drummer, I wasn't sure - made a decision and the music came on: Otis Redding, not what I'd expected.

The tone had been set, they wanted to relax, to chill out with some soul music and marijuana. I felt left out then. But I couldn't go back on what I'd said, decide I did smoke after all. They'd want me to skin up then. And even if I only had a few pulls I'd be out on the patio lying on my back. That stuff didn't agree with me. Rum agreed with me, though, it always had. It made me rowdy but in a fun way, and friendly to all. The more I drank of it the more I thought about going over to Gavin, chatting to him, breaking down whatever barrier had been erected between us. No one seemed to be talking to him, though. His only interactions were accepting joints and passing them on. I wanted to help him, to unlock whatever secrets he'd kept hidden away since returning from the army. Maybe he'd killed someone out in the Lebanon in a training exercise gone wrong. Or maybe he'd been raped? Those army barracks could be lonely places, I'd seen it in the films. One dark night, a room full of frustrated young men, who knew what fate could befall a small lad like Gavin? He'd be easy enough prey for a commanding officer with a horn.

Before I could make a decision on what traumas Gavin had witnessed in service to his country, Yvonne came back with Gabby who had recovered and was back to her talkative self. Undeterred by the established seating arrangements, she squeezed herself between Ashcroft and one of the band members and began flirting wildly with them both, taking the joints they offered her and laughing uproariously at everything they said. I couldn't help but like her; she was a circus. Better still, this left Yvonne at a loose end. Mutt vacated his seat for her but she declined and sat alongside me on the floor.

"Rum?" I asked, holding up the bottle.

"Fuck that," she said, making a face.

Instead she took the weed and papers and began skinning up. It seemed I was the only person in the room who didn't smoke the herb. I decided there and then that I would get some during the week, learn how to skin up, develop a tolerance for it and then announce I had relapsed at the next session - if there was a next session. I'd done well so far, behaved myself, impressed everyone with my lavish taste in alcohol, but I could feel myself slipping, my mind going, thoughts getting scattered. In my haste I'd flattened half the bottle of rum, and that was on top of God knows how many pints and the blast of whiskey back in *Cullen's*. This was usually the point where I'd stagger up to bed, but there was no bed here for me so I powered on.

For a while it was okay. I chatted away to Yvonne, told her she was great, jokingly arranged to call in to see her at the supermarket some time. Then the rum hit me. I remembered getting on my feet and annexing the stereo, shouting over at Mutt every time I saw a CD I liked, and I remembered he and I playing air guitar and head-banging in the middle of the room and everyone busting their arses laughing at us. I remembered complaining when someone suggested we create our own music, have a little sing-along while the lads strummed away on the guitar, and I remembered feeling insanely jealous when I returned to my seat to find Ashcroft in my place chatting to Yvonne. And I remembered going out onto the patio and looking at the stars while taking a piss.

Those were my only solid memories. There were blurred images of Mutt giving me a blow-back, of Gabby falling over and crying and of Gavin giving me a shoulder in the chest as we passed one another in the hallway. There was a ten-second clip of myself and Noel line dancing, a mortifying recollection of me attempting to sing an Ozzy Osbourne track and an even worse snapshot of me trying to dance with Yvonne and getting rebuffed. It was all sound-tracked by Motown, heavy metal, Abba, and shouting, excited voices which finally gave way to a calm, quiet hum and then silence.

*

I awoke in a panic. I'd left the fire lighting and forgot to put up the fire-guard. I rolled out of bed and landed with a thud on the floor. The floor wasn't where it was supposed to be, and I didn't even have a fire. There was a fireplace in front of me, though. Confused, I searched around the unfamiliar room for a fire-guard, bumping into objects and sharp things as I desperately tried to source this vital piece of equipment. I looked back at the fireplace. The fire wasn't lighting. More confused than ever, I looked for a way out and succeeded in finding a hallway and a bathroom. As I pissed I remembered where I was: in Mutt's house, at a session. I must have fallen asleep. Was the session over? And most importantly, where was Yvonne? A new panic overwhelmed me. What if she was in one of the beds with Ashcroft? Or what if he'd waited until I'd fallen asleep, then walked her home and was now in her bed, where I should have been? Well, it was too cold to walk to her house and anyway I didn't know where it was, so I went back into the living-room, got under the blanket and fell asleep.

When I next awoke, I found my new best mate smiling and full of the joys.

"Wakey, wakey, rise and shine," declared Mutt as he drew back the curtains.

I blinked against the sunlight, peering out through the patio doors at the unfamiliar terrain. This really was the cold light of day. I wanted my bed, wanted to be away from here and this strange man.

"How's the head?" asked Mutt as he shook one of the cans, realised it was half-full and took a sup.

"I'm okay."

"Some craic last night. You're some fucking dancer, Aidan," he said, creasing up laughing, adding to my anxiety levels, my paranoia.

"Was it bad?" I asked, fearful.

"Best dancing I've seen in years," he said, laughing some more.

Christ. What would Yvonne think? I'd made a tit of myself.

"Where did everyone go?"

"Home. Sure they only live down the road."

"Oh, right. Thanks for the blanket."

"No bother."

He made me a cup of tea, even offered me some beans and sausages, but I just wanted to get home, to get into my comfy clothes and be hungover in peace. His idea that we go back to Cullen's when they opened at noon tempted me for a millisecond, but I was bet to the ropes and just needed some time by myself. After being given directions to the bus stop and exchanging numbers so we could arrange the next night out, I descended the metal stairs, went through the side entrance and out onto the street.

There were people coming from Mass to get their newspapers in the shop, little kids with their hurleys and bikes and then me, reeking of booze, sick to the gills, in the same clothes I'd worn last night, the clothes I'd slept in. I made it to the bus stop, nodded a weary hello to a lad around my age who also looked the worse for wear, and waited patiently for the 380. When it came I hurried down the back, put my head against the window and let the numbness take over.

11

It had been a success. I was a success, the texts confirmed it. I hadn't made a show of myself, I'd been 'a riot'; Yvonne said so. She rang that afternoon to see how I was and took great delight in recounting the parts of the night I couldn't remember. In addition to my air guitar playing and line dancing I'd also done a Freddie Mercury impression (I didn't even know I had one), had a wrestle with Mutt and, worst of all, got my gut out and challenged the room to a 'big belly bounce-off'. If this was what happened when I got drunk in the company of others, it was just as well I'd spent all those years drinking alone. Although Yvonne found it all hilarious and was already talking about more nights out together, I didn't like where this was headed.

I had no desire to be the court jester, to entertain the masses with my high jinks and tomfoolery. I wanted to be popular for reasons other than my ability to make people laugh with my drunken antics. Those guys always ended up alone. Those fat, funny lads who could drink all night never had girlfriends. The tubby scoundrels who posed for photos with all the ladies in the club spent the rest of the week mired in self-loathing. They were all fun and laughter on the outside, but deep down they knew it was a sham. That was the role Yvonne and Mutt envisaged for me, the mad bastard who'd get naked if you filled him with enough drink. Well, I wasn't going to play their game. I wasn't going to be stereotyped like that.

So, for what felt like the millionth time I decided to knock the drink on the head. Not entirely, just during the week. From Sunday to Friday I would refrain, no more midweek madness. Come Friday evening I would have a few cans at home, and then meet up with the crew in Castleblaney for the Saturday night session. The effects would be manifold. I would lose weight, thus losing the tag of fat, funny man, and also when I did drink I wouldn't be able to drink as much. This time I was motivated, I had a woman to impress. By Monday afternoon I was hankering for a can, dying for just one sup of beer. Instead I went out walking, using all that negative energy, my anxiety, my addiction, as a source of energy. I walked and walked until my feet were sore.

It stopped me from drinking, stopped me from doing anything but flopping down on the sofa every evening and watching TV. The withdrawals began on the Wednesday, offering me the perfect excuse for one tiny little can. I resisted. Even on Friday, as I dealt with stomach cramps, cold sweats and headaches, I said no; there would be no drink in this house tonight. It got so bad I couldn't meet the lads on Saturday night, had to make up an excuse as to why I couldn't join them, but by the following week I had recovered. I'd dried out and could now resume drinking. This was how normal people did it, binged at the weekend and lived a quiet life during the week. I could do that.

This time they were meeting in a bar in Rún Derg. There was a bluegrass music festival on all weekend; local, national and international musicians playing in various pubs and clubs for two days and three nights. It would hardly be as good as Black Daze, but I was happy to accede to their choices.

"There he is now," declared Mutt when I poked my head in the door of an unfamiliar tavern. They were all there, a big crowd of them: Noel, Yvonne, Gabby, Conrad, Ashcroft, Dervla and the rest. There was no sign of Gavin.

"You're looking well," said Yvonne coolly as I slid into the booth beside her.

It was already working. If she was impressed after two weeks, she'd be positively blown away by the results in a few months' time. It had felt good depriving myself of a drink for that long. I'd purged and cleansed, and now it was time for my reward. That first pint tasted like victory, as did the second and third, and in no time I was back in the groove; the king of the drinkers, untouched and unmatched. It didn't take long for the banter to start. This was part of having a group of friends, the ability to take, and dish out, insults.

"We going moshing, Aido?" asked Mutt, a big grin on his face.

"Nah, not yet," I replied.

"Will I ask the band if they know any Queen songs?" enquired Conrad.

They all laughed and I laughed with them, but deep down I was furious. Conrad hadn't even been there, what right had he to take the piss? If it had been Noel I'd have accepted it, but not him.

"I don't know about ye but I'd love a big belly bounce-off," said Ashcroft to yet more laughter.

I took a slug of my pint, hiding my annoyance. I was so upset that I ordered two pints on my next visit to the bar and knocked them back fast. If they wanted entertainment, I'd give them entertainment. Before I could do so, someone suggested we go to another pub. I traipsed out with my so-called friends, falling in with Yvonne and Noel as we shielded ourselves from the spray coming in from the sea.

"Don't mind them, I think you're a lovely little dancer," said Yvonne.

I couldn't tell if she was serious or not. Noel just gave an apologetic shrug, too kind to comment either way.

"I go a bit overboard when I've had a few," I said.

"We've noticed!" Yvonne said.

"Going to take it handy tonight, though."

"Yeah, it looks like that all right."

Had she been monitoring my intake? It was flattering to think that she might. The strange thing was, if she told me to stop drinking, switch to fizzy orange for the rest of the night, I would have willingly done so. As it was, she gave me a mildly disapproving look when I returned from the bar in the next pub with a round of shots for everyone - a look which didn't prevent her from merrily drinking her own shot. There were more shots, more pints, a few trips outside to the smoking area, and after a while I forgot about the slagging they'd given me. Sure it was only all a bit of craic, back and forth between mates.

I even gave some back, calling Mutt a 'bald cunt', informing Ashcroft he was just a smaller, uglier version of Richard Ashcroft, and telling Noel there was no need to be so nice all the time. They seemed to take it in good spirits, apart from Ashcroft who got into a mild strop before Mutt told him to cop the fuck on. I liked that, now someone else was at the bottom of the pile, at least until I did something stupid again. But I was really behaving myself. It helped that the music was so loud and inoffensive. It was vanilla for the ears and did nothing for me. Some of the group, Dervla and her fellah, two of the other couples, had gone out dancing. We sat staring at them, transfixed, occasionally bursting into fits of giggles as they got really into it.

I was stoned. It had just crept up on me. I'd been smoking whatever they'd handed to me, not really taking any notice, and now I was fucking stoned. I liked it. I looked over at Mutt for confirmation, saw his big dopey grin and gave him a thumbs-up. Yvonne was sitting one table over on her own, looking wistfully at the couples out dancing. She was lonely, I could tell. I decided that this was the time. I still had enough of my faculties to judge whether it was a wise decision, and they all told me it was.

But just as I rose from my seat, a beefy guy in a check shirt came over and asked her to dance. He took her by the hand and guided her out on to the dance-floor, crushing every hope and dream I'd ever had. There it was, the alpha conundrum. No matter what I did, I would always lose out to a more handsome, more powerful man. Every time I met someone I liked, an alpha would appear out of nowhere and steal her away. I would have to settle for a Marion, for someone the alphas wouldn't ever consider.

I watched the two of them dance together, Yvonne's arse wiggling happily in time with the music, the alpha's beautiful backside doing the same, until the song ended and Yvonne came back to her seat; but not to the one she'd been sat on, to one beside me.

"Whew," she declared. "It's hot out there."

I didn't respond, just stared into the middle distance.

"Hello, Aidan! Anyone in there?"

She was waving her hand in front of me. I wanted to push it away.

"What?" I asked irritably.

"What's your problem?" she asked, equally irritable.

"Nothing."

"Jesus," she said, "you could have fooled me."

"Who was that guy?" I asked, unable to help myself.

"I don't know, just some guy."

"Oh, right."

She softened, her anger evaporating.

"We're not jealous, are we, Aidan?"

"No," I said, unconvincingly.

"Okay. That's fine. That's fine if you don't like me."

"I do like you," I blurted out.

"Do you now?" she asked, arching an eyebrow and studying me closely.

"A little bit," I said.

"This much?" she asked, extending her thumb and forefinger a couple of inches.

"A bit more."

"This?" she asked, extending them as far as they'd go.

"About that."

"That's a lot, Aidan," she said.

"If you say so."

She got up and went back to her original seat and for one wretched, sickening moment I thought that was it, that she'd had her fun and was now going to wait for the next alpha to come her way. But no, she was just getting her jacket and was walking towards me as she put it on.

"Come on, let's go for a walk," she said.

I silently got to my feet, picked up my own coat, calmly finished my drink and walked out behind her, not even looking to see if Mutt or Noel had noticed.

*

We walked along the seafront, neither of us speaking, the only sounds the waves crashing back and forth and the distant hubbub of the pubs and clubs. The last time I'd been here, I had been walking in the opposite direction, towards salvation. Yvonne had put up her hood and occasionally turned to look at me, her eyes full of mirth, like a child who's been told to keep quiet but is finding it increasingly difficult.

"Will we go on the beach?" she asked as the drizzle grew steadier.

I looked at her attire: tight jeans, a flimsy raincoat, mercifully flat shoes.

"You sure?"

"I grew up on beaches, boy," she declared, stepping nimbly onto the stony beginnings of the beach.

"Okay," I said to myself, following her.

"You love this beach anyway, Aidan," she shouted over the waves, slipping and sliding as she defiantly forged ahead. "Always hanging around here, so you are."

Despite her ungainliness she reached the flat, firm part of the sand long before me, proving that she had indeed grown up on beaches.

"See, it's fine here," she said when I eventually joined her.

A wave cascaded towards us and I instinctively backed away. Yvonne remained where she was, watching as the water halted a metre or so from her feet and retreated from whence it came.

"Come on, you big melon," she said, pulling me along so we walked side by side. Again she peeped up at me, her round little face illuminated by the lights of the promenade. Those looks meant something, I just didn't know what. Everything about this was a mystery to me.

"I wish we'd brought drink," she said sadly as we walked.

"Me too."

"And some weed."

"Yeah."

The sea air and the shock of suddenly being alone with her had sobered me up. I couldn't think of anything to say, was trapped inside my head. This felt like a moment in time which I would look back on for the rest of my life. I was afraid of letting it slip through my fingers, but also afraid to act out of turn. All I could do was keep walking and hope at least one of us knew what was going to happen.

"How far up did you go that time?" she asked.

"Miles. To the end."

"Why?" she asked, looking at me again. The rain had caused her fringe to stick to her forehead, her make-up to smear.

"Peace and quiet, I suppose."

Yvonne stood and looked around her, held out her arms, tilted her head back and then spun around in a circle until she fell into me. I grabbed her, preventing her from whirling head-first into the sand. She wrapped her arms around my waist and pulled herself upward so that her head lay on my chest. Then she settled into me, slotting comfortably into my embrace as if she'd been moulded specifically for it and was only now realising where she belonged. My heart was pounding, I was afraid she'd hear it, feel its rhythm as it vibrated against her perfect little head, but she said nothing. She held on tighter, squeezed me and made a sound somewhere between a sigh and a squeal.

It seemed she was content. And I was too. I would have been happy with that, happy to have just held her for a while, listening to the sea, waiting for the water to lap against my feet. Then she looked up at me again, the hood framing her features as she blinked away the rain. This time she held my gaze until there was no doubt in my mind what those looks were about. I leaned down and kissed her, paused just to make sure it was okay, and then kissed her again. When she kissed me back, forcefully and with a passion that matched my own, I felt happiness, true happiness, for the first time in my life.

*

After our kiss we walked a little more, holding hands at first, then with her pressed against my side. Every ten paces we would stop, she would give me that look again and I would bring her to me, until eventually we were no longer walking. We held one another, kissing, squeezing, sighing with pleasure and, in my case, relief. Yet for all its romance and spontaneity, an Irish beach at night in late autumn is not a place for lovers to linger.

"Will we go back?" she said in a tone I hadn't heard before, a sweet, affectionate tone with none of the edge or brashness she usually adopted.

"Yeah."

"You're drenched," she said, tousling my hair.

"It's okay."

"Do you want my coat?" she asked, all her old sass returning.

"I'll manage."

"Ooh, big brave man."

It was hard to keep up with these changes in her personality. So I did what I always did, stayed quiet and hoped it would reflect well on me. The closer we got to civilisation the more business-like she became. At one point she detached herself from me to check her phone and I felt my stomach lurch again; I'd done something wrong, she was bored with me and as soon as we got back to the pub she was going to ditch me for that bastard with the pert backside and checked shirt.

"Just seeing where the lads are," she said apologetically before suddenly punching me in the ribs.

"Ow, what the fuck!"

"I knew you weren't tough," she said gleefully.

Unless I was mistaken she wanted me to respond in kind, maybe hit her back. Perhaps that was why she'd grown momentarily cold. I reached out an uncertain hand, not sure how to proceed, and she dodged away from me, dunting me with her shoulder. I understood then, this was all part of the mating ritual, a way for me and Yvonne to get physical without letting on we wanted to feel one another up. So I sprang forward, surprising her with my speed, and held her firmly by the shoulders. She gazed up at me, a look of helpless excitement on her face, but I didn't know what to do next, we were on a beach, I couldn't slam her to the ground and jump on top of her. While I pondered my next move she jammed her fist into my crotch, firmly, but not so hard that it hurt. Then she scampered away, her shoes sliding from under her as she made the slowest escape in the history of modern warfare.

Buoyed by this new form of physical contact, I decided I would take a risk and see where it got me. I chased after her, caught her and brought her to the ground as gently as I could. I waited for the angry response, for her to chastise me for ruining her coat, her jeans, her hair, but it didn't come. Instead she pulled me on top of her and clamped her mouth over mine, her little hands wrapped round the back of my head. She was biting me, driving her lips, her tongue, into my mouth, pressing her face against mine. Then she was grinding into me, moaning as she bucked back and forth. I had begun to do the same, rubbing my erection against her stomach, moving my hips, thrusting in search of pleasure. Before I knew what was happening, *it* was happening.

She took my hand and guided it inside her jeans. I felt the soft material of her underwear, paused and then slid my hand inside it. There was hair, but not much, and there was wetness, a lot. I explored a while and then slipped a finger inside her. She let out an involuntary moan and I moved my head away to look at her; she stared at me with a desperation and an urgency I had never seen in another. I slipped another finger inside and continued doing what I was doing, nuzzling and kissing her neck as she pulled my hair. Her jeans had ridden down to her knees and her knickers were now thigh-high, allowing me greater room for manoeuvre. Like a seasoned pro, I slid my fingers in and out, keeping a steady rhythm, afraid to change anything, do anything different, in case I ruined it. And as I nuzzled and kissed, using my other hand to feel the outline of her breasts, she bit and bucked. The rain grew heavier, the water drew closer, and the night darker, as she let out a series of strangulated yelps, culminating in one loud, undignified grunt. The biting and bucking stopped. I stopped too. Yvonne was breathing heavily, slowly returning to the land of the living.

"Ha ha! Jaysus, I'm fucking soaked!!" she said, laughing with delight.

I removed my fingers, my arm drenched from the rain, and she quickly righted herself, getting back to her feet fully clothed, as if nothing had happened.

"The best thing about sand is that even when it's wet you can just brush it off," she said, beating the sand off my jeans to prove her point.

"It's some stuff," I said.

She gave me the broadest smile yet, grabbed me by the waist and we veered our way back to the pub.

*

They were all still there, little had changed. Mutt looked like he needed his bed, and there were a few more people out dancing, but in the hour we'd been away the dynamic hadn't shifted perceptibly. In contrast, I had left that pub a boy and was now returning as a man, a giver of orgasms and a pleaser of women. Technically I was still a virgin, but I'd engaged in a sex act, a proper one, and it had been an unmitigated success. As with any good news I wanted to share it with someone, perhaps celebrate over a few glasses of champagne, but out of respect for Yvonne I decided I would keep it to myself.

There was another reason too. I didn't know enough about her, whether she'd been romantically involved with anyone in this pub. What if I told the wrong person, discovered that she and some dusky hunk at the bar had been going out for three years? I was too insecure for that, couldn't bear the thought of her ever being with someone else. It was easier to imagine she'd been saving herself for me, even if she did have a fifteen-year-old daughter.

"Where the fuck were ye?!" asked Mutt belligerently.

"Out walking," replied Yvonne, not missing a beat.

He looked at me quizzically, I said nothing, and he went back to his drink.

Interrogation over, I went to the bar for a round, leaning against it with a new-found confidence, holding my money in the same hand, with the same fingers, that had been inside her. This was how real men must feel all the time, cocksure in the knowledge they could satisfy women. It was all-consuming. While I waited for the barman to serve me I found myself eyeing up a MILF, holding her gaze when she caught me staring. I was out of control. No, Yvonne was the woman for me. There was so much more to come now, I was sure of it. I returned with the drinks, even giving Conrad a friendly smile as I placed his fruity cocktail in front of him.

"Thanks," said Yvonne with a smile as I deposited the last of the drinks on the table and took my place beside her.

Unsure how to act, whether public displays of affection were permitted, I played it safe, sitting close to her, close enough so that people might presume we were a couple, but not engaging in any physical contact. Every so often she gave me a little look, her mouth curling into a slight smile, before averting her eyes once more. A thought struck me: what if we weren't finished? What if there was more to come later on? I could end the night an even bigger success - or, more likely, a failure. If we ended up in bed I'd just finger her again, stick with what I knew. I couldn't do that forever, though, eventually I'd have to try other things and show her how much of a disappointment I could be. It was no good. I was better off leaving this pub now, returning home and severing all ties, leaving her with the thought of what might have been, the memory of the enigmatic Aidan Collins and his magic fingers.

"Going out for a smoke?" she asked, nodding to her friends, to Dervla, Gabby and two of the other young wans. Girl talk. The thought of Yvonne telling them about me lifted my spirits considerably. I had to revel in my victory for as long as I could and forget about what might lie ahead. While they were gone, Mutt came over to me and we got to talking about music. He was banjaxed and wasn't making much sense, but it was good to talk to a man again, to escape from the mysterious world of women. Sure enough, upon their return Dervla and the others were definitely looking at me in a new light, looking at me rather than through me.

Yvonne sat beside me again, even closer than before, and put her hand on my thigh as she made herself comfortable. That was it, then; we were a couple. When the lights flashed and the band announced that this was their last number, talk turned to how we might continue the night. The day of drinking had taken its toll, however. Mutt was asleep, Ashcroft and his mate had left earlier, Conrad was arguing with one of the bouncers, and the entire group looked like an army squadron returning from battle having suffered terrible losses. Only Noel seemed with it.

"Someone's going to have to bring him home," he said, nodding at Mutt. "And calm him down," he added, as Conrad got right up in the bouncer's face.

A couple of the girls and their boyfriends were heading out in search of food. The singer and drummer from Black Daze had arrived, their eyes wide and unblinking, jaws twitching involuntarily, and Gabby was over in the corner with a group of lads, laughing hysterically, boobs spilling out of her top from all angles.

"We'll get a taxi with Mutt and Gabby," said Yvonne.

"Yeah," said Noel, momentarily distracted as the drummer slipped something into his hand.

"Noel, you're not to take anything," Yvonne said sternly.

"I won't," he said.

"Noel!"

"We're going into town," he said sheepishly.

"For fuck's sake."

By the time Yvonne extricated Gabby from her new friends the rest of them had deserted us. We were left with a stroppy, bellicose Gabby and a drunken, semi-comatose Mutt. The last I'd seen of Conrad, he had latched on to the Black Daze after-party and was studiously counting out notes while the singer patiently waited to complete their transaction. My job now was simple: as the most sober one among us, I had to get Mutt home and put him to bed. That would be easy. Then I had to help Yvonne bring Gabby to wherever she lived. Again, easy enough. What came after that I did not know. But it would be more difficult than the other tasks. We fell out onto the street, into a cold, wet and windy night. People were hailing cabs and buses from either side of the road, standing in front of cars that weren't even taxis, sidling up to windows and giving addresses to people who'd just stopped to get chips. It didn't look promising.

"Hold on," said Yvonne. "I'll ring Dessie."

"Aw, Dessie. I love Dessie," cooed Gabby.

Yvonne stepped away from us to make the phone call, sheltering under the awning of a nearby arcade. Meanwhile Mutt had regained consciousness and was wandering aimlessly about, mumbling obscenities under his breath, and occasionally breaking into song. People were actively avoiding him, giving him a wide berth. I moved in his direction, hoping to corral him away from the general public for everyone's safety. Before I could get there, however, someone else intervened.

"Get the fuck away from him," snarled Gavin, protecting Mutt as if we were his parents and I'd just lost custody.

"Okay, okay," I said, backing away, hands held where he could see them.

"Mutt, Mutt!" Gavin shouted, staring into his friend's eyes. It was a bit over the top; Mutt had simply had too much to drink, smoked one spliff too many.

"Don't worry, Mutt. I'll get you home," said Gavin, guiding his friend away as if I were the cause of all his travails.

Sadly, he chose to guide him in the general direction of Yvonne.

"The fuck are you still doing out?" Gavin barked at her. My pulse quickened in response.

"Gavin, not now," Yvonne said, shaking her hand dismissively.

"Are you with *him?*" he asked, nodding in my direction.

"Mind your own business, Gavin. Who invited you anyway?" she answered haughtily.

"I'm here with *my* friend," he announced, holding Mutt up as evidence.

"Oh, grow up," Yvonne said.

"He *is* my friend," Mutt declared, putting an arm round Gavin and ruffling his hair playfully.

"I don't fucking like him, Yvonne. I don't fucking like him!" Gavin shouted, loud enough for everyone to hear, for me to hear.

"I don't give a fuck what you like!" Yvonne bawled back.

"What about Izzy, then?" he snapped.

"What about her?" asked Yvonne, her eyes narrowing.

"Should you not be at home with her instead of out with that fucking weirdo?"

I'd been called a weirdo before, many times, but this one hurt for some reason.

"Look who's fucking talking. You're the biggest weirdo going!"

"How am I weird? How am I?"

They could have gone on all night, providing a show for those eating their chips and waiting for lifts, but, just as things threatened to reach a crescendo, Dessie arrived. He was a stout, elderly bald man with a taxi ready and waiting for four people. Unfortunately, there were now five of us. Gavin quickly escorted Mutt into the back and Gabby appeared from behind a chip van to take the passenger seat. It was clear I was the odd man out. Yvonne paused, looking towards the car, at its cosy interior and its promise of home and then back to me, the giver of orgasms, the man she still didn't really know.

"I'm sorry, Aidan," she said, giving me the most mournful of waves before clambering into the back with her brother and Mutt.

I watched them speed off, Yvonne's sad face peering out at me as the night came to an abrupt end, and all I could think of was whether there was anywhere I could get a drink at this hour.

12

There wasn't anywhere to get a drink. I traipsed round the damp narrow streets of Rún Derg in search of a late bar, but there was nothing but chippers and people huddled in groups waiting for taxis. Eventually, sometime after 4 a.m. I managed to find one willing to bring me home at a premium rate of €30, and made it to my front door before sunrise. I was soaked to the skin, footsore and exhausted. Myself and Yvonne on the beach seemed to belong to another time. I couldn't even remember what she looked like. After I'd taken off my clothes and dried myself, I took a quick look at my phone; there were texts and missed calls but I was too tired to read anything or call anyone. As soon as my head hit the pillow, I was out for the count.

The next morning it all felt like a dream. I'd spent my whole life praying for a night like that. What was this madness? Was I about to become one of those happy people? I had no idea what came next. The entire thing was so stressful, so anxiety-inducing that I almost wished the date had never happened, that I'd never met Yvonne and had nothing to concern me but the end-of-level baddie in my new Xbox game or the price of cider in the supermarket. That was loser talk, though. If you wanted to achieve anything in this life you had to take risks, and that's what I was doing: I was taking risks, I was living.

The texts she'd sent were mostly gibberish; apologies for Gavin's behaviour, flirtatious messages full of misspellings, other illegible nonsense. I opted to ring her, to cut straight to the chase. No answer. I wasn't concerned, the last text had been sent at 5.21 a.m., she was probably sleeping. There was also a chance that Gavin had murdered both her and Gabby (I reasoned he'd let Mutt survive) and then turned the gun on himself. He surely had a gun, those army types loved firearms. Despite his hostility towards me and the likelihood he owned a Glock 17, I wasn't particularly afraid of him. He just wasn't a fearsome guy. If he confronted me, became threatening, I would deal with it, but otherwise I would keep my distance. Yvonne didn't seem too bothered about her brother not liking me, in some ways it gave our affair an added frisson, like Romeo and Juliet, Taylor and Burton, Ann and Barry.

It was mid-afternoon before I heard back from Yvonne.

Sorry. I've been with Izzy all day. How are you?

Grand. Was everything all right after?

Yeah. That's just Gavin, I don't know what the hell is wrong with him.

He doesn't like me, anyway.

Well, I like you Aidan, and that's all that matters.

She liked me. She still liked me.

I like you too, I wrote.

Things got a bit wild there on the beach, she replied, adding a shocked smiley face at the end.

I know, it was great.

Three crying laughing emojis and then: **It had been a while, you know.**

Who was she telling? It had been thirty-one years for me.

It's good to be spontaneous, I replied.

It is, Aidan. Next time I won't be so selfish. More crying laughing emojis.

You weren't selfish. I didn't mind.

Okay. But all the same, we'll have to look after you too the next time.

When was the next time going to be? Were we strictly weekend lovers or was there a possibility of a midweek date?

Any plans for next weekend? I asked.

I have Izzy all weekend. Sad face. And then: **But I'm free Thursday?**

Great. What will we do?

Not the pub, anyway.

I waited for a further text, for her to suggest something, for the little dots which informed me she was typing, but there was nothing. She was waiting for me. I cast my mind back to our conversations last night, to the chain of text messages, our phone conversations. Cinema. Everyone liked the cinema. I hadn't been there for years, though. Cinemas made me anxious: the dark room, the loud sound systems, being trapped in your seat, afraid to move in case someone gave out to you for disturbing them. It would be different now, though. We'd go early when there was no one around, we'd have the run of the place.

I quickly scanned the listings in the local Omniplex. It would have to be something funny or scary, something fairly light with not too much plot. I really wanted to see *Straight Outta Compton* but Yvonne had shown little to no interest when I'd engaged her in the merits of east versus west-coast rap. *45 Years* had good reviews and promised romance and drama, but a film about a couple celebrating their 45th wedding anniversary seemed wholly unsuitable for our first official date. There were a few blockbusters on, a superhero comic-book reboot and then, finally, showing at 6.15 p.m. *Trainwreck*, a romantic comedy starring Amy Schumer with Judd Apatow directing. I read the blurb.

'Having thought that monogamy was never possible, a commitment-phobic career woman may have to face her fears when she meets a good guy.'

That sounded encouraging. I could pick up some tips, see what constituted a good guy in modern society.

Cinema? There's a film, *Trainwreck*, that looks good. It's a comedy.

Only if we can sit in the back row.

Deal.

So four days later I was once more busying myself in front of the mirror, looking for another fresh shirt, and applying more aromatic fragrances. I hadn't accounted for this; meeting her without alcohol to assist me. I thought about a hip flask full of vodka to pour in my Coke when she wasn't looking, but no, this was a test of my nerve, a potential turning-point in my life. If I could do this, I could do anything. With shaking legs and trembling heart, I walked the short distance to the cinema, all the while fighting the urge to retch, to lie on the ground and start crying.

She wasn't there when I arrived and for a moment my spirits lifted; she'd stood me up, I could go home and be safe again. No, I was just early. A couple walked past me and headed inside. They looked happy, comfortable with each other, maybe they were going to see *Trainwreck* too. Some other people went in, young lads, and it made me think; here I was, standing outside a cinema, waiting for a woman, my date. I wasn't hiding in the shadows or skulking in the corners. That felt good. Not good enough to calm my nerves, but enough to stop me from wanting to vomit.

"Am I late? I'm always late."

It was Yvonne. She'd appeared on my blind side, came through the car park instead of over the little bridge. She leaned in and kissed me gently on the cheek.

"You smell great," I said.

She responded with a simple smile and in we went.

"Did you get sweets?" she whispered, opening the top of her bag to reveal packs of Maltesers, Smarties, and those little mini Twirls.

"I usually just get popcorn," I said.

"You get the popcorn, I'll provide the sweets," she said, leaving me to queue up.

"What about a drink?" I called back.

She pointed solemnly at the bag. It didn't look that big. Maybe it was one of those bottomless bags I'd always dreamed about having as a child, the ones that never ran out of sweets no matter how many you ate.

I decided to get the biggest popcorn they had, the mega family size. It was so big I could barely see over it.

"For fuck's sake," she said, laughing, when she saw me coming. "You're already after dropping half of it."

Flustered, I rummaged in my pockets for my ticket while she stood on the other side, laughing away at me. Usually if someone was laughing at me like that I'd be upset, a bit cross, but it felt like we were in on the joke together.

"Come on, you eejit," she said when I finally made it to the other side of the barrier.

"What number are we in?"

"11. Up the stairs, come on."

I dutifully followed, happy to be an eejit.

There were five other people at the screening; a couple and three women around our age. It was one of those smaller rooms, the kind they use for films which have had their big opening and are slowly being phased out. The couple had taken the seats right in the centre and the woman were two rows from the back.

"Back row is free," Yvonne said, leading the way.

We sat on the inside of the row, towards the wall, with me on the outside. I felt safe there. There was room to stretch my legs, and if I needed to escape there was no one obstructing my path. Yvonne immediately opened a bag of Minstrels - I didn't even know she'd had those - and offered me some.

"Take a handful," she said when I emerged with one solitary little Minstrel.

I'd already placed the popcorn between us and she was dipping in and out of it, combining it with chocolate.

"Almost as good as crisps and chocolate," she said appreciatively.

The trailers started. I hated trailers, they showed too much and yet still managed to make you want to see more.

"Going to the toilet, I hate the trailers," I whispered.

"Grand."

I left her there, munching away. The bathroom was empty so, after relieving myself, I took a look in the mirror. I looked better than I remembered, I could almost make out the outline of a real person beneath the fat alcoholic mess. And the date was going well. I didn't even want a drink. I was looking forward to going back in there, to seeing what Yvonne would do next.

"It's just starting," she warned as I tiptoed up the steps back to my seat.

A plastic packet was thrust onto my lap: Fruit Pastilles. Had she smuggled them in as contraband? Hidden them somewhere she knew no one would look? There was no time to ponder that, because the film had indeed started and right from the off it had me squirming. Amy Schumer's character was funny, very funny in fact, but she was also quite promiscuous. There was nothing wrong with that per se, but it reminded me of my own untainted state. I still got the jokes, but I felt a fraud for laughing at them. Yvonne on the other hand, was in the knots. This concerned me. Was she remembering some of her own one-night stands, the good, bad and indifferent lovers she'd had during her lifetime?

This was a terrible choice of film. I should have gone with *Straight Outta Compton* with all its rapping and machismo. Thankfully, though, after an unsettling start, *Trainwreck* became a more conventional love story. Amy found a nice guy, abandoned her old ways and the two of them settled into a comfortable, monogamous relationship. I could manage that. I relaxed and set about making a dent in the popcorn. At one point I felt Yvonne's hand enter the tub at the same time as mine, I paused and moved my hand over to give her room. She grabbed my hand, twisted my fingers, tickled my palm and scratched my wrist before emerging with what seemed like half the remaining popcorn. I glanced over at her, she stared blankly at the screen as if nothing had happened. Well, if that was the way she wanted to play it . . . I lay in wait until she went back in for more.

As soon as her little paw came in I pounced on it, squeezing it so that the popcorn squished into pulp; but she fought back, wiggling free and pinching my wrist. It fucking hurt. A tussle ensued, a giggly teenage tussle which caught the attention of the women in front. One of them turned back and we momentarily stopped our scrapping. When the coast was clear we resumed in earnest, Yvonne catching me unaware and yanking my hand out of the tub. Unfortunately, my hand was attached to the tub and it came out of its holder, along with all the remaining popcorn, and up into the air, landing with a plop on one of the seats beside the three women. This time they all looked back, one of them muttered something which sounded like an angry warning, but Bill Hader's on-screen antics drowned it out. Yvonne elbowed me quite solidly in the ribs.

"Fuck's sake, Aidan."

She had adopted a stern expression, as if disgusted with me and my behaviour, but as soon as I caught her eye it set her off. We were both gone then. I had to put my head into her shoulder to drown out the laughter. She was shaking uncontrollably, no noise coming out of her, just little wheezes as she caught her breath. I had become one of those people who ruined films for others at the cinema. One of the worst kinds of people. We'd managed to compose ourselves by the time the film ended and the lights came up, and we averted our gaze as the women gathered their belongings, threw us dirty looks and left us alone in the auditorium.

Yvonne leaned forward, picked up the tub of popcorn and fired a fistful at my face.

"We should go," I said, worried the women would complain to the manager.

"Aw, you frightened?"

"No, just. We should go."

"I want to finish my sweets first," she said, not budging.

"I think you've had too much sugar," I said.

"You haven't had enough!"

Luckily no members of staff had been alerted to our shenanigans and we made it outside without being sent to cinema jail.

"Will we go for a drink?" I asked hopefully.

"Well, I'll need something to wash down all that sugar, won't I?"

Had I offended her? Did she think I was calling her fat? It was hard to tell whether she was joking or not. We went to a pub I'd never been to before, one of those oul' lad pubs which had been appropriated by a young, hip crowd and become a goldmine for its unwitting owner. There were a few hipsters in the corner drinking craft beer and a group of dishevelled, good-looking people lingering at the exit to the beer garden. Yvonne took a seat at one of the tables and sent me to get the drinks. When I returned she didn't even look at me, just scrolled on her phone, not saying a word.

"I didn't mean anything when I said about the sugar. It was just because you were acting hyper."

She turned to look at me with a face like thunder.

"I eat what I want and I drink what I want. If it's one of those skinny girls you're after, then look elsewhere."

"God, no, Yvonne. Honestly, I love your figure. I think it's - I think you're - I just like it, that's all. I really do."

"Which parts do you like?" she asked, deadly serious.

Fuck.

"All of it," I offered.

"Which parts?"

"Your. . . well, your. . . your boobs."

She immediately perked up.

"I do have great boobs. What else?"

"Erm, hips?"

"I have wide hips, Aidan."

"I know."

"And you like that?"

"I do."

She didn't believe me.

"I like a real woman," I continued. "Curvy, you know."

"So I'm curvy now?"

"Yes?"

That didn't help. She still looked cross.

"I like you, Yvonne. I can hardly say anything about weight, can I?" I said, gesturing at my own bulk.

"You're curvy," she said in a childlike voice.

"I'm a BBM."

"Big beautiful male," she grinned.

She poured her drink into the glass, took a long slug, and then gave me her most winning smile.

"What did you make of the film?" she asked.

Crisis over. Lesson learned. No more references to food, over-eating or curves.

"It was great," I said, smiling. "Amy Schumer is gas."

We left it at two drinks because Yvonne had to work in the morning. As we walked towards the bus stop she took my hand and swung it back and forwards. She seemed perfectly at ease but I was thinking about my next move and when and where I should make one. We'd gone through the entire date without even kissing. I lapsed into silence as we walked, my tension so apparent that she soon followed suit.

There were a few people inside the bus shelter, workers heading home after a late shift, a woman and her two kids, an older man with a scarf and flat cap. We stood away from the shelter, lingering in the background. A real man would have known what to do here, but I just stood to one side, looking at my feet.

"The bus will be along soon," she said abruptly.

"Okay," I said.

She sighed in disappointment. If I didn't do something now, we'd probably never see one another again. Panicked, I made a step towards her, angling my body for an awkward, unrequited lunge. But she responded in kind, and before I knew what was happening we were kissing again. It was even better than I remembered; urgent, passionate, full of desire and longing. People were walking past us, probably staring, wondering how anyone could let themselves be kissed by me. I didn't care, I was in the moment. I even brought my hands down to her waist and onto her arse, cupping her buttocks, enjoying their heft as my erection ground into her stomach.

"The bus," she said, disengaging.

"Ah, fuck."

She laughed. "Next time, Aidan. I promise."

"Okay."

While the others filed onto the bus, we kissed again, then again, then one more time, until the driver asked us if we were getting on or just standing there for the hell of it.

"Bye," she said softly.

"Bye."

I watched her get on, hand the driver her ticket and then almost catapult along the aisle when he drove off with a start. By the time she'd found her seat, she had to strain her neck to see me. I was still watching and waving as she disappeared into the night, the world in bright technicolour as my erection slowly subsided and my heart filled with joy.

13

THE NEXT TWO DATES FOLLOWED the same pattern. We had another pub date, this time on a Sunday, and again in Rún Derg. Once more it ended with a passionate embrace, an even lengthier bout of kissing and some general tugging and fondling. Yvonne got a loan of Noel's car for date four and we went to Mahon Falls, climbed up as far as we dared, had a little picnic and drove backwards up the hill (we argued about the science of this, but it was a good-natured argument, a discussion really). By the time she dropped me back into town it was evening, and I suggested we keep the date going with dinner somewhere.

"I can't. I've to get back."

I didn't question it but my disappointment must have been evident because she leaned across and gave me one of her best, most sensual kisses. This time it was accompanied by an excursion below the belt. She grabbed my knob, still outside the jeans, and then my balls, squishing and stroking them, then moving back to my knob and wanking it up and down. I whimpered in pleasure and felt her mouth part into a smile. I planted one hand on one of her boobs and gave it a little rub, the other on her knee and just left it there: a statement of sorts. She said nothing so I moved it up further, but she was wearing tights, making access very limited. As I fumbled around, looking for something nice to touch, she grew more vigorous with her wanking, really getting into it. My hand went to my belt buckle, I paused and looked her in the eye.

"No, Aidan. We're in the middle of the street," she said.

"It's dark. No one can see."

"Soon. Okay?"

"Okay," I said.

She kissed me goodbye and turfed me out onto the side of the road, leaving me with another erection, more sexual frustration. But it was okay because she'd said 'soon'. What did that mean, though? A hand job? A blow job? Sex? The first two would be easy enough, my role passive. The last one scared me. Technically I didn't even know how to put it in, the one time I'd tried, I'd got about halfway there before failing in spectacular fashion and that had been with someone I didn't even fancy. If I got naked with

Yvonne, got to see and feel all those parts I'd been admiring over the past fortnight, I'd go off like a fire hose as soon as she touched me. And if I didn't, if I somehow maintained my composure, I couldn't just jab it against her thighs until she showed me what to do. I had to at least act like I'd done it before. The only thing I knew for certain is that there would have to be drink involved, and just the right amount; enough to induce the wildness but not so much I lost the run of myself.

Her texts later that evening did nothing to reduce my anxiety.

You were getting fairly frisky there in the car. I think I'll have to sort you out soon.

I had a long, hard think about my response.

Whenever you're ready, I am.

I'm ready. she replied.

Cool. I answered, feeling anything but.

I could come round yours on Saturday night? she suggested.

Perfect. We could get a takeaway and watch a movie.

Yeah. I can't stay, though.

That's okay.

Will we say around six?

Okay. That sounds good.

Obviously, it didn't sound good. It sounded terrifying. Over the next couple of days our texts took on an oddly formal tone, the mischief going out of them as the hour of destiny drew close. I'd had my fingers inside her, touched her most intimate parts, but this was different, this was planned. We both knew what was ahead, what was at stake. If it went badly, which it surely would, there'd be no way back. I bought condoms and tried one on a couple of nights before. It went on okay but I couldn't tell if it was inside out or back to front. So long as it went over my knob and stayed there, I didn't care.

There was also the question of when to have my last wank before the event. If I left it too long I'd be dangerously aroused, in fire-hose territory, too late and I might not be aroused enough. I decided to have one on the morning of the day before, that would give me approximately thirty-six hours to replenish my load. On the day itself I bleached the entire apartment, had two showers, trimmed my pubes, cut my toenails and flossed my teeth and then sat on the couch like a child waiting to head off to his communion.

I had a couple of cans at five p.m. She arrived at a minute to six with a bottle of wine and a film she'd brought along, which both of us knew we wouldn't be watching.

"Wow, amazing views," she said, moving to the windowsill where Sonia used to sit.

The thought of Sonia gave me a twitch, but that had been an impossible fantasy. This was the real thing, and it was right here in front of me.

"What will we get to eat?" Yvonne asked, idly leafing through the menus on the table.

"Whatever you like," I said, sick with worry.

She rose with a smile and we hugged, exchanged a brief kiss, then looked into one another's eyes. Wordlessly we moved to the bedroom. She pulled the curtains while I half-kneeled, half-sat on the bed, and then we lay together side by side looking at one another again, taking a moment before the night took on an entirely different hue.

After we'd kissed for a while, gently, patiently, I made the first move, taking off my jumper and pulling down my jeans. She liked that. Feeling no need to follow suit, she continued to kiss me and then helped me out of my last item of clothing. My knob was behaving itself; it was fiercely erect, but with no sign of an eruption just yet. Yvonne casually held it, assessed it as if it were a piece of fruit in the supermarket and stroked it up and down. This was what I didn't want. If I came now before she'd even got her clothes off, the whole thing would have been for naught. I'd have failed. We'd have to do it all over again, unless she decided I wasn't worth bothering with and stopped answering my calls.

I gently moved her hand away and put my own between her thighs. She was wearing jeans this time, and a blouse. I got to my knees, pulled her up with me and began to unbutton her blouse. It was almost too much to bear. A black bra with fat, round boobs crammed into it. They looked humongous, like something from a porn film. Dumbstruck, I just gawped at them, not knowing where to begin. All the porn in the world couldn't have prepared me for this. She undid her bra and set them free. The areolas were large and brown, the nipples perky and pointy. I buried my head in them; as I did so, she laid on the bed and shimmied out of her jeans. I was happy enough with the tits, didn't really need anything else, but I felt her hand take mine and guide it downwards.

My finger slipped inside and I heard her moan. I was doing it, I was pleasing her again. She pulled down her knickers and lay before me in her magnificent glory. It was surreal, almost too much to comprehend. I ran my hand along her breasts, just to make sure I wasn't imagining it, and she smiled up at me. If only I could have left it like this, kept her like that. If only she didn't have to experience the disappointment that was to follow. I continued with my fingering and breast-sucking, not feeling confident enough to do anything else, until she shoved me away and gave me a look that could only mean one thing: your time is up, son, get out there and fight.

Hands shaking, I opened the door of my bedside locker and took out the condoms. The wrapper was tricky but I managed it and, after trying it one way with little success, I pulled the condom on and turned to face her.

"Hi," she said quietly.

I half-mumbled, half-cried in response.

She parted her legs and placed her arms round my neck. We kissed some more and then, lifting her knees, she slowly but firmly grabbed my buttocks and pulled me towards her. A series of strange erotic images flashed before me: lying on the sitting-room floor as a child watching Jet in *Gladiators*, seeing Ms. Moran's armpit one day when she was writing on the blackboard, a woman on the beach in Rosslare wearing a bikini, the outline of Sonia's tit as she sat on the windowsill, the wildness with Marion, the cool dullness of Ellen on the FÁS course - all the women I'd ever lusted over and fantasised about, and then Yvonne.

Yvonne. Yvonne. Yvonne, right here in front of me. Her smell, the vivid, earthy smell of her sex. Her boobs laid out before me, her creamy, supple thighs, her kind, patient face as we embarked upon this journey together. And then inside her. I was inside her. What ecstasy. What sweet, unbridled joy! This was Darwinism at its finest. My penis, having spent almost twenty years in the company of porn actresses and my own familiar hand, had finally found a home, a place where it belonged, a beautiful, warm and welcoming place designed especially for it. In it went, happier than it had ever been, not even a sheath of rubberised plastic capable of spoiling its delight. In again, and again, and again, and a couple of more times, before the pleasure spread from this one central point to the rest of my body, to my brain, my soul, my entire being.

I looked into Yvonne's eyes but they were closed, her head tilted to one side as she enjoyed, yes enjoyed, the moment. But that moment was about to end and there was nothing anyone could do about it. Hungry, ravenous for more, my penis gathered in speed, propelled forward by someone, presumably me, until the waves of wildness consumed me, turned me into an animal, a beast, a man, and I came - with a roar, a deep, masculine shout which the neighbours must have heard, which probably reverberated around the world. Unlike my usual ejaculations, where there was no one involved but myself, this one went on and on, as if it were coming from a separate store of semen reserved for sexual intercourse which had been building up for my entire life and was now being emptied in one rapturous release. It lasted an inordinate amount of time, my orgasm peaking and peaking, until I slowly returned to reality and found myself face to face with Yvonne.

She kissed me gently on the forehead.

"Stay," she said.

I lay on top of her until I felt my penis return to its dormant state. Worried about the condom and its contents, I pulled out, awkwardly cosying up to her, waiting for my assessment. How long had I lasted? Not long enough. She'd hardly been satisfied by that. Could I finger her until she came? Try giving her head? There was no question of me getting it up again, that ship had sailed, it wouldn't return to port for many hours. I quietly got up and went to the bathroom. When I returned Yvonne was under the covers, looking at her phone. I got in beside her, not sure whether the sex stuff was over. She immediately snuggled in to me, putting her head on my chest as I lay flat on my back.

"It'll be better next time," I offered.

"Shush."

"First time in a while."

"I'm taking it as a compliment."

I wanted her to tell me it was all right, that we had all the time in the world, that even if it took me years to get good at it, she didn't mind. But I'd fallen short, well short. As soon as she got home she'd have vibrators, rabbits, the whole lot of them out on the bed, stuffing them into her every orifice in an attempt to salvage something from this miserable night. We lay like that for some time, silent and naked. For a while I tried to summon another erection, reminding myself that I'd waited for a moment like this my whole life, that a woman with big tits and a nice face was right there beside me, but it was no use; the stress, excitement and exertion of losing my virginity had taken its toll. Then I got bored and hungry. What use was it lying in bed? It was too early to go to sleep, and we'd done what we came to do.

"Are you hungry?" I asked hopefully.

"Mmm," she replied.

"I could get us a takeaway?"

"Nah."

"There's rolls there, I could make us some."

"No, I've to go soon," she said, disengaging so she could check her phone.

"Oh," I replied, crestfallen.

She played on her phone for a few more minutes and then got out of bed. Being a gentleman, I didn't stare as she rummaged around for her clothes and only took a good look when she stood up to fasten her bra. As she arranged her tits inside it, I couldn't help but wonder if I'd ever see them again. When she was fully dressed she went down to the living-room and I quickly followed suit, hoping for something, a few words of encouragement or consolation to quell the growing panic in my chest. She was gathering her things when I walked in.

"I guess we're even now," she said.

Seeing my look of confusion, she added: "One each."

It was true. I'd satisfied her and now she'd satisfied me.

"I thought I was loud," she said, affecting a look of terror.

"You are," I said.

"Not as loud as you."

"Imagine how loud it'll be when we satisfy one another at the same time."

"The guards will probably be called," she said.

"And the army."

"There'll be ambulances tearing down O'Connell Street."

"We'll be on the nine o'clock news."

"Have to do a press conference with the taoiseach."

"Explain ourselves."

"Be banned from doing it during business hours."

We hugged one another in the middle of the room, remaining in a deep embrace which, the longer it went on, became almost more intimate than what we'd done in the bedroom.

"Nearly burst me eardrum, you fecker," she whispered.

"I could probably be louder."

"You're loud enough for now."

Eventually we separated and I walked her to the car.

"Text me later?" I asked.

"I will."

She drove off and I walked back up the stairs, more of a man than I had ever been. I had presumed I would never experience sex, that I would die without feeling the warmth of another, but I'd done it now; I could walk with my head high, a man of the world, no longer a thirty-something virgin. Now that I'd done it I wanted to do it again, and do it well. There was no point in having sex if I was going to be blowing my load after thirty seconds. That was all right for teenagers, young lads still finding their way, but I was supposed to be a grown man, a man of years.

When I got back upstairs I took a look at my penis, wondering if it had been transformed by the experience. No, it was still the same old penis: average length, average girth, slightly leaning to the left. Maybe in time I could teach it to be better at sex, to respond the way I wanted it to. There were other things, though; I could go down on her, try to satisfy her that way, ease some of the pressure on my untrustworthy penis. And if that didn't work, there was always the fingering, I was great at that.

14

Needless to say I awoke the next morning with an erection for the ages, the kind of diamond-cutter that would have satisfied Yvonne many times over. I looked at my stupid, happy penis as it peered up at me from beneath the blankets and wished she was here, that I could summon her for round two while the going was good. But, having brought our relationship to the next level, it was to be another ten days before we saw one another again. Efforts were made, overtures, but her life was far busier than mine; she had a job, a daughter, responsibilities. And, for now at least, I remained a secret. Our meetings had to be covert, with only a select few aware of our blossoming romance.

She was apologetic, promising to make it up to me, and I played the role of martyr effectively, telling her I understood how difficult it was, that she was worth the wait and so on. In all honesty, I didn't mind. Years of celibacy and loneliness had taught me patience. Just knowing she was out there was enough to sustain me. It was even enough to keep me off the booze, to have me walking the streets morning and night in pursuit of a trim, desirable body. I wasn't even that disappointed when it was confirmed our next meeting would be a group affair, a birthday party for one of her friends in *Cullen's*. Would there be sex? Who knew? It was in the hands of the gods. That took the pressure off.

With my waistline in retreat, I prepared for the night out by purchasing some new clothes: nothing outrageous, a smart shirt and a pair of jeans. Yvonne was already making me a better man. Now, when I stood naked in front of the mirror I didn't look like a clownish caricature or a giant, chubby baby. I looked almost normal, still fat, still foolish but not hilariously so. I even chanced a look at my arse, it was big and bulky, firming up from all the walking, the kind of arse a woman, a drunk, desperate woman might want to pinch. Best of all, the unsavoury emissions, the burps and belches, had tapered off as my digestive system adapted to this new alcohol-lite lifestyle. I didn't stink of cheese quite as much, and the nervous sweating was less of a problem too.

My head was clearer, thoughts less muddled, and while I could never be confident, I didn't hate myself with the same vehemence as before. The night ahead, meeting more of Yvonne's friends terrified me, made me so anxious I wanted to crawl under the bed and live with the spiders, but amid all the fear and paranoia there was a scintilla of excitement, anticipation and hope. It could be a good night, there was no reason why it shouldn't be. Armed with this new mindset, I boarded the 380 to Castleblaney ready to meet my pals, Mutt, Noel, Ashcroft, Gabby and the rest. And, most importantly, my woman. Because, by now, that was what she surely was.

My woman wasn't in the pub when I got there, though. None of them were. I got a pint and waited, only slightly paranoid. By the time I'd finished it and bought another I was beginning to feel a little uneasy. Was I being played for a fool here? Had she invented this birthday party as a joke, a way of punishing me for some transgression I wasn't aware of? I thought back to our recent text conversations and chats on the phone, but nothing stood out. There'd been no mention of curves, of food or anything to do with her weight. Maybe Gavin had stolen her phone and lured me here so he and his mates could beat the shit out of me. I shifted uncomfortably.

There was no sign whatsoever of a party in this pub, no balloons, no decorations, no music; just a few oul' lads at the bar and a keenly contested game of pool up by the toilets. I checked my phone. Her last text had been two hours ago, a simple **See you later xxx.** She couldn't be this cruel, not after everything we'd been through. Too proud to ring her, to send a message asking what the hell was going on, I ordered another pint, my mood darkening, heart sinking. I wanted to ask the barman about a party, but to do so would confirm my worst fears. Better to sit and wait, cling on to whatever hope I had left.

I was devising scenarios in which I stabbed her to death and fed Gavin her entrails when Yvonne suddenly appeared through the front door, all dolled up in a dress and high heels.

"I'm so sorry, Aidan. I totally forgot."

Life poured back into me, the sun came out from behind the clouds. I didn't care what she'd forgotten, what she was sorry about.

"We're in the function room next door. I'm such an idiot."

Pretending I'd guessed that all along, I took my pint and followed her into a function room I hadn't known existed. It was small, a self-contained pub all of its own, and was already packed with people. This was a family affair, a local affair, and everyone had been invited. It seemed like the whole village of Castleblaney had crammed inside this little room to celebrate one of its own. There were children running about the place in their Sunday best, jowly granddads with pints of porter, fat women with massive arms sipping on vodka whites, and lots and lots of young wans in figure-hugging dresses, some revealing more than the eye could take. They all mixed and moved freely with one another, a new conversation at every turn, bound together by generational friendships, school days, workplaces, marriage, hurling, football, fighting and drink. I knew I could never fit in here, never be a part of this, no matter how much I tried.

I could move in with Yvonne, marry her, father her children, have those children go to the local school and star for the hurling team, and I'd still be 'your man from Cruinníth'. I could shop in the newsagents, drink in the pub, join the men's shed, become a committee member for the tidy towns and they'd still say 'Yeah, young Collins, the fellah Charlie Comerford's daughter married'. That realisation filled me with immense sorrow. This room was full of connections, full of the blood and earth of Castleblaney and here I was, the eternal outsider, of no particular heritage, no particular anything.

Yvonne guided me to the corner she and the lads had partially managed to commandeer. As usual there were new faces, the never-ending cast of Castleblaney spitting out some more members for me to shake hands with, smile deferentially at. I hunched in against the wall, suddenly overcome with emotion. What was I doing here? How had this happened? Yvonne? I didn't know her. And she didn't know me. If she did she wouldn't have brought me here, among all these people. I wanted to sink to the floor, hold my head in my hands, close my eyes and burrow into a deep hole, where these people with their loud voices, shining eyes and sharp elbows couldn't get me. I wanted to burst out through them, shoving them to the ground as I made for the exit, bashing a few heads against the wall as I broke free into the night, maybe back to Cruinníth, to my own people: the Collinses, the O'Sheas, the Powers, the Foleys and the Aylwards. I was tired of being the outsider, of new people and new faces, of having to pretend, of fitting into their lives, their worlds. When would I ever get to be myself? To walk into a room and have everyone know me, my struggles, my battles?

No one knew me. No one had ever known me, least of all the patrons of this pub and the woman who had brought me here. Not that I told her that. I just waited for the sadness to seep out of me, smiled when spoken to and greedily slurped back the pints placed in front of me. Eventually I adjusted to my surroundings, drank enough to forget why I was upset and got into the spirit of the occasion. Fay Rourke was celebrating the big four oh. She was joined by her parents, her husband, two of her children and her three brothers, as the cake came out and everyone sang *Happy Birthday*.

It was a fine cake, a giant wheel-sized thing which could have fed the room and left enough for the few villagers who hadn't managed to make it on the night. But when a slice came my way I shook my head and refused the offer. I loved cake, even when I was drunk, but it wasn't my place, there were other more deserving recipients: Rourkes, Walshes, O'Briens, Duggans and even Comerfords. A Collins man had no right to come in here and take a slice off the plate of one of those families. With the main event over, the younger kids were escorted off the premises and the music started. They'd squeezed a DJ in under the television and he immediately launched into the radio hits of the day, part hip-hop, part electronic dance, part garbage, all fully endorsed by the crowd, especially the young wans in the figure-hugging dresses, some of whom looked distinctly underage. As usual, Yvonne was doing her thing, mingling, chatting and charming her way round the room, every now and then returning to check on me. Even though I was getting drunk and I could see Mutt over by the fag machine and Noel up on the windowsill, I was sticking resolutely to the wall, neither willing nor capable of sparking up a conversation and joining in the festivities.

"You okay? You're very quiet," Yvonne said as she came to see how I was getting on.

"I'm okay," I said, suddenly feeling very tearful.

"Mutt is over there," she shouted through the din as a popular song sent ripples through the room.

"Ah, later."

She studied me closely, her eyes peering deep into mine, and then she kissed me full on the lips, in front of this room full of her people. It was like a seal of approval. She no longer cared who saw us. She wasn't ashamed of me. I brightened up immediately and gave her a cheery little peck on the cheek on my way to the bar. After waiting an inordinate amount of time to get served, I shimmied my way over to Mutt, who met me with a toothy grin and a friendly jab to the chin. Everything was okay. I'd been dramatic for nothing. No one in this room cared who I was, except Gavin. He was developing a habit of turning up at the most inopportune of moments and here he was again, forging through the crowd, ignoring the friendly faces, his pygmy features tense and taut. As was his routine, he took up residence within a few feet of me, close enough to stare me down, not so close that I could ask him what was the matter. Someone engaged him in conversation, diverted his attention long enough for me to lean towards Mutt and pose a question.

"Is Gavin all right?"

Mutt smiled non-committally, like a politician batting away an oft-repeated question.

"He hasn't been the same since the Leb," he said eventually.

"In what way?"

"Ah, he's just not the same Gav. He's wound up tight."

"Do you think something happened?"

Mutt shrugged. "I've asked him. We all have."

I looked back at Gavin, he did look wound up; his shoulders were tight, jaw rigid and brow furrowed, as he distractedly listened to the middle-aged man who'd cornered him. He was anxious, Gavin was anxious. Our paths may have been different, but they'd led us to the same place. He was dealing with the same feelings I fought every day. It was no wonder Mutt, Noel or Yvonne couldn't help him. They didn't know what it was like, but I did. An image came into my mind of me and Gavin locked deep in conversation, heading out the back to get away from the noise. I could help him. I was an expert at this.

I stopped myself. I was drunk. This was a foolish idea. Just because he was anxious and I was anxious didn't mean we shared any common ground. Any attempts to engage Gavin would only inflame the situation. He'd already stated his dislike of me and, like Mutt said, he was wound up tight. Best to leave him, let someone else stage the intervention. Yet as the night wore on and the drink continued to flow, the idea of approaching my future brother-in-law wouldn't go away. When Yvonne came over and gave me a big hug followed by a sloppy kiss I looked for his reaction straight away: he had turned puce. I gave him what I hoped was a reassuring smile, the look I imagined Jesus gave his disciples before he was mounted on the cross. Gavin simply glared back at me.

I decided I would get a few whiskeys, one for him, two for me, and invite him to discuss the problem like men. But by the time I got served he'd done another of his disappearing acts. I asked the lads where he'd gone, but nobody knew. Not to worry, it just meant extra whiskey for me. Gavin didn't come back to the pub. As the DJ played his last song and the young and old drifted home to their beds, the crowd grew smaller and smaller until, with the staff pleading with us to drink up, just a few remained. Mutt and Noel were holding firm. Yvonne, although twisted, was requesting one for the road.

There was a couple in their forties with a man of similar age, and a young guy, perhaps early twenties, who wasn't really saying anything. He seemed out of place, more the type to be in one of those trendy late bars buying fancy glasses of gin for the women. But here he was with us, his hair perfectly styled, white shirt open at the chest, studiously watching us, listening in on the conversation, making no contribution. I still didn't know where I'd be spending the night, it hadn't been discussed, but Yvonne was being very touchy-feely. There had been several lunges at my crotch, a few slaps on the arse and one disconcerting moment when she tried to mount me right there in the pub. Wherever we were going it seemed likely we would go there together. I was ready for all eventualities, drunk, but not too drunk to perform, hopefully drunk enough to last a bit longer. When Mutt and Noel departed on their own with no mention of a session, I knew where my destiny lay.

"I should ring a taxi," I said.

"No taxis tonight, Aiders," Yvonne replied.

"Shouldn't we catch up with Mutt and Noel?"

"Leave 'em off," she said.

"I'll have to sleep on the beach, so."

She gazed at me with a big drunken head on her, and then hugged me with such force that it took my breath away.

"You're one of the good ones, Aidan, I think. Are you?"

"I'm only all right."

"No," she said, pulling away. "You are. Aren't you?"

She looked around the pub for someone to answer her question, but there was only the couple and their friend. The young lad was over at the cigarette machine slowly feeding coins into the slot.

"You are," she murmured as she stood on unsteady legs. "Mind me," she added, almost toppling onto the table.

I grabbed her by the arm and led her out of the pub, thanking the staff for their work, not even thinking to ask for a carry out. We'd barely made it outside the door when a voice called out in the darkness.

"Hey, where's the session? I have fags here."

It was the young lad from inside. He had followed us out and quickly fell into step.

"I'm Wheeler Tobin's nephew," he said by way of explanation.

"Ah, Wheeler is lovely," cooed Yvonne. "What's your name?"

"I'm Dean."

"Hello, Dean," she said, disentangling herself so she could shake his hand.

"I know you," he said to her. "You were going out with Paddy Tennyson years ago, weren't you?"

"Ugh, Paddy Tennyson," Yvonne said.

"His family are my neighbours," said Dean, his tone shifting.

"Shower of wankers," Yvonne continued.

I gave her a look but she barely noticed. "Tennyson knackers from East Court Terrace."

"What's wrong with people from East Court Terrace?" asked Dean indignantly.

"Knackers," Yvonne repeated offhandedly.

"You'd better control your woman," said Dean, switching his attention to me. He looked twitchy, unpredictable.

"I can control myself," Yvonne said truculently.

"I'm warning you, boy. Tell her to shut the fuck up."

I wondered where my temper was, the crazy animal which had emerged when I'd defended Marion in *The Three Sisters*. It was nowhere to be found. All I had was a sick feeling in my stomach and a deep fear of being beaten up in front of Yvonne.

"Come on, Yvonne," I said, guiding her away from the conflict, away from Dean and his loyalty to the Tennysons of East Court Terrace.

"Yeah, fucking run, boy, take her home before she gets you into trouble."

His words stung, but not enough for me to turn around and do something about it. I would take her home and, all being well, I'd have sex with her too. Far better to have sex in a nice warm bed than to be fighting young lads on the street at all hours of the night.

"You'll get us killed with that mouth of yours," I said affectionately as we left Dean behind.

"Hmph."

"What does that mean?"

"*You'll* get us killed," Yvonne said.

"What?"

I knew what she meant, though. I wasn't able to protect her, couldn't even protect myself. I was useless, not strong enough, masculine enough or powerful enough.

"Never mind, Aidan," she muttered.

"I thought I was a good guy?"

"You are," she said, tiring of the conversation.

"Well, I can't be all the guys."

"I suppose not."

We walked in silence, my temper now in fine order. What did she want? What did women want? A nice guy who treated them well, said all the right things and put them first at all times, but also a tough guy, a gallant hero who would happily beat the shit out of anyone who spoke ill of them. Did such men exist? If they did, Yvonne Comerford wanted one - no wonder she was single. I decided I would walk her home and then ring a taxi for myself. That would show her how tough I could be. As if sensing my intention she sidled up to me, snuggling into my arm like a baby chick. I left her there a moment, neither accepting nor rejecting her. I could never stay mad at her, though, I was too much of a good guy. I wrapped my arm around her and she gratefully held me close.

"My good guy," she said.

"Better than Paddy Tennyson?"

"Fuck Paddy Tennyson."

We laughed, mostly out of relief. We were back together, our disagreement resolved, the air cleared.

"Are you staying over?" she asked, fixing me with her most innocent stare.

"Is the spare bed made up?"

"It is."

"Okay, then."

More laughing, a little giggle.

"Izzy is at her dad's."

"I guessed as much."

"So you can sleep in my bed if you like."

"And put you in the spare room? No, that wouldn't be right."

"Stop it, Aidan," she warned.

"Oh, wait," I said, as if the thought had just occurred to me. "You want me to sleep in your bed *with* you?"

"Maybe," she replied, suddenly coy again.

We could easily have gone back and forth like this all night, neither of us brave enough to speak our mind, but the sight of a familiar housing estate quelled our chat. It was the first time I had been back since the night they'd dragged me off the beach.

"I've slept in your bed before," I told her.

"You have."

"Guess what?"

An arched eyebrow.

"I woke up with a big horn that day, in your bed."

"Eugh, you're disgusting!" she said, punching me in the stomach.

"No, I'm not," I said, grabbing her for another kiss. It was a long, meaningful one. That spare bed would remain unoccupied tonight. We hurried along to the house, frisky and excited, ready to charge up the stairs, to enter that bedroom together. It took Yvonne an unfathomable amount of time to locate her keys and even longer to open the door. Once inside, we haphazardly threw our jackets to the floor and continued to maul one another. I was ready to do it right there in the hallway but she resisted my advances, pushed me away.

"You go on up," she said, eyes full of devilment.

I did as I was told, taking the stairs two at a time. Maybe she was going to dress up for me, produce a pair of thigh-high boots from under the stairs and march in like a dominatrix? Whatever the outcome, I was prepared. It was different this time. I was loose and confident, my mind clear of doubt and troubling thoughts. I'd just flipped off my shoes, was considering lying flat on my back, buck naked, when the sound of raised voices came from downstairs. *Dean*! That fucker had followed us, had broken into the house and was now trying to steal my woman. Without thinking, without any sense of danger, I flew back down the stairs, ready to defend Yvonne and reclaim my manhood. It wasn't Dean at all, though. It was a more familiar foe. The pixie king himself. Gavin.

He was seated at the kitchen table, hands gripping its edge, knuckles white as he stared at his sister. His jaw was clamped shut and his skin had turned a pale, sickly colour. He looked unwell, like someone who'd taken too many drugs and was about to spend the next four hours crawling the walls.

"What the fuck?" I mouthed to Yvonne.

She was as nonplussed as I was, but unlike me she was deeply concerned about Gavin's welfare.

"Gav," she said, taking him by the arm.

He didn't flinch, just slowly and deliberately moved his head towards me, locking eyes with me so that I was forced to stare into the deep emptiness of his soul. With great effort he began to speak, enunciating his words carefully so there could be no mistaking their meaning.

"Tell me, tell *her*, what you were doing on the beach that night," he said. It wasn't a question, it was a statement, as if he already knew and simply required confirmation.

I looked at Yvonne, puzzled, hoping for a way out. She was staring at me too, now all ears.

"I told her already. I was with my friends and . . ."

"Cut the bullshit!" spat Gavin, gasping from the effort.

Was it possible he knew? How could he know? Did people who'd tried to commit suicide give off telltale signs? Did you learn how to spot them in the army? He was so insistent, so convinced, he must have found out somehow. Maybe he'd been further up the beach that night, wandering alone and had seen me enter the water, watched with interest as I floundered underneath, and then fallen back into the shadows when I emerged, minutes later, alive, but only just. Why the hostility, though? Wasn't suicide supposed to emit sympathy, compassion? When your sister was involved you had to be careful, though, even more so when there was a niece to consider. Well, I would confess, lay myself bare to Yvonne. It had been bound to come out eventually, you couldn't hide secrets like that if you wanted to have a healthy relationship.

"Tell her," said Gavin through gritted teeth. "Tell her what you were doing up there."

Yvonne looked worried. She may even have backed a step or two away from me.

"It's hard to explain. Maybe if we all sit down . . ."

"Don't!" growled Gavin when Yvonne pulled out a chair. "He's not sitting down in this house."

I was baffled by his attitude but felt a weight lift from my chest, a sense of liberation as I prepared to tell my story, to share the thoughts and fears I'd never shared with anyone.

"You know what they do up there, don't you?" Gavin asked, switching his attention to Yvonne.

She shook her head slowly, sombrely.

"Dirty bastards."

Now I was intrigued, so intrigued I forgot about my own story, wanted to hear more of Gavin's.

"Who, Gavin?" she asked.

"He knows," he said, looking at me with disgust.

Now they were both staring at me: the Comerford Inquisition.

"Aidan?" asked Yvonne, a chill in her voice.

I shook my head wildly, grasping for words, too panicked to divulge any details, to out myself as a dirty bastard.

"You think I don't know?" said Gavin. "I see them heading up there every night. Soon as I saw you coming, I knew what you'd been at."

"For Christ's sake, Gavin, just tell me," said Yvonne.

He took a few deep breaths, summoning up the monumental effort required to inform my beloved, the only woman I'd ever had sex with, that I was a mental case, an attempter of suicide, a sad little weasel who had apparently chosen a spot popular with many of the local menfolk.

"Dogging," he finally uttered. "Do you know what that is, do you? I'll tell you. It's a load of perverts watching wans getting fucked in cars."

His words bounced around my head like magic sparkles, entering the part which accepts sounds, finds their meaning, and relays them back to the logical, reasonable bit at the front. But my brain didn't compute. It took the words, jumbled them all together and rejected them as gibberish, unintelligible nonsense. I sent them back, asked my brain to have another go, to do the job it was built for. This time, with great effort, it accentuated one of the words: *dogging*. I knew what that was, had heard rumours about it going on at certain beaches but I'd thought they were just that: rumours. Surely there weren't people who actually did it, went out for the night with a torch and waited for couples to arrive so they could tug themselves off?

If I'd known that was going on in Rún Derg, I would never have chosen it as my suicide site. What if they'd been out that night, all gathered in a circle waiting for me to join them, to push in alongside and get my willy out. I wouldn't have been able to go in the water then. Having made sense of Gavin's words, of the sheer lunacy of the accusation, two further thoughts occurred to me. One: I didn't have to tell Yvonne I'd been up there trying to kill myself. And two: I had to quickly deny this allegation. Before I could do that, however, another part of my brain took over, the one responsible for happy feelings like relief and mirth. I started laughing, and not in a good way. It was uncontrollable, the kind of laughter you know you shouldn't indulge but can't prevent.

Aware that Yvonne was both repelled by my reputed perversion and appalled by my flippant reaction to being rumbled, I fought to suppress my laughter. I held my stomach in, caught my breath, as I tried to steady myself and find the appropriate reaction.

"No," I said, shaking my head. "I wasn't. I mean . . . fucking hell. No."

Tears were streaming down my eyes, but I could see a change in Gavin's demeanour. He was no longer the pixie king, more a silly goblin, as he regarded this shameless pervert who considered pulling himself in public to be a big joke.

"Yvonne," I said, moving towards her. She recoiled. "I didn't . . . I wouldn't . . . Jesus."

I took a seat and placed my head in my hands, trying to compose myself. Finally the shock and horror of the last few minutes faded out and normality returned.

"Yvonne. Gavin," I began portentously. "I didn't even know that went on up there. Me, dogging? I get stage fright if someone stands beside me in the urinals."

Yvonne still looked doubtful, Gavin slightly abashed.

"Come on, Yvonne, seriously? Do you think I'd get a bus all the way from town to walk along a beach and wank beside a group of dirty old men."

There was a softening in her stance, but she still wasn't convinced.

"And if I'd been dogging, why was I so wet? Is that part of it, Gavin?"

He was saying nothing, but I could tell he believed me.

"What were you doing up there, Aidan, really?" asked Yvonne.

There was only one way to resolve this, to clear my name; it involved the truth, the whole truth, and nothing but the truth. So I asked both members of the Comerford family to join me at the kitchen table and listen to my tale. Yvonne duly obliged, fixing me with a cautious gaze, half-terrified of what odd fetishes were about to be revealed. Gavin, by this point, looked defeated, as if he just wanted this whole thing to be over. I gathered my thoughts, searching for a starting point, a way to introduce the story of my life. I began at the end, sparing them my childhood woes, adolescent agonies, skipping right up to the day in question, the day I chose to take my own life.

I couldn't explain why, not in one sitting, so I simply told them I'd had enough, that my depression, my anxiety, had overcome me, made life not worth living. To my surprise, Gavin nodded his agreement, mumbled his recognition, as I briefly outlined the pain I was enduring on a daily basis. Then I took them through those final hours, those hours that were supposed to be my last. I told them about the bus, about meeting Mrs. M and having to change my destination. I told them about my search for alcohol, my intrepid journey through the town, and arriving at the supermarket where Yvonne worked.

When I got to the bit about the self-service checkouts being down, and being told to 'Go up there to Yvonne. She'll look after you', I looked at her to see her reaction; she was staring into my eyes, tears welling in her own. I told her how that simple conversation momentarily salved my wounds, made me believe in a future, and how I pushed those thoughts away and carried on with my mission.

As I continued my story, I was forced to confront my own reality for the first time. I had gone up there to kill myself. It had really happened, my intentions had been clear. I waited before saying it out loud, perhaps hoping they would interject and spare me my own truth. No, they sat there rapt, hanging on my every word, awaiting the outcome like a pair of kids listening to a scary story. So, I gave it to them. I told them how I'd drained the vodka, passed out, awoke to the water lapping at my thighs and, after a slight hesitation, strode into the sea.

At this juncture I paused, as much to gauge the mood as summon the strength to continue. In the space of five minutes, their dispositions had changed. Yvonne had leant forward, her hands reaching out to mine, body motionless as she looked on in clear discomfort. She took the interlude as an opportunity to move closer, switching seats so she could hold my hand. She began caressing it, stroking it as if were the paw of an injured animal, all the while looking into my eyes as if trying to pour her own goodness into me.

She had accepted me for what I was. It was too much to bear, I slumped in my chair, shoulders sagging, on the brink of collapse. Strangely, it was Gavin who gave me the impetus to continue. He placed a conciliatory hand on my shoulder and nodded his encouragement. I fought off my emotions, continued my story. And I began with one simple sentence, a sentence I'd never dreamed of speaking to another.

"I wanted to die. I was going to kill myself."

The squeeze of Yvonne's hand, the distant look in Gavin's eyes as he recalled his own demons, propelled me onwards. Sparing them nothing, I spoke of the shock of the water, the excruciating pain as it filled my lungs, stopped my breathing, did precisely what I'd asked it to do. And how it was this pain which forced me to act, to rebel, to opt out and search for salvation. I relayed in great detail my battle for survival, the failed attempts to find air, the kicking and screaming as my energies faded and my life-force dimmed. Then the great escape, the thrust towards the skies to a new beginning, which now seemed the stuff of legend, out of keeping with the sorriness of my tale. It had been me, though. From start to finish, it had all been me.

"Then I just kind of staggered along the beach until I felt the warmth of the fire. Suppose that was when ye found me."

Yvonne immediately sprang from her seat and enveloped me in a hug. She was crying, whether for me or herself I couldn't tell. Between squeezes she peppered my face with kisses, as if the power of her love could erase the sadness of my memories. When at last she retreated, her touch lingering as she hurried to boil the kettle, Gavin and I locked eyes. Immediately I knew. He had been there too. Maybe he hadn't yet reached his limit, but he had fought and was continuing to fight those very same battles. Unlike me, he had kept his battles to himself, fought in silence. He looked away, not yet ready to admit it, to speak up.

I thought about reaching out, physically, emotionally, whatever he needed, but it passed and we carried on, a tacit respect on both sides. Yvonne returned with the tea, pressed the mug into my hands, as she continued to hug and hold me, kiss me, protect me from the world out there and the terror in me. It was Gavin who broke the silence, revealing a hitherto unseen sense of humour.

"So you definitely weren't dogging, then?"

We all had a laugh at that, relieved to be able to laugh at something and break the tension. Gavin got to his feet, hugged his sister with renewed affection, whispered an apology in her ear and then stood to greet me.

"I'm fucking sorry, man," he said, holding out his hand.

"It's okay," I replied, shaking it. The gesture solidified our relationship. It was the most meaningful handshake of my life.

He went to speak again but nothing came out. I had rendered him dumbstruck.

"Sure I might see ye tomorrow," he said. Yvonne walked him to the door, told him to be careful on 'that road' and returned to me. Again I was taken into her arms, held tight, squeezed until there was nothing left of me to squeeze. Then, without a word, she took me by the hand and led me upstairs. When we got to her bedroom we slowly undressed and got under the covers. For a while we just lay there holding one another, not speaking, allowing ourselves a moment. She dozed off for a while, then I did too. When I awoke I was hard and she was kissing my neck, there was no great urgency in the gesture, it was a slow nibble, a gentle exploration. I placed a hand on her hip, pulling her towards me, onto me. She softly complied and I slid inside her seamlessly, as if I'd been doing so for years. There she remained, unmoving, content to just lie on my chest and look into my eyes. My resolve wasn't so strong, however. I lifted up my legs, just enough to get some purchase, and slowly began to thrust in and out. She responded in kind, again with no urgency, until we moved as one, a perfectly synchronised being driving gently and quietly to unknown pleasures.

We moved through the night, smiling as we resisted the temptation to rush towards that pleasure, content to let it come in its own time. When it came, it came as one great rush, immersing us both in an ecstasy so powerful that I wanted to scream, to roar like a maniac and devour my lover in one great ravenous mouthful. Instead I placed my head on her shoulder, my mouth on her neck, and drowned out my lust. She lay on top of me for a while, our bodies still connected. But the enormity of the night had taken its toll, there would be no round two, no heroic feats of lovemaking. We slowly, naturally disengaged and retreated to our own cosy corners of the bed, new bonds created, old barriers overcome. We were a couple now, for better or for worse.

PART FOUR

2017

1

"OKAY, THAT'S IT. I'LL SEE you all tomorrow, bright and early."

There was an immediate cacophony of desks being shut, chairs flipping up as the hundred or so students hurried to the exits, to their next destination. I took my time, slowly putting my notepad into my satchel, making sure my pens went in the front so I could access them with ease in the next lecture. Then I climbed the stairs to the back of the hall where the others were filing out. For them it had been an inconvenient interruption, a compulsory chore before they embarked upon another night of drinking and socialising. For me, the quiet, attentive guy in the front row who'd arrived with pre-printed slides and written down almost every word that had come out of the lecturer's mouth, it had been a life-altering experience. I was here. I had made it. I was a student, a proper one, as much a part of the university as the other twenty-two thousand enrolled learners.

My classmates may have been blasé about the first lecture of the semester, but for Aidan Collins, Student ID 4341681, First Year, Bachelor of Science in Information Technology, it had been a revelation. I walked out of the auditorium and I took it all in: the high glass ceilings of the giant building named after an Australian scholar, the bronze busts of famous professors and academics, the water feature in the foyer, the groups of young people splayed out in the grass enjoying the traditional Irish Indian summer, the wide forecourt with people hurrying backwards and forwards, and the sense of optimism and hope that can only come with attending an institute established to birth careers, to set its graduates on the road to jobs, cars, homes and families.

The majority of these people had a significant head start on me. I was almost double the age of the other first years, but while they had time on their side, they didn't have what I had: life experience, regret, a desire to make amends, to atone for previous mistakes and create a life I would never have thought possible. I crossed the forecourt, ignoring the lads handing out flyers for Frisbee classes, and headed straight for the library. I'd been inside it during my orientation day and had marvelled at the wealth of material on offer, all free and available for whoever wanted it. That was the other thing about university life; for mature students it was almost entirely free.

Yes, there were books I required and other ancillary costs, but all I'd had to do was switch my Jobseeker's Allowance to Back to Education Allowance, apply for a grant, and let the government look after the rest. It had blown my mind, and it still did. I suspected the government knew what it was doing, knew that by investing in people like me, people who'd frittered away their lives and were now on the path to righteousness, it would eventually get every cent back. It was right. I was going to be the best student here. Not just the best in my course or in my year, but the best in the entire college, number one out of all twenty-two thousand. I intended to hit the ground running.

Day one of lectures and I was straight into the library, thirsty for more information. It was predictably quiet; a few other eager first years, some postgraduates, and a group of international students trying to figure out the electronic loaning system. I went up to the third floor, planning on seeking out a book the lecturer had mentioned, one she'd said wasn't imperative for our course but would make a good companion piece for the other textbooks. But I'd been beaten to the punch. One of the girls from my course was in aisle 19 A-H, and she had the book in her hand, leafing through the pages, perusing it at her leisure.

"Oh, hi," she said. "Are you looking for this too?"

That was another thing about university: the young people and, in particular, the young women. This was only my second day on campus, and already I'd seen enough beautiful women to last me a lifetime. As their elder I had a responsibility to behave respectably, to keep to myself and avoid any creepy behaviour. My plan was to get through the full three years without talking to anyone apart from the other mature students, to leave the youngsters to their own devices. But here I was, confronted by a toothy little bobcat who looked as naive as they came.

"Ah no, it's okay," I said, waving her off and making to leave.

"It's okay, there's two," she said, pointing to the shelf. "That one is an older edition but it seems to have mostly the same text."

"Oh, great," I said, not budging, not wanting to go near her.

She moved along the aisle, apparently looking for another book, one not recommended by any lecturer. I took the chance to pry the book from the shelf. It *was* an older edition, the one she had was better.

"What did you make of the lecture?" she asked, not moving her eyes from the shelves as she squatted down for a look at the bottom row.

"Good," I said.

"Are you going to communication skills later?"

"Yeah."

"Have you been assigned a tutorial group yet?"

"No, they said that won't be till next week."

"Oh, yeah," she said.

She was still scanning the shelves, so much so that I wondered if I needed more books. Did these young school-leavers know something I didn't? Were they going to be miles ahead of me before the end of the first semester? Resolving to come back later when she'd gone, I said goodbye and went to find a quiet corner to read my book. However, there weren't many quiet corners on campus and those there were came with distractions. The little nook I found on the ground floor of the main building had appeared promising, but it wasn't long before groups of students began passing back and forth, disturbing my peace.

That was just an excuse, though. The book was boring, incredibly so, written in that sterile academic format which encourages one's mind to wander after a couple of lines. That was the old me talking. A person with no willpower, no drive, a person who was content to let his life fade away. He was gone now. So, I opened up the book again, blocked out all the noise, and concentrated for all I was worth. An hour passed. It was time for my second and last lecture of the day. Communication Skills, as the girl had said. Our group had been split into two for this module and we were in a smaller, more intimate lecture hall. I got there early, too early, my friend from the library was waiting outside on her own.

"There's a class in there," she whispered.

I nodded and stood to one side.

"Did you read the book?" she asked.

"Tried to," I said, grimacing.

"Very dense, isn't it?"

"Yeah."

"A bit like some of the lads on our course," she said, smiling.

She was marking us out as equals, the two frontrunners who could poke fun at our less intelligent colleagues. I was flattered.

"Where are you from?" she asked.

"Town."

"You don't sound like a townie."

"Well, I'm not from town but I'm living there."

"Got your own place?"

"Yeah."

"I'm on campus," she sighed, "sharing with three girls and two boys. They were up till all hours last night. *Very* noisy."

"That's not good."

"No. I might have to look for someplace else. Do you have housemates?"

"No, just me."

"Oh."

A couple of lads from our course appeared, loitering in the background, not sure what to do with themselves. I took this as an opportunity to peer through the window of the lecture hall. The group inside were readying to leave. We made way as they exited *en masse* and then went into the empty hall. I didn't want to sit beside the girl, was keen to nip this burgeoning friendship in the bud. If I didn't I'd be stuck with her for three years, trying to be a gentleman, a respectable, reserved mature student, while she divulged every detail of her exciting young life. I tried to wait until she'd sat down, tried to discreetly distance myself from her, but as soon as I'd taken my seat she appeared beside me.

"Might as well sit here. I don't want to be near those other eejits."

She was too close to me, we were almost touching. I angled my body away from her, trying not to appear rude. If the lecturer saw us he would immediately jump to the wrong conclusion, report me to some faculty, get me thrown out before the first week was over. Thankfully the room filled up and the seat on the other side of me was taken by one of the other mature students; now we just looked like a group of keen learners. The girl was an accomplished note-taker and I couldn't help but glance at her work. She was using headings and subheadings, different-coloured pens for each, her dainty hand perfectly attuned to the rhythm of the lecturer's voice. Even when he showed us a video, instructed us to leave down the pens and focus on the screen, she couldn't resist jotting down a few observations. She made me uneasy. I'd had aspirations of being the best but saw now that there was a certain level of dedication, of innate talent required to reach those heights. The sooner I shook her loose the better.

When the lecture ended I tried to immerse myself in the crowd, hoping to slip down a corridor before she caught up. The moment I got outside she was there once more, tagging along, talking about the lecture, about my plans when I graduated. She volunteered information about herself, unprompted. Her name was Laurie and she was from Carlow. She had wanted to go to one of the Dublin colleges, but had missed out in the points race and was now left here while all her friends were in the capital. It was her first time away from home and she was finding it difficult to adjust, as she didn't really like partying or going out. Clearly this was a girl in need of a friend. As we crossed the forecourt towards the bus station and pick-up points, she slowed down. She said she lived in Cosgrave Heights, all the way on the other side of the campus.

"Are you going into town or staying around?" she asked.

I had to laugh, inwardly, of course. In another life I would have invited her back to mine, taken advantage of her innocence, her loneliness in whatever ham-fisted way I could. Not now, though. Such irony. Opportunities presenting themselves when they weren't for me to take. As she looked at me hopefully, her sweet face having not yet witnessed the true horrors of the world, I saw the familiar navy hatchback across the road and its driver, the woman with the metallic red hair, the piercing blue eyes, scanning the throngs for me.

"Going home," I said. "There's my lift."

"Oh," she said, her gaze following mine as she saw the car and its sole occupant. "Well, I'll see you later, I suppose."

"Yeah. Bye."

2

"WELL, HOW'S MY LITTLE LEARNER?" asked Yvonne as soon as I got in the car.

"He's fine."

She gave me an enquiring look.

"It went well," I said, exhaling dramatically.

"Anxiety?"

"A little, but it was okay."

"And the lectures? Easy or hard?"

"Ah, they were grand. I got a book," I said, proudly displaying the tome.

"A book," she said reverentially.

"I know."

We manoeuvred our way round a couple of buses and let a gang of young lads in GAA shorts cross the road.

"Look at those lads," said Yvonne. "I bet they didn't get books on their first day."

"Too busy drinking and riding," I replied.

"The mature students have no time for that."

"They don't."

We drove in silence through the rest of the campus, down the tree-lined avenues full of students walking and cycling to their accommodation, to parties, part-time jobs, and discount supermarkets for the bare essentials. Their lives were completely separate to mine, their college experiences as far removed as they could possibly be. As we left the grounds of the university and stopped at the traffic lights, Yvonne leant over and gave me a peck on the cheek.

"You're a very brave man, Aidan Collins."

"Yeah."

"You are," she insisted.

"Okay, I am."

Although I'd been learning how to accept compliments and even to praise myself for jobs well done, I didn't feel brave. There was nothing brave about sitting in a lecture hall repeating a mantra to keep yourself calm, or having to continually remind yourself that thoughts couldn't harm you, that you had a choice whether or not to give them power. My bravery consisted of leaning heavily on Yvonne, my counsellor, the course director at the university, and on all the people who'd helped me to get where I was. I wasn't brave, I was a thirty-three-year-old alcoholic who'd been sober for nearly ten months and was slowly learning how to live like a normal person.

For reasons I still didn't understand Yvonne considered me a worthwhile investment, and I felt obliged to give her a detailed account of my day. So I told her how my legs had almost given way as I'd walked into the first lecture, how I'd slowly taken my seat, identified the source of my anxiety, casually examined it and told myself not to be afraid, not to will it away, but to leave it be. And how I became so engrossed in the lecture, in my note taking, that I momentarily forgot about the anxiety. How the second lecture had started in the same way, more nerves, more panic, and how I'd worked through it again, taking it in blocks of five minutes, praising myself the longer I went without unravelling.

I assured her the coursework was well within my capabilities, told her I'd taken pages full of notes and was going to purchase additional software for my desktop at home. She asked about my classmates, whether I'd made any friends, if there were any other mature students. I told her it was mostly young lads, that there was a core group of nerdy tech guys and a splinter cell of messers who probably wouldn't see out the year. I chose not to tell her about Laurie from Carlow. It was an unnecessary detail and would only have spoiled the mood.

We drove back to Yvonne's. She was making me dinner, a celebratory feast for my being so brave and heroic. It was almost two years since I'd decided to end it all, and in that time my life had altered beyond compare. I still lived in the same grotty flat, but there had been talk of moving into Yvonne's - I already had my own key - I was friendly with her brother, on good terms with her parents, and had been welcomed into the Comerford family and the wider Castleblaney community as a whole. I'd even managed to patch things up with my father. Truthfully, I couldn't remember if we'd fallen out, whether he was mad or me or I was mad at him, but I rang him one day anyway, told him about the changes I'd made, how I'd acquired a girlfriend, started college, given up the booze and was now a son to be proud of. He sounded put out, not as happy to hear from me as I'd imagined.

I suggested myself and Yvonne come visit some time and that perked him up, setting him off talking about the importance of family and how we had to stick together. I humoured him for a while, asked after Mrs. M, and made non-committal plans to meet. I didn't tell him it had all been Yvonne's idea, that I wasn't particularly fussed about seeing him or his live-in lover. As with most things, Yvonne had gently steered me towards reconciling with my father. She did that a lot; she'd found me a counsellor, got me the forms for college, sent me to the doctor to get my liver and kidneys checked out. She even came clothes shopping with me and picked out the stuff she thought would suit me. I didn't mind. It was like having a personal assistant, one you could have sex with after discussing what shoes to wear.

However, as I'd suspected, relationships were hard. Ours was healthy, with far more ups than downs, but there was another person involved whose importance far outweighed my own. I had been formally introduced to Isabel a few months after Yvonne and I started dating, invited over for dinner. The three of us had sat down at the table and made small talk until the younger Comerford excused herself and made a sharp exit. Even in that brief encounter I could see the potential for trouble, why they clashed. Isabel had her mother's wit, her easy charm, and her wickedness. She had her figure, the same figure which had drawn the attention of Isabel's father and was now drawing the attention of other boys, even men. Isabel had Yvonne's sallow skin, soft features, but she had something else, something she could only have received from her father.

At first I'd thought she was just a mopey teenager, dark eyes peeping out from beneath her hood, soft, barely audible voice speaking only in monosyllables. There was more to it, though. Her every movement, mannerism, was deliberate, as if she had to assess the effort involved before deciding whether to reach for the salt, fill her glass with water. It wasn't that she was sulking either, she seemed pleasant enough, was polite and hospitable and always spoke when spoken to. But there was a sadness in her, a sorrow, it seeped out of her, made you want to sit her down and ask if everything was all right, if there was anything you could possibly do to coax a smile out of her.

After that first introduction, Isabel and I became familiar with one another. She was neither hostile nor friendly. I wondered about Yvonne's previous boyfriends, whether any of them had become part of the family, formed an attachment with Isabel, left a wound when the relationship broke down. Perhaps she was reluctant to accept me in case I disappeared like the others. More likely, though, she was a seventeen-year-old girl with a busy life and my occasional presence in her home was an irrelevance. Yvonne and I tried to minimise the time I spent in the house when Isabel was there, restricting it to Friday and Saturday nights when she was out. But in a three-bed house with just one bathroom it was inevitable our paths would cross.

On a couple of occasions I'd left the bathroom after a loud, errant piss, to find her standing outside in her pyjamas, patiently waiting her turn. For that reason I tried not to go for a shit while she was there. It was embarrassing enough when Yvonne was subjected to my stink. One morning when Yvonne had left early for work, thinking I had the house to myself I sauntered downstairs in just my boxers, hoping to find some biscuits to go with a cup of tea. Instead I found Isabel at the kitchen table, poring over her phone intently.

"Oh, sorry, I didn't know . . ." I said, turning on my heels.

She absent-mindedly looked up from her phone, sniffled and returned to the screen. She'd been crying, her eyes were red, cheeks puffy. I paused, wishing I'd put on some clothes, wondering if it was appropriate to ask her how she was feeling while I stood there in my underwear.

"Erm, your mam's gone to work."

"I know," she said.

"Okay, then," I said briskly and disappeared back up the stairs. By the time I'd dressed and returned to check on her she had gone.

Over time I discovered that Isabel's situation was more complicated than I'd realised. She'd cried many tears in her young life. A shy, introspective child, she'd spent much of her youth in the middle of two bickering parents. Yvonne and Paul had officially broken up before Isabel was born, but there had been attempts to reconcile, spells when the family unit was reunited and mother, father and daughter lived in harmony. Yet each time Yvonne and Paul got back together the ensuing split was more severe. Accusations, invective and kitchenware flew from one end of the house to the other, the adults momentarily forgetting there was a child in the house, as they fought their corner, fought for justice, for supremacy. Finally, when Isabel was nine there was one last fight.

Their altercations had always been loud and abusive, but rarely had they turned physical. On this occasion Yvonne decided to forcibly remove Paul from the premises, to claim ownership of the house by being the last one standing. A scuffle had broke out, the former lovers tumbling into the garden and rolling round in the grass, until a neighbour intervened and Paul was quietly advised to leave. Isabel saw it all; she was standing at the door throughout, watching it unfold. A brief court battle followed before Paul acceded to the judge's wishes and arranged visitation and child support.

Peace briefly reigned. Isabel was no longer subjected to the sight of her parents quarrelling, she spent every second weekend at her dad's and her relationship with her mother improved. She remained a quiet, gentle girl who did well in school and had an aptitude for crafts. If she could have stayed right there, been frozen in time as that meek eleven-year-old who enjoyed drawing dresses and designer outfits in her sketchpad, everything might have been okay, but within a year there was fresh chaos in the Comerford house.

The transition from primary to secondary school did not go well. Isabel struggled to adjust to her new environment. Her friends had new friends and were in different classes. The teachers were stern and distant, the learning curve steep and unforgiving. Her first set of exams were a train wreck, the reports which followed like something from a horror novel. Isabel withdrew into herself, becoming uncommunicative. She spent entire days in her room, refusing to go to school. On the days she did go she returned in a frenzy, stamping up the stairs, refusing to divulge the details of her day, the reasons for her bad mood. The weekend visits to her father dried up, he became a peripheral presence in her life, unreliable and untrustworthy.

Aged fourteen, Isabel began cutting herself and was assigned a psychologist for the first time. The cutting stopped but she began drinking, staying out all night, flying into fits of rage when challenged on her behaviour. Yvonne was frequently summoned to the school to discuss Isabel's latest misdemeanour, until all ties were broken and they expelled her. She enrolled in a new school, became the new girl, the one with the mysterious back story. Secretly Yvonne expected her to fold, to succumb to the pressure and revert to her old ways. Against the odds, she rallied, put her head down and successfully completed her Junior Cert. She even began talking about the future, about a job in fashion as a seamstress. Then Max appeared.

Two years older than her and with an innate disregard for authority, he became a regular fixture in the house, so much so that Isabel refused to go to school unless Max could stay over in her bedroom, which was usually locked. There had been issues with the guards, a handful of court appearances for theft and shoplifting, and an emotional and violent break-up with Max before Isabel found a counsellor she liked, returned to school and stayed out of trouble. She was doing better now than she had at any point in the last two years but, as Yvonne explained, they had to take it one day at a time.

All this was revealed to me in small, palatable portions, drip-fed in subtle conversation over the course of a few months. With each revelation Yvonne's voice would falter and, having completed the story, she would turn away, fearful of my reaction. She worried it would be too much for me, that I would assess the relationship anew and decide it wasn't worth the hassle. Yet none of the stuff about Isabel concerned me. It wouldn't have bothered me if Yvonne had teenage triplets, ten foster babies and a secret family in the attic. A seventeen-year-old girl was scant baggage compared to the airport-sized load I was carrying around. I didn't mind being number two in her life, even three, or four; as long as I was in the top ten I figured I'd be happy enough.

I did think about Yvonne and Paul and what it was that made them get back together time after time. It must have been the sex. Their physical connection must have been so powerful that not even a saucepan into the face could keep them apart. I kept that to myself though, focusing on reassuring a suddenly insecure Yvonne, promising her it wasn't too much for me and I wouldn't run out at the first sign of trouble. During those moments she became fragile and exposed in a way I had never seen before. It brought out something new in me, a protective streak, a depth of feeling I hadn't known was there. I would have killed for her, would have put my body on the line to ensure her survival. Rather than drive me away, her disclosures brought us closer. I began to understand what a real relationship was about, how important trust was, how you had to sacrifice and compromise, set aside your own wants and needs every now and then. Yvonne was still the strong, confident, charming woman I had grown so attached to, but she had a delicate centre, a damaged soul which had to be nourished and cared for. She had done so much for me. And it was impossible for me to repay her.

3

A SEVENTEEN-YEAR-OLD DAUGHTER WAS OF little concern to me. Her father, however, her handsome, charming father who had a long history with her mother, was another issue. I had hoped never to meet Paul, but he was part of the family too and was currently in the middle of what Yvonne called his 'good dad spells.' He was paying his maintenance, showering Isabel with attention and generally being an all-round hero. It worried me. How could I ever compete with what they had? Yvonne and Paul were only ever one sweet exchange away from falling for one another once more. Them getting back together made more sense than having me around, confusing their daughter by walking round the place in my underwear.

I lasted almost six months before meeting him. I had called out to Yvonne one Saturday afternoon, a lazy weekend with my beloved at the forefront of my mind, when I walked into a fire storm.

"So much for the fucking 'good dad spell,'" said Yvonne by way of greeting.

She was standing by the worktop in the kitchen, staring at her phone. I placed a consoling arm on her shoulder.

"It's not me I'm worried about," she said.

"Where is she?"

"Upstairs. I tell her not to get her hopes up, but she never listens," said Yvonne sadly.

"She'll figure it out for herself eventually," I said.

We were interrupted by the sound of an excited young woman running triumphantly down the stairs.

"He's here!" shouted Isabel.

A look flashed across Yvonne's face, fleeting but telling; she was displeased, annoyed at being proven wrong. I heard the door opening and a man's voice. Taking a deep breath and clearing my throat, I stepped into the hallway to meet my rival. Naturally he was good-looking, they all were, but he wasn't an alpha and that somehow made it worse. He was a sigma or an omega, a strange class of man who couldn't easily be categorised.

"Aidan," he said,

He was shorter than me, maybe five foot ten, and built like a middle-distance runner, narrow but solid and sturdy. The smile he was offering me seemed sincere enough but behind it I sensed disquiet, mistrust, an edginess which unnerved me. Then there were his eyes. I saw Isabel there, saw all the sadness and sorrow in those dark mournful pools of blue and grey. Momentarily transfixed, I averted my gaze, and adopted a formal air.

"Yes. How's it going?" I replied, shaking a reassuringly sweaty palm.

"We meet at last," said Paul. He looked pleased to see me, pleased with my chubby discomfort.

Isabel reappeared.

"I told you, Mam," she said, cosying up to her father.

"Yeah, okay. Make sure she does at least some studying, she's doing her Leaving this year, in case you forgot."

"Okay, Yvonne," said Paul, mimicking a disgruntled teenager.

He took Isabel's schoolbag and led the way out to his car. It was a normal car, a 'good dad' car, nothing fancy or loud. I watched the two of them get in, Isabel almost rapturous, her father taking the acclaim in his stride. Yvonne stood beside me, making us look like concerned parents watching their daughter head out on the town with her troublesome friends. Yvonne sighed deeply, I pulled her close, relieved that we'd have the house to ourselves after all.

Our domestic bliss lasted until the following morning, until Yvonne's phone rang right in the middle of a surprise blow job. She ignored it the first time, but when it rang again she rose from beneath the blankets to take the call. I knew it was trouble right away, knew she wouldn't be returning to finish what she'd started.

"Why? What's up?" she said.

"I'm not coming to collect you unless you tell me what's happening."

"Are you surprised, Isabel? Are you really surprised?"

"I'll be there in twenty minutes."

Again I saw of flash of triumph in her eyes as she got dressed, my Sunday morning treat now forgotten.

"It's Paul," she said. "One of his whores called round last night after Isabel went to bed."

"Oh, yeah?" I said, letting the blanket slip to reveal my naked self.

"She walked in on the two of them at it."

"Fuck," I said, as Yvonne pulled on her runners.

"I won't be long. Do you need anything from the shop?"

"No, thanks."

A minute later the front door slammed shut. My erection was still intact but I ignored it, letting it slowly subside. It didn't seem right to do otherwise.

By the time the Comerford women returned I'd smartened myself up, put the kettle on and was ready and waiting to assist in any way I could. Isabel looked dejected and weary. Her mother was rallying round, hugging and holding her, stroking her hair as if she were a much younger child. I poured the tea as instructed and left them in the kitchen. I was insignificant. But this was what I'd signed up for, this was what Yvonne had told me might happen.

If I'd had my own car, was the kind of man who took command during moments of crisis, I could have marched out into that kitchen, taken them both under my wing and announced that I was treating them to Sunday dinner. They would have loved me then. Isabel would have wiped away her tears, said I was the kind of male role model she'd never had, and we'd have all gone to McDonald's for the happiest of meals. Instead I shuffled nervously in the living-room, wondering if I should poke my head in and announce I was getting the 380 into town.

They had been out there for more than half an hour when finally the kitchen door opened. I braced myself, expecting to be politely asked to leave, but the women had resolved matters and adopted an airy disposition.

"Why don't we do something, all three of us?" suggested Yvonne.

I looked at Isabel. She was observing herself intently in the mirror.

"Like what?" I asked.

"We could go for a drive."

"A drive?"

"A drive."

I checked with Isabel for affirmation, she smiled absently.

So we went for a drive with me in the front, Isabel in the back, and Yvonne in charge of both the destination and the music. Although the latter was up for debate.

"No, Mam! Come on, please," Isabel protested when Bon Jovi's *Slippery When Wet* found its way into the CD player.

I was with Isabel on this one. Her mother had terrible taste in music.

"What do you want, then?" asked Yvonne.

"Anything but that," came the response from the back seat.

After hearing the alternatives (The Corrs, The Stereophonics, *Take That's Greatest Hits*) we opted for the radio and the sounds of today with an annoyingly cheerful presenter. It was okay, though, the music was inoffensive and both mother and daughter sang along agreeably.

"Where are we going, then?" I asked as the car turned left at the roundabout leading to Waterford city.

"Just you wait," Yvonne smiled.

I checked to see if Isabel had any clues. She also smiled. Sometimes it was okay not to take command, to just go along for the ride.

Half an hour later, after briefly entering Waterford, Kilkenny, Wexford, Kilkenny, and then Wexford again, we pulled into somewhere called Tintern Abbey.

"Mass?" I enquired, wondering if the two of them had found God during that chat in the kitchen.

"No, dummy," said Yvonne. "It's lovely here, come on."

She parked outside the Abbey, it looked like it could hold a great Mass.

"You sure we're not going to Mass?"

"Will you shut up with your Mass!"

Isabel was already out of the car, stamping her feet and rubbing her hands as the cold, crisp air hit her.

"Come on, will ye!" she shouted.

Although it was a bright, sunny day, winter was in the offing as we bypassed the Abbey and trudged down the asphalt path. There was an information board on the trail, containing a map of the area and a list of all the birds which frequented it. The women had no need for information or maps, however, they were clearly regular visitors. Leading the way, they showed me the ancient burial site of some royal English types, a river which once ferried merchants to and from the estate and the bridge which led to the lush woodlands. Before we entered those woods, Isabel stopped and pointed proudly to a giant wooden statue.

"This is Isabel. She was married to the fellah who set up the Abbey. That's him there."

Another statue stood in front, this one of a man with a giant spear and shield: the great protector of women, proudly guarding his property against all invaders.

"They'll build a statue of you too someday, Izzy," said her mother.

Isabel rolled her eyes and continued on into the forest, past the playing children, the old mill and a group of walkers. We followed on, delving into this deep, luscious woodland. I'd never fully appreciated the great outdoors when I'd lived in Cruinníth, but after seven years of living in a city centre flat I'd come to yearn for vast open spaces, and this was better than most. With trails running in all directions and a fast-flowing stream splitting it in two, it was a hidden paradise. The further in we went, the better it got. You could forget yourself in here, forget that, just a few hundred metres away life was carrying on as normal; people were on their phones, in their cars, polluting the atmosphere and destroying the planet.

"It's amazing here," I said in awe.

"This is our favourite place," Yvonne said.

"How is she?" I asked, as I watched Isabel pause to pick up a stone and then continue her exploring.

"She's okay. She's tougher than you'd think."

"Wonder where she got that from."

"You *know* where she got that from."

"Yeah, Gavin is fairly hardy all right."

I received a solid dig in the arm for my insolence and we caught up with Isabel, who'd stopped at a seating area by the river.

"Look at the carvings," she said, pointing to one of an owl.

It was large and imposing, a fine piece of craftsmanship.

"Have any ye food?" Isabel asked. "I'm starving."

"You said you weren't hungry ten minutes ago," answered Yvonne.

"That was ten minutes ago."

"We'll go for something after this."

"That pub we were in the last day?"

"Good idea."

Yvonne looked at me in concern. "Are you okay going into a pub?" she whispered.

"I'll be grand."

I didn't like pubs any more. Once my favourite place in the world, now they just made me sad. It wasn't so much the booze, although that was a major part, as the atmosphere. That atmosphere was created by people drinking alcohol, and if you weren't drinking then you weren't part of it. I'd tried going out a couple of times since giving up drink completely, but it had been thoroughly depressing. It wasn't like the night out with Sonia years ago. I'd been on a mission on that occasion. Now I was just a guy who didn't drink, a guy who went to the bar and ordered sparkling water while everyone else knocked back pints and had a good time. Yvonne tried to shield me from it, told me she'd never really liked pubs anyway, but she was only saying that to make me feel better.

It was the only part of my new life I didn't like: the sobriety. But I had two choices. I could choose the life I had now, or I could choose drink. We continued our walk, going deep into the woods, crossing the river and then looping round to where we'd started. Isabel stayed out in front the whole time, perhaps afraid to walk with us lest she see or hear something emotionally scarring. We were holding hands, but the days of spontaneous bouts of passion were behind us now. When we returned to the entrance, she was waiting for us.

"Come on, will ye! I'm fucking starving."

"What about the walled gardens?"

"No, I'm dying here, Mam."

"Maybe Aidan would like to see them, Izzy."

Isabel looked at me expectantly. A walled garden sounded appealing but I wasn't about to add to her anguish.

"I'm kind of hungry myself now," I said.

"Great! Come on then," said Isabel, almost dragging us across the bridge.

The pub in question was situated right on the coast, a stone's throw from the ferry which brought motorists to and from the counties of Wexford and Waterford. As soon as we walked in the door, I felt it, that yearning. A pint would have been lovely, but it was more than that: I wanted to be in here all day, to drink a hundred pints, to experience the warmth and wholeness of others, to have that connection which bound Irish people together. The only saving grace was the number of families around, mothers and fathers with young children, older folk with their adult children, young couples enjoying a relaxing Sunday roast. They were still drinking pints, but it wasn't their sole reason for being there. The waiter found us a cosy little table by the window and left us with the menus.

"Ye want a drink?" I offered.

"Just a Coke," replied Yvonne.

Isabel screwed up her face awkwardly. "A bottle of cider?" she said tentatively.

"Have you ID?" her mother asked.

"Well, no, but Aidan has."

"What do you think?" Yvonne asked me.

"She looks eighteen," I said, keen to stay in Isabel's good books.

"I didn't ask you that."

"What are the staff like?"

"It's a country pub, they won't give a shite," said Yvonne.

"A cider it is, then," I said, sharing a smile with Isabel.

Just to be safe I got a bottle of Cidona and we placed the glasses side by side, ready to be switched at a moment's notice. The food was hearty and substantial, rich and heavy; after we'd finished we leant back into our seats, sleepy and sated. Isabel mooted the possibility of another drink and my heart panged at the thought of the creamy pint of Hoegaarden a lad in a golf jacket had just brought back to his table.

"No more drink. Let's pay up and go for a walk on the beach," said Yvonne.

At the mention of money I perked up, recognising an opportunity to earn brownie points. Silently I went to the end of the bar to the cash register and paid for the three dinners and drinks. It was more than €50, a significant expenditure, but being able to walk back and tell the two Comerfords that everything was paid for made it worthwhile. Yvonne did the usual thing of protesting, but I could see the admiration in her eyes. She huddled in close as we walked on the beach, not bothering to hide our affection from Isabel who had struck out ahead of us again.

"Thanks for this," Yvonne said.

"For what?"

"Just for today."

"I'm having a great time."

"Are you?" she asked.

"I am, honestly."

"She likes you, you know."

"That's only because I'm buying her drink."

"No, she does. She told me."

"Sure she's easy to get along with."

Yvonne let out a little snort.

"You know, I didn't think you'd be able for this," she continued.

"For what?"

"For the drama."

I thought about this for a while. It didn't feel like drama. I hadn't enjoyed meeting Paul, and I did worry about his presence in our lives, but the rest of it, Isabel, the odd argument between mother and daughter, was really only a minor inconvenience. The unfinished blow job had been upsetting but there'd be other blow jobs, especially if I carried on like this. And compared to my previous life, to the unending misery and despair of those dark, lost years, this was plain sailing.

"It's not that dramatic, Yvonne."

"You sure?" she asked, grasping my hand.

"Yeah," I said. And I meant it. We'd had a lovely day and Isabel had been part of that, even if she had spent most of it walking a safe distance away from us.

After loading up with chocolate for the drive home we lapsed into a contented silence until the signs for Maraghmor signalled the end of the day. Yvonne drove down Wolfe Tone Street, allowing me to point out where I lived to Isabel. She seemed impressed, her imagination not vivid enough to countenance what lay inside. She was less impressed by the clumsy kiss her mother and I shared as I got out of the car and let her in the front.

"See ye later," I said, waving them off.

They cheerily waved as Yvonne drove away, the two Comerford women looking more like sisters than mother and daughter with each passing day.

4

The lecturers made a great show of telling us not to worry, that these were only the first set of exams in our first year. But it was still important, and there was still pressure. Although I'd been proving my worth in the assignments, building up my average grade, the exams presented a fresh challenge. Lectures, tutorials and general attendance were my own responsibility, and while there were deadlines for assignments they were generous and flexible; for the exams you had to be at a certain place at a certain time, and you had to be ready. I hadn't suffered any major incidents, anxiety wise, since the course had started, but it was always there, lurking in the background.

As the date of my first exam drew close, I felt a familiar weight in my chest. It was accompanied by racing thoughts, a sense of helplessness and an overwhelming desire to just pack it all in, to email the course director and inform him of my decision to quit. Life was different now, though, I had people around me who could help. Yvonne had a sixth sense when it came to assessing my moods, sensing danger even before I was fully aware of it, like one of those magic dogs who know when their owner is about to have a fit.

"How you feeling about the exams?" she asked one evening as we lay on the couch at my place.

There was nothing ominous in her tone, nothing to suggest she'd been building up to the question, but the mere mention of exams caused my breath to falter.

I sighed deeply in response.

"Tell me, Aidan."

I didn't want to tell her, to even think about the exams, but I knew she wouldn't let up.

"Just anxious, that's all."

"Anxious about what?"

"I don't know."

"Well, let's try and figure it out, then."

"I don't want to talk about it."

"So, you'd rather wait until you have a panic attack, is it?"

"Stop, Yvonne, please."

She sat up and looked me in the eye.

"If you just avoid it it'll only get worse," she said.

I covered my face with my hands, trying to hide from her, from everyone and everything. I didn't deserve her attention. It would be far better for all concerned if she allowed me to be anxious in peace, to succumb quietly to my demons. As I felt her arm on my shoulder and was gently pulled into her chest I stifled a sob, the tension I'd been holding in gradually dissipating as I began to talk.

"What if I have a panic attack on the morning of the exam and I can't go in?" I asked.

"We'll just get them to reschedule it."

"What if the same thing happens when they reschedule it?"

"We'll explain it to the course director, they'll allow you to take it in your own time."

"What if I get in there, have a panic attack halfway through and have to leave?"

"We'll explain it to the course director, he'll arrange for you to resit the exam when you feel better."

"What if I get there and my mind goes totally blank and I can't write anything and I get an F?"

"This information is locked into your brain, Aidan. It's like your times tables, you can't forget it."

She had an answer for everything, a solution to each catastrophic scenario my embattled brain conjured up. After further analysing my greatest fears she suggested I discuss it with my course director, explain to him I had an anxiety disorder, that certain things triggered it and that I was feeling unduly stressed about the first set of exams. This sounded like a ludicrous idea, a sure-fire way of undermining my credentials, but Yvonne insisted it would help lighten my load and ease my stress. I took her advice. And she was right. Incredibly, she was right.

Once more the care and support provided by my third-level institute of choice blew me away. Not only was the course director sympathetic and understanding, not only did he offer me an opportunity to sit the exams in a quieter, less crowded auditorium on a day of my choice, he also recommended a handful of books designed specifically to help young scholars deal with exams and gave me his home phone number to call at any time, day or night. The relief at being understood, at having all these people by my side, was mixed with a degree of shame and embarrassment, but when I told Yvonne about that she reminded me that no one would be bothered helping me if they didn't think I was worth it.

I wasn't the only dealing with exam stress. Even though Isabel's Christmas exams wouldn't go towards her final results, they were seen as a good barometer of what lay ahead in the Leaving Cert. And like me, while she performed well in the day-to-day lessons and at home, Isabel did not respond well to pressure. With a week to go before her first exam she locked herself in her room, only coming out for the odd bowl of cereal and to yell obscenities at Yvonne. The last thing I needed was being around a stressed person, so I left Yvonne to it and focused on my first exam: Programming Concepts. Wednesday morning. 9 a.m.

Sleep didn't come easy but I got five, maybe six, broken hours before forcing down a few cornflakes, having a long shower and dragging myself to the bus stop. Reminding myself that if it got too much I could simply leave the examination hall and take a breather, I held it together all the way out to the college. The rest of the class were assembled in a tight corridor outside the hall. We were grouped with some other courses and everyone had their books out, poring over the pages, firing questions at one another in the hope of something sticking at this late hour. I half-heartedly flicked through the pages of my own notes, notes I'd read and reread so much the words didn't even make sense any more. I was interrupted by a tap on the shoulder.

"How are you feeling?"

It was Mr. Givens, the course director.

"I'm okay," I said, resisting the urge to ask him to hold me.

"No bother to you. You know this stuff inside out."

He was right. So focused had I been on getting to the college, actually making it into the examination hall in one piece that I hadn't really thought about the contents of the exam. After I was shown to my seat and we were instructed to turn over our papers, I had to contain my excitement. It was easy, it was so easy. All I had to do was write down the answers. They were all there in my head, just waiting to be transported to the page. So easy was it that I began to doubt myself, thinking that maybe I was missing something, but when I saw Laurie leave after forty-five minutes and two of the others ten minutes later, I knew it was all above board. I checked over my answers one more time and then alerted one of the adjudicators. It had taken less than an hour.

By the time I got the bus back into town I was finding it hard to remember why I'd been so anxious. We had two exams the following day, both went the same way as the first. It shouldn't have been this easy but, as Yvonne reminded me, it only appeared easy because of the work I'd put in during the semester. The ghostly faces of the lads who'd barely made an appearance all year was testament to that. Feeling jubilant, I called out to Yvonne on the Thursday evening, as my next exam wasn't until the following Monday. She was preoccupied with her other little learner. And it was bad. So bad that Yvonne, a woman who always seemed to have a solution to whatever life threw at her, was at her wit's end.

"She won't come out," she said, biting her nails as she stood by the mantelpiece in the living-room. "I've tried everything."

"Is she going in tomorrow? What's the first exam?"

"I don't know, Aidan. That's what I'm trying to tell you! It's English, her favourite."

"What does Paul say?"

"Paul doesn't say anything. He just tells her not to worry and it'll be grand."

A few months previously I wouldn't have dreamed of going near Isabel when she was in her room, but we'd developed a moderate friendship and, exultant from facing down my own demons, I thought that maybe I could help.

"I could talk to her," I said.

Yvonne gave me a strange look; for a second, I thought she was going to tell me it would be very inappropriate for me to talk to her daughter at this juncture and I should know better. Instead, she gave an indifferent shrug, a gesture which said, 'Go right ahead, but you're wasting your time.'

Ascending the stairs I felt like a gladiator from Roman times, sent to slay an unconquerable beast which had dispensed with the emperor's finest soldiers. If I could succeed where others had failed, I'd be acclaimed, if I failed, no one would bat an eyelid. I tapped gently on the door and waited for a response. I was met with silence. I tapped a little louder. Still nothing.

I got worried then. What if she'd done something stupid, had resumed her self-harming and gone too far?

"Isabel, it's me. Are you okay?"

There were some shuffling sounds from inside.

"Aidan?" she enquired, her voice sounding brittle.

"Yeah, sorry. I just wanted to have a chat, see how you are."

The door opened a couple of inches, exposing the top half of her head, the dim lighting inside.

"Can we do this another time?" she asked. "I'm not feeling well."

"I know, your mam said. I might be able to help."

"Is nothing fucking private in this house?" she said bitterly.

"She's just worried."

"Yeah," she sighed sadly.

"I had exams the last few days," I offered.

She gazed into the middle distance, her attention fading.

"And I had a massive panic attack last weekend."

Isabel's eyes darted back to mine, and then quickly cast downwards.

"I've had anxiety nearly all my life. I know what it's like," I continued.

Now she was looking sceptical.

"Honestly. Racing thoughts, palpitations, sick stomach, chest pains: all of that."

She opened the door wide and slumped back onto the bed. Accepting the invitation I gingerly entered her domain, mindful not to overstep whatever boundaries had been set. She was just as messy as her mother. I looked for somewhere to sit, found a chair and placed it at the end of her bed, leaving the door open behind me.

"You can close that out a bit," she said quietly, lying flat on her stomach, looking down at the floor.

I pushed the door out.

"English tomorrow then, yeah?" I asked.

No answer.

Dispensing with the small talk, I launched into what I hoped would be a helpful run-down of my own internal struggles.

"For a long time I couldn't even go outside. I'd turn to jelly as soon as I left the house."

"Jasyus," she said, suddenly light-hearted. "Would never have known."

"That's not even the half of it," I said. "I self-medicated with alcohol and pills for years; that was the only way I could function. I tried everything to stop the panic attacks, to make them go away, until eventually I realised I couldn't . . . make them go away that is."

She looked over.

"So, I'm going to feel like this forever?"

"No. It will go away."

"But you just said . . ."

"I said *I* couldn't make them go away."

She returned to staring at the floor. "Aidan, I'm not being funny but you're not helping."

"By fighting it, you're only making it worse. Once you accept that you can't get rid of it, it will go away by itself."

"Aidan, my head's not able for this. I just can't."

She rubbed her hands frenetically against her forehead, her breathing growing rapid and shallow. I was losing her, adding to her anxiety rather than easing it.

"You need to get out of this room and away from those books," I said.

"I can't," she whispered.

"Come on, we'll go for a walk."

"Please, just go."

"I'll wait outside while you get dressed."

"Please."

"Take your time. We have all night."

I went outside and shut the door behind me with a quiet click. A few minutes passed without any sound, then the shuffling resumed and she appeared fully clothed, woollen hat obscuring the hair which had been tangled up in knots a few minutes previously.

"A walk might be good," she said, the tiniest sliver of hope in her tone.

We went downstairs. Gavin had arrived and was in the living-room with Yvonne. They stopped talking when they saw us in the hallway.

"We're just going for a walk," I said.

"A walk! At this hour? Are you mad?"

Yvonne stopped herself.

But it was too late. Isabel was out the door and halfway down the drive, little legs moving at a blurring speed.

"Let me try," I said when Yvonne tried to follow her.

I caught up with Isabel as she was heading out of the estate and onto the main road. She accepted my presence wordlessly and we walked like that in silence for some time. We went past the petrol station, past *Cullen's*, the newsagents where Mutt lived, the beauty salon and the chipper, until we reached the church at the crossroads. To our right was a housing estate and on our left the bumpy, potholed road which led to the little stretch of beach Castleblaney called its own. Isabel hesitated, unsure of how to proceed.

"I sometimes go down there at night," she said, nodding towards the beach.

"Oh, right."

"It's kind of weird."

"Why?"

"Well, I mean I used to go with Max. That was where we went. It was our place. Now I just go on my own," she added sadly.

"We don't have to go there," I said.

"No, it's okay. We just won't go to *that* part."

We walked down the narrow road, the only light coming from the pale moon, the only sounds the crunch of our feet on the frosty concrete and our breathing as she set a rapid pace. I made sure to keep a respectable distance away from her, because it *was* weird. She had walked this road with her boyfriend, her first love. They had sought refuge here, spirited away from the rest of the world, their hearts light and full of joy as they held one another close. This had obviously been before Max had been granted a place in the Comerford household, when they'd still had to find somewhere private to do whatever it was teenagers did. Now she was bringing her mother's boyfriend down the very same path.

As if reading my thoughts, she let out a mirthless chuckle.

"Never thought I'd be walking down here with *you*," she said.

"Bit dangerous being down here on your own at this hour," I offered.

She looked at me briefly, her smile weak and empty.

"Thanks for this," she said.

"It's okay."

"I needed to get out of there, away from it all."

"A walk always clears the mind."

We reached the small parking area which accommodated a dozen cars or so on a busy summer's day, and made our way onto the beach. It was eerily silent. The waves, as if sensing the mood, were doing their best not to disturb us, barely audible as they crept in and out. There were no signs of life; no birdsong, no inquisitive critters come to see what we were up to.

"This way," said Isabel, jutting her head quite firmly towards the far end of the beach. I stole at glance at the short end, where the waves' progress was halted by the foot of a dark, rocky cliff. I could see a number of crevices along the bottom of the outcrop, indents carved out by years of erosion. It had probably been one of those, Isabelle and Max's place.

"Once I'm in there I'll probably be fine," she said.

"What?"

"The exam."

"Oh, yeah."

"English isn't too bad."

"You're good at English, then?"

"I'm okay."

We trudged forward towards more rocks, not a cliff this time but a collection of large boulders embedded in the sand. They looked slick and menacing in the moonlight.

"You can climb over these in summer," she said. "There's more beach on the other side."

"Not in winter, though?"

"No."

We found a dry, round rock and sat there, staring out at the sea. I tried to stop myself shivering as the chill settled in around me. Isabel didn't seem to notice it, though. She just sat there, hands crammed in her pockets, staring out at the water like an explorer contemplating her next voyage.

"It's that house, more than anything," she said.

"Your house?"

"Yeah, lots of bad memories. Fights," she added.

"It's okay now, though?"

She breathed in deeply.

"It stresses me out. *She* stresses me out."

"She doesn't mean to."

"I know. But I can't be around her, not at the moment."

"Because of the exams?"

"Yeah. She tries to act cool, but I see it in her face; she wants me to do better than she did. It's not my fault she got pregnant and ended up working in a supermarket."

"She'll be proud of you, no matter what."

"She won't, Aidan," said Isabel, turning to face me, a wisp of hair escaping across her face. "She thinks I have to be a success because she wasn't."

I hadn't been prepared for the intensity of the conversation, for this fragile young woman to so bluntly spell out all her troubles.

"I just want to do my own thing, without all this shite," she said, waving a dismissive hand in the air.

"You'll be able to, soon."

"When, Aidan?" she asked, suddenly tearful. "I'm fucking sick of them, sick of the two of them."

She began to cry then, now very much a lonely, confused child who felt like she had no one to turn to. Awkwardly, I moved in beside her and took her under my arm. The biting cold eased as her warmth combined with mine. Isabel cried whatever tears she had to cry and then gently, so as not to offend me, extricated herself from my grasp.

"We should get back," she said.

The return journey was conducted at a much slower pace, Isabel playing for time, reluctant to face the inevitable questions.

"How about I come with ye to the school in the morning?" I said as we turned into the estate. The plan had been for Yvonne to drive her to the first exam, which started at 9 a.m.

"It's okay, Aidan," she said.

"No, I mean it. If you like, I could go for a coffee somewhere nearby and wait until you've finished."

"What about Mam?"

"She has work at one. We could go for lunch somewhere and then get the bus back."

Isabel pondered this.

"Okay," she said.

When we got in Isabel quickly shook off her coat, hooked it on the banister and disappeared up the stairs.

Yvonne and Gavin were in the living-room, expectant, awaiting an update.

"We just went for a walk," I said, sitting in by the fire.

"Where? It's nearly eleven o'clock," Yvonne said.

"To the beach."

She shook her head in amazement. "This beats all. And what did ye do at the beach?"

"We just had a chat, Yvonne," I said, looking to Gavin for reassurance. "She's feeling the pressure right now."

"What did ye talk about?" asked Yvonne.

I made a face, the kind of face mobsters make when a cop asks them to rat on an associate.

"Sometimes it's good to get a different perspective on things," I said.

"Fucking hell, Aidan. Is she all right?"

"I think so. I might come with ye in the morning."

"To the school?"

"Yeah."

"Why?"

"Moral support."

She looked at Gavin, he prodded one of the logs with the poker and shook in a few knobs of coal.

"Whatever you like," said Yvonne, walking out to the kitchen, leaving me and her little brother staring into the fire.

*

It was icy cold the next morning, so cold that Yvonne had to go out and heat up the car to defrost the windows. Isabel and I waited in the living-room. She was a woman again now, the girl who had cried obscured by make-up and hair.

"How did you sleep?" I asked.

"Not bad, actually," she said. "I've decided I just don't care any more."

She let out a nervous laugh.

"That must be liberating."

"It is," she said, laughing again. "Are you still going to wait for me, like you said last night?"

"Yeah," I nodded.

"Good."

Yvonne appeared at the door, looking ragged and annoyed.

"Come on," she instructed.

For a second I felt Isabel's stress, saw the subtle mannerisms and gestures which defined their relationship.

"Take it easy," I whispered as I hurried past Yvonne into the car.

I got in the back, my role one of encouragement, of silent support. Yvonne glared at me as she waited for Isabel to do up her seat belt, my words of advice obviously not appreciated. She drove with a silent aggression, whipping down the sun visor when we dipped out from behind the hills, commanding her daughter to give her the sunglasses when it got too bright, flicking the indicator on and off with sharp, abrupt movements and surging past slower cars as we hit the bigger roads on the way into town.

"What are you doing, Aidan?" she asked, all formal, as we approached the outskirts and Isabel's school.

"I'm going to go for a walk in the park, maybe get a coffee."

"Not home?"

"No."

"So I'll let you out here, then?"

"Yeah."

I got a quizzical look in the rear view mirror this time.

"Okay, then. Best of luck, Izzy." Yvonne sighed as she pulled into the drop-off area.

"Thanks, Mam," said Isabel, flipping the door open and walking into the school grounds without looking back.

Yvonne stayed where she was.

"Are you getting out too?" she asked.

"I'm going to meet her after the exam, maybe take her for lunch," I said.

Yvonne undid her seat belt and turned to face me.

"Thanks," she said.

"I'd say she'll be grand after today."

"I hope so," said Yvonne, leaning back and kissing me.

I got out and hurriedly walked away from the school, conscious that I was neither a parent nor a guardian and there were teenagers everywhere. After a few laps of the park, I bought a newspaper and found a cosy coffee shop with nice scones and agreeable Christmas music. I'd had time to reflect on matters and thought I understood why Yvonne had behaved the way she had: she felt threatened. Here was I, bonding with her daughter, talking about God knows what, possibly even sharing secrets while the two of them fought like dogs. It wasn't just that, though. Isabel's ascension to adulthood brought a new threat.

She was about to steal her mother's crown, entering her peak years while Yvonne gradually left hers behind. As silly as it sounded, Yvonne was jealous, maybe even worried. She needn't have been, of course. Perhaps deep down most men fantasised about a younger woman, a teenage nymphet who'd satisfy their every desire, but it wasn't like with me and Isabel. I saw a kindred spirit, a tortured soul and just wanted to help. There was nothing sexual about it, nothing at all.

After I'd read every inch of the paper, tried my hand at one of the crosswords and completed half the Sudoku, I received a text message from Isabel.

Finished. Where are you?

In the *Coffee Pot*. You know it?

Be there in a few.

She was giving nothing away when she walked in; a little wave, a half-smile, before turning her attention to the barista. She looked calm, at ease, it had to be good news, people liked to wait when delivering good news. When she sat down, I glanced at her briefly and then returned to my crossword.

"In the popular song, what is given on the sixth day of Christmas?" I asked.

"Huh?"

"Five letters, second letter is E."

"Is that the Mariah Carey one?"

"Never mind."

She sipped on her coffee, taking in her surroundings.

"They do sandwiches here," she said.

"They do."

"And cake."

"Yeah."

We sat in silence, me pretending to be engrossed in my crossword, Isabel twitching in her seat like she had ants in her pants.

"For fuck's sake, Aidan, are you going to ask me how I got on or what?"

I looked at her in faux confusion, furrowing my brow, closing one eye, pretending to try and remember what it was I was supposed to ask her about. After looking into the distance for thirty seconds, I asked if she'd been to the dentist. Neither that nor my question about her taking surfing lessons were well received, so, before I got a belt in the mouth, I relented.

"Oh, you were doing exams or something today, weren't you?"

"Fuck you, Aidan," she said, laughing.

"Applied poetry, was it?"

"Stop it now."

"Foundation level spellings?"

"It's not funny," she said, folding her arms in frustration.

"Okay, okay, I'm sorry. How did it go?"

I had been right, it was good news, not fantastic, but good nonetheless. She felt she'd acquitted herself well, answered the questions to the best of her knowledge and had at no point been stricken with terror.

"Well done, Izzy. That wasn't easy."

She shook off the compliment.

"It's only the Christmas exams, no big deal, like."

"Yeah, but you can use this experience to help you in the Leaving."

She stuck out her tongue childishly, mocking my sincerity.

"I'm starving, though," she said.

"Get whatever you want. You've earned it."

She wandered over to the array of cakes on display and, after much deliberation, returned with a Toblerone brownie, a confection I hadn't known existed.

"These are fucking delish," she said, holding the large piece of cake in front of her mouth, savouring the moment, and taking a giant bite. As she chewed, she closed her eyes and breathed in through her nose.

"Christ almighty," she purred in pleasure. "Why don't you get one?"

"I had a scone."

"A scone," she said, as if comparing the two was utterly ridiculous.

"I'm fat enough."

"Ah, you're not that fat," she said as she took another bite.

"Cheers."

"You were fatter before, I think. Weren't you?"

"Thanks."

"You were though, when you and Mam first started going out. I think you were, anyway."

She was right, of course. I'd lost more than two stone in the past year, but I was too flattered, too bashful to admit it.

"Mam hasn't lost any weight, though. She's always on about diets or starting in the gym. Never does, though."

She was right there too. In the two years we'd been together Yvonne had announced on at least a dozen occasions that the following week would be the one where she implemented a new regime. I'd been careful how I responded to these declarations, being supportive but not *too* supportive, and telling her I liked her just the way she was. And I did. I was just as attracted to her now as I had been on the first day, but I did sometimes wonder what it would be like if she followed through with one of her missions, shed a few pounds and got toned up as she was threatening to do. Would I fancy her even more then? I blamed her for putting it in my head.

"I don't need to diet. I'm young," said Isabel as she finished off the brownie with a satisfied smack of her lips.

"If you eat one of those after every exam, you might change your tune."

"Well, I won't have you to buy me one after every exam, will I?"

Taking the hint, I went to the cashier and paid up. There was a bus stop across the road; we could be back out in Castleblaney in half an hour.

"I don't really want to go home yet," said Isabel when we came out of the coffee shop.

"Well, where do you want to go?"

"Into town."

"Do you not have an exam to study for?"

"You're starting to sound like my mother."

Keen to retain my cool status, I agreed to go into town with her but drew the line at walking round the shops. It was decided we'd go down by the quay, feed the birds and then she could spend half an hour in the shops while I went to the supermarket. As soon as we got off the bus, though, she started complaining, saying she was tired and didn't want to go to the quay and see the stupid birds. If this was what it was like minding a seventeen-year-old, I was glad I'd never been put in charge of an actual child.

"What do you want to do, then? Will we just get the bus back?"

"Can we go to your place?" she asked hopefully.

"Mine? Why?"

"Dunno, just an idea."

"It's a dump."

"I don't mind."

"It's only a living-room and a kitchen."

"I'd just like to see it."

Reasoning that the sooner she saw it the sooner we could get the bus back, I led the way towards Wolfe Tone Street, trying to remember what state I'd left the place in the day before.

"There's a lot of stairs," she said as we climbed past apartments Five and Six.

"How do you think I lost all that weight?"

She smirked in appreciation.

"What are your neighbours like?"

"I don't really see much of them."

A bang from inside Number Seven startled her. I nodded to tell her it was okay and we continued our ascent.

"Come in, then," I said, opening the door.

She was immediately drawn to the view from the window.

"Wow, cool."

She stood on the windowsill, opened the top partition and peered down at the street.

"Imagine living here," she said.

"It gets very old, very quickly."

"Want to swap?" she asked.

"Ha."

"I'm serious. You and Mam can shack up and I'll live here, have big sessions every night and work in that shoe shop over there."

"You have it all mapped out."

"I'd love it," she said wistfully. "I could stay here all day, just watching the people. Look at him, and her, and him, and them! Ooh, there's Emma McDonald. If she sees me up here, she'll freak."

"Don't," I said, moving towards her, afraid I'd be hosting a teenage disco before the day was out.

"It's okay, I'm not going to say anything."

The whole thing, her being in my flat, hanging out the window, seeing her school friends, was making me very uncomfortable. It had been a terrible idea. I should have been firm, insisted we get the bus and stopped trying to act cool.

"Come on, Izzy. You've had a look now."

"No, I haven't."

"Look, there's the kitchen, there's the couch and the clothes horse," I said.

"I want to see the rest," she said primly.

"No, you don't."

"Well, I'll just stay here and look out the window, then. Those boys over at the pizza place look familiar, maybe I'll wave over at them."

"All right, quickly."

She didn't have much interest in the bathroom, giving it a cursory once-over before I tentatively opened the door to my domain.

"Here it is," I said.

Isabel stood at the threshold, surveying the living arrangements of this hopelessly unsuccessful thirty-three-year-old man. She took a good look, her eyes running over the unmade bed, the dusty bedside locker, and the chest of drawers with my toiletries on top. She leaned round the door so she could take a gander inside my wardrobe, then, satisfied she'd seen it all, she nodded agreeably and signalled it was time to go.

On the bus back we talked about nothing, about Christmas and what to get for Gavin, idle chat with no particular purpose. As usual, she flew up the stairs the minute we opened the door to her house. Yvonne didn't finish work until eight so I was on dinner duty. This amounted to boiled spuds, a few clumsily-chopped carrots and chicken goujons out of the oven; but when she arrived, tired and cranky, my offerings were gratefully received.

"There's nothing like being served up your dinner," she said as she pulled up a chair and sat at the kitchen table.

"Don't get too excited."

"Is Izzy having some? ISABEL!"

Isabel's door opened upstairs.

"WHAT?"

"DINNER!"

A pause.

"COMING!"

This was how they communicated, bellowing from one room to another.

I dumped the potatoes onto the plates, pulled the tray out of the oven and did my best to make it seem as if an adult, and not a four-year-old child, had been left in charge for the day. This wasn't helped by Isabel immediately requesting brown sauce when she saw what was on the menu.

"Talk to me, Izzy," said Yvonne as we all tucked in.

"It was okay, not as bad as I thought."

"Really? That's very positive coming from you."

"I'm all about the positivity."

"And what about you?" Yvonne asked, turning to me. "Were you the emotional support for the day?"

"I was."

"Aren't the two of ye just great?"

"I showed Izzy my flat," I said, suddenly fearful, wanting to control the narrative, ensure everything was out in the open.

"Why?" Yvonne asked,

"I wanted to see it, Mam," said Isabel.

"Why?" Yvonne repeated.

"Dunno, I just did."

"Strange," Yvonne said quietly as she returned to her food. She looked hurt. I would have to explain. We ate in silence until Isabelle declared herself full and left us to it.

"I didn't see any harm in it," I said.

"It's okay."

"She seemed to get a buzz out of looking out the window."

"I see."

"I thought you'd be happy we were getting on."

"I am, but it's going to take a while to get used to ye being bosom buddies."

"If it bothers you, I'll spend less time with her."

"No, don't be stupid."

It wasn't until after we'd eaten, washed up and had tea, that she finally spoke up.

"It's just new," she said, when the credits rolled on *House of Cards*.

"Yeah, it was an English show originally. This is an adaptation, or a remake; I'm not sure which."

"No, not that. I mean you and Izzy being so pally."

"Oh."

"None of my previous boyfriends ever really took an interest in her, and she definitely never took an interest in them."

"We just get on," I said.

"I see that."

There was more, but she wasn't ready to come out and say it yet. It wasn't until we went to bed and we shared that look we always shared when it was time to decide whether we'd have sex or not, that she outlined her deepest, darkest fear.

"I can't tonight, Aidan."

"That's okay," I said, secretly relieved because, for once, I wasn't really in the mood.

We lay in the dark a while, neither of us sleeping, an unspoken issue casting a pall over us both. I hated when we fought or when there was any type of tension between us, but I certainly wasn't going to be the one to bring it up. In this scenario, it was far better to plead ignorance. I was just about ready to call it a night and sleep on it when she spoke.

"Do you still find me attractive, Aidan?"

"What?"

"Do you?"

"Course I do."

"But really?"

"Yes. I have from the very start."

There was another lengthy silence. I grew drowsy, almost drifted off.

"Isabel is a lot like I was at that age, physically, I mean."

"Ye're like sisters," I said.

She laughed pleasantly. "Yeah, people do say that."

I knew what she wanted to ask me, but I couldn't ask it for her. She turned towards me. I could make out her little face in the darkness, sad round eyes begging for consolation.

"Aidan."

"Yeah."

"Nothing."

"What?"

"It's just - I worry."

"About what?"

"About Isabel and you."

"How do you mean?" I asked.

"I don't know," she said. "I shouldn't think it, but I can't help it."

"I love you, Yvonne."

I thought I saw a faint smile in the gloom.

"I love you too, Aidan."

We held each other. It was an intimate embrace, an opportunity to remind ourselves of the bond we shared, and it was nice, affectionate, reassuring. As ever, though, my body misconstrued the meaning, presumed a prolonged spell of physical contact meant there were other opportunities to be had.

"Where did that come from?" Yvonne asked from beneath my shoulder.

I knew from her tone that it was a welcome development. And, having not been in the mood just minutes prior, I gladly rolled over onto my back as she slipped out of her nightdress and guided me inside her.

5

After completing the paper, I allowed myself a minute. I had finished my last exam and in the process finished my first semester as a college student. It seemed unreal how far I had come - from an alcoholic mess, a man on the brink of suicide, to a flourishing academic. There was still a long way to go, but I had come further than I could ever have thought possible. It felt good. I sighed contentedly and put my hand in the air.

"Finished?" whispered the invigilator.

I nodded solemnly, collected my pens and pencils and strode confidently out of the room. That exam had been like the previous ones: surprisingly straightforward. Everyone talked about third-level education and degrees and how hard it all was, but if you had any interest at all and applied yourself, the system wouldn't let you down. It was a simple transaction; the more you put in, the more you received in return. While I waited for the bus back into town, I watched the other students as they hauled bags and suitcases onto bigger buses for longer journeys. They all had that same glow, thoughts of home and family sustaining them as they queued in the pissing rain.

Soon they would be crammed onto their buses and curled into their seats, headphones on, as the buildings and halls of the campus were replaced by the city limits and then the countryside. With each stop at each village and town, their own little corner of the world would draw ever closer. After months of student accommodation, months of bad food, loud friends and late nights, their old room, the one they'd been so determined to escape, seemed like bliss. Their mammies, their daddies, or the equivalent, would be waiting for them. The dinner would be on, the house warm and the tree up, their presents underneath. Even their little brother or sister would be happy to see them. After the dinner, the tea and the chat, there'd be people to see, nights out to be had.

They were college students now and they had stories to tell, experiences to share. Their old friends who'd gone to other colleges would have stories too, and for those few days they would feel like conquering heroes returning from foreign climes. They would stride into their old haunts, the shop, the pub or the church, and see an ex, a former source of infatuation, see the remorse in their eyes as they spied this strong, confident figure who had been transformed after just three months away. It was almost enough to make them forget how badly they were doing in class, how after even one semester they were hopelessly behind, how they'd got blackout drunk and woken up beside a stranger just two nights previous, and how they weren't sure if they even liked college life. How they hated their part-time job, hated being broke, and hated all the responsibility thrust upon them. And how they secretly wished they could stay at home beyond the New Year and never go back, let January fade into February and never mention it at all.

This year, for the first time since I was a child, I was looking forward to Christmas too. It was myself and Yvonne's second Christmas together but our first as a proper couple. I had spent the day on my own for the past six years, barely marking the occasion. Before that, when I'd been living at home, I'd availed of the turkey and ham, exchanged hastily-bought gifts with my parents and then retreated to my room to either drink or eat myself into a stupor. This year was different. I had not one but two invitations for Christmas Day. The first came from Mr. and Mrs. Comerford, Frank and Pauline. There was a place for me at their table alongside Yvonne, with Isabel on one side and Gavin the other.

I would have been delighted to accept, but Christmas was about family; so I had accepted my other offer, the one from my father and Mrs. M. We were getting on a bit better now, my dad and I. He had met Yvonne, declared her a 'little dote' and spent the next six months trying to get us to go on a night out with him and Mrs. M. I wasn't ready for that, but we did call over occasionally and when Christmas came an invitation was extended to the two of us along with 'the little wan', meaning Isabel, whom my father had yet to meet. He sounded disappointed when he learned it would just be me, his only son, but he cheered up at the suggestion we all do something together on New Year's Day.

Before all that though, I had to purchase some gifts. Dad and Mrs. M were easy; a nice aftershave for him, a book voucher for her. I got Isabel a new cover for her phone and a pair of runners, a bottle of whiskey for Frank, wine and chocolates for Pauline. I even got my old pal Gavin a book about the Vietnam War, his favourite war out of all the wars. That just left Yvonne. I wanted to get her something good, a signature gift, the type of thing we would be reminiscing about for years to come.

At first I went too big, started looking up holidays to Paris, weekends in Venice, all well beyond my financial capabilities. Disheartened, I decided I'd make her something, a keepsake item created with my own hands; but then I remembered I was useless with my own hands. Jewellery was a minefield, vouchers too impersonal and even I knew that household items were a massive no-no. I could have just asked her what she wanted, but that was pathetic. I had to either get creative or pick up on whatever subtle hints she dropped. But after listening to everything she said for an entire week, remaining focused even during her most boring stories, I had to admit defeat. There were no hints, or if there were, I was too thick to pick up on them.

One of the bloggers, a wise lady blogger, recommended a book entitled *Ten Reasons I Love You*. It cost €30 and required me to write the ten reasons myself. It would have been a romantic gesture, something from the heart, but Yvonne was a practical woman, she would open the book and ask why I didn't just tell her ten reasons why I loved her. The blogger also suggested naming a star after your beloved, but Yvonne would look up at the sky, ask what the fuck she was supposed to do with a star and that would be the end of that. What I really wanted to do was go into one of those fancy shops, maybe Brown Thomas, and get the lady at the counter to pick something for me. They'd know exactly what to get her, that was their job. I'd only ever been in Brown Thomas once and had not enjoyed the experience. There were too many good-looking people and they all smelled terrific. I couldn't go in and ask one of those beautiful, fragrant people for advice.

So I thought about what Yvonne liked: cigarettes, her hair, make-up, perfume, bad music, her friends, her family, me, her home, sex, the sun, the beach, films from the 1980s, chocolate - and it finally came to me. From the time we'd first met she'd talked about her long-lost career, how, as a teenage mother, she'd been forced to abandon her dreams of college. Back then she'd wanted to study graphic design but now, as an adult, she had a keen interest in interior design, or was it furniture design? It was one of them. She loved those programmes on the telly where a tired, drab house is transformed into a modern, multi-functional residence by foppish architects and visionary designers. Yvonne got very animated during these programmes, throwing her hands up in frustration at regular intervals and critiquing the end results in the manner of someone who thought they could do better.

I called Isabel and asked for her expert guidance. She didn't even know Yvonne watched those programmes and suggested I get her some hair straightener thing that cost €300. I couldn't ask Yvonne's friends, they were all mad, so in the end I searched for interior design night classes in the south-east and found one which started in the middle of January. It took place in a secondary school in town, ran for ten weeks from 7-9.30 p.m. and included modules on colour trends, paint finishes and techniques, fabrics, wallpaper, accessories and, rather brilliantly, Feng Shui. The cost was €300, the same as the hair straightener. I booked her place and received a confirmation email which I then printed out and put in an envelope. She would love it. I was a brilliant boyfriend.

I spent Christmas morning in my own place, listening to festive tunes, glad the shops were closed because I really fancied a drink. Then I got ready to go my father's place. He was full of cheer in the car, excited to have me visiting for the dinner. I wondered if he was getting bored of Mrs. M, or she of him. To my eyes they had never seemed a good match, were wholly incompatible. Perhaps the entire thing was based on an animalistic desire which was now petering out. When we got to the house, however, they were as tactile as before, brushing up against one another, holding hands unnecessarily, more like a pair of youngsters in the first flush of love than a couple of adulterers who'd killed my mother and fornicated on her couch.

"It's great to see you, Aidan. Pity Yvonne couldn't make it," Mrs. M said as she handed me a glass of fizzy orange.

"Maybe next year," I said.

"Hear that? He's already thinking ahead, she must be a keeper," said my father.

I smiled weakly, content to play along. Although I was much happier these days, I still felt slightly nauseous whenever I entered their house or was in their company. My father on his own I could tolerate, but the two of them together was an issue and would remain so. It wasn't so much of an issue that I couldn't enjoy the food, all three courses of it, or the present of €150 from my dad and a book voucher from his good lady. There was much ribaldry when I reciprocated the gesture, handing her a voucher for the same store, albeit one for €20 less. For a split-second, as we laughed at how much we both liked books, it was just like before, when Mrs. M was my friend and my father hadn't ruined her for everyone. Then he broke the spell by spraying on some of the aftershave I'd got him and asking her to smell his pink, puckered neck.

They'd opted for an early dinner and it was all over and done with by two p.m. This was good on two counts, it meant I'd be able to go to Yvonne's parents' house earlier and potentially get a second dinner there too. Although my thoughts were already turning to the evening's entertainment, I did the decent thing and sat down with dad and Mrs. M in front of the telly. I estimated that an hour and a half was a reasonable amount of time to stay on, long enough for them to squeeze every last drop of cheer out of me but not so long they'd get bored of me.

"We're going over to Eddie and Jacinta's later," my father said as he sipped on his second brandy of the afternoon.

"Who?" I asked.

"Do you not remember me telling you about them? They live on the other side of the village. There's a few of us going over. We went last year as well."

I had no recollection of this conversation, and certainly none of my father ever having friends. I'd always presumed my mother had banned him from having friends on the day they'd met.

"What will ye do there?" I asked, genuinely curious.

"Oh, we have great fun, don't we, Tom?" said Mrs. M. "Drinks, some party games, cards - we were there till all hours last year."

A vision of a topless Mrs. M, sulking because she'd lost another hand of strip poker, flashed through my mind, followed by one of my father playing Blind Man's Buff and fondling Jacinta's arse, whoever the fuck she was. I looked at my fizzy orange, wondering if Mrs. M had any rum she could put in there to help me out.

"I don't know if they play games at Yvonne's parents'," I said, reminding them I had better places to be.

"I'm sure they do," said Mrs. M cheerfully.

Her tone rankled. She said it as if Frank and Pauline's games couldn't possibly be as good as Eddie and Jacinta's. It occurred to me that Mrs. M was a snob, that she'd always been a snob and she was turning my father into one too. I could only imagine the carry-on of the two of them over in Eddie and Jacinta's, the amount of simpering and showing off that'd be going on. Snob or not, she knew how to look after a guest, and after accepting the cheese board with a variety of patés, the biscuits, the sweets and the turkey wrapped in tinfoil for sandwiches, I gave her a well-meaning hug, said I'd see her on New Year's Day and got in the car with Dad for the drive back to town.

If that had been that, the day would have remained untarnished. I could have gone to the Comerford's house, enjoyed the evening with a family I already preferred to my own, and it would have gone down as one of my best Christmases ever. But after driving a safe distance from the house, my father dropped a steaming Yuletide log into my lap.

"Aidan," he said gravely.

I knew straight away, of course, was surprised it had taken this long.

"Yes?"

"I need to tell you something."

There was nothing stopping them, he was a widower, she a fair maiden. It made sense.

"What is it?"

"It's four years since your mother passed, now."

"The anniversary was November 16. Did you visit the grave?"

"I did, Aidan."

I hadn't, but that was beside the point.

"I'm not sure how to put this," he continued.

I remained silent. If he asked me to be the best man, I'd grab the steering wheel and drive us into the river.

"I've asked Beatrice to marry me."

I knew it had been coming, but it still knocked me sideways. Mrs. M my one-time neighbour, childhood pal, sharer of literature and occasional crush, was soon to be my stepmother.

"That's good, Dad."

"Really?"

"Yeah, why not?"

"I thought you'd be mad, Aidan."

"Sure what have I to be mad about?"

"You might beat me up the aisle yet," he said, in that jokey manner of his.

"Have ye a date set yet?" I asked.

"We're thinking autumn of next year."

"Okay," I said, wondering if I could enlist on a mission to Mars in the next nine months.

"She makes me happy, Aidan."

"Good, Dad. If you're happy, I'm happy."

"Are you happy, Aidan?"

"I'm ecstatic, Dad."

He shook his head affably. He wasn't a bad dad, really, he'd had to put up with a lot between myself and my mother. If Mrs. M made him happy, then who was I to rain on their parade?

*

The festivities were in full swing at the Comerford's. From the first time I'd stepped into their house I'd known it was a good place, a warm, welcoming place. I'd grown up in a house where each of the four residents kept to themselves and communal gatherings were avoided unless absolutely necessary, but the Comerfords did everything together. There was always something going on there, conversation to be had, people to see. If it wasn't Frank and Pauline themselves, it was one of their brothers, sisters, nephews, nieces or grandchildren. And of course there was Yvonne.

She seemed happiest in the presence of her parents. She doted on her father, waited on him hand and foot, kissed his perfectly bald head every time she entered the house. With her mother, she talked at a rate I had never heard her talk before. I had never heard anyone talk like they talked. It would begin the moment she arrived and continue until we left, several hours later. What they talked about I couldn't really say. It was impossible to follow, to fully decipher, like a secret dialect honed over years of communication. You could tune in for a spell and hear about a local woman's battle with cancer, gather some handy tips on how to make a good casserole, but if your concentration slipped for a second you were lost, wondering how they'd switched to a full run-down of the sartorial choices of the weather lady in such a short space of time.

As someone with not much to say for himself at the best of times, this was the perfect setting for me. I could watch and listen to all the goings-on, smile when Pauline's sister, Frances, came in and patted me on the shoulder, nod sagely when Frank and his best friend Moses railed against the government's decision to raise local property tax, and fade quietly into the background when one of Yvonne's attractive cousins dropped in unexpectedly during an episode of *Coronation Street*. I loved it there.

Bracing myself for the chaos of a Comerford Christmas, I walked into the small cul-de-sac which contained their house and seven others. There were cars everywhere: SUVS, saloons, family vehicles for sons and daughters to bring the little ones to see Nanny and Granddad before the day was out. This was the evening shift; those sons and daughters had spent the first part of the day with the other set of grandparents and now had to do it all over again, share the same stories, eat the same food, and refuse the same drinks in the hope that eventually they could get back to their own house and give the kids a few hours with the presents they'd opened that morning and barely had a chance to play with. I'd brought my presents with me and was feeling very pleased with myself as I strode up to the door and pushed the bell. The porch light came on and the door opened, revealing Pauline with a yellow paper party hat and a slab of Christmas cake in her hand.

"Jesus, Aidan, you don't need to knock. Come in, boy."

And that was it. I was in. Into that warm, illuminated house in which every room revealed new and unexpected surprises. My coat was taken and thrown into a pile under the stairs. From there I was ushered into the kitchen and handed a can of beer by Pauline's brother James, who seemed dumbfounded when he was politely informed that I didn't drink. Pauline then brought me to the utility room where all the minerals and alcohol were stored and listed the fare on offer, as if I couldn't see the contents of the boxes for myself. After much fuss and fanfare I was presented with a glass of Coke, some mince pies, and a chair at the kitchen table.

There were at least five different meals in progress at that table. Gavin, looking hungover and miserable, was stolidly chewing on his turkey and ham, a child aged around nine or ten was nibbling on a sandwich, with two more on the plate beside him, two of Yvonne's cousins, Jackie (mid-twenties, not attractive) and Karen (early-thirties, mother-of-three, confident, intimidating, beautiful) were having cheese and crackers, and Moses (who, to the best of my knowledge, didn't have any family of his own) was having a bit of everything: dinner, sandwiches, crackers, cheese and the can I'd just refused.

"How was your day, Aidan?" asked Pauline, taking time out from her endless cycle of asking people what they'd like to eat or drink to catch up with me.

"It was nice. Quiet, you know."

"I bet your dad was delighted to have you."

"Ah, sure."

"Cool as a breeze, this lad," Pauline said to James, who was still looking at me in awe following the non-drinking revelation.

"Did you ever drink, Aidan?" he asked.

"Yeah, a fair bit."

He nodded as if that explained everything, which I suppose it did.

"You could do with stopping, yourself," said Pauline, scolding her brother.

"How else could I fucking put up with ye," replied James, winking at me as he took a hearty slug of his drink.

"Fuck off," retorted Pauline, offering Moses an extra roast spud which he duly accepted.

I was purposely trying to stay with Moses and James, to keep my attention on them. Jackie and Karen were sitting across from me, the sandwich kid at the other end of the table. I didn't want to talk to any of them, didn't know what to say. I wished I'd been brought into the living-room, it sounded great in there, like there were loads of people. Jackie and Karen had opened a bottle of Prosecco and were trying to set up the Bluetooth speaker someone had bought for Pauline. I knew how to set them up, had done it for my father, but I didn't want Karen staring at me while I fumbled with the controls. The boy, who was obviously one of Karen's, was trying to butt in, telling them he knew what to do. They let him at it and returned to their drinks, bored with reading instructions and leaflets.

"What did you get Yvonne, Aidan?" asked Jackie.

I'd only spoken to her a handful of times. She was James' daughter and had inherited the plumpness of the Phelan side of the family, the same plumpness Yvonne had acquired from her mother. Unlike her cousin, Jackie didn't wear it well, seemed to resent it, dragging it round like a curse. All the Phelans had a bit of an edge, but Jackie was confrontational, almost aggressive. That wasn't my only reason for not liking her. Whenever she spoke to me or even looked my way, I felt exposed, as if she knew all my secrets, knew I was a phoney, undeserving of the warmth and kindness of her Aunt Pauline and Uncle Frank. The rest of the family extended that kindness unreservedly, but not Jackie; you had to earn it with her, and to date I hadn't done so.

"I can't say yet," I said.

"A secret!" she said with glee, elbowing Karen to ensure she was listening.

"If we guess right, will you tell us?" Jackie continued.

"You won't guess."

"We might."

Karen looked my way for the first time, her sad green eyes sympathetic and understanding.

"Is it an engagement ring, Aidan?" she asked. "We won't tell if it is."

"No, no, it's not."

"Will ye leave him alone!" called Pauline from her station at the worktop.

"We're only messing, Pauline. Relax," Jackie called back.

"Is it something sexy?" she asked, falling against Karen with a giggle.

"No, Aidan wouldn't be the type," Karen said assuredly.

I flushed. Jackie had found my weak spot and was keen to force home her advantage.

"I thought I saw you in Ann Summers the other day," she said with a guffaw.

"Did she not die last year?" asked Moses, momentarily looking up from his dinner.

"You're thinking of Mary Somers," said James.

"Did she not have a sister, Ann?"

"She did, but she went to England about thirty years ago."

Grateful for the interruption, I got up from my chair and moved towards the open-plan doors connecting to the living-room, receiving a look from Jackie which suggested she wasn't finished with me yet.

"Thanks for that, Pauline. Are the lads inside?" I asked.

"Yvonne and Izzy? They were here earlier, anyway."

I opened the doors and was greeted with the sight of various Comerfords and Phelans assembled on chairs, the arms of chairs, the floor and one another's laps, as a thousand different conversations bounced from one side of the room to the other.

"Aidan! Come in, lad," shouted Frank above the din.

I stood frozen at the door, desperately scanning the room for Yvonne or Isabel, for somewhere safe. All I saw were unfamiliar, albeit friendly, faces and standing room only.

"Yvonne?" I mouthed to Frank.

He looked around him like a general assessing his troops, before turning back to me with a vacant expression. She wasn't here, neither of them were.

"Might she be up in her room?" I asked Pauline.

"Who?"

"Yvonne."

"Could be, boy. Go up and look."

So I mounted the stairs, almost colliding with a little girl as she exited the bathroom in a flurry. Yvonne's old room had remained her room. With no one else to fill it, she used it as a temporary getaway/storage container. I had stayed over one night when Pauline and Frank had been away and needed someone to look after the place. Needless to say Yvonne and I had christened the bed, although the thought of having sex in the bed she'd slept in during previous relationships had affected my performance. But it held no memories for me, that room, it was the most remote part of the house, a cold, distant place with none of the warmth I associated with the Comerford family. The light was on inside, maybe Yvonne was just getting changed, perhaps we could have a sneaky fumble while the party went on downstairs. I tapped the door gently, hoping I might be a pleasant surprise, but it was Isabel, not Yvonne, who opened it.

"Isabel, what are you doing here?"

She had reindeer antlers on her head and gold glitter on her cheeks, but that aside she looked more grown-up than ever, her bright red jumper and dark skirt reminding me of one of the wholesome Midwestern American women in a Hallmark Christmas film. If it weren't for her make-up, the severe darkness of her eyes, she could have passed for one of Santa's helpers.

"Just needed a break," she said, taking a seat on the bed.

"It's crazy down there," I agreed.

"I can't cope with them all."

"Where's your mam?"

"Gone down for more chairs."

"Had a good day?"

"Yeah," she said, smiling for the first time. "It was actually. We got Nanny and Granddad a smart speaker."

"I know. Karen and Jackie were trying to set it up."

She rolled her eyes at that.

"I've presents for you downstairs," I said.

"Presents?" she asked, focusing on the plural.

"Nothing too crazy, don't get excited."

"I won't," she said.

It was clear that it wasn't just the noise and clamour which had driven her up here. My guess was her father had let her down again, broken another promise.

"Did you have a drink?" I asked.

"Some wine with dinner."

"Are you allowed more later?"

"Dunno."

We couldn't go for a walk on the beach on Christmas evening, that was out of the question, but I needed to do something to bring her back to life.

"Do you want your presents?" I asked.

"Yes, please," she said with a childish grin.

I went back downstairs, retrieved the bag of presents from under the kitchen table, avoiding Jackie's glare, and returned with Isabel's two gifts. Suddenly embarrassed, I took out the clumsily wrapped phone cover and runners and placed them beside her on the bed.

"Which first?" she asked.

"Maybe the smaller one."

I had picked out the phone cover online, purposely searched for one with Bernese mountain dogs on it. She was obsessed with that breed and constantly watched videos of them on YouTube. She opened the present slowly and deliberately, prising my handiwork apart with great precision. The sight of the distinctive Bernese colouring, its black, brown and white coat caused her to gasp in excitement.

"Bernies!" she said. "Oh, my God!"

Isabel ripped off the rest of the wrapping and the plastic box, holding up the phone cover in wonder.

"I hope it fits your phone. It said it's suitable for all Samsung Galaxies."

"It will. It will," she said, pressing it against her chest. "Aw, thanks Aidan."

She jumped up and hugged me with a force I wasn't expecting. I smelt her shampoo, the designer perfume she wore, but it was the physical sensations that lingered longest: the tickle of her hair as she grasped my neck, the cold damp of her cheek as our faces touched and, shamefully, most disturbingly, the solid weight of her breasts as our bodies momentarily joined as one. She pulled away, wholly unperturbed by our encounter, while I tried to compose myself and regulated my breathing, my animal instincts stirred into action by her closeness.

"I knew you liked Bernies," I said.

"I *love* them, Aidan, love them! This is my best present," she said decisively.

Thankfully, I hadn't chosen the runners. Those had been suggested by Yvonne who had in turn been tipped off repeatedly by Isabel, but they still elicited an excited response and another hug, briefer, not so disorientating. By the time she'd put the cover on her phone, tried on the runners, and given me my present (a hoodie I'd admired while out shopping with her mother one day), Yvonne had returned with the chairs and I was happy to go down and assist with the carrying and shifting.

"Oh, where did you come from?" she asked as I appeared in the hallway, ready to be assigned duties.

"I've been here a while."

She kissed me, revealing her own scents, the more familiar, safer aromas I had come to know and love. Like her daughter she had dressed sensibly for the occasion, opting for the jumper and skirt combo that all the women - bar Jackie, who was head to toe in sportswear - were wearing.

"Sorry, I had to go get the chairs," said Yvonne.

"It's okay, I've met everyone."

She raised her eyebrows and carried on into the kitchen. I brought in some chairs, was told where to put them by one of Pauline's sisters, then stood awkwardly to the side while the new set-up was organised and arranged.

"I've your presents here," whispered Yvonne.

She held a bag of perfectly-wrapped gifts, and I couldn't help but be excited about their contents. I had been dropping some hints of my own, talking about forthcoming gigs, a new laptop, the possible benefits of owning a Kindle or the complete series of *The Sopranos* on Blu-Ray. By the look of that bag I could have any number of those items, perhaps all of them.

"Yours are upstairs," I said.

"Come on, then," she said.

"Isabel is up there in your room."

"Well, we're not going up for a ride, come on."

She pulled me by the arm and led me into her room. Isabel was on the bed, playing with her phone.

"Look, Mam. Look at the cover Aidan got me."

Yvonne examined the cover, mildly perplexed. "Whose dog is that?"

Isabel gave me a look which conveyed frustration, disappointment and gratitude all at the same time.

"Never mind," she said, scooting off the bed, gathering her presents and leaving us to it.

"Those are her favourite dogs," I said. "Bernese mountain dogs."

"Okay," Yvonne said absently, scanning the room.

"They're here," I said, picking up the bag with her presents in it. I'd got her some perfume, a pair of earrings, and a voucher for a spa treatment along with the place on the design course.

"Ooh, how many are there?"

"You go first," I said.

She plucked out the perfume, shook it, sniffed it and then ripped off the paper.

"Good boy," she said, planting a kiss on my forehead.

I was next. The first item was heavy and bulky, a book, a hardback: 1001 Albums to Listen to Before you Die. A bit left-field, but I could work with it. The earrings were met favourably, a hug and kiss my reward, then I got a pair of lime-green chinos which I was informed I could change if I didn't like them. I did like them. I tried them on there and then, and it turned out that Yvonne knew me better than myself. The spa treatment made me three for three, and I was similarly pleased with both the shirt and jumper I got in my next package. It was down to the serious stuff then; the ace in the hole.

I'd printed off the confirmation email and placed it inside a Christmas card.

"Another voucher?" she asked suspiciously.

"Sort of."

Eyeing me warily, she slid open the envelope and took out the card. Cooing at the sight of the happy snowman on the cover, she carefully looked inside.

"What's this?"

"Just read it."

I was nervous now. She could hate it, tell me I obviously didn't know her, or worse, pretend to like it to spare my feelings. I watched her face as she slowly read the page and felt my heart leap as her features softened, eyes lit up and mouth spread into a beaming smile. The force of her hug told me I'd absolutely smashed it. She released me to read the email again.

"Aidan, what . . . How did you . . . When is it on?"

"It says it there," I pointed. "January. It's Wednesday evenings, so you might need to sort it with work."

Yvonne read it once more, her eyes glazing over, half-confused, half-delirious.

"Work," she said to herself.

"I mean, if it goes well and you like it, you could apply for something similar in college. It would add to your credentials."

"Credentials, yeah," she whispered, still staring at the paper. Finally she came out of her reverie. "Aidan, you're something else. How did you think of this? How did you know?"

"You like it, then?"

"I love it, Aidan. I've always wanted to do something like this."

"It's only a night course, it might not be great."

"It doesn't matter, Aidan. You're so good."

I smiled shyly, delighted with myself, delighted to be able to make her so happy. There was still one more present left for me: the top prize, the one she'd purposely left till last. I could see it in the bottom of the bag, it had a pleasing size and shape, brick-shaped and solid, possibly technology-related.

"Come on, open yours," Yvonne said.

I held it, feeling its weight. It wasn't a laptop, it was too small for that, and it wasn't a box set: too wide, too flat. I fancied it was something I'd always had a hankering for, without really feeling the need to purchase one for myself. The first tear of the paper confirmed what I'd suspected. I saw the familiar logo, the apple with the bite taken out of it, and I looked at her with joy and appreciation.

"Yvonne."

She grinned.

It was an iPad, the newest model, the shiniest, most lovely piece of equipment I had ever laid eyes on.

"But these cost a fortune."

"You're worth it, Aidan."

I took it out of the box, marvelling at how sleek it was, how polished and perfect.

"You can use it during your lectures at college. You're always saying the laptop is too bulky to bring with you every day."

She was right, I had said that. It hadn't been a hint, more of an observation, but the tablet would be ideal. I could use it to take notes, to view slides and download coursework. It would help me become an even better student, a modern, forward-thinking learner with all the advantages Steve Jobs foresaw. It could probably even double up as an e-reader. I surveyed my haul and declared it as good as I could have wished for.

"Will we go back down?" I asked as a cheer made its way up the stairs.

"Let's just stay here a while, have our own little Christmas."

We lay on the bed, side by side, occasionally kissing, but mostly just looking at one another. I could have willingly gone in for a ride but it was too risky, and anyway Yvonne seemed content to simply share the moment. I was too, but after a while I got bored, wondered what was going on in the sitting-room and whether it was too late to get in on the quiz I could hear being set up. After what seemed an age Yvonne smiled, stretched happily and suggested we head down. They were in the first round of the quiz when we walked in, our hair tousled, clothes unkempt.

"Oh here, look at these two," shouted one of Yvonne's cousins, one of the Phelans.

That set them off.

"Fucking hell, lads. Could ye not have waited a few hours?"

"And there children in the house, Yvonne. You should be ashamed of yourself."

"Ye dirty pair of feckers."

"Disgraceful behaviour."

"I wouldn't mind a ride if anyone is up for it?"

It was no use protesting. The evidence was there for all to see. I was incredibly embarrassed, worried that Pauline and Frank would think I was taking liberties in their house, but Yvonne seemed quietly pleased about it all, threatening to throttle her tormentors, but in an affectionate way.

"Can we fucking play or not?" she demanded, inserting herself into the middle of the room.

"I'm not having them on my team, sure you don't be able to think straight after the ride," piped up an uncle.

"That's just you," replied his wife.

Eventually, after a bit of grumbling and some rearranging, I was put on a team with Moses, Karen and Ray, a young lad in his early twenties who was a bit of a brain, according to the rest of the family. Which was just as well because Moses, who had appointed himself our team captain, wasn't worth a fuck. Every time a question was asked, he immediately wrote down his answer on our sheet and wouldn't show it to us until the end of the round. This led to lots of arguments, lots of crossing out his answers, and myself and Ray planning to stage a coup the next time Moses went to the toilet.

Karen was similarly ineffective, leaning in with intent every now and then to whisper something inaudible before drifting into the background once more. The more time I spent in her company, the more I wondered if she were sedated. She had that misty gaze, the distant smile and languid air. To the outside observer she looked like she had it all, the handsome, successful husband, beautiful kids, expensive cars, designer clothes, but people like that could be miserable too. Or maybe she was just pissed. Either way, she was no use to us in the quiz.

Yvonne was on a team with her mam, her auntie Eileen and one of the Phelans, an older man who ran an architectural firm in town. They were a strong team. That riled me. I wanted to beat them, didn't like how Yvonne had finagled her way onto the same team as Pauline, a woman who watched at least eight different quiz shows religiously every day. I made a face at Yvonne, informing her that, despite our personal relationship, we were now sworn enemies. Isabel was squirrelled away in a corner with Jackie, I couldn't tell if they were part of the quiz or not.

A question came up about Greek gods, asking who was Apollo's twin. I knew it straight away, it was Artemis, and a quick conferral with Ray confirmed it. Not that it made any difference to Moses. He turned his back on us, writing down his answer like a kid in a maths test. Karen watched on in a daze, nothing more than a passenger.

"What did you put down?" I asked Moses.

"Nothing. Shush."

"For fuck's sake!"

"I have it right," he said, reaching down for his can. I peered over his shoulder as he did so. He'd put down Pluto. Which didn't make any sense. I shook my head at Ray. We would have been better off with just the two of us. The same thing happened with the next question, about Ireland's largest lake; this time Ray knew the answer, was quite adamant it was Lough Corrib. Our captain had other ideas, though, and had Loch Lomond written down in large capital letters within seconds.

"That's not even in Ireland," protested Ray, his patience wearing thin.

"Course it is," replied Moses.

At the end of the round we had to wrestle the sheet from Moses, correct all his mistakes, and hand it up seconds before the deadline. He got put out then, said he wasn't going to play any more. It led to a stand-off. We would have been glad to be rid of him, but Moses was a bit of a legend in the Comerford house and the thought of him not playing was enough for a few of the guests to propose calling the whole thing off and heading home for the night. All the while Yvonne was sitting with her mother, Eileen and the architect, a strong, united team who'd been getting eights and nines out of ten from the start.

"Here," I said, handing the paper to Moses. "Work away."

"No, I don't want to now."

"Sure you were mad to play a minute ago."

"Bored of it."

"Go on, Moses."

"Nah. We're losing, anyway."

I had to coerce him, this sixty-year-old man who was single-handedly sabotaging our chances of winning, into rejoining us. The whole room was on tenterhooks, waiting to see if he'd relent, and the stupid cunt knew it. I could see why he had no family, or if he had, why they didn't invite him over for Christmas. He was a pain in the arse. A big baby.

"Okay, I'll play one more round," he said, as if he were doing us the biggest favour of all time. Immediately everyone relaxed, those who had been on the verge of leaving went out for more cans, Frank got some coal for the fire, and the kids were allowed to open another selection box. Needless to say, Moses made a balls of the next round. It got to the point where I wished I was out there in Karen's world, half of me here, the rest floating above the clouds. And without the quiz to distract me, I realised how sober I was and how drunk everyone else was. Even the kids were high on sugar. All I had was a tube of Pringles and some Maltesers Pauline had brought me. The designated drivers were on the dry but they were all engrossed in the quiz, on competitive, fully-functioning teams.

My spirits sagged. Could I just have one drink? Could I quietly go out to the kitchen, have a nosey round and find a can of something nice? And if I liked that one could I have another? Maybe one more after that, and leave it there? Three cans, enough to instil some festive cheer. That was all I needed. At the end of the sixth round, with Yvonne and Pauline's team in the lead and us second last, I decided I'd had enough and went out to the kitchen. A couple of the kids were there, heads buried in their consoles, I wouldn't have minded a game of something, but you had to be careful around kids these days.

A cousin, a neighbour or a family friend, was sitting at the table staring blankly into space, a glass of brown liquid in front of him. I sat across from him, saying nothing, hoping we could be miserable together. He took one look at me, picked up his drink and wandered out to the conservatory. That was me told. I suddenly felt very alone. I knew Yvonne was close by, Isabel too, I knew they cared for me and I knew that Pauline and Frank were the warmest, most welcoming couple ever to walk the earth, but I couldn't shake my feelings of detachment. It was all a sham, the whole thing. Me being here, pretending I was a normal guy, being nice and polite when all I wanted to do was scream at them and tell them to shut the fuck up. I probably didn't even love Yvonne. She was just a woman I had sex with. An hour previously I'd hugged her daughter and briefly thought about having sex with her instead. Was that love? The presents, the gifts, that wasn't love, it was just part of the game, something you did.

All these people, Christmas, getting dressed up, the big dinner: what did it mean? What was it really for? Same with me going to college, having a iPad, planning a future, getting a job, a house, a car, starting a family. It was laughable, a total waste of time. Why did I have to come in here, smile at these people and listen to them talk about their children, their jobs, their lives? I didn't care. If they told me that Santa had walked in and shat in their fireplace, I would have smiled and said, "Oh, that's nice, the kids must have been delighted." Why was I subjecting myself to this, playing along with this charade? So Yvonne would still like me, keep on having sex with me? Surely there had to be easier ways.

Mostly, though, I wanted to know why I couldn't have a drink. Who had decided that? All this pressure, this effort and hard work, managing my anxiety, staying sober, doing what's right, was a waste of time. All I ever really wanted was to sit down and watch TV, to eat what I liked and find someone willing to have sex with me. The rest of it was of no use, no use at all. Sitting in that kitchen, listening to those strange people play their quiz and to the beeps and whizzes of the kids' consoles, I knew I didn't belong here. I had willingly been drawn into this world, but it wasn't mine and never had been. My world was a much smaller one: a place of darkness and shadows, where there were no rules, no reason to be nice or polite. I yearned for its simplicity. I noticed myself standing up, but didn't question it. Nor did I query the walk to the utility room or the lengthy pause as I looked up and down at the mountain of cans. A hand reached out for one of the green cans. It was my hand. That hand wrestled with the plastic and called in another hand to help out. That one was my hand too. The first hand brought the can back and held it there in front of me like a reward. These were good hands, resourceful hands. And on those hands were fingers which deftly popped open the ring, creating that beautiful shucking noise which, when accompanied, by the metallic odour of the liquid within, gave me an immediate erection. The first hand brought the can to my lips and tilted it towards them.

An unholy shriek from the living-room stopped me there. It pierced the air, cutting through the drunken chatter, the squeals of the kids and their games. The house, all of its occupants fell silent, the quiet optimism of *Jingle Bell Rock* on the clock radio the only sound. I paused, wondering if it were the ghost of my mother, come to stop me from falling off the wagon. No, she wouldn't care about that, would be more likely to complain about me letting Dad sell the house to a vulture fund. I was just about to resume my journey into the heart of darkness when a sound to rival the shriek made itself known. It was guttural, throaty and menacing, like Linda Blair in *The Exorcist*.

"You watch your fucking mouth now, girl."

I knew that voice. It was Yvonne, or at least a version of her. I was aware a danger lurked within her, had seen flashes of it over time, but it had never been fully unleashed in my presence. Until now. The questions I'd been asking, the pointlessness of my existence, my reason for being, whether I was capable of love, of life, of living, were all flung to the back of my mind, to that dark place where they belonged, and I sprang into action like the loving partner I truly was. The open can was abandoned without a drop being taken as I hurried towards the action. There, I saw my beloved, my Yvonne, being restrained by her father, as profanities spilled out of that pretty mouth.

"You little cunt! You whore, bitch, cunt! Fuck you, I'll kill you, you dirty tramp. Fuck you!"

Her face, with its rosy cheeks and friendly, open smile, had become contorted and twisted, sneering and crackling with rage. It made my stomach lurch, my chest hitch. This was too raw for me. I wanted that drink now more than ever. On the other side of the room, gently held back by a smirking Jackie, was the younger Comerford, the one who sometimes looked like her mother's sister but right now was very much a drunken teen who'd gone too far. She was listening to the volley of insults coming out of her mother's mouth and smiling victoriously, as if each curse only vindicated her argument. Isabel nodded at Yvonne with a knowing smile, repeating: "Yeah, that's right," over and over again. One of the children, a little girl of six or seven, was staring up at Yvonne, all her Christmases flashing before her as she contemplated the evil of adults.

"Aidan, get her out of here, will ya?"

It was Frank, entrusting me with a vital role. I had been wrong all along. I was a part of this, an important part.

"No, not Yvonne, the other one," he said when I moved towards his daughter.

Summoning all the poise I could muster, I stepped across the room, avoiding the spilled drink and ruined quiz, towards Isabel and Jackie.

"Isabel, come on," I said.

"She's all right," said Jackie, grabbing her cousin.

I met her stare and she relented. Isabel came readily enough, perhaps glad to escape before her mother's rage was fully realised. We stepped out into the darkness, into the cold.

"Wait here, I'll get our coats," I said.

That was a mistake. In the time it took me to rummage around for the coats, Yvonne found her way out to the porch where the onslaught, thankfully only verbal, continued. Coats located, I squeezed my way through the scrum, not even looking at Yvonne, ignoring her entirely, and returned to my duty: escorting this dangerous young woman from the premises. I half-lifted, half-carried Isabel down the drive just as her mother's fury gave out and the flurry of insults faded, replaced by sobs and repentance. But there was no turning back, this remained a potentially lethal situation.

The sound of Yvonne's tears seemed to strike Isabel on a primal level, we'd barely left the avenue when she began crying too. Then she began wailing, loudly, very loudly. I tried to placate her, cajole her, fearful that a passer-by or a nosy neighbour would think I was the cause of her anguish and call the guards.

"Isabel, come on. It's okay. It's okay."

It clearly wasn't okay. She bawled like a mother who'd lost her child, a child who'd lost her mother, and everything in between. In the finish, I just held her tight, muffling her cries until she lapsed into a quiet sorrow punctuated by sniffles and moans. The walk to Yvonne's house was only ten minutes and when we got there I switched the heating on, boiled the kettle, got Isabel's favourite blanket and propped her up on the settee.

"What the fuck, Isabel?"

"What's this?" she asked, accepting the mug.

"It's tea."

"Make it Irish," she slurred.

"What?"

"The tea," she said, handing me back the mug.

"I'm not making it Irish."

"Make it Irish, Aidan," she warned.

"Isabel, stop."

"IRISH! IRISH TEA!" she roared, spilling half the mug's contents on her blanket.

I took the mug away from her and placed it on the side.

"Hey! Gimme that back."

"Maybe you should go up to bed?" I suggested.

"I'm going out," she replied haughtily, getting to her feet. "Where's me shoes? What the fuck you done with my shoes?"

She had kicked off her shoes the minute she'd got in the door; one of them was halfway up the stairs, the other in the hallway.

"It's too cold to go out."

"You're just like her," Isabel said, pointing an accusatory finger in my general direction. "You are," she added for extra emphasis when I didn't reply.

This was too much for me.

"Come on, Isabel, let's sit down. Will I get you a glass of water?"

"Glass a wata," she jeered as if it was the most ridiculous thing she'd ever heard.

Still on her feet she appeared ready for anything, capable of jumping out the window or rushing past me into the night in her stockinged feet. I held the doorway, guarding the exit like a sturdy bouncer at the most popular club in town.

"Why you being like this, eh? Eh?" she asked, looking at me in disgust.

"Sit down, Isabel. Please."

"Kay," she said theatrically, flopping down and wrapping the blanket round her.

"Are you going to stay there?"

She pulled a face, mimicking someone with special needs. I shut the door behind me, aware only that I had to keep her inside the house.

"You sit down too," she said, her voice changing, now amenable and pally. "Here," she continued, patting the couch beside her.

I sat down warily, preparing to grab her if she made a run for it.

"Why're you with her, Aidan?"

"Your mother's done a lot for me."

Isabel blew a raspberry.

"When you're older, you'll appreciate everything she's done for you," I said.

"Will I fuck," she said wearily.

She had curled up in a ball, was starting to flag.

"Sorry, Aidan," she said. "Sorry for everything."

I moved off the couch and carefully laid her down, ensuring the blanket covered her feet, using a cushion for a pillow. She was mumbling to herself, singing a quiet lullaby, as I tucked her in, made sure she was warm and took a watching brief on the chair opposite. My objective now was to protect her, to prevent any further harm from coming her way. I didn't know where Yvonne was staying tonight, whether she might erupt through the door and set the whole thing off again. An hour passed. Isabel was sound asleep and no one had come to the house. There hadn't even been a phone call or a text. The drama appeared to be over. Moving quietly, I switched off the light, went upstairs into Yvonne's bedroom and undressed. I lay there for a while, listening for any unfamiliar sounds, and only when I was convinced all was well, did I finally allow sleep to overcome me.

6

I AWOKE, INSTANTLY ON HIGH alert. Yvonne's side of the bed remained empty. That didn't mean she wasn't here. But downstairs there were no signs of life. The couch was empty and the blanket was gone. I opened the curtains, turned on the Christmas tree and decided to light the fire. I would make this a home again, create a warm, cosy environment for its occupants. They would be drawn by the warmth, it was hard to stay mad at someone when you were sitting by the fire. So I lit an absolute humdinger, made myself a cup of tea, got the Quality Street and watched the last hour of *Indiana Jones and the Temple of Doom*. Then I watched half an hour of *The Great Escape* and the Christmas edition of *Top Gear*. And still no Comerfords.

It was now 2.30 p.m., long enough to sleep off even the worst hangover. I went up the stairs, hoping that I'd been right and Isabel had dragged herself to bed in the middle of the night.

I knocked on her door.

"Isabel, are you okay?"

Nothing.

"ISABEL! Are you in there?"

I placed my ear to the door and to my relief I heard a slight rustling, like the sound of a tiny bird scouting for twigs on the forest floor.

"Can I come in, Isabel?"

A groan of anguish came from inside. I knew that groan, had groaned that groan. I opened the door a crack, just enough for me to see in. The curtains hadn't been closed. A mass of black hair was splayed across a pillow with no head in sight. Her feet stuck out from underneath the duvet. She still had her tights on.

"Are you okay?" I whispered.

"Ow, uw, ah."

"Will I get you something? A cup of tea? Glass of water?"

"Buh."

I moved in a little closer, worried she might have been sick and I'd have to clean it up. But the room appeared untainted, although it did reek of booze. I stepped around the bed so I could see her. She looked like a bag lady who'd been living on the streets for the past forty years.

"How are you?"

She whimpered and put the pillow over her head.

"That good, eh?"

"What happened?" she croaked from under the pillow.

"I'm not sure. Yourself and your mother had a row."

"Oh, God. The last thing I remember was drinking vodka with Jackie. Oh wait, oh no . . ."

"What?"

Isabel fell silent. She was recalling her actions, experiencing that growing sense of dread as fragments of the night returned to haunt her. She needed my support now. I sat on the bed, waiting to console her. Eventually she peered out from under the pillow, her hair askew, eyes puffy and cheeks ruddy, now looking like a puppet from a Jim Henson show.

"I've fucked it, Aidan," she said matter-of-factly.

"No, you haven't."

"I have," she whined as she flopped back onto the bed.

"I'll talk to your mam, it'll be grand."

"It won't."

"Sure ye're always fighting and ye always make up."

"Not this time."

"Why not?"

"The things I said to her. Jesus. I'm never drinking again."

"She said some things to you too."

"And at Nanny and Granddad's, in front of all those people! Oh, fuck," continued Isabel, now close to tears.

"I'll go up there and explain everything."

"I'm going to have to move out," she said with surprising finality.

"Don't be stupid."

"No. I've fucked it. Where will I go? What will I do? I'll have to leave school."

Despite myself I let out a little laugh. "Come on now, Isabel."

"Aidan," she said, deadly serious, "I called my mother a fat fucking whore in front of everyone."

Now I was fully laughing.

"And I think there was more," she said. "Something about a dirty ghoul bag and an unmerciful bitch."

I stopped laughing, suddenly concerned. Why was she calling her mother a whore and a ghoul bag? Was there something I didn't know?

"Why did you call her a whore, Isabel?"

"I dunno. I didn't know what I was saying."

"You're a liability," I said, returning to my jokey manner.

"I really am," she said sadly.

"The fire is lighting downstairs. I'll make you soup."

"Ugh, I can't eat," she said.

"Well, come down anyway. It's a duvet day if ever there was one."

"I can't, Aidan. I have to get out of here. Can I come live with you?"

"For fuck's sake, Isabel."

"Seriously," she said, looking completely bereft. "Just for a few days, a week or two, until I find my own place."

"You're not coming to live with me."

"Well, I'm just going to have stay in here, then."

"That's no problem. If you get hungry or need anything, just give me a call."

She lay face down on the bed, no longer interested in anything I had to say.

With the wellbeing of one Comerford now assured, it was time I checked in with the other one, found out how she was taking the events of the previous night.

I called her, hoping for a stress-free conversation, a contrite Yvonne ready to make amends.

"Well," she said, giving nothing away.

"Where are you?" I asked.

"At Mammy's."

"I'm at yours. The fire is lighting."

"And the other wan?"

"Still in bed."

"I bet she is."

"Was it that bad?"

"Yes," Yvonne said firmly. My hope of reuniting the family was diminishing with each new conversation.

"She was drinking vodka, sure she didn't know what she was saying," I said.

Yvonne let out a big sigh. She had probably been discussing it all night with her parents.

"What you doing? You staying there?" she asked.

"Yeah. I've the fire lighting, I told you."

A pause. Even in the silence I could feel her mood soften.

"Will we get a takeaway?" she asked. "I can't eat any more fucking turkey."

"Whatever you like," I said.

Half an hour later, Yvonne had changed into her comfy clothes, had a cup of tea and provided a brief summary of the night's events: Isabel got drunk, started ranting and raving, Yvonne lost it, the children cried and everyone went home.

"Pizza?" suggested Yvonne, as we looked through the menus of the local takeaways.

That was fine with me. I made my selection and passed the phone to her. As she added toppings and considered the deals, I thought about Isabel. She had to be hungry by now. Even the sickest stomach needed food eventually.

"What about Isabel?" I asked gently.

Yvonne glared at me a moment, long enough for me to wonder if she could really be that cruel.

"Go up and ask her sure."

I did as instructed, knocking on the door once more. Little had changed since my last visit, the room was darker, a bit chillier, but its inhabitant was still prone on the bed.

"Iz, are you hungry?"

She sat up in the bed, looking like she'd survived the worst of it.

"What did Mam say?"

"It's grand. We're getting pizza."

"From where?" she asked.

"Gino's."

"I'd love a Mediterranean Madness."

"We'll order you one."

"And some chips."

"Okay."

"Coke?"

"Yeah."

"Will you bring it up to me, Aidan?"

"Will you not come down?"

"No, she'll kill me."

I went downstairs and informed Yvonne that her daughter was in one piece and also very hungry. When the food came, I delivered the pizza and chips to the bed-bound patient. She was sitting up and had turned on the bedside lamp.

"Ah, thanks, Aidan."

"Need anything else?"

"Will you bring up the salt and vinegar when you're finished with it?"

"I will."

The smell of greasy chips, hot tomatoes, onion, garlic and cheese wafted through the house as all three of us horsed into the food; myself and Yvonne in the living-room, Isabel in her bed. For twenty minutes there wasn't a word spoken, no one was angry with anyone else, no one felt any emotion, we were just animals fulfilling a need. And when the food was eaten we lay back in satisfaction, our needs sated, the rush of excitement and anticipation giving way to a bloated lethargy.

"Pass me over the Roses, will you," said Yvonne.

I didn't feel like eating anything else, certainly not chocolate, but I helped her all the same. The two of us put a sizeable dent in the tin before she pushed it away, straining from the effort. I joined her in the crook of the L-shaped couch, in that little corner we took on our nights in. *Men in Black* 3 was on. I'd seen it before. Yvonne thought she might have too, but it didn't matter; it was the only kind of film we were able for right now. I got biscuits, made another cup of tea, and we lounged in a half-stupor, enjoying the simplicity of a big-budget movie where the good guy always wins and life returns to normal no matter what happens.

Will Smith and Tommy Lee Jones did what they always did, flirted with danger and wisecracked their way through spectacular set pieces before ultimately, inevitably, saving the planet. Just before they did that, however, something altogether more surprising occurred. The living-room door slowly opened and a shadowy, shabby figure slipped inside. It headed straight for the armchair beside the television and wrapped itself in a blanket. There it remained, staring at the film as if it had been waiting all its life to see it. After a while Yvonne lifted herself up, located the tin of Roses and wordlessly slid them towards the new arrival. The blanketed one, startled by the sound, looked over at us appreciatively, picked up the tin, placed it on her lap and steadily emptied it as she watched the rest of the film.

7

THE MIDDLE DAYS BETWEEN CHRISTMAS and New Year's Eve were spent in relative harmony. Yvonne was working, Isabel was out with her friends and I was at my own place. They had dealt with The Incident in their own way, absorbing it, communicating first with subtle, unseen gestures before transitioning to quiet, cautious, mostly practical, conversations. There would be no risk of a repeat performance for New Year's. Yvonne and I were staying in, Isabel spending it with her friends in Rún Derg. That in itself was a point of contention, an arrangement Yvonne wasn't entirely happy with, but with neither party keen to renew hostilities Isabel's attendance at the party was confirmed by default. She would be expected home by 2 a.m. Dessie's taxi had been booked in advance.

I had my own reasons for wanting to stay in. While the two of them had been licking their wounds, I'd been dealing with some demons of my own. That blip on Christmas night, the moment when I'd decided that I needed a drink and nothing was going to stop me from having one, had been more than just a blip. I'd come seriously close to falling off the wagon several times since. I had even bought a six-pack of cans, placed them in the fridge, poured one into a glass, stared at it, smelled it, gone as far as putting it inside my mouth, but I hadn't swallowed. I was still chaste.

Under normal circumstances I would have told Yvonne I was struggling, but she had enough to deal with. I couldn't burden her, not this time. There was no one else, they probably had addiction services at the university - they had everything else - but I wasn't due back there until the middle of January. So I toiled on in silence, making it to New Year's Eve by sheer force of will, hoping Yvonne's presence would subdue this sudden urge for booze. She was questioning her own relationship with alcohol. Despite several overtures from her friends, she was resolute in her determination to stay in for New Year's and had vowed to have only one bottle of wine over the night. When I arrived the house was awash with perfume, music blared from upstairs and every light in the place was on. I thought Yvonne had changed her mind and we were going out, but then she appeared in her pyjamas, face clean of make-up, hair scraped back against her forehead.

"This is going on with two hours," she said, nodding to the ceiling.

As if on cue a door opened and Isabel's voice carried down the stairs.

"MAM!"

"WHAT?"

"WHERE'S YOUR HAIR DRYER?"

"IN THE SPARE ROOM ON TOP OF THE IRONING BOARD."

There followed the stomping of feet as Isabel hurried from one room to the next, a brief pause as she plugged in the device, and then the familiar whir of the dryer as she continued her pursuit of beauty.

"I've to drive her to Rún Derg. Are you coming for the spin?" asked Yvonne.

"Yeah."

"We can order food on the way and collect it on the way back."

"Grand."

This was what I liked, domesticity. Just the two of us. No pressure, nothing exciting, just a normal, uncomplicated life.

"IZZY?" she called up the stairs.

"YEAH?"

"HURRY ON!"

"OKAY."

"Where's the party?" I asked.

"Prospect Heights. Apparently the parents are gone away for the night and there'll only be a few there, she says."

Prospect Heights was, as the name suggested, one of the seaside town's more affluent areas, not the kind of place likely to be overrun with local hoodlums, as safe a spot as you could hope to send your underage daughter for a New Year's Eve party.

"Could be worse," I said. "Town will be full of kids her age tonight."

"Don't give her any ideas," warned Yvonne as her daughter slowly descended the stairs.

For someone who was going to a house party where there'd only be a few people, Isabel had gone to extraordinary lengths to look nice. Maintaining the elegant look she'd mastered on Christmas Day she wore sleek, black leggings and an oversized beige jumper, possibly cashmere, with a black, gold-trimmed belt. Her hair was piled high on her head with a handful of thick black curls spilling across her face, which was delicately made-up, most of the focus on her dark eyes and lashes. She slipped a short black leather jacket from the rail in the hallway, popped her phone and small bottle of vodka into her bag, and sat on the edge of the couch, ready for the world.

"That all the drink you're bringing?" I teased.

"I think they might have punch there."

"Very fancy."

She made a face.

I wanted to say something paternal, to offer some advice about the perils of alcohol, but I was too shy, too embarrassed. Instead I scuffed my feet and asked her who she knew in Prospect Heights, and whether this meant she was too posh to talk to the likes of me. She was just explaining that not everyone who lived there was posh and that the young people of today didn't judge others based on where they lived when Yvonne appeared with her jacket and runners over her pyjamas.

"For fuck's sake, Mam. You're not going out like that?"

"What's wrong with me?"

"You look like a tinker."

She did look like a tinker or, at the very least, someone who hadn't bothered to get dressed that day.

"Sure who's going to see me?"

Shaking her head in annoyance, Isabel got up and went out to the car. "You're not to drive up to Shell's house. Drop me at the bottom of the hill."

"That's me told," said Yvonne as she ushered me out the door.

With four hours left of 2017, the roads were busy as cars, taxis and buses ferried people to their final destination, the place where they would see out one year and begin the next. Even Rún Derg, traditionally a seasonal town, had flickered into life for the occasion, with traffic jams at both ends of the strip.

"Jesus," muttered Yvonne as she ground to a halt behind a lengthy stream of cars.

"Mam, why don't you go up by Davin's Terrace?"

Isabel's suggestion was met with silence. Yvonne did not take kindly to back-seat drivers.

"Mam?" repeated Isabel, in case she hadn't heard her the first time.

"We'll be grand here," came the terse reply.

"But, Mam . . ."

Realising she was wasting her time, Isabel muttered some expletives of her own and then, to make up for the time she was losing, opened the bottle of vodka she had in her bag. She winced as she took a sip.

"Any of ye any Coke?"

Yvonne stared straight ahead, severely unimpressed.

"No, sorry," I replied.

"Ugh," she said, taking another hit.

"Take it easy, Isabel," said Yvonne sternly.

"Well, I wouldn't have to start drinking now if you'd gone the right way."

Finally the traffic broke and we got onto the promenade, stopping to let a group of girls in high heels totter across the road. From there we bypassed the centre and all the amenities and headed up the hill towards the fancy houses with the views, the ones far enough away from the beach to avoid the undesirables who came here in their droves every summer.

"Remember, Mam, the bottom of the hill," teased Isabel.

"You sure you'll be able to walk from there?" Yvonne fired back.

"I will, thanks."

Now self-conscious about her attire, Yvonne did as requested, coming to a halt at the foot of Prospect Hill. Somewhere up there was a house with punch and a handful of Isabel's friends, perhaps a Bluetooth speaker and the number of the local pizza delivery store. It sounded so innocent.

"Dessie will be here for you at two," Yvonne said.

"I know, I know," said Isabel, already halfway out the door.

"Wait," said Yvonne.

"What?"

"Look after yourself, okay?"

"I will, Mam. See you. See you, Aidan."

"Bye, Iz."

We watched her walk up the path, as regal and refined as a seventeen-year-old with a naggin of vodka in her bag could look. As the hill curved upwards she rounded the path past the first few houses and disappeared from sight.

"It's just up there, Shell's house," said Yvonne as if to herself.

"We can follow her if you like," I said.

"Not funny, Aidan."

She turned the car and headed back towards town.

"It's going to take us ages to get food," she said.

*

It did take ages. I was standing in the queue for twenty minutes and had to wait another twenty for the food to arrive. Fortunately Yvonne took the short cut by Davin's Terrace on the way back and we were in the front of the fire, telly on, eating our food by 9 p.m. It should have been a nice night in but Yvonne was distant, preoccupied with the goings-on at a house party fifteen miles up the road. I thought maybe a shag might take her mind off it, but despite an incredibly erotic back rub - including a gentle poking with my semi - and a playful fondling of her boobs, she wasn't interested. She didn't want a drink either, which I suspected was because she feared she'd have to drive at some stage during the night. So we just sat there, her worrying about Isabel, me trying to stop her worrying about Isabel.

"Will we watch a film?" I asked.

"Nah."

"Jools Holland is on."

"I don't like that."

"Let's see what's on RTÉ. I think they have a New Year's countdown," I said.

"It's only half ten now."

She did this thing when she was upset – she stared vacantly at the television, remote in hand, going from one channel to the next, lingering for a minute on each programme and then switching over. Occasionally, she would stay a little longer, two or three minutes, and I'd ease back, content to be watching something even if it was just a repeat of an old sitcom I'd seen hundreds of times. And then she'd change channels again. Her TV package wasn't as comprehensive as mine, so it didn't take long before she was returning to shows she'd already flicked past. This didn't matter, though, she'd pay them the same amount of attention, pausing just about long enough for me to get the gist of what was going on, and then she'd carry on to the next show.

"What about that thing we were watching on Netflix?"

"Which one?"

"The serial killer one?"

"Who?"

"It's about the two detectives."

"Oh, yeah."

"Will we watch that?"

"Nah."

So that was my night sorted; I would sit beside her on the couch, trying to make her horny, while she hopped from one channel to the next. Salvation came when she nipped out to the toilet, allowing me to grab the remote, put on Channel 4's New Year's Eve show and then hide the remote down the side of the couch. I braced myself for her reaction but she simply sank back into her chair, glanced at the television distractedly and began scrolling on her phone. As midnight drew close, the presenters began whipping up the live studio audience, cutting to outside broadcasts in central London, Cardiff and Edinburgh where merry, ruddy-faced revellers answered banal questions and screamed gaily into the camera. I'd never understood the hype surrounding New Year's Eve, but for the first time in my life I could now reflect upon twelve months of significant growth, a year in which I'd made great strides. 2017 had been the best year of my life, no question. My relationship with Yvonne had gone from strength to strength, I'd started college, stayed off the booze and managed my mental health successfully. That was cause for celebration, reason enough to partake in this communal commemoration.

I thought about doing something dramatic when midnight struck, clasping Yvonne close to me, telling her how much I loved her and how special the last year had been and then ravishing her as the crowds cheered. I gave her a little poke as the comedian hosting the party announced there were just five more minutes till 2018.

"What?" she asked.

"It's nearly midnight."

"Mmm."

"It's been a good year, Vonnie."

No response.

"The best year of my life."

She was on Instagram, watching her make-up videos. I got annoyed then. I understood she was worried about Isabel, but I was here too and this should have been a special night for us. The crowds had gathered at Big Ben, thousands of them, tightly packed for warmth, their icy breath visible from a distance. They'd surely been drinking, there were probably hundreds of them with hip flasks and bottles up their sleeves, their beery voices louder than the rest as they leaned lazily against the person in front, not caring who they offended. Maybe I'd get a drink, celebrate the New Year with the folks on the telly. I shifted up to my end of the couch so that we weren't touching any more.

The countdown began in earnest "...twenty...nineteen...eighteen... seventeen..." still no reaction. She was still stuck in the phone like a teenager. Fuck her. As soon as midnight struck I was going to bed and I wasn't putting out, no matter how hard she tried. "Nine...eight...seven...six... five...four...three...two...one," a big cheer went up in London, Cardiff and Edinburgh. There was confetti, streamers and a big electronic display with 2018 flashing on and off. The crowds began singing *Auld Lang Syne* and the camera honed in on the younger people, the happy couples, the groups of lads, the women in unseasonably short skirts swaying back and forth, arms locked, as they sang their songs and looked ahead to a new year and a fresh start.

There would be someone there in one of those British cities, in one of our Irish ones, who felt like I did, who could hardly believe how far they'd come and hoped and prayed they would continue to move forward and make 2018 every bit as good as 2017. And there would be people everywhere who barely registered the beginning of another year, who were lost in addiction, depression and loneliness, intent only on survival, on making it through another day. Even though Yvonne didn't care, I was glad to be here, glad to have left that life behind, to be looking forward with genuine optimism.

"I'm going to head to bed," I said.

She glanced up from her phone and saw the scenes on the television.

"I missed it."

"You did."

"Happy New Year, Aidan."

She hugged me and kissed my face. Immediately she was forgiven and I wondered if the new year might begin with sex. I snuggled up beside her and rubbed her toes as some B-list celebrity outlined his goals for the year ahead.

"Are you going to bed?" she asked. "It'll save me having to bring a hot-water bottle."

Defeated, I slunk up the stairs, vowing to be tougher, less of a pushover in 2018. I lay in bed a while, fantasising about Yvonne coming up, repentant, wanting sex, and me saying I wasn't in the mood. That would show her. I would be more mysterious this year, keep her guessing. She was starting to take me for granted, presuming I would always be this nice, gracious guy who put up with her moods, was always there for her and could never resist the opportunity for a go on her tits. Yes, 2018 would be the year of the new Aidan Collins: a dark, capricious character, capable of anything. And if Yvonne Comerford didn't like that, that was her problem.

I didn't hear her coming to bed. I heard nothing until almost three hours later when I was shaken awake by Yvonne.

"Aidan. Aidan."

She was looking for sex. Despite my resolutions, despite being mostly asleep, I was ready, I was always ready. But it wasn't sex.

"Izzy isn't back yet."

"What?"

"It's three o'clock and she's not back."

An image of a clock floated through my mind, a big electronic one with red numbers. Midnight. Isabel had stayed out too long and lost her slipper.

"Who?"

"Aidan, wake up. It's Isabel. She's not back yet and I'm worried."

I sat up in the bed, rubbing my eyes, blinking against the light of Yvonne's bedside locker.

"What time is it?"

"Three. The taxi was booked for two."

"He's probably just running late. It's New Year's Eve."

"No, Aidan."

"Sure ring her and find out where she is, or ring Shell."

"Will I?"

She looked uncertain, as if making these phone calls would automatically escalate this mild disturbance into a code red event.

"Ring the taxi rank, see if he's been yet," I suggested.

"Okay."

Yvonne dialled the number and waited. I watched her face, listening to the tone as it rang and rang, till it rang out.

"No answer," she said.

"There's not going to be at this hour. Half the country is looking for taxis."

"Will I try Izzy?"

"You'll have to."

She swallowed and scrolled down to her daughter's name. Again I watched her face and listened to the phone as it rang, praying for the sound of Isabel's voice, to hear her familiar sardonic tone as she answered her mother's call. But there was no answer.

"Call again," I said.

Dumbly, Yvonne did as instructed. For the third time in quick succession, there was no reply.

"Leave a message."

"What will I say?"

"Just tell her to ring you when she gets the message."

Yvonne went through the process again, waited for the beep and then shakily told her daughter to call her straight away.

"Now what?" she asked.

"Check her WhatsApp, see when she was last online."

She fumbled with the phone.

"11.51," she said, looking at me expectantly.

I thought it over. What could she be doing? The most likely scenario was that she'd got pissed and fallen asleep, been too drunk to get in the taxi when it arrived, and was now totally oblivious to the phone calls and messages pinging in on her phone. That was just one scenario out of many, however. For all we knew she'd gone into town, or into Rún Derg, and was traipsing round the streets with a group of strangers, some fellah she'd just met, on her way to a house party where there'd be drugs, drink, all sorts. She could be anywhere, doing anything. Although she liked to act as if she were a fully-grown woman, she was still just a kid, a seventeen-year-old girl who had no business being out and about at 3 a.m. on New Year's Day.

"We'd better go to the house," I said gravely.

Yvonne's face crumpled, her worst fears realised.

"It'll be okay," I said. "She's probably just fallen asleep, we'll have to carry her into the car."

She nodded, watching me as I got out of bed and began getting dressed.

"Come on," I said. "You're going to have to drive."

So for the second time that evening, we ventured out into the cold January night on our way to Prospect Heights. The windscreen of the car had frozen over, we should have waited, allowed it to thaw, but Yvonne hastily reversed out of the drive, completely blind, over the speed bumps in the estate and onto the main road. I wiped the screen with my sleeve but she still had limited visibility. Mindful of her aversion to back-seat and passenger seat drivers, I said nothing, silently grimacing as she sped along the country road. We made it to Rún Derg in record time, slowing down as we hit the centre of the town. As we cruised along the strip, I surveyed the scene.

Even at this hour the streets were busy, with gangs of people huddled outside chippers; those who had received their food sat on wet footpaths gorging on sloppy burgers and those who had no need for food engaged in intense, animated conversations at the entrance to Rún Derg's only late-licensed bar. There were a few casualties on display, a woman in her bare feet nursing a cut head, a young man hunched under an awning, head to one side, a pool of vomit beside him, and another man, slightly older, with a bloody mouth, who was arguing with his girlfriend. Of course, our presence didn't go unnoticed. A leering drunk walked out in front of the car, forcing Yvonne to stop, then came up to the window, his big obnoxious face staring in as he sang a song about a football team. Yvonne nudged the car forward, gritting her teeth, resisting the temptation to mow him and every drunk on the street down.

Once we cleared the crowds she flew up towards Prospect Heights, this time going straight up and around the bend, following the path Isabel had taken some six hours earlier. Any concerns we might have had about locating the house were immediately eased, replaced by new ones as we saw and heard the goings-on at the miniature castle on our right-hand side. It was built on a slope, facing out onto a large, ornate garden. Even from the road, we could see this was no small gathering of people. Youngsters filed up and down the long, winding drive, some arriving, some having had their fill. The less fortunate ones would have to walk home but there were plenty of lifts on offer, plenty of cars around if they were willing to wait for the owners.

Others had assembled in the garden, their purpose unclear, perhaps taking a break from the heat of the party, seeking some fresh air before returning to the fray. The house itself seemed to visibly throb, a heavy bass emanating from somewhere deep within its foundations courtesy of a sound system turned up all the way to eleven. It was lit up like a spaceship, like Blackpool illuminations, lights on in every room, fully occupied as the party extended into every corner of the building. Beneath the bass came the unmistakable hum generated by a large group of people, the clamour of a hundred drunken voices. Yvonne pulled up on the side of the road and paused. I had expected her to whip off the seat belt, hotfoot it into the house and drag her daughter out by the ear. But she remained in the car.

"Will you go in?" she asked.

"Okay."

"Hurry," she said, her hand brushing against mine.

She needn't have said anything. I understood the gravity of the situation. This was a rescue mission. Without any thought for my own safety, I marched up the drive, ignoring the youths coming the other way, the sudden shouts and roars that only a drunken mob can generate, and made my way to the front of the house. It really was a fine structure, an elegantly crafted piece of architecture; the walls were made of solid, brown brick, with steps leading up to the long, wide porch which contained heavy, wrought-iron seats to relax upon, to watch the sea below and ruminate on what had brought you to this point in your life. Those seats were not currently being used for that purpose. They were occupied by young men and women in varying states of disarray; one of the women, or girl to be more precise, wore nothing but a small, figure-hugging dress and appeared on the brink of death. Her face was as white as snow, body trembling, teeth chattering as she fought the cold and whatever chemicals she had imbibed. She was not my concern, though. The front door, a large, imposing black construct which looked heavier than Yvonne's car, was wide open, a blast of heat and noise funnelling out through it. I stepped inside, half-expecting an angry young man to ask who in their right mind had invited me to the party. No one came. The stairs stood before me, deserted, there was more noise coming from the upper floor, a more intimate noise, the sound of considered conversation, romantic liaisons.

Like a veteran soldier in search of their target I decided to clear the ground floor first, to go room by room until I found the person I was looking for. To my left was a living area of sorts, one of those additional rooms that people with money had but barely used. It wasn't so popular with the party crowd either. A young lad was unconscious on the couch, a few others loitered at the fireplace, smoking cigars, drinking what looked like hard liquor. My presence didn't even register with them. Across from there was a dining-room, a massive space with a long oak table capable of seating a family of thirty or more. The walls here were panelled, like something from an American cabin, I half-expected to see a bear head above the dining area.

At the end of the table was an entrance into a kitchen, open-plan, with more drunk boys, one of them rummaging in the freezer. This led into another living area, a snug spot with armchairs and couches placed close together in front of an electric fire and a massive, wide-screen television. Some lads had started up a game of cards on the table, looking like a proper bunch of hustlers as they threw in their chips and smoked yet more cigars. Where were they getting all the cigars? Someone had hooked up a laptop to the TV and had found the most violent, most hardcore porn imaginable. The boys watching laughed in unison as the action took another depraved turn.

At this point it seemed like a frat party, like the girls had left the boys to be boys and found their enjoyment elsewhere. But as I left the dining-room, through the glass doors which connected it to the main living room of the house, I saw that the women were definitely still here and were definitely enjoying themselves. It was from here that the music emanated. A set of decks had been placed on a table in the corner of the room, a room which had surely played host to far more agreeable gatherings than this: resplendent family occasions, birthdays, wedding receptions, christenings and Christmases. It had a high, cavernous ceiling and once more the walls were wood-panelled.

Unlike the other rooms this one had carpet, a red plush material which felt like walking in marshmallow, and a real, functioning fireplace. There were white leather sofas and chairs set around a vast table which housed bottles, glasses, ashtrays, cigarette lighters and all the flotsam and jetsam of a teenage party. These weren't just any teenagers, though. These were the elite. I saw it in them. These people went to the private schools that you only got into if your lineage was of the right calibre. They were well-dressed, healthy young men and women. Even in their inebriation you could see it. The lads in their shirts and chinos, their sturdy, well-fed bodies built for sport, for excellence on the field of play. Their hair, sensible yet stylish, ensuring everyone knew they were of a certain class. It was apparent in how they carried themselves, how they danced, there was an ease to it all, a happy, self-belief which momentarily jarred.

The women, the young women, most of whom were either slowly sashaying with their partner of choice or dancing in small, compact groups, wore tight dresses, revealing lithe, graceful figures, delicate limbs, fragile necks and varying degrees of cleavage. There were no fat people. It was as if science had assembled all those with a genetic advantage for a covert experiment, possibly for breeding. It got better. There was a swimming pool out the back, the water shimmering as males in their boxers horsed around like children. A couple of the braver girls had joined them, their underwear protecting their modesty as they were repeatedly dunked underneath by oversexed lads. I walked across the living-room floor, eyes fixed on the swimming pool, still searching for Isabel but also fascinated by what I was seeing. I reached the doors and saw there was also a hot tub to the left. It was bubbling away, more than a dozen people crammed inside, more girls than boys. Again, the lads had cigars.

Seeing them all, semi-naked, beautiful and alive, made me painfully conscious of my own physical appearance, of my age, my ugliness. I was shamefully out of place. But aside from the odd quizzical glance, no one seemed to care that I was here. They were too far gone, too deep into the party, to pay me any heed. I took one last look at the swimming pool and its surrounding areas, and turned back into the house. There was still no Isabel. I couldn't decide if this was a good or a bad thing. After waiting to check the two downstairs toilets I stood at the foot of the stairs, straining my ears, hoping for an excuse not to go up there.

While I'd been gawping at young wans in a hot tub, Yvonne had been waiting outside in her car, half-frantic. How long had I been gone, five minutes? Long enough. I ascended the stairs, my intention to quickly search every bedroom. If people were in bed, doing things, then I would have to ascertain their identity, ensure that none of them was Isabel and move on. If I stopped to think about what I was doing, of the potential consequences, I'd never go through with it, so I cleared my head, focused on Yvonne, on Isabel and opened the first door. A shriek caused me to slam it shut again. There had been people in bed, two of them, a boy and a girl. The girl hadn't been Isabel. I would have to assume she wasn't asleep under the bed or in one of the wardrobes. The next bedroom didn't have a copulating couple, but it did contain a group of stern-looking young women who were deeply unhappy at being interrupted by a thirty-something bozo with enquiring eyes.

I took a breath and stared down the hallway. There were five more doors, all of them shut. That wasn't all. At the end of the hall the corridor turned left, presumably to more rooms, more doors. The next two doors were of no use: one containing a dozing male receiving vicious head from a determined female, the second a lovestruck couple asleep in one another's arms. Door three was a bathroom, unoccupied. When I opened door four, I was met with looks guiltier than my own from three young lads who were elbow-deep in someone's drawers. I left them to it, wishing my own needs were so basic. There was a lot of noise behind door five, too much noise. With my heart thumping in my chest, I crouched down and looked through the keyhole. More than a dozen youngsters were in a state of semi-undress. It was a game. They were playing Truth or Dare, or a derivative of it. I felt an aching jealousy. I reached the end of the hall and looked to my left. Just two more doors. If she wasn't here I could get the fuck out of this madhouse, scurry back to Yvonne and discuss our next move.

It was quieter in this part of the house, perhaps designed that way, allowing the master and mistress to retire to their quarters in peace. This allowed me to listen before entering, to take my time before making my next move. I waited outside the first door, ears straining, head cocked. There was a sound, but it was muffled and far away. I edged the door open.

The room was dim, a faint light coming from the far corner. Both doors belonged to the same room. This was the penthouse, a bedroom bigger than my entire flat. The en suite was to my right with a walk-in closet up ahead. Slowly I scanned the room. I looked across the vast expanse of floor space, the breakfast bar, the desk and chair, the wide drapes which fluttered in the wind, revealing the balcony behind them, and the bed, with lamps built into the walls above the headboard, both lit, enabling me to see its occupants, not in their entirety, but well enough to recognise them, or at least one of them. It was Isabel.

She lay in the bed, her head on the pillow, turned to one side, eyes closed, as the slow, steady rhythm of flesh upon flesh played its tune. Above her was a man, his shoulders arched, back tensed as he moved patiently towards his goal. He was panting, peppering his performance with words of encouragement, whether for her or him I couldn't say. "Yes, oh fuck, yes ... that's it ... come on ... oh, yes!" I could only see the back of his head, his short hair and muscular arms, but I didn't need to see any more. I knew exactly what was happening. The thing inside me, the hidden beast, slowly unfurled in my stomach. Roused from another lengthy slumber it took its time, gently travelling up my spine, caressing my nerve-endings as it passed through my core, through my heart, my lungs and into my throat. It dallied a while, considering its next move, before racing at breakneck speed to my brain, where it exploded, turning everything to dust.

Logic, rationale, right and wrong were scattered to the wind and in their stead came one overriding certainty: I had to save her, to protect her at all costs. The moans and grunts from the bed intensified, the sickening rhythm increased, that slapping sound, the creaking and squeaking of the bed as he took what he wanted. The last semblance of control slipped from my grasp and I sprang to my feet, searching for a light switch. I succeeded only in illuminating half the room, not enough to distract them. The shout as I announced my presence, launched myself in their direction, wasn't quite what I intended either, more a strangled yelp than a booming roar. It wasn't until I was almost upon them that they noticed me.

I paused, dimly aware of how unusual a situation this was, but as the man turned to face me. his torso slick with sweat, penis angry and erect, I continued onwards. The bed was so big I had to clamber aboard, momentarily joining them in a threesome of sorts before I grabbed him by his bare shoulders and shoved him off. It was like a child's game, the king and queen of the castle. He quickly regained his balance and got to his feet, more annoyed than afraid.

"What the fuck? Who are you?"

Isabel was still on the bed, only her eyes moving as she watched the action unfold. I dismounted, scrambling, intent on destroying her tormentor. Like the others he was ripped, a strong physical specimen, but he was naked and off-guard and when I ploughed into him he smashed against the patio door and brought the drapes toppling down on top of him. I leapt forwards, ready to answer any response with a barrage of punches, but a voice stopped me in my tracks.

"Aidan. Aidan!"

Isabel was sitting up in the bed now, blankets covering her modesty. Her make-up had run down her cheeks, her lipstick smeared across her face. It wasn't about the man, about punishing him for his actions, I had to get her out of here and end her ordeal. Leaving him as he swore and shouted his annoyance, tried to extricate himself from the curtains, I pulled Isabel from the bed and lifted her into my arms, the blanket coming with her.

"AIDAN!" she shouted, but there was no time to talk. Surprised at how light she was and how strong I was, I carried her out of the room down the hallway. The blanket snagged on something, slowing us down. I pulled at it, panicking, and then let it unravel, let it fall to the ground. A girl coming out of the bathroom almost knocked us over, cried out in concern when she saw Isabel's naked body, but there was no time to explain. We forged ahead, ignoring the girl as she called after us. She would surely alert her friends, as would the guy I'd thrown into the window. This situation was threatening to spiral out of control. Holding Isabel close to me, protecting her as if she were my newborn child, I steadily descended the stairs.

People were still streaming in and out of the house, the party remained in session. Some of them stopped and stared, their eyes burning into me, as I kept my head down and made for the door.

"Hey, what the fuck, man?"

I felt a hand on my shoulder, solid and uncompromising. I shook it off, growling at its owner, hoping I wouldn't have to expend any more energy fighting. The bodies before me parted respectfully, allowing us to continue our journey.

"It's going to get cold, Isabel. Sorry," I said as we left the house and went into the night. Sleet had begun to fall, its icy droplets splattering onto Isabel's skin as I hurried down the drive, around the cars and towards salvation. Someone shouted after us from the house, loud and threatening. They were coming. They would reclaim her and destroy me. Afraid to look back, I hunched into the sleet and finally reached the end of the drive. Yvonne's car was where I'd left it, haphazardly parked on the other side of the street. I staggered the last few feet, grateful to see Yvonne emerge from the car, to be able to return her child to her.

"Jesus Christ, Aidan! What happened? Get her in the car!"

Now almost on my knees, I bundled Isabel into the passenger side, ripping off my jumper and placing it over her. Yvonne got in and shut the door, turning the heating up full blast.

"Get in the back!" she shouted at me as I stood over Isabel, determined to make sure she was all right.

There were coats and tops, jumpers and hoodies littered over the back seat; I chucked them all over Isabel. As Yvonne started the engine and edged round the BMW that had parked in front of her, I saw three young men come running down the drive. I recognised one of them. It was strange seeing him with his clothes on.

*

By the time we got back to Yvonne's house, the car was like a furnace and Isabel had nine different items of clothing on her. She had remained entirely silent throughout the drive home, ignoring her mother's questions, her breathing slowly returning to normal as the warmth spread around her body. Yvonne parked the car and prepared to escort her daughter inside. I waited in the back seat, eager to offer my assistance. As her mother fussed over Isabel, hugged her, rubbed her, did everything in her power to revive her, I felt like an intruder, an outsider who no longer belonged. Yvonne turned to me.

"Go inside, will you?"

"Okay."

I was no longer required. My duty was done. It was time for the women to take over now. I stayed in the living-room, kept the door shut as they came inside and went up the stairs. Hours passed. I thought they'd gone to bed, wondered if I should just sleep on the couch. Eventually, Yvonne came back down, peeping into the living-room, as if hoping I'd be gone.

"Can you get a taxi home?" she asked.

That hardly seemed fair. I thought about protesting, reminding her what might have happened had it not been for me, but it was easier to just agree - more noble too.

"Is she okay?" I asked.

"She's fine."

I searched Yvonne's face for answers. She looked sad, close to tears, but not distraught like I'd thought she would be. I got up and hugged her, holding her close. She hugged me back, but not with the kind of force I was used to. She wasn't there. It wasn't Yvonne. Reminding myself that in situations like this I had to put my own needs on hold, I released her and went to stand outside. It was after 6 a.m. now, the rush for taxis would probably have died down.

8

We had been supposed to spend New Year's Day with my father and Mrs. M, but that didn't happen. I spent the day alone and afraid, a painful curdling in my stomach. Yvonne wasn't answering her phone or replying to my texts. Neither of them were. And I knew why. I had known from the moment I'd awoken with a unshakeable sense of foreboding. I'd often woken up with the same dread, a feeling of having fucked up, but I'd been drinking on those occasions, had never been able to pinpoint the cause of my concern. There had been no alcohol consumed this time, my memories were sharp and in focus, instantly accessible. I didn't want them, but I couldn't escape them.

I had stormed into that house and roamed brazenly from room to room. I had lingered too long in the back garden, staring at the girls in the swimming pool and the hot tub, and I had mounted the stairs and painstakingly continued my investigation, interrupting private liaisons. If that had been all, I could have coped; but I had gone further, much further. I had crept into the master bedroom, spied the young couple making love in the bed, interrupted their union, attacked the man and dragged the woman out of the bed. I had clasped that naked young woman to my chest, holding her tight, the scent of sex still clinging to her body and I had carried her, carried Isabel, down the stairs, through the crowds and out the door, depositing her into the car as if I were a heroic soldier and she the only daughter of a stricken king.

At the time I had felt just like that: a heroic soldier. My warped mind had convinced me I was on a mission of justice, a crusade against the tyranny of mankind, when, in reality, all I had done was barge in on a pair of love birds. Whatever had been going on in that room had been consensual, I understood that now. I didn't need to be told. If I'd been of sound mind I would have known straight away. If I hadn't been on some vengeful quest I would have quietly slipped out of the room, returned to Yvonne and explained the situation. We would have sat in the car, discussed what to do and then driven back home to await Isabel's arrival. If I had only confronted them, instructed them to get dressed and meet me down in the living-room for a serious chat, it might have been okay. That was what a normal, sane adult might have done.

If I had simply cast the boy aside, threatened to throttle him as Isabel watched on in terror, it still could have been salvaged. If I hadn't chosen to whisk her from the bed, take her in my arms, it could have somehow been explained. But I had exceeded every possible boundary, broken every rule, spoken and unspoken. They were a pair of teenagers, and I had invaded their world; an ugly, abhorrent man in his thirties, the kind of oddball you read about it in the news, saw hurrying out of court, their face obscured by a newspaper. Isabel was the daughter of my partner, and with that came a responsibility, a duty of care. My role was one of gentle guidance, quiet alliance. The serious stuff was not my terrain.

More than that, there was an understanding - one which had nothing to do with Yvonne - that I would remain entirely unaffected by Isabel's burgeoning sexuality. I had to behave as if she were my daughter, my flesh and blood. That was the law of the land. Anything else and I would be no better than the nonces and sex pests in the maximum security wing of Mountjoy. That bond had to remain sealed. I had to see past her physical characteristics, become blind to her charms, restrict the part of my brain which automatically sent eyes wandering where they shouldn't. Had I been doing that? No, I hadn't. I could admit that now. The only consolation was there had been nothing sexual about my rescue act. That wouldn't be how Isabel would see it. I had broken that bond, tore off the seal and, no matter how hard I tried, it couldn't be put back on.

When New Year's Day passed without any communication I knew it was over. Yvonne was playing for time, deciding how to deliver the fatal blow. The silence wouldn't last, and when it was broken it would break me too. All I could do was wait, a condemned man. On the second day of 2018, I chose to make the waiting go by a little quicker. I went to the supermarket, stocked up on cans, a bottle of wine, and returned home. I placed the alcohol on the worktop, looked at it awhile. Such an innocent thing, a dark bottle, some fancy French writing on the label. And the cans, elegantly decorated, colour-coordinated, no hint of the danger which resided within. Once I'd emptied their contents into my body my world would change, perhaps irrevocably, but I needed them. I needed them to help me wait and to help me deal with my future.

Those cans and that bottle had been replaced by others, bolstered by some vodka, when the lines of communication were finally reopened on January 4. A text.

We need to talk.

Between the start of the drinking and Yvonne's text message, I had lost all control. There had been phone calls, lots of them, and accompanying voice mails full of anguish and sorrow, indignation, hysteria, and finally irritation. I recalled using the phrase 'How dare you?' more than once. There had been tears, shouting, maybe a little song, until I gave up and resorted to lengthy, punctuated text messages, outlining my case, my argument, why this needn't be a big deal. And with each unanswered call I grew more frustrated, more despondent. My hesitant, almost dainty, return to drinking quickly progressed until I was mired in a sea of empties, half-dressed as music blared out of the stereo. And now we 'needed to talk'.

Well, maybe I didn't want to talk. Maybe I wanted to keep drinking, to keep listening to whatever the hell I was listening to, and march to and from the toilet in my stockinged feet. But that wasn't the case. I did want to talk. As drunk as I was, I knew we had to talk, and talk as we'd never talked before. Sighing deeply, acutely aware of my dramatic fall from grace, I began tidying up, first the flat, then myself. I filled up some black sacks, mopped the floor, stowed away the remaining drink and took a shower. Curious as to how much damage I'd caused, I took a look in the mirror. There wasn't that much change, a bit puffy round the eyes, red around the gills, but it was still salvageable, I didn't have to go back. But already I was thinking about how I'd deal with the talk. I couldn't do it sober. Not now. Not when I knew what was coming.

Okay. I replied to Yvonne's text.

I can come into town and meet you in that café on Plunkett Street.

I looked outside, it was still daylight. She wanted to meet today, right now.

What time? I asked.

2.30?

All right.

It was the formality that killed me. This was a woman I'd been to war with. We'd been in love, were still supposed to be. I'd kissed every part of her body, put my tongue, my face, places I hadn't even known they could go. We'd stared deep into one another's eyes, exposed parts of ourselves more intimate than anything physical or sexual, and now she was like a secretary confirming my doctor's appointment. I looked around, searching for some way of making this better, and all I could think of were the cans in the fridge, the half-bottle of rum in the press. They were all I had, and so I drank them. I drank right up until 2.25, at which point I got my heavy winter coat, left the apartment and made my way to Plunkett Street.

9

Town was busy. People hadn't gone back to work yet, or maybe it was the weekend. I didn't know. The sales were on. I had planned to buy some new clothes, but that money had been spent on drink. When I got to the café, it was busy, too busy. The seats by the window were all taken and as I approached the door I saw a queue by the counter and crowded tables in the middle of the floor. I wanted to turn around and just keep walking until I sobered up and my legs grew tired, until there was nothing left to do but lie on the ground and wait for sleep or death to take me. Yvonne had spotted me, though, she was at a table on the far side of the room and had stood up to try and catch my attention.

My heart crumpled in my chest. I didn't want to do this. I wanted her to hold me, tell me it was okay and bring me back to her place. I wanted to sit beside her on the couch for the rest of my life, just flicking through the channels, watching whatever she wanted. I wouldn't even look at Isabel, let alone talk to her; she'd surely be moving out soon, going to college. We could get over this and make it work. I walked towards Yvonne, trying my best to look sober, to glide past the chairs and tables blocking my path. Instead I bumped awkwardly into a waitress, jammed my knee into someone's back and caught my foot in the handle of a lady's bag. By the time I reached Yvonne she knew, she had probably known from the minute I appeared at the door.

"Aidan," she said sadly, with a hint of the old Yvonne.

Maybe getting drunk would work in my favour, remind her of my vulnerability, how I couldn't cope without her.

"Some crowds around," I said airily.

"Aidan, what have you done?"

"Nothing," I said, looking at her directly.

"Jesus Christ," she whispered.

While I dealt with my shame a coffee was ordered on my behalf, a strong one for the day that was in it. I sipped on it out of politeness as Yvonne asked questions about my drinking. The responses were stock: it was only a couple of cans, a once-off, I don't know what came over me. I could lie to her now, it didn't matter any more. With the niceties out of the way, she began her spiel. Unlike me, she had something prepared.

"First, I want to apologise," she said. "I should have got in touch sooner."

I wordlessly accepted her apology and waited for her to continue.

"It's been a mad couple of days. Izzy hasn't been well."

My hopes lifted. Maybe Isabel had contracted pneumonia and they'd all been in the hospital. It had been a massive misunderstanding.

"Her anxiety," Yvonne continued. "The other night. What happened. It wasn't good for her. She's in a bad place, a really bad place."

I tried to form a response, offer sympathy, ask a question, assemble my thoughts into a meaningful sentence, but it was too hard.

"Aidan, what you did was far from okay. You know that, don't you?"

I nodded dumbly.

"I mean, what the fuck were you thinking?"

I wanted to tell her about the night in Dublin, about the girl on the bed and the big bear man, but I was getting confused now. The youngsters on the table next to us were looking at me strangely; they knew I was pissed and were probably talking about me, saying I was weird and ugly.

"I thought there was something wrong," I said eventually.

"You walked in on her having sex and attacked some young lad," Yvonne hissed. "Then you dragged her out of the bed and carried her through the house with not a stitch of clothing on her."

"Is he all right, the young lad?" I asked, my mind thick, thoughts muddled.

Yvonne screwed up her face in irritation.

"You're just lucky Gavin hasn't found out what happened."

Gavin, my old pal. I'd miss him too.

"Do you know how long it took us to get her to where she is now?" Yvonne continued. "A long time. It took a lot of counselling, a lot of medication and an awful lot of hard work. Then you just fucked it, you fucked it all up."

She was getting upset now, people from the table to our right, not the youngsters, had begun to notice us. Yvonne took a deep breath, steadied herself and went on.

"We can't see one another any more, Aidan. I can't have you near her. Even the mention of your name has her in tears. I'm sorry. Maybe you meant well and misread the situation, but what you did wasn't normal."

There it was. I wasn't normal. She'd finally figured it out. So fixated was I on my abnormality that it took me a moment to realise she'd just broken up with me. Time was against me now. She had said her piece and wouldn't want to hang around much longer.

"Yvonne, we're good together though, aren't we, me and you?"

She snuffled into a hanky, eyes brimming with tears.

"Why don't we go for a walk?" I asked, pulling out my chair and backing into an oncoming customer.

Hastily apologising to the injured party I got up, rounded the table and tried to get Yvonne to her feet. If I could just walk her out of the café, away from all the people, we could have a proper conversation, go down to the river, look at the Christmas lights. But she beat me to it, was up and away before I could intercept her.

"Aidan, just leave me alone. Okay?" she pleaded through her tears, through the crowd as she slowly edged away from me

She was trying to make it painless, trying to avoid a scene, avoid further humiliation for both of us. In that moment, through my drunken fog, I saw the woman I loved, saw all her kindness, her generosity of spirit and the toughness which masked her deep insecurities. I saw a woman who just wanted a quiet life, wanted her daughter to be happy, to have someone nice and normal to come home to after a hard day's work. A woman whose life had been beset by complications for far too long, who had made many mistakes and had now reluctantly accepted that she had made one more. I stood in the middle of that café, unsteady on my feet with nothing to hold on to, and I watched her leave.

As the door shut behind her I moved in its direction, not to follow her, but to take one last look. I watched her as she hurried through the crowds, that unmistakable red hair making her easy to pick out until she disappeared down one of the side streets, out of view, out of my life. And then I left the café, stopped, went back in to leave a tip and returned home. When I was certain enough time had passed for her to have made it to her car, negotiated the traffic and got out of town, I picked up my reusable bags, went back out to the supermarket and did some shopping. Mindful that I hadn't eaten in a while, I bought some bread, milk, rashers and beans, but most of the money went on drink. I was going to need every last drop, and when that was all gone I was going to need even more.

EPILOGUE

The lonely man walks the streets. He walks them at night, walks them alongside the other lonely men, but not alongside them, not with them. The normal people, the people of the town know him, but they don't *know* him. They don't know his name or what he does but he's part of things, a familiar face in the crowd. Were he to disappear they might wonder about him for a moment, ask themselves whatever happened to that guy, the one they sometimes saw going in and out of the supermarket, but he would quickly fade from memory into anonymity, another forgotten face in the crowd. That's okay. He doesn't want to be known or to be seen. He has everything he needs now, has it all figured out. He tried to become one of the other people, the normal people, to escape his loneliness, but it wasn't for him. It was too hard, took too much effort. If that was normality, they could keep it.

He has found his place in life, a quiet, comfortable existence he can call his own. It isn't perfect and has its drawbacks, but it's his and his alone. And he isn't alone, not really. He has the only true companion he's ever known, a reliable friend who never lets him down. This friend carries him through the nights, blurs out the days, softens the edges and straightens the creases. A good friend. He knows that one day this friend, like all the others, will eventually betray him, turn its back on him, but until then he's happy enough with their arrangement, pleased to have any kind of friend at all. So they carried on like that, the lonely man and his wicked, reliable friend.

They had some laughs, some tears as they slowly sank to the bottom. It took some time, longer than the lonely man expected, but once they got there, once his friend revealed his true colours, the lonely man fought hard for that friendship, that doomed, wretched friendship. He grasped his wicked friend, looked it dead in the eye and asked for one last night, one last party for old time's sake. Understanding its role, the wicked friend gave the lonely man all the love it could spare until, finally, there was no more to give. Only then, when the final betrayal was revealed, did the lonely man say goodbye to his friend. And then, as his friend departed into the night in search of other parties, other lives, the lonely man said goodbye to it all: to his sad memories and distant dreams, but mostly to the life he had never lived.

Previous works by this author

And the Birds Kept on Singing (2017)

About the author

Simon is a journalist by day and an author by night (and occasionally on the weekends). If given the choice he would be an author by day, night, weekends, and everything in between, but he must persevere with the journalism while he waits for his books to become best-sellers. He currently lives in Co Wexford and *A Place Without Pain* is his second novel.

bourke.simon79@gmail.com